The author's name is Gabor Bartos. Born in Budapest seventy years ago, he is a retired ex-piano tuner, inventor, and former mayor of Poynton in Cheshire. He loves reading books and he has managed to collect a very eclectic collection of mainly factual and historical books, particularly biographies of interesting people. He has never planned or thought that he should write a novel. He has been inspired to write this novel after a terrible spiritual and emotional experience during a visit to the concentration/death camp at Auschwitz.

Gabor Bartos

STIGMATA OF AUSCHWITZ

*Szeretettel ajánlom
nektek Lívia*

AUSTIN MACAULEY PUBLISHERS™
LONDON • CAMBRIDGE • NEW YORK • SHARJAH

A CIP catalogue record for this title is available from the British Library.

ISBN 9781398463103 (Paperback)
ISBN 9781398463110 (Hardback)
ISBN 9781398463127 (ePub e-book)

www.austinmacauley.com

First Published 2022
Austin Macauley Publishers Ltd®
1 Canada Square
Canary Wharf
London
E14 5AA

I would like to thank Gabor Olah who designed the cover artwork.

The Tree of life ©

Two beautiful trees have been planted next to each other
Some decades ago, in the middle of the field so carefully, well planed
A hawthorn tree and one oak tree; they were magnificent looking creations
I am the hawthorn, and you are the oak tree
With many broken missing branches
Torn, beaten by the rough weather, but still proudly standing
In every summer sheltered travellers, who rest under its rich thick leafage
Giving shelter and protection for their nests to all the birds from the burning heat
All the songbirds repaid the tree welcoming with their choral singing
The hawthorn whispered with the wind some love poems to the oak tree
The oak tree leaves blushed hearing the love poems from its neighbour
The two trees' crowns grow close to each other
Their branches reached and danced to the rhythm of the gentle breeze
When the autumn came, they took off their clothes and drifted into sleep
Dreaming of their beautiful memories they have spent together
In the morning of the next spring they wake up by the singing choir of the birds
And both dressed up in the most colourful clothes again, ready for the coming
year
These are the trees of life which have been planted by the good gardener, the
Creator
But one day an evil people came along with axes and fire
They looked at these magnificent living gifts for all of us
In sheer hatred they killed the two trees along with the forests of millions
After the mindless killings, they set all of these magnificent creations on fire
They burned all the wood but in their sheer hatred, they could not destroy them
In the next spring these trees' roots brought shoots of new life again to grow up
Serve, and please us and make the ultimate perfection enjoyed by all
No one can destroy what the Creator planted.©

By Gabor Bartos
Copyright Registration ID: 2120114

Genesis: Chapter 12, verses 2 and 3

2: I will make you into a great nation,
and I will bless you;
I will make your name great,
and you will be a blessing.
3: I will bless those who bless you,
and whoever curses you I will curse;
and all peoples on earth
will be blessed through you.

Celtic horoscope

Gabriel; Hawthorn – The Illusionist
May 13-June 9
Hawthorn signs in Celtic tree astrology are not at all what they appear to be. Outwardly, they appear to be a certain persona, while on the inside, Hawthorns are quite different. They put the term "never judge a book by its cover" to the test. They live seemingly average lives while on the inside, they carry fiery passions and an inexhaustible creative flame.

Rebekah; Oak – The Stabiliser
June 10-July 7
Those born under the Celtic tree astrology sign of the Oak have a special gift of strength. They are protective people and often become a champion for those who do not have a voice. In other words, the Oak is the crusader and the spokesperson for the underdog—nurturing, generous and helpful.

Gabika; Holly – The Ruler
July 8-August 4
Among the Celtic tree astrology signs, Holly is one of regal status. Noble and high-minded, those born during the Holly era easily take on positions of leadership and power.

Chapter 1
Call from the Rabbi to Go to Munkács to Teach

In the early spring of 1938, Rabbi Simon Hevesi called me aside after the Sabbath services at the Budapest *Dohány utca* (Street) Main Synagogue. He invited me for lunch at the nearby Kosher restaurant on *Dohány utca*. The restaurant owner, Mr Reisz, was well known for his specialities of Cholet and clear chicken soup with gnocchi. Not to forget his poppyseed, honey and crushed walnut cakes. (Hevesi Simon and Chief Rabbi Immanuel Lőw)

I was curious what such a great and well-respected scholar could want from me; he was the editor of *Magyar Zsidó Szemle* (Hungarian Jewish Review). We had known each other as I had been doing some work for the Synagogue but nothing more to it as we had met in the Synagogue and some years ago, he had lectured in my semester. He was a well-known person worldwide with his studies which he posted regularly in his magazine. I was just one of the irregular members of the Synagogue.

As we were walking down *Dohány utca* before we got to the restaurant, we were just discussing art and music and what was happening in the theatres or what musical recital had been on recently in Budapest and what would I recommend to him at the present.

A short distance to the restaurant from the Synagogue and we were welcomed by the owner, Mr Reisz, who led us to Rabbi Hevesi's favourite table. We placed our order with Mr Reisz, and when the food arrived, it looked appetising and the taste was truly delicious and plentiful. Washing it down with a lovely *Hárslevelű* (Chardonnay), Rabbi Hevesi told me about the history of how the Jewish people got to Hungary.

'You know, my boy, for almost as long as the Jewish nation has existed, it has been persecuted and forced to wander from land to land around the world to find a home on the promised land: since they have left Shinar (Mesopotamia) and Canaan with the leadership of Abraham. Later, they ended up in slavery in Egypt where they lived for many generations till their Exodus under the leadership of Moses.

'You know, Gabriel, we've been called the "Wandering Jews"—while searching for our homeland, Moses needed 40 years to make the 720 km (450 miles) journey from Egypt to the Promised Land.

'After the Jewish Bar Kokhba revolt against the Romans, the depopulation of Jewish communities had begun, barred them from Jerusalem and many Jews scattered, exiled, and escaped to freedom among other nations. The captives that were not sold as slaves were deported to Gaza, Egypt and elsewhere, greatly adding to the Jewish diaspora to the destruction of both Temples in Jerusalem, till the Crusades.

'However, there was always a glimmer of hope, as the Jewish people began to adapt to their new surroundings. The Jews began to flourish everywhere as they were setting up communities, building synagogues and ritual baths and establishing "Yeshiva" schools and higher education *Gimnázium* (Gymnasium). The secret of the success for the Jewish people was in education and strong family traditions and faith in the true God: Yahweh.

'Jews arrived and settled in the capital of Buda after the Tatar invasion of the country in 1235, but it was King Béla IV *(IV. Béla)* who granted a charter of freedom to the Jews; the right to live under the protection of King Béla IV himself and he made a Jewish financier Henuk the Count of the Royal Chamber. He dealt with all the king's commerce and trade offers. This important post has been fulfilled by Jewish financiers ever since under the successive kings of Hungary. The first Jewish Quoter was established at the West End of Castle Hill, then later a second Jewish Quoter was founded in *Óbuda* (Old Buda) North outside the castle of the Castle Hill of Buda.

'As the Jewish community grew in the 1700s, they established a new business quarter in Pest at *Király utca* in *Erzsébetváros* (Elisabeth Town), the 7th District of Budapest. And here we are, in the late 1930s and we are still fulfilling this very important position in the area of trade and commerce, and this is the result of Jewish educational traditions.'

After lunch, he suggested that we should walk up to the *New York Kávéház* (coffeehouse), walking off the heavy dinner we had at Mr Reisz's restaurant.

While we were walking towards the coffeehouse, he said, 'You know, my boy, I cannot trust anybody with what I am telling you now, I don't want

10

somebody else to hear it or maybe someone is just spying on us. You know some dangerous times are coming towards us, to Jewish people.'

I was very surprised to hear what he was telling me. You just don't read this in the press.

'The Hungarian Educational Authority are going to send teachers to reform the school's curriculums at Munkács and Ungvár, basically in the Transcarpathian, Ruthenian region in the next months or so. They want to force all the Jewish Gymnasiums' teachers to teach pupils in Hungarian and not Yiddish or Hebrew. As you know, there are many very well-established Jewish schools and universities all around in that region.

'I know your qualification, Gabriel, and your high standard of teaching and lecturing. I have done some investigation on you. You speak several languages, you even work for the Synagogue to translate important and secretive documents and I am satisfied with your standard; you would be the best person to carry out this work for us in this mission. Furthermore, you are Jewish so you would not upset the Jewish community or the authority with your qualification. As you know, a large number of Jews have emigrated to Transcarpathia from the mid-1600s, and particularly 42% of the population of Munkács are Jewish and they are very influential in the areas of trade and commerce.'

'You know, Rabbi Hevesi, I don't do politics and I am not even a member of this new Zionist or other organisation; they don't pay my bills. I know they are doing tremendous, good work, but I do what I believe, and I should stick to things which nobody can object to or criticise. So, I stick with art, poetry and music and projects for the common good. For example, there is a beautiful building which has been built and completed in 1913 just right opposite the Synagogue. It's the First Army Insurance Company who commissioned it.

'I know the architect, Mr Guido Hoepfner, he visited the Synagogue from time to time, mainly for the Jewish Holiday celebrations. He told me there is a cellar in the lower part of the building big enough to build a small theatre in it with a good-sized stage and space for an audience of 560.

'I have been involved with the moving pictures industry for some time and we could have the opportunity to turn this cellar into a *Barlang Mozi* (Cave cinema) where we could play Hungarian-made films with Hungarian artists or some old silent movies. Or we could call it the *Filmmúzeum* (Cinema Museum). Just look at the tremendous success of all those great Jewish Hungarians who made Hollywood as great as it is now: the Korda Brothers, Michael Curtiz, Adolf

Zukor, William Fox, and many, many more. We only need some wealthy businessmen to invest in our project.

'You know so many industrialists and bankers, Rabbi Hevesi. Do you think you could introduce us to them to arrange a business meeting so we can present our project? Our team is full of real professionals in their fields like the well-known architect, Mr Ferenc Domány who has the design plan for the theatre.

'You know, Mr Árpád Ódry is a good friend of mine, the actor and director of the National Theatre. I was part of that group of enthusiasts with Mr Ódry, who believed we could build a small repertory theatre somewhere in Budapest where we could perform Hungarian writers' materials. We don't want Austrian or German musicals or light operas, as they do at other major, financially well-supported theatres. Hungary has many great talents, most of them just hanging out at the *New York Kávéház*, hoping to be able to sell their original materials, so we should give them a chance to have their plays/music/opera performed in Hungarian to Hungarian audiences.

'Finally, we have set up this little independent repertory theatre in the 8th district of Budapest, on 2/c. *Vas utca*, just off *Rákóczi út* (Avenue). The plays and the performers; actors and actresses are all young, very talented, some of them have never played in any theatrical production. Some of the talented ones have later been given parts in big theatres in Budapest or in other major towns in Hungary or in Transylvania. Mr Ódry later founded a Theatrical Academy where he teaches the secret of acting and performing. Later, he became the managing director of this Academy.'

'Gabriel, I promise I will investigate what I can do for this movie theatre project.' Rabbi Hevesi nodded. 'But, back to my project...Look, Gabriel, we believe in you because you are not married, and your existential situation is not very promising at present. We know about your little flat on 31 *Király utca*; a three-room flat is not good enough to raise a family. If you accept the offer, we, the Jewish Joint Distribution Committee (JDC) and the OMZSA *(Országos Magyar Zsidó Segítő Akció*—National Hungarian Jewish Help Action) would be very grateful and would meet with all your expenses.'

The New York Kávéház building became visible to both of us and as we stopped to cross *Erzsébet körút* (the Grand Boulevard of Elisabeth), we admired the architectural beauty of this magnificent "feminist" looking design. The doorman, *Józsi*, saluted us on our arrival and welcomed us by calling our names and instructing a young waiter, '*Marci*, table for two on the balcony...'

The true beauty of this building exceeded all expectations of anything it could compare with. The room inside sparkled like a jewellery box. There were twisted marble columns, and crystal chandeliers were hanging from the richly decorated painted ceiling, marble stairways and balconies of the upper floor; beautifully designed and finished with polished brasswork everywhere. There was no surface left bare on the wall and on the ceiling without being covered by gold leaf or paintings. A gipsy band was playing on the first floor.

No wonder this coffeehouse was the home of all Hungarian poets, novelists and composers, journalists, hoping to pick up fresh gossip from the floor which they can report to various leading magazines. Some of them were genuine talents who worked on their books or poems while they earned a day to day living as journalists. Basically, all the elite of the Hungarian art world and those who were still hoping to be discovered with their work met up here.

We had the best table in the house on the balcony, from where we were able to oversee the whole coffeehouse and its guests, who's who as they worked. Some of them nodded and waved at us on our arrival and confirmed they approved of our presence with a smile. My friend, poet Miklós Radnóti, walked past our table and greeted us in a familiar manner, 'How is your yellow canapé, Gabriel?' with a cheeky smile and a wink in his eye.

I felt a bit embarrassed at his question which Rabbi Hevesi picked on and reacted with a smile. 'Well, well, I thought I knew a lot about you. Never mind it, back to business again.

'Would you be able to accept our offer and move into Munkács? We will take care of all your expenses here in Budapest and in your new post in Munkács. You won't regret it, Gabriel!'

'I am really flattered, Rabbi Hevesi, Yes, of course, I will take up this offer of this new position knowing who is backing the project and more importantly, it's coming from the Hungarian Education Authority. Enjoying both "worlds" support from authority and from my faith without any prejudice. I am considering this offer not as a proposal but a privilege that you have chosen me. Thank you!'

The rest of the conversation was mainly on Rabbi Simon Hevesi's academic publications and the opportunities that we all had for the coming years. Also, he had an invitation from USA for a lecture tour in some major American universities.

Later on, he was discussing some more social-political issues like this new right-wing political movement called the Nazi Party was formed in Munich, they put unfair pressure on the Jewish community all over in Germany.

Rabbi Hevesi mentioned that his friend in Vienna told him that there was some kind of conspiracy going on between the corrupt government officials and the Nazi Party to create a "Greater German Fatherland". We were all hopeful that we wouldn't be affected with this development.

It was late on that Saturday evening, and I got a kind of headache from the cups of strong coffee and the cigar-smoke-filled room. Rabbi Hevesi called for a taxi, and he offered me a lift to my little flat. I thanked him but declined his kind offer, I needed a walk to get my head clear from the smoke. Walking all the way to my apartment to 31 *Király utca*, all my thoughts were trying to work out the day's developments, full of excitement. And what an important task I signed up for!

That night, I just turned in my bed and couldn't get to sleep at all, my only comfort was the familiar smell of perfume left in the bedding and the memories on the "Yellow Canapé". I tried to recreate these events which eventually drifted me into sleep.

Chapter 2
In Transit to Munkács [מונקאטש]

On Monday, the following week after my meeting with Rabbi Simon Hevesi, I had an appointment with some officials from the Hungarian Educational Authority in the back of the Synagogue's lecture room. I recognised the Chief Rabbi Immanuel Lőw, and some of the elders at the Dohány utca (Street) Great Synagogue of Budapest. I have seen them, always well protected from the rest of us, they sat in a special place in the oratory. I felt very impressed that Chief Rabbi Lőw and these elders and officials were gathered there to meet me and share their plans with me as to what I should carry out in Munkács, Huszt, Ungvár Beregszász and Eastern parts of the Transcarpathian Region. It was definitely the humblest experience of my life so far. My legs were shaking, my palms were sweating and my mouth dried out.

I was introduced to them by my mentor, Rabbi Simon Hevesi. It seemed that they had been briefed by Rabbi Hevesi, while I was outside the lecture room, waiting to be called in for interrogation on my political views. The government official was studying my diplomas and qualifications. Only questions they were asking of me was why I was still not married. I think they accepted my answer that I 'am still looking for the one arranged for me by the Lord. I will know the one and my heart will reveal her identity.'

Rabbi Hevesi came in with some explanation to them that I was very involved with the Hungarian art world as a critic for the Nyugat (West) Literary Journal, particularly the new cinematic (moving pictures) industry. It was a very promising new kind of entertainment and educational media to the masses. The group of movie directors regularly meeting at the Uránia Scientific Theatre. Just look at our influence in Los Angeles, Hollywood movie centre of the world, with Adolf Zukor (Paramount Film Studios), William Fox (20th Century Fox Film Studios), Korda Brothers, Michael Curtiz, Bela Lugosi and many more.

They advised me that they will report back to the ministers at the foreign and educational office at the Parliament that we were satisfied and happy with the proposed candidate quality and professional approach to leadership.

'Well, definitely we have the right and a well-qualified person for the task, who can deliver and oversee our plan in the Transcarpathian region. Within a week, you'll receive the official letter of authorisation from the parliament for the task and you must leave more a less immediately, so be prepared for it.'

Rabbi Simon Hevesi escorted the government officials to the door and turned back to us with a relieved smile on his bearded face. 'Well Gabriel, now is a more important and personal task we are going to take you through. Of course, this is the most secretive and confidential part of your vocation. After this training, you will be ready to help us achieve an agreement for the transformation of the Transcarpathian Jewish community's future.'

As we sat around the table, I was told by Rabbi Hevesi that while I was away on this mission, all my expenses will be jointly taken care of by the Jewish Committee and the Education and Foreign Ministerium as they told me so. Also, the accommodation in Munkács and around the Transcarpathian Region. My mission with the aim of all the places in the region that the Jewish communities had to be built into a more centralised organised manner, which will be controlled from Budapest.

'After your arrival and when you are settled in Munkács, we will send you some helpers and contacts with information and orders to be implemented into the Jewish community's welfare benefits.

'Just an advice, Gabriel, remember this—always keep your head down. Be humble and keep your dignity and integrity. Well-established locals don't like someone like you as a newcomer telling them what to do. If you have a problem that you can't control or deal with, you should always take it to the local Rabbi; he is the best communicator between you and the congregations. We will let them know about your mission, preventing any misunderstandings.

'Now Gabriel, please sit on this chair here so we can bless you and pray.' I sat on this chair in the middle of the room and all of them stood around me and laid hands on me. The Chief Rabbi Immanuel Lőw lead the blessing on me for this mission's success and for my safety. Unusually, I felt really special and uplifted as if I was floating while he prayed the Baw-rahk. I had never been a regular visitor of the Sabbath services, but I had never experienced this powerful emotional feeling before despite having celebrated year after year the Jewish Holidays at the synagogue, like many of my contemporaries.

At the end of the meeting, Rabbi Hevesi gave me some paperwork in a briefcase with instructions and contact names and addresses that 'memorise them, it will help you a lot. Also, here is some money for travelling and other expenses.' He said there will be more financial support transferred from the Hungarian Government and from them as well into the Bank in Munkács. 'We have opened a bank account for you in Munkács where you can draw them out for expenses, paying for printing and administrative materials costs. Never travel with lots of cash on you, it is not wise. You won't be alone, trust us, we won't let you down when we have invested so much in you.'

At last, I had all the necessary documentation for my task. Finally, the big day arrived for my journey into the unknown. I was travelling to Munkács on 9 April 1938. I notified my neighbours at my little apartment asking them to keep an eye on the place while I was away. I wasn't sure the time I had to be away, but they assured me that won't be a problem. I left the key with my neighbour aunt Évi, just in case if there was a problem with water or electricity or just to collect the post or if she would need access to the place.

I picked up my suitcase and my briefcase and I was ready to leave my apartment. Just one more time, I looked around the room before I shut the door behind me and wondered when, if ever, I will see this little place again.

I locked the room and said goodbye to my neighbours. With a heavy foot, I walked down the stairs and to the Astoria Hotel, where I caught the tram to the Eastern Main Railway Station; at my arrival, I went to collect my pre-purchased ticket to Munkács.

Walking past the magazine shop, I picked up a Magyarország (Hungarian Nation) titled newspaper, so I would have something to occupy myself during the journey. Settled in the train coach, I felt the steam engine slowly move forward with a jerking motion. I opened my newspaper and right on the front page in large typesetting was the headline: "Zsidótörvény Javaslata" New Jewish Law proposed bill … in the house of parliament.

I had a cold shiver run through my body! What an earth was going on? There was no sign of this draconian bill. None of my friends at the press would know about it or mention even the suggestion of such a law to be introduced in Hungary. Everything seemed to be normal and peaceful. I had just signed up for this job in a foreign country. Was I doing the right thing leaving my apartment, my home, my country for an unknown one, where I knew no one? At a time when uncertainty was all around us. Nothing much I can do about this now as I was here on a moving train, all the way to Munkács.

Well, at least the Lord God of Israel was with me on this project as the Rabbis had prayed for me. I know that He will protect me. He called me to do this job and I had faith in Him.

Jewish Law 1: "The companion and host on strengthening the balance of life" 1938: XV.tc. Since the mid-1930s, it had been gaining in strength; influenced by this, and at the same time demanded a far-reaching Hungarian far-right, the need to settle the Jewish question on TV korm.pol. the forefront. The proposal you put on me referred to → in his speech announcing the Győr program, it was submitted to the → Parliament by the → Darányi government, but the TV (29 May 1938) → Béla Imrédy was the head of the government.

The TV ordered the setting up of chambers (press, lawyer, medical, etc.) on the intellectual and freelance fields, where members max 20% could belong to the Israelite denomination. This rate also applied to corporate intellectual jobs. Religious discrimination abolished the principle of equality of citizenship. Released from the restrictions were widows and children of war invalids, heroic dead and those who died on 1 August 1919 before converting to any other established denomination. In December 1938, the Hungarian Israelite Probation Office was established to support tens of thousands of those affected. • SZPJ, 1285

Chapter 3
Arrival to Munkács (in Yiddish Minkatch)
[מונקאטש]

My two-day journey from Budapest to Munkács started. I had to change trains a couple of times and at last I arrived on the 10th of April in the late afternoon to a very impressive, structured building of the Munkács Railway Station.

Dr Sándor Fried, Attorney, welcomed me at the end of the platform; he had been notified of my arrival by the Hungarian Authority in Budapest. He also welcomed me as a fellow Jew in Yiddish, and from then on, we continued the conversation in Yiddish.

He looked a warm friendly person, wearing a dark double-breasted overcoat and a matching coloured fedora.

Mr Fried explained to me that he had booked me for a week in the Csillag Szálloda (Star Hotel), it was only fifteen minutes from the Main Railway Station. 'You will find Munkács is a small but very vibrant little place; everything is just a walking distance. After you have checked in, maybe you would like to have a drink just to wind down from the long journey. But if you think you would prefer to want to refresh yourself then I understand. There is a lot of opportunity to have a drink together.'

Politely, I declined his offer. The last thing I wanted was alcohol. As we said goodbye, he said he would be there at nine in the morning and take me to my future office and then look for a place to rent 'for you as I believe you will be based here for a long time in Munkács.'

My mentor in Munkács, Dr Sándor Fried, a local lawyer, arrived at 9 am as promised and collected me from my hotel to take me across the road from my hotel to the town hall to introduce me to the officials, and also to the educational department and then to my office where I will work until my mandate will be ended by the Hungarian Government.

Dr Fried briefed me on the history of the Town Hall. The building is truly a magnificent example of art nouveau style right on the main town square. City Hall is made in the Art Nouveau style, designed by the famous Hungarian architect János Granny Bush. Construction was completed in 1904. Since then, it serves as the administrative building of Town Hall. Inside is as beautiful as outside, full of marble floors, stairways, very high ceilings and large windows, polished steel on all the decoration and chandeliers.

By midday, I managed to brief my two helpers, Andre and Victoria. Requested some maps of the Transcarpathian region of Czechoslovakia to fix it onto the wall and some marking pins for the maps. Asked them to mark out the locations of schools that I had to visit. I had a brief chat with them to find out their background and qualifications and basically just find out the current political situation among the different nationalities as to their interest in art and culture as well as in the Subcarpathian region.

I invited Sándor for lunch; we casually had a conversation over a cup of coffee, and I pulled out the newspaper from my briefcase and showed the headline to Sándor, waiting for his response.

He told me as a solicitor he had heard of it but wasn't sure of the outcome, as it was a proposal. He said the ministers in Hungary will debate it and will have some amendment to it before they will be ratifying it and that will be final, the law/statute. Sándor said that he wanted to study it before he would make a case out of it.

Sándor brought it to my attention while I was travelling from Budapest to Munkács, probably I didn't know what had happened in Austria. I had no knowledge of what had happened. Sandor lowered his voice and told me that Germany just annexed Austria. I just couldn't respond to Sandor's announcement. A cold shiver ran down my spine as if I'd just seen a ghost.

I was surprised at the news, but I didn't expect this Anschluss to happen so quickly.

'Rabbi Hevesi told me at our New York Coffeehouse meeting some weeks ago that this will happen.'

Sándor was surprised to hear my comment that the Anschluss was known to some well-informed people in the Viennese Jewish community, which will be the outcome of the German expansion plans.

'Sándor, I would like to ask for some favours, one is that I would like an introduction to the Chief Rabbi of Munkács, and two, I have to find a place or room to rent. The Hungarian Treasury will not pay for a hotel room for the rest of my stay while I am employed by them.'

'That is no problem as Rebbe Baruch Yehoshua Yerachmiel Rabinowitz is expecting you. I will organise the meeting with him tomorrow morning in the synagogue. After the meeting with Rabbi Baruch, I can take you to see a couple of properties to choose from.

'One particular property belongs to Elisabeth Schwartz. Elisabeth has been widowed for some years; her husband used to be the community kosher butcher. The husband died before they could have children, now Elisabeth is struggling on her own and financially, she needs some support. She lives not far from the centre in the outskirts of Munkács.'

Next Tuesday morning, Sándor promptly arrived at my hotel at eight am and guided me to meet Rebbe Baruch, at the Hoif Complex Synagogue on Munkácsi Mihály utca, in Munkács, a very large building near the Latorca, River Bridge.

Rebbe Baruch was standing at the top of the stairs in the main entrance of the synagogue, talking to some members of his parish. He looked in his thirties, a person who demanded attention and recognition with warm affection when he spoke to people peeping over his round reading glasses. There was an obvious reason why he was chosen to be the Chief Rabbi. Instantly, I felt very positive towards Rebbe Baruch as he welcomed us and invited us into his office.

He said, 'Let's get over the business first then I will show you around the complex. Should we carry on speaking in Yiddish or on Hungarian?' I suggested speaking in Yiddish. He offered us a cup of coffee and a glass of water.

Rebbe Baruch asked me if I found Munkács a progressive-dynamic small town. I said I would have to see a bit more as I had just arrived in Munkács two days ago.

I presented him with a letter from Chief Rabbi Immánuel Lőw and expressed the Chief Rabbi's good wishes. Rebbe Baruch said, 'The last time I saw him at my wedding, he was our special guest.'

'Yes, I would like to congratulate you as well to your wedding of the year to Chaya Frima Rivkah, daughter of Rebbe Chaim Elezar Spira.'

He told me that he will read the letter from Chief Rabbi Lőw and talk to me at length, and he would like it if I would accept his invitation for supper at his house tomorrow evening at six and meet his family as well.

'Now let me guide you through the Synagogue, the bath and the school buildings which hopefully, you visit as often as you can in future, like Sándor does.'

After showing us around the Synagogue, he walked us to the door and said goodbye till tomorrow evening at 6 pm.

Sándor organised the meeting with Mrs Elisabeth Schwartz, so I could have a look of the room that I was going to rent. Leaving the Synagogue behind after the meeting with Rebbe Baruch, I felt a very strange observation—clean air; it was a refreshing experience; living in Budapest's well-polluted environment everywhere on the street or in coffeehouses. I was commenting on the freshness and clean air to Sándor, who with a smile responded, 'Yes, we are really blessed with this clean air; it comes from the hills of the Carpathian Mountains.'

As we walked out of town on Latorca utca (Valanberha Street), the landscape changed from townhouses to nicely maintained typical suburban private houses with gardens.

Sándor knocked on the door knocker and a sophisticated lady in her late forties-early fifties dressed in full black, opened the door and invited us into the house. Two dogs appeared from the back of the garden; one called Floki and the other one Szuka.

Mrs Schwartz asked us if we had something to eat that morning. She had prepared some salami with fresh bread and fresh milk. We had some of her salami which was very nice and just saved us to going to have lunch in a restaurant. She showed me around inside and outside of the house.

I liked the cleanliness of the house and I decided to rent a room from her for an unknown period. I told her that I will have to travel on business around Munkács, and to a more distant town like Ungvár so I wouldn't be home every night.

It was getting late and Sándor walked me back to my hotel and said goodbye till tomorrow.

Chapter 4
History of the Rebbes of Munkács
Dinner Invitation at Rabbi Baruch's House

I had bought a nice bunch of flowers and a bottle of vintage Tokay wine that I had brought with me from Budapest to present to the host, Rabbi Baruch, and his wife, Rivka. I arrived sharp at 6 pm as my invitation advised. (*I always arrive to appointments just a bit earlier as it is important to be prompt.*)

Rabbi Baruch's house was near the Synagogue, a modest yellow-painted townhouse with a large gate in the front allowing a car or horse-pulled cart to get through in comfort.

The housemaid let me in and led me to the living room where the Rabbi and his wife welcomed me with such warmth. I felt genuinely astonished with their affection towards me. The conversation was in Yiddish from the minutes of my welcoming and we have carried on with our conversation in Yiddish.

Rabbi Baruch introduced me to his wife Rivka, and I presented her with the flowers, which she accepted with a smile. I gave the bottle of Tokay wine to the Rabbi, which he accepted with the comment that it was a good vintage year for this particular Tokay wine.

The Rabbi recommended that I should sit down in a very comfortable easy chair till the dinner was served. He offered me a small glass of Unicum, 'It will help set our appetites.'

Rabbi's wife Rivka asked me if there was a Mrs B, left behind in Budapest. I said, 'Not just yet, the Lord will provide me with the one whom I will marry.' I explained that in my early years, I was dedicated to university studies and later on my involvement with art, mainly theatrical and with the new movie industry as well. So, I could not make commitments which I knew that I couldn't dedicate to the partner I loved.

Rivka said, with a twinkle in her eyes, 'You know, there are some beautiful young ladies living in Munkács.'

I said, 'Yes, I have been here only three days, but I have noticed some of them.'

The housemaid interrupted our conversation and called us to the table as supper was to be served.

Rabbi Baruch said the Kiddush, *Berachah,* blessed the meal and the wine and gave thanks for its Maces dumpling, followed with stuffed goose breast. I was congratulating Rivka's cooking standards. The Tokay Szamorodni was well chosen for the poultry-based meal.

He lifted the glass of wine and said, '*Baruch atah A-donay, Elo-heinu Melech Ha'Olam borei pri hagafen.*' And toasted us L'Chaim.

During the meal, I was commenting on their wedding ceremony, and so many very important guests from the Jewish communities around Europe had celebrated the wedding ceremony with them. 'Your wedding made the press interested in many countries with the headlines: "Wedding of the year" of the daughter of Rabbi Chaim Elazar Shapira in Munkács, 15.03.1933.'

Rivka said it was a special unforgettable event because her father was a well-respected Rebbe among the Jewish communities in surrounding countries. 'He comes from a dynasty of Rabbis. And he has done so much for the community of Munkács. In 1925, he laid the cornerstone of the new Hebrew *Gymnasium* in Munkács, and Rabbi Chaim Elazar Shapira become the first director and teacher of the gymnasium. He nicknamed the *Gymnasium* the *Beit Hatfela* (the House of Frivolity).'

We finished the most delicious meal with an even nicer Flodni, full of all the layers of poppyseed, apple and crushed walnut. At the end of meal, Rabbi Baruch said *Berachah Acharonah.*

After this beautiful supper, we retired to the lounge again. Rivka gave her excuses and retired to leave us alone to talk business.

Rabbi Baruch opened the conversation, saying, 'I have read Chief Rabbi Immanuel Lőw. Yes, truly a very interesting time ahead for Jews. What do you feel? I can't even ask what you think is going on in the West, as you just can't follow or predict the way the politics are developing. I heard that Germany has taken over Austria and made themselves a very important and powerful nation in Europe.'

'Yes, it is very strange that I have dined with Rabbi Simon Hevesi in Budapest, and he told me that some of his connections in Vienna were predicting this Anschluss, as corrupt Viennese politicians had made a pact with the Nazis in Germany. Now I hope you can understand why I am here in Munkács, as a Jew and representing the Hungarian Cultural / Educational Ministerium with a plan.'

'Yes, Gabriel, I have read Chief Rabbi Lőw's letter you handed to me at our first meeting at the Synagogue. I have read it twice because I just couldn't believe the content of his letter.'

'As far as I can work out, there is some kind of a deal going on between the Hungarian Regent Horthy and Ribbentrop, aka the Nazis, over the future ownership of the Transcarpathian Region.'

'Like what, Gabriel?'

'I think the Horthy regime are going to make an agreement / pact with the Germans, so the price of that pact is that Subcarpathia will belong to Hungary again. I am not saying that is the fact but why on earth have I been sent to Munkács, by the Hungarian Government to arrange and negotiate the future of educational standards. Maybe Horthy is making a deal with some evil organisation which he cannot see the outcome of. I don't know.'

'What is wrong with our educational systems, Gabriel?'

'As you know, there is a very strong lobby coming from the military of promoting more physical education in schools and a strong nationalism about the dominant Hungarian language on this proposal has been agreed by all MP's in the House of Parliament, and they made it as law. This will affect all faith, private and state schools, the educational languish has to be done in Hungarian, and also to introduce more sports lessons in a weekly curriculum.'

The 1843/44 2nd act ordered Magyar to be the language of the letters coming from the King, the text of acts, the conversation of parliament and the juridical bodies. The 1843/44 9th act ordered it to become the language of the schools.

'Now I understand your position and the reason you are here in Munkács, to sell this change to everybody in Subcarpathia by you as a Jew and as a teacher. Very smart. Please don't misunderstand my comments. I do like you very much as a fellow Jew and the Jewish Communities will welcome you too.' Rabbi Baruch apologised to me, but he still had to prepare for the next week's Passover ceremony which began on the 15th to 23rd of April. 'Please come along to celebrate with us.'

'I'll try, Rabbi Baruch, but I still have much to organise here in Munkács. Thank you for this assurance, Rabbi Baruch, I am sure that we will be able to find something which will satisfy the Hungarian Authority and we will be able to keep our tradition. If there is a will for compromise among us, we will find the way for that.'

'How about if we are still able to teach our history and the Tora in Hebrew? What do you think, Gabriel? And we can teach the rest of the subjects in Hungarian.'

'With regards to the extra physical education per week, I think a bit more physical exercise will do the children good. We could create sporting competitions between schools at the regional level.'

'I am very pleased to meet you, Gabriel, I like your company and your energy. I can promise you that I will organise a meeting with all the Hebrew school leaders and Rabbis from other town parishes, and we can present them with your mission and our proposal just as we worked out tonight.'

'Rabbi Baruch, thank you so much for this evening, and please thank your wife, Rivka, for the fantastic meal and her warm welcome that I have experienced in your house today.'

'You are more than welcome, Gabriel, and I hope we can have you again, but for a more relaxed and friendlier discussion. Not just business matters which I understand are very important indeed and which have to be done. I will let you know about the meeting with school principals and our friends from other Jewish communities.'

'That will be a great help. Thank you, Rabbi Baruch.'

'If you need some help while you are in Munkács, please do not hesitate to get in touch with me. Goodnight, Gabriel.'

'Goodnight, Rabbi Baruch.'

After this beautiful supper and with the great company of my host, I was walking back to my hotel on the cobblestoned and gaslit street. I felt that this was a good exercise working off the extra weight which I must have put on with tonight's meal.

Chapter 5
Lvov and Rebekah

Finally, I checked out of the hotel and moved into Mrs Elisabeth Schwartz' house on Latorca utca, in the district called Kert Város (garden town) of Munkács.

It wasn't difficult, as I only had with me a medium-sized suitcase, some shirts, underwear, cleaning and shaving kit. The rest was my books and paperwork for my mission.

The room was nice and clean.

Mrs Elisabeth Schwartz' house:

Leaving the Latornya bridge, walking on Latorca utca, leading out of town towards the meadow. It is a very wide road, an elevated part which is like an embankment of the river Latornya, it's wide enough for two carts to pass each other at the same time. Both sides of the road, there is a row of houses, all the roofs are thatched, with large double wooden doors nicely carved with bright coloured painted flowers decorating them. Next to the gate is a small door which is also well decorated. The front of the houses is in level with its boundary; they are all built away from the road. All of them have two double windows facing the road with a flower box fixed to the wall under each window and they are full of geraniums and pansies from spring to early October.

These houses are uniformly designed and built in the early 1800s. Typical Eastern European Houses built by straw and clay with very thick walls and every one of them is regularly whitewashed with lime not just to look pretty but to keep the flies away from the households.

The back of the houses has attached stables, agricultural storage place and room for the wooden spoked wheeled carts (szekér) and various small poultry and pigsties. In front of the building is the driveway and yard, in the middle of the yard there is a gemes kut "nodding well". Yards are always full of livestock and dogs for security and protection from the wildlife, foxes and wolves come in as far as the middle of the town, particularly in wintertime.

Every day in the early morning, the herdsman comes with his sheepdogs first, followed by the shepherd with his dogs, ringing the bell in the middle of the road and collecting from every household all the cattle, sheep and geese, taking them to the fields/pasture. A really strange practice was that every herdsman has his own distinguishing sound of bell which the different kinds of animals recognise and without any encouragement, they just come out of each house and join the herd/flocks. In the evening, the same well-trained practices as the cow, sheep or geese arrive to their household and go into stables for the night without any mishaps or encouragement.

This area is not the wealthiest part of Munkács, it is a well-mixed population culturally and within their religious heritage. Ranges from Slavic, Polish, Hungarian, Jewish, German and Russians.

Most of them are farmers / small holders, supporters of Munkács Town with food, vegetables and dairy products at the town marketplaces.

They live in a harmonious existence, tolerating each other with respect and support each of their community's traditional celebrations.

Elisabeth was originally from Debrecen, Hungary. She was a youngish-looking woman which I would guess was in her late forties to early fifties.

She lived alone since her husband passed away some years ago (I've never asked why or in what circumstances); she went into mourning, wearing black clothing, covered her head with a (kendő) kerchief all the time. She told me that her husband was a well-respected kosher butcher, his slaughter room was still in the back of the house. Elisabeth used it only when she slaughtered some poultry for herself or some of the locals, otherwise the room was always locked.

She showed an instant acceptance of me with a kind of older sister caring from her attitude. Then she showed me a photograph of her and her husband and then I understood the reason of her affection towards me. There was a very strong resemblance between her dead husband and me.

I just looked at her as she had some tears rolling down her cheeks; was it a kind of emotionally charged feeling with her as sympathy or just my upbringing which made me stand up from the kitchen table and give her a hug. She embraced me for a while. I felt her body gently shaking as she cried on my shoulder.

I felt that I had ripped open some of her memories which she had buried for a long time.

She said the first time when we met, when Sándor brought me to see the lodging room at her house, she felt that this was some kind of omen that will compensate for the loss of her loved one.

I tried to explain to Elisabeth the reason why I was there in Munkács, just the basic reason that I was doing business there in the whole Subcarpathian region. She understood that and afterwards never questioned me about my work. But she said that if I had a favourite food or if she could help me with information on people in Munkács, or anything I would need like laundry, ironing or anything else. I thanked her for such a homely welcome and I said that I would like to ask if somehow, I could return all her kindness to me.

She said, 'I am just happy that you are here.'

On the following day, I went to the office at the Town Hall and tried to get things moving as my work had slowed down a bit while I was moving from the hotel to Elisabeth's house.

I had a message from Rabbi Baruch, that he had made some progress over our future meeting with the Jewish community leaders.

Viktoria and Andre were back to working in the educational department office as they were only loaned to me for my work here in Munkács.

'Dear Andre and Victoria, would you please organise a meeting? I want to request the local authority to arrange a meeting with all the state and faith schools' headmasters in Munkács, to do my presentation to them corporately and individually as well.

'I have suggested to them the meeting in one week and to organise it either in the town hall or in the Drama Theatre, if it is possible by the end of May, but not the 28th because that is a Sabbath. So, let us have it on the 30th of May, at 9.30 am. It should be a 6 to 7-hour consultation, and at midday we will have a break for lunch then continue in the afternoon when I will answer questions from the floor.'

I told Viktoria and Andre that I had to go to Lvov for four days and should be back to get ready for the meeting. I asked Viktoria to book me onto the next train tomorrow morning from Munkács to Lvov.

Viktoria told me later that she booked a room for me in the Grand Hotel in the centre of Lvov. Near to the University where I was going to have a meeting with Professor Mihály Schlesinger.

I was tired by the time I got home to Mrs Schwartz' house. Elisabeth was waiting for me with my favourite soup kept warm on the stove, with freshly baked bread. She asked me if I would call her Elisabeth, instead of her married name. I felt it made me comfortable and homely. I told her that I was going to travel to Lvov for four days and had to get up early to catch the first train to Lvov. I asked her if she would like me to get something for her from Lvov. She said with a quiet voice just to get back home safely.

She said, 'I will wake you up on time to get you to the railway station to catch your train to Lvov.'

I packed some fresh shirts and underwear in my case and went to bed. My head was buzzing with the day's events and finally, I fell asleep.

Next morning, as I was leaving the house, Elisabeth was standing in the gateway and waving goodbye as if she knew something would happen to me in the big city.

Sitting on the train, I was making up some theories to find an explanation for her behaviour. The train was going through some magnificent scenery, the countryside and the landscape was breathtakingly beautiful. As we pulled into Lvov main railway station, I asked some of my fellow passengers if they could tell me the directions to the Grand Hotel.

After I checked into the hotel, immediately I headed to the famous Lvov University to meet up with Mihaly Schlesinger. It wasn't difficult to find the University as it stood out with its sheer size among other buildings, and it was in the heart of Lvov.

The Lvov University was built at one end of a very large rectangular park named Kosciuszki Park, full of bushes, flowers and well-maintained garden features; they named it Jesusita Garden, and at the opposite end of the park was the Lvov Polytechnic School. This beautiful building shows the whole splendour of its architecture as it is facing the park.

At the entrance I asked for my contact, Professor Mihaly Schlesinger. With a short wait, the professor walked into the waiting room where he greeted me in his typical black university cape with a big smile on his bearded face. He hadn't changed since I had met him all those years ago at the Dohany Uti Rabbi college in Budapest.

'It's been a long time, Gabriel, since I've seen you last in Budapest,' he told me in Yiddish.

'Yes Sir. Those were the days. We were in much more security and freedom to learn with great plans for our future.'

'Yes, I enjoyed lecturing to your class, it was full of energy which I felt influenced me as well encouraged me to pass more information to your class than was on the planned subject matter of instruction. But what are you doing here in Lvov?'

I explained to him my mission and promised him that I will fully brief him about it. I asked him if we could meet up for a coffee or a meal later that evening.

He said, 'Let me show you around the university, Gabriel, it is truly a well-designed purpose-built building for higher education with all the different faculties.'

As we were walking past his lecturing tiers, there was a group of pupils of different ages standing in the corridor and you could hear among them all kinds of debates going on. I asked Professor Schlesinger if these pupils were waiting for him. He looked at his pocket watch and said, 'My goodness, is that the time! I will have to show you around some other time, Gabriel.'

I couldn't really hear what he was saying because a young lady I guessed to be one of the professor's pupils just turned around and looked at me. As our eyes met, I felt my heart "explode" and start beating with tremendous speed. Our eyes just locked on and I felt something special which I had never experienced before. Neither of us turned our heads away, just absorbed the energy that was being created by both of our spirits. We both smiled at each other, and I think she winked at me or maybe I just imagined it.

I was brought back to earth by the voice of Professor Schlesinger. 'Gabriel, are you all right?'

It took me some seconds to recover myself and with a flushed face, I turned his way and said, 'I have just seen an angel.'

Professor Schlesinger didn't force what had happened, my face was a picture. He said, 'Why don't you come to my lecture and we will have a chat afterwards.'

I jumped at his invitation and went up to the top of the seats in the tiers where I could keep my eyes on this mysterious "angel" who had touched my heart with such emotional energy.

She must have felt my energy as I was watching her from the top of the tiers because she turned in my direction without searching through her classmates as if she knew I was there and smiled at me. I don't think she concentrated on Professor Schlesinger's lecture as her mind was on me.

At the end of lecture, neither of us stood up, just absorbed each other's presence. The Professor walked up to me and called for her to join us. Without hesitation, she stood up and we were being introduced to each other by Professor Schlesinger, my old teacher. 'Rebekah, let me introduce you to my dear ex-student from Budapest, Gabriel.'

As I stretched my shaky hand towards Rebekah, I felt a huge fire was burning in me and I could only say to her, 'It is my pleasure to meet you.' She was in a similar state. When we touched each other's hand to shake, it was like an electrical charge had gone through our hands and sealed our future forever.

The Professor politely excused himself and claimed that he had a prior engagement and with a smile he left us to work out our moment of privacy and future.

Chapter 6

It Is Us — Rebekah and Gabriel

I just did not know how to start the conversation; I was starstruck (angel-struck) or I had forgotten which language I was speaking out of the many that I speak.

In the end, Rebekah opened the conversation in Yiddish. She said, 'I do not mind what language you would like to speak in. I can speak Hungarian, Slovakian and Rusyns (Ruthenian) and of course, Yiddish as well. When your country has been ruled by so many other countries, speaking different languages is easy in our little Transcarpathian Region of Munkács. Let us carry on in Yiddish.'

At last, I gathered my thoughts and confidence. I agreed that Yiddish will be good to carry on with. I asked Rebekah if she had any more lectures to attend that day. She said, 'Yes, one more which is the history of ethnic migration from Asia to Western Europe.'

I asked if she would mind if I joined her. 'I would like to invite you for a coffee or a supper later where we could just have a chat. I would like to know more about you. Since I saw you in the lecture hall and have been introduced to you by Professor Mihaly Schlesinger, something has happened to me, and I would like to understand my feelings. I am not a young man as many in the university. I have had relationships before, but I must admit I have never felt this dramatically emotional experience like I went through today when I looked at you among the crowd of people. You have touched my soul and I feel I have touched yours as well because my energy has been absorbed by your energy. Also, your energy has been settled in my physical energy, there were no clashes or any negative vibes, just peace and rejoicing.'

Rebekah said, 'I have never heard someone like you who would explain an emotion which has spontaneously touched two completely strange individuals' reaction to a first-time meeting such as this. I have to say that I am like you. I have never experienced that your energy would "strip me naked" emotionally and so openly reach right into my heart just with our eyes which have locked in without any build-up or warning. Yes, of course, I would like to dine with you this evening. I have to find out why this amazing experience has happened between us, and I want to understand it.'

I think it is better just to accept it as it is, without analysing it or trying to find a "logical" explanation for it. There is no explanation to this when two emotions and a supernatural energy takes over our mind and our free will and accepts it. Some scientists would just deliver a simple analysis that it is called LOVE.

After the lecture on ethnic migration, we both walked out of the university building and decided to enjoy the sunny April afternoon in the beautiful park. Luckily, we found a free bench as these benches were very popular among students. As we sat down, how romantic it was, the sun, the flowers and their perfume in the air. Birds singing like a well-rehearsed concert before they call it a day and retire into their nests. You have to be a poet to recreate the atmosphere, the company and the place as of this moment. This was so romantic and I felt really blessed with all of this and I will remember it till the end of my days. It was so beautiful to remember the nice things in life that should encourage us that it was worthwhile to go forward and fight for your everyday life.

While Rebekah was telling me her future plans and her involvement with a woman's liberation organisation which started from Manchester, England, called the "Suffragettes". She was very active with lots of energy in and it was called the Ukrainian Women's Union.

I just absorbed her beauty. Her jet-black wavy hair down below her shoulders, her mesmerising black eyes. Her little nose and her very sexy lips covering even snow-white teeth. She was wearing a two-piece of reasonably with the fashion and a white blouse, high heeled shoes. I just could not take my eyes off her beautiful bosom forcing her jackets buttons to burst open. A mid-length skirt showed her delicate long legs.

Just chatting on the subject of immigration as it was still fresh in us, we both agreed that the whole world moved into the land that we all call our "home" country. We both came from a Jewish background from different parts of the world and its ancient traditions, our faith in our Lord God, and the law of Moses, which was keeping us together, this was our identity. It didn't matter where we came from, the Lord had given us a free will to decide and adjust it into our life and we were offering Him all of our success for a blessing and humbly giving Him all the glory for his grace.

The temperature started dropping a little bit, feeling the cool air drifting from the Carpathian hills. I suggested to Rebekah that we should go to have our supper in the hotel where I was staying, I knew they offered a great variety of food. She agreed on the restaurant, and she collected her books from the bench. I offered to carry her books. I can put them into my briefcase; she nodded and thanked me for my offer. I reached out for her hand to help her stand up. Automatically, she accepted my gesture and put her soft little hand into mine. When she stood up, we looked into each other's eyes and I felt the same emotional feeling again and from that moment on, I never let her hand out of mine.

We walked to my hotel restaurant hand in hand as two lovers for a long time. I felt her energy, her heartbeat through her fingers and very hot palms of her hand.

At the restaurant, the waiter sensed our state, it was not difficult, it was written all over our faces and he offered us a more privately positioned table. I was very grateful for his action. The restaurant had a gypsy band who sensed the romance between us; they did not approach us in respect of our intimate conversation, but they were playing very soft songs.

The waiter took our order and in a short while, he brought our wine and poured the wine into our glasses.

Rebekah was very impressed and felt a bit embarrassed as she had never been in a restaurant with a strange man. But she knew (told me later on) she was not in control of her actions. While we waited for our meal, we started talking about us.

She said to me, 'You know, Gabriel, I never expected this, it is not happening to me as I have passed the age 23 which in a Jewish woman's life in a particularly small town like Munkács, counts as an unwanted person, too old to have children and look after the family. I thought this would never happen to me but in my very secret dreams, I believed that someone like you would come along with a true and unconditional love. So here I am with you; do not spoil my dream.

'You know, my mother died when I was a young girl, my father never married again, this is the reason I have no brothers or sisters, I have just remained as a one-off. My father worked very hard looking after me. I know he has spoiled me because I reminded him of my mother. He hired a nanny who looked after me while he was still building his small engineering business at the Latorna riverside industrial area which he made very successful employing many people.

'After I finished the Jewish Gymnasium, he brought me into his business to do the administrative work and bookkeeping. I became very good at that and became a freelance bookkeeper for other Jewish businesses as well as ours. But I felt I wanted more in life, not just bookkeeping. I wanted to learn more at a higher educational level; that is why I ended up here in Lvov University. I love music, theatre and read as much as I can. I have not had real friends as all of them have now been married with children and family commitments. But if I do meet up with them somewhere in Munkacs, I do not really have anything in common with them. Do not know what to talk about with them. How about you, Gabriel?'

'Well, let me tell you a story, a certain man who was born as the youngest one into a family of four children and knew for a fact that his heritage out of the family is very little. You could say nothing. So, he has to make it on his own with the Lord's blessing. He has studied, read as many books as possible so he could educate himself and focused on what he tries to achieve in his life in an existential standard. He tries to be near where his beliefs and dreams lead him. As he managed to achieve all those things successfully that he dreamed of, but the years have passed above his head.

'So, here is that once little dreamer who has now passed thirty years of age in his life. He has been in some relationships in the past, but they were really just casual ones, but never met anyone who would turn his flickering light into the fire which would burn with a passion. Yet here I am now, this is you, Rebekah, you are the one I was dreaming of. I just cannot control my emotions and my desire for you. Just holding your hand and being with you for the rest of my life. I had the most enjoyable meal that I ever ate because of you, Rebekah.'

It was really just a *Töltött káposzta* (stuffed cabbage) and Kindli for sweet. Rebekah had a duck leg with rice and red steamed cabbage, and we shared a bottle of Tokay wine.

We lost track of the time, it was past ten at night. The gypsy band was packing up ready to go home; the waiter had set all the other tables for the next day and he was waiting for us to leave.

As it was so late, I looked into Rebekah's eyes and asked her if she would stay with me in the hotel room for the night. She closed her eyes and in a very quiet voice replied, 'Yes, I would like that.'

I settled the bill for the evening and helped her out of her chair, held her hand and walked up to my room. It was not a big room but was everything a businessman or a tourist would need. A double bed, a wardrobe and a bathroom. I drew the curtains and asked Rebekah if she was all right. She nodded and I went close to her, held both of her hands and kissed her on her cheek. I felt a tremendous heat coming from her. I felt she approved the situation and I kissed her on her lips. She let my hand free and with the same motion she put her arms around my neck and kissed me back. I pulled her waist to me so closely as my body was feeling her firm bosom; her nipples hardened, and our lower bodies were on fire, and we kissed passionately.

I unbuttoned her jacket and lowered it off her shoulders. We started kissing each other again with the same passion; she forced her lower body to mine which was by then in a dangerously built up position, but she enjoyed it as she was rubbing her body with mine. I undid her skirt zip and let it slide down and drop to the floor. We were shaking so much with excitement we could hardly breathe; our hearts were beating at an amazing speed for each other's love.

Rebekah broke away from my arms and went to the bathroom and came back with a towel which she laid down on the middle of the bed then she let her slip fall and got out of her knickers. She said in a bashful way, 'I have never ever been with a man before. I have always kept my virginity for the one I am longing to be the true one.'

She laid down on the bed and reached out towards me. She looked like an icon in Michelangelo's painting. Absolutely perfect body waiting for my love. Her breathing sped up and her bosom was rapidly moving up and down; her body started shaking as her breathing rhythm speed increased. I laid right next to her on the bed and started kissing her on the lips. She pulled me on her and by that time we were both shaking in the excitement; from my touch finding her on top of her emotion without any assistance, she was dripping wet, so it was not hard to enter Rebekah; just a gently slide in but there was a sudden impediment which made me push a bit harder, then I realised that I had just broken her virginity, she moved a little bit upwards and cried in pain and joy.

A while later I felt hot from our satisfaction and laid on the wet sheet. Her tears were running down her cheeks and with a smile she whispered in my ear, 'That's all that I had, my innocence, my virginity, kept it for so long and now I have given to you.'

We just lay next to each other, wet through and absolutely exhausted. I said, 'Rebekah, this was the seal to our future. We were one body when we made love and hopefully will remain one for the future. Rebekah Grósz, will you please marry me?'

She looked me in the eye and said with tears running, this time of joy, and said, 'Yes! Gabriel, I promise you I will never leave you and I will love you forever.'

We made love twice that evening, which became morning of the next day. What a beautiful feeling to wake up in your lover's arms with her kisses.

Chapter 7

Rebekah and Gabriel in Lvov

In the morning, we both woke up absolutely exhausted but in each other's arms, which made us realise that the night we had spent together wasn't just a beautiful dream. It finally happened for both of us at last, we found treasure and we were holding onto it with passionate protection. Just looking at each other with beaming smiles and we kissed again. I said jokingly, 'Well, my dearest, this is my wakeup call. This is what you will be getting from me every day in the future.'

Rebekah said, 'Can I have an extra portion of this delicious wakeup call?'

I looked at my watch and in a panicking voice I said, 'My goodness, it is seven o'clock already.'

Rebekah said, 'Oh dear, I have to attend an eight o'clock lecture.' She was panicking now and in a rush we both had a quick shower to refresh our body from last night's passionate lovemaking. We didn't have breakfast, just quickly got dressed and grabbed our books with the briefcase and rushed downstairs towards the university.

Rebekah had her lecture; I had an appointment with Professor Mihály Schlesinger. We had forgotten everything in last night's sensual pleasure. It was time to get back to earth from heaven. Luckily, as the university wasn't far away from the hotel, we managed to make it on time; maybe there was some second or two to spare for a kiss we were able to plant on each other's cheeks and I whispered into Rebekah's ear that 'I'll see you later.' She nodded with a playful smile and went into the lecture hall.

I had to wait for Professor Schlesinger in his office as he was held up in a meeting at his superior's office.

He greeted me and offered me a cup of tea which I was grateful for as we had not had breakfast. Then he asked me if I had a relaxed evening. With a blushing smile, I replied, 'Yes thank you, it was a very pleasant one.'

He told me the reason for his late arrival. He had a briefing with his superior, the Head of the University, over the developing political situations in Europe itself.

I said, 'Professor Schlesinger—'

He interrupted me and asked me to call him Mihaly, in a more familiar manner in private, of course. I understood and thanked him for being so generous.

'Yes, this is the reason I am here in Lvov, I just wanted to brief you about the speedy political changes which are happening particularly in Hungary, but generally in Europe. I have been commissioned by the Hungarian Education Ministerium to travel to Munkács, Ungvár, basically all over the Transcarpathian region to prepare all the state schools and faith schools as well that a new curriculum will be implemented for the new educational year. Also, I have been appointed by the Chief Rabbi of Budapest, Rabbi Immanuel Lőw, that I have to brief the Jewish community over the forthcoming changes and prepare them for this event. As a member of the Jewish Community of Budapest, I hope my fellow Jews in the Transcarpathian region will listen to me and accept the advice which is coming from the Chief Rabbi of Budapest.'

'When can we expect this "change", Gabriel?'

'The negotiations are already at hand. Horthy and his ministers are negotiating over the takeover of the region. Since the Anschluss on the 12[th of] March this year, Nazi Germany is testing its influence and power over the future of the so-called Sudeten Land. Horthy and the Hungarian Ministers are already negotiating the takeover program. It looks like it will happen before the end of this year.

'Was this development that I've just explained to you the subject of your superior's briefing, Mihaly?'

'Yes, more or less. But he also emphasised that this will not affect us here in Lvov, as Lvov is in the Ukraine.'

'It is just proof and very sad to know the fact that history as always is repeating itself. Germany has never given up the colonialist attitude to rule the whole world. How many innocent people lost their lives in the last conflict? Thank God that I am at this ripe old age, and I don't have to get involved with idiots in the army killing people on the other side. Perhaps I would kill some of my friends in other university colleges on the opposite side's army. It is not a human attitude.'

'How long are you going to stay here in Lvov, Gabriel?'

'I am going to travel back to Munkács the day after tomorrow. I would like to visit some of the beauty spots of Lvov before I leave.'

'So, we could have dinner or supper together and catch up on the latest gossip of Budapest. I know you are very much involved with the theatre scene and with the movies' progress in Budapest. I know a very good Jewish kosher restaurant here in town next to the Golden Rose Synagogue. I know you would like the food there.'

'I have an engagement already for this evening, Mihály, with that young student of yours; she's called Rebekah.'

'Well, why don't you bring her along with you? She seems to be a very nice young lady. She would bring our age group down.' He smiled and gave me a wink.

I said, 'Yes, why not? I am pretty sure she would enjoy that.'

I was meeting Rebekah in the university at two in the afternoon. She was there promptly, and she rushed to me almost like she had wing s and just wanted to avoid any loss of time for us to be together.

Rebekah said, 'I just couldn't concentrate on the lecture. I was daydreaming about us and particularly about what happened between us last night. I am not a virgin any more and more than anything, I am in love with you, Gabriel. And it is you who is the one that has been chosen to be gifted with my innocence. I was always just trying to imagine what would it be like to lose it. Well, yesterday morning I thought it is just another day at the university. But when I saw you chatting to the Professor, I thought I am dreaming; I have just seen an angel.

'You stood out from the crowd of students. Your head was shining as if you had a halo around your head, I just couldn't take my eyes off you. And when Professor Schlesinger introduced me to you and you told me your name Gabriel, yes, it's truly one of God's main angels. The Lord has answered my prayer and surely sent me one who I will love for ever. And you have proven over last night that you are truly my angel.'

Rebekah linked my arm, and we were walking through the park just sitting down on a free bench and having a relaxed chat, maybe a kiss (like many other students do on the benches). Maybe the flowers and the birds singing in the park or just the month of April and May makes it so romantic for everybody.

I asked Rebekah if she had something to eat today. She said yes, she had a cheese sandwich and a cup of tea in the university canteen. She asked me why I was asking, and I told her that Professor Mihály Schlesinger had invited us for supper at his favourite kosher restaurant near the Golden Rossa Synagogue. 'He asked me to bring you along with me, jokingly, just to keep our ages down. No, truly he would like to meet you in a different environment, not just as a teacher and pupil.'

She said with a blush on her face, 'Why did you tell him about us? Of course, gentlemen don't discuss such things together.' She just looked at me and it was written all over on my face.

'Don't forget that he is a professor of psychology as well.'

She was relieved and said sorry, she didn't want to accuse me of gossiping.

'Yes, I would love to dine with Professor Schlesinger and with you. It would be my greatest honour.'

I said that he will come to the Grand Hotel to collect us in the lobby at six.

We still had some hours till the appointment with the professor. 'Let's go up to my room and have some time for us. I couldn't think anything else today but you and the perfume of your skin, the stroking of your hair and of course, the fire of your love.'

Rebekah's eyes sparkled and she whispered in my ear, 'Yes please. I want you to fly me up to heaven.'

We just couldn't control our emotions and our passions; the same energy was set free as we embraced each other on the bed and made love in such heat as if we hadn't made love for a long time, although it was only just a few hours ago.

As our energy finally completely drained out of our bodies as a result of our passionate lovemaking, I held her shoulder as she laid in my arm, we were resting on the bed in a pool of sweat and she asked me, 'Will it be always like this, Gabriel?'

I nodded and said, 'Yes my love, it will be as long as the Lord God may give us enough energy to do so.'

We went down to the lobby to meet Professor Schlesinger five minutes early. As the clock turned six, the Professor walked into the lobby and with a beaming smile greeted both of us. He made a special charming greeting to Rebekah as he kissed her hand. He said he had reserved a table for three of us for half-past six.

'So, let's go, we can take a tram or just walk.' I suggested that we take a taxi as arriving on time was important to me. There was a taxi in front of the hotel. Professor Schlesinger asked the driver to take us to the Golden Rosa Synagogue.

The head waiter greeted the Professor by his name and led us to our table, helping Rebekah with her chair. 'Is it the usual wine, Professor?'

'Yes, please,' he replied, turning to me to say he hoped I would approve of this local wine; even the Rabbi next door at Synagogue drank this one for the Sabbath. Rebekah ordered the pike with crushed walnuts and mashed potato; I ordered the stuffed gooseneck with steamed potato and boiled eggs. The Professor ordered half a roast duck stuffed with walnuts and raisins. He suggested to both Rebekah and me that we should call him just Mihaly in the restaurant.

He turned to Rebekah and said, 'I know very little of you, my dear, as I don't socialise with my students, where are you from?'

Rebekah opened up and felt so special that her well-respected professor was asking about her.

'I am from Munkács, I am not married,' as she briefly looked at me then continued, 'I believe the Lord God has created men and women for his image as the Tora tells us. I always wanted to study, educate myself as many of my contemporaries around the world. I believe knowledge is a gift from the Lord. I am really blessed as I have a very supporting, helpful father who is encouraging me to study and be more than he has ever been. I am also a member of the Union of Jewish Women, the Union of Ukrainian Women in Munkács, and of course, I am attending their meeting here in Lvov.'

'I am very impressed with your attitude and drive, Rebekah; you will make a great partner to your future very lucky husband.' Mihály briefly looked at me and smiled.

Our food was served and we started to enjoy the flavours, it was very delicious. Also, it was very impressive that all the diners in the restaurant knew Professor Schlesinger as many of them nodded to him or just said hello to him. We felt very proud to be in his company.

The whole evening was very pleasant. Professor Mihály kept recalling the years he had spent in Budapest, and the lecturing years in the Dohány uti Rabbi College, and 'I do remember you, Gabriel, you never stopped asking questions from me about everything and you've been busy organising something around theatres and art. Are you still writing reports in magazines and newspapers?'

'Yes Mihály, but not as much I would like to do. In the last few months, I have been involved with this governmental mission.'

'What is that, Gabriel?' both Rebekah and Mihaly asked at the same time.

'Well, basically, it is the new curriculum which will standardise the method and the language to be taught in all the state and faith schools in the whole Transcarpathian region. Of course, this will have no effect in Lvov.' Rebekah asked me why.

Mihaly knew the answer from our earlier conversation. I said to Rebekah that, 'I will tell you this on the way home to Munkács.'

I felt Rebekah had enjoyed the wine tonight and rather not discuss that subject in the restaurant under the influence of alcohol.

Professor Schlesinger asked for the bill, and he insisted on paying for it. I thanked him for the wonderful meal and evening. 'I haven't had such delicious cuisine for a very long time. Truly, I'll treasure this experience.'

Rebekah said the same praises and asked if she could kiss Mihaly on his cheek. The Professor encouraged her, of course. 'I have enjoyed your company all evening and have learned a lot about you tonight, particularly your commitments,' he said with approval. 'You will be a great partner and wife to a very lucky man, Rebekah,' as he winked in my direction.'

Rebekah blushed again and with a smile, she nodded, looked at me and said, 'Yes, I will.'

Professor in great spirits suggested why don't we go to the Sztuka Café. 'I don't think either of you've ever been in this great social and cultural gathering place for artists, musicians and poets. It is a mini New York Kávéház here in Lvov.'

'That is a great idea, Mihaly, I have heard of this place being mentioned by a pianist friend.'

Mihaly suggested, 'Let's walk to the coffeehouse; it isn't far just on Teatralna str. 10. It will do us good to work off the evening meal.'

Chapter 8

Rebekah, Professor and Gabriel at the Coffeehouse

It was a nice warm late April evening, the flickering gas streetlights were giving us some help preventing us from falling over on the uneven cobblestones. We took the backstreets which shortened the distance from the restaurant to the coffeehouse. Finding our way to the Sztuka Kavehouse, Rebekah got in-between us and linked her arms with Mihaly and I. It seemed the Professor had no objection Rebekah's gesture and to her girly attitude.

Finally, we arrived at the Sztuka coffeehouse at Teatralna str. 10, we could see it from the distance; wooden walls and large windows. It occupied the whole grand floor of this very attractive Art-Nuevo building. It looked as if we had arrived late to the coffee house as the "party" was in full swing.

The room was pretty full up with some very interesting people and some beautiful women all dressed in the latest Parisian or Viennese fashion. A poet had just read a poem in their native Ukrainian language. We just stood in the doorway waiting for the artist to finish his performance in the hazy smoke-filled room. The audience appreciated the performance warmly with great applause.

The waiter recognised the Professor, waved us in and squeezed us around a table which some couples had occupied already. They didn't mind our intrusion as one particular couple were students of Professor Schlesinger from the university. With beaming smiles, they greeted him and nodded in our direction.

Rebekah recognised one of the women from her feminist movement and greeted her with a kiss on her cheek.

She said, 'I have never seen you here before, Rebekah.'

Rebekah introduced me to her, 'This is my friend from Budapest, who is just visiting me here.'

I introduced myself saying, 'I am very pleased to meet you; my name is Gabriel.'

She said, 'Welcome to Lvov.' She introduced herself as Magda, and she turned to Rebekah and said, 'You have a very nice boyfriend.'

Rebekah blushed again as she said thank you. Professor Schlesinger did not need to be introduced as most people in Lvov knew him. The word of our presence quickly passed around to other tables and that I was from Budapest.

The waiter announced us and told everyone that our guest with Professor Schlesinger was from Budapest, it was a bit of an embarrassing situation as I didn't expect such a warm welcome here in this coffeehouse. It was even more embarrassing when Professor Schlesinger stood up and introduced me as a leading art critic and member of the New York Kávéház writer's guild. I had to stand up and say hello to the cheering crowd.

'I apologise for my poor knowledge of the Ukrainian language, so I hope you don't mind if I greet you in Yiddish or Slavic. I am really grateful to my ex-professor from Hungary, that he brought me here this evening with Rebekah, to this most perfect place where you can cultivate your culture in your own native language. This is laudable and I encourage you to be much braver and more creative to let the next generation know and appreciate what you are doing now which is for the benefit of the future generation. It is their cultural food and all of you here tonight whatever you are creating now will be called original and classic for tomorrow.

'This is what we are aiming and trying to achieve at the New York Kávéház, we don't need German or Austrian foreign art, music or poetic genre to dominate our theatres when we have so many great talents in Hungary. They are the ones who need to be supported by all of us because they are the gift for our future generation. And this is yours here in Lvov, and all over the Ukraine, but you have to be pure and honest. Remember the originals of the past; Nikolai Gogol, Alexander Pushkin, Andrey Rubljov, Leo Tolstoy, Pyotr Ilyich Tchaikovsky, Ivan Petrovych Kotliarevsky, Markiyan Shashkevych. I could name many other great ones, who are now listed as classics, they didn't know what they were doing at that time, but they will be remembered as today's classics.'

After my speech, I had great applause and some of the artists came to our table and shook my hand and welcomed me as one of the rebels who wanted to protect the purity of their native culture without any political influence of a different kind.

We received a lot of free drinks offered by the newly acquired friends. Luckily, we had heavy food in the restaurant this evening which was able to absorb the glasses of extra alcohol and the coffee which helped clear our heads.

After my speech as I sat down in my chair, Professor Schlesinger turned to me, tapped me on my shoulder and said, 'Well Gabriel, you haven't lost your touch. I can see that all my efforts to teach you psychology and proficiency were not in vain. You are still a rebel, and you will not allow people to categorise you into a box.'

Rebekah looked at me with a happy face, tears of joy were running down her beautiful cheeks. She grabbed hold of my hand and said, 'I am so, so proud of you, Gabriel. I have seen that shiny halo around your head again while you spoke to the crowd of people here. This is not just my opinion, this is what my friend Magda commented on you and your charismatic speech. She said to me, "Rebekah, you are a lucky girl. Truly he's been guided to you by the Lord God, he is the Lord's gift for you. I am so very pleased for you, my friend, you deserve him. You'll be a great couple and I wish you to have a lot of children. Just think what rebellious children you two will have and they will have a great drive to protect humanity."'

Rebekah felt she was walking on air. Two days ago, she had met the man of her dreams and fallen in love with him, and the very night she met him she gifted this man with the precious gift of her virginity. 'And what a night it was, as he had taken me to heaven and brought me back to earth. I swear I have heard the angels singing. Truly he is the one I have prayed for, since I have learned that I am the only girl from my gymnasium year who is still a virgin and not married. I am thanking the Almighty God for hearing my prayer and He has sent me this amazing man. The Lord has gifted me with a much greater gift than I asked from Him in my prayers.

'I feel his true love is in my soul, he's reached into the very deep inner self of me. And here, in a strange town Lvov, far away from my comfort zone of a little town of Munkács. I don't feel a stranger now anymore, like I felt before, as just another university student among the hundreds of others in the Lvov university.

'I have dined with and been entertained by the most respected University Professor of Lvov. I have been welcomed and entertained here, in the famous Sztuka Kávéház by the creme of artists, musicians and the most famous individuals of Lvov, because of these two men.'

I asked my friend from the feminist movement, Magda, 'I am just dreaming what is happening here now? Am I?'

'No Rebekah, you are here with us in the coffeehouse, and this is a special evening for all of us. Someone like Gabriel, who came here tonight and shared his vision with us and reminded us that we shouldn't be ashamed to be ourselves and be creative without being influenced by any ruling authority and be free from any political pressure from their regulations. This is what our organisation is working on so hard to force the male dominated world to accept the fact that we women are equal to men.'

I said to Rebekah and Magda, 'I agree as this fact has been demonstrated to all of us in the Book of Enoch, that the Lord God has created the first man and woman at the same time, called them Adam and Lilith.'

Magda said, 'It looks like Gabriel has read this book too. You are a lucky girl, Rebekah, there won't be any discord between you two in the future over equality or women's emancipation issues.'

It was half past one at night when I said goodbye to the Professor and to our newly acquired friends at the coffeehouse. Professor Schlesinger asked us to stay a bit longer, as the atmosphere was still on the highest of excitement.

Magda came in with her defence to protect our decision to leave the party, and with her comment 'it looks as she is the only one who understood the reason why we wanted to leave before the end of the party.' She looked at us and winked to Rebekah and said to just enjoy it.

Rebekah nodded and replied with a red face, 'Yes, Magda, I promise you that we will.'

I called for a taxi to get us back to the hotel, as quickly as we could, and being so late, I had to awaken the night porter as the main door was locked at midnight. I gave him a tip which he appreciated, and he gave me our room key.

We just couldn't wait to get into our room as Rebekah clung to my neck with a passion. Eventually, we got into our room, and I let Rebekah walk in front of me into the room, I noticed she started to undress herself, unbuttoned her blouse; suddenly, her well-shaped large breasts were visible through her satin slip. We did not switch the light on as the streetlight was filtered through the curtains and lit up the room, it was just right in that moment which made everything so much more romantic. Rebekah let her slip slide down over her body to the floor, but her hard nipples stopped it to fully slide off her body.

She said to me quietly, 'Now you have to help make it fall.'

I stepped closer to her, and I said, 'It is my privilege to unveil the statue of this beautiful goddess.' I freed her slip and touched her firm breasts and I started to stroke them gently.

She pulled me to the bed as we both lay down, she still held onto me. Her entire body was shaking in a sexual reaction to the foreplay, her breasts was moving so fast in the excitement as she was breathing, she whispered into my ear, 'Take me up, elevate me to high heaven again, my love.'

I climbed higher with our emotions when Rebekah was in ecstasy with one hand bracing me hard with her arm and with the other one she grabbed the pillow and gripped it so hard that I thought she would rip it open. As she flowed with the pleasure then the climax as we had it sometimes before I made love to her.

I felt in such pleasure then her body completely relaxed; I said, 'My love, we have now just become one body.'

After the joyful act, we remained together as one body, just relaxing from exhaustion. I stroked her face and her hair and said to her, 'Just let me stay in as we are now and start again when you ready.'

She said, 'I can feel you are ready again to make love.' She embraced my body again firmly and whispered into my ear, 'Yes please, do it all night long. I am ready, and I'm yours; you have taken me to heaven again. I've lost count of my journeys.'

This time I tried to make it more pleasurable for Rebekah and let her dictate the tempo and the level of pleasure. It was a great feeling to experience her tempo and her sexual pleasure the way she built it up to the crescendo to her full climax. By the time we stopped making love all night long in total exhaustion, we just laid on the bed in silence, just holding each other's hands. The dawn had just broken, and the early sunshine filtered through the curtains.

'How romantic is this moment, my love? I'll remember this night for the rest of my life.'

She didn't look at me, just sighed deeply, 'Yes, it will be our most remembered night that we have made love together.'

I said it was just like a scene out of Shakespeare's Romeo and Juliet; it wasn't the song of the Lark, who broke the silence of night with his song of the dawn, but the early tram wheels' distinctive noise from the front of the hotel.

Rebekah smiled and said, 'It is so peaceful and wonderful being with you. I feel so happy, safe and secure with you, Gabriel. You'll never leave me, will you?'

I just looked into her frightened beautiful eyes and assured her, 'Till death take us apart.' I just held her hand and kissed her on her lips. 'I would like to meet your father and ask him if I could take his daughter as my beloved wife.'

I felt warm tears from her eyes as they dripped down on my face; we laid close next to each other on the bed, and she bent over my body and looked in my eyes and the tears were running down on my face from her sparkling eyes, and with an emotional voice, she said, 'Thank you for that, I know my father will love you as his own son.'

'I apologise for my ignorance, love; I don't even know your father's name.'

'His name is Isaac Grósz.'

We both fell asleep in total exhaustion.

In the morning at the hotel restaurant, we were having breakfast together and I asked Rebekah when will she going back home to Munkács.

She said, 'I am planning to leave with the four o'clock afternoon international express train.'

I said, 'That is great. I will be going back to Munkács on this train too, so I'll be with you on the train journey as well. I have some very important meetings in Munkács for the next week, so I have to get ready with my presentations.

'Also, I have been invited to attend at the Hoif Complex Synagogue by the Rebbe Baruch Rabinowitz, for his Sabbath service. I have to be there on time in my best.'

'You know, Gabriel, in this case you will meet with my father on the Sabbath in the synagogue as he is the member there, at the Hoif Complex. That is the one where he'll be on Saturdays.

'I will be accompanying him and after the service I will introduce him to you. Praise be to the Almighty God of Israel. The way He has arranged everything in our life, we just don't have to worry for our future, if we trust and believe in Him, He is arranging everything in our life.'

'May I suggest to you, my dear Rebekah, please bring your belongings with you here to meet up in the hotel and we will go to the station together. I'll see you later, Rebekah, and this time, please take some notes from the lecture. I will test you about your subject on the train.'

We both smiled and she rushed off to the university with her books under her arm. I popped into the university to say goodbye to Professor Schlesinger for the fantastic evening we both had experienced the previous night.

I set off sightseeing, some of the most magnificent architectural buildings of Lvov. It is truly very diverse in styles and showing off its wealth from their successful business activities. As their cultural activities benefit from the financial wealth of the city. Like the opera house and ballet theatres and religious buildings. Like the Golden Synagogue which has been built in the early 1700s.

Different ethnic communities in multicultural Lvov had their own communication centres. Coffeehouses also became important hubs for intellectual life. Artists, painters, actors and filmmakers came together to share plans and dreams with people of different origin and status.

Lvov has many historical buildings, such as churches and palaces. The city's architecture shows the best of European styles from various periods. Walking through the streets of Lvov, you see baroque, renaissance and classic architecture.

The Secession was developed in Lvov due to the influence of Vienna and, in particular, of the Otto Wagner architectural school. Compared to such centres of the Secession (Art Nouveau) style as Paris.

Chapter 9

On the Train with Rebekah to Munkács and Home with Elisabeth

I was having a cup of tea at the hotel cafeteria, just relaxing; I should say that I was recovering from the previous evening's excitement at the Sztuka coffeehouse and the "steamy night of sheer pleasure"! I will never forget this first three days of meeting and falling in love with my future wife. Just being in her presence, holding her soft hand and listening to her voice as she told me stories of her involvement with the women's liberation organisation as she was trying hard to establishing that movement in Munkács too.

My Lord, I am missing her all ready. I never loved a woman in my life so much as I love her. I feel like a young schoolboy who is in the deepest love of his life! I suppose I am. I thought as walking on the streets of Lvov, absorbing the splendour of its building's magnificent architectures, I couldn't really think about anything else but Rebekah.

Just as I was trying to picture her face in my memory, there she came towards me on the hotel terrace with a beaming smile. My God, she looked beautiful. The gentle breeze blew her long black hair like a victorious flag. I stood up and embraced her, kissing her on her lips and told her, 'I was thinking about you wondering what you've been doing.' She just smiled. I said, 'We have to leave now to catch our train to go home.' She agreed and I picked up my small travelling case and we set off to the main railway station of Lvov.

She put her arm into mine and squeezed it so hard as if she was frightened of losing me.

Rebekah said, 'I have so much to tell you about what people at the university were talking about us, our last night appearance at the Sztuka coffeehouse.' Her eyes sparkled, and she was giggling over the stories of her fellow students at the university about us at the coffeehouse and our contribution to the evening discussions.

She was almost dancing with excitement like a little girl whose character and talent was suddenly discovered and recognised with merit.

I said with confidence, 'Yes, my darling, this is just the beginning of our partnership which will make people start to take notice of us together. Sorry Rebekah, may I call you Darling? I feel that little word is more personal to me, with much more meaning to me. There's nothing wrong with your lovely name, but this is us, you and me. My Darling.

'You know the meaning of Rebekah is captivating beauty. It comes from Hebrew Rivkah, it is perfectly fitting, well chosen by your parents. They must have loved each other so much to choose your name, you are a true captivating beauty. Rebekah is the name reserved only for the best women on earth.'

Rebekah stopped me on the road and turned to me, tears of joy and happiness in her eyes and said, 'Yes, please, my dearest angel. That is the meaning of your name and that's what you are to me. My Angel! As Gabriel is an angel who is sent by the Lord God.'

I said, 'You know that Rebbe Baruch Rabinowitz' wife is called Rivkah— Rebekah. Just like yours.'

She kissed me on my lips again in the street.

I said, 'Darling, we have to hurry to go to the station as our train will not wait for us.'

We got to the station, collected our train tickets from the ticket office, and the man behind the glass urged us to hurry as the train will leave on time from platform three. We got into our compartment and settled in our seat for a long journey to our home, to Munkács. The train slowly started, pulling out of the main station building. We just looked at each other with a relaxing smile, getting excited on the train ride like two juveniles. We were going home. Traveling in the train is always an uplifting and exciting experience when you do it in comfort. Travelling into the unknown with great expectations.

Rebekah sat next to me at the window; she put her lovely soft hand in mine, put her head on my shoulder and sang something very pretty. Unfortunately, I didn't know the song, so I just looked at her beauty and harvested her glowing joy with a smile. I kissed her on her head and asked her of the origin of this pretty lullaby.

She said, 'My mother used to sing this song when I was a little girl, this lullaby helped me sleep every night. My angel, I have to get some sleep because I will completely become a zombie. All that excitement of last night! I have struggled to be awake and concentrate on the lecturer. Sorry my love, I do need some rest.'

I said, 'Of course, I understand, you just keep your head on my shoulder and have a rest. I will guard your dreams. I love you, my darling.'

The ticket conductor woke us up from our sleep, announcing our approach to the main railway station of Munkács. I woke up to the announcement and looked at my darling Rebekah; she was still sleeping on my shoulder, her beautiful pitch-black hair covering her face. She must have dreamed of angels, or just reliving the past few days' excitement as her lips were smiling like a little girl. I combed her hair away from her face with my fingers, kissed her on her head and said, 'My Darling Rebekah, we are approaching Munkacs station, let's get ready to depart from this train otherwise we will end up in Budapest.'

She opened her sleepy eyes and looked at me and said, 'I can't believe I have to get down back to earth, into reality. I have to leave you and I have to sleep alone tonight, without being in the comfort of your protecting arms. I just can't wait to do it again.'

The train stopped and I helped her step down the coach steps. I took her luggage and started walking to the station exit to catch a taxi to get us home as it was just after 8 o'clock in the evening. She was clutching my arms still with a sleepy eye. Got in the first available taxi, gave Rebekah's home address first then my address. Rebekah lived just off Corso, in a nice apartment block. She held my arm so hard as if she would never see me again.

I said, 'Darling, I will see you tomorrow at the synagogue.'

She said, 'I know that, but I have to sleep on my own, without you and the only thing I can cuddle up with is my pillow. And I will miss your loving body.'

We kissed discretely in front of her house then I waited for her to open the main door and just one more kiss she blew to me. I got back into the taxi and gave Elisabeth's address as the end of our journey.

It was 20 minutes past eight, I knocked on the front door and Elisabeth let me in. The two dogs rushed to the door too, wagging their tails as they recognised me by my voice as I greeted her.

Elisabeth welcomed me home and I noticed she had waited for me as she had set the table for me. She said to me, 'You must have a nice soup. You must be hungry.' She had made me my favourite clear chicken soup. She just looked at me from the other end of the table and said, 'I am not going to join you as I had a meal before you arrived.'

Elisabeth looked at me while I had my late supper. I felt her eyes were studying me. When I finished my supper, she asked me, 'Are you alright, Gabriel? Everything went well as you planned it?'

I just looked at her with an innocent look like little boys do something and now it all has come alight. 'What do you mean, Elisabeth?' I asked. I think my face was read while I responded to her question. As a big sister would do, she asked it straight to the point.

'Have you met someone in Lvov?'

I felt my face was on fire, at least I must have looked like a beetroot. With some hesitation, I asked her, 'How did you know that?'

She said, 'You are a different person now since you have moved here. You look as someone is daydreaming because he is in love.'

I started to be worried, used to be I managed to hide my feeling better. I said sheepishly, 'Yes, I have met a young woman in the university of Lvov.'

She said, 'I thought that's the case as it's written all over your face. Is she local to Lvov?'

I said, 'No, she is from Munkács.'

'What is her name, Gabriel?'

'Her name is Rebekah Grósz.'

She sighed and a smile came on her face and she said, relieved, 'Good. I know her and her family. Very nice family, hardworking honest people. God-fearing, respectable well-established old local family. I think you have chosen well for a wife, Gabriel, without the help of the Shadchan (matchmaker).'

Elisabeth laughed and said, 'Well, you both saved some money on the matchmaker.'

I said, 'You know, Elisabeth, I am not a young man; I have had partners before, but I have never felt anything like this. I have fallen in deep love with Rebekah without being introduced to each other.

'We just simply looked at each other and fell in love. I just wanted to look at her all the time while we were in the lecturing hall, she looked at me all the time. I don't think we listened anything of the lecturer's presentation. I just felt we were communicating with an electric wave as we constantly looked at each other.'

Elisabeth sighed again and said, 'I am very pleased for you, Gabriel, you have been sent here by the Holy Spirit to find you future wife. One thing is true; there are no coincidences in the world, this match has already been arranged by the Lord. Well, you will meet her father tomorrow at the synagogue.'

I said, 'Yes, she has promised that she is going to introduce me to her father after the Sabbath Service.'

'My goodness, you two are moving really fast. I know it is too early to ask if you two will move back to Budapest or you may settle here in Munkács? If you decide to stay here in Munkács then just to let you know, my next-door house is for sale. It's been on the market for some time. I think it will be a good starting property for you. And I would have a good neighbour. Hm, my little adopted brother.'

'Well, I haven't really thought of that, Elisabeth, let's see how tomorrow will be thought out. Dear Elisabeth, please forgive me but I am going to bed as I have to get up early in the morning to get ready go for the synagogue.'

'Of course, Gabriel, I understand. I will prepare some cleaning things for you in the morning.'

I stood up and said, 'You know, Elisabeth, you are like a big sister to me.' I walked to her and kissed her on her cheek and said goodnight.

She had some tears in her eyes and said, 'You know, Gabriel, since my husband died, no one did this to me. And now here you are, and you have brought a family atmosphere here to this house again; yes, we are like good brother and sister. This is giving me a new energy and meaning to look after someone.' She smiled and said, 'Goodnight, my little brother.'

The name Rebekah is a girl's name of Hebrew origin, meaning "servant of God". It derives from the Hebrew name Rivkah. The biblical Rebekah was the wife of Isaac and the mother of Esau and Jacob.

The name of Gabriel means "devoted to God", "a hero of God" or "God is my strength" in Hebrew. Gabriel is one of the main seven angels who stand before God. In the Bible, Gabriel is the angel who tells Mary she will bear the son of God, Yeshua Messiah.

Chapter 10

Sabbath Shalom

I managed to wake up at six in the morning (it wasn't difficult to ignore the rooster's crowing) to get ready for the big day at the Synagogue and the meeting with Rebekah's father. I tied my bowtie as I always did when going to important places or meetings, got my fedora hat and I was ready. Elisabeth looked at me and said, 'You look just like my husband used to look.' I kissed her on the cheek and stepped out for this special day in my life.

I walked along from the house of Elisabeth, properly dressed for the service, where I met a couple of Jewish men as we walked along towards the synagogue. They greeted me with the Sabbath Shalom, I returned their greeting with a Sabbath Shalom. They introduced themselves and said that they hadn't seen me there before. I said, 'Of course, as I've just moved into Munkács.' They welcomed me and updated me with all the local gossip you should know.

In Munkács, the Sabbath was holy... everything was shut and all who had walked along the quiet streets of the town in the morning were on their way to the synagogue. The scene was heart-warming—men wearing streimels [Hasidic fur hats] and talleisim [prayer shawls] on their shoulders, softly singing different melodies. The women looked splendid in their elegant dresses and the children were adorned in Sabbath clothing. The atmosphere was serene and festive, and the aroma of cooked fish and cholent wafted out of the houses.

It was a good experience and a learning to be careful about everything that I did or said to strangers and also to officials everywhere in the region. I had been sent to Munkács on a consignment with a very important task.

We arrived at the synagogue very quickly as these two kept me company. When I got to the synagogue door, I guessed a helper welcomed me and noticed that I didn't have a Tallit (prayer shawls and Siddur), he offered me one for the service. I thanked him and stood in the back of the room as I always did in the past (the sinner's place).

I was looking for Rebekah and her father; if I would be able to see her just for a minute and tried to scan people's faces among the congregation if I could recognise him through Rebekah's facial identity. It was not easy when all the people were facing forward.

But I had no luck in spotting her in the gallery either.

The service started with Rabbi Baruch Yehoshua Yerachmiel Rabinowitz entering the room and welcoming us. He started the service, the usual welcoming, with Birchot Hashachar, followed it with a Yotzer (praising God for creation and praising God for his revelation).

He read the Shema, passages from Deuteronomy 6:4-9, Deuteronomy 11:13-21, and Numbers 15:37-41. After the recital of the Shema, the service concluded with a third blessing, Emet V'Yatziv, praising God for redemption.

The Sabbath Amidah (which contains petitions for individual's need). Then the Torah scroll was removed from the ark and the weekly Torah portion was read. After the Torah reading came the Haftarah, with the weekly reading of Torah portion. Once all readings were completed, the Torah scroll was returned to the ark. Then he said the Aleinu prayer and we all said Amen, and he concluded the Sabbath Services.

Surprisingly, the whole Sabbath Service lasted only fifty minutes.

At the end of the Sabbath Service, I was approached by a man who introduced himself as Ishmael Cohen. Mr Cohen asked me that Rabbi Baruch would like to invite me to his office in the back of the synagogue.

I thanked him and I asked him to lead me to the Rabbi's office as I had never been there before.

Mr Cohen asked me to call him Ismael. I said thank you. He said, 'May I call you Gabriel please?'

I said, 'Of course', then we shook hands and I followed him to the Rabbi's office.

I walked into his office and with a big smile he welcomed me and offered me a chair to sit. He said, 'I have invited some people for you to meet later. But I have heard some interesting news about you.'

I felt, *My Lord, what can that be*!

He sensed that he had embarrassed me with his comment and said, 'Sorry, it is not a bad thing at all. Right opposite of that. I think it is quite a positive, an encouraging one.'

He led me into a large room almost like a theatre with a good-sized stage. It was full of people chatting away. Rabbi Baruch with a lifted voice asked the congregation for some attention and he said, 'I would like to introduce our friend from Budapest, who has been sent by the Chief Rabbi of Budapest, Rabbi Immanuel Lőw. Please welcome Gabriel Bartos. Some of you are going to attend his presentation on Monday, so here is Gabriel for you.'

I thanked Rabbi Baruch for the warm introduction as he welcomed me in his Synagogue. Many people came to me, introducing themselves and letting me know that they will attend my presentation on Monday. Some of them had queries asking me what my presentation will be about, but I suggested to find out on Monday.

At the end, a slightly grey-haired sophisticated gentleman walked to me and introduced himself, 'My name is Isaack Grósz.' He pushed his hand, offering a handshake which I automatically welcomed, and we shook hands and said Sabbath Shalom.

I didn't know what happened to me, but I thought it was only Rebekah's father and I in the room alone. I was completely frozen. It was unusual that I couldn't find a word. We were still shaking our hands when I finally managed to say, 'You must be Rebekah's father.'

He said, 'Yes, I am, and I would like to welcome you to Munkács, Gabriel. Also, I would like to invite you for an afternoon tea or coffee this afternoon.'

I said, 'I am honoured, Mr Grósz.'

He said, 'Please call me Isaack.'

I asked him what time he would like me to arrive. He said about four. I said, 'Thank you. I will be there promptly.'

'I asked him, 'Rebekah must have told you of our meeting in Lvov.'

'Told me? She has never stopped talking about you, Gabriel. There must have been something very powerful between you two which I would like to find out. Don't worry, it is not negative, quite opposite.'

'Sir, sorry Isaack, I look forward to coming and sharing my thoughts with both of you.'

On my way home from the synagogue, I stopped at a florist on the corner of Corso and ordered a nice big bunch of flowers nicely arranged. Also, I got a box of Rebekah's favourite bonbons. I got home to Elisabeth where the table was set for a lunch for two this time.

Elisabeth said, Welcome home, Gabriel. How was the service? Have you met Rebekah's father?'

I told her that the service went on pretty well, everybody welcomed me, and I told her about my meeting with Rebekah's father Isaack. And? He invited me to their house for a tea at four.

Elisabeth was pleased as things were developing for my future.

'But now sit down to have dinner with me as "families" do together.' She served breaded chicken legs with chips and sauerkraut and a glass of dry white wine. I thought what she was doing was more than my expectations and I had to appreciate her effort in some way.

During the dinner, she told me that her brothers were killed in the Great War, and she had no relatives left. After she got married to her husband, they were building up his butchery business and saving up to pay for the house; he died before they could have a child. It was a very sad story to hear.

I thought, *I will make her life a bit less dwelling on the past and tried to encourage her to be more optimistic of her future.*

She sighed and said, 'Yes, we will see it as it develops. But you have to hurry up to get ready to meet your future father-in-law.'

I put one of the bottles of Tokay Szamorodni wines in my briefcase that I brought with me from Budapest and went to the florist where I ordered the flowers and the Bonbon chocolates from earlier on. Also, I ordered a bunch of flowers and asked her to deliver it to Elisabeth this afternoon. I thanked the florist for her good services. I know that flowers would make Elisabeth happy.

I walked to Rebekah's house on the Corso. It was five minutes to four in the afternoon and I pressed the bell under the name of Grósz. A very nice lady in her late fifties opened the door. I introduced myself and she said, 'I am Rita, the housekeeper.' She walked me up the stairs to the first floor and led me into the front room then to the lounge. As we walked into the lounge, there was Rebekah's father Isaack.

He greeted me with a warm handshake and offered me a chair to sit on.

I was very impressed with the style of the deco and the furniture; nice expensive paintings on the wall; one of them made me pause and look at a woman's portrait that strikingly reminded me of Rebekah. I guessed it was her mother's portrait. I put the flowers and chocolate on the side table and sat on the opposite side of the coffee table to Isaack. He started the conversation straight to the point.

'Look Gabriel, I don't know if Rebekah told you the sad story of the loss of her mother, my wife Rivkah. I have brought her up with the help of her nanny Rita whom you've just met. We are a very close family where we, Rebekah and I, have a strong bond together; we are both very supportive of each other as father and daughter. Rebekah from the age of eighteen was working in my business as an accountant. We went on a holiday or out for an evening, we have done all these things together.

'I guess that is the reason she never had a boyfriend or never sought a husband. As she is becoming twenty-three years old in July, I thought she has become too old to make a relationship or there was no one who would marry anyone at her age, so she has dedicated her life to looking after me. And now here you are, and I feel as a daunting father seeing that you are taking my little girl away from me.

'Last evening after you brought her back from Lvov, I have seen her as a changed person, she was singing to herself and looked very happy. I asked her what made this change in her life as she went to the university in Lvov, as she did it all the other times and now, she came home as someone who is walking in the clouds. She told me that she has met you and she has fallen very much in love with you. She just couldn't stop talking about you. I hope you don't judge me with jealousy but as her father, I really want to know what happened, what is the present situation.

'So, I ask you, Gabriel, please tell me what is happening between you and Rebekah.'

'I do understand your fear and your concern, Isaack, this whole situation has blown apart your accustomed life with your daughter. I have never been married before, neither do I have any children, so I don't really understand what you are experiencing in this circumstance.

'I have been sent here into the Transcarpathian region with a task or a mission to deliver the task they have commissioned me with. When I arrived here to do the work and when I have finished with that, I will going back to Budapest. I haven't had anything else in my mind to look for a relationship, neither a casual one nor a serious one at all. I am now over thirty-one years old. My priority in life was to educate myself, get a diploma and get a good job which would set my existential position. As the years have gone by, I felt I have become too old to get married and have a family as all of my contemporaries have happily settled.

'I became involved with supporting and promoting Hungarian cultural establishments like theatres and the movie industry and become an art journalist, art critic. My reputation as a scholar, someone like me who is able to speak in several languages, I was in demand to do translations of documents and literature. I was doing some work for the Budapest Main Synagogue when I was approached to do this important job for the benefit for all of us.

'This job has become a task, conjunctions with the assignment of the Hungarian Foreign and Education Ministry and as me being Jewish, and by the Main Synagogue of Budapest. I went to see my ex professor from Budapest, at his new post in the Lvov University. It was here where I noticed an angel who shined, stood out of the crowd of people and that was your daughter Rebekah. I asked Professor Schlesinger to introduce us to each other and we both in that moment of shaking hands just fell in love.

'I have never felt such a strong and pure emotion before that I felt at that meeting with Rebekah. There is not an explanation to our reaction which went through our bodies at that moment but that powerful energy which suddenly discharged from both of us was extraordinary. I just can't make such an excuse or say this is destiny, I can't offer you any reasoning for this situation, the fact is that I have deeply fallen in love with your daughter, Isaack. So here I am now in front of you and respectfully asking for your blessing for us. I would like to marry your daughter Rebekah.'

Isaack was stunned at my direct straight approach asking to marry his daughter. He said after my request, 'You know, Gabriel, for years I have waited for someone to make this request and deep down, I hoped it will never happen. So here I am and not ready for it. Let's have Rebekah here with us. I would like to hear from her what is her response to your request.'

Isaack stood up and walked to the dining room and called her into the room. 'Come in and join us,' and asked her if she heard our conversation through the door. She nodded as she couldn't speak, she was full of emotion and again her tears were running down her cheeks. Isaack asked her, 'What do you say to his request, Rebekah?'

She ran to her father and embraced him and said, 'Yes, Papa please, I am very much in love with Gabriel and would like to marry him.' Then she walked to me, reached out for my hands, she grabbed both of them and then turned to

Isaack, and pleaded with him, 'Please Papa, I love him with all my heart, I am happy with him. Please give your blessing to our marriage.' I kissed her hand and turned to Isaack.

'In the presence of the Eternal One, The Lord God of Israel, I promise you that I will love and protect your daughter Rebekah. I will provide her with comfort, care and wealth with all my strength and with my soul.'

Isaack sat down in his chair, looked at his daughter with a confused eye. He didn't know what to say or do after this event in front of him.

Isaack suggested after this emotional state, he would need something much stronger than a tea or a coffee. As we all sat around the coffee table, I picked up the flowers and Rebekah's favourite chocolate bonbons from the side table and presented them to Rebekah. She looked at me with her sparkling eyes still full of tears. She thanked me for the gifts then looked at her father who smiled at her and approved the gifts.

She looked strikingly beautiful in her long dark skirt and a white lace blouse which was buttoned up to her neck. I presented Isaack with the bottle of Tokay wine and said, 'I hope you will enjoy it as you can see on the label, it is a limited-edition reserve wine.'

We settled down to a szilva pálinka, a plum palinka, and Isaack toasted it L'Chaim, drink it for life. L'Chaim.

Isaack just looked at us and smiled and with a sigh, he said, 'I have dreaded this moment in my life, but I remember this kind of experience. I went through the same emotion when I asked your grandfather to let your mother Rivkah marry me. Just a minor note, we spell her name the Yiddish way, as Rebekah.'

I thanked Isaac for this correction, I will remember this.

'I don't think I have to think any longer on your request, Gabriel, I am giving my blessing to your marriage.' Rebekah jumped up and rushed to Isaack, hugged him and kissed him for his blessing.

I stood up and said, 'Sir, I respect you for your decision. I know it is very hard for you as you have explained it to me earlier on. I promise you that my love for your daughter Rebekah will never die. I will love her and will be her protecting husband.'

He stood up from his chair, shook my hand and embraced me and said, 'I can feel the purity of love in between you two. I welcome you to be my son.'

Isaack invited Rita into the room and told her the news about our future engagement. She burst into tears as she hugged and kissed Rebekah and said, 'I dreaded this moment, my dear Rebekah. It will be hard to accept that you are sharing your love with someone else, not just with me. May thy Lord bless both of you with all his gifts of life.'

Isaack said, 'Why don't you stay for a supper with us, Gabriel, so we can discuss the engagement arrangements between the three of us.'

Rebekah suggested, 'What about having the engagement celebration on my birthday on the fourteenth of July? We still have enough time to arrange everything necessary for the engagement ceremony.'

Isaac looked at me. I said, 'Yes, that is a good time for me so I can complete my mission to the region of Transcarpathia.'

Isaack looked at me with questioning eyes and said, 'Is it a very important change which is going to affect us, our system? Can you tell me all about it or it is secretive?'

I said, 'Well, it isn't secretive to the Jewish community, but I can tell you about all the changes which will affect everybody here in Munkács and in the surrounding areas. Actually, I am going to do my presentation to an invited guest list at the synagogue on Monday morning, would you like to come along with me?'

Rebekah's voice was filtering through the door from the kitchen where she was helping Rita in the supper's preparation. She sounded so bubbly and happy.

Isaack and I were discussing the present development in Germany and in Russia as well. I said, 'Hitler and Stalin have made a pact to divide Poland, basically the Sudeten Land area, included Bohemia and Moravia. Within a few weeks, Hungary will take over the administration of the of the whole Transcarpathian Area.'

'Is it that much in progress, Gabriel?'

'Yes, it is a matter of weeks. This is the reason I am here. I have been commissioned to do the preparation for the transition of the new Hungarian administration, mainly for the changes of the education standard and its direction. The Hungarian language will be the official one for teaching and administration. I have been sent here in advance to get all local authority for the changes. I have been chosen as Jewish and someone who speak several languages by the Jewish Joint Distribution Committee (JDC) and the OMZSA (Orszagos Magyar Zsido Segito Akcio) to get the messages first to the Jewish Communities in the Transcarpathian region.

'But please, Isaack, let's talk about of our future now, Rebekah and I have a beautiful future which we are looking forward to. There is far too much aggression going on; if there are any changes that you should know, I will update you immediately.'

'It looks like the supper has been prepared so let's sit down and have our hopefully first of many suppers as a family.'

My Darling Rebekah's eyes were sparkling from joy through the evening at the very day of her engagement. The meal was exquisite. I just couldn't take my eyes off her all through the supper. I just wished if I could kiss her again, but I had to be patient. Isaack opened a very classy champagne to celebrate his beloved daughter's engagement news.

The dinner and conversations at the table was flowing so freely, running late in the night.

I thanked Isaack that he was so understanding and accepted my marriage proposal to his daughter Rebekah. And his warm welcoming into his close family. Rebekah volunteered to walk me to the main door and let me out. Isaack shook my hand and said, 'I will come to your presentation on Monday. So, I'll see you there. In some way I am very proud of you what you are doing for us Jewish people.'

I said to him, 'Thank you very much for the praise, Isaack, but I am Jewish origin too, so I am doing this for the benefit of all of us.'

Rebekah got her arms around me, and she closed her apartment door and started kissing me with such passion as if we hadn't kissed for a very long time; she said, 'Gabriel, I am feeling you have satisfied me again, I am wet all over.'

I said, 'I came very close to that too.' I told her how pleased I was to learn that her father gave his blessing for us to marry. 'He is a very good man and I do respect him for everything he achieved in his life without his beloved wife to support him. And he brought you up in such dignity.'

After we parted with a long kiss goodbye, she said, 'I hope I will see you very soon. I just don't feel that I should go back to the university so far away from you. That place will be empty without you.'

I said, 'I have a job to do here in Munkács and go to visit all the places in the region and to do the work I have been sent over here for.'

'Just one more kiss from my angel and I will let you go. I love you, Gabriel, now even more as you achieved to secure my hand from my father. Now in only a matter of time, we will be together forEVER!'

'Goodnight, my darling, sleep well and dream about our future. Take care of yourself in Lvov.'

'I will, my angel, I will. Goodnight.' She blew me a kiss as she closed her front door.

I just realised that I was singing all the way home, to Elisabeth's house. That had never happened with me before. Anyway, I just had to accept things when you are in love. I opened the gate and the two dogs recognised me and they were running towards me with tails wagging.

I got into the kitchen. Elisabeth was still up and she asked me if I was hungry. I said, 'No thanks, Elisabeth, I had a meal already, I was the guest at my future father-in-law's house.'

This comment made Elisabeth wake up and start asking many questions.

Politely, I replied, 'I will tell you all about it tomorrow as I won't be going anywhere.'

She pointed to a bunch of lovely flowers in a vase on the table and said, 'I haven't had flowers delivered to me for a very long time, Gabriel. You are an angel. Thank you.'

I said goodnight to her and went into my comfortable bed alone without my darling Rebekah.

Elisabeth said, 'I can't wait till tomorrow. But it looks I have to. Goodnight Gabriel.'

Chapter 11

Presentation to the Jewish Community of Munkács

Getting up early at Elisabeth's house was easy, you didn't need an alarm clock when you had Elisabeth's rooster. You can set your clock to his timing in the morning, it's perfect. Not for the day when you had just proposed a marriage to the father of your sweetheart and you were still dreaming of the exciting future and planning the number of children we were going to raise. And that was it; the horrible little thing just broke halfway through my dream of having one child, a boy.

I had to get ready with my speech for tomorrow, Monday. Later on, today I was having a meeting with my helpers, Viktoria and Andre, to catch up with the instructions I had left with them and their arrangements for my presentation in other towns in the Transcarpathian region while I was away in Lvov.

After getting ready for the day, I walked into the kitchen and found Elisabeth sitting at the table and looking at the vase full of lovely flowers. She had set the table for two people already, and she stood up as I walked into the kitchen. 'Please come to me,' she said and gave me a hug and a kiss on my cheek. 'Are you going to spoil me with things like these beautiful flowers? I feel really good and happy. Thank you for it.'

I said, 'You are giving me a much more comfortable position than what I would expect from my landlord. I have to appreciate all these extras. Maybe I should offer you more rent money for all these extras.'

She said yes, it would be welcome as her only income was from the town market selling agricultural products.

I suggested to double the rent and I hoped that would cover all the extras like breakfast, laundry, etc.

She said, 'Thank you, my little brother.' We both had breakfast and a very nice cup of tea. After we finished breakfast, Elisabeth looked at me with an eagle eye and said, 'You have spoiled my night's sleep as you wouldn't tell me the full story of what happened at Rebekah's house. So now we will not be getting up from the table until you tell me all that. What did Rebekah's father say in reply to your request to marry his daughter, will it be a wedding, Gabriel?'

I said, 'Yes, hopefully as he accepted my request with a heavy heart. I felt it was painful for him to realise that this would happen to his beloved daughter when she was at that age and as him and Rebekah had been resigned to the fact that she will end up looking after her father and remaining celibate for life.'

A sincere tear of joy and happiness burst out of Elisabeth, and she said, 'I knew that you would be going home to Budapest with a wife. I am so very pleased for you both. This house next door to me is still up for sale. You never know what is in the future.' Elisabeth said, 'I can arrange for you to have a look at it. No pressure, Gabriel, but I can see some benefits to you in just viewing it.'

'Just please slow down, Elisabeth. I am here only on a business commission from Hungary. Who knows how long this commission will last?'

She accepted my point and left it to be discussed at some other time. She said someone was knocking on the gate, she looked at me and asked, 'Are you expecting someone?

I said, 'Yes, my helpers from the town hall.' She went to the gate to let them in.

When Viktoria and Andre turned up with their information, Elisabeth said, 'I will leave you to get on with your work as I have to get on with my regular work around the farm.'

One thing I noticed that some kind of close bond had developed between these two youngsters, it was a refreshing observation. I think I was responsible for this as they had been working on my project, maybe that brought them close together. Just like Rebekah and I, it must be some kind of powerful energy that drifted in with the spring breeze.

I asked them if everything was going on well with the meetings. I requested them to organise with all the local authorities in the Region. Andre reported first and told me that they had a confirmation from all the local authorities whom Andre had approached. He said that all of them wanted to know what it was about.

I thanked him and turned to Victoria to report back on the businesses who would support us with the printing of stationery and more complicated things like books and mainly what to expect in cost.

Viktoria had a meeting with Munkács Town Educational committee and asked for a meeting with the three of us sometime this coming week. 'I will be coming into the Town Hall on Tuesday the 31st of May and will draw up the plan for visiting all the major towns' local authorities in Transcarpathian Region. Maybe you two can come with me to do the administration and it will be very helpful for me as you know the local customs and traditions.'

After the meeting with Viktoria and Andre, I went out for a walk along the River Latornya, just to get some fresh air and a bit of peace to get my thoughts together from everything, all of the excitement I had gone through in the past few weeks since my arrival to Munkács from Budapest.

I just wondered what was happening at home in Budapest, and particularly that of the New Jewish Law which was proposed at the time I arrived here in Munkács. I didn't have access to Hungarian newspapers, and it made the situation more worrying for me and my future. And for my protection as a Jew in Hungary.

The walk did me good, it captured the beauty of this countryside in the beginning of summer. The river walk was full of people, young, old, all ages. Absorbing the lovely landscape, the flowers and freshness of the clean air drifting down from the Carpathian hills.

The next day, on Monday morning, I walked to the Hoif Complex Synagogue of Munkács, where I was going to giving my "unofficial" presentation with all the information I received from the Chief Rabbi Immanuel Löw, with regards to the forthcoming developments in Transcarpathian Regions.

I was welcomed by Rabbi Baruch Rabinowitz on my arrival and invited into his office. He said, 'I have a mix of guests from all kinds of business and education backgrounds.'

I thanked him for his effort in organising this important and confidential meeting. We walked to the main hall (where I had met Rebekah's father on Saturday) into the room which was full of people. The Rabbi and I went to the top table on the stage, and he introduced me to the audience. I stood up, looked around and I noticed Isaack and my new friend Dr Sándor Fried in the crowd. They had managed to come along to this meeting.

I welcomed the attendant representatives of various organisation and others as individuals. I nodded towards Isaack and Sándor and got all my paperwork out of my case. I said, 'Please note this meeting and my presentation materials are very confidential and important to all of us with Jewish origins. I have received this information from the Chief Rabbi of Budapest, Dr Immanuel Lőw.

'As some of you know, the following act of the Anschluss some weeks ago brought political and social influence in Central Europe, as power has shifted from a moderate position to a more radical and aggressive situation. Germany becoming a more dominant power, are ready to expand their territory over other sovereign communities and countries to dominate their attitude for land grabbing. Their foreign policy and its minister Ribbentrop are collecting supporters for their Greater Germany plans.

'Russia has put the original Molotov-Ribbentrop pact and its secret protocol as a very important move for both countries. Alongside, Moscow is ready to accept the German invitation and the 1938 Munich agreement plan of the occupation of Czechoslovakia. To the approval of this agreement, the Germans are bribing some of the neighbouring countries governments, to sign up to their illegal sinister plan. I repeat myself, *please note this information is highly confidential.*

'The Hungarian Government leadership of Horthy has been already convinced and is ready to agree to this treaty and the reward will be, the annexation of the Transcarpathian Region back to Hungarian administration.

'I am not sure of the timetable, I haven't received any authority to comment on this, and mainly NOT to speculate on the final conclusions on this event. This means that the Hungarian administration and control will be coming directly from Hungary. All the official, educational and business languages for the future will be conducted in Hungarian.

'Please try not to draw conclusions or panic over this change; it may well be beneficial for our community, and it may be that a more watered-down version will be getting here as we are so far away from the main administration centre of Budapest.

'So please brush up on your Hungarian. We will still continuously be supporting you with Jewish Joint Distribution Committee (JDC) and the OMZSA (Országos Magyar Zsidó Segitő Akció) and National Hungarian Jewish Helping Committee. Thank you to for your attention and this concludes my presentation. If anybody would like to raise a point or ask a question, please feel free to do so.'

One gentleman asked me about the New Jewish Law.

I handed the full paragraph of this proposal to everybody in the audience. I added that this was influenced by the right-wing organisations lobbying the Members of Parliament, encouraged by the German influence in Central Europe.

I thanked Rabbi Baruch Rabinowitz for his help in making this presentation attended so well. Also, I presented him with my shopping list, particularly for printers specialised in printing books and also others for leaflets, stationery, etc. I explained the main reason I was concentrating on printing issues to Rabbi Baruch:

It can be said about each of the publishers that (practically) they are financed and the support is coming from Hungary. Only governmental publishers are state supported, but this is too little for regular book publishing, and these, too, bring out most of their Hungarian volumes by getting support from Hungary. Transcarpathian Hungarian book publishing is virtually sustained by the Ministry of Culture and Education of Hungary that annually conducts a competition for Hungarian book publishing for Hungarians.

Rabbi Baruch Rabinowitz said he understood and he had some names already in mind for these works.

After the presentation, I was talking to some members of the audience and trying to calm them down from being so overexcited and worried for their future.

At the end, Rabbi Baruch invited me and Isaack to his office. This was the first opportunity to greet Isaack. I shook his hand and we both smiled each other.

Rabbi Baruch Rabinowitz offered us some tea and he started the conversation. He said, 'I've just been talking to Isaack, and he told me a great news that you have proposed to marry his daughter Rebekah. Does it mean that you might end up settling here in Munkács?'

'Yes, Rabbi Baruch, I had the pleasure of asking Isaack for his blessing for my request to respectfully marry his daughter Rebekah. And to my delight, Isaack gave his special blessing for our marriage. For your second question, I can't just answer to you with yes or no.

'This proposal has only happened on the last Sabbath afternoon. There are many things that we have to discuss over the marriage arrangements.'

Isaack suggested that the engagement and the wedding should be here in Munkács, and of course, he will stand the costs of both ceremonies. We both shook hands on the marriage deal in front of the Rabbi, who put his hand on top of our handshake and gave his prayer of blessing on our agreement. At the end, with a beaming smile, he said Mazel tov!

'You have saved a lot of hassle for our Shadchan (Matchmaker).' Then he got out a bottle of Kosher Plum pálinka from his office desk and poured it into three glasses and lifted up the glass and said, 'L'chaim!' We both replied L'chaim and drank it. Rabbi Baruch shook Isaack and my hands and repeated, Mazel Tov.

As Isaack and I were walking out of the Rabbi's office, Isaack put his am in mine and said, 'Please come for a supper sometime this week to celebrate Sabbath with us, and we will arrange the engagement and the wedding details. Gabriel, you have made my beloved daughter so very happy, and I am so grateful for you coming into our life, into our family. I can see your true quality and importance and I am very proud of you for it.'

Dr Sándor Fried joined us and asked, as a typical solicitor does, he was sensing something unusual in our behaviour. 'I didn't know that you two know each other in such a personal way.'

Isaack replied, 'I would like to introduce you to my future son-in-law.'

Sándor was speechless for a second then he looked at us with his beaming smile and said, 'Mazel tov! We have to celebrate this, Isaack, don't you think. We going to have a very valuable new resident friend in Munkács.'

Isaack nodded, and looked at me with pride and said, 'Yes Sándor, we have a valuable son here among us.'

The administrative-territorial division of the region: 13 administrative districts, 10 cities, including 3 cities of regional subordination (Ungvár, Munkács, Huszt), 20 towns and 579 villages. The administrative centre was the city of **Ungvár.**

Transcarpathian Local Authorities

County/District	County Council Towns
Beregszász District	Beregszász
Huszt County	Csap
Ilosva District	Huszt

Munkács County	Munkács
Nagyberezna District	Ungvár
Nagyszőlős District	
Ökörmező District	
Perecseny District	
Rahó District	
Szolyva District	
Técső District	
Ungvár County	
Volóc District	

The First Jewish Law: "The companion and host on strengthening the balance of life, 1938: XV.tc. Since the mid-1930s, it has been gaining in strength. influenced by this, and at the same time demanded a far-reaching Hungarian far-right, the need to settle the Jewish question on TV korm.pol. the forefront. The proposal you put on me. referred to → in his speech announcing the Győr program, it was submitted to the → Parliament by the → Darányi government, but the Béla Imrédy was the head of the government. And the Government Decree has ordered the setting up of chambers (press, lawyer, medical, etc.) on the intellectual and freelance fields, where members max 20% could belong to the Israelite denomination. This rate also applied to corporate intellectual jobs.

Religious discrimination has abolished the principle of equality of citizenship. Released from the restrictions were widows and children of war invalids, heroic dead, and those who died on August 1, 1919. before converting to any other established denomination. In December 1938, the Hungarian Israelite Probation Office was established to support tens of thousands of those affected.

Chapter 12

In the Office

Next day, Tuesday 31 May, I turned up in my temporary office in Munkács Town Hall at 8.30 in the morning.

I was the first so I could get organised. I took my paperwork from my briefcase and was going through those files before my meeting with Andre and Viktoria. Five minutes to nine, my helpers, Andre and Viktoria, arrived. Viktoria brought in a pot of tea with cups on a tray. She said, 'If I remember right, you don't take sugar?'

I said no and thanked her for the drinks. She poured tea for the three of us and we started the meeting.

I asked them to arrange my meetings in geographically nearby areas within each county. 'I want to start at the administrative-territorial division of the region: 13 administrative districts, 10 cities, including 3 cities of regional subordination in Ungvár and Munkács. I am going to start the meetings at the administrative centre in the city of Ungvár.'

After the long meeting, I realised that it was half past twelve, I felt sorry for Viktoria and Andre as they only had some cups of teas. So, I invited them for a lunch on the Corso. 'Well, I think I need some help from you as I don't know Munkács so well, so where would you recommend having something to eat on the Corso?' Both of them recommended any of these two restaurants.

'We could go to the non-kosher Homdi Café on the Corso that is the favoured afternoon gathering place for 'the elite'—wealthier ladies who meet there elegantly dressed in hats, gloves and Persian lamb coats.

'Or we could go to the Úri Kávéház (Posh Coffeehouse); it is on the Corso too. This one is frequented by the better off, the self-employed, basically the professionals and the educated people. This included the Jews as well. Also,

74

there is the Moskop Restaurant downstairs in the Town Hall building, mainly for the town hall office staff.

'The more orthodox is the one for mainly Jewish families, including the more religiously observant, at the kosher Sternbach Café. Well, the choice is yours, Gabriel. But I think you would like the Homdi Coffeehouse.' Viktoria agreed with Andre's suggestion.

I said, 'Alright then, let's go to the Homdi Coffeehouse.'

It was very nicely decorated with pastel coloured wall with lots of paintings on the wall (I guessed from local artists), very modern art nuevo chandeliers and nice comfortable deco chairs.

When we sat down, I noticed that Viktoria and Andre were welcomed by some younger waiters. I asked them, 'Do you come here often?'

There was a bit of an awkward silence then Andre broke the silence, 'Since your arrival, Gabriel, as you chose both of us to work for you, we have become much friendlier with each other, and we started to socialise together, and this is the place where we come to meet up after work.'

I thought that it seemed I had another mission, that of bringing these two young people together, maybe it will be ending up in marriage. Hopefully, they will achieve that. Definitely there was something in the air, here in Munkács. Rebekah and I and Viktoria and Andre. Well, it's written that God's way is unpredictable.

I felt sorry to embarrass them with my blunt manner. So, I suggested, 'Let's order some food as we all have worked so hard, and you must be hungry and in need of some energy.' Firstly, the waiter served our coffee with a glass of water then a little later he brought our sandwiches.

I was just listening to these two young ones chatting about themselves and their backgrounds. Telling me all about the latest gossip and the trendiest place to go to. Andre said that at the end of the Corso, there was a more romantic tryst under the bridge to Oroszvég Restaurant Coffeehouse!

Viktoria said, 'We are both Jewish but not very orthodox or Zionist as many of our fellow pupils are. The Jewish Highschool is really responsible for converting them to it.'

I said, 'I am like you, I am Jewish too, keeping and honouring the Chumash and my faith in God but I do not criticise the more religious ones, I accept them with respect. If that is what they chose to be, that's all right with me. I am more liberal-minded and open for discussions and open with life in general.'

I felt that this conversation was needed to understand Andre and Viktoria a bit better as we were working so closely together in such important and confidential matters. My mind was on how I can meet up with my Rebekah, my God, I am missing her very much.

I wrote a note in the coffeehouse and, on my way back to the office in the Town Hall, I put it through her letterbox as her house was on the Corso, near to the Homdi Coffeehouse. Sometime later, as we got back to the office, we started to set my programs for Ungvár.

I had a call from the porter at the front door that a lady would like to see me. I asked him to send her up to the office. My heart was pumping faster as I knew who that lady can be.

It's my Rebekah, she's got my message I put through her letterbox. I am relieved that she got it herself. Viktoria let her in as she responded to the knocking on our office door.

Rebekah walked in, wearing her two-piece costume, she had the same lace blouse on that she was wearing in Lvov. (My God, she looked beautiful!) She asked, 'Are you Viktoria?'

Viktoria replied, 'Yes, I am. But how do you know?'

Then Rebekah turned to Andre and greeted him by his name as well then she said to me, 'Hello Gabriel.'

I could have rushed to her and kissed her, but I had to control myself, I just couldn't do it in front of my helpers. I just stood up from my desk and said, 'Andre, Viktoria, this is Rebekah, my future fiancé.'

The two kids just looked at me with surprised faces then they looked at Rebekah. Andre couldn't take his eyes off Rebekah, her beauty had mesmerised him. Both of them shook Rebekah's hand and greeted her. I stood up and kissed her hand and her cheek as well. I was knocked over from her perfume. I can recognise that perfume in a dark room.

Andre politely offered his chair to Rebekah and in his embarrassment, he asked me if we wanted some privacy. Then Andre asked Viktoria if she would help him get the report that they prepared for me earlier.

I thanked them both for being so polite and they left the room and now Rebekah and I stayed in the room together. (Thank you, Lord, for answering my prayer.) I rushed to her, she just dropped her handbag and shopping on the chair and put her arms around my neck and flooded me with her usual passionate kisses. I held her at her hips and pulled her body close to mine. We both got overheated from our desire to make love, but I forgot to lock the door. I broke up from her squeeze and I went to the door to lock it with the key.

As I turned back from the door, I saw her taking her jacket off and starting to unbutton her blouse. Her beautiful curves were visible through her slip. We embraced again in the deepest passion as we both felt each other's bodies. We were on fire again! We just couldn't think of anything else but to take it to the top of satisfaction as we always managed to take it to the limit. Again, we flew to Heaven and back as we made love in a different, very unusual place. But under the circumstances, that was all that we could improvise on the location just to satisfy our lust. But we didn't care about anything embarrassing with our action; there was no common-sense. When you are in love in such a desperate way as we were, in this difficult circumstance you just can't hide your emotions. Luckily, I was blessed with such understanding helpers like Andre and Viktoria.

Rebekah and I got ourselves dressed respectably again and I telephoned Victoria if they would bring coffee with them for all of us on their return.

Rebekah said, 'I have to go to the university in Lvov for two days tomorrow. I should be back home on Thursday evening like last week. I'll be sitting in for Professor Schlesinger's lectures and as soon as he finishes, I'll be rushing to the railway station to catch the train back home to you. I miss you, my love, for two days already.'

Gentle knocking on the door signalled that Andre and Viktoria had arrived back to our office with the drinks. It was embarrassing for a minute as I realised that I had left the door locked.

I rushed to the door to unlock it and let both of my helpers into the office with four cups of coffee. I appreciated their intimacy. I shook Andre's hand and got on with our planning where we had stopped at the arrival of Rebekah.

Rebekah was chatting to Viktoria, in a kind of girly chat, as they giggled sometimes. Andre and I concentrated on our plan of my next week's presentation meeting for Ungvár's local authority and one for the Jewish community's Grand Synagogue of Ungvár, just like the one I had given at Rabbi Baruch's Synagogue.

Rebekah stopped with her chatting on hearing that I was going to Ungvár and looked at me then the two girls carried on chatting. I broke up our meeting at four o'clock, it was a busy day and we achieved much today. I shook hands with them while Rebekah kissed Viktoria on her cheek like girls do. I thought Rebekah was an amazing entertainer and my delightful partner in any society. I loved her so much. I would like to show off to my friends at the New York Kávéházban.

When Andre and Viktoria left, we both rushed to each other's arms and kissed again passionately. I said, 'I find it difficult to cope with each minute I spend without you, my darling Rebekah. I hope this suffering is just a temporary one as we can't go out publicly as engaged fiancées. I do not wish any bad mouth gossip or defame should affect you and your father. I have to ask your father if he would allow us to go out to a restaurant or coffeehouse together here in Munkács.'

'But I miss you, my angel, I find myself daydreaming every day.'

'I know, my darling Rebekah. I feel the same way, missing you desperately. Just the touch of your hand, never mind the rest of your beautiful body. I want you every minute of the day, I feel and act like a teenager who is in desperate love. I have to let you leave first from the office and from the townhouse because people will talk. It is only four days, and we will see each other again. But you know I'll be there at your house for the Sabbath. Please be patient, my darling.'

'Gabriel, I was thinking to arrange our engagement on my birthday. What do you think?'

'When is your birthday, Rebekah?'

'It is on the 14th of June. I was born in 1915.'

'That is great, my darling Rebekah. It is now only in two weeks' time. This is fantastic!'

'When is your birthday, Gabriel?'

'Mine is on 19 May 1907. We will discuss everything with your father on the Sabbath at your house, my darling Rebekah. Praise be to God, the Almighty one.'

I dried the tears from her eyes with my handkerchief, kissed her again and said, 'You have to go, my darling. I'll see you on Saturday at your house at 5 pm.'

Not willingly but she understood the weight of our responsibility, and one more time she kissed me on my cheek. Just before I closed the door behind her, I harvested my eyes on her fantastic body. *Well Gabriel, she is a great gift from the Lord, the answer to your prayers.*

I reminded myself of that ancient wisdom of Celtic prophesy about each month of the trees.

Rebekah is Oak, and I am Hawthorne. Let's look into that, it would be interesting to know the meaning of them.

Oak—The Stabiliser

June 10-July 7

*Those born under the Celtic tree astrology sign of the Oak have a special gift of strength. They are protective people and often become a champion for those who do not have a voice. In other words, the Oak is the **crusader** and the spokesperson for the underdog. Nurturing, generous and helpful, you are a gentle giant among the Celtic zodiac signs. You exude an easy confidence and naturally assume everything will work out to a positive outcome. You have a deep respect for history and ancestry, and many people with this sign become teachers.*

*You love to **impart your knowledge** of the past to others. Oak signs have a need for structure and will often go to great lengths to gain the feeling of control in their lives. Healthy Oak signs live long, full, happy lives and enjoy **large family** settings and are likely to be involved with large social/community networks.*

Hawthorn—The Illusionist

May 13-June 9

*Hawthorn signs in Celtic tree astrology are not at all what they appear to be. Outwardly, they appear to be a certain persona, while on the inside Hawthorn's are quite different. They put the term "never judge a book by its cover" to the test. They live seemingly average lives while on the inside they carry fiery passions and inexhaustible **creative flame**. They are well adjusted and can adapt to most life situations well—making themselves content and comforting others at the same time.*

*You are naturally curious and have an interest in a broad range of topics. You are an **excellent listener,** and people seek you out as an outlet to release their burdens. You have a healthy sense of humour and have a clear understanding of irony. You tend to see the big picture and have **amazing insight**—although you typically won't give yourself enough credit for your observations. Hawthorn signs match up nicely with Ash and Rowan's.*

Social life of the city the prime venue for socialising other than in people's homes was The Corso, a main walkway through the centre of town, running from the main square where on each corner a magnificent building which are the Town Hall, the Star Hotel and two theatres. On one corner of the main square is a fiakker (open horse carriage) stand and on the opposite corner of the main square is a modern-day taxi rank.

The council always kept the cobblestoned wide street clean and the flowerbeds in the middle, lined by several elegant fashion shops, many of them Jewish-owned. Offering the latest fashion, inspired by Paris and Vienna. Walking on the Corso was just like walking in Budapest's elegant downtown shopping street. Elegantly dressed ladies wearing gloves and some in a larger and some in smaller, Parisian style hats were carrying their shopping.

The restaurants and coffeehouses placed tables and chairs in front of their premises to attract people who preferred to sit outside. This was frequented on weekend afternoons or weekday evenings by people, many of them the more secular Jews, walking around in groups or in courting couples as well as families. Teenage girls walked around the Corso with their girlfriends carrying books with them working on the pretext in order the boys would approach them chatting them up.

The flirtations sometimes led to lasting relationships and some people ended in marriage. Different kinds of music was played in restaurants, coffeehouses and on the weekends, there was a bandstand for mainly military style music. The Grand Theatre had entertainment for five days a week with drama and instrumental performances. In the cinema, the locals had the latest Hungarian and films from Hollywood, America. There was entertainment for everybody; for the preference of the classical audience and for choice of light entertainment.

After the conclusion of Sabbath, Jewish families, including the more religiously observant, gathered at the kosher Sternbach Café.

Summer was also the time of year of long twilight when the café was beautifully lit up and became a place for a younger crowd in the evenings. The Corso itself had two parts, reflecting the prevailing class distinctions. The Úri (Posh) Corso was frequented by the better off, the self-employed, the professionals, the educated populace. This included the Jews. Then there was the Baka (Soldiers) Corso, where young soldiers, maids, unskilled hired 'help' strolled. As with the Úri Corso, this was a venue for young groups and courting couples to meet, stroll and talk. The two parts were separated physically by a strip of park with flowerbeds and a bench, and mentally by an awareness of one's place.

More romantic trysts happened under the bridge to Oroszvég, away from the bright lights of The Corso.

The Hasidim avoided walking anywhere near The Corso area. Most of their social life seemed to have revolved around their synagogues, their homes and their large extended families.

Chapter 13

Week in the Office, Meeting with Education Officials of Munkács

On the next day, Wednesday morning, I had a meeting with the officers of the education department at the council room. Andre and Viktoria came with me. Viktoria was taking the minutes of the meeting and Andre helped me with the presentational paperwork.

There was Cllr Cohen who was the Chairman of the Educational committee. I recognised Cllr Cohen from my presentation I had given to the Jewish Community representatives on Monday.

I thought this will be some help as Cllr Cohen had heard my presentation but how wrong I could be. When you were dealing with councillors, you can find yourself with very strange and self-important kind of small-minded politically driven characters.

After I welcomed members of the Educational Authority and the representatives of the Councillors, I described the importance of present guidelines recommended by the Hungarian Educational Authority for the forthcoming changes for the Transcarpathian Region. It came from a higher Government-level initiative from Hungary, which was in a process to introduce the new future Regional Governor, in Baron Zsigmond Perényi, who will be the newly appointed Governor for the Region of Transcarpathia. He will take his office very soon.

Now, the guideline for the adaptation and implementation of the new curriculum act was:

The 1843/44 2nd act ordered Magyar to be the language of the letters coming from the Regent, the text of acts, the conversation of parliament and the juridical bodies. The 1843/44 9th act ordered it to become the language of the schools.

'As you know, there is a very strong lobby coming from the military of promoting more physical education in schools and a strong nationalism about the dominant Hungarian language on this proposal has been agreed by all MPs in the House of Parliament, and they have made it a law. This will affect all faith, private and state schools, the educational language has to be done in Hungarian, and also to introduce more sports lessons in a weekly curriculum.'

Cllr Cohen asked me, 'When would you propose these changes, when there is the Slovakian curriculum still in practice?'

'Cllr Cohen, there are fundamental changes on the way. I would expect that as you are a Councillor, a man in the political environment, you would hear about these changes.'

'I understand, Gabriel, that changes are coming but exactly when will it be in place? We are in June already; there is no way that you would be ready with your changes for the new school year which will start in September.'

'These are not my changes, Cllr Cohen. I am here representing the Hungarian Education Ministerium. As you know, this region has had changed control by many other countries, from Hungarian to Polish, then Austro-Hungarian and now for a time Czechoslovakian. Very soon, it will be Hungarian control again.

'Probably, you are aware of the proposed plans which are being negotiated at this moment in Vienna, by the Czechoslovakian team led by Mr Andrey Bródy and Mr Avgusthin Voloshin. Just let me explain it in a plain manner.

'As you know, every builder plans the outlook of a house first, then they set up the foundations of that house. At this moment, I am the one who is setting up the foundations here for you, getting it ready for the builders who will complete the house on these foundations itself.

'I am here to help you get a smooth transition for the changes, Cllr Cohen. I am not a politician or anything of that kind, neither an activist nor member of any political party, I have been appointed to deliver these regulations to you by the Ministry of Education of Hungary. So please don't expect me to get involved with any political debates. Thank you.'

My response to the councillor made the atmosphere a bit frosty as he tried to lead me down on his path of politics, but I managed to crack a joke which made the officials smile again and brought the attention back to my presentation. I asked them if there were any questions. There were none and I said, 'I will come to your office on a later date to finalise the details with you.' I thanked them for their attendance and closed the meeting.

We broke up for a lunch break and I invited Andre and Viktoria again to have a lunch together of their choice. Their choice again was the Homdi Coffeehouse. Then we sat down at the same table as we did yesterday.

Andre started analysing the event and particularly the way I handled Cllr Cohen. Andre said, 'He is a well-known troublemaker, typical minor politician who is always looking for some argument over anything. Nobody really likes him as he tries to get involved with people's private business uninvited.'

Viktoria said, 'You should have seen his face as you told him off in your diplomatic manner.'

I turned to Andre and Viktoria with a much more serious face and told them how grateful I was for their considerate manner yesterday in the office when Rebekah came to visit us.

Viktoria replied first, 'Are you two really engaged, Gabriel?' She was quite excited that I had found such an elegant lady here in Munkács so quickly.

Andre smiled and said, 'Yes, she is really beautiful.'

Viktoria gave him a critical look. I said, 'Thank you both for your approval, it looks as if we all found her attractive with the same credit.'

Viktoria said, 'Andre, please don't forget me. I am here with you.'

Andre smiled, nodded and said, 'Of course, we are one too, like Rebekah and Gabriel.'

I asked them in confidence if they were going to get engaged too. I embarrassed them as both of them blushed. Quickly, I apologised and said how pleased I was for them.

'Back to business, would you like to come with me to Ungvár for two or three days where I am going to do the same presentation?'

They just looked at each other then they both answered in unison, 'Yes please, that would be fantastic.'

I said, 'I need your help there just like you gave me today. Well then, we would need to get some rooms booked for all of us in Ungvár. Can you do that please?'

Viktoria asked how many rooms.

'Three rooms please. You know I have to keep up appearances. I hope you understand.' They smiled and said of course.

The three of us went back to the office, Viktoria typed up my report and Andre had letters to send out with an invitation to all major schools in the region for my presentation here in the town hall on the changing curriculum in Transcarpathia.

It was 4.30 in the afternoon when we finished for the day, and we went on our way as it had been quite a busy and eventful day.

Walking home from the Town Hall to Elisabeth's house, I realised that I was whistling some happy Hungarian melody. Everything looked so romantic, the trees full of blossom and the birds just singing nonstop a happy song. How beautifully romantic was this afternoon. I just wondered what was Rebekah doing without me in Lvov at this time? I do miss her.

I got through the gate at Elisabeth's house and the two dogs were running towards me with their tails like a flag in the wind. They knew that I had something for them again. Yes, a piece of marrowbone for each of them. Elisabeth came to the kitchen door as she heard the dogs' excitement. She said, 'Gabriel, you are spoiling these two.'

I said, 'It's only a bone from the butcher's scrap bin, just look at them how happy they are, and how much good these bones are doing to their teeth.'

Elisabeth said, 'Excuse me, Gabriel, I can hear the cow and sheep's bells getting nearer,' so she went to open the gate to let the cows and the geese in as the herdsman were leading them back from the pastures. Elisabeth waved to the herdsman and shouted, 'I'll see you tomorrow morning.'

After having a meal with Elisabeth, she went to milk the cows, getting the milk ready for the evening collection. When she finished with the milking, she said, 'Let me show you around this house next door while it is still daylight. I have the key.'

I said, 'Alright but I have to get on with my paperwork.'

When she opened the door, I smelt a smoky atmosphere; the owner must have been a smoker. Elisabeth noticed my finding and she confirmed that the old man was a pipe smoker. 'So, what do you think, Gabriel?'

I said, 'It needs a lot of work on it to get it up to the standard where I would move in. It needs modernisation in the rooms, like a bathroom, separate kitchen, dining room and so on.'

'Yes, I agree with you, Gabriel, but the house is bigger than mine and there is room to do the alterations. And the main thing is the property price is right. You couldn't get a house here in the *Kertváros* anywhere near this price.'

'Yes, I can see that, Elisabeth, I will think about it.'

I was putting my report together to make it ready for Viktoria to type out for the printer. I learned out of today's experience with Cllr Cohen, do not argue. I just had to be sure that the message will be understood by everybody at my presentation in Ungvár.

Guideline for the adaptation and implementation of the new curriculum act is:

The 1843/44 2nd act ordered Magyar to be the language of the letters coming from the Regent, the text of acts, the conversation of parliament and the juridical bodies. The 1843/44 9th act ordered it to become the language of the schools.

As you know, there is a very strong lobby coming from the military of promoting more physical education in schools and a strong nationalism about the dominant Hungarian language on this proposal has been agreed by all MPs in the House of Parliament, and they made it as law. This will affect all faith, private and state schools, the educational languish has to be done in Hungarian, and also to introduce more sports lessons in a weekly curriculum.

The removal of Latin, as the language of instruction, from the schools happened only by passing a general act. In 1832/36 an act ordered to the registration births in Magyar, an 1839 act declare the use of Magyar in the letters sending from the parliament and municipalities to the King, in the work of governing body, and the Hungarian military troops. The next step was the use of Magyar in the circle letters of churches, and prohibition of the employment of clergymen who could not speak Magyar. The 1932nd act ordered Magyar to be the language of the letters coming from the King, the text of acts, the conversation of parliament and the juridical bodies. The 1938 act ordered it to become the language of the schools.

In the 1930s, the sport-club initiated the local (district, county) sports races. The acceptance of this initiation depended on the support of the directors and educational administration After 1937, only the national centre of school clubs could give permission for this.

The expansion of the role and power of physical education teacher is important concerning not only the military but importantly the sport education, this issue is a general aspect of school-administration.

The government needs "commissioners" in the schools, who were independent from the traditional elite of the schools, from the director and who reported about the school life as not an element of intellectual society, but as an element of political society, who concentrate not just for scientific values but concentrate on physical values as well.

Next morning, Andre and Viktoria walked into the office; they looked very cheerful. I thought something very exciting must have happened to them last night. I was very happy for them, they looked very impressive together, would be a great married couple.

Viktoria said that she had a confirmation from her parents that she can come with me to Ungvár. I asked her if she had told her parents that Andre was coming with us to Ungvár too. With a smiley face, she said yes.

I said, 'That is great; now I can understand your happiness. Now, back to business. Viktoria, would you please type this N 8a, information in a leaflet format and get it out to the printer and ask them to make a thousand copies and get it ready by Friday morning. Andre, would you please send an invitation to all the heads of middle and high schools to invite them here for the end of their school year for my presentation on these changes. You can get the names and addresses of each school here from the educational office. By the way, when is the end of the educational year?'

Andre said it will be in the last week of this month.

I said, 'That is good; we have enough time to talk to them before they'll be gone for their holidays. Sorry, but I can't take you to the Homdi Coffeehouse today as I have to see a friend.'

Viktoria said, 'Oh, that is all right; we would like to get on with our jobs.'

I walked across to the Star Hotel from the town hall, where I knew that was where Isaack usually had his lunch every day. I walked into the restaurant and noticed that Isaack had arrived already, he was just reading the local paper before his meal. I called the waiter and asked him to go to Mr Grósz and ask him if he would accept me at his table. The waiter came back and led me to Isaack's table. Isaack stood up and greeted me with a smile. He asked me to please join him and take a seat.

I said, 'Thank you for welcoming me to your table, Isaack.'

He said, 'Please Gabriel, hopefully, we will be soon becoming a family, this is just natural that we are dining together. Hopefully, this will be our regular daily event.'

I said, 'Yes, that will be very nice, discussing all the events and business opportunities for both of us.'

Isaack insisted that I was his guest today.

'Thank you, Isaack, there will be many future opportunities when you'll be my guest for lunch or dinner.'

Isaack congratulated me for putting Cllr Cohen into his place at yesterday's presentation; he said, 'I am very proud of you, Gabriel. This news has spread very quickly that someone is brave enough to stand up to him. That man is a troublemaker, he doesn't get on with anybody and he is a bully. He thinks he's running this town of Munkács.'

I said, 'Goodness me, news travels very quickly, typical small town. I have to be careful what I am doing, I just can't afford to make mistakes. I try to be friendly with people like you, Rabbi Baruch and Sándor. I was going to ask you about Dr Sándor Fried, is that his given name?'

'No, his name is Samuel, he just doesn't want any aggravation over his name with the other minorities.'

'I see, thank you for this information.' I started the explanation as to why I was here seeking his company and I would like to learn his plan or suggestions for my forthcoming engagement to Rebekah.

Isaack said, 'I appreciate that you have come to me with this subject before our Sabbath dinner at my house. It makes your whole engagement organisation much easier for us, to have a pre plan that we will discuss together with Rebekah.'

'Am I right, Isaack, that Rebekah's birthday will be on the 14th of June? Do you think we could arrange the engagement for that day? It would make Rebekah very happy, and we would have much more time and opportunity to plan for the wedding itself.'

'Yes, that is a good idea, Gabriel, it would work; that would be Monday, the 14th of June.'

'Good, we could do it either on Sunday the 13th or Monday the 14th.'

'But why this rush, Gabriel? I hope you are not forced with time for some other reason. I hope Rebekah is not expecting a child.'

I said, 'No, Isaack, she is not expecting anything. I give my word and honour to you. I would not do unorthodox actions like that where I would compromise the one I love so much to allow others to gossip about her. She is a real lady, and

I would not allow this to happen to her; I will fight for her dignity to be preserved if I have to.'

'I know that you are a gentleman, Gabriel, and thank you for your confirmation.'

'You know, Isaack, I am getting on; I am 31 years old now, I have found someone as beautiful as your daughter Rebekah, and I have fallen in love with her. I know this feeling is mutual between us. I just can't let this last opportunity pass me by without settling down and having a family of our own. This is a simple human urge or your body's reaction that is telling you don't leave it too late. I have never been in love with a woman like I am now and whom I would like to share my life with forever.

'So, this is the reason, Isaack, it may look like a rushed decision, but I have to go back to Budapest and report to the education secretary on my progress. After that, I can return here to Munkács to follow up and guide the implementation with the education officials that I am setting up now.

'My landlady Elisabeth, here in Munkács, has been taking me around a property next to her house which I like, and I am thinking of purchasing it. While I am in Budapest, I am going to sell my apartment and buy this one here in Munkács Kertváros (garden city). It is close enough to the centre of town and I have fallen in love with the view of the beautiful landscape and with the fresh air.'

'Well Gabriel, you have convinced me now with your sincerity, commitments and with your plans for the future, I promise you that I will help you whatever way I can.'

After the "constructive business dinner", Isaack reminded me of his invitation to celebrate Sabbath in his home at 5.30 pm.

I said, 'I will be there on time.' We shook hands at the end of our lunch then as I looked into his face, I noticed the sparkly moisture gathered in his eyes. I didn't want him to be embarrassed to see a grown man in tears, but he hung onto my hand for a long time and finally, we said goodbye to each other, and I said, 'I'll see you on Sabbath.'

I went back to the office and finished my work for today. My two helpers had gone all ready, so I just locked up, said goodbye to the cleaner and repeated the same walk all the way home to Elisabeth's house.

Chapter 14
Building Up to the Sabbath and Engagement

One of the directors from the education department popped into my office as we were studying the map of Transcarpathia to arrange our plans for Ungvár and its county's schools in order to see which authority and which schools we should go to see first, second and so on. He asked if I would join him for a coffee down on the Corso.

I said yes, why not. I could do with a bit of caffeine to revive me. We walked down to the coffeehouse on the Corso next to the theatre. János started the conversation and said that the Mayor called him in asking about yesterday's presentation I gave to the education department and to the councillors.

Cllr Cohen made a complaint about me to the Mayor about my manner and the politically inspired material I was "spreading" to the audience.

I said, 'Well, I haven't been disrespectful to anyone and furthermore, I did not spread anything which could be branded as "politically inspired". The information I gave, and I emphasise that this information is available from the local newspaper too.

I found Cllr Cohen's behaviour as the representative of the Council of Munkács wasn't helpful. Or I would say, it was aggressive. I am not a member of any political or faith organisation. I am delivering the changes which will come by soon. I am representing the Hungarian authority; I am only a civil servant who has been commissioned to carry out a difficult job. It may well be Cllr Cohen has some personal issues with me, then he should have addressed them to me yesterday.'

János sensed my disappointment with the council as a politically driven "busybody" had made a complaint against me and said, 'Please Gabriel, there is no complaint from the Mayor; he only wants to know what really has happened. Look Gabriel, I am a civil servant like you, I have to deal with councillors all the time, with an attitude like that of Cllr Cohen, we make an extra effort to be more uncooperative with their requests. If they can't deliver what they promise to the residents whom they represent, well, the complaint reflects on the councillor's incompetence. But these kinds of minor politicians think they run Munkács.'

János smiled and said, 'Don't worry, we are all behind you. You have made a good impression on everybody here in the town hall and we like you.'

I said, 'Thank you for your honesty and your support, János, but I will present my report to the Mayor, and to your department as well. My poor helper Viktoria had so much work and she still hasn't finished the minutes of that meeting I gave which is in question.'

I got back to my office and asked Viktoria to make the minutes she had taken to be her priority. She said it would be done by tomorrow. Viktoria's minutes report was on my desk, typed and well presented on the following morning. I made the effort to hand deliver it to Janos's department and Mayor's office as well. I asked the Mayor's secretary if the Mayor could accept me to present my report to him.

She walked into the Mayor's office and within minutes, she came back to me and said, 'Yes, please the Governor / Mayor Konstantyn Hrabar and Deputy Mayor Iván Parkányi will see you now.'

'Good morning, Mr Mayor and Deputy Mayor. I hope I didn't disturb your meeting.'

'Of course not, Gabriel, may I call you Gabriel?'

'Yes of course, that would be very kind of you.'

'Please take a seat. Would you like a coffee or tea? So, what can we do for you, Gabriel?'

'Mr Mayor, I understand that Cllr Cohen reported me to you for my being disrespectful to him when I gave my presentation over the new proposed School Curriculum. I believe my conduct was to a professional standard with retaining the expectation of my authority's guideline; to be respectful as I am the representative of the Education Ministry of Hungary.

'So, I would like to present you with the minutes of that meeting which was taken by one of your administrators who is my secretary at this moment. This report is the true record of the meeting. Also, these minutes have been read back to the officials at the end of meeting as a standard procedure to check the contents correctness of that meeting. All members of the representatives voted unanimously that it was a correct record of the meeting. So please, you be the judge if I have conducted my presentation in a correct, professional manner.'

'Dear Gabriel, we know that your position means your conduct has to be in the highest level as you are the representative of the Hungarian Education Ministry. We also learned of your character from the people who you have been communicating with. Everybody is speaking very highly of your knowledge and diplomatic attitude, and the respectful manner you in which you are conducting yourself. You are a credit to your employer, the Ministry of Education of Hungary.

'With regards to Cllr Cohen, he is member of the Židovská Strana (Zionist Jewish Party). He is well known as the kind person who likes controversy if any project is proposed by the Council, and if he doesn't like it, he would argue and argue on anything just to abandon the project or do it in his way. A kind of control freak. He would disrupt any meeting in the council chambers when he is not even a member of that committee. But it is a credit to you for the way you have silenced him with your knowledge and your charmed manner. Many people at your meeting were very pleased that you have put him in his place. I guess that is what he just can't accept. This is the first time when there is someone who dares to stand up to his bullyish attitude.

'Before your arrival, we made some enquires about you. Just the usual standard check for our own security. I have to say that you have a very distinctive record in Budapest, with all your involvements with art, mainly with the theatrical and movie fields and the distinguished membership of the New York Kávéház Circle. Also, your inspiring speech you gave to all the artists at the Sztuka Coffeehouse in Lvov. Encouraging them to create more of their work in Ukrainian. Very patriotic!

'We would be happy to welcome your energy and knowledge here in Munkács, of course, if you would decide on that kind of offer.'

'I am amazed at the knowledge and information you have collected on me, Mr Mayor. How do you know about my Sztuka Coffeehouse speech?'

'Well, my wife is a member of the Union of Jewish Women of the Munkács branch like your girlfriend Rebekah Grósz. And she told me of your fiery encouraging speech that you made to the artists of Lvov.'

'Well, I am speechless, all that information and facts you know about me.'

'And there is more, Gabriel, the waiter from the Star Hotel overheard your conversation with Isaack Grósz, Rebekah's father, that you were discussing an engagement plan with him, and also, that you were looking at a property in Munkács to purchase. Is that true, Gabriel?'

'Well yes, I've almost choked on the tea. Yes Mr Mayor, that is true there was a conversation of that subject with Mr Grósz.'

'Do you think you could have a plan to settle here, and make your home in Munkács? If you would settle here in Munkács, we would be delighted to offer you a position to be the director of the Education and Art Department of the Council, to modernise and promote a much active cultural life here in Munkács. Actually, we can offer you that position. Just think of the opportunity you could offer to local artists with your knowledge and your charisma.'

'Mr Mayor, thank you very much for this great opportunity you are offering me. Certainly, flattering of your trust put in me and I will consider it carefully. Truly, I found Munkács is somehow a very special place in the world, attracting very much in many ways.

'At this moment I am still employed by the Hungarian Government, and who knows how long my contract will last with them. But I guess it will be terminated at the completion of my mandate for the changes to be adopted which I am presenting to the region's education authorities. Please give me some time to think it over before I decide.'

'Yes of course, Gabriel, we do understand your situation and are happy to wait for your answer. I hope it will be a positive one. It would be mutually beneficial and very fruitful for both of us.'

I shook hands with them and on my way out, the Mayor asked me, 'Is your Rabbi is Rebbe Baruch?'

I said yes, and Governor / Mayor Konstantyn Hrabár gave me a wink and said, 'I'll see you there on the Sabbath.'

I nodded and said, 'Yes, I look forward to seeing you there.'

Getting back to my office, I just couldn't get the Mayor's conversation out of my head. Viktoria asked me if the Mayor was happy with her minutes.

I said, 'Yes Viktoria, he was pleased with them. Would you please post these weekly reports on to the Education and Foreign Ministry officials in Budapest in the usual way. Thank you.'

On Friday morning, I found a note in a familiar perfumed envelope. I knew it was from Rebekah. She said that there was some very exciting news she was going to tell me. I was worried about that the news that she was pregnant. Oy vey, now I am in big trouble; I've just told Isaack yesterday that Rebekah is not expecting. Oy vey, Oy vey. Well, let's wait until the evening Sabbath meal.

I picked up my bouquet of flowers for her birthday from the florist and set off to the lion's den—Rebekah's apartment! I was concerned that Rebekah will announce her pregnancy during the evening. I hope not! This was her birthday; she wouldn't spoil that, surely not.

I rang the bell and Isaack welcomed and invited me in, as Rebekah was busy with the preparation for the Sabbath meal.

The table was beautifully set for the Sabbath Celebration; two simple silver candlesticks, two loaves of challah covered with a light blue striped cloth and a big glass full of red wine. Isaack and I went to the bathroom to wash our hands then we returned to the dining room where Rebekah was ready for the Mitzvah.

She looked beautiful and like an angel in pure white with the lace scarf on her head. Rebekah lit the candles as we stood around the table; Rebekah, Rita (her nanny), Isaack and me.

After Rebekah's lighting the candles, she waved her hands over the candles, welcoming in the sabbath. Then she covered her eyes, so as not to see the candles then she recited the blessing:

Barukh ata Adonai Eloheinu, Melekh ha'olam, asher kid'shanu b'mitzvotav v'tzivanu l'hadlik ner shel Sabbath.

Blessed are You, LORD our God, King of the universe, Who has sanctified us with His commandments and commanded us to light the Sabbath candles.

She removed her hands from her eyes, and she looked at the candles, completing the mitzvah of lighting the candles.

Isaack held the Kiddush cup and thanked the Lord for the wine:

Wine: Baruch Ata Adonai Eloheinu Melech Haolam Borei P'Ri Hagafen.

Wine: Blessed Are You Lord our God Sovereign of All Creator of the fruit of the wine.

Then Isaack removed the cover from the two challah loaves, lifting them while reciting the blessing:

Barukh ata Adonai Eloheinu melekh ha'olam hamotzi lehem min ha'aretz.

94

(Bread: Blessed are You, Lord our God, Ruler of the universe, who brings forth bread from the earth.)

The challah was then ripped into pieces and passed around the table, so that each of us may have a piece. The family meal may now begin. Sabbath Shalom.

Then Rita went to the kitchen, and she brought in the clear chicken soup with dumplings. I have to say it was clear as it should be, I was praising Rita for such a tasty soup.

She said it wasn't me who cooked it, Rebekah did it, as she remembered that this was my favourite soup.

I looked at her and said, 'Rebekah, you are not just beautiful but a great cook as well. Thank you for this surprise.'

She smiled and quickly looked at her father who smiled back at her and said, 'Yes Rebekah, you are just like your mother, she was a great cook too.'

The main dish was a roast duck with beetroot and roast potatoes Then came the gourmet of the evening, Flodni (crushed walnut with poppyseed and grated apple).

The atmosphere in the room was truly relaxed and happy. Rita stood up to clear the table and I asked her to stay with us as I had an important announcement to make. I got out a little box from my pocket, the one I had purchased from Dr Sándor Fried's jeweller friend, Mr Ernő Ungár.

I stood up from the table and walked to Rebekah, went down on my knee with an opened jewellery box and proposed to her, 'Rebekah Grósz, would you please be my wife? This is my special birthday present for you!'

Rebekah looked at me with tears running down her cheeks. Then she looked at her father who nodded with approval; she looked at me and said, 'YES, YES and Yes.'

I got the engagement ring out of the box and put it on Rebekah's finger. It was a very well-designed engagement ring, one big diamond in the middle and some smaller ones around the larger one. She lifted the ring in front of her; she hardly could see the ring as her tears were running unstoppably. She kept looking at the ring which looked very pretty as the flickering candlelight reflected on the sparkling diamond. She held me on my shoulder and kissed me on my cheek and on my lips. Then she turned to Isaack, showed her engagement ring with pride and hugged him, kissed him on his cheek. She said with joy to Papa, 'Aapukám, I am going to get married!'

Isaack walked to me and shook my hand then he hugged me and said, 'Thank you for making my daughter so very happy.'

In the meantime, Rebekah rushed to Rita, showing her engagement ring. Rita was crying aloud and she kept saying to Rebekah, 'I always told you so that your angel will come one day, and he will be one with you forever.'

Rebekah sat back into her chair and kept looking at her new ring. Isaack suggested that we should go to the lounge and celebrate the engagement. He pulled out a bottle of fine dry Hungarian champagne from the cold box and served it to four of us. He toasted us and to family. I thanked him for welcoming me into his family. 'I am feeling at home in your company now. Thank you very much. I promise you, Isaack, that I will be faithful and will protect your daughter Rebekah, may the Lord God give me strength and wisdom to be your worthy son-in-law.'

Rita was working in the kitchen, hiding her tears of joy and we were having a chat in Isaack's comfortable chairs. I told them what happened in the Mayor's office. I told them that our discussion in the Star Hotel restaurant was overheard by the waiter and that gossip got to the Mayor. I was surprised by the speed of that gossip, but I should know people in high places have a good information network. But anyway, from tomorrow, it will be known by the whole of Munkács that Rebekah and I were engaged. Isaack smiled and responded, 'Welcome to Munkács.'

I related what Mayor Hrabar told me this morning. When he found out that I had looked at a property to be near to my landlady Elisabeth, he asked me to stay and settle down. The Mayor and the deputy Mayor offered me a job here in the town hall to be the director of the education and art department. Isaack and Rebekah both looked at me with amazement and great interest, curious of what was my reply to the offer. I told them that I was honoured to receive such on offer but I was still contracted to the Hungarian Education Ministry, and I knew this contract would be terminated in November 1938.

Isaack said, 'If you are looking to buy a property and you've just gotten engaged to Rebekah and been offered such a respective appointment? So that means that you have made your mind up already.'

I looked at Rebekah and said, 'Wherever Rebekah is, that is where my place is too.'

She smiled at me and said, 'My Lord, it isn't true, is this happening to me? I have met the man of my dreams a couple of weeks ago; we have now gotten engaged and I am learning that he is moving from Hungary to Munkács just to be with me, with us. This is a true miracle. I hope I don't wake up and find that this is just a dream.' She came to my chair, crouched at my chair, holding my hand, looked into my eyes and asked me, 'Is it true, you are going to move over here?'

I said, 'Yes, I have instructed an estate agent in Budapest to sell my apartment so I can purchase this property next to Elisabeth, where we could live together.'

'What attracted you to that house, Gabriel?' asked Isaack.

'I have lived in Budapest for a long time, and I find living in the capitol city is not very healthy. It is crowded, the air quality is very poor. Compared with Munkács, where the air quality is healthy and clear, the magnificent landscape of the Carpathian Mountains. I can't imagine a better place for our children to grow up carrying on with our genes to the future generation. I have found myself deeply in love and at my age with no one to communicate with.

'And finally, it has happened I have found someone who loves me and wants to share her life with me. This is the reason, Isaack. This is where I feel home, with you, with my newly found family, who are giving me the most beautiful wife I could ever have dreamed of. People say we just can't understand the Lord God of Israel, His ways are unpredictable.

'I have just accepted it as it is. It is good to be led by Him as His plans are perfectly prepared and delivered. Yes Rebekah, I would like to share my life with you till the end of my life.'

'With many children, like you said, Gabriel.'

'Yes Rebekah, with as many as the Lord will bless us with. Our genes have to be carried on.'

Isaack said regarding the property purchase, we don't have to worry about it, he wished to be helpful in our future.

'Thank you, Isaack, I know you will be a fantastic grandfather to our children.'

He smiled. 'While we are planning the future, we have to concentrate on our most important thing, of your wedding arrangements. When and where would you like to get married?'

Rebekah suggested the Handelsman Restaurant. She said of all her friends' weddings have been held in that place.

(The Handelsman restaurant and reception hall is the venue for many Jewish weddings.)

'That is all right, Rebekah, it will be as you wish. But when do we have to book that place? I heard that it is very busy with bookings, I will organise that. I suggest that you should get together with your friends and find a wedding dress of your choice.'

I said, 'I will arrange it with Rebbe Baruch to do the wedding ceremony and also, I would like if he would bless our engagement as well sometime soon.'

'That is a very good idea, Gabriel, and I will ask the Rebbe to announce your engagement in the Synagogue tomorrow morning at Sabbath services.'

'It should bring you some pride and joy, Isaack, with all those well-wishers from the congregation.'

'Yes Gabriel, and more importantly, you are the one who is marrying my daughter Rebekah. Someone with your quality and pedigree.'

'No Isaack, Rebekah has made her own career in respect to looking after you, and also as an important member of the community who is there to protect the interest of Jewish women's equality and rights of Munkács.

'By the way, Darling, do you know the Mayor's wife, Mrs Ester Hrabar?'

With wide eyes, Rebekah asked me, 'Why? Yes, I do know her, she is a member of the Union of Jewish Women of the Munkács.'

'The Mayor was telling me of my Ukrainian patriotic speech at the Sztuka Coffeehouse.'

Rebekah said it was probably Magda who told her the story about my speech.

I said, 'That is no problem. I have only appraisal for my effort from the Mayor. Only thing troubling me is that wherever I go, or whatever I do or say it will be known by everybody here in Munkács. It worries me that next week I have to go to Ungvár to do the same as I do it here in Munkács, and my reputation will arrive before me.'

'When are you leaving for Ungvár, Gabriel?'

'We will be leaving on Tuesday morning by long-distance bus.'

'Who is we, Gabriel?'

'It will be me, Viktoria and Andre. Why, would you like to come with us?'

Rebekah looked at her father and asked if he would mind if she went with us. She said that she will share a room with Viktoria, Gabriel's secretary.

Isaack said, 'Yes, I think it would be all right if you are going to share a room with Viktoria.'

It turned half past midnight and I said to Isaack and Rebekah, 'Forgive me, but I have to walk all the way to the Kertváros where I stay.'

'I understand, Gabriel, shall I see you in the morning at the synagogue?'

'Yes, you will, Isaack, and we will talk to the Rabbi to arrange our wedding date.'

Rebekah walked me to the front door to let me out. She looked at her new engagement ring again and said, 'After you have gone home, I am going to my bed and will continue the dream that I have been involved in this evening.'

We kissed again in the usual passionate way then I started my journey back home to Elisabeth's house on the dark cobblestoned street; no lights as after 10 pm, all streetlights switched off. I just hoped that I wouldn't disturb Elisabeth being so late.

Chapter 15
Rebbe Baruch, Property Viewing and Journey to Ungvár

My usual alarm clock, Matyi, the rooster, woke me up and got me out of bed. There was no thick enough pillow in the whole world which could silence his early morning crow!

Anyway, this time I appreciated Matyi's wake up call, it was quite late by the time I'd gotten home. I got dressed and I was looking for my bow tie, I just couldn't remember where I had put it overnight. I went to the kitchen to look for it and Elisabeth lifted it up from the back of the chair and she said, 'Are you looking for a bow tie, Gabriel?'

I said, 'Yes Elisabeth.'

She said, 'I had to clean it as it was covered with red lipstick; it would be a bit embarrassing for a bachelor to turn up in the synagogue like that, don't you think?'

I kissed her on her cheek and thanked her for washing and ironing my shirts.

'It is a pleasure, my little brother; it's made me feel good that I am taking care of a man's everyday needs; it reminds me of the days when my husband was around. At least have a cup of tea, Gabriel, before you go to the synagogue. So, how did the last night Sabbath meal progress? Did Rebekah say yes?'

'Yes, Elisabeth, she says yes, and she was so very happy, she couldn't see the ring for her tears.'

'Mazel tov, Gabriel, Szivböl gratulálok (congratulations from the bottom of my heart)! I am so happy for you and of course, for Rebekah as well! Somehow, I felt that you will settle here when you met Rebekah. She is a well-respected lady; she didn't get married because she looked after her father since her mother, Rivka, died when she was only a young girl. So, Gabriel, are you going to buy this property next door?'

'Yes, Elisabeth, it looks like it, but I would like to bring Rebekah with me to let her see the property for herself to see what it is like. If she likes it then I will get my friend, Dr Sándor Fried, to arrange the purchase of this next-door house.'

Elisabeth clapped her hands with happiness and said, 'In this case, we will be neighbours with you and Rebekah. I volunteer that I will be the nanny to your children while you are at work or you two are involved with some official engagements and entertainment.'

'Slow down, Elisabeth, deal with everything on time as they are progressing.'

Well, I think I made her day. I didn't tell her that I was selling my apartment in Budapest, and I had a job offer by the Mayor of Munkács.

On my way to the synagogue, I bumped into the same two men whom I met a week ago. We greeted each other with Sabbath Shalom. They were telling me what they heard about the changes coming to the Transcarpathian Region. I just listened them and their conversation. I didn't volunteer to contribute anything at all. Just let them speak and learn about the latest gossip which was very interesting and colourful. I knew it was nothing like the way I presented it to the community.

When we neared the Hoif Complex Synagogue, we bumped into a lot of Jewish people; some of them were Orthodox, or Zionists and many of them like myself more liberally in modern clothing. After all, 42.4% of Munkács population is of Jewish origin. Munkács has 30 synagogues and prayer houses (Shtibelach).

I noticed Rebekah and Isaack walking towards the complex. She looked absolutely stunning in a navy polka dot dress and a large, brimmed hat. Isaack had on a double-breasted dark suit with a black Fedora hat, and like me, he always wore a bow tie. Rebekah spotted me and waved as they were coming towards me. I kissed her hand and shook Isaack's hand and we all greeted each other with a Sabbath Shalom.

Rebekah proudly showed me the engagement ring on her finger and said a thank you with a smile and praised how beautiful it was. 'I hardly slept for the joy and happiness which overwhelmed me. I couldn't even see the beauty of it because I couldn't see through my tears.'

The three of us walked to the main door of the synagogue. Isaack and I walked in together. I sat next to Isaack and Rebekah went upstairs to the balcony with the rest of the women. I noticed that she was showing off her engagement ring to her friends with a beaming smile. I was so pleased at making her so happy, she does deserve all the happiness.

After the service, the Rabbi was looking for me and wanted to congratulate me.

I didn't know the reason, but he called Isaack and me and said, 'I don't know, Isaack, if you have met the Mayor of Munkács, Mayor Konstantyn Hrabar. Rabbi Baruch said I know you have had a meeting with him during a week, but I am not sure about you, Isaack.'

Isaack shook hands with the Mayor, both said Sabbath Shalom.

Rabbi Baruch turned to me and he said, 'I believe you don't need a Shadchan anymore; can I congratulate you for your engagement, Gabriel, Mazal tov.'

I felt so embarrassed; so many things went through my mind; how did he know that I was engaged to Rebekah, as it was only last night at Isaack's house only a few hours ago. I saw Isaack shake his head as it wasn't him who had told the Rabbi of our engagement.

Everybody was looking at me, the Mayor Rabbi Baruch and Isaack. Also, some people started to listen to our conversation. Rabbi Baruch said, 'You just don't purchase an engagement ring from the jeweller without people starting to put two and two together and the guessing game is started immediately, who is the future bride? Well, now I can see the reason why you and Isaack sat together in the hall. I am very pleased for you and Rebekah. Mazel tov!'

Then more and more people came to shake hands with Isaack and I could hear the loudness of Mazel tov in the room.

I looked up to the balcony where the women sat and saw a crowd of women standing around Rebekah and they were congratulating her on her engagement.

Mayor Hrabar turned to me and asked, 'Does this engagement mean that you will accept my offer?'

I said, 'Yes, it looks like I will accept your kind offer, Mr Mayor Hrabar.'

He shook my hand and said, 'Please come and see me in my office on Monday.'

Isaack looked at me and said, 'Gabriel, I am very pleased and proud of you. Mazel tov.'

I asked Rabbi Baruch if he could bless our engagement with Rebekah and me.

Rabbi Baruch said, 'Just get in touch with me next week and I will arrange the special engagement.' He put his hand on my head and blessed me as a new member of his congregation. I felt that my feet didn't reach the floor, it was such an uplifting experience which I never experienced before.

Rabbi Baruch said that he had had a word with the Chief Rabbi of Ungvár, Rabbi Yosef Elimelech Kahana, with regards to my presentation to the Jewish Community of Ungvár. I thanked him for his help and support and said I will come and see him in his office on Monday. As Isaack and I walked out of the synagogue, we saw Rebekah with a ring of women around her, hugging, kissing, shouting Mazel tov, Rebekah, Mazel tov.

She spotted us walking towards her and she told the women around her, 'This my fiancé, Gabriel.'

I felt a bit embarrassed, then greeted all Rebekah's friends.

Isaack said to Rebekah, 'We have to go, my dear.'

She broke away from the ring of her friends who surrounded her and waved goodbye to them. Rebekah came between us and put her arm into Isaack's and mine as we were walking back to Isaack and Rebekah's house for a dinner that Rita had prepared already.

We, as a new extended family for Isaack, sat down for the Sabbath dinner then Isaack said the Kiddush. I think (judging by his voice) he was at the top of his spiritual mode, he was so happy and proud as a father who is happy for his daughter's new partner and for the son he has just received through this engagement and all the special uplifting experiences at the synagogue and being propelled into a level of society which he had never been involved with because his and his daughter's priority was paramount and his business which supported all of his family with comfort.

Isaack lifted his glass to the painting of his wife and toasted her and said, 'In the presence of your spirit, my dear Rivka, I am thanking and praising the Almighty God of our fathers, who is controlling and blessing us with joy and hope to fulfil his promise to Abraham about his son to be born. So, here is to you, my Rivka, this is the continuation of our love for Rebekah, and through her love with Gabriel, our future is well protected. Let's all of us drink to life. L'chaim!'

We all repeated l'chaim!

I said, 'Isaack, this was a very emotional speech. Thank you for your kind acceptance of me into your family.'

'Gabriel, I am very pleased to have you as my son-in-law, as you bring so much pride and quality into our family, it is overwhelming. The best gift the Lord could have given to my daughter Rebekah is you, Gabriel.'

'You flatter me, Isaack, I wouldn't have all these qualities if the Lord God hadn't chosen to gift me with them. The energy and wisdom I have is from Him. He chose me to do things for his glory. And I will not claim or hold onto these achievements for my glory. He is my glory.'

Rebekah looked at Isaack then looked at me with tears in her eyes and said, 'I am not superstitious at all, but we should have a chair for my mother.'

'Isaack said it's not needed, Rebekah; she is looking at us as we speak, and I feel her spirit, her presence is among us.'

During the meal, Rebekah was telling us her exciting experience up in the synagogue balcony with all the women when they spotted her engagement ring. She just couldn't stop talking about the well-wishers and who said what.

I told my new family that I put my apartment up for sale in Budapest and was thinking of purchasing a property in the *Kertváros* (garden city) of Munkács, next to where I was staying now on Latorca utca. 'I would like it if you both could come along and give your opinions. It is a large house; in need of some modernisation with a large garden and it's very close to the town centre.'

Isaack said, 'It looks to me that you have decided that you are going to settle here in Munkács. I am very pleased for that. It will give me an opportunity to see and play with my grandchildren.'

Rebekah said, 'Thank you for this, Papa, you are making me so happy and encouraging me for this marriage with your support and your blessing.'

Isaack asked us, 'And when do you plan your wedding?'

We just looked at each other and I said, 'It would be great if we could do it before Rosh Hashanah. As the time is ticking for both of us and we are committed so I hope that will be acceptable for you, Isaack?'

'I can see both of your commitment, I am not concerned about that, it is all written on both of your faces that you just want to get together but to do things in the traditional way. Tradition is very important in keeping us together, identifying us, as we are Children of Abraham, and upholding the Chumash.'

'I think there is enough time to organise everything. Don't you, Isaack?'

'Yes, I do but we have to book a place for the wedding reception.'

Rebekah chipped into the conversation, 'Yes, Papa, I would like our wedding reception at the Handelsman Restaurant as this is the best place for weddings,

104

Rózsi Neumann had her wedding there. You remember, Papa, we were guests at that wedding. Handelsman Restaurant has the best reception hall, and it is the venue for many Jewish weddings.'

Isaack said, 'Yes Rebekah, you will have your wedding reception at Handelsman, for you will get the best. It will be a very special day for such an important bride and groom like the two of you.'

Rebekah rushed to her papa at the dining table and hugged and kissed him. 'Thank you.'

'You are my only daughter, I would get you the very best.' He looked at me and said, 'I expect some very important people to be among the guests, Gabriel, are we not?'

'Yes Isaack, I will have all the very important people from Munkács and from Budapest as well. But don't forget all those very important people who are Rebekah's friends.'

By the time we finished the Sabbath lunch, it was well into the evening.

Isaack said, 'Gabriel, why don't you come here for Sunday lunch, and we will discuss more of our plans for this big occasion. It just has to be perfect.'

I thought that would give me a better timetable to solve my situation in my mission and also my apartment sale in Budapest.

Rebekah was so excited to see her plans unfolding; she had met her true love, lost her innocence to him in such an amazing experience, been introduced to the cream of society, been engaged and now they were planning their wedding. And this all happened within three weeks. It was truly a miracle. *And on top of it, his name is an angel, Gabriel. I love him so much; I can't have enough of his love and affection.*

Rebekah went into the kitchen to help Rita with the work she was doing on her own.

I was telling Isaack that I was going to Ungvár for four days on business to meet with the County Officers to deliver my task of presenting them with the Hungarian Education authority's future plans for the political and educational changes. 'I am going to have a meeting with the Chief Rabbi of Ungvár, Rabbi Yosef Elimelech Kahana, and deliver my presentation to the Jewish Community of Ungvár. I am going to be very busy with this mission and I will need some help on this trip. I am taking both of my helpers, Andre and Viktoria, but I am afraid that this workload is too much for the three of us. May I respectfully ask you if I could take Rebekah with us to help with our workload? We would have a hotel room for each of us and will be travelling together there and back by train.'

Isaack looked at me for a minute or two as he was considering his decision.

'When would you leave, Gabriel?'

'On the first train to Ungvár on Tuesday morning. I'll have a meeting with Rabbi Kahana in the early afternoon and I will do my presentation to the Jewish community of Ungvár in early evening. Then the following day, I have a meeting with the County Education Officers and we should be back home at noon on Friday, just like she gets back from her university in Lvov.'

'Sound like a very busy schedule, Gabriel.'

'Yes, it is, Isaack, I like my helpers. I think they going to have a good career with their dressing style and knowledge. Furthermore, Rebekah has never been in Ungvár before. It is a big city, the capital of the Transcarpathian Region, and we are going to meet many interesting and important people there.'

'Look Gabriel, I know Rebekah is not a young girl, she knows what she is doing, as we both have engaged, and you are going to a city where no one would know you. I agree that she can join you for this trip. I trust both of your judgements to be respectable to your engagement agreement.'

'That is fine, I can promise you, Isaack; after all, I am representing with my representing the Hungarian Government. I understand the weight of my mission is a great responsibility, and I am living up to that weight.'

At the end of the lunch, Rebekah walked me to the door and I told her that her father agreed that she will be joining us for the trip to Ungvár. She jumped and kissed me on the lips as she always did passionately. She worried about me leaving her.

I said, 'I'll see you tomorrow for Sunday lunch, my love, and I will tell you more about the trip to Ungvár.'

'Goodbye, my love, my fiancé!'

I arrived at Rebekah's House on Sunday for lunch and for the planning meeting of our wedding. I arrived on time again with a bouquet of beautiful carnations—Rebekah's favourite flower. Rebekah thanked me for the flowers and gave me a kiss then she put the flowers into a vase, the carnation perfume was just overpoweringly dominating the living room atmosphere.

I showed Isaack the proposed plan for Ungvár and asked him when we should discuss it—before the meal or after. He suggested after dinner.'

Rita invited us all to the dining table as she was ready to serve the food. As we sat down, Isaack said the Kiddush again and we started the family lunch. The meal was delicious again as usual, and Rebekah showed off, 'I cooked the main goose roast.' She wasn't just beautiful and smart but a great cook as well.

Isaack looked at me with a smile and said, 'Her mother Rivka was the same; that is where that quality comes from. I felt we can discuss our plans with the wedding arrangement.'

Isaack said, 'So, you and Rebekah would like it to have it before Rosh Hashanah.'

'Yes Papa, I do would like it before that.'

'How about you, Gabriel?'

'That will be all right with me. Hopefully, the modernisation on the property will be completed by then on the house I am hoping to purchase now. But firstly, I would like if you and Rebekah would come along and have a look at the house.'

'I know the area, Gabriel, yes, of course, I will come along with Rebekah to have a look at it.'

'I approached an estate agent in Budapest to put my apartment on the market. I hope it will sell very quickly as it is in a very good location right in the heart of Budapest. It is in the Jewish quarter, there are lots of synagogues and theatres and very good restaurants around of my apartment. How about if we would walk to this house to view it after dinner. My landlady, Elisabeth Schwartz, has the key for the house so we can have a look at it.'

Rebekah got excited and said, 'Yes Papa, I would like to see this house.'

Isaack agreed to walk to the Latorca utca property to have a look at it. 'Soon as this part of planning is completed then we can progress with all the wedding arrangements, like the booking of the Handelsman Restaurant and Gabriel and I will see the Rabbi for the wedding ceremony.'

After the lunch, the three of us walked down to see this property and Rebekah said, 'And also, I can meet up with the other lady in your life.' We all laughed at Rebekah's joke.

'I hope you are not jealous of Elisabeth.'

Rebekah smiled and said, 'Of course not, it was just a joke.' We all smiled again.

As we arrived at Elisabeth's house, she was sitting on the veranda and looking at the livestock which was running around her feet. When she realised that I had Rebekah and Isaack with me, she stood up and said, 'You could have told me, Gabriel, that you were going to bring this beautiful lady with you.' Elisabeth welcomed Rebekah and Isaack and invited us into the house, but we said that we all would like to see the property.

Elisabeth said with a smile, 'I am glad that you are bringing your future wife to see the property where she would call home.'

We all went to have a look at the property and Elisabeth showed us from room to room then she showed the garden and outbuildings as well.

Rebekah commented, 'Papa, I am feeling a good vibe in here, I like it. I know there is a need to modernise it to rearrange things to suit our requirements and make it a bit more luxurious.'

Isaack said, 'Yes, there is some kind of peace in here.' Then he pulled me aside and said, 'Look Gabriel, if you are stuck with money until you have sold your apartment, I will lend you the money to pay for this property before somebody else buys it.'

'Thank you, Isaack, that will be a great help, and as soon as the apartment is sold, I will repay your money to you. Thank you again. That would give us much more time to get the alterations ready for our wedding.'

Elisabeth put her arm in Rebekah's arm and said, 'I remember your mother, dear; you are as beautiful as she was. And she was a well-respected lady. She always helped the poor in the Jewish community. Many people loved and missed her. She was gone too soon; God bless her soul.'

I thanked Elisabeth for her help showing us around the house; we went back to Isaack's house to continue our planning for the wedding and now there was a new project, the house. At the end at the family plans, I presented my timetable for the trip to Ungvár.

I asked Isaack if he would agree with me to ask my friend Sándor to start the negotiations to purchase the property.

Isaack said, 'It is a good idea; let's get the business rolling.'

'I am feeling truly home now here in Munkács, all our plans are coming together. Miracles are happening around us but sometimes we are so busy with our everyday life's minor details, we just can't see the whole picture on the canvas.'

Chapter 16
Ungvár

History

Old city and Roman Catholic church, Greek Catholic Cathedral, Ungvár. The best known of the first city founders are early Slavs. One of their tribes—White Croats—settled the area of the modern Uzhhorod in the second half of the first millennium. In 895 AD, Hungarian tribes, headed by their leader Árpád, stormed the Hungvár fortress. The forces were not equal and Laborec was defeated and beheaded on the banks of the river. There was not much of a settlement when the Magyar tribes arrived, having left Kiev (then known as Kevevára) and encountering no resistance.

After the arrival of the Hungarians, the small town began to extend its borders. In 1241-42, the Mongols of Batu Khan burnt the settlement. In the early 14th century, Ungvár showed strong resistance to the new Hungarian rulers of the Anjou dynasty. Although the majority of inhabitants were Hungarians, they wanted more freedom. From 1318 for 360 years, the Drugeths (Italian counts) owned the town. During that period Philip Drugeth built Uzhhorod Castle. The name Ungvár in Hungarian meaning Castle of Ung. Together with the castle, the city began to grow. From 1430, Ungvár became a free royal town.

During the 16-17th centuries, there were many handicraft corporations in Ungvár. In this period the city was engaged in the religious fight between primarily Protestant Transylvania and Catholic Austria. In 1646 the Ungvár Union was proclaimed and the Greek-Catholic church was established in Subcarpathia, in a ceremony held in the Ungvár castle by the Vatican Aegis. In 1707, Ungvár was the residence of Ferenc II Rákóczi, leader of the national liberation war of Hungarians against Vienna.

Twentieth Century

According to the 1910 census, the city had 16,919 inhabitants, of which 13,590 (80.3%) were Magyars, 1,219 (7.2%) Slovaks, 1,151 (6.8%) Germans, 641 (3.8%) Rusyns and 1.6% Czechs Since Jews were not counted as ethnicity (as defined by language), rather only religious group, this Austrian-Hungarian census does not specifically mention the Jewish population, which was significant, and consisted of about 31% in 1910 In the same time, the municipal area of the city had a population composed of 10,541 (39.05%) Hungarians, 9,908 (36.71%) Slovaks, and 5,520 (20.45%) Rusyns.

The First World War slowed down the tempo of city development. On 10 September 1919, Subcarpathia was officially allocated to the Republic of Czechoslovakia. Ungvár became the administrative centre of the territory. During these years Uzhhorod developed into an architecturally modern city After the Treaty of Trianon 1920, Ungvár became part of the eastern half of the new Czecho-Slovak state.

After the First Vienna Award in 1938, Ungvár was given back to Hungary from which it was separated after WWI.

In 1941, the Jewish population reached 9,576. Ungvár during this time was an important centre of finance and industry, areas in which Jews played leading roles. In the twentieth century, Zionist and non-Zionist organisations gained a firm base; the city became a stronghold of the Židovská Strana (Jewish Party). Some Jews, however, continued to support pro-Magyar circles.

Chapter 17

The Build-Up to the Trip and
We Are in Ungvár

On the Monday morning, I asked Andre to collect the information sheets from the printer on Rakoczi Street and bring them to our town hall office.

I called in at my friend, Dr Sándor (Samuel) Fried, solicitor's office and asked him to start the negotiation with the vendor of the property on Latorca utca. Sándor shook my hand then he hugged me and said, 'I knew that you will be going stay here with us when Rebekah came into your life. Welcome to Munkács, Gabriel! Yes, I will deal with the case immediately. I guess Elisabeth Schwartz has all the details for me.'

I said, 'Yes, she has them all. I am going to Ungvár on business for the rest of this week and I should be back by Friday around midday.'

Sándor said, 'I owe you a dinner to celebrate your engagement. Well, you made my day, Gabriel; I have gained a very good friend who is now going to settle here with us in Munkács.'

I left Sándor's office and rushed to get back to my office.

Andre just got back from the Rákóczi utca printing plant with all the A4 and A5 leaflets which we had to hand out at tomorrow's presentation at the Ungvár Synagogue and at the Ungvár Educational Department meetings. I felt sorry for Andre as these leaflets were quite heavy, luckily it wasn't far away from the town hall. Viktoria reported to me that she had managed to organise tomorrow's trip to Ungvár.

She said, 'I have booked four rooms at the Hotel Korona, which is right on the Theatre Park, in the heart of the city. It in the best location, two beautiful theatres on both sides of the square, there is a theatre facing the Ung River. Everything is in walking distance. The synagogue is just right behind the theatre, the Corso Street is full of restaurants.'

'Thank you, Viktoria, do you have a confirmation for my presentation from the Education Department of the Ungvár Town hall with the Russian Autonomic Governments, Minister for Education, Stefán Avgusztin?'

'Yes, I have manged to organise the three meetings you've planned for the officials, for the teachers and at synagogue, and a private one with Rabbi Yosef Elimelech Ungvar Kahana, in his residency.'

'Very good, Viktoria. Are you ready for the trip? We are going to be very busy for this week.'

Rebekah called into the office as we agreed we were going to have lunch together with Isaack at the Star hotel's restaurant. She looked very elegant again as usual, she had a large, brimmed hat with lace gloves and a flowery patterned summer dress. She looked stunning and she was the one I was going to marry. I was very proud of her taste of modern dressing.

She said, 'I've just bumped into the Mayor/Governor Mayor Konstantyn Hrabar's wife at the entrance hall. She was congratulating me on our engagement, and she said your wedding will be the "society wedding of the year". She said I hope I shall receive an invitation for that.'

'I didn't know, Rebekah, that you know Mrs Hrabar.'

'Yes of course, I know her; she is a member of the women's organisation, also she is running many charities for the poor, all over the county of Beregszász.'

'Well, well, I learn something every day about who knows whom in Munkács.'

I had forgotten that Viktoria and Andre didn't know that Rebekah and I were engaged. Both of them just stopped and looked at Rebekah and me. It was a bit embarrassing. Rebekah and I explained to them that we weren't engaged officially; we were going to have the engagement party on Rebekah's birthday on the 14th of this month. Actually, this coming Sunday. Rebekah told them we were going to tell you about this news in Ungvár as we were going to spend some days there together.

Viktoria recovered first from this announcement and gave a hug to Rebekah and wished her all the best. Rebekah thanked her and said, 'Well, Viktoria, next will be yours with Andre.' Andre shook my hand and congratulated me on the engagement.

I suggested to Rebekah that we would have to leave to meet up with her father at the Star Hotel restaurant for lunch. Walking out of the building together, you could hear people were whispering about us, our engagement.

Rebekah said, 'Why are you surprised; this is a small town and many people know us through our social and professional lives.'

'Yes, you are right, Rebekah. Where should I book for your birthday and our engagement party? Would you like it at the Handelsman restaurant, or somewhere else?'

She said, 'Let's see papa first and we will discuss it later.'

Isaack was sitting at his usual table; he stood up at our arrival and greeted me, Rebekah kissed her papa on his cheek.

Isaack asked me if I was ready for the trip.

'Yes, Isaack, I hope we are. We are taking a lot of printed materials with us; they should have been printed in Ungvár. But as it is still very low-key news as I am just presenting these initiatives for changes which will eventually become a law, I have to have some discretion from the printer.'

'Well Gabriel, you have to hurry up with these presentations as things in the "political theatre" are moving very quickly. I was just reading in the Kárpáti Magyar Hírlap newspaper (Carpathian Hungarian's News) that the Hungarians are putting pressure on the Czech Government. But let's talk about your engagement and also our other plans have to be discussed.

'Rebekah would like to have her birthday and our engagement celebration in our house on Sunday. Would that suit you, Gabriel?'

'Yes, Isaack, that is good with me, but we are going to be in Ungvar till Friday half past eleven, it is a big workload for you and Rita, as Rebekah is coming with me to Ungvár.'

'Don't worry; it is better this way as I am going to make this occasion a special one. It will be a surprise for both of you.'

Rebekah looked at me and we both said thank you; Rebekah said, 'I just can't wait.'

After lunch, I excused myself as I still had much to do before the trip tomorrow morning and I said goodbye to them.

'I will pick you up tomorrow morning from your house to go to the railway station.'

Rebekah said, 'I will be ready for you in the morning.'

I got back to the office and got on with the preparation for the trip and my speech. I suggested to my helpers that they should leave earlier today as they had to get up early in the morning to get here to the town hall first to collect all our printed materials for Ungvár. 'I will organise a taxi from the taxi rank next to the town hall to take us to the railway station.'

I was still organising my presentation speeches for different meetings in Ungvár. It was a nice walk home. I enjoyed the scenery of the blossoming trees and the birds' chorus and the main thing that attracted me so much to Munkács was the clean fresh air. Arriving home, Elisabeth hugged me as I walked into the house and kissed me on my cheek.

I said, 'Why did you do that, Elisabeth?'

'Because you are going to be my neighbour, my little adopted brother. You and Rebekah are going to be my neighbours, I am going to have two beautiful people next to me. It looks like my prayers have been answered, I won't be alone. I promise you, Gabriel, that I won't be interfering with your life, but I will be here for you when you need me any time. You are truly Godsent. Since my husband passed away, I have found myself in a very strange place far away from where I have grown up. It is his memory and the wealth he has left behind that I enjoy.

'Sándor came to see me this morning and I gave him all the documentation and the details of the vendors. It looks like you'll get it very soon at an amazingly low price.'

'Yes, Elisabeth, thanks to you for all your help to enable me to get this property for so cheap a price. I know there is a lot needed to be done but that will be to our specifications.'

'You know, Gabriel, you have arrived here at Munkács some weeks ago and it appears to me that you know all the important people in this place, it seems to me you are more important than you allow people to believe who you really are.'

'Just let's leave it to that, Elisabeth. I am what you want me to be. I'll go along with that.'

'I understand you, Gabriel, I just accept you as you are; my little brother I always wished for. And furthermore, you have the most beautiful lady that I have seen in a long time. I hope and wish you two will have many children to recreate the beauty and love which is in you to be implanted into your offspring. To Rebekah's and Gabriel's future.'

I just kissed Elisabeth on her cheek, said goodnight and went to bed, I was shattered from the busy day. The taxi arrived at Elisabeth's house on time at half past seven. I was ready thanks to Matyi the rooster's crow. When we got to the town hall with the taxi to collect all the administrative packages with the printed flyers, Andre and Viktoria were there already with their little hand luggage. I noticed that Rebekah was walking to the town hall to join us. She looked very elegant in her two-piece skirt suit and a small, brimmed hat. She looked as if she had just stepped out of a Vogue fashion magazine. I said, 'We were going to collect you from your house, Rebekah.'

She said, 'Sorry, I am so excited about this trip to Ungvár, so I just walked. It's only a few meters from my house.'

I took her small travelling case and put it into the taxi. We all got in the taxi and headed to Munkacs railway station.

Viktoria collected the tickets from the station ticket office, and I picked up a Kárpáti Magyar Hírlap newspaper at the newsagent's shop. I just had a quick look at the headlines with a report of Milan Hodza Czechoslovakian Prime Minister in Praha received a delegation; Mr Géza Szüllő, Andor Jaross and János Eszterházy Members of the Hungarian Parliament who handed over an 81-point declaration which demanded the region autonomy.

On the same day, Prime Minister Hodza received a delegation from the Hungarian Nationality. Part of Transcarpathia members were Endre Korláth, Károly Hokky, Aladár R. Vozáry, and Károly Köszörű who handed in the minutes of the memorandum Committee meeting which was held in June 1938 in Munkács.

I felt a bit uneasy as I read the headlines. Well, it's already started. Thinking the worst of these rapid developments, I just hoped there won't be any bloodshed resulting from these meetings. I was aware of these developments as I was part of these changes on the educational side.

Rebekah looked at me and asked me if everything was alright. I just turned the front page of the newspaper; she read it and looked at me to explain this headline. I said, 'I will tell you all when we will be alone.'

We got on the train and got settled into our first-class train coach. The two girls sat at the window and started chatting to each other. I asked Viktoria if the hotel booking was confirmed.

She said, 'Yes of course, I told you yesterday.'

I said in an embarrassed voice, 'Yes of course, you did tell me. Sorry about this, Viktoria, it is just the last-minute checklist.' I just couldn't tell her about my being off the track which was caused by the headline in the paper.

I said, 'Well, there is only two and a half hours to Ungvár, so have some relaxation.'

Finally, we arrived on time at Central Station of Ungvár. We all had to carry some packages with us off the train as it was continuing its journey on to Kassa.

We got into a taxi; luckily, it was a large Skoda so all our belongings fitted in well. Arriving at the Hotel Korona's entrance, we had a porter who took care of all of our belongings. Enjoying the scenery from the station to the hotel, I have to say Ungvár is a very nice prosperous city. Crossing on the River Uzh bridge, we arrived at the main square where there were two theatres on both sides of the square and the Korona Hotel was facing us. I have to admit that I have never been in Ungvár before, but I was very impressed with it. Everybody shared my enthusiasm, none of them had ever visited Ungvár before.

Viktoria was checking all of us in and as we received our keys, I asked them to come down to the cafeteria in ten minutes' time and I will brief them on our schedule in Ungvár. Luckily, Viktoria had booked four rooms next to each other, so it made it easy to communicate with each other. After we settled in our rooms, we all met up at the cafeteria as agreed.

I said, 'I am going to have a private meeting with the Chief Rabbi of Ungvár, Rabbi Yosef Elimelech Kahana. I don't know how long that will take. So, please have a sightseeing trip in downtown Ungvár. Would you please take care of these two young ones, Rebekah?'

With a smile she said, 'Yes, of course, I'll be their big sister. It looks like there are some very nice shops in their Corso Street.'

I said, 'Please take this money with you to spend but I do need receipts for everything.'

Rebekah said, 'Yes, I know, as you know I am doing my father's business account. I am used to it.'

'Oh yes, you do, I know that; my apologies, Rebekah, this is just a habit.'

My appointment was at 1 pm with Chief Rabbi Kahana at the Rabbinical residency. I rang the bell at five to one, I have always been prompt as this is how you show respect to people with your timekeeping.

Mr Stern opened the door for me and led me to the Rabbi's office.

Rabbi Kahana looked more like a professor than the Chief Rabbi, a very friendly face showed wisdom and a tremendous peace flooding from him. I was not surprised that he had been chosen for this highly important position. He welcomed me with a handshake, holding my hand with both his hands, I felt a very powerful energy through his hands. It was similar to the one I experienced from Chief Rabbi Immanuel Lőw, in Budapest.

I introduced myself and handed to him the envelope I received from Chief Rabbi Immánuel Lőw, from Budapest. I felt it when he looked into my eyes and said, 'You are just like Chief Rabbi Lőw described you. I sense your mission in your spirit, it has been given to you from beyond of the human order. You have been well chosen for this task, Gabriel. This task is within your name; Gabriel, the messenger who came to us from the Almighty One.'

He invited me to sit opposite him around the small coffee table. He said, 'I have received a letter from Rabbi Lőw, in which he explains all about your mission. I know why the Hungarian Government has sent you on this mission. I am hearing of these so-called changes on the radio, reading it in the newspapers, but I have a nervous feeling about this change. What is the truth behind this mad rush, Gabriel?'

'Rabbi Kahana, I think the Horthy regime has drifted too much to the far right with some negative racist groups who are aggressively lobbying the members of the parliament in Budapest. Like Szálasi, the anti-Semite leader of the Arrow cross fascist party. Horthy is going to make an agreement / pact with the Germans, so the price of that pact is Transcarpathia will belong to Hungary again. I am not saying that this is the fact but why on earth have I been sent to Munkács and Ungvár by the Hungarian Government to arrange and negotiate the future of educational standards here in Carpathia. Politicians from Czechoslovakia and from Hungary are having meetings in Vienna over the future of Transcarpathia.'

'What is wrong with our educational system, Gabriel?'

'As you know, Rabbi Kahana, there is a very strong lobby coming from the military of promoting more physical education in schools and a strong nationalism about the dominant Hungarian language on this proposal has been agreed by all MP's in the House of Parliament, and they made it as law. This will affect all faith, private and state schools. The educational language has to be done in Hungarian, and also to introduce more sports lessons in a weekly curriculum.'

The 1843/44 2nd act ordered Magyar to be the language of the letters coming from the King, the text of acts, the conversation of parliament and the juridical bodies. The 1843/44 9th act ordered it to become the language of the schools.

'I can see why Rabbi Low has recommended you, Gabriel, to the Hungarian Educational Ministry.'

'Yes, Rabbi Kahana, as I am of Jewish origin, a teacher, and I speak several languages, mostly Slavic and Yiddish, of course. I am not married so there is less cost to the Hungarian Government for sending one person away from home and less expenses to the treasury.'

'So where are you going to stay here in Ungvár, Gabriel?'

'We have been booked into the Korona Hotel for three nights.'

'Who are the "we", Gabriel?'

'Andre and Viktoria, they are my helpers / secretaries and my fiancée, Rebekah Grósz.'

'Nobody told me that you are engaged, Gabriel.'

'Yes, Rabbi Kahana, I have met an angel in Munkács, and we have instantly fallen in love with each other. I truly believe that the way I have met my Rebekah was something special, it has been arranged by a higher order. You just don't meet someone in such circumstances, getting engaged to her and planning a wedding within the next month or two. Glory to the Highest, the only God of our father, the God of the Israelites.'

'Please introduce me to her, Gabriel, I want to give my blessing to you both. Mazel tov! Let us drink to it, you know, Gabriel, this kosher plum brandy is twenty years old, so enjoy it. L'chaim, to life.

'Now back to business, I have invited some Jewish teachers and some prominent businesspeople for your tomorrow's presentation. Please bring your Rebekah with you and of course, your helpers too. Thank you very much, my boy, for your special company, I have enjoyed to talking to you. Mr Stern will show you to the door, until God be with you, Shalom Gabriel.'

Well, the time passed by with so much to discuss at our meeting, which I will truly treasure as long as I live. Rabbi Kahana truly was a man with many gifts of charisma and energy just flowing from him. I made my way back to the hotel. I felt that I wasn't walking on cobblestones but drifting on air.

By the time I arrived back to the hotel, it was half past four in the afternoon. I saw my delegation having a good time in the cafeteria. I was so pleased that

Rebekah was so relaxed and happy. She had never done anything in an official capacity like this one. I noticed that she was getting on with Viktoria and Andre so well.

I said, 'Can I have some room around this happy table please?'

Rebekah replied, 'Well, if you are going to order the next round of coffees, then you can.'

They all smiled at me and the joyful atmosphere became a bit more serious, as the boss had turned up.

I said, 'I won't be buying the next round of coffees, but I will buy you an evening meal for all of us.'

I asked them where they would like to have supper as they had time to look around in downtown today. Rebekah recommended that there was a restaurant attached to the theatre overlooking the river Uzh.

I said, 'Ok, just let me refresh myself then we can go together, it is just across the Theatre Square from the hotel. We all agreed that so we will meet up downstairs in the hotel lobby and will walk across into this Csárda (restaurant).'

We all went into our rooms to get refreshed for the evening meal.

I pulled Andre aside and said, 'I don't care if you are sharing the night in one room but do it in a more discreet manner.'

When Andre and I arrived in the lobby on time, there was no sign of the two girls. Then suddenly, Rebekah arrived with Viktoria, giggling all the way from the staircase to the lobby. Andre and I just looked at them, we were stunned at the transformation and the entrance of these two beautiful ladies. By that time, the hotel residents were following them with their eyes. They both had bright red lipstick on, and I have to say it was tastefully done. The two models stepped out from the Parisian Vogue magazine.

I was so happy to know she was my fiancée; I looked at the face of Andre and he had his mouth open on Viktoria's look.

Rebekah broke the silence and with a confident voice she said, 'Let's go; we are hungry.'

When we got to the restaurant, the gipsy band started playing my favourite song—*Monti Chárdás*. The waiter introduced himself as Mihály, he thought that we were some kind of celebrities and offered us the best table in the room overlooking the illuminated river Uzh. I tipped Mihály, and he brought the menu for us. He asked me, 'Are you from Budapest? I can tell by your accent.'

I said, 'Yes.'

He said his cousin was the doorman in New York Kávéház. I said, 'Is he called Józsi?'

He looked at me if I was a mind reader. He said yes he was. 'Do you know him?'

I said, 'Yes, of course, he is a very nice man with his son called Marci.'

Mihály just looked at me and became very emotional and shook my hand for so long that it was a bit embarrassing. Mihály whispered in my ear, 'The band will play for us exclusively and the evening drinks will be on him.' He treated us as some important celebrities.

I thought this was something unexpected but went along with it.

The "primas", the lead violinist of the band called Tibor Rácz announced that we have a very important guest from Budapest New York Kávéház. Then he came over to our table and welcomed us to Ungvár and asked if he can play for these beautiful ladies their favourite songs. It was a bit embarrassing; I only wanted a romantic evening for all of us, and now this unexpected fame.

But anyway, the main thing was that the girls enjoyed it very much. Yes, it was special. At the end we had a great meal and a very romantic evening which I had to credit to Mr Tibor Rácz and his excellent band. My personal thoughts were that our appearance at this restaurant this evening will be known by everybody in this small town.

By the time we were leaving the restaurant, it was quite late before we arrived back at our hotel; we just walked to the bridge and enjoyed the scenery of the flickering lights reflected on the flow of the river Uzh. We slowly made our way back to our hotel. I felt a bit tired; it was a busy day for us, at least for me.

Rebekah followed me to my room, and I noticed that Andre had sneaked into Viktoria's room. Rebekah and I just smiled as the events were played out in front of us by these two lovely youngsters.

Rebekah put her arms around my neck and whispered into my ear that tonight she had the most romantic evening of her life. She asked me, 'Please undress me again and let's finish it with a firework!' She kissed me on my lips, and we made love with such passion that I felt my tiredness was a figment of my imagination.

We all made it to breakfast and were ready for the hard day, only Andre wasn't complete; he had no tie on. I asked him where his tie was and he replied, 'I have been given a bowtie like yours, but I just can't tie it for myself. Would you please teach me how to do it, Gabriel, I am very impressed with the way you look with the bowtie. Viktoria said that it would look great on me too.'

Viktoria said, 'I bought it for Andre yesterday; we chose the tie with Rebekah.'

I said it would be my pleasure to teach you to tie your bowtie. We both went to the gents bathroom, and I made him stand in front of the mirror and showed him how to do it.

'There you go now, look how sophisticated you look; it suits you, Andre.'

Rebekah commented on Andre's new look, 'I do like you better with the bowtie on compared with the normal one. It makes you stand out from the crowd of ordinary office workers.'

Finishing breakfast, I asked Andre to bring the printed materials for the Jewish Community.

'So, I'll see you all in the lobby in half an hour.'

Chapter 18
Presentation in Ungvár

Four of us arrived at the Great Synagogue of Ungvár on time, with all the printed materials which included my report and all the official proposals from the Minister for Education of Hungary. We set up a small stall designed for the Jewish Community of Ungvár.

Rebekah and Andre stood at the promotional stand at the back of the hall where they were both handing out information leaflets to all the people who attended this designated meeting exclusively to the Jewish community. Which was informing the members of the Jewish community on changes in education and on top of that information which was the social political issue of the "New Jewish Law" issued on 29 May 1938. *by the new Prime Minister of Hungary, Imrédy Béla.*

Chief Rabbi Yosef Elimelech Kahana opened the meeting and welcomed us all, the ones who attended this very important meeting. He introduced us by name and thanked us for taking time in our busy schedules to deliver this important message especially concerning to the Jewish Community here in Ungvár and for Jews in the whole of the Transcarpathian Region.

I stood at the front of the hall with Viktoria who sat behind me at a table and took the minutes of the meeting. I have thanked Chief Rabbi Kahana for the warm welcoming words and the members of the Jewish community who attended.

I gave the identical presentation here in the Great Synagogue of Ungvár, as the one I gave in Munkács some days ago. Only adding more news items which resulted from my presentation that I gave in Munkács, which has developed since that Munkács Educational Committee Meeting members have agreed on that, the Local Authority of Munkács will request on the implementation that the Hungarian language should be used in education and should be experimented in the Gimnázium of Munkács, the one which has been banned in 1919 by the Czech Authority. And furthermore, to establish a teachers educational training college in Munkács, From the 1st of September 1938.

I had a mixed reaction to this news but also, I sensed the resignation of acknowledgement that the changes are here, and we have to adopt them even here, in Ungvár as well.

Learning from my experience of the Munkács meeting I didn't invite anybody to raise questions with regards to my presentation. (I have now learned from the mistakes I've made with Cllr Cohen in Munkács.)

After the meeting Chief Rabbi Kahana, has invited us all to a working buffet where we all have an opportunity to interact and raise some questions or comment on the substance of our presentation.

Some of them were helpful to form a positive view on the composition of my report to Chief Rabbi Immanuel Lőw at Budapest Main Synagogue.

After the end of the event Chief Rabbi Kahana invited Rebekah and I to his office for a brief social chat.

Rabbi Kahana just held Rebekah's hand in the same way as he held mine yesterday and he looked into her eyes and said, 'I can see a deep commitment and passion in your eyes Rebekah. Your child will be a very important person in his future life, you and Gabriel are truly blessed with wisdom and passion. But as I look at you, I know the Lord has blessed you with a great beauty as well.'

Then he laid his hand upon of both of our heads and said, 'I bless you for protection from any harm you are facing in the spirit of our Lord of Our Gods.'

I felt that Rebekah's legs were giving in, and she fell to the floor by the power of the Holy Spirit. I was very close to that emotion, but Rabbi Kahana had finished with his blessing. He said, pointing to Rebekah, who was still on the floor, to just leave her to "spend time with her Angel".

I looked at her lying on the floor with a smiling face, which was shining like an aura. By the time she came around from her experience, I helped her up and I was having one of Rabbi Kahana's special kosher plum brandy. I helped Rebekah to the chair and The Rabbi offered a glass of the brandy to Rebekah as well which she happily accepted. The Chief Rabbi Kahana lifted his glass and saluted us and thanked us for the presentation with a second round of kosher plum brandy and said, 'L'chaim for Life!' And we both repeated L'chaim! We both thanked Chief Rabbi Kahana for everything he had done for Rebekah and for me, particularly for his blessing. With Rebekah we said goodbye for today and added, 'Shall we see you tomorrow at the town hall, Chief Rabbi Kahana?'

'No Gabriel, I won't be going. I have other commitments to attend for tomorrow, but there will be someone who is going to represent me in attendance.'

By the time we got back to the main hall to join up with Andre and Viktoria, they had packed up already. Mind that there weren't many things left to take back with us. We left all the Jewish community concerned leaflets behind in the synagogue with the organisers of the community event.

Four of us were walking back to the hotel and commenting how warm the temperature really was, that we noticed how much cooler the temperature was in the synagogue at this time of summer. Andre and I took our jackets off; the girls didn't share our actions, Rebekah said, 'We are keeping our dignity and our traditions as we should.'

I suggested that we should freshen up from the busy day of work we had, and I gave the afternoon off to Andre and Viktoria. 'I'll see you later if you would like to join us for a supper.'

I asked Rebekah if she would like a cup of coffee with me on the hotel terrace.

Andre said that they would like to have a sightseeing tour in Downtown Ungvár and probably they will have supper somewhere else in town. 'But thank you for your offer, Gabriel, at this time we will decline from it. You should have time together with Rebekah.'

I said, 'That is fair enough, Andre, but be ready for tomorrow, we are going to have a very heavy program this time with the political elites of Ungvár.'

Relaxing on the hotel coffee terrace with Rebekah's company and a cup of coffee with soda water and some delicious cake, the "taste of Hungary's" Dobostorta.

Rebekah said, reflecting on the day's events, 'I feel I have been truly blessed today, Gabriel. Physically, through Rabbi Kahana's prayer. Over two months ago, I would have never believed anyone if they would have told me that my very quiet life in Munkács, will be transformed into events of a tornado. The speed of this lifestyle, and the weight of its importance and I have suddenly found myself that this activity is taking a lot out of my energy.'

'I am so sorry, my darling Rebekah, if I put you into such tiring activities.'

'Oh, no I didn't mean that way, Gabriel, I feel still young and capable to take this kind of workload. I have just never done anything like this before in my whole life. This is a completely different kind of world I am used to dealing with, I am dealing with people of such high level of social and political importance, it is new to me, and I have to learn quickly, to not let you down with my inexperience.

'I want to support you as a good Jewish wife is expected to do to her husband. I am a liberated Jewess, but I am still following my Jewish tradition, such as what is the role of the wife, and how she should support her husband. I want you to be proud of me! You made me a woman and that is very important in any girl's memoir of life.'

I kissed her hand and held it for some time and said, 'My Darling Rebekah, I am very proud of you indeed! What you are doing for me unpaid, your contribution is immeasurable!

'You are the first woman in my life who has given me all the support emotionally, physically and your knowledge is of the highest of intelligence among all. I am the luckiest man. I have the pleasure of your knowledge and with all of your qualities and furthermore, of your beauty, and a fantastic taste of style and your sophistication.

'I can have a conversation with you about music, drama, and poetry as well as business. Not to mention of both our beliefs in education for all, humanity, and justice for the downtrodden. All this noble quality in you I have received far from above us from our Lord. And I am so grateful for it. I don't really know how I have deserved you as my shining darling pearl.'

'Pearl, Gabriel?'

'Yes Rebekah, Pearl! That is your birth stone. Pearl! Pure white like you are. You have gifted me with your purity on that fantastic night in Lvov. And that is my gift from you, and I will treasure the memory of that till the end of my life.'

'How can I forget that night, Gabriel, when you took me in your arms and introduced me into heaven? And ever since I am still feeling that joy each time, we are together I am in heaven again with you Gabriel, my personal Angel! Would you take me up in your arms into high heaven? Right now?'

I called the waiter and paid for the coffee and cakes. I held her soft hand helped her out of her chair and hand in hand we walked upstairs into our rooms. People in the cafeteria who spoke Yiddish guessed of the outcome of our departure.

I felt Rebekah's hand was shaking again, the sign of her excitement and I knew that our clothes would litter the floor from the door to our bed. Well, our passion is gentle but exquisite, we take poetry with our master sculptor's perfection into our earthy satisfaction.

Just to hear her breathing, next to me, the taste of her lips when she kisses me the touch of her velvety skin, and the silkiness of her hair, just look at her, Lord, she is Your perfect creation.

'Thank you for Your gift, my Lord.'

We both fell asleep after our "journey to heaven" and when I woke up to the banging noise of our next room door, I opened my eyes and looked at her, she was buried into my arm, resting her head on my chest, with a smiling face and probably she was dreaming with angels. What a scenery and what a beauty and she is in my arms. Hmmm!

I kissed her on her forehead and said gently, 'It's time to go to have a supper, my love.'

She looked at me, still sleep in her lovely eyes and said, 'Please just give me some five more minutes, my angel.'

Eventually, we managed to refresh ourselves and get dressed for the evening.

'Where would you like to have your supper tonight, Rebekah?'

'Yesterday I have seen a little restaurant on the Corso, where a very talented pianist was playing along with a harpist. It looked very romantic, and it has a good menu as well.'

I asked the hotel receptionist if he could secure a table for us there.

The young man phoned the restaurant and booked a table for us, he said it is not as busy now as it is on the weekend.

We walked through on the narrow cobblestoned street towards the restaurant in the warm summer evening. A cocktail of trees and flower perfumes drifted into town on the summer breeze. Oh, what a night, it's starts very romantic already.

The music was echoed through the narrow street followed with a burst of applause appreciating the musician's performance.

The waiter welcomed us and walked us to our reserved table.

It was a smallish room big enough for an upright piano and a harp, and some tables inside and some more tables on the outside in front of the restaurant on the street.

Seated at the window we had a view of the restaurant, and the people out on the Corso.

I suddenly changed and became excited.

'What's happened, Gabriel?' Rebekah asked with a worried voice.

'There is my favourite concert pianist friend from Budapest.' I said to Rebekah, 'Would you please excuse me.' I stood up and walked to the table of a sophisticated lady dressed in a black dress, her hair in a chignon. I stood in front of her and said, 'Hello Annie.'

With surprise on her face, she looked at me and with a smile she said, 'Gabriel, what are you doing here in Ungvár?'

She raised her hand and I kissed it (amazingly long and muscular fingers). 'I am here on business at the Great synagogue and with the Ungvár City Council Officials.'

She was surprised, and said, 'You have never been involved in politics.'

I said, 'I don't, but it is a long story I will tell you later. But what are you doing here, Annie?'

'I am performing at the theatre this evening of Franz Liszt, Hungarian Rhapsody.'

'That is fantastic; what time does your performance start?'

'At 8 pm.'

'We have to come along to hear your performance, hopefully we will be able to get a couple of seats.'

'Who is we, Gabriel?'

I waved to Rebekah to come and join us. She walked to us with an embarrassing mood.

'Dear Annie, may I introduce to you Rebekah Grósz, my fiancée.' I turned to Rebekah and said, 'Rebekah, may I introduce to you Miss Annie Fischer.'

Annie looked at Rebekah and said hello to her. Then she turned to me and said, 'I have never known that you have been engaged, Gabriel? The born bachelor. Oy vey! Well, I have to come here to Ungvár to find this news.'

'It is too complicated, Annie. May I see you after the concert please. I will explain to you the reason I am here, and I am engaged to one of this most beautiful woman in my life.'

'Wow I would like to hear all about your story Gabriel. I am staying in the Korona Hotel so I expect we could talk there after the concert.'

I said, 'That is great Annie, that is where we staying as well.'

'Even better Gabriel. I tell you what, I will arrange a complimentary ticket for you two at the theatre under your name, then we will remember of the parties we all had in the New York Kávéház.'

'I am sorry, but I have to go for a final rehearsal on stage. It was a pleasure meeting you, Rebekah.'

'Same here, Annie.'

We walked back to our table and continued to order our supper.

Rebekah was still shell-shocked, and she just looked at me with her big eyes and said, 'What else am I going to learn about you Gabriel?'

'Nothing bad my love I promise you I have never done anything bad to anybody in my life which you should be ashamed of me.'

The musicians who recognised Miss Annie Fischer, the world-renowned concert pianist, then they turned their attention to us, I guess, wondered who on earth we were to talk to Miss Fischer in such a familiar way.

The musicians started to play more classical Hungarian music. I have to say they did it with perfection. I guess they wanted to show off with their talent. They were good.

All the way through our supper, Rebekah was unusually quiet. 'I hope I didn't embarrass you, my love.'

She shook her head and said, 'I am just beginning to recognise your hidden quality and Gabriel, the member of high society in Budapest.'

'I promise to you my darling that I am not a member of any society particularly not the high society at all. I am just a person who would be there for friends when they would need help. Simple is that.'

Rebekah slowly started to relax. I am not sure if it was to the result of the wine we had with a delicious meal, or she was just accepted the fact that I know some famous people. Before we left from the restaurant, I asked the musicians if they would accept a round of drink to appreciate their performance for tonight. They returned my offer to them with a smile.

We walked out the restaurant as people was following us with their glance. May well be, they were admiring Rebekah's perfect shape? She well deserved that attention as she looked again perfectly dressed to innkeeping with her stunning body.

She held my arm so very closely to her body as I felt her firm bosom. I asked her if she liked classical music. With a beaming smile, she nodded. 'Yes, I do love classical music. I never expected to attend to a classical recital tonight and particularly with an artist who you know Gabriel. All my girlfriends in Munkács and Lvov will be very envious when I will be telling them this story.'

'By the way, Lvov. My friend Magda, and all the members of the Sztuka Kávéház sending their regards and asking about us when are we going back to visit them? I am having my examinations next week at the university Gabriel. Would you come up with me please. Just giving me a moral support.'

'When is your examination, Rebekah?'

'Next Wednesday and Thursday.'

'I have to check my appointment diary Rebekah. But yes, of course I will come with you to support you, not to mention of recreating of our first night's lovemaking.'

'Yes please, is that a promise?'

'Yes! It is.'

We couldn't continue with our conversation as we arrived at the theatre, for Annie's concert performance. There was a big sign above the theatre entrance and some smaller posters with pictures of Miss Annie Fischer performing Frans Liszt Hungarian Rhapsody.

I know these pieces of music. It always makes me emotional, a true nationalist Rhapsody. It truly reflects on this small nation of Magyar's struggle to surviving in the world with the mood of its ups and downs. I can't wait to hear this masterpiece performed by Annie; she is the very best in the world.

Walking to the box-office to collect our complimentary tickets and getting a program book as well. Some very well-dressed couples lining up at the concert hall. Rebekah and I, we always dressed appropriately for any occasion, so we didn't stand out from the crowd.

Just looking into the program book and noticed that the whole evening is dedicated to the greatest Hungarian Composer to Franz Liszt. Annie starts with the Rhapsody No; 14, then the Hungarian Rhapsody No.12, the Hungarian Rhapsody No. 9 "Pesther Carnival" then she is finishing her performance with Hungarian Rhapsody No. 2.

Recognised a couple of wealthy Jewish industrialist and a banker from my morning presentation session. They just greeted us with a smile and tipped their hats. I returned the greeting in the same way. One of them commenting on the rich program and telling us that he had heard Miss Fischer performing in Budapest.

Rebekah quickly responded to that claim with, 'My fiancée is a good friend of Miss Fischer.'

Some people stared at us and the one who made the comment said, 'That is very nice.'

I whispered into Rebekah's ear, 'Just let them show off with their own memories, as they are so proud of them. We are different, it is better to sit in the back row in the theatre then been in the front.' She smiled and squeezed my arm tighter.

Handing my tickets to the usherette and she asked us to follow her. She showed our seat at the middle of the second row. I felt a right hypocrite as I'd just said a couple seconds ago that I prefer to sit in the back row, and now we were seated in the stall here in the second row. Well, I think I have spoken too soon. I felt a right smack.

A familiar voice greeted me from behind us, we both turned around and there was Rabbi Kahana.

He said, 'You two look very good together, it was my pleasure meeting you both today.'

I said, 'No Rabbi Kahana, the blessing was ours.'

The auditorium light turned down and the stage light turned on. A compere came to the stage to introduce Annie.

A gentle applause as she was walking to her Bösendorfer Concert Grand piano.

Annie's fingers hit the ivory and ebony keys her fingers have run through on the whole keyboard in such a force that have always amazed me of a gentle lady with a delicate finger can put so much force on a piano key that sound like a thunder. As she finished her program the audience jumped on their feet applauded in such enthusiasm, shouting Bravo, Bravo! Truly she gave a tremendous performance I haven't heard her putting so much passion into her performance. As she walked off stage the shouting volume increased until Annie came back and gave her encore, and she performed Hungarian Rhapsody No. 15 – Rákóczi Marches. Well, the audience went crazy *(as Rákóczi is a local noble family to Ungvár and Munkács).*

It was a great choice of music, certainly it "brought the house down".

At the end we said goodbye to Rabbi Kahana and made our way back to our hotel Korona. We sat in the hotel bar just relaxing after the perfect ending of this exciting and full of activity of this day.

An exhausted Annie walked into the bar where we agreed to meet up.

'You look absolutely exhausted, Annie dear.'

She said, 'Yes, I am' as she sat down at our table.

The waiter opened the champagne, which was on ice for a while, so it was well chilled.

We toasted and I kissed her hand and said with an emotional voice, 'Dear Annie thank you for the tickets and for your performance tonight and dedicating your program to our hero, Franz Liszt.'

'O, Gabriel you are a big softy so much Hungarian nationalism in a Jew, come, come.'

Rebekah said, 'Miss Annie you have mesmerised me with your performance and most importantly not just an amazing artist, but a Jewish women artist. Thank you for this "journey" you have taken me this evening, I will never forget your performance and giving us the best seat in the theatre.'

'Thank you, Rebekah, this is very nice of you. You have emphasised the Jewish Woman. May I ask you why? Are you involved with some kind of women's liberation organisation?'

'Yes Annie, I am a member of the Ukrainian Jewish Women's Organisation. We are fighting for women's equality encouraging young girls to be educated and standing up for themselves in the man's world.'

'That is very good I respect the work you ladies putting into bringing feminism into the twenty's century. Just look at me I fought hard to be accepted in my profession on the same level as the men. Tell me something Gabriel how did you two met did you ask a Shad Chan to find you such a sweet woman?'

'No Annie, I have seen a vision of an angel through the crowd at the university of Lvov and I just couldn't take my eyes off her.'

'Well, this is very romantic, I have known you for some time, helping me with my English lessons I thought that you are going to stay a bachelor. How is your poet friend Miklós Radnóti? Has he married that young lady (Fifi), Fanny Gyarmati?'

'Yes, Annie they have, back in 1935.'

'Well Rebekah, these two, Radnóti and your Gabriel been well known in the Budapest cocktail parties scene. If you forgive me but I feel tired and I have to get ready to travel back to Budapest in the morning.'

'Certainly, Annie, I mustn't keep you I can understand it you've been working very hard tonight. Sending my regards to our friend in Budapest. I should be back to Budapest in the second part of July. May well be I could catch up you at the Kávéház if you are in town.'

We said goodnight and all of us went to our rooms. I asked Rebekah if she would like to share my bed, or she would choose hers as we both were very tired in this eventful day.

'I would like to sleep in my bed Gabriel if you don't mind?'

'Of course not, goodnight my darling Rebekah, see you in the morning.'

'Goodnight Gabriel, sleep well my love.'

Chapter 19

My Thoughts Alone, Reflection on My Life

After a very busy stressful day, I tried to wind down in my bed alone, I just can't get to sleep, turning in my bed and my mind in overdrive, reflecting on the past day's events.

Meeting with all those interesting people at my presentation. The genuine ones, and the calculators whose only interest is to get rich through obtaining information does not work or achievement. Stepping all over humanity and getting higher on the social perches taking more away from the downtrodden selfishly not sharing their earthly wealth.

Your achievements away from home what people accepting what you are and what you've achieved and respect you for that. Until someone like Annie, comes along who have "walked the walk" has comes from the same humble background and achieved great respect from people for her contribution to society criticising and questioning others who are making their way up on the perches of life. Try to "thumb you down" as you have no right to achieve greater thing in life. You should be staying in your place where you've been born that is where you belong to.

My thought should be more positive and uplifting for my tomorrow's presentation to politicians and to civil servants of Ungvár.

I am dreading of having another "bully" councillor like Cllr H. Cohen. An ex retired army man who has a chip on his shoulder. He's got kicked out from the army for bullying a junior officer. So, he found himself in another opportunity where he can obtain power with, which he can carry on bullying others with" Power" He accept the authority from above him as long as he can exercise that little power on others to satisfy his corrupt and sick mind. Hypocrites all of them they lying to the people who put them into that position so they will be supposed to protect them. Like the famous teaching of Vladimir

Ilyich Lenin what he said: If you want to convince people of your interpretation of "facts" just tell a lie again and again until the public will believe in that lie is the true fact.

So why am I doing this? Haven't I been happier in my little world doing humanitarian work where I have made people happy? Or taking on a consignment like this; Does "Schmuck" shine so brightly on my forehead? Or the usual thing: "Gabriel will do it".

The dawn must of have broken by the time I have fallen asleep. I woke up like a "zombie". Getting dressed for this heavy day again have met up with my helpers in the breakfast room. I asked where was Rebekah. Andre said, 'We thought she was with you.'

'No, she stayed in her room.'

Viktoria said, 'Gabriel you need some strong coffee you look very tired.'

I was telling them of the last evening concert story, the reason of being late for breakfast.

Viktoria turned to Andre and said, 'So, I was right Andre, I have recognised her, that lady was Annie Fischer who had a breakfast and she just left a half an hour ago.'

'Did you have a good time last night?'

'Yes, we went to a small restaurant in downtown where a band was playing jazz.'

'I didn't know that you like Jazz.'

'Yes, we do very much.'

Rebekah just walked in and joined us she looked as someone who had a better night sleep than I have had.

'Good morning Rebekah, did you have good sleep?'

'Yes, thank you, like a little girl curled up and thinking of the last night and piano recital, what a fantastic pianist Annie is. And what a lady, working on the same principle as I do. For women's equality in the man's world.'

'What do you mean Rebekah?' asked Viktoria.

'I could take you to our next Jewish Women's Union meeting in Munkács, if you would like to know of the kind of works, we do for women.'

Viktoria looked at Andre what would be his reaction to Rebekah's invitation.

Andre said, 'We will have a chat on the way back home from Ungvár.'

I said, 'Have we finished with our breakfast? I do not want to be late for this very important meeting.'

The porter called a taxi from the rank next to the hotel entrance. We managed to get all our presentation materials in the boot of the taxi, and we fit in the car without discomfort.

We went to the Transcarpathian Parliament / County Hall for our ten-clock presentation. We still have to set up our stand in the room and organise for all the printed materials for this meeting.

At our arrival, the porter of the town hall asked for our paperwork as they have some very important people coming from Hungary. When he learned of those "very important people from Hungary" was us then he apologised and quickly added that security is very important. Then he called on his deputy gatekeeper to carry all of our packages upstairs into the council chamber and to help us whatever we would need for this presentation. I heard he was telephoning the organisers that the delegation has arrived from Hungary.

We have been escorted into this beautifully furbished council chamber. All the walls covered in wooden panels and the furniture's are made out of the same finish wood.

Rebekah said that all the interior and furnishing has been custom made by a Munkács base company; Sutyai Béla Furniture Factory. Rebekah's father's engineering factory was making some of the fixings and metal works for the Parliament building.

I said, 'This is very impressive Rebekah. Your father Isaack has never told me that.'

'No, he is a very modest man.'

'Yes Rebekah, he is a very modest man.'

As we started to set up our stand, a very nice gentleman walked to us and started to talk to Andre and Rebekah, while I was setting up my speech in front at the main councillor's lectern.

The gentleman came to me and introduced himself of Andrew Bródy.

I introduced myself and added, 'It's very nice to meet you Mr Bródy. Are you the Member of the Transcarpathian Parliament?'

'Yes, Gabriel I am the minister for education and the Regional Prime minister of Transcarpathia.'

'I am very sorry Mr Bródy for my ignorance. I don't know much about you, but I have read some interesting facts about your noble work for the peace of the region, and I have to say I am saluting your commitments and the bravery you are demonstrating it in the political fields. Thank you to showing interest in my presentation.'

'I am very interested of you as well, mainly following your work, I have heard much appraisal from Governor Konstantin Hrabar, now he is representing Munkács. I believe you have met him at the Munkács Town Hall. He has told me that you are going to settle in Munkács with your charming fiancée. It could be very useful for us of your knowledge and your quality here in Transcarpathia.'

'Yes Mr Bródy, there is a big possibility of that commitment through marriage. But at this moment I am working for the Hungarian Government. I have to return to Budapest in middle of July with my report and consult the ministers on the result of my finding and experience I have learned about the education here in Transcarpathia.'

'When you do plan you return to Munkács Gabriel please let me know.'

'I promise Mr Bródy, you'll be the first to know. But having said that Munkács is a small town and there is no secret kept longer than an hour.' As we spoke with Mr Bródy, people started to coming into the chamber for my presentation.

Mr Bródy smiled and said, 'Yes, that is true. Then he called a gentleman to join us, and he introduced him as the Mayor of Ungvár Mr László Megay, and Ernő Dudás, and Volosin Avgusztin MPs.'

(I had a very negative, aggressive vibe from Volosin I felt he doesn't like Hungarians or Jews.)

The mayor asked Mr Brody to start the presentation as we were getting late for the start. Viktoria sat at the councillor's place at the top table, and she was ready to take the minutes of the meeting.'

As we all settled, Mayor Dudás introduced me to the audience and asked me to begin with my presentation to the relevant department of the county officers and of the county and Town councillors.

I had pre-timed my presentation so it shouldn't take longer than on hour and a half so it will give opportunity to ask questions at the end of my presentation. The subject on the presentation sheets Rebekah and Andre had handed out to all the attendants was the same as it is based on in my speech of the footnotes; N15 and N22.

Only adding more news items which resulted from my presentation that I gave in Munkács, which developed since Munkács Educational Committee Meeting members agreed on that, the Local Authority of Munkács will request on the implementation that the Hungarian language should be used in education and should be experimented in the Gymnasium of Munkács, the one which has been banned in 1919 by the Czech Authority. And furthermore, to establish a teachers educational training college in Munkács, From 1 September 1938.

There weren't many questions unlike I had in Munkács. At the end, the Mayor of Ungvár Mr Ernő Dudás thanked me and our delegation by naming us for the excellent presentation on behalf of the Hungarian Education ministry.

Mayor Dudás invited all of us for a buffet and a private chat in his cabinet office. I noticed that Mr Bródy was chatting to Rebekah during the buffet. She looked so elegant with her body language she demanded respect. She is a real professional businesswoman a great asset for me during my meetings with officials, professionals, and politician's.

By the time we finished for the day the mayor offered that his official car will take us back to the hotel. We thanked him for his offer, and he's instructed his secretary to organise the car for us.

He said goodbye to us with the seeing you in Munkács sometime later on this year.

The mayor's official driver gave us a tour around Ungvár which was very interesting as none of us been in Ungvár. After we got dropped off at our Hotel Korona we still had enough time to do something together. I asked jokingly, 'As we have finished earlier would you like to go home?' Everybody's face was a picture.

Rebekah looked at me and she asked, 'Are you serious Gabriel? Could we not stay here for another night as we planned it originally, please?'

Everything was written on Andre and Viktoria's faces.

I laughed and said, 'Of course NOT! I am enjoying myself with you. Very much we have done all the work which was required as my job description from my employer. Just a note; it doesn't matter who is my employer. I, we, still have to deliver our job to the highest standard, as people expect it from us.

'If I may say this Andre and Viktoria, for your future to remember this; if you are doing anything in your life, you must do it to the highest and more professional standard as you can the expectation is not just for your employer but also you should have a job satisfaction out of it as well.

'So, I shall see you at five and will going to have a nice meal somewhere and then we are going to find a jazz club or a classical one any of them which you choose. We deserve a relaxed evening after the hard work we have done.'

We all had two hours free time to relax or may be doing some more pleasurable exercise. Andre and Viktoria quickly disappeared Rebekah and I just smiled and thought that we could follow their idea as well.

When we got into our room the temperature was a bit warm from the heat of the day, we had the window opened a little bit enough fresh air to get in. Luckily, we had a ceiling fan which was placed right above our bed. We both said that will be helpful to keep us in the right temperature.

Rebekah walked to me embraced her arms around my neck and slowly she pushed her lips and her body closer to mine and she kissed me in such passion as she did it in Lvov. Then she whispered in my ear, peel me my love think of me if I am on orange, do it Just slowly, bit by bit. What a pleasure to making love, the way poets or painters would describe it in words or express it on the canvases. It is magical.

When we got downstairs our faithful helpers were in the hotel's cafeteria all ready.

Rebekah said, 'How can they do it so quickly?'

I said, 'Just look at them they are much younger than us they do everything in a speed.'

She just laughed. Andre suggested, 'Why don't we have our supper here in the hotel restaurant. I've seen the menu it looks very good.'

I looked at Rebekah and asked her if that would suit her.

She said, 'Why not, let's give it a chance.' Andre asked the waiter if they would have a table for four of us. The waiter came back with four menu and handed out to us and recommended the Hungarian fish soup with cottage cheese pasta. 'I can recommend any fish dishes they are freshly delivered from the fisherman.'

'Do you have any Tokay Szamorodni?'

'Yes sir, we get a supply directly from the winemakers as Tokay is so close to Ungvár.'

'Alright I would like a bottle of chilled Szamorodni and some sparkling water as well.'

'Would you ladies like some liquor as aperitifs?'

Rebekah and Viktoria asked for a glass of Unicum, Andre and I ordered a glass of Kosher Plum Brandy. We all chose different kind of fish dishes from the menu and kept our appetite low for having room for the puddings.

The food was absolutely delicious and plentiful. We all had different desserts; Rebekah and I chose the Dobostorta, Viktoria and Andre's choice was the *Gesztenyepüré*.

We decided that we will have a coffee at the jazz club later on.

After the lovely meal we all four of us walked to the jazz club arm in arms. Andre lead us to this place where he and Viktoria has been last night. The volume of the music was getting louder as we were getting nearer to the club. It is looks to me the club is a cafeteria during the day, and it has been transformed into a club for the evening. Stopped in the doorway waiting to find a table for four of us. It wasn't just the music flown out into the street but the smoke as well. You didn't need to smoke a cigarette you just inhaled it and that was terrible. I don't smoke neither Rebekah. I suggested to Andre that I would rather go to this Cafe where the pianist and the harpist were playing. I don't mind if you want to stay here but we are going. The waiter came back to us and told us that there was no table available at all.

So, we all four of us went back to this Classical Coffee where we met up with Annie Fischer the night before. As we walked into the coffeehouse, the waiter recognised us and offered the same table for four of us. The musicians did welcome us with a hello to our direction.

Viktoria said that she preferred this place rather than the jazz club. This was much more romantic.

Rebekah said, 'I am glad you say this Viktoria,' and she touched Viktoria's hand looked at her and gave her a wink, then the two girls giggled again. It was a very pleasurable evening for all of us in particularly for the two girls they were having a great gossiping "match" about all the famous politicians and the wealthier residents and their wife's of Munkács.

I noticed there was a program leaflet pinned on the notice board, promoting:

In July 1938. Sereghy Andor Theatrical Group will be performing at the Grand Theatre of Ungvár, guest performers Muráti Lili, Törzs Jenő.

Well, well, well. I will have some good idea for the Hungarian Cultural Minister next month when I have to deliver my report and my recommendations to them for promoting Hungarian artists in Transcarpathia as culturally promoting the Hungarian language through entertainers from Budapest.

In fairness many great artists originated from Ungvár like the Latabár Brothers, Manyi Kiss, of Munkács. I was very pleased with my idea and promised myself that I will work out a promotional study for the cultural minister.

I chipped into the conversation with a much serious subject. I suggested to Andre and Viktoria, as they had first-hand experienced through our work in Munkács and here in Ungvár as well that the local authorities getting ready for the changes.

'I would like to suggest to you and to your close friends and members of your families that they should apply for the Hungarian Citizenship as soon as it will be available. Just to avoid the rush for passport applications.'

They all looked at me with an open mouth and I felt I had to explain to them thoroughly. I said, 'I will explain it to you in the office next Monday.'

I sent a couple of drinks to the musicians I have paid for the bill and started to walking back to the Hotel Korona in this warm summer evening one more time and then tomorrow back home again to the treadmill in Munkács.

I said goodnight to Andre and Viktoria and told them that our train will leave at 9.45 am so we should be ready at 8.30 am so we won't miss our train back to Munkács.

Viktoria thanked Rebekah and me for the nice meal and for the evening.

I said, 'It was truly a pleasure to be with them during the past few days.'

Walking up to our room with Rebekah, I asked her if she would like to share a bed with me.

She said, 'I am very sorry my angel, but I have just started my period this evening, I need to attend it and it just wouldn't be the same as last night. So, goodnight my angel.'

I said, 'I understand,' and I kissed her goodnight. 'Goodnight my Darling Rebekah.'

Chapter 20

Back to Munkács to Prepare Reports and Wedding Plans

I checked out from the hotel for all of us at the reception and asked them to call for a taxi to take us to the railway station.

All of us were in quite cheerful mood at the thought that we were going home. I noticed that Andre managed to tie his bowtie on his own. I was complimenting on his looks, 'I have to say Andre now you look a sophisticated young gentleman with that bowtie. It suits you Andre.'

Rebekah added, 'Yes, I think you should keep this image from now on.'

'Thank you, Rebekah, you bought it for me, it shows your good taste.'

We all managed to get into the taxi this time only with light hand luggage as we left all the printed materials, leaflets behind at places where we gave our presentation.

Again, the two girls were arm in arm and having a conversation on they own. I am glad to see that Rebekah got on so well with Viktoria. (Probable Rebekah will introduce Viktoria to the Union of Jewish Women's Organisation) Why not Viktoria should put herself more forward as she is very quick minded, she is able to do anything, I don't think Andre would mind if her name would be known as an activist for a good cause in Munkács or even further afield. I think Rebekah is caring for Viktoria as a big sister. Since Rebekah first came into our office and she has met Viktoria there is a strong bond which has been developed between these two girls. (sorry women).

We had half an hour to get on the train. The Railway between Ungvár and Munkács is just over one year old, they opened it on 15 June 1937, for some reason it's bypassing Szerednye. It's really reducing the travelling time to two and a half hours and also a big help to bring business closer together between the two major towns.

I just got the local newspaper at the station's trafik (news agent) to look through what has happened in Transcarpathia, in particular Ungvár and Munkács. I was glad that none of my engagements were published as it is still primary status in governmental level.

On the way home to Munkács the girls had the same arrangement; they sat at the window chatting all the way to Munkács.

Rebekah bought two copies of the latest fashion magazine one for herself and one for Viktoria.

I was analysing the three-day engagements we had one for the Jewish community and one for the council's which was more political based engagement.

I asked Andre, 'What was your feel between the community presentation and from the political one?'

Andre said, 'It is my intuition that the community leaders and businesspeople were more open and welcoming for the changes from the Czechoslovakian to the Hungarian style administration. They still have fond memories of the Austro-Hungarian administration.'

'Yes, I know what you mean, Andre, under Emperor Franz Joseph the Jewish people were welcomed and Jews have contributed immensely to the wealth and prosperity to the Austro-Hungarian Empire.'

Franz Joseph was a visionary leader and a strong believer and follower of the Lord and put his faith into practice to support and protect God's chosen people like in; Genesis 12, 1-3.

'Do you think Andre that the politicians at the Ungvár Town Hall have understood, and accepted the reality of what they are facing?'

'I am not sure Gabriel, as I have been listening in the back of the room with Rebekah, and listening to your presentation, which I have to say it was straight forward explanation of the meaning of the changes which is the main message of your presentation.

'I felt some of the Russian pro Czechoslovakian Nationalist politicians have been visually worried and concerned I guess of their positions, influence, financial benefits and mainly of their power in the Transcarpathian Region.'

'Yes you right Andre, Czechoslovakia, has never existed before it was the creation of the Following: The **Treaty of Versailles** was of the peace treaties that brought the World War I. to an end by the Pittsburgh Agreement of May 1918, the Czechoslovak declaration of independence, created in Washington was published by the Czechoslovak National Council, signed by; Masaryk, Štefánik, Beneš David Lloyd George, Vittorio Orlando, Georges Clemenceau and Woodrow Wilson on 18 October 1918 in Paris, and proclaimed on October 28 in Prague.

'Towards the end of the First World War which led to the collapse of the Austrian-Hungarian Empire, several ethnic groups and territories with different historical, political, and economic traditions were blended into new state structures. Czecho-Slovakia was a sovereign state in Central Europe that existed from October 1918, when it declared its independence from the broken state of the Austro-Hungarian Empire, until its peaceful dissolution into the Czech Republic.'

'I didn't know this Gabriel.'

'Yes, it was a conspiracy to break up the Austro-Hungarian Empire with a "manufactory created country" called Czechoslovakia, by some members of an international secret society without the consideration for the ethnic communities' traditions and cultures.'

Andre was amazed at the points I have presented him with. 'Have you never learned of these historical facts Andre?'

'No, I haven't heard of them or been taught of these facts Gabriel.'

'Well, it's well known that there is always the winning team (country) who is to rewrite the history.'

We got back home in Munkács very quickly, just turned eleven in the morning, this is it, when you have some interesting subjects to talk about. We really couldn't enjoy the beautiful landscape scenery of the hills and woodlands.

Luckily, there was a free taxi at the station, so we didn't have to wait for one to turn up for the train arrival. We dropped off Rebekah at her home kissed her and said will see you later, and we all went to the town hall to drop off all our official paperwork. I asked Viktoria to type out the minutes of both of my presentation and the conversation I had with the audience. From both meetings, the one I gave at the Great Synagogue of Ungvár, and the other one which is the most important is the one I gave to the politicians and the civil servants at the County Hall in Ungvár.

I had to complete my report now which I started last night in my room at the Korona Hotel, but I couldn't complete as we had such a busy program. 'I hope you can read my writing Viktoria, just ask if you get stuck with it, then I have to post it today to the officials at the Education Ministerium in Budapest.'

We all finished with our work by 3.30 pm. giving an opportunity to Andre and Viktoria to get home on time and ready for the Sabbath.

I walked to Munkács main post office to post my reports in express with a courier service so the officials will receive it by next Monday at the Education Ministry in Budapest. The lady at the courier office recognised me as I have been sending my reports to the same place with their services. From the post office I have dropped into the butcher to pick up some marrowbones for Elisabeth's dogs as they are now waiting for those goodies from me.

I had to take my jacket off as the summer heat was unbearably hot, luckily Elisabeth's house wasn't far away where I could refresh myself and get back to Rebekah's house for the Sabbath supper.

I still hadn't had the opportunity to look into the newspaper the one I bought it in Ungvár.

I think the dogs must have sensed my steps as I got nearer home, they started barking. As soon as I have opened the gate, the two dogs were running around me as they smelled the bones in the brown paper bag. I got the bones out of the bag the dogs were sitting passionately next to each other and waited for the bones.

Elisabeth came out to see what the dogs were barking about. Both of the dogs rushed off with the bones to their favourite spots and started the joyful chowing of the marrow bones.

Elisabeth with a beaming smile greeted me, 'Welcome home "Neighbour"!'

First, I didn't know what she was on about neighbour, then I realised that before I'd gone to Ungvár, I'd asked my friend Sándor to arrange the exchange the paperwork for the purchase of the property next to Elisabeth's house.

Elisabeth was delighted that she had gained a good neighbour and assured me that she will keep her eye on the property if we ever go away on business or for other reasons.

I got refreshed, changed into a summery suit and I went to Rebekah's house to celebrate the Sabbath. On my way I collected the flower arrangement for Rebekah, and for Rita, and a bottle of *Egri Bikavér* (Bulls Blood) for Isaack.

At my arrival Rita opened the door for me. I kissed her on her cheek, and she was kinder to me than in previous other times.

When we got through the apartment door Isaack welcomed me, we shook hands. I presented him with the bottle of red wine and Rebekah rushed out from the kitchen with a beaming smile. I presented Rebekah and Rita with the flowers and Rebekah gave me a kiss on my cheek thanked me for the flowers and asked Rita to put them into the vase then she put her arms in Isaack's arm and said, 'Papa has something to show you Gabriel.'

Isaack opened a small briefcase and pulled out the sales document of the property which is the one next to Elisabeth. Also, he presented us with a gold coloured key in a box of the property on Latorca utca in the Garden District of Munkács.

Rebekah jumped like a little girl and shouted joyfully, kissed, and hugged her Papa then did it to me as well. I thanked Isaack offering my hand to shake it, but he declined and gave me a hug and kissed me on my cheek too. Isaack turned to me and said, 'Now I can call you my son Gabriel!'

I was finding difficult to hide my emotion as I felt my tears were running down on my cheeks too. Only word I could say was 'Thank you Isaack!'

Realising my embarrassment, Isaack changed the subject slightly and said, 'While you were away Sándor came in with the official sales contracts and the key for the property. We had a very good chat and on Thursday evening we both went over to the Star Hotel for a meal and for some drinks. I have to say we both have enjoyed it and we agreed that we will repeat of the getting together once a month in the same place.'

I said, 'Thank you for lending me the money for the property, I've been told from my estate agent that I have a buyer for my apartment in Budapest. Soon that money will be transferred into the newly opened Magyar Kiralyi Bank I will pay it back to you.'

Isaack told me, 'I know you will Gabriel, but at this moment we have the most important first step in your union is you and Rebekah's own property here in Munkács. Actually, now I am very excited over that to know that you and Rebekah will be living so close to me.'

Isaack got out a bottle of champagne and said, 'Let's celebrate this joyful news! L'chaim! L'chaim!'

Rita reminded Isaack that it's getting late for the Sabbath. Isaack said, 'I am so happy I say a special kiddush for this Sabbath.'

We all stood around the Sabbath table and Rebekah did the Sabbath blessing.

Rita brought in the food from the kitchen and Isaack served us with the wine and said the kiddush, it was so beautiful just as I remember of my childhood. It was so special, almost Holy. Yes, it was our family who celebrating Sabbath together in unity with our Lord and Creator.

'My mother used to say a wisdom at our Sabbath meal in Hungary… "Never trouble your mind for anything that shall happen to you in this world. Nothing can come but what God wills." (by St Thomas More)'

'That is so profoundly beautiful, Gabriel.'

'Yes, it is. It is pure, just like God's timing which is not always understood by humans, and this is the reason for so many conflicts among us.'

After the meal we just chatted around the cleared-up dining table discussed our plans.

I suggested to Isaack and to Rebekah, 'As I can see of these changes are coming into practice now that I would like to marry Rebekah at the registrar before I have to travel back to Hungary as I am now completing my mission here in Transcarpathia, and hopefully with a new mission I have been promised from the Cultural Ministry of promoting Hungarian cultural events in Munkács region.

'During this time while we are at the Foreign Ministry in Budapest, and if I can prove that we are officially married then I can apply for Hungarian Citizenship for Rebekah with a Hungarian Passport. And also, I can complete the sale on my apartment in Budapest, so I don't have to travel back again for that alone. I can use my connection in the Foreign Ministry, for obtaining a citizenship, for Rebekah, after all I am working for the Hungarian Government.'

'But what about our wedding Gabriel that we have planned?'

'That will happen the way we have planned it Rebekah, it's only we will have an official document to prove that we are married in the eye of the law. It is purely a great unmissable opportunity for both of us. A Hungarian citizenship for you my darling is better than a Czechoslovakian one.

'As these changes, the one what I am presenting here is shows that the time is now here, at the doorstep for Transcarpathia to be part of Hungary again.'

Isaack said, 'What Gabriel is saying does have merit, if anything would happen then you Rebekah have a well-recognised citizenship which will protect you all around the world. I can see that this would be for your benefit my dear daughter. And when do you think of this official registrar wedding should be done before that trip to Budapest.'

'I think it should be done in the middle of next month on the Thursday, 14 July 1938. As I have an appointment in the ministry on Tuesday, 19 July 1938.

'I will explain the whole reason of this rushed marriage contract to Rabbi Baruch as this is just an official deed of recognised by the state law and has been registered here in Munkács. I hope he will understand it as this is an opportunity for all of us. We are not going to break Chumash the law of Moses. I have to see him to update him on Monday with my finding during my presentation at the Ungvár synagogue.'

Isaack said, 'I like the idea, what do you think Rebekah?'

'I can see the benefits of the citizenship and also going to Budapest at the same time. Yes, I like it. Papa, I am having my graduation ceremony next week at the university in Lvov, I would like to arrange that tonight as well.'

'Of course, Rebekah, all of us are going to go to this special event with you to Lvov. I want to see for myself my daughter receiving her diploma from the university director. After all those years of hard work you have put into studies and travelling forward and back to Lvov.'

'My goodness I can't even follow both of your speed. This is it, now is the time for the future generation to fight for their existence and us to sit back, slow down a bit and let your youth energy to succeed. I guess this is the way I've done it with your mother Rebekah when we got together. Well, those were our times now it is two of yours.

'I just can't express to tell you how happy I am for you two. Looking forward to take my grandchildren for a walk, playing with them. The main thing is in our life is to survive and secure our genes for the future generation for growing up with dignity, respect of our traditions and for the love for our Lord God of Israel.'

'What about our engagement party Papa and Gabriel?'

'My dear daughter I haven't forgotten. How about on the week on Sunday, so we could celebrate your engagement and your graduation altogether?'

Rebekah and I thought that was a very good idea. Then Rebekah immediately started making a list who she should invite to this engagement party.

Isaack said, 'I thought that we only invite some close relatives or friends Rebekah. Our apartment is limiting the number of people we can cater for even if it is just a buffet.'

Rebekah said, 'Yes Papa, you are right maybe we should just do that.'

Chapter 21

Sabbath at Rebekah's House and Plans for Lvov and Our Wedding

On the day of the Sabbath, I arrived at the synagogue much earlier (as my alarm clock rooster croaked earlier or he couldn't sleep so he decided to wake everybody up). I met up with Dr Sándor Fried. I thanked Sándor for exchanging contract in such a speedy way, it helps me immensely with my plans.

'What do I owe you for your work Sándor?'

'Well, Isaack lent you the money for the property and for the transfer fee at the land registry. My cost is, well, let's see, that will be my wedding present for you two.'

'Thank you very much Sándor! You are a gentleman, and I am honoured that I can call you my friend.'

In the meantime, Isaack arrived with Rebekah. She looked stunningly beautiful again in her large flower print summer dress and a matching hat. I noted there was no gloves this time as she was showing off her engagement ring. I still can't believe it I shook Isaack by the hand, and kissed Rebekah's hand and on her face. (It was quite difficult to get near to her face from the large brims of her hat.)

By that time more people were getting together and making their way into the synagogue. Rebekah joined all the ladies and went upstairs to the balcony.

Three of us were sitting now next to us, greeting some of the people we knew. My tallit was slipping and a helpful hand behind me lifted it back on my shoulder, I turned around to thank the person for his assistance and with a big smile Mayor MP Hrabar greeted me. 'He said congratulation on your new property Gabriel.' I thanked him for his comment, but our conversation has stopped as Rabbi Baruch Rabinowicz entered into the hall and the service has started.

After the service we men were chatting in the hall waiting for the special Bar Mitzvah Ceremony for Zachariah Grünwald's son.

This meant that I couldn't even speak briefly with Rabbi Baruch.

Isaack asked me to try to talk to the Rabbi Baruch tomorrow because Rita had cooked my favourite dishes of *Töltött Káposzta* (Stuffed cabbage) and *Mákos Beigli* (rolled pastry stuffed with poppyseeds) as you know she is very keen with the dinner time.

'Oh NO, I wouldn't upset her by being late, particularly when she is cooking my favourites dishes. She is really spoiling me Isaack, she is a good woman.'

'Yes, you're right Gabriel, I don't know what I would have done without her. She has been looking after Rebekah as her daughter, they are very close. And she looked after me as well I couldn't of have built up my business without her help.'

By the time we got outside Rebekah was again the centre of attention among her girlfriends and some more mature ladies.

As we got to the group of ladies Isaack, and I tipped our hats and greeted them with Sabbath Shalom. They returned their good Sabbath greeting and asked me 'when is the "Khasene" (wedding) going to be Gabriel?'

Just jokingly, I replied, 'Next week.'

There was a bit of surprising faces but some of them understood the joke of it and laughed it off. Mrs Singer said, 'Hopefully we will be invited to it?'

I said, 'That is up to Rebekah, it is her department.'

Isaack just smiled and said, 'This is the answer you get to your curiosity.'

Walking back to Isaack's apartment both of Rebekah's arms held us tight to her body; she said: 'You know I have suddenly become a kind of celebrity. Everybody is fussing me and being so nice to me. I have been going to this same synagogue for all my life and I have just been the one who was still not married. Poor girl.

'But now since you come along Gabriel and with your status and "fame" they just can't believe that you have chosen me, the "poor girl" who has not married to anybody.'

'Get above them my Rivkah! Just gossip and women's talk.'

'Yes Rebekah, your Papa is right. Now I am here for you as your Knight and Angel who will protect you from "evil tongues". You should tell them my train from Hungary was running late, and that held you back, but now I am here to stay with you.'

Isaack and Rebekah looked at me and he said to her.

'You see what you have now? they have never dreamed of it in they life, just quickly get married and have children. That is where their life end. You are blessed with all of that what they don't have.'

'Yes, you are different than any of them. You have and have your Papa's support to educate yourself be more than others around you. You have represented freedom and knowledge, that they have never been offered, so this is just common jealousy. I promise you I will treat you as an equal partner and encourage you to be a modern wife and mother as the Lord God created man and woman to be equal.

'By the way, Sándor told me that he has a client who is a builder, and he could do all the alternations on our new house. Rebekah, would you please look for some magazines for the modern home interior designs.'

'Yes of course I will happily.'

We stopped the conversation as we arrived at Isaack's house.

Rita welcomed us and even if we were late, for the dinner I defused her anger with a big hug and kiss on her face. I said, 'You have to stop spoiling me Rita I know you have cooked my favourite dishes, but I have chosen Rebekah already.'

She laughed at me and said: 'I would not challenge Rebekah for you or for anybody.'

We all laughed, and Isaack and I went to the bathroom to wash our hands and went to the dining room where Isaack said the kiddush for the food and for the wine then we four of us held hands and said Amen.

The food was truly excellent (not because it was my favourite) but it somehow now becoming a relaxed regular and blessed family occasion. I haven't experienced this feeling for a very long time.

Rebekah started to organise the trip to Lvov for this coming week for her graduation celebration. She said her graduation day is on Thursday at eleven in the morning and she has suggested that if we would leave on Wednesday morning train to Lvov we could stay in the Grand Hotel in the centre of Lvov, not far away from the university where we could walk to the event casually. Spending one more evening in Lvov, we could get back home to Munkács on Friday.

I said, 'That is a good idea Rebekah.'

Isaack thought it would give some opportunity for him and for Rita to look around in Lvov, as it was some years ago since he came with Rebekah to arrange her scholarship in the university.'

I just looked at Rebekah, in my mind that the same hotel where we made commitment for each other for life. She looked at me with her bright eyes and I realised that was she was thinking along with me.

'Apukam, I don't really know how to thank you for all the great gifts you have given me. This opportunity at the university and all the way of my life you were there to support me, and of course you Rita as my "second mother" cared for me. Thank you very much for all of the love and support. Here is the result with my graduation at the university and here is with my future husband.'

Rita needed a handkerchief which I put into her palm and started wiping her tears.

Isaack touched Rebekah's hand and squeezed it, 'Yes, my beloved Rivkah, I am—we are very proud of you and very, very pleased for you two.'

I suggested that I will ask Viktoria to book the hotel in Lvov, and the train tickets in the name of the Council of Munkács as I can get a discount for being an official from the council.

I can save some money for the Golden Rosa Restaurant, near the synagogue.

Isaack just looked at us and he thought we must have some sentiment at that place.

The conversation moved onto the restoration of the property what we've just purchased and credit to Sándor he has completed not just the contract for the property but also arranged the change of new owner's registry at the council's Land Registry Office.

'He is a good friend Gabriel,' said Isaack, 'he is just like us keeping our traditions but accepting the changes of modern times.'

'Yes Isaack, I am very fortunate with his friendship from day one. Since my arrival to Munkács I felt he was the one I have felt common spiritual brotherhood with. I will try to see Rabbi Baruch Rabinowicz tomorrow. I have planned it for Monday, but I think he wouldn't be able to see me as on Munday is always the market day and he will be busy with all the livestock in the marketplace.

'Like I said I will arrange the booking for the "civilian" marriage registry for the 14th of July. As I said it should be done in the middle of next month on the Thursday, 14 July 1938. I have an appointment in the ministry on Tuesday, 19th of July 1938. in Budapest. We don't really have a lot of time to organise everything, but we will manage.

'Isaack, I have met a Jewish businessman in Ungvár who is looking for an engineering company who could make/supply an Archimedes principle screw conveyors/elevator for moving semi liquid and solid materials. I told him that I know an excellent engineering company in Munkács owned by my father-in-law and I will pass his enquiry to you.

'He is based in Ungvár, but here are his contact details in Ungvár. I wasn't sure if it would be of any interest to you Isaack, just mention my name so that he'll be remember me.'

'That is very good of you Gabriel, we can design anything whatever the specification would be and also, we can manufacture it as well. I have a very good knowledgeable workforce they can do anything depending on the specifications. Thank you for this Gabriel I will get in touch with him on Monday. You could be a good salesman for me.'

'With respect Isaack, I am not good of being a salesman no disrespect to your offer, but I would rather stick with the field I can understand and am good at, and that is art and entertainment. This is what I have done in all of my life.'

'Was your trip to Ungvár successful Gabriel?'

'I hope so Isaack. The reception at the Great Synagogue was a kind of positive from one group of people from the Local Jewish Community, and some others who had some concerns of the developments in central Europe, in particularly of the Austrian Anschluss, and the political and economic pressure from the "Greater" Germany's expansion in Bohemia.

'And this new Jewish Law has just been passed in the Hungarian Parliament in May, is a concern to many Jewish resident in Ungvár and also here in Munkács as well. Some people have welcomed Hungarian controlled administration in sentimental memory of the old Austro-Hungarian Empire. The memory of the assassinated Emperor Franz Joseph.

'At my presentation to the political, administrative side I sensed some very negative vibe of resistance, opposition from particularly from the Pro-Praha party. From the Russian party supporters were mixed reaction. I have met a very nice Russian politician Dr András Bródy, originally, he is a teacher like me, but he has found a calling to represent his people's interest in the political world of "Hyenas". I have felt an instant spiritual resemblance.

'But there was an objectionable negative politician a pro Czechoslovakian Politian (like Cllr H Cohen of Munkács) I felt he is a troublemaker. Awkward and objected to everything that I have said. His name is Volosin Avgusztin MP. and minister of Transcarpathia. Not a very nice man, full of hate a typical career politician.

'I had a conformation of that from the Ungvár Council's Education Committee, that they will open a Hungarian language Gimnázium from the first of September 1938. They have a very strong lobby group from the; PRMKE (United Hungarian Party) urged the Hungarian nationality parents to send their children to dominantly special Hungarian language schools. A call to all: "We have to protect our culture."

'Sounds like this party is putting pressure on the Munkács Local Authority as well. I do not have any guidance from Budapest on this issue so I cannot comment if this has merit or not along with my mission. Despite I am sending my regular reports of all my experience and my assessment to the Ministry in Budapest in conjunction with my mission, I have not received anything regarding this political lobby group of; PRMKE.

'Actually, Isaack I think I have done everything what the Hungarian Ministry commissioned me with, so I think it is now time for me to move on.'

Isaack told me, 'Well Gabriel, I am very proud of you not just as my son in law, but all the good and positive things that you do for the Jewish Communities in this region. I think you was the right choice from Chief Rabbi Immanuel Lőw, of Budapest.'

'Thank you for your trust in me. This mean a lot to me, not just in loyalty but in kind of real fatherly character. With regards to the money, you've lend me for the house, I will pay it back to you as soon I have sold my apartment in Budapest.'

'I know you will Gabriel, just don't worry about it, you have a lot more things waiting for you to solve them.'

'Yes, Sándor told me as well that he has some clients who are trusted builders are and they will do all the alterations on your house. They can start the work as soon as you two will give them a plan you want.'

'I leave that for Rebekah to decide on, she is very practical, and she knows how she want to arrange the kitchen, the bathroom and so on. Rebekah has excellent taste, and she is good of these home making plans.'

Rebekah came into the lunch where Isaack and I had a conversation and she said, 'I heard my name was mentioned what was all about it.'

I said, 'It is my belief that you are the best to redesign the new house the way you want it to suit your good taste.'

'Yes Papa, I have some good ideas. I have seen some modern designs of the latest Viennese Art-Nuovo magazine. It will be some opportunity to shop around in Budapest to see some nice ideas and may be get them to deliver them there.'

'Yes, we can do that Rebekah, I know a friend from my university in Budapest who is in the shipping business he can arrange whatever you would choose for the interior my love, like wallpapers, tiles and so on.

'My goodness just look at the time, it's evening all ready. I have to prepare some reports for Chief Rabbi Lőw, in Budapest, and try to organise a meeting with Rabbi Baruch over this marriage arrangement. I have to explain to him the reason why we are having to take this decision. I hope he will understand my reasoning. Also, I will ask him some available dates for our wedding which we would like to be held in his Hoif complex Synagogue before the Holydays of Rosh Hashana, which is on the Monday, 26 September 1938 (in our Jewish calendar, 1 Tishrei 5699). So any Sunday before that date. What do you think Rebekah?'

'Let me see the Sundays in September; it is on the 4th, 11th and 18th of September. Really any of them will do. Would you like me to come with you Gabriel?'

'If you don't mind Rebekah no, not this time, when we will have the available date then we will go in together to secure the date for our wedding.'

'Of course, I understand Gabriel, I'll leave that with you.'

'Before you go Gabriel have one more plum brandy, one for the road.'

'For your good health Isaack, L'chaim.'

'To both of you L'chaim.'

Rebekah walked me to the front door, and we kissed so passionately as we always do before we say goodbye to each other. It was a very natural goodbye because we knew that we would see each other in the morning, but I know I won't see Rebekah for a couple of days only on the Wednesday when we will be leaving to Lvov. We have to accept that It is only the kiss left for us.

'Thank you for this perfect day my darling Rebekah. Come and see me in the office sometime if you have some free time. Goodnight.'

'I will come in to see you my angel Gabriel. Goodnight.'

Chapter 22
Meeting Rabbi Baruch for the Wedding

First thing in the morning, I called into the Hoif Complex Synagogue just to ask Rabbi Baruch if he could have an hour of his time for me. It would be important.

'Good morning Gabriel, yes, I always can spare some time for you. What can I do for you? How did you get on in Ungvár with your presentation?'

'Thank you for your time Rabbi Baruch. Firstly, Chief Rabbi Yosef Elimelech Kahana is sending his kind regards to you and he thanks you for those bottles of Plum Brandy which you have sent to him.

'I don't know if you are aware that my mission will be ending at the end of this month, so I have to go back to Hungary to present my report and update the officials with my findings at the Education and Foreign Ministry.'

'No, I didn't know this Gabriel. But I have just heard that you have completed a purchase on the property on Latorca utca. I thought you will settle here in Munkács, because of the engagement to Rebekah Grósz?'

'Yes, both of them are correct. I think you may find this a bit complicated, but I will try to explain it to you in brief. Rebekah and I are going to get married here in Munkács, and if it is possible, we would like to get married by you Rabbi Baruch. We have some dates for the wedding any Sunday in September; it is on the 4th, 11th and 18th, before the Holy days of Rosh Hashanah, which is on the Monday, 26 September 1938 (in our Jewish calendar, 1 Tishrei 5699). We would like to find out if any of these dates would be available to have the marriage ceremony.'

'I have to get back to you on that may be later on today.'

'As you know we all have to register birth, death and marriage at the Towns, Cities Councils Registry Offices. We are, Rebekah and I are going to get married in the Registry Office in Munkács before we are going to Hungary as a married couple in the eyes of the civilian law. So, with that marriage certificate We are going to apply for a Hungarian Citizenship for my Rebekah, with the help of my connections at the ministry. Gaining a citizenship through marriage I believe is an asset to having dual nationality. As situations are developing here in the Transcarpathian Region I believe a Hungarian Citizenship is more beneficial than just the one Czechoslovakian/Russian.

'We have to rush this registry through as the timing is essential for us to make the application look as if it is not driven by any political agenda but purely is a result of being married. I have discussed it with Isaack, and he gave his blessing to this decision what we have to make.'

'Well, I can see the way you're thinking Gabriel that you want to protect your new wife from any inconvenient actions which could accrue in the future. I also understand that the civilian side of the registry, but my only concern Gabriel is that I am representing the Chumash, the law of Moses.'

'Rabbi Baruch I do understand, marriage is the legal union/contract of two people, who are joined together after they obtain a marriage license from their authority and take part in a ceremony. This type of marriage is called a "common law" marriage. Being married also gives legitimacy to sexual relations within the marriage. I do respect the Chumash and do not wish to compromise our tradition. Isaack and Rebekah Grósz are like me we are both practicing a more Liberal way of influenced/interpreted Jewish traditions. Both of us mature individuals I am 31 and Rebekah is 23 years old, we have passed the kinyan (engagement ring) ceremony with Isaack. Our commitments for each other is to fulfil the codes define it by these two categories: ishut and kiddushin (persons and process.)

'We both have the same respect and commitment to uphold the Chumash. After the marriage, our household will be Jewish, and we will bring up our future children according to the law of Moses and keep the Sabbath Holy.'

'Well Gabriel, I know and understand both of your family's commitment to our faith and I also know your background. I can see the sincerity of you wish to be blessed of your wedding under any circumstances. It is my duty to bless any union of marriage for anybody who is following the Chumash faithfully, is qualified for their marriage to be blessed according to the law of Moses. I will let you know the date you've given me tomorrow after the market day. But tell me Gabriel, what are you going to do on your return from Hungary?'

'I've been offered a job by the Council of Munkács to build up our cultural life here in Munkács and in the County of Beregszász. Promote Hungarian Culture and of course support our Jewish Culture with all our holidays as well.'

'That is very encouraging Gabriel they couldn't chose a better person than you.'

'Yes, this is the other reason I am going to Budapest I'll try sell my idea of this and to get a commission from the Cultural Ministry to promote Hungarian movie films, musicians, actors' entertainers, and circuses in the region. Hopefully, they will be supporting these events financially as well by the Cultural Ministry.'

'Excellent idea Gabriel, I can't wait to see a bit more classical cultural life here in Munkács. Look Gabriel, I am busy right now, but I will come into your office at the town hall around 12.30 in the afternoon with the booking and anything you should need for your wedding.'

'Thank you, Rabbi Baruch, and see you later. Shalom'

'Ye Gabriel, Shalom.'

Walking back home from the synagogue my mind was wondering in the beautiful Summer day tipping my hat to many people I have met already since I have moved here, some of them were walking back from their church services. Very friendly people all of them as they are so well mixed ethnically, they don't have any prejudice against each other.

Turning the keys in the front door the two dogs were rushing towards me, but they were greatly disappointed as I offered no bones to them. But nevertheless, they still welcomed me with great affection. It looks as Szuka is favouring me as I always stroke her on her head and really, she's getting the biggest bones with more meat on it.

Elisabeth just finished the work with the cattle in the barn laying fresh straws for their bed and fed them with a freshly cut hay.

Elisabeth gave me an extra key for our new house. The position of this key gives me some kind of security of this is "my place it's my home" feeling. I remember when I bought my first-floor apartment at 31. Király utca. And now I am going to sell that lovely place which gave me a home, comfort and so many fond memories of a very special kind of excitement on the "Sárga pamlag" (yellow bed).

I noticed that Szuka is following me to the house another thing I have noticed that the dog behaviour was relaxed, her waging tail was like a flag in the wind, I sensed that was a good thing may be a good omen? Someone told me in the past that dogs sense spirits in properties, if they are happy and feel comfortable the house is blessed with positive spirits. If the dog is backing off from the room, there is unsettled bad spirits there.

I just stroke her head and tell her well Szuka, this house will be your new home as well from now on. She looked at me if she would understand what I have just said to her I guess she really does sense me spiritually.

Elisabeth just walked into the house and said, 'I can see that your Rebekah will have to organise some changes to this old-fashioned house.'

'I hope so Elisabeth, it needs a lot of changes, like running water, a proper bathroom with hot water and all the facilities. A proper kitchen with all the built-in modern facilities for a future young family.'

'When are you going to start the alterations Gabriel?'

'I leave that to Rebekah, Elisabeth. She is a very modern minded woman and I know she will go for the latest fashion and the fashionable style design and comfort. My Rebekah has an excellent taste for comfort, not to mention for the future generation.'

'Or will it be the next *generations*, Gabriel?'

'Who knows, Elisabeth?'

'Well, you have a ready-made nanny for them Gabriel.'

'Yes Elisabeth, we will take up your offer indeed!'

'I am so glad Gabriel that you are my next-door neighbour. And just look at Szuka, she is going to be your security dog for life.' We both looked at the dog and smiled. 'Come on Gabriel I have cooked for both of us a Sunday dinner.'

I gave Elisabeth a hug and kissed her on her face and said, 'Thank you, my big sister.' Szuka just looked at us with jealousy on her face, Elisabeth and I just stroked her on her head then her tail was going fast again, she made sure that she had not missed out of our affection.

On Monday morning at eleven, Rabbi Baruch called into my office. I was surprised as I had not expected him to call on me before the end of the market.

'Yes, Gabriel, I have good news for you and for Rebekah, the 11th of September is booked already for your wedding.'

'Thank you so much Rabbi Baruch I should say that we are, Rebekah and I, two of the happiest people now in Munkács. She'll be so happy when she'll find out this great news. Rabbi Baruch, may I invite you for lunch please, just across the road at the Star Hotel restaurant. I believe they do cook kosher food as well.'

'I will be delighted to accept your offer.'

I knew that Isaack will be dining there at this time of the day. As we walked into the restaurant, Isaack spotted us, and he stood up and waved us to join him for dinner at his table.'

Isaack was delighted to see us in the restaurant, particularly as I was companioned by the Chief Rabbi of Munkács. 'What a privilege and honour.'

As we sat down at the table, Isaack has ordered the finest plum brandy for a glass of aperitif.

I started the conversation with the good news. 'Isaack, I am glad you are sitting as this news would probably make you sit down. Rabbi Baruch has given us a date for our wedding which will be on the 11th of September in the Hoif Complex Synagogue and will be conducted by the Chief Rabbi of Munkács.'

Isaack said, 'I am a strong weathered man, but you are right I need a drink for this news.' Isaack said in an emotional voice, 'Rabbi Baruch Rabinowicz, I am so happy for these two young people one is my daughter and the other one is my new son!' He couldn't continue with his speech as Rebekah just walked in with Viktoria, and with a lot of magazines under their arms. She was very surprised to see us with her father in the restaurant.

She said, 'I hope I am not interrupting you now?'

Isaack said, 'Far from it.' Then he looked at Rabbi Baruch and said, 'I hope you don't mind if they are joining us for dinner.'

Rabbi Baruch said, 'Of course not. I would like to talk to Rebekah, or Rivka? Over the wedding contract with Gabriel.'

Rebekah's legs went jelly-like and she sat down on the chair. She said, 'So, will you able to do our wedding Rabbi Baruch?'

'Yes Rebekah, and it is booked already for the 11th of September at the Hoif Complex Synagogue. So, you can start the planning for your wedding now.'

Rebekah said, 'This must be a dream I am seeing, am I?'

'No, my darling daughter Rivkah this is it! This is what you have always dreamed of for many years and now it is here at your feet you just have to pick it up and hold on tight to yourself it is truly yours.'

Rabbi Baruch said, 'I am so glad for this unplanned opportunity to see both side of the bride and the groom together so I can judge the commitment in both parties. To have the bride's father at present is even better to see it for myself the legitimacy and the commitment of all parties. I will announce your wedding in the first Sabbath of the 6th of August.

'Also, I had prayed about you to obtain a marriage license from the authority to allow a later time to take part in our Jewish tradition of the wedding ceremony. I believe you are not disobeying the low of Moses. The law doesn't specify the time delay from the Authority's Marriage license to the law of Moses Marriage Contract. So, it is correct from me to say as your faith leader to accept your explanation and I grant your request for getting married in the Hoif Complex Synagogue on the 11 September 1938. And now let's order our dinner as I am getting hungry.'

The happy Isaack asked the waiter to bring more chairs for Rebekah and Viktoria and placed the order for our dinner.

Rabbi Baruch asked Rebekah, 'Are you the same age as my wife Furma? She is called Rivka or Rebekah like you.'

'I think Rabbi Baruch your Rivka was two years above me in the Hebrew Gimnazium. I remember her well; she has always been our hero. She is very highly educated, knowledgeable and she always won the arguments against the boys.' (Both Rebekah and Viktoria were giggling.)

Rabbi Baruch said, 'Yes, she has never lost that quality. But I believe there are congratulations in place for your university graduation.'

Rebekah blushed for a minute and proudly said, 'Yes thank you Rabbi Baruch, we are all going to Lvov for that celebration. You see, I believe just like your wife Furma who has encouraged girls to get more higher education than just accept the elementary one. Your wife Furma encouraged us girls in the gymnasium to become the members of the Ukrainian Jewish Women's Organisation.'

'Yes, I have heard about her activities, she was always there for the people who have needed some kind of help like her father Rabbi Chaim Elazar Spira.'

Andre walked into the restaurant with the news that he had booked us into the Grand Hotel in Lvov and also the return railway tickets for all four of us.

I introduced Andre to Rabbi Baruch and to Isaack and said, 'Rabbi Baruch, these two young ones here, Viktoria and Andre, are going to get in touch with you in the future to make their marriage commitment too. We've got one more chair for Andre to join our table as well.'

'What a day and blessing we are having today all the things that we have planned for our future the way we wanted, and it's happening, we are thanking the Lord for His blessing and support for us.'

A little later as we planned everything it was due to the fantastic dinner we had with Rabbi, Isaack and with Rebekah, I was walking back to my office with Andre and Viktoria, and they were both unusually quiet.

I said, 'I hope I didn't embarrass you two in the restaurant with my comment to Rabbi Baruch?'

Viktoria said very quietly, 'No, I don't think you have done anything intentionally, but I had an argument with Andre over the weekend.'

I just looked at them and said, 'Well, this is just the beginning of your relationship trust me there will be many more disagreements going in the future between you two. Andre, thank you for organising and booking the hotel and the railway tickets. I appreciate your help.'

'It's my pleasure Gabriel.'

Rebekah stayed with her father in the restaurant then afterwards, she called in at my office with all those magazines she had collected today with Viktoria.

She said, 'Just look at them Gabriel what fantastic designs these are, the latest deco styles from Vienna. I would like to go through these magazines with you to have some ideas for our new house.'

'I think there will be plenty of time to do that on the train to Lvov, we can look through of them all. Sándor told me that he has a very good builder who is his client, who could do all the work, so I don't expect he would do a bad job for us. Also, we can look around the shops and get some more ideas in Budapest as we are going to be there for some days.'

'That will be fantastic Gabriel, I can look for some ideas for wedding dresses in downtown of Budapest.'

'I can't do that, but I promise you that I will introduce you to my friend Miklós Radnóti's wife Fanny, she is known as Fifi. She is the same age as you and Fifi will help you do some shopping.'

'And how about you Gabriel? Are you not going to be there with me?'

'Of course, Rebekah, I will be there with you, but I do have some very important meetings to attend in the Ministry. But when I can't be with you Fifi will be accompanying you. Rebekah, you speak Hungarian and Fifi speaks Yiddish as well so I am pretty sure that you girls will get on very well together. She is only three years older than you, but I can tell you that, to be with her is fun. She knows all the best shops in the Belváros (downtown) Budapest. I will meet you and Fifi at the Gerbeaud Coffeehouse when I have finished my meetings at the Ministry. Anyway, the shops in the Belváros and the coffeehouse are not far away from my apartment it is only in walking distance.

'I am sure she will know where to get the best wedding dress for you, and just think nobody will know in Munkács what you are going to be wearing for your special big day. No gossip!'

'Yes Gabriel, that is a great idea, I had never thought of it. All the people in Munkács can just guess about the style of my wedding dress. Yes, this thought makes me very happy indeed. And besides, you should not be able to see my wedding dress before our wedding day.'

'Yes, that is true, it is custom that the groom should not see the bride's wedding dress before the big day. Sorry my darling for my thoughtlessness. Now darling Rebekah, I don't want to be rude but Andre, Viktoria and I still have a lot of things to organise. We can plan of our Hungarian trip some other time.'

'I am so sorry Gabriel for my selfishness I am just excited. We will discuss more of our Hungarian plan on the way to Lvov. I'll see you Gabriel at the station, thank you for this exciting day.'

Rebekah said goodbye to Andre and Viktoria and whispered to Andre try to be easy with Viktoria.

'Yes, Rebekah I will see you at the station on Wednesday morning. Goodbye my love.'

Chapter 23
Trip to Lvov for Rebekah's University Graduation

I was really lucky to have such great helpers than Viktoria and Andre. I could not have managed to solve all the mail enquires and correspondences we have received from all the local authorities and from faith schools all over the Transcarpathian Region.

I was just finishing my weekly report for the Hungarian Education Ministry when I have just heard the news from Ungvár. Mr Bródy has officially confirmed this very important news that in Ungvár as a follow up of my presentation' there will be a new Hungarian Gimnázium from the first of September just like here in Munkács.

I took my report personally to the Post office to send it on by a special courier to the officials of the Hungarian Education Ministry.

I left Viktoria and Andre in the office to send out all the remaining correspondence to all those headmasters with an application form for schoolbooks and a level of national standard for examinations, to those who were requesting forms and information on the points system for further educations like for trade colleges and to universities.

I reminded my helpers that I wouldn't be back until Monday next week so they should get on with the work that I have ask them to complete. I said goodbye to them, and before I left, I called Andre outside of our office for a chat with me. When we were outside in private, I put some cash into his pocket, and asked him to take Viktoria out for a dinner somewhere in the Corso and make it up with her. 'You know Andre we all have to work here in this office, and it is much more pleasant to have a good working atmosphere around us then this sombre tone.'

He looked at me and quietly said, 'Thank you. I will do that Gabriel. Thank you again.'

'Enjoy it and put all the bad feeling behind you. You two have been made for each other.'

I picked up my overnight bag from my office and walk to the taxi rank next to the Town Hall and collected Isaack, Rebekah and Rita with their light overnight cases.

At the Station I went to collect the return tickets to Lvov. Rebekah said, 'Gabriel you don't need a newspaper this time as I've got all the interior design magazines. You said on Monday that we will have time on the train to look through these magazines and decide on how we are going to redesign the inside of our house.'

'Yes, you are right Rebekah, we have to make a decision very quickly to let the builder be able to start the work as soon as possible and finish it for our wedding day. And there is no time to waste as the wedding is now only three months away.'

Isaack said, 'I will look after the project while you are away in Hungary. And I am sure Sándor will keep his eye on the builder too.'

As we passed the newsagent at the end of the platform I couldn't resist to get the local newspaper as I've seen on the front page which alarmed me in a way it was written, I think it is too aggressive the approach: The PRMKE (United Hungarian Party) urged the Hungarian nationality parents to send their children to a dominantly special Hungarian language schools. A call onto the parents: "We have to protect our culture".

'Is it bad news, Gabriel?'

'I think it is, Isaack, it will flare up some anger among the other ethnic groups. I wonder, Isaack, where has the inspiration originated from? Is it locally thought out or was it some guidance that has come from Hungary? I don't know Isaack, but they should have done it in a much more diplomatic way.'

The Budapest Lvov express train just arrived at the station platform, and we found our coach easily and finally settled in our pre-booked seats. Just as we settled in our seats the train started slowly to move on.

Rebekah and Rita sat opposite to each other in the railway carriages, studying the brochures.

Isaack told me, 'Thank you for your introduction to that businessman in Ungvár about the conveyors and elevators. He is very interested, and he will come and see our factory facilities next week. It sounds a very interesting project to be involved with.'

'Yes, it is Isaack. I thought there is a tremendous wide range of areas where businesses can use those kinds of machines. From the food industry to the waterworks, sewage works, agriculture and really anywhere where you have to move something in a sealed unit.'

Rebekah looked at us in a not very pleasing way, so we stopped talking politics and business as well. She got out her university cap out of her hatbox and she put it on, showing off. 'Do you like it?'

'Yes, Rebekah I like it you look so sophisticated with that hat on.'

She put the hatbox back on the rack and went straight into the house redevelopment plans.

Isaack said, 'I have seen it many times Gabriel the plans look modern and comfortable to me it is much more fashionable than my house. I have to admit it has changed very little since my wife Rivka passed away. She was very good of designing and arranging things like this. Rebekah has inherited her mother's taste and her look.'

'Rebekah, I have great ideas, but I will not be going to get involved with that after all it will be you are the one whose kingdom it will be.' As we were planning the changes on the house, the time went very quickly. The guard came into our carriage and warned us that we were arriving to Lvov in ten minutes' time.

We collected our cases and were getting ready for our arrival to Lvov.

Rebekah and I just looked at each other with a cheeky smile and we understood what we were thinking about. We were going to revisiting of that unforgettable nights that we enjoyed so much in the Grand Hotel. That night sealed our future life. Can we do it again when Isaack and Rita here with us? I don't know. The temptation was great. But I don't want to spoil our time here for everybody and particularly for Rebekah's sake; it was not fair on her. We asked the taxi driver to take us to the Grand Hotel on Svobody Boulevard. To the place that both of us will remember for ever. I had been given the most precious gift a man can have from a woman, which is her innocence.

As we were checking in, the receptionist recognised me and discretely welcomed me back to the hotel. He smiled and he asked if I would like the same room. 'No thank you but we have booked four rooms if possible next to each other.'

The receptionist said, 'Yes, I will arrange it for you as you wish.'

The way Isaack arranged the room I was next to him then Rita and at the other end Rebekah.

I was very happy with the arrangement, but I sensed Rebekah wasn't happy with it but when I looked at her and shook my head then she accepted the room arrangements. We agreed to meet up in the hotel lobby in fifteen-minutes time and we will go out for a sightseeing walk.

As we walked past the Sztuka coffeehouse on Teatralna Str, the tables were nicely set in front of the coffeehouse. Rebekah suggested to sit outside and have some sandwiches or cakes with a cup of coffee or tea.

After we settled at a table in the front of the coffeehouse and Rebekah said, 'Papa you must come and see the decorations of this famous place in Lvov,' she invited Rita as well.

I stayed outside and unhooked a local newspaper from the magazine stand and tried to catch up with the latest headline news: … The Czechoslovakian Government is not happy with the Reginal Government of Ungvár's pro Hungarian stance. Volosin Avgusztin accuses Dr András Bródy the Prime Minister of treason… I couldn't manage to read through the article as Rebekah came back with Isaack and Rita to the table. Rebekah looked at me with an angry eye and commented that we were on vacation so I should forget the politics for the time being.

I apologised for being so thoughtless.

Isaack looked at me and without a word he asked me what was happening. I showed him the news headline as I was going to hang the newspaper back on the magazine holder. Silently signalled to me "is that bad news"? I nodded with a grim face.

Isaack suggested we should have a sandwich and a supper later on somewhere.

I said, 'That is a good idea Isaack, I can recommend a fantastic restaurant where our Professor Schlesinger took me with Rebekah some weeks ago where we had a great meal, it is right next door to the Original 1030's Golden Rose Synagogue of Lvov.'

Rebekah was very excited again just to hear the name of the restaurant, after that meal we came here to the *Sztuka Kávéház* and I had given that speech encouraging artists to create and promote local artworks of Ukrainian origin and make them a masterwork.

'It sounds like you Gabriel and Rebekah have found each other matched well; two revolutionaries,' Isaack said.

'It may sound that way Isaack, but I believe local art and cultural tradition is very important and should be kept for the future generations, just like our Jewish inheritance of tradition which is keeping us together in unity as a nation.'

'Papa, we are just voicing what the people want but they can't or are too frightened to speak out for themselves. We are only representing those people's voices; I am speaking out for the wellbeing of women with the Union of Jewish Women's Organisation and Gabriel speaks up for the artists communities.'

'I didn't want to disagree with you Rebekah, just saying that you with Gabriel are matched well in one voice and one belief. I hope people will acknowledge your effort as the one who protecting their interest.'

The conversation was interrupted by the waiter who brought our order—a mixture of cheese and tuna sandwiches, and some very delicious looking cakes and coffees.

Getting back to our hotel in exhaustion from our sightseeing of Lvov, Rebekah and Rita went up to their rooms first. Isaack asked me to have a drink with him and a short chat over that newspaper article. We both had a local beer on the restaurant terrace.

'What was it all about that news from Ungvar Gabriel?'

'I don't know Isaack I couldn't read it fully as Rebekah interrupted me with my reading. I don't know if I told you that I have met this very nice and honest politician who has started his career like me as a teacher. Then he's got onto journalism and other things like politics. He is representing the people in the Transcarpathian Region who have elected him into that position. He has realised that the local Russian, Hungarian and a big majority of Jewish people would favour the old Austro-Hungarian administration as you know which has been taken away by the Czechoslovakian elite all those years ago.

'Czechoslovakia has never existed before it was the creation of the following. The **Treaty of Versailles** was of the peace treaties that brought the World War I. to an end by the Pittsburgh Agreement of May 1918, the Czechoslovak declaration of independence, created in Washington was published by the Czechoslovak National Council, signed by the Freemasons; Masaryk, Štefánik, Beneš David Lloyd George, Vittorio Orlando, Georges Clemenceau and Woodrow Wilson on 18 October 1918 in Paris, and proclaimed on October 28 in Prague.

'Towards the end of the First World War which led to the collapse of the Austrian-Hungarian Empire, several ethnic groups and territories with different historical, political, and economic traditions were blended into new state structures. Czecho-Slovakia was a sovereign state in Central Europe that existed from October 1918, when it declared its independence from the broken state of the Austro-Hungarian Empire, until its peaceful dissolution into the Czech Republic.

'One major mistake, which I believe is that they have created a poison for the ethnic situation. Probably that was their original intention in Prague to destroy the harmonious unity among ethnic communities. If there is no unity only hate and disagreement then they can control among the disunited communities as peacemakers.

'Dr Bródy Prime Minister has understood what is going on in Central Europe has been created and now it looks like the dominating "power" comes from Germany. Just look back at what happened in Austria in March, the Anschluss. Now Germany is demanding the return of the Sudetenland and claims the Protectorate of Bohemia and Moravia which has been lost in the Treaty of Versailles.

'Dr András Brody is a good man we both had a good understanding of each other's mission in our life.'

'This is terrible Gabriel, will it affect us Jews, here in the Carpathian Region?'

'I don't know Isaack, I hope we are an unimportant region, and we are far away from the centre of power, like Hungary. I pray and hope we will be safe here in Munkács. I am not a politician, so I don't have the "twisted mind" like they have developed, I am only a civil servant who only picks up some news in places which is not meant to be broadcasted to the public.'

'Let's talk business Gabriel, I am a reasonably established businessman. My motto has always been; look after your workforce educate them and pay them well and they will be staying with you for life. I have set up a very good (apprentices) program. I have a good continuous workforce who are capable to make anything for you. When I discussed the possibility of manufacturing Archimedes principle "Screw conveyors and elevators" they were quite excited as some new challenges for them. I have done some research on the demand for that type of system and the demand is enormous very encouraging to explore this with a good salesman.

'I know that is not your field but I would always leave room for you to come into join my business as you are now member of the family Rebekah is already in the business as my accountant so it may well be you could manage and take over my business. You have a managerial quality and an open minded for new opportunities in different fields of industry or agriculture as well. We can build this business for our future generation.'

'Isaack I am flattered with your offer but at this moment I am still in different kind of industry called entertainment. Of course, I would come into your business and try to find some use of myself and for both of us and for the benefit of your company.'

Isaack stood up came to me and gave me a fatherly hug. 'Thank you, Gabriel. Thank you, my son.'

Rebekah just walked into this action, and she was stunned; she couldn't understand the meaning of this emotional hugging between her father and her fiancé. She asked with suspicion in her eyes, 'Did you talked about politics?'

'No, my daughter it was business for a change.'

Her face lit up and she said, 'I am glad to hear that. I am ready now for the evening. Are you ready too?'

As we spoke, Rita came to joined us. Isaack and I just looked at her with an open mouth.

Rebekah said, 'So, what do you think of Rita's new look?' We both looked at Rebekah. 'Yes, it was with my help to turn her into a younger woman of course with a bit of my makeup.'

We all smiled, and it was a good introduction to our evening enjoyment.

I had never seen Rebekah such a confident and motherly character. Well, it suited her.

Isaack and I said simultaneously, 'You ladies look stunning.'

Isaack said, 'Well Gabriel we have to do something to match up with the ladies.' We both went into our rooms to get changed for the evening.

By the time we got down to join them at the terrace, Rebekah commented on our outlook, 'So, what did you do to change from the day clothing; you still have the bowtie and the hat on?'

'We both have a fresh shirt I guess,' said Isaack.

I said, 'I just couldn't find my make up, so I am afraid you have to put up with both of us without lipstick.'

Rebekah and Rita laughed at my comment and from the next table a couple chipped into our conversation and the lady offered us to lend us her lipstick. More laughter from tables around us. We said goodbye to the people at the next table to us, they asked us if we could recommend a good restaurant.

I said, 'If you like a good Jewish style food then I can recommend the Golden Rose Restaurant.'

They thanked me for the recommendation and said we may see you there later on.

I called for a taxi and told the driver the name of the restaurant (as I had forgotten the name of the street) and the taxi driver said, 'Oh I know the place well; have you booked for a table?'

'My God, of course I didn't, just please wait a minute while I ask the receptionist to book us a table.'

The driver said, 'I know the head waiter they are using me to bring customers to his restaurant. So, don't worry he will get a table for you through me.'

'I will appreciate your effort for that help.'

'Just pay me for the fare as I will get the backhand from the headwaiter anyway.' He smiled and made a cheeky wink at me.

When we arrived at the restaurant it looked as if the waiter recognised me from our last time we dined here with the professor.

He said, 'Would you like to join Professor Schlesinger again or you would prefer to sit somewhere else?'

I asked the waiter, 'Is the professor is dining here tonight as well.'

He said yes with a smile on his face, 'Of course, he is here most of the time, this is his second home. I have to ask the professor if he would welcome you at his table.' The waiter came back to us with a smile and said, 'Yes, the professor would be delighted to share his table with you.'

I looked at Isaack and asked him, 'Would you like to meet your daughter's professor and share a table with him?'

'I would be delighted Gabriel.'

Rebekah's eyes sparkled from the joy she will dine with the professor again, here in this restaurant.

When we got to his table, I did the introductions. 'It is my pleasure to see you again Professor. May I introduce you to Isaack Grósz, he is Rebekah's father, and to Rita.'

'It is my pleasure to meet you Mr Grósz, you must be a very proud father to Rebekah, she is one of my favourite students. My name is Michael Schlesinger.' He gave a hug to Rebekah and said, 'Well, I can do this to you as your graduation ceremony will be done tomorrow. So, there is no favouritism for you. It is good to meet you all.' He kissed Rita's hand and asked us to have a seat with him.'

The professor was telling Isaack what a talent Rebekah was, 'I am going to miss her for the next semester.'

I said, 'Michael, I think you will be seeing us much sooner as we would like to invite you to our wedding on the 11th of September.'

The professor almost choked on his drink at my surprised announcement.

'You Gabriel the born bachelor?' He looked at Rebekah and then he looked at me and said, 'Now you are going to call me a Shadchan! As I am the one who has introduced you to Rebekah.' We all laughed on his comment. 'Well, Mazel Tov to you all. I am very pleased for you Gabriel, as I have followed your career since you were my student in the rabbinical college in Budapest all those years ago. I will be delighted to accept your invitation for such a lovely couple whom I have educated in my long career.'

Isaack and the professor clicked on in a very friendly turn which amazed me, and it exceeded my expectations. We all had a great meal and a lot of alcohol. Even Rita put some drink behind her bun too. The whole evening went into a small party as the guests we had been talking to at the hotel joined us with a joined extended table. The noise decibel of our group of people was well amplified but the management ignored our noise as regular clients. Árpád the owner of the restaurant was happy, and he put up with the noise we created because he made a very successful deal with our newly acquired table friends who were the owners of the famous vineyard of the Tolcsvay wine estate, Mr and Mrs Tolcsvay.

As the evening turned into night well past the closing hour, Michael (Professor Schlesinger) excused himself with a reason as he was going to present the graduation awards to all his graduates in the next morning at the Lvov University. We ordered a couple more taxis and made our way back to our hotel.

Our new friend Mr Tolcsvay suggested we should have a goodnight drink before we retired for the night. 'Would you try my Törkölypálinka (distilled wine brandy) this is my specially distilled one?' He poured a glass of brandy for all of us. It was one of the best brandies I ever had which is made out of the pressed grapes. In fact, you could taste the grape flavour in the drink. I can remember I had a similar drink in Baja (South of Hungary) but never been so clean and refined drink like this one.

After the drink we all said farewell to each other and retired into our rooms.

The next morning, I had a kind of headache, at the breakfast room we all came done with the same kind of heavy heads. The communication was minimal, as we all tried to recover from the previous night's drinking experience.

Rebekah urged us to be ready for ten in the morning as the graduation ceremony will begin at eleven and she didn't want to be late.

We all made the effort to be there on time. Rebekah was fully dressed in her Graduation Gown and the Mortar Board (Cap). She looked very distinguished and sophisticated. She had taken her Mortar Board off stopping it from blowing off in the summer breeze. Isaack and Rita were so proud of Rebekah as she looked great in that graduation costume.

We walked to the University from our hotel which helped our bodies recover.

Rebekah had gone with the rest of her fellow students in front of the main stage where all the professors and officials were sitting, we sat in the back with the other relatives. The ceremony was held in the open air on the University courtyard lawn. The organisers were very precise on time and followed the traditions of the Lvov University rules. I noticed that all the Professors were at present on stage while the Headmaster of the University handed the diplomas to each graduate by calling them out by their names. When it came to Rebekah Grósz, we all stood up and shouted Bravo! She looked so very proud, and her eye sparkled from the joy or was it tears I am not sure. She turned to our direction and said, 'I have made it.'

At the end of the ceremony, they had some group photos taken then she joined us with such happiness she could have walked on the clouds. Isaack had ordered some flowers which the teaching assistants handed to all the parents who had ordered them. Isaack said, 'My dearest daughter I am so very proud of you for graduating from this famous University.' He handed the flowers to Rebekah. 'This is for all the hard work and energy you have put into the studying, now it has resulted with this graduation diploma. Mazel tov Rebekah.'

Rita and I joined into the congratulations. 'Mazel tov Rebekah!'

At the end we managed to have a quick word with Professor Schlesinger as he was going to celebrate with his fellow professors in the university building. I asked the Professor, 'Dear Michael please keep in touch with me.' We exchanged our addresses and we said goodbye to him.

We went back to our hotel for a special dinner which Isaack had organised all ready. Rebekah was still wearing her gown; Rita was clutching onto Rebekah's hat. Rebekah received many congratulations from her friends and from the Union of Jewish Women Organisation.

Finally, we made it to the dining room where spontaneous applause greeted Rebekah. You instantly recognised our table because it was decorated with those beautiful flowers. This was part of Isaack's organised dinner for his beautiful university graduate daughter. Rebekah's eyes were sparkling from joy and happiness. The last time I'd seen her like this was on that unforgettable first night we enjoyed together here in this hotel.

We had champagne and the finest wines which were on the menu. Truly it was a special day for Rebekah. All the hard work she has put in for all those years commuting for the lecturing for two years and now it has been completed. Rebekah said, 'I am glad it is now over, but I will miss all the friends I have made through the years in the university and in Lvov.'

After the meal we had a relaxed time on the restaurant terrace. Isaack decided that he and Rita will take a leisurely walk around the park and went to see some of the most impressive buildings of Lvov.

When Isaack and Rita left the hotel, Rebekah looked at me and said, 'My angel, we have some time for our self why don't you take me up into "heaven" in your arms.'

I didn't need any more invitation to complete Rebekah's day, with my contribution for her, to complete this fantastic day. We both rushed up into my room and as the door shut, she was clinging in my neck and kissed me with such passion las if she never done it before she has been so excited for the pleasure which we both enjoyed and to the crescendo of fulfilment in love making.

From the door we didn't even get to the bed dressed as we ripped all our clothed off from each other and there we were already stark naked. I felt her breath was like a fire when we kissed, her bosoms were pounding from the excitement. I have pulled her body close to mine and felt the full of her whole body next to mine. We both disappeared into the highest, most satisfying pleasure of lovemaking that possible we could reach.

Rebekah said at the end as we were lying on the bed dripping wet, 'We've both been exhausted of lovemaking. You know Gabriel this is the second time I have felt exactly to the same extent of satisfaction since the night I have gifted you with my innocence at that wonderful and beautiful hight. I love you my dear angel. Remember this, I will love you for ever, even in heaven too. I want to be your wife, lover, and the mother of your children.'

Later on, Isaack and Rita got back to the hotel, they looked absolutely exhausted. They spotted us sitting on the hotel terrace and they walked to us, crashed into the chairs and called for a beer to recover from the sightseeing trip in Lvov. Isaack asked me if we had relaxed and recovered from the day's excitement.

'Yes, Isaack we have been relaxing here in the hotel and now we have a couple of *fröccs* (spritzer) and enjoying the nice cooler breeze on the terrace.

Rita was studying Rebekah's face if she would know what happened with her. But she just smiled and gave her a wink. Rebekah regained her confidence from that sign from Rita and she was leading the conversation again as she did it all day long. She looked very happy and a strikingly beautiful woman! And she is my fiancée. What more a man can ask for?

'I could do with an early night tonight as I am exhausted.'

Rita looked at her and with a smile she said, 'Yes, it must have been an exhausting day for us today.'

Rebekah blushed and put a peck on Rita's cheek and whispered into her ear, 'Thank you.'

I managed to peck Rita's cheek and whispered into her ear, 'Thank you for your politeness.'

She gave me a hug and said, 'Anytime Gabriel. Anytime.'

'Goodnight to you all.'

Chapter 24

Back to Munkács, Builder Starts the Work on Our House

Rebekah put all her interior design magazines on display again. At this time, she was sitting opposite of me in the carriage, we left Rita and Isaack to sit at the window while we were discussing the plans. I said, 'My Darling you have amazingly great taste for style and practical arrangements, not just the way you dress but the way you are redesigning properties too.'

'Yes Gabriel, I have inherited these qualities from my mother, she was very good at doing these kinds of things in such perfection.'

She was showing some sketches and saying, this is the kitchen and the bathroom that I have designed.

'I thought that we won't be needing the stable so we could put our bathroom and our bedroom together en suite, and we could have a smaller bathroom in the middle of the house to support the front bedrooms. The kitchen can be put next to the bathroom and the dining room, and the lounge can be put in the middle of the house. What do you think?'

I said, 'Yes, it is really a very good plan indeed. You're right that the stable can be turned into our master bedroom en suite. After the Sabbath tomorrow we have to ask Sándor to introduce us to his builder client.'

'That is a good idea Gabriel. Maybe we could go to our house together with him and explain it to him our design and ask him that can it be done and how soon could he complete the works?'

Isaack and Rita nodded off from the sightseeing of Lvov, and from the excessive drinking we all had. They were woken up by the ticket officer calling to passengers who are getting off in Munkács.

I helped lift off the cases from the rack and got ready for our departure from our compartment. The late June weather was unusually hot, fortunately we didn't have to wait too long for a taxi to getting us home from the midday heat to Rebekah's cool apartment.

Isaack asked me if I was going to be with them to celebrate the Sabbath?

I said, 'Yes please I would like that, but I have to get back to my room at Latorca utca to have some fresh clothing as I feel a bit sweaty from the travelling.'

'That is great Gabriel, so we will see you at our usual time for the Sabbath meal.'

Getting nearer to Elisabeth house I could hear the dogs barking. They must of have sensed me or recognised my steps. As soon as I got through the gate there, they were with all excitement for the bones. I made them to sit and wait until I have given them the bones. Elisabeth came out from the house hearing the barking. When she saw the two dogs were sitting patiently for their bones, she said, 'Well Gabriel you have trained them well. You could take them to the *cirkusz* (circus).' Then I gave them the well-deserved bones one by one, immediately they have run to their favoured place, and you could hear the way they enjoyed those bones.

Elisabeth said, 'I have seen Sándor was showing a man around the house, I guess that man was probably your builder. He was measuring the whole building inside and outside too.'

'That is fantastic Elisabeth, we have got a plan for all the alterations for the whole property. Rebekah has showed me her plans as the way she wants it to be done. We were planning to have a meeting with the builder here on Sunday to discuss the plans with him.'

Elisabeth asked me if I was going to go to Rebekah's house to celebrate the Sabbath.

I said, 'Yes Elisabeth, but I will be coming back here for the night, then I'll go to the synagogue tomorrow for the Sabbath Service. There is some business I have to take care of with other traders.'

Elisabeth asked me in a kind of embarrassing manner, 'Gabriel I know you've been very busy in the past weeks, but would you please give me the rent money for June?'

I felt really embarrassed and I went into my room and brought the rent money and apologised to Elisabeth for being so forgetful.'

'Don't worry Gabriel I am surprised that you still know where you live. I think you are doing too much; you will be burning yourself out for your wedding day.' We both smiled at her comment.'

'Or for the wedding night?' She laughed at my comment.

After the Sabbath service at the synagogue Sándor introduced me to the builder; his name was József Klein. Mr Klein said, 'I have heard a lot about you Gabriel I didn't really need the introduction from Dr Sándor Fried. I have been visiting your house with Dr Sándor and I have to say it is a bit of an old-fashioned building. The house itself is in good condition only the inside which needs modernising like connecting to the main water supply from the road, installing water pipes into the kitchen and to the bathroom, also installing waste pipes to the septic tank outside in the back of the garden. Rewiring the house, painting, and decorating. I don't know if you would like to move or alter rooms to redesign inside. You would need a wooden or parquet covered floors right through the house.'

'Mr Klein, could we have a meeting in the house itself because my wife has done all the design and she could give you her drawings that she has made all ready and the magazines she looked at as she would like it to complete the work to those styles.'

'Yes Gabriel, I can meet you and your wife at your new house on Latorca utca tomorrow, let say at ten o'clock in the morning would that be convenient?'

'Yes, that will be great Mr Klein.'

During our Sabbath dinner at Rebekah's house, I was telling her that I have managed to speak to the builder about our house project.

'Rebekah would you please come with me to meet the builder Mr József Klein so, we can speed up the project on our house. He told me that Sándor and he went to see the house two days ago and he has some idea what is needed to be done to update it for today's modern standard.'

Rebekah was getting all excited over the way we were progressing on the property.

She said, 'I am going to get all my drawings and plans after we've finished with the dinner, and I want to sit down with you Gabriel and to have an agreement on these plans. I do want to know what your input over the designs is and if you are happy with them.'

'I have told you Rebekah on the train that I like your designs and plans for the alterations in particular I like the arrangement of the kitchen. I still want to see more ideas from your magazines for the bathroom. Mr Klein told me that they have to connect to the main water pipe which is running in front of the house. Also, he has to lay and hide all the water pipes to the kitchen and to the bathroom. Then he has to lay a waste pipe from the kitchen and from the bathroom to the sewage pipes and to the septic tank outside at the back of the garden. So, he has to know where the sink in the kitchen is and where are the toilets and the bath going to be placed.

'Do you know traders in Munkács Rebekah, who could supply us with all these items for us from these catalogues?'

'Yes Gabriel, I have been visiting some plumbing shops who specialised on complete kitchen and bathroom accessories. And I would like if you would come with me next week to see it for yourself. If we like any of them, they will order it for us.'

'Yes, you are right Rebekah I wasn't paying enough attention to all your hard work but as you know I was extremely busy, I know this is not an excuse to be so passive on this front. Very sorry my love.'

'So, I will come to the house for 10 am and will set the whole alteration works into action.'

'But I would like to know Rebekah what the complete work and materials will cost us at the end of it.'

'Yes, you are right Gabriel.'

'Rebekah, I will take all the magazines and your drawings with me, so you don't have to carry it tomorrow with you.'

Mr Klein arrived promptly on time (I thought that was a good sign) before Rebeka did. While we waited for Rebekah, I pointed out that I would like of the driveway and the paths to be covered either with bricks or stone as far as the fence from the end of the outside buildings.

We were in the back of the garden checking where would be the best place for the septic tank when Rebeka walked in. I introduced her to Mr Klein and I said, 'Rebekah made all the designs so it would be better if she will explain to you how we want the alterations in every room of the house. And also, Rebekah has taken a lot of idea from BAUHAUS Magazine, and with László Moholy-Nagy designs.' Rebeka was very precise with the plan and made Mr Klein follow her wishes clearly.

Mr Klein commented on Rebekah's taste for modern styles. 'Miss Grósz you are a true follower of the todays interiors styles, and I can see that, if I may say so you are someone out of a fashion magazine, you are a very elegant lady.'

Rebekah looked at me and I winked at her and said, 'You see that is a compliment I am not sure if it is for your taste and feel for the styles or your being trendy.'

It looked as if we all agreed with Rebekah's plans and Mr Klein said, 'Yes, these plans can be done as Miss Grósz has put it into her plans. Of course, I would like to advise you to order the kitchen and bathroom's furniture and accessories from those importing companies as I can see some of those brochures are coming from Budapest or from Vienna.'

'That is all right Mr Klein, we will order them from Bauhaus Magazine as soon as this coming week but now as you have some idea of the amount of work would be required for this alteration what would be the final cost for completing this project?'

'Of course, I know you can't give us an exact figure and there is a tolerance in percentage. So, would you please give us an idea of price for the project.'

'I can't give you an exact price for the work like you said but as you are the friend of my solicitor, I will make some preferable costing for you. The tolerance will not even be 2 or 3%. I can confirm the cost to you now, but I will have to make a proper costing for all the works we are going to carry out. Look Mr Klein I can pay you in Czechoslovakian Korona or Hungarian Pengő?'

'Dear Gabriel, I would prefer to be paid by Hungarian Pengő.'

'Would you like it in cash in your hand or a transfer it from the Magyar Királyi Bank to the Moric Ulmann bank in Munkács?'

'I would like it in cash please.'

'That is all right Mr Klein if I pay you in cash would you able to give us some discount?'

'Dear Gabriel, I am sure that we will be able to give you a very good discount, even furthermore reduction if you don't need an invoice.'

'Yes, that is an option we can discuss Mr Klein.'

'Please Gabriel would you please call me József in private, but in front of other people you can call me Klein, it makes the communication much easier for me.'

'All right I will call you József, but please call my fiancée Miss Rebekah.'

'Yes, of course, I will. Is there is anything else you would like to discuss with me Miss Rebekah?'

'No thank you Mr Klein, I think we have really gone through our designs and alterations on the house. I can see it will be a very modern luxurious home. It's a credit to your taste you should be an interior designer, you are that good.'

'That is flattering Mr Klein. Thank you, but this house will be our home for a very long time, I hope. The main question is how long would it take you to complete this project Mr Klein?'

'I believe Miss Rebekah it would take me a good four weeks. It's the preparation which is the most time demanding like removing walls and building new ones. Digging trenches for pipes and for electric cables and so on. As long as all the necessary accessories for the kitchen and the bathroom will be ready to be installed.'

'Mr Klein I am going to order the bathroom accessories like bath, toilet, washbasin, and the kitchen sink as well. All the woodworks like kitchen, bathroom furniture's will be done by my father's friend in a Munkács based company; Sutyai Bela Furniture Factory. Also, they will do all the flooring works for all the and doors as well. My father's engineering factory will be making all of the fixings and metal works.'

'Well, I didn't know that your father was associated with Sutyai Furniture Company, Miss Rebekah.'

'Yes, Mr Klein my father owns the Grósz and Co, Engineering Company on *Partalja utca*. I will be going to place the order for all the bathroom and kitchen accessories where I've been told by the owner of Mr Swartz that all the accessories will be available within ten days.'

'That is very well organised. I am impressed Miss Rebekah.'

'We are all professional people Mr Klein; I hope we all will be satisfied with each other's commitments.'

'I am a respected tradesman in Munkács Miss Rebekah, I guarantee you quality work and I will complete all the work we agreed on time, and I will be giving you a good price for the work.'

When Mr Klein left, with all the drawings with him of the project, I was speechless on Rebekah's standard of professionalism. 'My darling Rebekah, I am very impressed with your leadership quality.'

'Don't forget Gabriel that as I have been growing up and involved with my father's business since I was a young girl, as you know I did all the accounts and paid the wages to our tradesmen and to the suppliers.'

'My darling Rebekah I just can't find the words, only thing I can say to you is that I love you.'

I just lifted her hand and kissed it then I said, 'This kiss is our first kiss in our home.' Then I pulled her to me and held her tight she put her arms around my neck, and we kissed as if we had never kissed before.

She said at the end of our long kiss, 'Yes, my angel and we will never stop doing this, a beautiful and a pure love what we have for each other. Yes, I feel peace in this house like you said, we will have a kind of love which our future generations will be teaching to their children to follow.'

Rebekah said, 'Gabriel, someone is walking in front of our door I have seen a shadow.'

'Just stay inside Rebekah, I'll have a look.'

As I opened the door, Szuka was laying in front of our door, the dog just jumped up and with a tail wagging welcomed me, as I shouted to Rebekah, 'My darling it's your competition Szuka.'

As Rebekah came outside, Szuka immediately rushed to Rebekah and rubbed her head to Rebekah's legs. Rebekah bent down and stroked the dog's head and said, 'Well Gabriel we have the best security arrangement we could ask for and she is only costing us a big marrowbone.'

We both smiled and I said, 'Yes, and I thought that she has favoured me for all the bones and now this, there you go she has found a soulmate with you. Girls always stick together against the fellows.'

We both laughed and walked to the back of the garden and Rebekah almost shouted, 'Look Gabriel there is a small vineyard here and all of those lovely fruit trees. I have never been this far back of our property before when we have only just come to have a look at the house itself with Papa and with you. I really like it now even better my angel and the air is so clean and fresh what a place to bring up a family of four!'

'Did you say four children Rebekah?'

'Yes, please Gabriel, we have a big enough house and there is room for all the children on they own.'

'Yes, we have a very large house that is all right, but you would be very busy with four children.'

'Yes, but we can have a nanny to look after of them.'

'Yes, you are right we could do that. Just looking of these stables and outside buildings we won't need them, we could turn them some extra rooms at later time.'

'Yes Gabriel, I have a plan for them already.'

Wherever we walked Szuka shadowed us, and she was always on Rebekah's side and kept looking at her just try to catch her attention. I said, 'Elisabeth will be jealous of us; we pinched her dog. I know we really didn't because she has a gate between the two properties where both dogs have access to move freely.'

'Just look at the time Gabriel, we have to hurry back to our house as Rita has prepared the Sunday dinner.'

We both briefly called into Elisabeth's house to say goodbye and walked back to Rebekah's house in the centre of Munkács. Rebekah had taken me by my arm very tightly and being so excited of our new property, in particular, her new discovery of the large land with all those fruit trees and with the grapevines.

'You know my Rebekah; this property was part of the Heavenly plan that we have met in the university and fallen in such poetically deeply love and that has led us to getting married. The sheer speed of this "love story" should be written in a book for the future generation to see how our Lord God works in His mysterious way. I believe our destiny has been arranged by both of our protecting Angels.'

Chapter 25

Alteration on the House Begins

I enjoyed the Sunday with my new family we shared the meal that Rita had prepared for us. This Sunday dinner was unusually noisy we were very excited to hear and discuss Rebekah's plan for our new house on Latorca utca. Rebekah led the conversation enthusiastically and we all just listened to her with amazement at her knowledge of interior designing and enhancing old properties to a more modern lifestyle. We all were captivated with her enthusiasm she was telling us all the details which will transform the old country farmhouse into a model catalogue finish show house.

Rebekah said in an excited voice, 'Aapukám, did you know that there is a large field at the back of the house which is part of the house? There are many fruit trees and a small vineyard in the back of the property. There is a fence with a gate on it I guess it was to stop all the animals—livestock to get into there to damage the vegetables or the strawberries.'

'No Rebekah, I didn't know that the land was part of the house. I haven't really had time to read through the land register deed. In this case your property is worth much more. Like you always say Gabriel there are no coincidences in our life the Lord knows what we need and what we can cope with. His way and His timing are always perfect, as the Lord God for himself is perfect!'

'Yes Isaack, I do believe in Him without any doubt I do it with all of my heart and mind.'

I said to Rebekah, 'I am going to be very busy this coming week in the office I have to assess all the contacts from schools, names, and responses; comments I have received from them. I will try to make one report for the Chief Rabbi Immanuel Lőw, and also the one which I am going to present to the officials at the Education Ministry in Budapest. Also, Rebekah you and I are going to meet with Mr Klein at the house on Tuesday the 28th of June when he is going to present us with the quotation for the work. You remember he asked us to be there so he can explain everything to us on site.'

'Yes, Gabriel I remember I will be there, but I would like you to come with me to the Zloch es Partner plumbing and bathroom main dealer to place an order with them and to choose the colour and the style for the tiles as well.'

'Yes of course I will come with you and will transfer the money from my account with the Móric Ulman Commercial Bank Branch here in Munkács.

Isaack was surprised to hear from me mentioning the Móric Ulman Bank name. 'I didn't know Gabriel you are banking with Móric Ulman Commercial Bank.'

'Yes, I have been for some years as his bank was sponsoring some of the theatrical and film projects I have been part of. I thought it was fair to use their facilities as they are so generous with me.'

'I bank with them for my business account and for my private one as well. By the way Rebekah as you have now graduated from the university, I would need you to come into the office and complete the end of month's account book and you have to transfer some payments to our suppliers.'

'Yes, Papa I will be there I will come in with you tomorrow morning and will do all these jobs I have left behind because of my education and travelling days to Lvov.'

I went into my office early in the morning as I had so much to organise as I was going to lose my office from the end of July. Andre and Viktoria hadn't arrived yet, so I am just beginning to collect all the important invoices and bills which covered all my expenses for travelling and for my accommodations in hotels and at Elisabeth's. I just couldn't let either Andre or Viktoria to do that, it was private.

I had a knock on the door and the mayor's secretary walked in and asked me to come with her as the Mayor would like to see me. She walked me straight to the Mayor's office and to my surprise, there was a new Mayor who was there some weeks ago as the Deputy Mayor, Iván Parkányi, and there was another gentleman with him. I greeted both of them, and I said, 'So sorry being so uninformed, but I thought Mayor Konstantyn Hrabar is still the mayor. Well in this case there is congratulations in order. Congratulations Mr Mayor on your new post. So, who is your deputy Mr Mayor Parkányi?'

'My secretary will take you to his office and will introduce you to him. But in the meantime, I would like to introduce you to Mr József Nemes who is the new Commissioner of Munkács. It is my pleasure to meet with you Mr Commissioner Nemes.'

'No, it is my pleasure to meet you Gabriel, I have heard a lot of good things about you. I have just been told by Mr Mayor Parkányi that you are about to get married to a local lady Rebekah Grósz, and you are going to settle here in Munkács. We can use someone with your quality and connections.'

'I am flattered, Mr Commissioner. Thank you for your kind words. Yes, I have purchased a property on Latorca utca which at this moment is in a process of being modernised. Also, Mr Mayor Párkányi offered me a position to run and manage the cultural department to promote cultural events in Munkács. I hope that offer is still available for me, Mr Mayor Parkányi?'

'Absolutely. Yes Gabriel. I know you have to report back to the Education and Foreign Ministry in Budapest, but as soon as you get back from Hungary, I would like to discuss this position with you. So, my secretary now will introduce you to my Deputy Mayor and hopefully see you soon.'

'Yes, it was a pleasure meeting you both. Goodbye.'

The deputy unfortunately couldn't see me as he had a visitor in his office, he instructed the secretary to make another appointment with me.

I thought this new Commissioner is a nice enough person and it seems that he knows a lot about me. (Just keep away from the politics, Gabriel!)

On my way back to my office, I called into the marriage registry office and asked for a day for my wedding to be registered. The registrar told me that they were very busy with applications, but the only available day they had was the 14th of July. Well, what can I say?

I can't really complain as I still had enough time to get all the necessary paperwork's from the registrar to obtain a marriage license from their authority for a civil marriage certificate.

Walking back to my office I was thinking of how lucky I am to be able to have the date of the 14th of July it has been offered. As I got into my office I was buried in my thoughts, and I noticed that my helpers were there already. Viktoria had red eyes and I thought, *My goodness they have had an argument again.* But Viktoria came to me and gave me a hug and said, 'I am sorry to lose you Gabriel. I believe you are going back to Hungary and won't be coming back; Andre and I like you so much not just as our boss but more of as our big brother.'

I felt touched with their genuine expression of their feelings for me, and I told them, 'Look yes, I am going to Hungary just for ten days then I will be coming back here to live. As you know Rebekah and I just have bought a house on Latorca utca. Yes, my mission is over, and I have completed my contract, but I will be working here in Munkács. So, I will still need some helpers for the future, so you never know how the future will be turning out in the end.'

Her face lit up and both of them smiled again, and I said, 'Now you know the truth from me and now get back to work we have much to catch up with.'

On Tuesday morning Rebekah arrived at our new house earlier than our appointment was made with Mr Klein.

Her newfound company, Szuka, rushed to Rebekah and made a fuss of her. I said, 'I would like to know my love what your magic secret with this dog is? Elisabeth was telling me that Szuka keeps going over to our house and then walking back to Elisabeth with her head down. Obviously, she is always looking for you.'

Rebekah smiled and suggested that we should walk around the garden at the back of the house as she would like to look at it properly not like we did on Sunday morning just in a rush.'

'Look Gabriel we can turn all these outside buildings like the style and the hen house into a storage building and the stable will be turned into our bedroom en suite. We can strip the ceiling right through the house back to the bare wood and just varnish it. Natural wood colour floor and wooden ceiling.'

As we got to the low wooden fence at the end of the courtyard, Rebekah went through the gate to the field at the back end of the house and excitingly said, 'Look Gabriel, strawberries still on the plants.' She picked up a couple of good size bright red strawberries and she gave me one and she had the other one; she said, 'My goodness, this is so sweet and juicy and look at these plum and apple trees. I can see that in the future we won't have to go to the market on the Mondays because we can have fresh fruits at any time of the day from our garden.'

Elisabeth was in her garden and overheard our conversation and said, 'Why don't you take some strawberries home with you Rebekah? I can lend you a bowl to pick some; rather you have them than the birds.'

Rebekah thanked Elisabeth for her offer but in the meantime, Mr Klein arrived with his quotation, Rebekah and I joined Mr Klein who explained the necessary work we had already agreed with him on the first visit to assess the work on the house. Rebekah and I found Mr Klein's quotation acceptable, and we gave the work to his company to get it started as soon as possible. Mr Klein told us that he can start the work with his workers on Wednesday. We shook hands over the deal and Mr Klein promised that all the work groundworks plumbing rearranging walls and the electric works, will be completed in three to four weeks. He pointed out that the septic tank had to be put into the back of the building where the strawberries are. We agreed to that and gave him a set of keys to the house and to the gate as well.

When Mr Klein went, Rebekah picked a bowl full of strawberries and we walked back to her house where she left the bowl of strawberries with Rita then we went to the bathroom showroom at Zloch & Partner place on *Rákóczi utca*.

As we were walking to the showroom, I said, 'I have to tell you my love that I have booked our wedding date at the town hall registry office for the 14th of July.'

She stopped and looked at me, tears were running down her beautiful face then she kissed me on the street and said, 'Now I can see that the time is finally here, and I don't know how to react to it. I have always fantasised about how I am going to react to this announcement what you've just made, and I can't believe this is happening to me right now. I will be married to my love on the 14th in two weeks' time.'

'Yes, my darling Rebekah, I never thought that I will ever be getting married as I have passed that time some time ago when a man is usually getting married. And here we are.'

'You and I going to get married. You have made my day Gabriel and thank you for that. Thank you to make me grow up. Don't forget we are going to celebrate our engagement on this coming Sunday at our place.'

'Of course not. How could I?'

'Gabriel let's see my Papa first then we can go to the bathroom showroom later on. We have to tell this news to your Papa as well when we are going to meet him at the hotel restaurant.'

'But we have to let him have a strong palinka to cope with the news.'

Isaack was in the Star Hotel restaurant sitting at his usual table and reading a local newspaper. He stood up at our arrival and welcomed us and we all sat down at his table to join him for dinner. Isaack invited both of us to share a glass of wine with him before the dinner.

Rebekah said, 'Aapukám, I think you should have something a bit stronger than a glass of wine because what I am going to tell you now you might need a stronger drink.' Isaack was speechless and he looked a bit confused on what

Rebekah was telling him. 'Aapukám, it is all happening now Gabriel has booked with the registrars for our wedding date which is going to be on Thursday, 14 July 1938.'

Isaack was visibly shocked and the only words he could say were, 'Yes, please I need a double *Szilvapálinka*. You know Rebeka I had given up the hope as the years have gone by and you still haven't been married that you will stay with me as father and daughter for ever. I had given up that I will have an opportunity to be a grandfather and accepted the fact that there would be no future generation to take over the successful business I have built up with your help Rebekah. But now I am very touched my prayers and dreams have now finally answered there is a continuity to the Grósz Engineering Company. When are you expecting Rebekah?'

'Papa you are misunderstanding us. I don't expect anything just, yet this is purely the wedding arrangement for my Hungarian Citizenship application. Yes, we are going to have our proper marriage ceremony at the synagogue on the 11th of September, but this is just for the "common law" marriage for the certificate. It's a kind of official registration document or a license of acknowledgment that we are officially a married couple in the eyes of the law.'

Isaack drank all the palinka from the glass at once and finally he remembered that we had explained to him this reason once already. At the end when Isaack recovered from the strong palinka, he said with an emotional voice, 'Well, Mazel Tov my children! He reached both of his hands to us and gripped our hands for a long time. My children, Mazel Tov! You have made me a very happy father. Well, it is all happening now. We are having an engagement party in our house on this coming Sunday the 3rd of July. Well, well, well, it is all happening. Mazel Tov to you both.'

Rebekah and I were both feeling Isaack's energy of emotion as he was still holding on to our hands. Rebekah's eyes sparkled from the tears which were building up and burst onto her face like a mountain stream. I felt a bit emotional for myself as well without a tear, but I understand what a shock it is to a grown-up man; what is going through his mind with the realisation of losing his daughter.

At the end Isaack said to me, 'Just look after her Gabriel like I did for all these years.'

'I don't have to promise you that Isaack as your daughter Rebekah already has my heart in her hand, I have given it to her some time ago.'

'Thank you Gabriel I know you love her very much and you would do anything to protect her from everything because I can feel that you are not just in love with her, but you love her very much. I am, a good judge of character and I love you Gabriel as my own son. You are the one I have wished to marry my daughter, all my life.'

'Isaack, I don't know how to thank you for welcoming me into your house from the first day when Rebekah has introduced me to you. This warm welcome made me to decide to settle here in Munkács, with the love of my life and not to take her with me to Hungary where I have all my friends and where I have established myself in my field of the art and entertaining business. But what you offer me here in Munkács is a kind of my chosen new family life which I believe in, and I know I won't regret it.'

Rebekah just couldn't stop wiping her tears with her handkerchief of joy from her face to seeing the genuine affection between the two grown man whom she loves so much in her life. Only words she could say, 'Now I know that I have chosen you well in Lvov Gabriel to be my partner and my husband for life.'

At the end of our dinner at the restaurant we parted from Isaack as we were going to place an order for our bathroom and kitchen accessories, and Isaack was going back to his office.

Isaack stopped me for a minute asking me, 'Please come and have a meeting with my foreman to discuss your idea of the Archimedes principle screw conveyors, he is very keen on the idea and wants to manufacture them.'

'My dear Isaack I was in the entertaining business all in my life, I can present or sell items, but my knowledge is based on what I have heard from a person I know at the Ministry of Agriculture, which is very little, but I will come and talk to him. In fact, I have never been to your company before for whatever reason. May be, I have never been in one place for longer then one day since I have arrived here in Munkács. If I will come into your factory tomorrow morning would that be the convenient for you?'

'Please come along with Rebekah she will show you around my small engineering company. With all my hope our family, three of us will build it up into a more prosperous business specialising in products that other people don't or can't do. I am ready for the expansion! We are going to be a great team a manager, a financier, and a salesman, we are a dream team.'

'Papa I will see you later on this afternoon in the office. Now I am going with Gabriel to the Zloch és Partner's plumbing and bathroom main dealership on *Rákóczi utca* to choose the colour of the appliances and place an order with them.'

'All right Rebeka, I hope you still know where we are, as you haven't been there for some time.'

'Very funny Papa, of course I know, and you will know that I am there when I am going to ask you about the bills you want me to put through the account book.' Both of them smiled at the jokes.

What a nice and modern shop here on *Rákóczi utca*, as we walked in the manager welcomed us, he recognised Rebekah and he kindly offered us a chair and a cup of coffee; he said, 'Mr Zloch will be with you in just a moment.'

A middle-aged gentleman came and greeted us; he was probably my height with thinned hair and a modern suit and a bowtie like mine. He also recognised Rebeka and said, 'I am so pleased to see you again.' He kissed Rebekah's hand than he introduced himself to me as Dávid Zloch and he joined us at the coffee table and put all those brochures on the coffee table that he brought with him and said, 'I hope Miss Grósz these are the makes and the styles you have chosen?'

Rebekah said, 'Yes these are the ones Mr Zloch just like in the pictures. I have come in with my fiancé to decide on the colour of the bathroom, of the kitchen and as well of the dining room.'

'What about the wallpaper Miss Grósz?'

'We looked at the wallpapers and have decided on Number 2, the British, William Morris designed wallpaper please.'

'Yes, these are a very nice choice it is unique to Art Deco style, your friends will be very impressed when it's finished. By the way Miss Grósz may I ask you who will do the installations for you?'

'We are using a local builder Mr József Klein, to do the building works, but we have no installer in our mind. Could you recommend a tradesman who does all your installation and the tiling?'

'Yes, Miss Grósz we do have good tradesmen who work for us, they are precise and very good. I guarantee that you will be satisfied with our workmanship. We will do all the plumbing work for your connection to the main waterpipe from the street to your house as well. We also have a master carpenter who will fit all the wooden panels and the fireplace and all the tiles as well. We can guarantee all the appliances for the kitchen, bathroom, and your dining room and the installation for five years.'

'Mr Zloch, I hope you have some costs for us?'

'Yes of course here it is, it covers all what we discussed with you.'

'Mr Zloch, would you please give us some ten minutes to discuss it with my fiancé.'

'Absolutely, perhaps would you like some fresh coffee and maybe some cakes with the coffee?'

'Yes, Mr Zloch that would be very good of you, thank you.'

We looked through the invoice and felt it was reasonably priced. 'Mr Zloch, we have decided on your package as it is on the pictures including the tiles as well and with all this included, we are accepting your price. One more thing; would you able to cooperate with Mr Klein for the successful completion?'

'Of course, we know Mr Klein and will be in touch with him over the work.'

'In this case we have a deal Mr Zloch. I will transfer the money from my account to your account from the Móric Ulman Commercial Bank Branch here in Munkács. I believe these are your bank details on your invoice. I will pay for the two thirds of this invoice now in advance and the remaining will be paid into your account on the works satisfactory completion.'

'That is fair enough Mr Gabriel. It was a pleasure to do business with you.'

I was going back to my office and Rebekah was walking in the other direction to her father's factory.

I kissed Rebekah and said, 'I will be coming to your house tomorrow morning at nine.'

'All right my angel, I am so happy to see our dream house will take shape. We will love that house, which is our home now for ever, with you and with all of our children as well! I can fly now with joy.'

Chapter 26
At the Factory and Our Official Engagement Party

On Wednesday at half-past eight, I knocked on Rebekah's door as we agreed as she is going to take me to their factory. Rebekah came down fully dressed for the working environment of the office. She still looked elegant, and she kept her dignity as a middle-class lady despite her being a working woman. Isaack has already gone to work so it was only two of us who were going to work at that time of the morning. The rest of the shop floor workers had started already at six in the morning. So here I was visiting Isaack's company for the first time, as we walked down the road with Rebekah the company was just down the road from the Star Hotel at the back end of the theatre at number 7. Partalja utca.

As we arrived at this small (its looks like a family house in the front with a large yard in the back of it) company, we got through the front gate and were heading to the office. Some of the workers who spotted us were greeting us lifting off their caps and saying have a good day. Isaack welcomed both of us kissing Rebekah on her cheek, and he had shaken my hand and said welcome to this little 'gold mine', Gabriel.

The office wasn't really a large one, but you didn't expect to take more space out from the shop floor only as much as you need for two office desks with a telephone and a small wicker basket for the letters he kept and a filing cabinet. Some pictures on the wall and one photo in a silver frame on his desk particularly captured my attention. It was a slightly faded photo that I have recognised; it was Rebekah's mother. I thought he might be missing her as he had built a shrine of her at home, and it looked here in the office as well.

He asked me if I would like a cup of coffee before, he would take me to the shop floor to introduce me to his tradesmen.

I said, 'If you don't mind Isaack, I would rather go to see your business.'

Rebekah sat behind her desk already and opened the company account book. She buried herself into the world of bookkeeping just as she was trying to catch up with it, to bring it up to date.

I walked out with Isaack to the shop floor; it looked much bigger than you would expect from the outside. Some very precise tools and machines with a full welding facility.

Isaack called his master engineer who is the foreman for himself. 'He introduced him as Samuel Steiner. Samuel lifted his cap and said I have heard about you Gabriel from Isaack that you have some very interesting proposals for Isaack. This screw conveyor?'

Isaack suggested to go to Samuel's office and had a chat about my idea of this possible new project for the company. Both looked at me waiting to hear my proposal.

'Well, I must tell you both that I know very little about engineering or particularly technical machinery. I have overheard a conversation at the Agricultural and Ministry's buffet in Budapest where two officials, one was from the Ministry of Industry were having a conversation that they are planning to control the riverbed of the Tisza. Make it much straighter cutting through all its bends making the river flow free and excavating the riverbed deeper to make it available for larger heavier ships and barges to sail on as far as they possible can into Transcarpathia.

'I understand the government target is Hust. These two officials were talking about a company in England that has specialised in an 'Archimedes Principle' machine which can move solid, semi-liquid, and liquid materials. This machine can bring up water from the well or elevate from the river or lake into an agricultural watering canal. As I said I can't tell you any more information now, but I must go back to Budapest in ten days' time, and I can obtain more information on its technical design.'

Isaack asked Samuel, 'What do you think could we make a machine like the one Gabriel described?'

'I must see a drawing, Isaack, basically it is a simple mechanism it can be done but there is a strict distance between the blades of how fast or how much material should move,' said Samuel.

Isaack suggested that we should have a proper meeting between three of us after Gabriel's return from his trip to Budapest than in the meantime, I would make some information with my old friend at the Móric Ulman Commercial

Bank over the changing situation and of what business opportunities through the Transcarpathian Region. Isaack showed me around the factory introducing me to all the tradesmen and to their inas (apprentices).

I were crediting to Isaack that they were a very nice and respectful workforce, altogether of them nineteen and six inas (apprentice). One thought I had noticed on their work clothing was they were wearing one piece overall and a wooden sole shoe called 'klogs' with a metal strip on its hill. I asked Isaac, 'Why are they all wearing this wooden based shoe?'

'Because the leather sole shoe would be destroyed by the oily floor and of all these metal bits on the floor would cut in the leather sole. The metal strip is giving more durability to the shoe itself, it works like the horseshoe.'

Isaack said he is very proud of these tradesmen and, he is encouraging them to take a mester vizsga (master grade) in their fields, and they are very proud tradesmen as it will give them more respect and credibility within the trade. 'This means that I must pay them more wages, but this is helping me to know that the standard of work I am supplying is up to the highest standard. My engineers are the highest-paid workers in the county, and they are very proud of that.'

I am very impressed with Isaack's introduction to his company and his workforce. I can see that they could deliver the work on that conveyors which has brought so much interest and enthusiasm from Isaack and his foremen Samuel. In fact, it made me a bit excited over this new venture as well.

Isaack looked at his pocket watch and said, 'Oy vey, just look at the time my boy it is already dinner time, would you join me and Rebekah for a lunch at the Star Hotel?'

'I appreciate that Isaack, I accept your invitation, but I must leave at 1:30 as I have a meeting at two this afternoon in my office with an Education Officers delegation from Huszt.'

Isaack said, 'I understand Gabriel as you have been sent out by very important politicians from the Hungarian Government to deliver their instructions and complete your mission in Transcarpathia.'

On Isaack's invitation, Rebekah just stopped and said, 'I didn't realise the time has gone so fast, and it is dinnertime already. She closed her accountancy book and grabbed her handbag and her hat.'

As we walked down the street towards the Star hotel, Isaack put his arms into Rebekah on one side and into mine on his other side and said, 'You know my children I just can't sleep properly since you Gabriel put that conveyor business into my head. I am so excited at the great opportunity that we have with a project like that. We can achieve any of our dreams if we will stay together as a team.'

'But Papa we are a team.'

'Yes, we are, but you don't understand the way my mind is working. I have two young energy around me, and I feel that as we are one unit, we can do all those great things to achieve like other Jewish families achieved in the past when they work together.'

'God has blessed the family units throughout history, family is the most important and holy unity since creation.'

'Please Gabriel try to get as much information as possible through those people you know at the ministerium on this conveyor manufacturing as you possibly can.'

'I will Isaack, as it is now a matter of time as I am going to Budapest with Rebekah on the 15th of this month its two weeks from now. I promise I will make some more enquires for getting parts supplied for the complete conveyor unit like power to drive those conveyors. I know some of my old school friends work for the Ganz RT, and they are the best in the whole world with innovative power machines like electric power motors. Also, we would probably need good bearings for the shafts. Just leave it with me.'

Rebekah just turned her head from her father to me as we had the conversation over our plans.

Finally, she had managed to get a word for her own and said, 'I think Papa we would have to look for larger premises if we are thinking of taking this project on we have to think how we would be able to cope with the sheer size of these machines.'

We both have left our mouths open in our surprise at what Rebekah was saying, 'Yes, she was right with her comment.'

I said, 'Yes Isaack your daughter is right you do need much larger premises to cope with this project. But here we are, argued Isaack it is just purely a managing and organising quality.'

'Here is Gabriel who is one of the best salesmen here you are who is looking after all the finances and here I am with decades of experience and respect from the trade. If you don't step out in faith we will never know if we could or not succeed with a project like this.'

Rebekah still was adamant about the expansion and the financial projection. 'We've just bought our new home, and I don't want you to be in a situation of losing your hard-earned financial support.'

'Yes, you are right Rivka, I agree, you sound like your mother as if I would just hear her through and through.'

'I promise you I will not do anything before you two get back from Budapest.'

I had kissed Rebekah on her cheek, shook Isaack's hand and had left the father and daughter disagreement behind as my appointment was pressing me to be ready for my meeting. But I had to side with Rebekah's argument and not rushed into expansion plans without really working out the facts and possibilities of obtaining these orders in the first place.

I got in my office before I said I would be there as I'd walked into my office, I found Andre was kissing Viktoria. I had to admit I was a bit embarrassed and stepped back from the room. I just didn't know what to do I felt I have embarrassed this lovely young couple with my entry into my office so early. I have given them five minutes just to let them organise themselves.

I knocked on the door and entered my office and saw this lovely young couple bright red with embarrassment. I said, 'My apologies but please don't be embarrassed this is just natural between such young couples like you two. So please help me is there anything I should know of these people who we are going to meet?'

Andre said, 'Yes, Gabriel, they are very keen on your presentation and with the changes for the new educational directions. I think they are a bit of too right wing based set up.'

'Thank you for reminding me of this, Andre. It is always good to have you in meetings with me as I can't often read peoples as you do. It is always good to go into a meeting with an 'army of supporters' like you and Viktoria. Thank you.'

After this meeting, I really wasn't looking forward to doing it turned out very well they are very big supporters of the Hungarian culture and accept their present situation as a minority ethnic group under another cultural administrational dominance. When I told them of my future plans to bring Hungarian artists to Transcarpathia like theatrical plays, operatic performers, poets, and musicians from Hungary.

And not to mention my pet program the Hungarian films along with silent films from Hollywood USA. I think our meeting on education was only a few minutes and the rest was discussing entertainment as further education of Hungarian culture and language. I thought their reaction has just proven that there is a common hunger for an up to date cultural interest to catch up with Budapest. I planned to use this experience at my presentation to the foreign office officials.

I was so exhausted by the time I've got home I have even forgotten the bones for the dogs. I felt guilty as I walked past the closed doors of the butchers sadly, I could not spoil them with their regular bones. It made me smile as I thought of that, if in some hundreds of years' time an archaeologist would find these bones in this garden, they would think it was a ritual burial place for some weird ancient cult.

Elisabeth welcomed me with a leftover clear chicken soup with galuska (dumpling).

We had just a short chit-chat and we've both gone to bed early. In particular, Elisabeth has to let her cattle and geese out with the kanasz.

I just couldn't get sleep for a long time as my mind was grounded in my brain in such a busy day's activities. As I had sensed the quiet time of the night some noise was coming from the floor. I had investigated the origin of this noise I had noticed that Elisabeth had laid down some newspapers as a carpet over a freshly wet clay floor, just to protect my feet from getting muddy from the wet clay.

This little mouse was running over the newspaper and its nails made this distinctive noise that would alarm any hungry cats to make a kill. But not Elisabeth's fat cat (I don't like her) had been spoiled so much that she wouldn't know how to hunt for her food for survival. I had to say as I talked to this little intruder when he lifted his head up and looked at me as I was speaking to him, then the mouse in such confidence just walked on to do his business of finding food.

I had had this kind of sleepless night feeling when I was in my bed in Budapest some weeks ago when I had been still deciding to accept this consignment to Munkács or not. I was trying hard to remember the familiar perfume now which had been absorbed into the fabrics of my '*Sárga pamlag*'. Eventually, I managed to drift away into a deep sleep.

I woke up from my dream which was broken by our official 'alarm 'rooster'.

I thought, my goodness, it is Thursday already, as I was getting dressed up, I could hear the bells of the Kanász who were calling and leading the livestock to the pasture field.

Elisabeth came into the kitchen and said, 'You look worse than before you went to bed last night.'

I said, 'Thank you, Elisabeth, for your honesty yes you are right I had a soul-searching night if I have made the right decision to come here to Munkács?'

'Just stop searching for the answer Gabriel please accept your destiny which has been laid before you. Stop feeling sorry for yourself, when you have a beautiful fiancée and a prosperous future with many future children around you. You are old enough to think more maturely, be wise.'

'Yes, you are right Elisabeth I just should get on with my destiny as it has been written for me, I know my bachelor years have ended when I have fallen in love with my beautiful Rebekah. I think I have grown up with that thought. I shouldn't have regrets over that gift from the Lord. I truly love and greatly miss her, Elisabeth. It's only a couple of months, and we will be moving into our new home.'

'Listen to me my little 'adopted brother' I have just seen that Mr Klein, your builder has just turned up with his workers starting the work on your house. He doesn't waste time.'

'That is fantastic Elisabeth. It means that he will be finishing with the work on time (hopefully).'

Enjoying the early morning clean and fresh air which is drifting down from the mountains making all of us happier just smiling and polite to one other. But the heat has slowly started to rise, and everybody is trying to get on to their workplace. Children are already going to the River Latorna for either fishing or just have a swim in the cold water. The *strand* (swimming pool) is always busy, and it costs money while the river doesn't so poorer families rather have a swim and a picnic on the riverbank.

I have made my way to order our wedding ring from, Ernő Ungár Goldsmith Master's jewellery shop.

Mr Ungár greeted me at the door as he just opened up his shop and asked me in, 'Well, Gabriel, are you ready now for the wedding rings?'

'Yes, I am. How did you know that Mr Ungár?'

'Well, I am in the kind of business where I hear and know all the small-town gossip. No in fact I have a friend who is working at the Registrar's Office in the

Town Hall who is recommending my shop to newlywed couples to purchase engagement or wedding rings.'

'Yes, Mr Ungár that makes sense.'

'I believe your wedding is on Thursday next week.'

'No, Mr Ungár, it is on Thursday the 14th two weeks.'

'Ah Gabriel, then we have plenty of time to make you a very special wedding ring. I know a person like you who is in such a position where everybody can see their wedding ring will admire my workmanship and that should give my business a free advertisement. Of course, I can offer you a bigger discount if you could put some appraisal for my business. You know how that is Gabriel? I help you, and in return, you are helping me.'

'I tell you what, Mr Ungár.'

'Please, Gabriel, just call me Ernő.'

'Yes, thank you, Ernő. With all that hope I can do more than just that, but at this moment I can't tell you more about it, but definitely, we can work well together you won't regret it.'

'I can see, Gabriel. We are going to work well with each other. You have style as you come from the big city where there is fame and pomp and of course all the wealth of Budapest.'

'You are flattering me, Ernő, but it feels good to hear a bit of positive mentality.'

'So down to business Ernő, show me the best styles which you could turn into your masterpiece.'

'Just leave it with me Gabriel you will be well impressed with the style and with the finished product.'

'Thank you, Ernő, I know you'll give me a special one as you are the best. So I'll see you next week.'

Chapter 27

Getting Ready for Our Engagement Party

Walking to the Town Hall in the morning, I was assessing all the things I had to complete with mainly my reports to both to Chief Rabbi Lőw (this would be a special one in confidence) and the other one for the authority who appointed me with this mission in the first place.

I thought that I had achieved the goal that I had set out for myself at the standard that politicians would expect from me. I thought that I'd been respectful and diplomatic with everybody with my behaviour and my politeness. I knew that for sure I'd got the message through what my appointees expected from me. But far from it, I still had to cross the bridge when I got there, i.e., the judgement was in the hands of the officials at the ministry.

The officials in Budapest must have been informed by the officers of each community where I had given my presentation. I knew one particularly Cllr H Cohen who hated me, and I thought he still did. I didn't know why, I had never given him a reason to behave against me the way he does. Probably I dared to disagree with him in a meeting and had also been spoiled at the synagogue by Rabbi Baruch.

Just stopped analysing the past Gabriel and just looked forward and concentrated on your future.

The time had gone very quickly while I was analysing my mission here as so far out of my comfort zone. Lord knew that I was missing the exciting evening in various parts of the Budapest art scene. Particularly missing Miklós's company and those wild nights.

By the time, I got to the main entrance, I noticed that Viktoria had arrived at the same time. She looked very pretty I guessed that was Rebekah's where influence reflected on her.

As we got into the office it was only the two of us first, we had a cup of coffee and a chat.

'Viktoria has opened up; Gabriel, I know it is not really your concern, but you and Rebekah are treating me as a younger sister, so please hear me through; I am very much in love with Andre, but I think he is far too closed up like a mussel he is too serious. I thought when we went to Ungvár he was charming, and I sensed he did feel the same affection for me as I've felt for him.'

'Look Viktoria, Andre is a very reserved and conscientious young man who takes things around him very seriously. But it doesn't mean that he is not in love with you. In fact, he is absolutely adoring you, and he only wants to provide you with the very best not just for now but for the future too. He is very serious about your relationship. He does love you very much indeed.

'As you know after the Bar mitzvah every Jewish boy becomes an adult and thinks in a mature mentality. Which mean that the man must be the provider of his newly married wife. Andre is like you as neither of you have brothers or sisters so he is the one who will inherit the family wealth and so he has to grow up quickly as he will automatically become the head of the household, and all responsibility is going to be on his shoulders to provide you with comfort and security.'

'You know my case is entirely different, I have come from a family of four as the youngest I knew that my eldest brother would inherit the family business, not me. So I have to find my own way to create a career for myself to be successful in life generally. Being the youngest I had a different, more tolerant upbringing with less responsibility. The only opportunity I could see for my future was to get the best education for myself as I could. So I have studied art and drama and business, and I had a feel for languages so I found it easy to learn a language as much as I could so that is the situation when you come from a large family.'

'We have to stop this conversation as Andre has just come through the door.'

Andre pecked a kiss on Viktoria's cheek and shook hands with me.

'I told them that it looks like we have come to our short but very constructive working few weeks together. I want to thank you for your true professionalism and the diligence you have demonstrated. I noticed that Viktoria became emotional, so I tried to get a bit more positive and cheerful telling them, but this is not the end of our 'partnership'.

'As you know I have to get back to Budapest reporting on my mission to the officials who have sent me here in the first place. But I will be coming back to Munkács as you know Rebekah, and I have been engaged and now we are going to get married more precisely we are going to get married here in the Town Hall on the 14th of this month I hope you would be able to come to this registrar ceremony.'

Viktoria and Andre became much happier after I told them of my future plans.

'And furthermore, I have been offered a job here, and I would need some helpers again. But please keep this information in confidence. So please both of you don't rush into finding a new job because there may an opportunity for you to work with me again, I promise you won't regret your patience. But for now, please get back to work.'

I buried myself in work just like my helpers I didn't even realise that it is dinner time already.

Rebekah dropped into the office she reminded me that I have agreed to meet up with her to discuss Sunday's engagement party at her house. She greeted Viktoria with a kiss and said hello to Andre. Politely my helpers have excused themselves again and gone down to the sandwich bar to have something to eat.

As soon as my helpers left the room Rebekah has rushed to me, and we kissed so passionately we've almost knocked the ink vessel all over on my desk.

'I have been missing you Gabriel so much, every day is a punishment without you. As she was holding me even tighter as if she would be so scared to lose me.'

'Be patient my love.' I've kissed her on her forehead and stroked the hair from her face so I can kiss her again.

'I have almost forgotten how sweet your lips are my darling Rebekah. I think it is cherry, am I right?'

'Yes, it is and mixed with a bit of honey as well.'

'Yes, you right, it tastes like 'milk and honey' and, with a bit of extra cherry in it.'

We both smiled, and I suggested that we should walk down to the Corso to have a sandwich and a coffee at the Homdi Coffeehouse. I have a lot to discuss with you, Rebekah.

We managed to sit outside at the coffeehouse under an umbrella just staying in the shade.

'Firstly, Mr Klein has arrived at our house this morning, and he has started the work.'

I couldn't go further on with my story as Rebekah become very excited, 'That is good news, Gabriel. I am happy to hear this news.'

'Very good, now the second important thing is that in two weeks from today on 14 July, you and I are getting married in the Town Hall Registry. Who would you like to invite to that celebration? Also, we would need two witnesses for the ceremony. Who would you like to invite besides your father and Rita? I am thinking to invite Elisabeth, Sándor, Andre, and Viktoria.'

'Yes, that is very good Gabriel I have to think about who else I would like to invite. But Gabriel I think this wedding should be a small number of members of the family and close friends.'

'Gabriel you haven't forgotten this Sunday our official engagement party in our house of course not. I have not. I think we could discuss it there who are we going to invite to our registry's wedding celebration.'

'Good idea, Gabriel.'

'I would like Dr Sándor Fried to be my witness of course if he would accept it. Would you mind darling if I would invite Elisabeth, Andre, and Viktoria to the wedding ceremony.'

'Of course not. But what do you think Gabriel if we would ask Andre and Viktoria to be our witnesses at the Town Hall Registrar's ceremony? We still can ask Dr Sándor to be your witness at the Synagogue of our official ceremony.'

'Yes, this is a very good idea Rebekah we won't upset anybody with this move as this is just as the 'common law marriage what we are exercising by the law of the land.'

'How would you feel if I would ask Professor Mihály Schlesinger to be my witness and yours Gabriel would be Dr Sándor Fried for our proper Synagogue celebration of marriage?'

'As my Papa will walk me to the Chuppah and where Rabbi Baruch will conduct the ceremony.'

'Yes, it is a good idea, Rebekah. My goodness, you have worked out everything for that day, haven't you?'

'Yes, I can't think of anything else but that day. My old girlfriends are all giving me some advice for my wedding night already. I just smile at them for their small talks I wouldn't dare to tell them that I am well over that experience.

And what an experience that was! Hmm, yes please, I would like that all the time from my 'husband'.'

'Thank you, Rebekah, now you are making me blush which is unknown to me. Yes, you are the ever best I ever had. But please change the subject.'

'I can't believe that I have made you blush, Gabriel.'

Rebekah behaved like a giggling little schoolgirl, I didn't recognise her after the way she has dealt with the builder and Mr Zloch at the bathroom place in such a dominantly confident businesswomen manner. And now she is behaving just like she was in the Grand Hotel in Lvov on that beautiful night.

'Rebekah darling, I have to get back to my office. Would you come back with me to ask Viktoria and Andre if they would consider being our witnesses for the registrar's ceremony?'

'Yes, I'll be coming with you, and we both can ask them if they would do it.'

Rebekah put her arm into mine and held it so tight as I felt her firm bosoms through her thin Summery dress. She looked stunning again just as if she would have stepped out of that French '*Vogue Magazine*'. She is strikingly beautiful, and she is going to be my wife well what a lucky man that I am!

Andre and Viktoria were in the office already. They have sensed something very special when we've walked into the office.

Rebekah spoke to them first; I don't know if you two know that there is something very special going to happen to our life? Well, Gabriel and I are going to get married here in the Town Hall Registry Office on 14 July.

'Viktoria said yes, we know that as Gabriel has told us all ready, we are very happy for you. Mazel tov, we hope you'll have a great day.'

'Yes, Viktoria, thank you. But what we would like to ask from you two is if you would be our witnesses for both of us.'

'They have lost their voices on Rebekah's invitation announcement. Viktoria has rushed to Rebekah and hugged her in such great affection just as sisters would do to each other at news like this. Then she looked at Andre who was a bit embarrassed then Viktoria just nodded and both of them said; yes, of course, gladly. What an honour. Is that true that both of you would like us to do that?'

I said, 'Yes, we are both, Rebekah, and I, would like you to be our witnesses for our wedding.'

Rebekah added more to my request, 'Let's hope that one day sometime in the future Gabriel and I can return the favour to you both.'

They both turned bright red-faced at this time Rebekah hugged Viktoria just to comfort her.

Then she said, 'Well, you two must have thought of this step of marriage, haven't you?'

Andre and Viktoria both nodded and said very quietly yes, we have thought of it. It was really coming up as a possibility of getting married when all four of us went up to Ungvár.

Rebekah said, 'You see Gabriel, this is all our achievement. All four of us laughed at Rebekah's comment.'

'My goodness,' Rebekah said, 'I have to run to organise the food and cakes for Sunday's party.' She pecked a kiss on my cheek waved to my helpers and rushed out of the office.

Then both of them Andre and Viktoria thanked me for choosing them to do the honour to be our witnesses for our wedding.

I said, 'Yes.'

Rebekah said, 'It rightly that you two should think of your future don't take us as an example because we are too old for that commitment. When you are younger you can cope with married life better than when you get much older and more independent like me who has lived life as a bachelor. At least you are both young, and it is much easier to accept the growing together period with your partner or as husband and wife.'

'So get ready for that day and now get back to work.'

At the end of the day on my way home, I have picked up the two marrow bones from the butcher for the dogs.

As I got nearer to Elisabeth's house, I have noted that the builders are digging and working on our house. The thought that the completion date will be met made me very happy as from now on it won't be long until I could sleep in my bed in my house with a bit more luxuriously than this present arrangement.

The dogs recognised my steps and become more excited. When I walked through the front gate, they were sitting next to each other, and both have focused on my briefcase. Elisabeth was sitting on the shady veranda and looked at the dogs' performance, and she said, 'Well, Gabriel undoubtedly these dogs are yours for life, I have them since they were only puppies, but they have never shown such affection to me as they do it to you.'

I took the bones out of the brown greasy wrapping paper and handed it to them one by one, and they have run to their favourite places and that was it. So

I have pointed out to Elisabeth the fact, 'Just look at them Elisabeth their affection has only lasted until they have received their beloved bones.'

We both laughed at my assessment.

Elisabeth told me, 'These builders work so hard and the way they are progressing, and their working hours is just tremendous. Aren't you going over to see them?'

'No, Elisabeth. I don't want to interfere with their work, and besides, it is nothing really to see there it doesn't mean anything to me what they are doing frankly it is just a big mess to me. It will be more interesting at a later stage when the project will show some shape of a liveable house.'

I got a chair on the veranda next to Elisabeth's chair and was just relaxing from the day's events.

'You know Elisabeth as my contract from the officials in Budapest is coming to an end, and I look back how things already have changed or are in progress of changing.'

'I know you are originally from Debrecen, you have married the kosher butcher from Munkács. You have been living here for a long time even after the loss of your husband you have never returned to your birthplace Debrecen. What was the urge to remain here in Munkács?'

'Well, my little brother I have fallen in love with a man who was well respected here within the community he was a very good butcher. When he went to the animal market, and he looked at a bull he knew how much meat was in that beast, more a less he knew how much meat he would be able to sell out of it. But I don't really want to talk about why or how he has died it is still very painful. So I think it is the community which made me stay and settle here.'

'I know many people here in Munkács as I am taking eggs to the market once a month. You know the eggs are very sought-after items in particularly goose eggs. People come to see me regularly at the market and look for me if I am not there, I have become well and truly a resident of Munkács. Besides, it was so long ago when I lived in Debrecen, and all those friends have moved on or some of them have passed away. I do like this place here it is smaller than Debrecen, but you have everything here that I used to enjoy there.'

'Yes, I can see that Elisabeth for myself, I thought that I will miss all that buzz, excitement, and opportunities I have enjoyed in Budapest, but all those material things you can have here as well. Yes, they are in a much smaller size and quantity, but you can have access to them. What has become most attractive to me is the strong community spirit and a strong family unit among everybody. Families are sacrosanct it is not just among our Jewish community families, but it is in all ethnic background communities as well.'

'By the way, Isaack is organising an engagement party for Rebekah and I on Sunday after midday would you be able to come along with Elisabeth as my guest?'

'Also, Rebekah and I are getting married at the Town Hall Registrar on 14 July and after that ceremony, we are planning a finger buffet at the Star Hotel conference room.'

'Thank you for your invitation, Gabriel. I will come to support you at your wedding and will go to the Star Hotel 'finger buffet' reception but I can't make Sunday's party. I thought you have been engaged for some week ago.'

'Yes, we have been engaged some time ago, but Rebekah has insisted to make it an official event. I know some people have questioned our rush from us having met a couple of months ago then engaged for a month since our first meeting and now we are getting married. Gossip is flying already that Rebekah is pregnant and that is the reason for this quick marriage. It is unfair for her sake of this bad and negative gossip. I feel since I have come to Munkács I have brought the 'Decadent' Hungarian lifestyle, and I am poisoning the youth with this liberal mentality.'

I can categorically deny and promise you that my Rebekah is not pregnant, yes, we have seen each other before our engagement. In fairness, Elisabeth both of us are adult persons with the knowledge and take full responsibility for our actions. The fact is I am desperately in love with Rebekah. She is a strikingly beautiful woman, and she is smart and educated whom I can have a conversation with on any subject.

I don't want a wife whose interest is to be a mother of many children and would be tired out at the end of the day before we could have time for ourselves. I always wanted someone like her, but I have never found one in Hungary, and look at me I am a 31-year-old man I think it is my last chance to have a family.

'Yes, I can understand you my little brother fully, and I am wishing you all God's blessing!'

'But now come and have a meal with me as the dining table has been set already.'

'Thank you, my big sister. I am coming. We both laughed at our brother and sister's invention, but it shows our family respect for each other.'

Chapter 28

Kiddushin – Engagement Party at Isaack's Place and a Surprise about Sándor

I haven't seen Rebekah for a couple of days as I had so much to catch up on my reports, and I am still responding to all enquiries from the lower primary, junior schools, comprehensive high schools Gimnazium and faith schools. They are all asking the same question; what will be the consequences if they refuse this guidance which I have sent them well in advance.

I just keep repeating myself to them as if they would be children who have to be told many times before it would sink into their minds. Anyway, this is the reason I am here as a former teacher who knows how to deal with them without upsetting their self-esteem.

I just managed to go to Rebekah's house on Friday evening to celebrate the Sabbath, but I couldn't make the synagogue on Saturday. I asked Isaack to express my apology to Rabbi Baruch as I can't make the Saturday service. Rebekah was panicking over Sunday's engagement party worried that everything will go well as she has planned it.

Spending the Saturday at Elisabeth's house sitting on the gang (terrace) in the shade and composing my reports. After dinner that Elisabeth has cooked especially for me 'Töltött káposzta' (Stuffed cabbage) covered with tejfel (sour cream) and freshly baked bread.

Truly heavenly food you can have that any time of the year as cabbage is a very popular main ingredient in Central to Eastern European regions gastronomical dishes.

I noticed the builders were working from early in the morning and finished for the day at 2 o'clock. After when they have left, I went over to see for myself what progress they have made since Thursday morning.

I could see the great amount of progress they have made. The septic tank is in place already where Mr Klein told me where he was going to put it and the pipes were connected into the septic tank which was leading to the stable which will be our bedroom en suite. Not much work inside of the house itself but the water pipe from the street main waterpipe was excavated and the pipe was laid into a junction that will distribute water to the house itself and to the garden and for the front yard.

My faithful dog just looked at me if she would understand what is happening. Seeing my happy and satisfied face she must sense my happiness. Elisabeth came over to see the progress on the property. After I explained to her the plan, she said, 'My goodness, this will be a big house, Gabriel.'

'Yes, Elisabeth, we need it this big as we have plans for our extended family to be accommodated.'

She looked at me with a smile and said, 'Well, Gabriel, if you would need a nanny for your children here I am. I will be their second mother while you are both at work and going out for an event.'

'I wouldn't choose anybody else Elisabeth but you. At least you are remaining with us Elisabeth if I would erect a gate between our house and yours, which would make it easier for you.'

'Yes, I think that is a good idea, Gabriel.'

I had gone back to my paperwork and reports with the recommendations the officials in the ministerium over how different regional education officials had responded positively to my presentation, and they were ready for the changes.

My Lord, this is the worst part of my mission, I can't write everything down in my report which would cause mistrust and maybe more draconian measures to the implementation of the future National Curriculum. Be more diplomatic Gabriel keep the peace and make those sentences with words that have more meaning and with a positive upbeat attitude.

Leaving Elisabeth's house in my 'Sunday best' to attend our 'official engagement party' Rebekah has insisted on this party as an official engagement. If those people who are members of the family or our friends know perfectly well that we are engaged. From the evening when I have put her engagement ring on her finger, Rebekah has been showing off with it the following morning at the synagogue. So everybody has seen through her ring or heard about our engagement already in town. (I guess this is just an excuse to have a party)

The cobblestone street was watered down I guess just to keep the temperature cool As I was getting nearer to the town hall and turning to the Corzo to Rebekah's house I could hear all the church bells ringing for their Sunday services.

I rang the bell at Rebekah's house on time as we agreed at half-past eleven, Rita came to the door her face was beaming with joy I have pecked a kiss on her cheek as she let me in. When I walked into their lounge, I have recognised some faces whom I knew already and some I haven't met before. Rebekah rushed to me put her arm around my waist and in a loud voice introduced me ladies and gentlemen please welcome Gabriel he is my fiancée, my future husband.

I felt a bit embarrassed as this kind of practice is not customary in Budapest. (or I haven't been to many engagement parties before) Anyway just let's get over with it. Rebekah has introduced me to her mother's sister from Hust, Rachel and her husband Robert and to her father's brother Itzhak from Beregszász. The only person I have recognised was Dr Sándor my friend who does all of my legal documents from day one of my arrivals at Munkács. Later on, when we had time to talk to each other he said, 'Gabriel you didn't come to say hello when you went to see the new mayor.'

I was a bit confused. 'What do you mean Sándor I thought that your office is on the *Korzó*?'

'No, Gabriel, my new office is next door to Mayor Parkányi. Sándor must have seen my embarrassment and said, 'I would like to introduce to you the new Deputy Mayor Dr Sándor Fried of Munkács to you.' I couldn't say a word as I never knew that Sándor would be involved in politics.'

'Yes, Gabriel I am a non-political Deputy Mayor, I am representing the Jewish Community's interest I always tried to make Governmental Authorities recognise the Jewish people as an Ethnic group like the Russians or the Hungarians. There are 144,000 Jewish people living in Transcarpathia, and the Jewish community here is 13,488 this is representing 42.7% of the total population in Munkács. So this is the reason I have accepted this title.'

'I salute you Sándor what you do I can promise you that you can count on my support whichever way or that would be. But I didn't know that you were the deputy when I was introduced to the new mayor. I have tried to say hello to the Deputy Mayor, but you have had a guest with you in your office.'

'Yes, Gabriel I have been notified of your intention to meet me in my office, but my visitor was Rabbi Baruch who has been praying for me and for the opportunity to bring the Jewish amendment in the constitution of a recognised ethnic group.'

'Well, Sándor Mazel tov! Does this mean that I will have that job at the cultural department in the Town Hall?'

'Yes, Gabriel, you are the best person for that position we all agreed that with all of your connections and with your experience you will make Munkács culturally lively again.'

'Thank you, Sándor, you are truly a great friend who's always is full of surprises.' We both smiled and our conversation has been interrupted by Isaack.

'Isaack got a glass of champagne in his hand and said please congratulate my beloved daughter Rebekah's engagement and also to celebrate our unification as a family today.'

'I am very proud of Rebekah's chosen her future husband Gabriel who is now a very important member of our community here in Munkács. I have always prayed and hoped that one day my son will take over and further my little business and will make a success out of it. But now I have not just my daughter but my son in law who will succeed in my dream. Not to mention the next generation of my grandchildren who will take it to much higher perfection and to great success.'

'But now please congratulate my daughter Rebekah and Gabriel on their engagement.'

'Mazel tov-Mazel tov! Repeated by everybody drinking to our good health and to our future. L'chaim, and L'chaim. Yes, for life we all drink to that!'

Rebekah responded to her father's speech with, 'Thank you for bringing me up and adjusting my feet to love my Lord God with all my heart and trust Him in the promise He has made in the scripture to Sarah in **Genesis 18 words 10**: *…Then one of them said, 'I will return to you about this time next year, and your wife, Sarah, will have a son'.'*

'And here I am my beloved friends and relatives I am getting married to this wonderful man at the Town Hall Registrar on 14 July for our Lawful wedding and our proper wedding will be on 11 September, at the Hoif complex Synagogue with Rabbi Baruch Yehoshua Yerachmiel Rabinowitz. Our reception will be at The Handelsman restaurant and reception hall. So you are all welcome to that wedding on 11 September 1938.'

Rachel asked us to get together for a group family photograph and (she has kept crying over if my sister Rivkah would have been here) finally we managed to get together for this photo shoot.

Many of Rebekah's relatives came to me with a welcoming kiss to our family slogan. Isaack's brother Itzhak asked me if I was in engineering as Isaack mentioned that you are going to join his firm.

I have to explain to him, 'I am not into engineering, but my position is to be the salesman for the company. I am in the entertainment business and at this moment I am on a mission commissioned by the Cultural and Educational Ministry from Budapest. Ah, I can see the potential quality in you. You must have some good connections in high places?'

Rebekah came to my rescue her eyes were sparkling like her diamond ring. She looked stunning again in a long black skirt suit and a beautiful lace blouse. I still can't believe in that she is going to be my wife.

'I am sorry Gabriel I have left you on your own I should have spent more time with you, but you know what this family gathering is like I haven't seen them for a long time, and they have taken the time to come and wish us a happy future. They just wanted to share their joy with us like Rachel my mother's sister she is so emotional, and she keeps repeating that if your mother would be here.'

'Well, Rachel, must be missing her sister it is understandable.'

'Yes Gabriel, she is seeing me as her sister, she keeps saying that my movement my look is reminding her of my mother. Yes, they have been very close together as sisters.'

'Well, Rachel is a very attractive lady. If you going to be at her age and will look like her, I will be a very happy old man who has a young wife like you. We both laughed at my comment.'

The party ran into the early evening when friends and relatives started to leave Isaack's house, Rebekah's aunts and uncles have been booked into the Star Hotel which wasn't that far to walk.

Isaack looked absolutely shattered him and Rita were working very hard to entertain everybody makes sure that there was enough food and drink for the guests. Rebekah was still in her form she is rushing around I was helping her to clear off of the cutlery plates and get them into the kitchen. She advised Rita to have a rest with a glass of szilvapalinka, while I did the washing up and Rebekah did the drying and putting all plates into their place in the cupboards. Is this is how we are going to do this in our house, Gabriel.

She stopped for a second and looked at me with her beautiful eyes waiting for my answer I stopped and kissed her on her lips for a bit longer than we expected to do we forgot where we were, and I said, 'Yes my darling I promise you that it will be like this in our house every time I believe equality and partnership we are partners and lovers. I won't let your delicate hands be ruined with the washing up water I will do that just like now and you can dry them up.'

As Rebekah and I were going to join Isaack and Sándor, but in the kitchen, Rebekah pulled me to her so close to her body that I clearly felt her heartbeats, and we kissed so passionately in her kitchen as if only two of us stayed in the house without fear of anybody would walk into the room.

'I have suggested to her to button her jacket to cover up her nipples which were bursting through her blouse. I didn't want Isaack to note her state.'

We both joined Isaack and Sándor for a drink. Rita called Rebekah to the kitchen she didn't know the reason but when they got to the kitchen, I noticed that Rita cleaned Rebekah's lips with her handkerchief as her lipstick was all messed up with our kissing. Then Rita came back to the room with a smile on her face. Rebekah went to the bathroom and came back with fresh lipstick on.

'Sándor turned to me and asked me; How are you getting on with your report, Gabriel?'

'Which one would you like to know Sándor?'

'Why how many of them do you have to present to your authority?'

'Well, I have to present one to the Education Ministry which I am working on the moment. I try to be much more upbeat and positive with some facts which are already happening like a Hungarian language Gimnazium here in Munkács and also in Ungvár too. I try to encourage them to be a bit more gentle with their demands as there is a need for a Hungarian languages education system here in Transcarpathia, but I feel there will be a protest at faith schools, as the Latin and the Hebrew language teaching will be ending with this new curriculum.

The other one is the one which is much more complicated. This one I have to report back to The Chief Rabbi Immanuel Lőw I am afraid I have to tell him the true picture of what is happening here. The conversations I had with many Rabbis here in Transcarpathia are not very promising. 'But I expect they know it already as they have a very good network'.

'I am not very comfortable with this new Jewish law which passed at the Hungarian Parliament in May this year it won't be welcomed here in the region I think it will cause a revolt among our communities. There is a kind of nostalgic hope as it will be the same just like it was under Emperor Franz Joseph, at the Austro-Hungarian times. Well, just look at what happened in Austria the last March the Germans have annexed Austria through some very corrupt political leadership betrayal.

'Germany is now demanding more of the pre-WW1 territory's which it lost at the Treaty of Versailles, it was 20%, but most of the major territorial loses of Germany after WW1 were actually territory it had previously annexed from other countries. The defeated Germany the aggressor in the war and consequently made Germany responsible for making reparations to the Allied nations in payment for the losses and damage they had sustained in the war and set an amount of $33 billion in 1921.'

'And look at them now they are rich again, very powerful and demanding the lost territories back again. I wonder if they will be ready for another war to achieve these very valuable territories full of minerals and woodlands.'

'Well, Gabriel, it sounds like you learned the history very well. You should be in politics.'

'I am sorry to disappoint you Sándor, but I have no intention to take up that minefield territory. I will be staying with art, culture, and entertainment, that is my world, and I know that I am good at that.'

I noticed that Isaack's eyelids were closed a couple of times as he had a very tiring but successful party for his beloved daughter's engagement.

'I thanked Isaack for this memorable and warm welcoming day and for accepting me into his family. I know we are all very tired, and we are all facing another week's work. So thank you again for everything Isaack I am very touched by your kindness.'

Sándor and I said goodbye to our hosts and made our journey back to our homes. Sándor said at the door, 'Please come and see me tomorrow sometime in my office, Gabriel.'

'Yes, I will come in and have a chat with you Sándor over your and my plans here in Munkács.'

Chapter 29

Last Minute Organisation at the Town Hall Marriage

I called Sándor's secretary at the Town Hall to make an appointment with the Deputy Mayor.

Mr Deputy Mayor will see you at 10:30 a.m. was the secretary's answer.

I turned up on time to my appointment as arranged. Sándor's secretary let me into this large office its windows were facing the main square on the front of the building.

Sándor welcomed me with a long handshake and offered me a chair as we both sat down Sándor offered me some kosher plum brandy which I have declined and settled with a cup of tea.

Sándor started the conversation, 'I was very impressed with your speech last night at your engagement party over the present situation in Germany.'

'I am sorry Sándor I didn't want to come across to be so politically driven a person is particularly at my engagement party. My only interest is an art as you know but I am not a fool like many others who would accept any propaganda lies which the radio has been wrongly broadcasting not to mention in the press they are basically the propaganda news media. The public is very forgetful, and they have already forgotten the terrible hardship we had as a result of the great war which has been started by one nation alone with annexing lands from neighbouring sovereign countries.'

'I am absolutely understanding you Gabriel and I am sharing your views over these facts.'

'Yes, the public can be easily manipulated mainly on the nationalistic 'carrot' mottoes. It is all reflecting on the education system's misinformation from a young age. Brainwashing the simpleminded public.'

'Yes, Sándor, it is true Vladimir Ilyich Lenin always taught us just to tell a lie and repeat it as many times as we can and in the end the people believe it. The trick is that you have to promise everything that the people are asking for, and they will follow you like sheep all the way to the abattoir without a single question or a complaint.'

'You should be a politician Gabriel you have a moral overview on certain situations with humanity.'

'No, Sándor, I know my place, and I am feeling very comfortable there. We have a good politician, and his name is András Bródy MP.'

'Yes, Gabriel, and he is a good ally. I don't know if you are aware that I am working alone with the OZSMA organisation in fact I am their main contact here in Munkács.'

'I didn't know that Sándor but looking back I had a feeling that you are one of us when you came first to meet me at the Star Hotel and helped me through ever since every difficulty that I was going through and am still facing here in Munkács.'

'Before I have left Budapest, Rabbi Simon Hevesi introduced me to **'OMZSA'** *Országos Magyar Zsidó Segitő Akció* (National Hungarian Jewish Aid Association) and **JDC** Jewish Joint Distribution Committee.'

'So I am already involved with them and keep reporting back to them on a regular basis. They keep advising me on many issues mainly assessing the present situation and collecting information as I am having a meeting with Jewish communities all over in the villages and towns in the region.'

'Also, I've been advised to contact my old Professor Mihály Schlesinger at Lvov University where I pretended to be a mature university student. That is where I have met Rebekah and I believe she was truly God sent a gift to me.'

'Yes, Gabriel, you are right your mission has been organised from day one in such a perfect way that only the Lord can be so precise. Everything has fallen into places, and I believe Rebekah is the gift for your obedience from the Lord. I believe in that Gabriel that you are an asset for our organisations.'

'We want you here Gabriel helping our courses within the entertainment world so we can sell our ideas to the public.'

'Just let's go back to the ex-Mayor Hrabar's suggestion, he has offered you a position to work here which is based on your experience and your quality to run the Art and Entertainment Department for the Council of Munkács. This activity will give you a free hand to promote Hungarian artists and movie films to perform here in Munkács and in the whole of Bereg and Ugocsa County.

'But basically, you would be just like being a theatrical agent but with more authority and much bigger budgets. This is what you did in Budapest as I heard, and you've done it very successfully. Besides this is the program that the Hungarian Foreign Ministry is planning for Transcarpathia, to promote the Hungarian culture to the public on the Hungarian language.'

'I am flattered Sándor, and also, I am delighted to know that I will have authority to enhance and influence the entertainment here for the people's interest on demand in a much more perfected classical standard. This will not limit me to bringing in an up to date more modern style of music like jazz and Dixieland as well as movies from Hollywood. Widening the people's views of the big wide world we are living in.'

'You have made my day with this news Sándor, thank you. I am looking forward to this challenge.'

'I have to go to Budapest as I have to verbally present my report at the Educational Ministry on Tuesday, 19 July. Probably Count Pal Teleki will be present for my presentation as he is the Minister of Religion and Education. I know he is not very friendly with us, with the Jewish community. I know he is the one who was introducing the Jewish Law on 29 May.'

'Also, as you know Rebekah and I are having a registrar wedding ceremony here in the Town Hall which I hope you could come to along to support us. We want a marriage certificate to take with us to Budapest where we are going to apply for Hungarian Citizenship for Rebekah with this legitimate claim as she is my wedded wife. I believe this is a kind of protection and security for her.'

'Tell me more about this application Gabriel I might just have a friend at that department in Budapest. But let's have something to eat first. I invite you for a dinner at your and Isaack's usual place at the Star Hotel Restaurant.'

Walking into the restaurant Gerzson the headwaiter welcomed us by name and asked if Mr Grósz is going to join you at your regular table? Would you like the newspapers, Mr Deputy Mayor?

I said, 'Probably Gerzson, but Mr Grósz may be a little bit running late from his meeting.'

'Sándor suggested talking while we wait for Isaack. So who is Isaack having a meeting with?'

'He didn't tell me this yesterday.'

217

'He is at the Móric Ulman Commercial Bank he is seeking to have a larger overdraft facility.'

'Why? his business is quite profitable for him he is a well-off man.'

'It is all my fault Sándor I was telling Isaack that I have overheard at in the Agricultural Ministry that there is a big governmental investment is going to the River Tisza and its surrounding lowland where there is a plan to turn the area which follows the river all the land is to be irrigated with water channels making the agricultural products much more officiant. Elevating water from river level to higher level lands.

'Also, they want to excavate the riverbed allowing the river to be used for shipping as far as Huszt. Now the authority needs specialised machines for this work. They were telling me about this company in the North of England, who manufacture these so-called Conveyor and Elevators to move solid, semi-solid and liquid format with this Archimedes principle mechanism.'

'I told this news to Isaack that I have overheard in the ministry and his mind went into overdrive with the plans that he can manufacture these machines without any problem. I promised him while I am in Budapest, I will make an enquiry over the possibility that the Agricultural ministry will use Isaack's company with a ready-made product and would be able to manufacture to any specification as the Ministry would require. He would be in the best position to obtain a contract from them.'

'Well, you know Gabriel with what you have just told me that would make Isaack's company into a very prosperous and very large company. Just think of how Munkács itself would benefit from this opportunity with employment and wealth for everybody.'

'Yes, this is what I would call the 'business deal of the century'. Maybe even I could help Isaack as a business lawyer who would oversee the contracts and represent all the legal protection for the company.'

'I think Sándor that would be the perfect completion to the management setup. But this appointment has to come from Isaack not from me as I am only the salesman of this new venture. I would recommend you for that position Sándor. But I think we would be a dream team with this project if it will ever materialise.'

A very tired Isaack walked into the restaurant after Gerzson showed him to our table he asked for a pint of beer. He told us the bank manager's room was so warm and the only refreshment he could offer was water. Well, I just have to accept a glass of water to satisfy my thirst. Isaack turned to me and said Rebekah has gone to the Town Hall to see you she is probably on her way nowhere.

As soon as Isaack had finished his sentence Rebekah has just walked into the restaurant. All the fellas have followed her from the door to our table. She looked as stunning as ever in her linen pale blue summer dress and a short bolero type of top, high heel shoes and her ever-changing selection of hats.

She gave me a kiss on my lips shook Sándor's hand and sat down next to me.

She said, 'I thought that you would be in your office then later I remembered that you were going to see Sándor in his office then I thought that you will be here as it is dinner time already, and I was right here we are together again.'

'Isaack was telling me the good news about his meeting with the bank manager.'

I said to Isaack, 'I have mentioned the reason to Sándor why you were having a meeting in the bank.'

'I thought for such a big contract and on expansion on a business probably you would need a good lawyer like Sándor.'

'Isaack told me that he had discussed this already with Sándor yesterday with a possible legal support from him.'

'Sándor told Isaack that with his project he would be one of the biggest employers in Munkács.'

Isaack said, 'Yes, Sándor, I will call a meeting after when Rebekah and Gabriel will return from their trip from Hungary.'

First, let's see if my future son in law will be able to achieve that contract and bring me all the other information that we would need for this project. They all looked at me if I was the origin of this whole excitement, yes this is really my fault. It was just a comment I've made, and Isaack is hooked on the possibility for his engineering company's future, and it is now all in the centre of this planning.

At the end of our lunch, Sándor picked up the bill and asked Isaack if he could have a moment for him.

Rebekah quickly grabbed the moment of privacy with me as she has put her hand on my thigh and whispered, 'Rita is going to the hairdresser and also she is doing some shopping tomorrow morning from ten just think at last we could have a good couple of hours for ourselves, Gabriel. I am missing you so much my love we haven't been together for so long.'

I felt the same way for her, and how desperate I am now for private time with my fiancée. 'Without any hesitation, I whispered back; yes, my darling I will be there in the morning I can't wait much longer I am missing you every minute of the day. Only just a few more days, and we will be a legally married couple who do not have to hide our emotions and affections for each other anymore.'

Sándor came back to our table and said, 'We have to have a serious meeting tomorrow afternoon over the financial distribution to the poorer members of the Jewish community, I need your record and the list of the most needy people that you have collected. I will come to your office at 2:30 in the afternoon.'

'Yes, Sándor, I will be ready for you with that information as they are all in my office.'

Rebekah's face was a little bit concerned as our precious time together would be cut short.

'Don't worry, my love, we will have enough time for ourselves I promise.'

'Isaack turned to Rebekah and said, I am going to the factory are you going to join me?'

'No, papa, I am having a coffee with Gabriel then I will be going home to get changed.'

'I have to go back to my office soon my darling as most of the morning I have spent with Sándor.'

'That is all right, Gabriel. I understand it, but I am desperate for a big hug and a proper kiss.'

'All right, darling, but not here. I will walk you home, and we can do it behind your front door.'

Rebekah's eye sparkled again at the thought of having a hug in the middle of the day in reasonable privacy as you can have in a small town where everybody knows you. At last, we are able to achieve our most desired wishes. We walked towards Rebekah's house where we let loose our short and passionately embraced emotions for each other in our short and limited way.

Back in my office, I found Andre and Viktoria were doing the same cuddling just like I did it with Rebekah a few minutes ago. Poor kids, I felt for them I know what they are going through its a similar situation to mine. I said, look I am really happy that you two are getting on so well I hope it will develop into a serious and proper conclusion. But be careful it could have been somebody else coming through this door and you are in trouble.

I said, 'To them, let's make a deal I want to be your witness Andre on that special day. I want to return your gesture at my 'big day'.'

'Don't be sorry I am not criticising your actions at all, but for the next time please lock the door.'

A sigh of relief from them. 'I asked them and now please back to work.'

Viktoria would you please get me the list that I have collected through my meetings with Jewish Community leaders.

I was instructing Viktoria to write down all the names from the list the one with the 3 crosses only. Politely she didn't ask a question for the reason over the importance of the crosses. Also, I asked for their attention; this is not official, but I have been confirmed that the council is going to appoint me to run the cultural department for the whole of Beregi—Ugocsa Counties including Munkács Town.

'My office will be here in this room, and you will have your own room with some other helpers to carry out all the necessary administration. You two will be deputised to me with the running of this big and comprehensive project.'

Great jubilation from both of them is not just that they will still have work, but they will work with me on this exciting project.

'But please I am emphasising this do not tell anyone this news as it is not finalised yet and passed by the council as a body for itself.'

'There is one more very important matter which is they have to take an oath from you that you will not speak to others about this I am telling you now.'

'We do swear Gabriel that we will keep it secret and thank you for your trust for both of us.'

'Thank you, I feel much more comfortable to carry on giving you two a more confidential task.'

'I have to explain to them the OMZSA project and the importance of this plan.'

(N 37) OMZSA: *Országos Magyar Zsidó Segítő Akció* (National Hungarian Jewish Aid Association)

Both of them went into an emotional mood on hearing of how we are going to help the downtrodden fellow Jews all over the region.

Andre spoke first, 'Thank you, Gabriel, for telling us the work of this very important organisation, and I feel Viktoria and I definitely want to be part of this noble organisation.'

'This organisation is not just a Hungarian one, but this program is a worldwide project through JDC.'

I felt much relieved that I have cleared it with them I know that they are going to be true allies with this program, and I can rely on them of how much they will be committed to being involved with this noble project.

Well, just look at the time as it has gone so quickly it is home time now, so I'll see you tomorrow.

It is sad to know that the youth of today has been driven in wrong direction away from humanity and faith. I don't point fingers at anybody for the misleading of the youth into a politically manipulated direction, but I believe they should be leading them back to the Tora, and to search for their Lord God first through faith instead dogmas and schisms.

I know Andre and Viktoria are much more sensible than many other youths of their own age group, but I am not sure if I have influenced them at all within this short time, I have spent with them here in Munkács. I hope I have.

My usual journey home has now become a ritual exercise for me to collect our dog's goodies of their marrowbones from the butcher. I have to stop at the front of my new house to see the progress that the builders have achieved already.

Which was vaguely visible from the outside of the building but as we both went into my driveway of the house it was more evidence of the progress what the builders have achieved.

I went up to the back garden with Elisabeth and picked some strawberries and took some more with us to have after supper.

At the end of supper, Elisabeth and I have sat outside on the terrace and just relaxed from the very busy day's pressure.

As we sat on the bench Szuka came to me and put her head on my lap and waited for me to stroke her head and back she was seeming to enjoy the affection while Floki did the same with Elisabeth.

Chapter 30

Build-Up to and the Wedding Itself

On my way into the office leaving Elisabeth's house, I bumped into Mr Klein in front of my house he was giving instructions to his men. When he spotted, me he invited me into the house to show me all the progress he is making on our house alterations. I was curious but also, I didn't have much time to spend with him as I am going to have a very busy day today. I noticed that they have successfully connected to the main water pipes from the road which gave them access to water to get on with their work. He told me that he is going to see Mr Zloch at the Bathroom-Kitchen place today to collect some of the pipes and measurements of layouts for laying the waste pipes for the bathroom kitchen fittings.

'Mr Klein said by the end of this week they will complete all the electric cabling sockets and light fittings inside and outside of the house as on the plan. Plastering on the outside and inside of the house also they will place all the new door and window frames in as well as the setting of the base for the floor so the carpenters can come in hang the doors and windows and also the wooden parquet floors in the next three weeks.'

'I asked him what about the cleaning up of the ceiling of all the rooms to bare wood and varnish it and also the paintings and tile works?'

'Oh, Gabriel, they will be done at the very end when everything is in place and completed. Everything will be completed by the time you return from Budapest. I will be able to present you with the key to your new home and new driveway.'

'That is very good, Mr Klein, and I will pay you in cash Pengő when we are all satisfied with the work.'

'I can guarantee you Gabriel that you won't be disappointed with our workmanship on your finished property. And please call me József.'

'Thank you, József, but if you forgive me, I have to go to work now.'

Andre and Viktoria were in the office all ready and working with the windows wide open just letting the early morning cool air in as the temperature, later on, will heat up the room into such unbearable state that will make you sweat all day long.

I reminded my helpers that Sándor, The Deputy Mayor will come to visit our office for the information that I have described to them yesterday.

I have advised them please call Sándor on his official title as Mr Deputy Mayor.

To respond to their panicky face, I have to calm them down, and say, please don't worry he is one of us. I said to my helpers that I have to go out for a meeting now and should be back at 1 pm.

I have rung the bell at Rebekah's house at ten as we agreed with her yesterday. Immediately she let me in probably she has seen me through the window. She had her dressing gown on and a slip only. The smell of her favourite perfume filled the whole room with that dazzling aroma. As I have closed the door behind me, she has jumped into my neck embraced my waist with her legs like little children do to their parents and kissed me on my lips. She said, 'Please carry me upstairs 'to heaven' my love please do not lose valuable time that we could spend together.'

I walked upstairs with Rebekah hanging onto me like a child and kissing my neck. (She knows that I like that) When we got upstairs, she led me into her room. and she laid on her bed with an opened dressing gown, with that move she has revealed her firm breasts which were shaking from the sexual excitement, as she stretched her hand out towards me and said, 'At last, it's only you and I again, my love.'

I have started freeing myself from my clothes, my heart was pounding like a big drum from the accumulated sexual desire for this woman I love so much I didn't care about anything about the world just to fly with my love into the highest point of heaven and keep her up there as long as I can then cover her with my wings and with my energy, then slowly and gently I return to earth with my Rebekah in my arms.

What a beautiful gift I have been given from the one I most care about in my life. We've relaxed on the bed in the pool of our body's sweat of exhaustion as she has rested in my arms on the perfume filled bed I just whisper into her ear to say, 'My darling this is the kind of our journey we will be experiencing every time in Budapest. I can promise it to you.'

She has turned on top of my body I felt her firm breasts on my chest, and she looked into my eyes and said, 'I know the angel, and I just can't wait to be with you at all the times of the day.'

'Neither I can wait for that my darling Rebekah! And just think of our new life together in our new house. We don't have to hide and be ashamed anymore for our actions. Just you and me forever.'

I was refreshing myself in the bathroom washing my face when I felt her naked body on my back as she has embraced me from behind and is holding me tight she put her head on my shoulder and said, 'I want you again and again my angel.'

I turned around kissed her on her forehead and said, 'You know the time today is 'not our friend' anymore as Rita could come home at any time soon.'

'Yes, I know Gabriel, with her lip down she said I know that but thank you for this morning 'flight' my angel it has given me a fulfilment of my desire which I will treasure this satisfying moment till we get to Budapest.'

It was the hardest goodbye to make to my future wife at her front door, but the time was pressing on for both of us.

Back in the office, my helpers were busy working, paperwork all over on their desks and some empty coffee cups. I said let's have a break I will buy you lunch down at the cafeteria in the basement. At least there was a few Celsius cooler temperature than in our office.

Back in our office, Viktoria has closed the windows as the Sun has started bursting through the windows. Sándor has arrived on time as he promised. I have introduced him to Viktoria and Andre.

I was explaining to Sándor that I had told my helpers about our aim and commitment with OMZSA, as both of my helpers were already directly involved with the collection of the information.

Sándor looked at them and said, 'You know that this is not a political or a secret society, we are working for, but we still expect the most cautions from every member.'

'I suggested to Sándor that we need to deliver the information for the younger generations if we want them to understand the way they are thinking is wrong and also how they can bring their help to achieve our goals.'

'Yes, Gabriel you are right we do need them as we are building their future too.'

Sándor told, 'My helpers that he will ask them to visit his Deputy Mayor's office when Gabriel will be in Hungary so he can have a much deeper chat with them.'

Viktoria said, 'Yes, Mr Deputy Mayor, we look forward to seeing you whenever you wish.'

'Yes, Mr Deputy Mayor, we are understanding of the kind of secrecy this work is requiring, and we just want to assure you that we will be discrete and supportive to this agency. As you are aware that we are Jewish as well, so we are just helping our own people.'

'That is good, Viktoria and Andre. So I will see you soon.'

'Just to let you know Mr Deputy Mayor that Andre and Viktoria will be our witnesses for our wedding.'

'Very good, so I'll be seeing you much sooner.'

'Dear Mr Deputy Mayor, here is the requested information with all the list of names whom I thought are in the direst financial and health situation. They are the neediest ones on the list with the record of their names addresses and health requirements.'

'Very good, Gabriel, this information is very much needed to arrange the emergency support for the neediest cases. (He just briefly looks into my report and says, Yes Gabriel it is a very comprehensive and very helpful collection of data). Well done.'

'Well, Mr Deputy Mayor, I have a great and valuable help which has been contributed by Viktoria and Andre.' Both of my helpers blushed as I am giving them some credit and recognition of the hard work they did.

Sándor looked at them and said, 'Well, we are going to have a very good and long working relationship with you two. He offered his handshake to both and said well done and left our office.'

They have been still standing and looked at me. 'Viktoria spoke first and said, it is our pleasure to work with you Gabriel, you are taking us onto your journey, with care and protection, and we are really thankful for your trust in us.'

By Tuesday, 12 July, everything has gone crazy just two days to our wedding date at the registrar, and we are going to Budapest on the following day on Friday, 15 July.

I have a meeting with Chief Rabbi Immanuel Lőw on Saturday in the Main Synagogue in Budapest. I am having an appointment with the Officials at the Education and Foreign Ministry on the 19th.

Well, I pray and hope the Lord will bless me with the energy and the travelling safety to get through safely in this coming two weeks.

Right, so where am I now? I've just tried to organise my coming week's program.

Tomorrow on Wednesday I am going to the station to collect Rebekah's and my railway ticket for the express Pullman direct from Munkács to Budapest. Collecting our wedding rings from Mr Ernő Ungár Goldsmith shop and ordering some flowers for Rebekah's wedding. Collecting my double-breasted navy suit and shirt with a new pair of shoes from Mr Neuman's Gentleman's Tailoring Salon on the Corzo. When we get to Budapest, I will wear my old clothing from my mothball smelly wardrobe.

I still have my Tallit Shal, so I don't have to take the one from Munkács.

'Ask Rebekah to find her passport and let's hope it is still valid.'

Collect all my separate reports from my office safe, one for the government and one for Chief Rabbi Immanuel Lőw which is similar to the one I have given to Sándor, but the one for Chief Rabbi Lőw is a more comprehensive one.

I have crashed down on Elisabeth's balcony onto that wooden bench on a very warm Tuesday evening. My faithful friend Szuka joined me again she kept looking at me with those big eyes if she would have sensed that I am going away for some time. Elisabeth has joined me, on the balcony, and she was updating me on the builder's progress on my house. She brought me some freshly picked strawberries from my garden and some cherries from her garden.

'She asked me if she should ask Mr Tóth to take care of my back garden all the vines and trees need some attention and removing of all the weeds as it is getting out of hand the way they grow. I have agreed with her, and I have given her some money to pay the gardener and also, I have paid her in advance for my rent.'

'This is too much Gabriel you won't be even here for over two weeks.'

'I know Elisabeth but please take it you are so kind to me with many other things what you are giving me which are not in our rental contract.'

'I am very pleased Gabriel that you are my next-door neighbour with your beautiful wife Rebekah she has so much class and at the same time such humanity as well. Yes, both of you are a great match.'

227

Well, that night again I just couldn't get to sleep as my mind was just running around in circles.

I thought that my little friend the mouse will come and will keep me in the company. Yes as I've just thought it there he was running across the newspaper on the bedroom floor, and he stopped again halfway through the paper just like last time and looked at me with his little button eyes as if he was greeting me and wishing me a safe journey to Budapest. Then he just went on his business, and I couldn't remember anything until Matyi our alarm rooster woke me up in the early morning.

Well, I must have been sleeping so deep as I didn't know for a minute where was I. This time, I was grateful to Matyi to wake me up so early as I have to get on with my daily plans.

Now, one more day, and I still have a lot to organise I have to get everything spots on as we have planned it with a precise timetable and efficiency. So just get on with it, Gabriel.

Chapter 31

The Wedding at the Registrar

I woke up with the thought that I will be married to the most beautiful woman in the world. I found myself whistling all morning, well I have never done that before in my adult life.

Elisabeth noticed it and with a smile she said, I am very pleased for you Gabriel and added that you look very handsome as a movie star.

'Thank you, Elisabeth, are you sure that you wouldn't like to come and support me on our big day?'

'I can't Gabriel thank you for you asking me again, but I will be coming to your wedding which will be held at the synagogue.'

I kept checking the time on my watch. My goodness, I don't want to be late. I was checking the rings in the box and my wallet with my passport in it. My jolly feeling suddenly changed into a panicky mode. My God, please give me strength and confidence to get through this ceremony.

'Gabriel, please do not panic, everything will be fine.'

'Thank you, Elisabeth, I know but I have never done anything like this before, this is my first, and I promise you the only one for my life. I have been at other weddings, but I have never thought that this is such a nerve-wrecking experience until it happens for yourself.'

I have picked up my travelling cases and my briefcase with all the documents and reports in it, and I will take them into our room at the Star Hotel where we have booked in for one night for us, Rebekah and for myself. It is for tonight only as we can get to the station together to catch the international express train to Budapest.

Finally, when everything has been organised, I have decided to leave just to be there earlier. I can always go into my office and wait for the right time. I hope the florist has delivered the flower for Rebekah that I've ordered. I just hoped that I would not be spotted by Mr Klein the last thing I wanted was to listen to his achievements on how he was progressing on the extension and on the other things. Yes, It is important to know these things but not right now, particularly in this kind of mental state of my mind.

I have dropped off my luggage at the hotel room and headed to the town hall.

When I walked through the town hall gate the security man has congratulated me on our marriage which has been repeated by many others whom I have passed on the corridors. One of the officers told me jokingly, 'Well, it is not too late to change your mind, Gabriel.'

We both smiled at his remark, and finally, I got into my office where a friendlier face of Viktoria and Andre welcomed me and were just having a cup of coffee. Viktoria has seen my state and offered me a cup of coffee which I was very grateful for, it has calmed me down a lot. Andre was trying to cheer me up with a funny story which I have appreciated.

'Andre was asking me if I am ready?'

'Yes, Andre I think, I am. I have handed the box of two-wedding rings to Andre and asked him if he knows of the choreography of the ceremony, when is he has to hand it to the registrar.'

'Yes Gabriel, you have told me many times already.'

'Sorry, yes, you right I have told you many times.'

'Well, Gabriel, are you ready? We have to go now it's nearly 11:00. Viktoria and I have signed your marriage certificate earlier on, now it is all yours and Rebekah's signatures are required for the document and then you are officially married.'

We are walking from our office to the downstairs Council Conference Hall with Andre and Viktoria. When we got into the room, there were some chairs facing the Registrar pulpit which has two chairs and a table with some documents on the top, an inkwell and a penholder. I have to say the room was modestly but tastefully decorated. As we walked into the room I went to the stage, and I sat down. Andre and Viktoria sat at the front row chairs facing the stage. Just then when I have turned around, I was able to see the faces who were present to witness our wedding.

It was good to see Sándor was sitting in the front row of the right-hand side chairs companioned by Rita next to him. I have noticed some faces whom I had not expected like Mr Klein, my builder, and Mr Ungár the Goldsmith. For a big surprise, I noticed Councillor H Cohen was sitting with some of the Officers from the Town Hall. My attention was disrupted with the entrance of the Registrar Lady who has been taking Rebekah's and my details when I have applied for a date for our wedding.

We both smiled and greeted each other. Then the main entrance opened and there was my fiancée Rebekah, arm in arm with her father Isaack. (Then we have been asked by the Registrar lady to all stand up). Isaack walked Rebekah all the way to the front stage; then he joined Sándor and Rita on the front row and Rebekah came up to the stage next to me.

Rebekah just lit up the room with her entrance, she looked like my favourite Hollywood Movie Star, Hedy Lamarr (Hedwig Éva Maria Kiesler) as Rebekah was walking down on the red carpet to her latest movie premier.

Everybody's face was a picture as they all have been mesmerised by the beauty of Rebekah.

'Yes, and she knows how to walk on her very high heel shoes to get the maximum attention. She was dressed in a white silk dress with a white silk lace Bolero on her shoulder, white gloves and her signature clothing of the large brimmed white hat and a ribbon from the hat floating behind her like a cape. Her perfect body in the white dress has even amplified her pear-shaped figure. What scenery for all to remember. ('Even the Registrar lady Mrs Cohen whispered to her you look very elegant Rebekah.') (So that is the reason Cllr H Cohen is in the room with us as he is the Registrar's husband.)'

I whispered to her, 'You are my movie star. You look absolutely just stunning.'

She whispered back to say, 'Thank you for the flowers the one she was holding onto as something to comfort her hands in her embarrassment over the ceremony.'

Mrs Chen the Registrar welcomed us all, the members of families, friends, and guests then she has turned to us and welcomed us separately by our names. And she went into her routine speech.

Marriage is also called matrimony or wedlock, is a culturally recognised union between people, called spouses, that establishes the rights and obligations between man and woman, as well as between them and of their children, and also between them and their in-laws.

The state registration of marriage is established with the purpose of ensuring stable relations between man and woman. Registration of marriage also provides protection of rights and interests of married couples and their children, as well as protects the interests of the State and society.

The state registration of marriage is certified by the Marriage Certificate. The specimen of the Czechoslovakian Marriage Certificate is approved by the Cabinet of Ministers of Transcarpathia and Czechoslovakia.

I do solemnly declare that I know not of any lawful impediment why I Gabriel Bartos may not be joined in matrimony to Miss Rebekah Grósz.

(Then Mrs Cohen looked at Andre and ask him to bring the rings and place them on the embroidered cushion that Mrs Cohen held in her hand then she asked us to stand in front of her, and she asked me first to pick up Rebekah's ring, and she continued with her speech and asked me to repeat it after her.

I give you this ring as a sign of our love, trust, and marriage. I promise to care for you above all others, to give you my love, friendship, and support, and to respect and cherish you throughout our life together. I repeated her with the vows she just said and pulled the wedding ring on Rebekah's finger. I looked at Rebekah's face and I've seen the bright sparkle of tears just roll down on her face. I have slipped my handkerchief into Rebekah's hand to wipe the tears from her face.

Then Mrs Cohen turned to Rebekah and repeated the same vows to her which she also had to repeat and asked her to pull the wedding ring on my finger and put our hands together, then Mrs Cohen wrapped 'Blue and White coloured ribbons' around our hand and said.

I call upon these persons, here at present, to witness that Gabriel Bartos do take Rebekah Grósz to be his lawful wedded wife.

The registrar asked me first then Rebekah to sign the marriage certificate document that was on the table to be witnessed in front of the roomful of people present.

Then she turned to me and said, 'You may kiss the bride.' (Well, it wasn't easy to do from Rebekah's hat as I have to take off my Fedora to be able to get to Rebekah's lips to kiss her.)

Instant applause and shouting from the room full of guests Mazel tov. Mazel tov!

Then Mrs Cohen the Registrar told the guests, and with this, the ceremony of the marriage vow has been concluded, and I am wishing the newly married couple all God's blessing. Then she shook our hands and encouraged all the guests to do the same to congratulate us for our marriage.

It was a very touching moment when all the guests came to congratulate us, and it was a great blessing as Rabbi Baruch and his lovely wife Rivkah came to congratulate me and gave me a quick blessing than I saw he did it to Rebekah as well.

Councillor H Cohen came to me with his wife shook our hands and congratulated us. He said, 'Please allow me to introduce my wife Maria who was conducting your ceremony.'

'Yes, I have thought of the coincidence of names when I have seen you here after we had a different interpretation at times.'

'I hope there is no ill-feeling for each other I believe that we serve a different system.'

'Councillor Cohen, I do respect the work you do for the community, but I have to emphasise that I am serving my only Lord God of Israel.'

'I am not in and God willing I will never be involved in politics. It's my Lord and the world of art that is my life and of course from now on is my future is with my wife.'

Mrs Cohen gave me our marriage certificate in a hard-bound booklet. She said now you are officially married and this certificate here that has the seal of proof from the Authority.

'I thanked them and invited them over to the Star Hotel for a finger buffet and a drink.'

Isaack just stepped on the stage, and with a loud voice, he asked for some attention. When everybody had his attention, he invited everybody for a drink to celebrate his daughter and my marriage just across the square at the Star Hotel's bar.

'Rabbi Baruch and his wife Rivkah have declined the invitation and said that they have some prior engagement, and they have left the room.' I have noticed that earlier on my wife Rebekah and Rabbi Baruch's wife Rivkah was chatting at length and hugging each other as they were leaving the room.

I went to Isaack pulled him aside and said, 'I would like to thank you for bringing up a beautiful child and making her into the most beautiful woman you could imagine and now you have presented her to me. With all my heart I promise to you that I will treat her with the highest honour and respect may God be my witness. You know how much I love her and how much she means to me.'

'I know Gabriel, and I am very grateful that you will provide her with all that I couldn't do for her as I had to work hard work in the business without my wife's support and for a man having to deal with a girl's emotions without a mother. I know Rita through the years has taken some of those weights off my shoulders as much as she loves Rebekah, but it isn't her flesh and blood.'

'I like you Gabriel, and I know she will be a bright starlet on your side wherever you will take her in high societies.'

We all went over to the hotel bar for a drink, it was good to see that Sándor was talking to Andre and Viktoria at length, and at last, I managed to get my message through to Cllr Cohen that I am not his enemy. But he is in politics, and you never know which direction the wind will blow him.

Everybody had a good time at the Hotel Bar as Isaack paid for the drinks. Luckily, he set the time of the free bar, and it has closed down very quickly. Only a handful of people have been left behind who were much closer family or business associates of Isaack. I have managed to have a last-minute meeting with Andre and Viktoria instructing them for their next two weeks' works agendas. Viktoria told me that Sándor will take over their workload, and they will report to Sándor.

Then Sándor told me, 'Remember, those important meetings with our contact in Budapest.'

He said, 'Don't worry, Gabriel. I will oversee all of your commitments and works here with the help of Andre and Viktoria.'

Isaack and Rita gave me a hug before they were leaving the hotel and wished us good luck in Budapest. 'Isaack asked me to come home with a good and prosperous business deal through my contacts.'

I promised, 'I would try to do my best for all of our benefits.'

Rebekah and I have been absolutely tired out with the day's excitement and on all the worries we both were building up that everything should be done as we have planned it in the first place.

As finally, we've just gone upstairs into our room where a bottle of chilled champagne was in the ice bucket and two glasses awaited us on the table we were so tired so we agreed that we will compensate tonight's lovemaking until we get into our little apartment on *Király utca* in Budapest.

We have kissed each other goodnight, and she said, at last, we are now legal to make love, and we have to postpone it till tomorrow. Good night my dear wife I love you till the end of our life.

'Yes, goodnight, my husband, and I will love you even beyond our life, it will be forever!'

Chapter 32

On the Way and We Are in Budapest

Early in the morning, I have gone into the bathroom to refresh myself for the journey and when I was finished I pulled a single carnation out from the bunch of her wedding flowers, walked to her bed, and woke her up with a gentle kiss on her lips and put the single carnation on her pillow.

'Good morning, Mrs. I hope you have slept well? This is your prince who has come to wake his 'Snow white' with a kiss.'

Rebekah looked at me with her big eyes stretched her arms towards me and said, 'Here, I am my 'prince' kiss me again and again until the evening.'

'I just can't do that my love we have a fast train to catch at the station. We are going to have a very long day ahead of ourselves.'

I think that little word has convinced my newly wedded wife, she did get ready within minutes. While she was in the bathroom refreshing herself and getting dressed for the long journey, I was gathering her yesterday's clothing that she was wearing for our wedding.

'Don't pack those Gabriel I am going to be leaving them behind Rita will collect them from the reception along with my hat. I am only taking the smaller brimmed hat with me to Budapest.'

By the time we've got down to reception János, the receptionist told us that the Taxi is waiting for us at the front entrance to take us to the station. János called for the bellboy to take our luggage to the Taxi.

As we were getting into the Taxi to our surprise Rita and Isaack were in the Taxi already, they welcomed us, and Isaack said, 'We just have to wave you goodbye at the station.'

Rita said, 'I've never been without you, Rebekah, for such a long time.'

She was drying her eyes with a handkerchief then she has turned to me and said, 'Please look after her, Gabriel.'

I just touched Rita's hand gave a gentle grip and said, 'I will Rita I promise you that I will protect her.'

At last, we all got to the station with ten minutes to spare before the train's arrival so we could have more time with Isaack and Rita on the platform. Rita was holding onto Rebekah's hand and kept giving her advice as to what to look out for in Budapest. She said to Rebekah, 'She will collect her wedding dress from the hotel reception on their way home. Isaack asked me if I had enough cash on me?'

I said, 'Yes, Isaack. Thank you, I have plenty.'

He gave me a couple of envelopes and said, 'It's been handed to me yesterday during the celebration at the hotel bar with the request to give it to you before your departure. So here it is.'

Our discussion was interrupted by the station master's announcement with a warning to all the travellers that our train is now arriving at the platform where we stood.

Rebekah and I said goodbye to her father and Rita. then I collected all of our luggage and took them into our coach compartment and joined Rebekah at the window waving to Isaack and to Rita. Rebekah with tears in her eye shouted' look after yourself, Papa. 'I love you both!'

As the train was slowly pulling out of Munkács main station Isaack and Rita's size was getting smaller and smaller in the distance than their bodies have just melted into the horizon.

Soon as we left Munkács we were crossing the bridge of the River Latorna and leaving the mountainous hills of the Carpathian Mountains behind and heading towards Hungary.

The train guard checked our tickets then he invited us to the dining coach for a complimentary drink and told us that the dinner will be served at 12:00 noon sharp.

Rebekah held my hand, almost crushed it and said, 'My darling, I am so excited as I have never been out of the Transcarpathian region. My longest journey was to Lvov and back to Munkács. The only other time I went to Ungvár was with you. And now I am going to that beautiful big city of Budapest with my husband where we are going to live for an exciting two weeks.'

'Will you take me to all those beautiful theatres and coffeehouses?'

'Yes, of course, my darling Rebekah. Of course, I will take you everywhere wherever I go you'll be coming with me. I want everybody to see what a beautiful woman I have married who is really my secret movie star!'

We are heading to the dining car to have our well-earned dinner and claim our complimentary drink too. Rebekah whispered to me, 'Gabriel, I truly feel like a movie star as the way people look at me.'

'Yes, my darling, they are seeing something in your presence which is called charisma and class. You just have it many others in this dining coach don't. They have impressive stylish clothing, but they don't know how to wear it. You have the star attitude, and furthermore, you have been well educated while these women are just wives, they are just trophies for their husbands.'

We went straight to our dining table and the waiter immediately brought us a bowl of Beluga caviar and a glass of champagne. I noticed that all the other guests have it on their table too, so I thought this is our complimentary welcome drink. I like it. Thank you, Sándor this is your present, for us. 'Let's drink darling for Sándor as this is his present for us. He purchased the tickets for us in the first-class coach.'

Look through the window from our table and see that the train is crossing the River Tisza at Tiszaszentmárton which is the border town where we are crossing into Hungary as the river Tisza is the natural border between Hungary and Czechoslovakia. Then heading towards; Nyiregyháza, Füzesabony then Hatvan and at the end is Budapest. 'My God, it was over three months ago when I had this journey in the other direction towards Munkács. Well, darling, the landscape from Nyiregyhaza will be just flat lowland. As we are passing Füzesabony and Hatvan towards Budapest the landscape will be much hillier, not as hilly as it is around Munkács.'

A bearded gentleman who was dressed like me with a double-breasted navy blue suit and a bow tie at the opposite side table companioned with a lady he has overheard that I have mentioned the name of Munkács and politely asked us if we are from Munkács.

'Yes, we are, my wife is a native resident, and I have just been working there for the last four months.'

The gentleman said, 'I am a native of Munkács too, and I have been brought up and educated at the *Sugár uti* (Sugár Str) Jewish Gimnázium in Munkács.'

'May I introduce myself my name is Dr Zoltán Hacsek, and this is my wife Johanna.'

'Pleased to meet you both I am Gabriel, and this is my wife Rebekah.'

Rebekah responded to Dr Hacsek, 'I have graduated from the Jewish Gimnázium too.'

'But I don't think I would remember you, Rebekah, probably because you were much younger at that time when I was graduating. The Gimnazium was still under the directorship of Rabbi Chaim Elazar Shapira.'

'I am originally Czech, but I have learned Hungarian at the Jewish Gimnazium which was helpful for me when studying at the university in Budapest.'

'My parents sent me to study at the Corvinus University in Budapest where I have graduated in business administration, and economics, then later I have gained my doctorate. Were you visiting Munkács?'

'Yes, Rebekah, just for a couple of days as I was on business in Kiev and Lvov. I am working for the Kandó Kálmán and Ábrahám Ganz's, *Ganz Works* Factory in Budapest on finding and developing new markets for the company in the Eastern parts of Europe. As I am speaking several languages, they have chosen me for that position to promote the electric motor products for the company's export market.'

'This coincidence is amazing, Mr Hacsek.'

'Please, Gabriel, I think I am the eldest so please just call me Zoltán.'

'Very well, thank you Zoltán. You know one of the reasons I am coming to Budapest is to find a supplier of electric motors for a system which is needed to be powered by electronically.'

'You know Zoltán my father is the owner of an engineering company in Munkács and for his next project we would need some power to operate his system.'

'You see Zoltán we thought of the more traditional method of steam power, but we have to move on into the modern world the future is electric.'

'My goodness, Rebekah, you are so knowledgeable of technology.'

'Yes, Zoltán, I have a university diploma from Lvov University and also, I am running the accounts for my father's engineering business.'

'Forgive me, Rebekah. I thought that you must be an actress the way you are dressed.'

Johanna said, 'Yes, I agree with Zoltán you look different I am impressed with your confidence, Rebekah.'

'Thank you, that confidence is coming from my involvement with the Feminist Movement of the Ukrainian Union of Jewish Women. As you know The Union of Jewish women existed in Lvov from 1925 and its aim was 'to guarantee Jewish women a decent quality of life'. One of the founders of this organisation was Professor of Philosophy, Miss Cecylia Klaftenowa.'

Zoltán said, 'I am very impressed Rebekah. I have heard something about it, but I have never met anyone from that organisation. It explains your confidence and your charisma.'

Johanna got excited at the story of the organisation and asked Rebekah, 'Would you mind telling me more about this feminist movement I am very interested to know all about it mainly if there is a branch or an office in Budapest. It seems to me this kind of work gives meaning to our life to help women with their needs.'

'Sure, I would be delighted to do that Johanna.'

'Look, Gabriel, as your father in law is looking for products which would complete his project, I can help you with that. As Kandó Factory have no representatives in Munkács that I could help you set it up and to supply you with the right products you require. On the other hand, at the same time, your Rebekah could discuss the Union of the Jewish Women's Organisation with my wife Johanna. She looks very interested in that organisation.'

'Perhaps we could get together for dinner at our house I live on *Rózsadomb*, *Vérhalom Tér*, which is in the second district of Budapest.'

'Yes, I like the idea Zoltán, it would be great to have that opportunity, but I have a very busy coming week as I have several meetings with the Közoktatásügyi Ministry Officers and with Gróf Pál Teleki Education and Faith Minister.'

'Look Gabriel here is my business card and when you are ready and you have completed your engagements then perhaps, we can arrange the get-together.'

This unexpected meeting with Johanna and Zoltán was an unprecedented piece of luck. I shouldn't say luck as everything is happening with a pre-planned reason beyond our control.

As we did dine together with our newly acquired friends we have been drinking good wine and excellent food, the conversation has flowed, so has the time, as we were just passing the town Hatvan, and we all have to go back to our compartment and get ready for our arrival to Budapest Keleti Main Station.

Our train has arrived precisely at the timetable, and I really didn't feel the weariness of the long journey. Or it is just the first-class travelling in an uxorious coach which gives a much softer and comfortable ride. I don't know but we have enjoyed it.

As the train pulled into the station, it wasn't difficult to find a porter as they were swarming around the first-class coaches. We finally got outside the main building and there a very hot Budapest welcomed us in the mid-afternoon's summer heat.

I hired a taxi, and at the first moment, I have to think of my address. Then to my embarrassment, as I couldn't remember that we are not in Latorca utca. in the Garden City of Munkács, but we are now at home, in Budapest.

'At finally, I said to the taxi driver *Király utca* 31 please.'

The driver set the taximeter, and we have set off to my little apartment in the Jewish quarter, of Budapest.

When we got out of the taxi, I got my key for the house gate to open it I have felt a strange feeling that I am doing these routines as I am home again.

My apartment is on the first floor facing the courtyard where is a couple of leafy trees which gave some refreshing shade from the heat of the sun.

When I opened the door, I went into the apartment first, there was lots of mail which I'd picked up from the entrance floor, and I felt a kind of stale smell in the room as there was nobody to open the windows for months.

'I turned around to Rebekah and said, my darling welcome to a onetime bachelor's apartment I know it isn't a luxurious place, but this will be our home for the next two weeks. It is in the heart of the city we can walk to any theatre, opera house, to *Erzsébet* Park and to the main synagogue as well.'

I picked her up on the balcony into my arms and carried her inside into the apartment as you see it in the movies. She kissed me while she was in my arms, and I said, 'Welcome home, my darling wife.'

Rebekah looked around in the apartment while I have opened the windows to let fresh air into the rooms.

I just looked at her and said, 'I know we have a small kitchen, but we can always go out for a meal a small bathroom, but I have a large lounge and a large bedroom with a large bed.'

Rebekah sat on the bed she said, 'Yes, it is comfortable. She looked at me and asked; Is this, is that famous '*Sárga Pamlag*' (Yellow Canapé)?'

With a kind of embarrassment, I have answered Rebekah, 'Yes, it is.'

'That was at the time when I have never thought of you or even dreamed of your existence my darling Rebeka. But now I've got you and everything is you and yours.'

'We are selling this apartment now with all of its furniture with the exception of my books and my paintings they are coming with us to Munkács.'

'This place is my past, what you don't want to know.'

'But now we have the future together which is only you and I and with all God's blessing will belong to our children too.'

'Yesterday when I have made my vow to you, I have given up and forgotten my past, and it is now our future.'

'So why don't we go down to get some food and drinks before the Sunset at Mr Katz's delicatessen shop that is just down in the next block and get our kalach and the wine for this evening to celebrate our first Shabecz together here in our little apartment in Budapest.'

'Yes, I would like that, Gabriel.'

Before we managed to be gone to the shop my next-door neighbour Évi néni, just knocked on the door and welcomed me back home. I have called Rebekah to the door and introduced her, 'Évi néni this is Rebekah who is my newly wedded wife.'

Well, Évi néni just couldn't believe what she has heard and with great surprise on her face, she asked me, 'So when did you got married, Gabriel? I thought that you will remain a bachelor.'

'It was yesterday, Évi néni.'

'She was embarrassed, and she said I have collected some important letters for you so I just thought that I would give them to you.'

'I thanked her, and I apologised for that we have to get ready for the Shabecz and also, we need to get some food for us.'

She said, 'Yes, of course, Gabriel. I will come and see you after the Shabecz.'

'Have a good Sabbath Évi néni, Sabbath Shalom.'

'Yes, Shalom to you both.'

We have left our luggage in the lounge and went to do some shopping at Mr Katz shop.

Walking downstairs and Rebekah asked me about this elderly woman.

'Yes, she always had a crush on me, but she is fifteen years older than I, so she was my neighbour who has taken all my parcels in or my other important mail from authorities. She always kept her eye on my apartment like a kind of security person. We both laughed at my security comment.'

As we were going through Mr Katz shop door there was a small bell fixed on the door, so the bell rang and gave Mr Katz a warning that someone has entered the shop.

Mr Katz welcomed me back and said, 'Oh, it's good to see you, Gabriel. I have a lot of news that I have to tell you but not just now as the Shabecz will begin very soon.'

I have introduced Rebekah to Mr Katz as she is my wife. I thought he would faint immediately then he recovered himself and shook Rebekah's and my hands and said a 'Mazel tov'.

He said, 'I still can't believe it Gabriel, but Rebekah is a beautiful lady, Mazel tov my boy, well done.'

'I guess you want some food for tonight to celebrate the Shabecz. Just hang on I will get the very best Shabecz meal for you two. I still can't believe Gabriel that you are married now. Well, it is time now.'

'I look forward to serving you, Rebekah, at any time of the day whatever you want I can get hold of for you, my shop will be at your service.'

He quickly moved and came back to us with a big bag full of food and bottles of drinks. 'I have paid for them and left, thank you for these goodies Mr Katz and see you tomorrow at the synagogue. Good Sabbath.'

'Yes, Gabriel and Rebekah, Sabbath Shalom to you too.'

We went back to our apartment with all the food and drinks Mr Katz has packed for us.

Back in the apartment Rebekah has started to get her clothes from the suitcases and looked at my two wardrobes and then looked at me with a smile. 'Why do you have two wardrobes Gabriel when you hardly have any clothes in one of them at all.'

I looked speechless as I have no answer to Rebekah's question and try to make a joke out of the situation, I said, 'Well, I have kept it for your clothing my darling.'

She laughed for a minute then she walked to me and hugged; then she kissed me and said, 'Yes, you were a typical bachelor, my love,' and she carried on with emptying the cases into the wardrobe. When she had finished with the unpacking she went to the bathroom, came back to the kitchen, and prepared for the Sabbath celebration.

I have refreshed myself in the bathroom and joined Rebekah around our dining table.

After Rebekah lit the candles, she waved her hands over the candles, welcoming to the Sabbath. Then she covered her eyes, so as not to see the candles then she recited the blessing:

Barukh ata Adonai Eloheinu, Melekh ha'olam, asher kid'shanu b'mitzvotav v'tzivanu l'hadlik ner shel Sabbath.

She removed her hands from her eyes, and she looked at the candles, completing the mitzvah of lighting the candles.

Then I held the Kiddush cup and thanked The Lord for the wine:

Baruch Ata Adonai Eloheinu Melech Haolam Borei P'Ri Hagafen.

Then I removed the cover from the two challah loaves, lifting them while reciting the blessing:

Barukh ata Adonai Eloheinu melekh ha'olam hamotzi lehem min ha'aretz.

I have ripped the challah into pieces and gave peace to Rebekah then I said, 'My darling, Rebekah, this is our first family meal together as wife and husband now it may begin.'

'Sabbath Shalom, my dear wife Rebekah.'

'Sabbath Shalom, my dear husband Gabriel.'

Chapter 33

In Budapest Synagogue and Ministry

The Sabbath wine did help us to get a goodnight's sleep or may well be because of the long journey we had today. I have left the top window open just to have some fresh air which would help to clear that stale smell from the room. It was a strange feeling to be sleeping in my own bed again.

I woke up before Rebekah did as I looked at her laying in my arm her breathing was balanced for a rhythm. She looked like a little girl who is cuddling up in her fathers' arm.

My Lord she is beautiful, in her sleep she is smiling like a little cherub. I tried not to disturb her when she is must of dreaming of a wonderful dream.

She must have a telepathic feeling as I had a feast on her face, she just opened her eyes and never stopped smiling from her dreams. Then she pulled my head too close to hers until our lips have touched, and we had one of the gentlest kisses we ever had with so much feeling.

She said, 'Let us lay in bed just as we are my angel it is so nice and romantic.'

I agreed as it was so beautifully romantic almost poetic. If I could write a poem, inspired by this moment it would be a masterpiece.

As we were just holding each other's hand, and she was still in my arms. I started to be worried after a few minutes that we could be late for the Sabbath morning service. I wanted her to meet up with Fifi, to look after Rebekah and guide her to the Synagogue balcony while the services were on.

I pecked a kiss on her lips and got up to organise a cup of coffee for both of us. I asked her if she would like to eat something now or she would rather leave it for after the service then we could dine properly in a restaurant somewhere with Miklós and Fifi.

She asked for a cup of coffee for now.

I have suggested to her, 'Just stay in the bed my darling I will serve your coffee in bed.'

'You are really spoiling me, Gabriel. Thank you.'

'Yes, I want to spoil you forever.' I just looked at her as she was lay in bed just a thin nightdress, the curve of her perfect body was like Michael Angelo's painting.

I said, 'My darling you look like Venus who just been posing for Michael Angelo.'

She smiled and said, 'Gabriel, you are always so gentle and you treat me like I am a princess.'

'Yes, Rebekah, you are my princess my goddess and my greatest lover! And all in all, you are my wife!'

'Our love with all God's blessing will live for generations to come. The way we have met in the first place it was not just an ordinary boy meets girl.'

'I believe in this Gabriel our meeting was arranged by the Lord Himself through his angels.'

'I know my darling I do believe in that too, our life has been arranged even before we were born. We were meant for each other. He is a good God, He wants to give the absolute best to His children, do not forget that He has created us in the first place.'

'But please my darling Rebekah we can continue this conversation later as we have to be on time for the service. I know it is just a short walk to the Synagogue, but I still like to be there on time.'

We have got ready very quickly (I guess the cups of coffee helped us) to walk to the Synagogue on *Dohány utca*. Just as we are walking in the gentle Summer breeze, which is coming from the River Danube, and also the street has been cooled down overnight with a watering lorry.

Suddenly Rebekah asked me, 'Gabriel, you have left all your paperwork and reports behind in the apartment.'

'My darling, this day is not for business this is the day for your introduction to the Budapest elite the leaders of OMZSA and some other important people and my friends from the art world.'

'I will be having a meeting with Chief Rabbi Immánuel Lőw tomorrow Sunday morning.'

'My meeting is at the Ministerium is on Tuesday, 19 July.'

Rebekah said, 'How tall these buildings are, they are much higher stories than anywhere else I have ever been.'

As we were walking on *Károly Körút*, approaching the synagogue the main building has suddenly emerged and Rebekah stopped from the sheer size and of the magnificent architectural style.

She asked me, 'Is this is the Great Synagogue of Budapest?'

'Yes, my love, it is. It is magnificent, isn't it?'

'Yes, it is Gabriel, just like in the photo I have seen before we left Munkács.'

By the time we have got to the main entrance, some familiar faces were already gathering and greeting each other.

Some of them stopped their conversations as we were getting nearer to them and followed us with their glanced attention. Luckily, I spotted Miklós and Fifi among the people at the main entrance of the Synagogue. Miklós came forward to greet us and asked, 'Gabriel, who is this beautiful pearl on your arm?'

'Miklós, I would like to introduce you to my wife Rebekah.'

Miklós was absolutely speechless which is unusual with Miklós. By that time Fanni has joined us too. I turned to Rebekah and said, 'Darling, I would like to introduce you to my friends; Miklós Radnóti and his wife Fanni.'

'Miklós with amazement in his voice has repeated my word; darling? Your wife? Since when?'

'Since the past two days ago on the 14th Miklós.'

'Fifi broke the silence first, and she congratulated us then she hugged Rebekah and said Mazel tov.'

Miklós shook my hand and said, 'Well, another one who gave up the bachelor's life.'

'Well, Mazel tov to you my friend. She is beautiful like a movie goddess. Miklós kissed Rebekah's hand, and he just held onto Rebeka's hand and looked into her eyes and said, how could I have missed this goddess, Gabriel.'

'She is from Munkács, Miklós.'

'As strange as it is, I feel some familiar resemblance in her presence.'

But, in the meantime, other friends have joined us as they overheard the news and offered their congratulations on our wedding.

'Fanni gave me a kiss on my cheek and said, I am incredibly pleased for you Gabriel, yes, she is truly a lovely lady, I like her you have well-chosen.'

'Thank you, Fifi, yes, she is lovely, and I am an incredibly lucky fellow with her. Would you please look after her during this morning service then we will get together after the Sabbath Service?'

'No problem, Gabriel, it is my pleasure. Fifi asked Rebekah, come on let us leave these fellas alone I will take you up to the balcony where I am going to introduce you to some other girlfriends of ours.'

Miklós just could not get over the fact that finally, I have decided to get married.

'Never mind, Miklós, I believe this was the right time for me, and I have the perfect girl for it I just could not miss this opportunity. I am well pleased with my decision.'

We both went into the hall and sat together like we always did in the past.

At the end of the Sabbath Service Chief Rabbi Immánuel Lőw spotted me as we were walking out of the hall.

'He called me over and said Mazel tov Gabriel, I am incredibly pleased for you It is good to see you again. I would like you to come and see me discuss the situation at *Kárpátalja* (Transcarpathia) please bring your wife as well I would like to meet her too.'

'Rabbi Lőw would tomorrow morning at 10 a.m. be convenient for you, and I will bring all my reports, and I will update you with my findings.'

'That will be perfect Gabriel, so10 in the morning. Sabbath Shalom.'

'Sabbath Shalom Chief Rabbi Lőw.'

By the time I got free from talking to Rabbi Lőw, I noticed that Rebekah was in a ring of people around her some members of the Synagogue. I just stood there and waited for her I did not want to interrupt her moment of 'fame'. When she realised that I was standing in front of the gate she excused herself, and she said to the newly found friends, 'Forgive me but my husband is waiting for me.' I think my chest has grown to double its size. A lot of admiring comments she received as she was walking to join me.

Then Miklós and Fifi joined us, and we try to decide where we should go to have our dinner.

I turned to Miklós for a suggestion as I have not been home since April. Miklós suggested, 'How about the Pilvax or 100 Éves Restaurant?'

Pilvax is nearer to the Synagogue on Pilvax köz but then again the food is better at the 100 éves Restaurant.

'Then Fifi suggested we can walk up on Váci utca to the Café Gerbeaud that is my favourite place she was telling, Rebekah.'

'Yes, I would like that Fifi.'

Miklós said, 'All right, so have we decided?'

He said, 'Let us go to the *100 Éves Étterem* on *Piarista utca.*'

Rebekah and Fifi arm in arm walked in front of us and chatted away we could hear some girly giggles. Miklós, and I walked behind them. 'I asked Miklós if there would be room at the restaurant for us as it is Saturday?'

'No problem Gabriel I know the headwaiter.'

The temperature started to get warm at midday, and I thought it would be better if we could have a table inside in the cool restaurant.

It is just a short walk from the Synagogue to the restaurant walking down on Kossuth Lajos utca towards the Elizabeth Bridge.

When we got to the Ferenciek tér (Square) on the corner of the Parisian Yard building Rebekah has stopped as she spotted the emerging view of the beauty of the bridge.

She asked, 'What is that Fifi?'

'That is the Elisabeth Bridge Rebekah'.

Rebekah was mesmerised by the view of the bridge. 'What beautiful scenery! I still cannot believe that I am walking in this romantic city of Budapest with my husband and with these wonderful friends I have just met this morning. I hope I will not be waking up and realise that this is just a dream.'

We walked all the way to the corner of Kossuth Lajos utca and Váci utca just to let Rebekah enjoy longer the scenery of the bridge and the statue of St Gellért at the other end of the bridge.

Miklós jokingly said, 'Well, Rebekah, you must have been an exceptionally good girl in your previous life to receive all of this beauty in life.'

We all smiled, and I said, 'Let us have something to eat as my stomach is telling me it is time for a *Székely káposzta* and a cold *Dreher sör* (beer).'

Miklós agreed with me, 'Yes, let us get into the restaurant I feel thirsty too.'

As we got into the restaurant, we noted that it was already terribly busy as it is Saturday and lunchtime. Miklós spotted Pista the headwaiter from the door and got his attention the head waiter winked at him. Miklós showed four of his fingers to Pista to let him know we need a table for four of us then Pista waved towards us saying, 'Good to see you Mr Radnóti your table is ready for you.'

As we finally sat down, Pista the waiter with an apron wrapped around his waist rushed to us and took our orders for drinks. Miklós and I have ordered a pint of Dreher beer and Fifi suggested to Rebekah to try a glass of *Unikum* for the start and a couple of glasses of *Fröccs.* (wine and soda).

Rebekah and Fifi ordered the *Schnitzel* with *kovászos uborkával* (gherkins) I ordered a *Székely káposzta* with fresh bread and Miklós ordered a *Babgulyás* (Cholet with weal).

While we were waiting for the meal Miklós asked both of us about how we met up and why such a speedy wedding. 'I remember Gabriel you only left in April so tell me how and why this marriage was so important to you two.'

'Well, you see, Miklós, when I have met Rebekah, I felt I love this girl, and I just cannot let anybody take her away from me. The only way I can secure her is if I marry her.'

Miklós was a bit confused.

Rebekah understood my sense of joke, and she said, 'You see Miklós I have seen this fella in Lvov, and I had fallen in love with him, and I didn't want anybody to take him away from me, so I have married him.'

Fifi understood the joke from us and turned to Miklós and said, 'My darling husband these two are in love. Can't you see? I guess they have fallen in love at the first sight just like you and me back in 1935.'

Miklós in his embarrassment just ordered another round of drinks and asked me, 'How long are you two are going to stay in Budapest?'

'Only for two weeks Miklós.'

'That is great I have an evening with me I will be reading my poems and having some actor friends who will help me to make this event successful this event is called: An Evening with Miklós Radnóti at the Ódry Theatre, next Thursday evening at six.'

'Oh, that is great, Gabriel. I would like to be there.'

'You see, Gabriel, I have convinced your wife already.'

'You have convinced me as well, Miklós. You know I like your thoughts in poems and rhymes. We have been friends for a long time, and we always supported each other's work.'

'Great, then we will end up in our usual place at New York Kávéház after the evening.'

Rebekah looked at me with her big eyes, and she repeated with a question mark, 'Is this is the famous artist's coffeehouse?'

'We all said yes.'

Fifi asked Rebekah, 'Have you never been there before?'

Rebekah said, 'Fifi, I have never ever been in Budapest never mind of the New York Kávéház.'

'I cannot wait to be there.'

Our dinner was a real success it was a good choice to have our dinner there. The food was good and plentiful. At least we can work it off on the way of Váci utca to the Gerbeaud. We kept stopping in front of dress shops as the two girls were discussing the latest Parisian fashions in the shop windows.

Rebekah asked Fifi if she could help her to locate a wedding dress for her.

Miklós said, 'I thought you two are married?'

'Yes, Miklós, we are, but our marriage was at the Munkács Registrar was not in the Chuppah at the synagogue.'

'Oh, I see so you have an explanation to Rabbi Lőw tomorrow.'

'Yes, Miklós, I do. But I have a good reason for that which I am not going to tell you now.'

Finally, we got to the Gerbeaud and found a table at the front under the large Platánfa (Platán tree).

Rebekah said, 'Everything is so pretty and elegant here. The people are well dressed and polite. Look somebody is waving to us.'

Miklós turned to the direction where Rebekah pointed and waved back and said, 'Oh, he is just an artist friend of ours.'

We finally managed to get an order I had an *Eszterházy Szelet* (slice) and Rebekah and Fifi have settled with a *Zserbo* and four coffee with soda water. We must have spent a couple of hours at the Gerbeaud when Miklós said, 'I am so sorry, but we have to go as we are running late for visiting Fifi's parents this afternoon.'

They said goodbye to us and said, 'I look forward to seeing you at the Odry Theatre on Thursday.'

'Yes, Miklós, we will be there at six, look forward to it.'

When they left, Rebekah and I have walk down to the river Danube promenade just passing the Vigadó Theatre building and there we were on the promenade. I thought Rebekah had fainted as she caught the sight on the hilltop of the King's Palace which is on the opposite side of the river Danube.

She said, 'Gabriel do you have any more beautiful scenery for me in one day? It looks so big and magnificent I have to buy some postcards to send to my friends in Munkács and Lvov.'

'I am truly walking on cloud nine. My Lord, I feel that I am in heaven.'

'Yes, my darling, and all this that I am giving up for you and for our future in Munkács.'

Rebekah has tightened her grip with her arm on me and looked into my eyes and asked the question, 'And am I worth it, Gabriel?'

'Yes, my love I would give up everything and would follow you to the end of the world for your love.'

Walking back home through the Elisabeth Park to my Király utca apartment and feeling a kind of tiredness in our body. May be due to the heat of the day and of the excitement of the day with Fifi and Miklós.

On our way home I remembered that I have not ordered any ice for my refrigerator box, it is useless to keep cold drinks in there if is not filled with ice. So we called into Mr Katz shop again and got some fresh bread, paprika and Pick salami, and a bottle of Hungarian Brut Champagne to celebrate our first full day with friends in Budapest.

As we walked through the apartment door Rebekah jumped into my neck and kissed me.

I said, 'Please let me put these foods into the cupboard.'

'I have opened the bottle of champagne poured it into two glasses and said. My dearest wife we are at home now, and we do not have to worry about anything or anybody. We are legally married and what we are doing now is perfectly normal for any married couples' life. I have drawn the curtains and as I have just turned around Rebekah was halfway off stripping off her clothes in the middle of our bedroom.'

She asked me, 'Please peel me off like a banana.'

I have finished my drink put my glass on the table and walked to her in the shaded room. Her body was shaking again from the excitement. When we were both naked I have picked her up in my arms and walked to the 'Sárga pamlag', Gently placed her on the bed then I have stroked her body with my fingers from her toe to her head and back. Then we made love again and again as we have never done it before.

It was pure emotion on the loose and the pleasure was immense.

We were exhausted by the night and the only thing has left behind is to fall asleep in each other's arms till the morning.

Chapter 34

Meeting with Chief Rabbi Lőw and Budapest Sightseeing

After a most memorable night, Rebekah and I have enjoyed still laying in each other's arms just before seven in the morning we both are woken by the heavenly choir of the songbirds which are nesting resident in those two large trees in the middle of our apartment block courtyard.

I have pulled her body closer to mine until our lips have touched, and we kissed just to seal the end of the most pleasurable night we had and welcomed the secretive new day's continuity of our love.

I whispered in Rebekah's ear, 'You just stay in bed, and I will bring your cup of coffee to you in bed.'

She stretched herself and started to sing a lullaby just like a happy and satisfied little girl.

My Lord, she looks absolutely beautiful, like a Madonna, and she is laying in my bed.

Bringing her cup of coffee to the bedroom, and I noted Rebekah hugging the pillow with such affection as she would hug me. As she noted that I was bringing her coffee she has sat up and leaned back at the head of the bed. She pulled the duvet covered herself then I have given her the drink.

I have sat on the opposite end of the bed, and we must have looked comical having a chat about her yesterday's experience with Fifi, Miklós and with other people at the synagogue.

'You know Gabriel as I have been growing up in a small town in the region far end of the country and do not have the benefit to be able to travel it is hard to imagine a big wide world is existing out there.'

'We are both extremely fortunate people that we have the opportunity to travel and see how beautiful some other parts of the world, not just the one where you live.'

'I guess we are truly fortunate Rebekah, but this is our nature we Jewish people are always on the move travelling all the time. Just look at Moses he was galivanting in the wilderness for forty years.'

We both laughed at my comment.

She turned into a much more serious look and said, 'Gabriel, I do not know what I would do without you. It is so peaceful, and I feel so much fun and security with you. I will always love you even from beyond the grave. I am thanking the Lord for every minute I am able to spend with you.'

'I know, my darling Rebekah, and I feel the same affectionate way about you. You are the love of my life! I had to search for this pearl everywhere, but it has been worth it. Like my friend Miklós portrayed you.'

'Yes, he is right you are a beautiful pearl Rebekah, and you are adorning my crown! My pride and joy. You know it is so strange that here we are in this apartment as wife and husband.'

'For years, I have resigned to becoming a bachelor as I have done all my cooking, washing ironing cleaning for myself. Now here we are you and me as a married couple, and I still feel that I still have to do everything now for both of us. I have suddenly realised that you are home with me here in this little apartment comparing with yours in Munkács, and I feel a tremendous responsibility towards you.'

'I know Gabriel as I feel this care and protection coming from you. This is the reason I am feeling so relaxed and feeling that you are spoiling me.'

'I am not spoiling you. Yes, you are right I am spoiling you but on top of it, I just feel a kind of responsibility towards you. Here you are with me in a strange country, and even the architecture is completely overwhelming you compared with the places you have been before.'

'I just want to let you know that here in this big city you are under my wing as I am your Angel Gabriel. 'God is my strength'.'

'Gabriel's energies can help us overcome the fear of procrastination and may enhance our dreams and further aspirations!'

'Gabriel, this is so beautiful what you just have told me, yes, I am your ever-loving wife Rebekah.'

'I feel safe under your wing, may the Lord God keep me there forever. I just love you, my angel.'

'Now my darling wife we have to get ready as Chief Rabbi Immanuel Lőw is expecting us at 10:00.'

This morning we were walking on the same road again to the Great Synagogue with a different person. I felt she was so relaxed as if she were walking on air on my arm. But today it was I who was a little bit nervous to do my report by word and present it to the committee in a written report.

But today we entered the synagogue on the *Wesselényi utca* side entrance.

I have arrived promptly at 10:00 am, and to my surprise, I have not seen Rabbi Simon Hevesi. (Later on, I have learned that he is away lecturing.) Rebekah has been entertained by the Chief Rabbi's secretary in her office.

Chief Rabbi Immánuel Lőw started the meeting with an introduction to some of the members of OZSMA and officials of the Jewish Community. Also, he told to the officials that they have sent me on this mission, and it looks like we have lost him from Budapest to Munkács where he has found a very attractive Jewish lady and now, they are married.

I have received some positive and encouraging good wishes and Mazel tov's from the members of the committee present.

Before I started my presentation to the members of the committee, 'I thanked Chief Rabbi Immánuel Lőw for the introduction and the support I have received through him right from my arrival to Munkács, from Dr Sándor Fried. Or I should name him by his new correct title as Deputy Mayor of Munkács Dr Sándor Fried. He asked me to express his kind regards to you all.'

'I was also expressing the good wishes of: Chief Rabbi of Munkács Rebbe, Rabbi Baruch Yehoshua Yerachmiel Rabinowicz and also of Chief Rabbi of Ungvár, Rabbi Yosef Elimelech Kahana.'

'May I present the confidential letters they addressed it to you Chief Rabbi Lőw, so here they are.'

The meeting went on for over two hours where much good news has been acknowledged by the committee present from my report over the changes which have been positively accepted by local authorities in the region and the way it has progressed through Transcarpathia.

I have expressed that the communities in the major cities are genuinely concerned about the news of the Jewish law which has been passed by the Hungarian Parliament.

At the end of the meeting, I have explained that I am going to settle in Munkács. I have purchased a property already, and I have been offered a position at the Munkács Town Council to be the director of art and entertainment. As the changes in Transcarpathia are coming into practice Dr Sándor Fried offered this position to me through my connections and experience in the entertainment business that I would be the best person to control this department. I could invite some famous Jewish Hungarian entertainers not just to Munkács but to the region as well as these artists would promote Hungarian Culture in the Hungarian language to the public. I would expect we could be in a much more favourable position with the Foreign Ministry.

There were some very encouraging and positive comments from the members of the committee present over on my new position in Munkács. Hopefully, officials in the Foreign Ministry and the Cultural Ministry will see the constructive development I could influence on the public opinions through art and musical culture.

'Mr Swartz recommended that they should get in touch with their contacts at the relevant Ministries and encourage my proposal as I am in that position to deliver and promote their agendas.'

At the end of the meeting, Mr Mayor called me over and asked me, 'Is it true that I am selling my apartment at the Király utca?'

'If I do, he can help me to sell it within a couple of weeks. I heard that you just have bought this new house in Munkács, and I know you could do with some financial help.'

'Yes, Mr Mayor, that is true it would help me tremendously as I have to pay all the contractors, and I have borrowed the money for the house from my father in law.'

'Look I am a member of OZSMA, and we have friends at many places I have heard your good works for OZSMA in Munkács so do not worry we will be behind you. And thank you to reaching out to the younger generations and bringing them into our work. We like and support people with visions and you have that quality Gabriel you are an asset for us.

Dr Sándor will take care of your financial situation. I will take care of your apartment sale and will transfer the money to your account at Móric Ulmann Kereskedelmi Bank, in Munkács.'

'Thank you very much, Mr Mayor. You really are coming to my aid when I need it the most.'

In the end, Chief Rabbi Lőw asked me and Rebekah to join him in his office.

We both joined Chief Rabbi Lőw in his office as he requested. I have to say that I had a kind of bad feeling about our marriage in Munkács. He may disapprove of our actions of marrying at a municipal authority level. But I was not rushing to conclusions I will wait for him to let us know the reason for this private meeting with him.

'Look, Gabriel, I was not 100% sure about your choice to send you on this mission. But all the feedback I have received from all of our friends and associates from Karpatalja I have to admit I was wrong for my concern for your appointment. You have represented us and our agendas in such a professional way that we are immensely proud of you for your professionalism and as a diplomat you have proven you were the right choice for this important mission.'

'Thank you, Gabriel, for all what you have done for us in Transcarpathia.'

'Who are you going to see at the Ministerium on Tuesday?'

'It is Grof Teleki Pál Magyarország Vallás és Közoktatásügyi Minister. Just be careful with him Gabriel he is not a Jewish friendly man. He was the one who proposed the *Jewish Law: 'the companion and host on Strengthening the Balance of Life'*.'

'Thank you for your valuable advice, Chief Rabbi Immánuel Lőw. In this case, I will need a special blessing for this meeting.'

'Yes, I will remember to pray for you on Tuesday.'

'But now let us talk about your marriage arrangements with Rebekah.'

'I can see you have chosen well for an attractive and supportive new wife from our family. But wasn't this authority wedding a little bit rushed?'

I have explained the whole reason for our 'rushed' marriage and of the reason for that action we have chosen.

'Look now, it makes sense, and I can understand as you have explained to me so well. I will ask some of the officials at the home office to issue a Hungarian Nationality for Rebekah and then you will be able to acquire a Hungarian Passport under her new married name. I trust you have brought the official marriage certificate.'

'Yes, I have all the documents here with me Rabbi Lőw would you like to see them?'

'No, thank you, Gabriel. I trust you. You are an honourable man.'

'I cannot see that you have done anything wrong, or which would against the Chumash, Law of Moses with regards to your marriage vows.'

'Now please come to me and stand in front of me both of you I want to bless your marriage of **Sheva Brachot**.'

We both felt as if we have been lifted out of our physical body while he has his hand on top of our heads. Rebekah has been in tears of joy or was it the powerful words of Chief Rabbi Immánuel Lőw.

'I know it was the Spirit of our Lord God which has touched us.'

We can say that our marriage has already been blessed by the Chief Rabbi Immanuel Lőw.

There was no Chuppah above us, but I have felt that the Rabbi's hand was the Chuppah above our heads.

'Thank you, Gabriel, for all that you have done for us in Transcarpathia.'

'Now my boy go in peace on your business and come and see me sometime before you are going to have a meeting with the ministers.'

It was well into midday when we left Chief Rabbi Lőw's office, and I suggested to Rebekah to have some sandwiches on our way home then we can refresh ourselves and put on fresh clothes.

Rebekah was still wiping her tears after the Sheva Brachot. She said, 'I just cannot understand what is happening with me. I did not expect a blessing for our marriage and particularly from the Chief Rabbi of Budapest. Well, if I tell that we had a **Sheva Brachot** from Rabbi Lőw to my friends in Munkács.'

'I asked Rebekah to keep this story to ourselves as the Rabbi has conducted a blessing on us with an unofficial ceremony. We could tell our family or to our close friends, but I do not want to gossip before 11 September. I hope you understand what I am saying. I do not want to upset Rabbi Baruch with this news of our blessing by Chief Rabbi Immánuel Lőw.'

'Yes, I understand it, Gabriel. I will wait after our 11 September ceremony.'

'Now, Rebekah, I will take you up to Castle Hill which is the historically the Old Buda Vár (Castle).'

'But please my darling come in comfortable shoes as we are going to walk a lot this afternoon.'

Leaving our apartment on Király utca behind us and heading towards the Széchényi Chain Bridge at Count István Széchényi Square. Rebekah almost shouted in her excitement which overwhelmed her on the scenery in front of us, 'Look, Gabriel, what a beautiful view of the whole scenery of the Chain Bridge, the King's Castle on the left of the bridge and the Fisherman's Bastion and the tower of the Mátyás Templom (Mathias Church) to the right what a spectacular scenery.'

As we were walking through the bridge Rebekah kept looking over the railings of the river as it flows, and she said this is much wider than I thought of. As we were getting to the Adam Clark Square roundabout Rebekah asked, 'What is that thing next to the tunnel entrance climbing up the hill?'

'Oh, that is the Funicular'.

'Are we going to ride on that Funicular?'

'Yes, my love of course we will. Unless you want to walk all the way to the top of the hill.'

'That is fantastic, Gabriel. What an experience. I hope there will be some postcards available on the top of the hill.'

'I have to buy as many as we can as I have forgotten to bring my camera with me because of the chaotic last two days before our departure from Munkács.'

'Do not worry, darling. There will be another day when we will come up here.'

'I have seen a camera shop on Király utca next to the *Rothouser Testvérek* (Brothers) shop just on the way to the synagogue.'

'You know Gabriel I feel as if we are on our honeymoon.'

'Yes, my darling you are right, I suppose we are on our honeymoon, and with a bit of business as well.'

So we just enjoyed the view of Pest which was laid before us.

Rebekah said, 'I have to say I have not been in any other capital, only I have seen them by photos or on film footage, but I have to say Budapest is one of the most beautiful and romantic cities in the world.'

The cool breeze has just blown up from the River Danube to the top of the hill, and it was refreshing us from the summer heat. 'What spectacular scenery Gabriel I just can't believe that I am seeing this.'

We walked all the way towards the Szent Háromság Tér (Holy Trinity Square) where the Mathias Church stands its tower was visible since we have stepped on the bridge.

One of the most beautiful buildings in Budapest the Mátyás Templom appeared with its tall tower.

'This is St Stephen's statue. He was the first Hungarian King who has established the Hungarian Kingdom. He was the Grand Prince of the Magyars. He has established the Hungarian Statehood in AD 1000. And turned the

Magyars to Christian faith from a nomadic tribal nation, and he accepted the Holy Crown from the Catholic Pope Sylvester II. King Stephen's statue has been erected on the Fisherman's Bastion'.

'And now my darling wife, Rebekah I am leading you to the most feminine architectural building you have ever seen, and this is the famous Fisherman's Bastion'.

'Yes, it is magnificent. Gabriel, it is just breathtakingly beautiful. How much elegance and fragility in the stone carvings?'

We walked up on the sparkling white stone bastion wall and again the view was just truly breathtakingly magnificent. From the top wall, we have the view of the Hungarian Parliament building which has been modelled on the British House of the Parliament.

'I can tell that, Gabriel. You have learned your history well.'

'I always favoured my history lessons as it is an important subject which shows that the world history keeps repeating itself, and we should learn from the mistakes, and we have to see these historical facts.'

'I feel I am tired out from all of these amazing historical buildings. I feel I am walking back in time with you. Just wait till we get into this very old restaurant, it is just a short walk down on Országház utca that was the first Jewish Quoter in Budapest.'

As we walked on the cobblestoned street to the restaurant which looks like an old house from the outside but going into the restaurant was a different picture. Rebekah just could not stop absorbing all the artefacts and old pictures on the inside of the restaurant's wall. The waiter walked us downstairs into the cellar and offered any table we would like to sit at.

It was nice and cool and refreshing from the summer afternoon heat.

Rebekah was excited with everything that she has seen in such a short time on the Hill of Buda, as we have spent most of our morning at the Great Synagogue with Chief Rabbi Low.

It is so good to have a sit down now, I was getting very tired with all the walking we have done today. And mostly walking on these cobblestoned streets it is tiring you out.

'Do not worry my darling we will have a taxi back home after our supper.'

After a nice meal we had, we were ready to get back home.

Before we went up to our apartment, I have to go into Mr Katz shop to buy a new bottle of chilled Hungarian Champagne.

Walking up the stairs was much slower than our previous night. We were both tired out with the sightseeing of old Buda Hill.

Rebekah said, 'If you do not mind my darling angel, I will fall asleep due to all of this physical exercise we had today. I think this champagne is helping me to drift away in your arms.'

'Yes, darling, sleep well; goodnight, my Rebekah.'

'Goodnight, my darling angel. See you in the morning.'

'I have kissed her on her forehead, but she was asleep already.'

The walking has tired me out as well, so I have just followed my wife just asleep too.

Chapter 35

Relaxing and Sightseeing in Budapest

After yesterday's very tiering program we just had the luxury of staying in bed till ten in the morning.

Rebekah was naughty again (but I have enjoyed it too). This slight delay made our departure of another day of sightseeing.

While I was waiting for Rebekah, to get ready I have searched my drawers for a camera. I knew that I had bought one some time ago, but I have never used it. Finally, I have found it, but I still needed a film for the machine. That is no problem there is a lot of shops on Király utca where I can buy a couple of 36 shots films.

'Rebekah darling, would you please wear a flat-heeled shoe, as we are going to walk a lot in the Városliget today.'

As we walked out from our apartment block onto Kiraly street, which was already busy with deliveries to shops, by the '*kofák*' (woman market trader) bringing their fresh eggs, vegetables, cheese, and milk products etc to shop owners.

'I have never seen this road so busy Gabriel, all those shops and people everywhere.'

'Yes, it is Rebekah, as it is Monday now not just the Jewish, but the Hungarians are out shopping or selling their products.'

We walked down to the undergrad station of the Opera House stop and were heading to the Városliget.

I said, 'We will be there very quickly darling it is only five stops to Hősök tere (Heroes Square) from here.'

'I cannot wait to see that big park Gabriel I only have seen the square in magazines.'

'Yes, it is very impressive my love it is a very large park and there is the Hungarian National Zoo, the Fairground, and the Budapest Circus and two museums.'

The train has arrived very quickly and Rebekah was very impressed with its impressive Art Deco-styled tiled stations all the way to Heroes Square. As we were walking out upstairs from the station Rebekah has to hold down her full summer skirt as the draft lifted it up for a second. She has turned around if anybody has seen her legs in this incident.

'Then she turned to me and told me off not giving her a warning about the possibility that this accident would occur in this situation. She was quite relaxed as I have explained to her that I was walking behind her, and I have covered the view of her legs from others.'

As we got out from the station, the pure brightness of these white stone monuments was just amplified by the sheer size of it. She just had to stop absorbing the scenery of this gigantic open space. Two neoclassical design buildings were inspired by the Greek Temples. The classical front with massive Corinthian columns and sculpted tympanum forms a nice complement to the Palace of Art – from the same architects – at the opposite side of the square flanked by the Museum of Fine Arts and right opposite is The Műcsarnok which is an exhibition hall, mainly used to host temporary exhibitions.

Rebekah held onto my hand so strongly like a little child who is getting frightened in the huge open space.

She put her head on my shoulder and sighed, 'Gabriel you are so good to me, this is just so romantic, and at the same time, it is monumental scenery.'

Hand in hand we walked to see the statues of all the kings of Hungary starting with Saint Stephen then we walked to the centre of the square where all the Seven chieftains of the Magyars are with the Chief Chieftain Árpád in front.

'And who is on the top of the column surrounded by these Chieftains?'

'Oh, that statue is 'I am' Rebekah.'

'Sorry? So who is it?'

'My apologies darling, it was just a joke. It is Angel Gabriel!'

'Directly behind the cenotaph is the column topped by a statue of the archangel, Gabriel. In his right hand, the angel holds the Holy Crown of St. Stephen (István), the first king of Hungary. In his left hand, the angel holds a two barred apostolic cross, a symbol awarded to St. Stephen by the Pope in recognition of his efforts to convert Hungary to Christianity. In Hungarian, it is referred to as the double-cross or the apostolic double-cross.'

'Allegedly, some historian tells us that the tribe of Abram, when he left the land of Shinar (Mesopotamia), at the same time when the sons of King Nimrud; Hunor and Magor were leaving the land of Shinar, too according to the Book of Genesis and Books of Chronicles; 'the son of Cush, the grandson of Ham and great-grandson of Noah. So the Magor's believe that the Magyar's are one of the lost relatives of the Jews.'

'Oh, I see why the name of Gabriel is so important to the Magyar. But I know why is my Angel Gabriel is so important to me. Because he is my husband, and I love him!'

'Thank you for this comparison, my darling Rebekah.'

'Yes, I am your messenger and my message to you is that I love you with all of my heart!'

'Yes, my love, and I bring the message to you of joy and the most important message that: 'Gabriel is madly in love with Rebekah'.'

I noticed that Rebekah's eyes are wet again.

'I am so sorry, Rebekah. I did not mean to make you cry. So let us move on there are so many more beautiful things to see.'

Rebekah replied, 'it is the tears of joy my angel. It is. Yes, let us move on.'

Rebekah held my hand as we walked towards the Budapest Zoo building. 'As we walked in front of this building on our left Rebekah asked, what is this impressive building, Gabriel?'

'This place is the world-famous iconic Gundel Restaurant since 1894.'

'Before we go back to Munkács I promise you that I will bring you here for an evening meal.'

As we got to the entrance, I thought that it would be better to book a table for next Sunday, 24 July. As we walked into the restaurant, I have recognised Morris Hofmann from the synagogue who kept his efficiency and called me sir. 'I have called him '*Főpincér Úr*' (Headwaiter) I would like to book a table for two for Sunday the 24th.'

Morris replied in his official manner, 'Yes, sir. I have booked you in for seven in the evening.'

He gave me a wink and said I will get you the best table, Gabriel. Morris kissed Rebekah's hand and said, 'I look forward to welcoming you into our establishment.'

It was impressive Morris's improvisation in front of Rebekah and in front of his staff.

Then we walked past the entrance to the Zoo, and have something to eat at the restaurant as we were hungry enough to stop and have some food and some refreshment in the mid-July heat.

The next major building was the Main Budapest Circus. I suggested to Rebekah that we should get a ticket for the mid-afternoon Circus performance.

'You know my darling when I was a young boy, I used to love to go to travelling circuses. I think that experience which has stayed with me, and I now follow my instinct of experience to measure what would entertain people.'

'It is so strange, Gabriel. I had the same experience with travelling circuses. I always thought that I will run off with them, and I will dance on the ropes in a very pretty and colourful dress. But it has never happened to thank the Lord for stopping me from ever considering doing that. Otherwise, I would have never met you in my destiny.'

'Yes, my darling. You have captivated my attention from the moment I have seen you the first time at Lvov University.'

'You have a charismatic attitude like the so-called movie stars have. It is called Charisma!'

As you noticed wherever you go people are following you with their attention It is a gift my darling.

We both stopped at the Grand Circus entrance and reading through the program we noticed that there was a 2 o'clock matinee.

'I looked at Rebekah and with a smile she said, yes please I would like to see the matinee performance.'

As soon as we sat in the middle row of the auditorium the performance started. The circus auditorium was almost full of adults and screaming children.

We were like two adult children getting more excited from the atmosphere as the entertainers were all marching into the ring.

'You know Gabriel this moment I feel that I am a child again, it brings back to me all those memorable times. Holding papa's hand when the trapeze artists did, their acts. And when the tigers roared, that was very frightening. But I always loved the clowns.'

'I like the clown too. You know they are not just funny, but they are incredibly talented musicians as well. When they are not performing in the ring, they are sitting in with the musicians playing for the other artist acts in the ring.

Everybody is multi-talented artists. This is the love of their life to entertain people and make them feel happy just making them to forget they problems.'

'I remember Papa, and I used to feed the animals in the intervals. You see we never had a zoo in Munkács, the circus gave us a chance to see live wild animals closely.'

After the end of the circus experience, we ended up with a large ice cream, and still talking about the various acts performances we had seen in the circus. We walked past the Széchenyi Medicinal Baths and Swimming Pool and headed to the lake to see people rowing along with their little pleasure boats. The lake was full of wildlife swans, ducks, and some gulls. On the grassy bank of the lake people were having a picnic in the heat of the day.

While I was taking some photos of Rebekah a nice couple offered to take a photo of me together with Rebekah, then the man asked me if I would take a photo of them too.

Everything was so peaceful and relaxed people were genuinely nice to each other truly it was a good choice to come to the Városliget today.

When we got to the castle which is the replica of the original castle in Transylvania.

It was built in 1896 as part of the Millennial Exhibition which celebrated the 1,000 years of Hungary since the Hungarian Conquest of the Carpathian Basin in 895.

Rebekah said, 'What a magnificent and yet so scary a Gothic building.'

'Yes, darling, that was a scary time too, when the nations of the regions of Europe, were at war with each other all the time. So many killing in the name of God's and for what?'

'Please, Gabriel, I do not want any photos here in this 'spooky' place.'

'That is all right Rebekah than let us make our way back home to get changed before we go out for our supper. What kind of food would you like to eat tonight my darling, is it kosher or non-kosher or a Hungarian one?'

'I do not want to have kosher food tonight. Where are you taking me for a dinner?'

'It is a secret my darling wife.'

We were walking back to the underground station in front of the square at the end of Andrássy Street, as we were just passing the Műcsarnok, and Rebekah visibly looked tired.

We should be home very soon darling, 'I am so sorry that I have made you walk so much.'

'But please remember this time to hold on to your skirt when we walk down to the underground station. You do not want the same experience again.'

'Thank you to remind me Gabriel I have forgotten that already.'

When we got down to the station a nice cool drift of air was blowing on us by the arrival of the train.

'Oh, I like this, Gabriel. She was still holding her skirt down stopping the same experience to happen with her skirt again.'

We have arrived back to the Opera House stop again, and it was only some five minutes' walk back to our apartment.

I have called into Mr Katz shop for another bottle of Hungarian Champagne and a freshly baked Fonott *Kalács* (Kalach).

Mr Katz asked me, 'Is its true Gabriel that you are moving to Munkács? Are you selling your apartment?'

'Yes, Mr Katz I am moving, going to live in Munkács.'

'A friend of mine, David Krenczberger, would like to have a look at your apartment. Would you let him come and see it?'

'Yes, Mr Katz, but when? I am going to be busy tomorrow all day. Would it be all right with your friend to come and see me on Wednesday? Just to let you know that I have put it into the estate agent's hands already.'

'I will ask him, as he is a *Rőfös* (textile seller) he has a haberdashery shop just in the next block.'

'Well, in that case, he could come and have a view it this afternoon before seven as Rebekah and I are going out to have our supper.'

'I tell you what Gabriel I am going to see him now, and we will be with you in twenty minutes. If there is a deal than you can save the estate agent's big commission or maybe you could gift me something for my effort for the introduction if there is a sale.'

'That will be alright, Mr Katz. I will get you a commission for it if there is a deal with Mr Krenczberger.'

Walking up into our apartment with Rebekah she has stopped me on the stairs looked into my eyes and said, 'You look saddened my love?'

'Well, yes, I have lived here for some time, this was my home and now I am selling it the one which has brought me so much fond memories. It is like a kind of part of me is disappearing or has been taken away. But it had to be done as we are making our new life in Munkács together with you.'

'You know Gabriel I feel the same way moving out of my papa's apartment where I have lived all of my life. I understand that I am still staying in Munkács the town where I grow up. But it compares with you where you are leaving this wonderful City of Budapest and all of your friends behind.'

'And you are doing it because of me.'

'Yes, my darling, I am doing it for you. But you are worth it. I would give up everything for you, Rebekah, just to be with you. But just let us go up and get the room ready for a visitor who is interested to buy our apartment.'

Rebekah has quickly made the bed and made the room respectable for receiving a visitor.

Just as Mr Katz promised they have turned up in fifteen minutes with Mr Krenczberger. He looked the same age as I am. He is an Orthodox Jew who is renting a room just above his shop which he finds too small to share with his wife and a young son.

Mr Katz has stayed with Rebekah in the kitchen while I was showing Mr Krenczberger around the apartment.

A young man has knocked on my door while we were discussing the apartment sale, and he told me, 'I have been sent by the Chief Rabbi Immanuel Lőw, and he asked me to hand this letter to you in person. So here it is, and Rabbi Lőw doesn't need a reply to his letter.'

I have thanked the young man for bringing the letter to me, and I have sent my kind regards to Chief Rabbi Lőw.

I went back to the conversation I had with Mr Krenczberger over the sale of my apartment.

Mr Katz and Mr Krenczberger looked at me with surprise on their faces as they did not know what is in that letter, the one I have just received from Rabbi Lőw.

'I did not know Gabriel that you knew Chief Rabbi Lőw so well?'

It is an omen I thought this well-timed over my position as I was just about to crack a deal with the sale.

Mr Krenczberger said, 'I like your apartment Gabriel as it is so close to my shop and to the synagogue where we are attending as well. But I think it is more expensive than I could offer you.'

'Look, Mr Krenczberger, I can understand it, but I am moving out to Munkács, and my belongings will have to be removed and that is costly as you know.'

'Unfortunately, I just cannot accept your offer as I have just been notified by Rabbi Lőw that there are people who are willing to pay my asking price.'

Mr Krenczberger asked Mr Katz to have a word in private outside on the balcony.

About five minutes later the two gentlemen came back and Mr Krenczberger said, 'I will accept your price, and I want to go ahead to buy this property.'

'That is well, Mr Krenczberger. We are agreed, and we have shaken hands on the deal. I tell you what Mr Krenczberger I will leave behind these two wardrobes and kitchen furniture as well for you at least you will be able to keep your clothes.'

'That is very good of you, Gabriel. Thank you very much. If anything, you do not want to take with you to Munkács I would be very happy to accept it from you.'

'Very well, Mr Krenczberger, I will decide on what I will take with me, and I will leave the rest behind with you.'

During this week, I will ask my attorney to arrange the transaction with you over the sale.

'Yes, that will be good just well in time as I have not paid my landlord my rent for this month. So it will save us to pay for another month's rent.'

'Thank you for your assistance, Mr Katz, I will see you after the deal.'

'I know you will, you are a good man, Gabriel. I will miss your spending at my general store.'

'He is a good man, Rebekah. It was my pleasure to be at your service.'

'We haven't gone yet, Mr Katz, so we will come to your store and will spend more money with you.'

Mr Krenczberger turned to Rebekah, 'I have the latest lingerie from England. They are to the latest fashion excellent quality fabric it is the same they sell at the big London department store of Harrods. My cousin Hymie, he lives in Golders Green he supplies me from London, he is telling me that this fashion is much more modern and better quality than the ones from Germany or Austria.'

'I certainly will come into your haberdashery store and maybe we can see your latest stock from London. In fact, I will come in to see you Mr Krenczberger tomorrow morning, and I will bring my friend Fanni with me.'

'Excellent, Mrs Rebekah, I look forward to serving you and your friend. I will get you the best price just for you in Budapest.'

After when Mr Katz and Mr Krenczberger left, I have uncorked the Hungarian Champagne poured it into the only two glasses that I have in the apartment, and I said, 'Let's celebrate I have just sold my apartment today.'

'Well, darling, this is it. Now we are homeless here in Budapest.'

We drank our drinks, and I stepped close to Rebekah and Kissed her on her lips. When we have finished our celebration, Rebekah went to the bathroom to have a shower and at last, I have the opportunity to open Chief Rabbi Low's letter.

In the letter, he advised me that his contact at the Budapest Home Office will see us at ten on Wednesday morning. Please take your and Rebekah's official marriage certificate, and they will record your marriage in the Hungarian Registry, and at the same time, they will issue a Hungarian Nationality Document and a new Hungarian Passport for Rebekah. Please have two photographs of Rebekah with you. After when you have finished with all this formality then come and see me as I have more news for you which I want to discuss with you.

This news made me even happier. I joined Rebekah in the shower which was a little bit tight for two people but who cared when all the things we set out in the first place it was now all happening in a positive way.

I surprised Rebekah as I joined her in the shower, and she said, 'Gabriel, I have never done this before, but I like it.'

I held the soap-filled sponge in my hand and started to rub it onto Rebekah's beautiful body. I did not believe what we just did in the shower, but it was unbelievably beautiful.

At the end of our joint showering, Rebekah squeezed her body to me and said to Gabriel it was heavenly.

By the time we dressed and we were ready to walk to the restaurant, it was dusk and much cooler than during the day when the temperature was in the high thirties.

We walked hand in hand on Király utca, still that special joint shower was in on our minds as we have walked silently all the way to the Zur Stadt Wien Restaurant which is just up from our apartment on number 40 Király utca. As we walked into the *fogadó* (restaurant) Miska Kovács welcomed us and said, 'It is good to see you Gabriel, I have not seen you for some time. I hope you were not ill.'

'It is good to see you, Miska too. No, I have been working in Munkács in the last four months.'

'And who can I welcome in your company?'

'This lady with me is my wife Rebekah.'

'Oh, I am sorry if I was tactless, I did not realise that you have been married. Many congratulations. Even Mr Gyula Krúdy was asking about you, and I could not tell him of your whereabouts.'

'Well, I am here now, and we are very hungry for your delicious food.'

Miska walked us to my usual table and brought my regular kosher plum brandy one for me and for Rebekah as well.

As soon as we finished our drink the menu was presented to us.

'What would you like to drink my darling?'

'I would like to tray the Harslevelu dry white wine please.'

'That is an excellence choice, Mrs Rebekah.'

Miska has brought the wine in a clay jug and put it on the table with some pogácsa (cheese salted scone) in a small wicker basket.

'Who is this man who has been asking about you?'

'Oh, it is Gyula Krúdy he is an excellent journalist and a prominent writer. For his older years he always comes down here for a drink or two. He is a very nice person.'

We had an excellent evening supper, and we didn't stay late as we are tired out from the walking in the Városliget and the intimate excitement in the shower. I still cannot believe in that we have done it there.

Just a short walk back to our apartment from the restaurant from number 40 to 31 Király utca.

Rebekah has held on tightly to my arm and said, 'I have really enjoyed the meal tonight, thank you.'

'You are welcome my darling. I am not sure if the walking has tired me out or this wine got into my head, but for sure I will sleep well tonight.'

'Yes, Gabriel, I feel the same way as you do.'

We managed to get upstairs and just fallen into our bed. Rebekah has embraced me and fell asleep first before me. As I looked at her satisfied peaceful face, she looked like a little cherub again.

'Goodnight, my darling Rebekah, sleep well.'

Chapter 36

Meeting at the Ministry for Me and Rebekah Has Gone Shopping with Fifi

Once again, I have been woken up early in the morning by the birds before my alarm clock would set off.

I have switched off the alarm setting on the clock to stop waking Rebekah up at that time of the morning. She slept as a little girl curled up holding on to the corner of the duvet, and she was dreaming with little angels. (not like me).

It has given me enough time to get ready for my meeting later on at the ministry. I have gone through all the relevant paperwork, reports, and my recommendation on the progress I have achieved and that has been already made and the welcoming of the changes on the educational lower and higher levels. I just went through my speech and memorised my presentation. I knew that I am going to have a hard day inarticulacy from Gróf Teleki Pál *Magyarország Vallás és Közoktatásügyi Miniszter*. (Minister for Education and Faith)

I have made a fresh coffee for myself in the kitchen and made a preparation for Rebekah's coffee so she does not have to waste time for that when she will get up. But as I was ready to leave, she just called me from the bedroom, and she just walked into the kitchen. My goodness! She had her silk house coat unfastened and the silhouette of her perfect body shape showed through her nightdress. And here I am, I have to go to work.

'Are you leaving me so soon, Gabriel?'

'Oh, my darling I am not leaving you, I am just going to do my duty for the very reason we have to come to Budapest. I think this will be the end of my contract with the Ministry of Education.'

'My mission is in the Transcarpathian Region has been completed.'

'So now you are free from the Hungarian Authority Gabriel?'

'Yes, I am, but I am working out that plan which I have discussed with you.'

272

'By the way, Fifi will come and collect you at 9:30 and will look after you for the day while I am dealing with these officials.'

'So when shall I see you my darling?'

'I should be finished with everything I have planned by two in the afternoon. You know I have to see my contact at the Agricultural Ministry over that 'Conveyor and Elevator' business.'

'Oh, yes, I remember of that now.'

She embraced my neck and kissed me. 'See you later, my love.'

'Please do not forget to go to see, Mr Krenczberger, and Fifi will be here at 9:30 my love.'

'How can I forget him? He is such a nice character.'

'Here is some money for you my darling do not be without it. Fifi has an expensive taste for clothing like you my love.'

'I have enough money Gabriel you should not be worried. My Papa gave me plenty of money for my wedding dress.'

'All right my darling, enjoy the day, and I will see you later at the Gerbeaud.'

'Here is a good luck kiss from me my angel.'

'I love you my darling wife.'

'And I love you my darling Husband.'

We both laughed at what we have just said, and I kissed her on her lips.

When I have stepped out on Király utca the street it was as busy as ever. I was heading towards the St Stephen Cathedral and heading in the direction of the *Báthory utca* where the Education Ministerium are.

My appointment was 9 o'clock in the morning so I can walk to the ministry as the temperature was nice and cool from the overnight watering every street and the granite cobbles have kept the air temperature cool. Also, they have to regularly water the tram's tracks as it is getting deformed in the heat of the day.

Again, as always, I have arrived early for my appointment. I was sitting outside the meeting room waiting to be called in.

At last as my Omega pocket watch turned nine, the door opened, and the secretary asked me to enter into the meeting room. There were four officials whom I have never met before. They all introduced themselves, and I began my presentation. As I have got halfway through with my presentation.

Gróf (Count) Teleki, walked into the room, and he has sat at the side of the table.

As I have finished with my presentation, and I was waiting for questions from the panel of officials they all looked in Count Teleki's direction waiting first for his reaction.

'He has thanked me for my diligent and helpful contribution to implementing their agenda's in Transcarpathia and for all the useful reports I was sending them every week.'

'Count Teleki told me that he has read my reports, and it was encouraging for their plans for that region. It was very comprehensive and encouraging to further develop it and adopt my method for other regions like Erdély (Transylvania) and the Délvidék (Slovenia).'

Count Teleki has promised that he will visit Munkács and Transcarpathian Regions.

He asked me, 'Is that true that I have just recently married to a local woman in Munkács?'

'Yes, sir, I have, and hopefully I am moving and settling in Munkács to be with my wife and also, I have been offered a position at the Munkács—Beregszász County Hall to be the Officer of Art and Culture. Which I have accepted, and I will take up that position on my return to Munkács.'

'I was hoping for this opportunity to bring to your attention that I will be in position to promote Hungarian Culture and Art of course in Hungarian language right through the Transcarpathian Region.'

Count Teleki walked to the table joined the other officials and told them I like his approach and his ideas, that is very good and very helpful to our agendas this is what we are planning for that regions. Hungarian Culture along with education.

'Then he has continued to the officials and said, I do want this young man to be promoted from a ministerial level to be helped in financial ways and with access to artist we are promoting for this agenda.'

'I want to minute these words we have just discussed at this meeting. I want the minutes to be sent to me and to the officials at the Foreign Ministry.'

'I want to issue him with a ministerial command and with all the official endorsements on government document. I will consult with the officials and with my friend the prime minister.'

'I am pleased to meet you Gabriel, and very encouraged with your fertile pro Hungarian patriotic drive. I think I will be going to visit Munkács in the near future, and of course, I would like a welcoming of a pro Hungarian entertainment to be organised by you. Well done, Gabriel.'

All the officials were very upbeat after the approval of Count Teleki.

The meeting with the officials has ended much earlier than I have expected so I still had enough time to visit my friend Móric Hlébly, at the Agricultural Ministry.

We went out for a dinner and a drink at *Kossuth tér*, where we could talk in private, he gave me many good leads on and contacts and information on the Conveyor and Elevator that I would need to move forward with our project.

He gave me all the technical details of the workings of the conveyors and furthermore he gave me the details of address of the company who manufacture conveyors. One company that he has brought it to my attention was the one from Accrington, in England, Conveyor & Elevator Co. the Managing Director is Charley Wood and his Daughter Miss Jenny Wood.

Also, he gave me some names and contacts from the River Tisza program which was a complex project of the irrigation of the Puszta and generally the Nagy Alföld water supply for agriculture purchases.

The other part of the regulation of the navigation of the River Tisza.

'I have thanked Móricz and promised him a handsome appreciation if and when the contract will be awarded to us in Munkács.'

'You are a good friend Móric we have never forgotten of our friendship from the time we were children and when we had nothing but both of us have the determination to make success out of our lives.'

Well, I think I had an amazingly successful day. I was not expected all this promotion and appraisal from such high places. It looks as if we are in business with the conveyor manufacturing side of the business.

Let's just think and think in a rational manner.—While I was waiting for the number 2 tram in front of the House of Parliament many exciting theories have gone through my mind. Yes, there is an opportunity everywhere just have to speak out, may well be cheeky to ask for the job, or just be at the right time at the right place. (of course, with the right friend in places).

Finally, the tram has arrived, and I was making my way to meet up with my friends, Fifi and Miklós Radnóti at the Gerbeaud. As I got off the tram, at the Vigadó stop then I have to walk past the concert hall, so I have stopped just checking out the programs if anything is on for the time we are in Budapest. But

I have noticed that the season has been closed and there would not be any performances until mid-September.

The temperature was getting unbearably hot, but I would refuse to arrive to the Cukrászda without a jacket. It is not the custom so I have decided that I would rather sweat than look like a tourist who does not care about etiquette. I always can take off my jacket under the umbrella on the terrace of Gerbeaud.

I have immediately noticed Rebekah and our friends in front of the terrace facing the Square.

I have turned up with a couple of bunches of flowers bought from the *kofa* (Street florist) on the corner of the Vigadó building. I have noticed that Rebekah and Fifi have some boxes at their feet on the floor. I thought that she must have found a wedding dress so I shouldn't ask her what she bought. I know Rebekah will tell me what ever she has purchased but not her wedding dress. She is very good at keeping secrets.

After presenting the two ladies in our company with the flowers, and I was my greeting our friends, Miklós commented on my entrance: 'My goodness, my ever-romantic friend Gabriel. He asked me with a big smile. What was your day like, was it successful?'

'Well, I don't know where I should start.'

'From the beginning my friend, we don't want the prose you should know that I am the poet here.'

We all laughed at Miklós comment.

'Well, I have told them everything as it happened including the meeting, I had with my friend Móric about the agricultural business as well.'

'Well, my friend we have to celebrate this. 'Garcon, please', Miklós called for the waiter and told him in such a confident and loud voice that many people around us immediately recognised Miklós voice that their followed the outcome of the Miklós Radnóti's ordering Garson Champaign around!'

'Fifi was questioning Miklós order; don't you think Miklós is it too early for that drink and in particular in the heat like this?'

'Just one bottle, my dear Fifi.'

'This drink is on me, Miklós.'

'Alright, Gabriel, but we still have to celebrate your day of success.'

'Miklós my dear we have to go to honour your engagement this evening and you have to prepare yourself for the event.'

'Yes, you are right my dear wife as always. What would I do without you?'

I have collected the heavier boxes and Rebekah has held on to the one I guess with her wedding dress.

For a Tuesday afternoon Váci utca was unusually busy. 'I suggested that we should take the underground from Gerbeaud to the Opera stop, and it is much less walk from that stop than from here all the way to our apartment on Király utca. And it is much cooler than walking on these hot granite blocks.'

It was a good decision we have taken as we got home very quickly with the underground train.

I have looked at the box in Rebekah's hand, and I have recognised the name of Róthberger Jakab, *Váci utca Kristóf tér sarok* (corner of Váci utca and Kristóf square).

I didn't make any comment on that as I have recognised the shop by the name which has been printed on the box. I knew that Rebekah's wedding dress will be a talking point in Munkács as this shop the Rothberger Jakab, offers the best and the most fashionable wedding dresses in Hungary.

Walking home from the Opera underground stop to our apartment Rebekah pointed out to me that is Mr Krenczberger Haberdashery shop.

'I have to call in to collect all the lingerie that I have bought from Mr Krenczberger this morning. I just did not want to carry it with me to the *Belváros* (Downtown) when I have to pass his shop on our way home. You know Fifi has bought the same style and coloured one like mine. Isn't it strange Fifi has the same taste as I have?'

'Yes, darling, I knew that you would become a friend with Fifi, she has the same kind of background as you.'

'Fifi's father owns a big printing company here in Budapest, so she had all the benefit to be educated properly like you have. This is not a criticism my love I am just drawing a comparison between you two and her personality is just like yours. Both of you are very clever and a well-mannered lady.'

'Thank you, my angel.'

Rebekah walked in first into Mr Krenczberger shop a little bell rung as we opened the door and immediately there was Mr Krenczberger who greeted us. He called his wife to introduce us to her. 'Look Rachel this is the gentlemen and lady whom we bought the apartment from yesterday.'

Rachel looked to be in her late twenties, but she was dressed in a dark indigo coloured full dress and the same indigo coloured scarf to cover her hair.

'Thank you, Gabriel, for your kind offer to donate some of your furniture to us, you know everything is a help to us as we are renting this flat all the furniture's are belongs to our landlord.'

I felt good as I have offered the wardrobes to them as I've just heard from Rachel that they have nothing to furnish the apartment what they have just bought from us. Rebekah just looked at me and then she turned to Rachel and said, 'Look we will only going to take our clothing, books and the paintings from the wall which are personal to us, but we will leave all the furniture, duvet, pillows in the apartment for you. Whatever you don't want you can throw it away but hopefully that will be helping you with the moving in process. You will be able to have a bed to sleep on and a kitchen where you can prepare food for the Sabbath.'

'Yes, Rachel, I will leave my Mezuzah on the doorpost for you, so you'll remember us when you touch it and thank the Lord for each time you cross the door that He is a good providing Father to his people.'

Rachel burst into tears and embraced Rebekah they both thanked us for our generosity to help them to be exempt from a problematic removal into their new premises. I felt the atmosphere becoming emotional, and I didn't want them to be embarrassed, so we picked up Rebekah's shopping and said goodbye to them.

As we were walking home we both become quiet and when we got back to our room Rebekah with tears in her eyes embraced my waist and said, 'Thank you my dear Angel, we just have helped a family to start their life in their ready furnished premises without having extra cost to furnish their apartment so they can sleep and cook for themselves. That was noble of you to offer your furniture to Mr Krenczberger. I am immensely proud of you, Gabriel.'

'We have done it together my darling Rebekah. You are the one who recognised the desperate need they are facing with the nightmare moving circumstances. We are one body and one mind Rebekah we both feel for and help the downtrodden ones and with the help of our Lord God we will carry on with this kind of support for others and with this exercise we just help others with our deeds.'

'You know I have chosen well Gabriel when I have said 'Yes' when I married to you. I know that you are the one whom I want to be father my children. And those children will be blessed by the Grace of our Lord and with the gift of our energy.'

'We have to have an early night tonight Rebekah, we will have a busy and an important day tomorrow Wednesday morning at 10:00 a.m. We have on appointment at the Home Office and the at the Foreign Office. I have to get in touch with Dr Zoltán Hacsek with regards to the electric motors to power the conveyor and elevators. I was just checking his business card which I have kept along with the information I have received from him on our train journey from Munkács to Budapest.'

'Why don't we go out to the same restaurant to night to the Zur Stadt Wien Restaurant where we dined last evening at 40 Király utca. I have to phone Zoltán and find out if he is available to meet up either tomorrow evening or even, we could invite them to Miklós's poetry evening on Thursday evening at the Ódry Theatre.'

'Yes, that would be a good idea Gabriel let's do that.'

'Yes, I will do that. Then I can use the public telephone in front of the restaurant.'

It was a sheer luck that Zoltán and Johanna had nothing planned for Thursday evening, and they are delighted to attend Miklós Poetry Evening. I have suggested that after the theatre we all going to end up at the New York Coffeehouse for a drink. That even more excited Johanna as she can dress up for that place.

I felt that will be the best opportunity to talk business with Zoltán as we are in a much more relaxed situation not in his office.

After a successful telephone call with Zoltán I encouraged Rebekah to have a drink to celebrate the successful day. As we walked into the restaurant Miska Kovács welcomed us again and said, 'It is good to see you again, Gabriel. Would you like your usual table?'

'Yes, please, Miska.'

Miska automatically has brought out the kosher plum brandy as an appetiser, and he put the little wicker bowl full of Pogácsa on the table.

Rebekah said, 'I wish if Miska would stop tempting me with this pogácsa, it is so nice I have to ask him for the recipe so I can make it at home.'

Rebekah has ordered a Viennese Schnitzel with pickled cucumber, and I ordered a Töltött Káposzta (Stuffed cabbage) with fresh bread.

Rebekah asked Miska if she could have the recipe for the Pogácsa please.

'So tell me, Gabriel, how did your day go on?'

'I was explaining that I have received a positive response for my report and also I was telling her that our plan of promoting Hungarian art and culture to the Subcarpathian Region and also my new position I have been given in Munkács has been welcomed by the panel and promised of their full support, and they will be authorise me the maximum just to make my plan successful.'

'This is fantastic Gabriel it looks as all what we have set out at the first place will happen at the end.'

'Yes, my darling, and I have to report to Chief Rabbi Lőw with this deal I have managed to achieve.'

'Oh, I am so proud of you Gabriel, so far, I feel that I am still dreaming what is happening around me here in this fantastic City of Budapest. So many shops and amazing styles in the shops and the peoples are kind and helpful.'

'You know Gabriel I have bought the latest Bauhaus Household and Textile Magazine latest edition on Váci utca, and I believe there is a furniture shop where these Art nuevo style furniture is on display.'

'Do you think we could order furniture and household goods like wall lights and chandeliers direct from the factory or we should look for light shops in Munkács?'

'I think, darling, we should buy them in Munkács. But then again, we could ask the Sutyai Béla Furniture Factory in Munkács to supply us with everything that we need.'

Miska served our meal with a bottle of Hárslevelű and a handwritten recipe for the Pogácsa.

Rebekah thanked the chef for the recipe, and she asked for the menu again.

She said, 'I would like to try the Flódni (cake).'

I have stopped with my dinner and looked at Rebekah. 'Is everything is alight with you, Rebekah?'

'With a smile she replied, do you think that I am pregnant because I want a cake? No, don't worry my love I am not expecting a baby. I just would like to try a Flódni and that is it.'

'Well, it was a worrying feeling because I have promised to Isaack that there won't be anything like this and also, we are just not ready for a baby.'

After the meal we enjoyed the walk all the way back to our apartment. That time in the evening the temperature cooled down from the regular watering of the streets in the area. Rebekah put her arm into mine and laid her beautiful head on my shoulder, and it was so romantic which I have enjoyed as a perfect evening of the perfect day.

When we got back to our apartment, I have opened the remaining bottle of Hungarian champagne from my ice cabinet, and we drank all of it.

'You know my love we have to be at the Home Office for ten in the morning just to get your naturalisation papers registered and applying for your Hungarian Passport too.'

Well, this is it now for today as she was nodding off, and I whispered into her ear sleep well my love. Rebekah has cuddled into my arms and fallen asleep within minutes. May be the effect of the champagne or she was just genuinely tired out after the busy day we had today. I have kissed her on her forehead and whispered to her goodnight.

Chapter 37
Rebekah's Naturalisation and Passport Application

Another day of official business but this time it is for Rebekah's naturalisation to become a Hungarian Citizen. As she is married to a Hungarian citizen, automatically she has all the rights to apply for this privilege.

First, we have to take a taxi to the Hungarian Ministry of Foreign Office at Dísz tér, Buda Vár.

Then we looked for our contact at the Registry, Officer Mr Schneider he was expecting us, firstly to get Rebekah's application case to be registered than filing her citizenship application to be backdated so he could speed up her procedure.

We have handed over Rebekah's birth certificate and our official Marriage Certificate which we have received from the Registrar in Munkács after our wedding.

I really appreciated Mr Schneider's process of back dating her application as it usually takes at least three weeks to get it through the bureaucratic process.

When he entered Rebekah's signed application into the official record book Mr Schneider went out of his office with Rebekah's Application form to his colleague then he came back with a countersigned and stamped accepted Naturalisation document and along with an application form for the Hungarian Passport.

Rebekah has handed over her Passport photograph signed the back of her photos Mr Schneider dried the excessive ink with blotting paper and turned to us and with a smile he said, 'Well, congratulation, Rebekah, now you have officially become a Hungarian Citizen.'

Then he turned to me and said, 'I will bring Rebekah's Passport to the Dohány utca Grand Synagogue where Rebekah has to sign her new passport in front of an official person like Chief Rabbi Immánuel Lőw.'

'Well, this is it, Rebekah now it's all done.'

I shook Mr Schneider's hand and said, 'Look I will appreciate your help on Saturday after the service.'

'That is very kind of you Gabriel, but it is not necessary you are my fellow OMZSA member, and this is the very least I can do for you. I know your record of activity that you've done in Munkács, and I have to say I am impressed with your work. Shalom.'

Mr Schnyder kissed Rebekah's hand and one more time congratulated her on becoming a Hungarian Citizen. 'I'll see you both on Saturday.'

'When we finally got out of the Ministry, I have checked my Omega watch and told Rebekah; my darling it has just taken two and a half hours for you to become a Hungarian Citizen. Congratulations my darling, you are now a Hungarian Citizen and protected by an Internationally recognised nation for every country in the whole World. Our children will automatically become Hungarian Citizens and hopefully they will enjoy all the benefit of this great nation.'

'My angel, Gabriel, I still cannot think straight I feel I am walking on clouds. I am intoxicated with this morning's experience it is so surreal that it has taken two and a half hours, and I am now a Hungarian Citizen.'

'My dear, Rebekah, what you have experienced this morning shouldn't be discussed with anybody else as Mr Schneider could end up in prison for what he has just done for you.'

'I promise you Gabriel I won't even tell this story to anyone only to my Papa. I know the kind of risk involved with this procedure. I know it was officially done but it's only the timing that was speeded up for my application.'

'Let's have a lunch to celebrate the success that we had achieved today. I know a very good restaurant on the Danube Parade, which is overlooks the Kings Castle, the food is excellent.'

We have got a taxi from the Ministry at Disz tér Old Town Buda to Eötvös tér at the Chain Bridge Pest side.

We walk on the Parade (Ferenc József Rakpart) from the Chain Bridge towards the Elisabeth Bridge the midday heat was unbearably hot. Fortunately, the Platán trees given some comfort with their lush leaves. As we are passing the Duna Palota Hotel there were tables with parasols, and it was full of people having a drink in front of the hotel. We both felt thirsty just looking at the drinks on the tables.

'We are almost there Rebekah just on the corner of Vigadó Square. As we got to the Restaurant luckily there was some free tables, and we have settled at the front row of tables where we have a better view of Buda Hill and the panoramic view from the Citadels on St Gellert Hill all the way to the Fishermen's Bastion. Not to mention under the parasol and the cool breeze from the River Danube we have felt the comfort we were seeking from the Summer heat. I have started with a pint of Dreher beer and Rebekah ended up with a spritzer just to kill our thirst. My goodness, we had finished our drinks in one. Rebekah just couldn't get over of the magnificent view we had from the restaurant terrace.'

'I suggested to Rebekah that she must try the fish soup, which I am going to order for myself, it is a today catch from the river Danube and cooked with carp fish and served with fish filets in the soup and fresh bread.'

'Yes, I would like to try it.'

'Would you like it hot? They will bring out some Hungarian hot chilly paprika on the side plate which you can mix with your soup to a taste of your choice.'

'I do not want the paprika in my soup, but I'll have a spoonful to taste from your plate.'

I ordered a bottle of Hárslevelű and a bottle of soda water too.

As we lifted our wine glasses, I made a toast: 'Here is to you my dear wife Rebekah who has just become a Hungarian Citizen today. Congratulations to you my love.'

The waiter just overheard our conversation and walked to us kissed Rebekah hand, and he said, 'I am very pleased for you Madam. I know how pleased you feel at becoming a naturalised Hungarian Citizen, you know my wife is from Déva, Sothern Transylvania, and she has just become a Hungarian Citizen too it has taken us some eight weeks to get her citizenship, but it has worth every minute. She was the happiest women in the world. Where are you from Madam if I may ask?'

'I am from Munkács.'

'Well, may I offer you this bottle of wine on the house to just share your celebrations, this is our gift for your new Hungarian Citizenship.'

We have spent some two hours at the restaurant than we were heading towards Váci utca, passing the magnificent architectural building of the Vigadó,

Theatre and Concert Hall. Passed Gerbeaud and heading towards Apponyi tér direction on Váci utca.

As we've just passed Klára Salon, Rebekah made me stop and said, 'I would like to go into the salon with you please. I went in with Fifi in the other day and the lady does know you as her teacher of French language. Is that true?'

As we walked into the salon there she was, with a big smile she welcomed us and congratulated us on our wedding.

I have kissed her hand, and I turned to Rebekah, 'May I introduce you to Miss Klára Rothschild the most elegant Lady in Budapest and in all Hungary.'

'Well, Gabriel, I have always told you that there is a very pretty young lady is waiting for you, somewhere and here we are. It is good to see you, Rebekah, again.'

Miss Klára turned to me and said, 'I am sorry, Gabriel, but I have found another French teacher all ready as you have left me for this beautiful young lady Rebekah. But I don't blame you for it she is beautiful and very smart too.'

'But I think Rebekah could do with some up to date Parisian fashion dresses, don't you think? I can offer you ten percent discount just to you as an old friend.'

'You, Gabriel, just sit yourself on the couch, and you, Rebekah, just come with me.'

They went into the back changing rooms, and I noted one of the salesgirls were carrying some clothes into the changing room. Rebekah kept coming to show me the dresses she has tried on, and at the end, we have decided on two of the dresses which we thought would still turn some women red-faced with envy to see Rebekah in these dresses, and it is still modest enough for Munkács standard.

'I only could say that they all look beautiful on you, Rebekah.'

When I paid for the dresses Klára said, 'I am going to miss you, Gabriel.'

'I have kissed her hand and with a kind of emotion I have remembered her parties which I will miss greatly.' But I have now a purpose in my life with Rebekah in Munkács, and I am focusing on that.

As we walked towards Kígyó street, I told Rebekah that she could wear the pink and soft green dress with that funny little hat for Miklós poetry evening at the Ódry Theatre than as we were going to the New York Kávéház she would look wonderful in that new dress.

We walked on our way home to Király utca. We called into Mr Katz shop to get some salami and fresh bread with pickled cucumber and a couple of bottles of Hungária champagne.

Mr Katz came out from behind the counter and gave me a hug and kissed Rebekah's hand.

'You know, Gabriel, I knew you for a long time, and I always liked you but what you and your dear wife Rebekah have done to help Mr Krenczberger is absolutely noble as this family can move into their newly bought apartment without any worry about how to get their new apartment furnished. Please accept this bottle from our Orthodox community as a gift.'

'When you drink it with Rebekah think of us, L'chaim to you both, and may the Lord bless you with many children like you two.'

'Thank you very much, Mr Katz. This is really good of you, we will remember you when we drink this champagne. I would like to ask your help to get me some boxes where I can pack all my books and papers. I have hired a removal company to ship our belonging to Munkács, but I would rather pack these personal things on my own.'

'Yes, certainly, Gabriel. I can get these boxes for you, but you know these boxes will cost you, and I as a poor store owner I just can't finance it for you.'

'You have miss understood me Mr Katz of course I will pay for them.'

'Oh, that is alight, Gabriel. I will get them for you by tomorrow.'

'That will be great, Mr Katz. Would you like me to pay now?'

'No, Gabriel, I don't know how much it is going to be. I will let you know that.'

Back in our apartment I have started to collect all the books and other important documents and photographs. Rebekah has helped me when she picked up some of my old photos she laughed when she asked me, 'How old were you on this picture Gabriel? You look like the one who likes nice clothing. What a handsome little boy you were!'

All my other clothes I had were handed down from my two brothers.

Once I have told this story in a circle of good friends, János Grűn replied, 'Well, Gabriel, you are lucky as I have only sisters so can you imagine what could I have inherited from my older sisters?'

'So I have never mentioned this story again to anyone.'

Rebekah smiled and said, 'I promise you I will not mention it again. But it is a very funny story.'

It is a kind of upsetting feeling while I was taking down all my 'comfort' which is really my past as I knowingly am giving up, everything that I have collected which they has given me a pleasure to be around me. But these things are just materials and 'dead idols'. I think the time is now, to move on.

Rebekah has sensed my emotional wrestling then she walked to me and put her hand around my neck and kissed me without saying anything. We just stood in the middle of the room with my past memories around us on the floor and tables then she just hugged me cheek to cheek. She has wiped a tear from my eye which was running down on my cheek with her fingers and said, 'I love you, Gabriel, and I will make it up to you in our house in Munkács.'

I have felt embarrassed as I have never shed a tear in front of anybody. I have always believed it is a kind of sign of weakness for a man to cry.

'I am so sorry, Rebekah, but I just wasn't ready for this kind of emotional reaction.'

'Never mind, Gabriel. How about if we open this bottle from your icebox and just stop meditating on the past and let's plan our future in Munkács. I believe this will be a positive move for both of us.'

'We will prove it to the world that with our hard work we are special ones, and we will create it and that will be our success story.'

'When we are ready then we will have many little Gabriel's like the one you were on this photo.'

She held my old photo close to her chest with both hand and said, 'I will give you an identical little boy who will be a joy to both of us.'

I hugged Rebekah close to me, and we have kissed in such passion that we have forgotten the packing and everything else in the world around us. She whispered into my ear, 'My dear angel, please take me into heaven again.'

It was seven in the evening, and we have decided not to go out for our supper, but we should have some sandwiches and open that bottle of champagne from the icebox.

We only have house coats on us, as we didn't expected any visitors for this evening. At the end of our light evening meal Rebekah said, just wait here for a second. She went into the bedroom and came back still in a housecoat. Then she stood in front of me and with a slow motion has opened her housecoat and there she was in the latest French lingerie. I just couldn't say a word from the stunning look of my wife in that lingerie. She looked like someone out of Vogue Magazine with an absolutely perfect shaped body. She looked so sexy but as an elegant 'Lady goddess'.

At finally I have managed to speak only I could say, 'Darling, you look absolutely gorgeous.'

'Where did you buy this 'blood boiling' lingerie from?'

'It was your friend Klára who has chosen it for me today at her Szalon on Váci utca.'

'Well, thank you, Klára. You know what men appreciate and can feed their eyes on their wives.'

I just couldn't get over Rebekah's new lingerie, and I was kept looking at her housecoat which is now fastened and have no more view of that very sexy underwear.

'You know, Gabriel, I have some other items, but I just didn't want to give you a heart attack with that.'

'Well, there is always another day to indulge in your tempting body.'

By the time we have finished with our supper it was 8:30, and I guess the alcohol got into both of our heads, and we had decided that we are going to bed early. After this exciting day as Rebekah has become a Hungarian Citizen and all that walking, we had in the hot day which has tired us out for the day. Again, as usual tomorrow will be a very busy day for both of us as we have on appointment with Chief Rabbi Lőw in the synagogue and of course meeting up with Zoltán and Johanna and Miklós's poetry evening. Then a long partying into the night at the New York Kávéház.

Chapter 38

Meeting with Chief Rabbi Immánuel Lőw and Business Leaders at Synagogue

Around nine in the morning Mr Katz has knocked on our door, Rebekah has opened the door and invited Mr Katz in. He brought four fairly large, unfolded carton of boxes.

Good morning to you both as I have promised you last evening that I will get you some boxes for your books. He looked around the lounge and saw all those papers and books on the floor all over the place. 'My goodness, Gabriel you do have some books I hope these large boxes will take all of it.'

'By the way, as the news got to the rest of the Orthodox Community about your kind help to Mr Krenczberger family these boxes have been given free of charge from the Rothouser *Testvérek* (Brothers) shop at 6 Király utca, and they have thanked you for your kind support for the Krenczberger family.'

'Oh, Mr Katz, anybody would do the same for their fellow Jews.'

'No, Gabriel. Unfortunately, not everybody is thinking the way you and Rebekah do.'

'Thank you, Mr Katz. Can I offer you a cup of coffee?'

'Thank you, Rebekah, but I have to dash back to the shop you know if people see that I have a closed the door they might think that I have gone bust so I can't afford to lose business.'

We have started to pack my books and the photos along with my important papers. The room has looked already tidier.

Rebekah has made a couple of sandwiches and had a much more relaxed morning compering from the time since we got here to Budapest.

On the way to the Dohány utca Synagogue I have called into my attorney Dr Schwartz to arrange to the exchange of the deeds for the sale of the apartment. I have made the point that all furniture will be included in the sale of the apartment.

'I have given Mr Krenczberger details, and I asked specifically Dr Schwartz that the purchaser wishes to move in before the end of this calendar month not later than Sunday, 31 July 1938. It would save Mr Krenczberger a substantial amount of money to pay out for another month of rent to his landlord.'

'I have heard of your kind support for this family, and I will make all the effort to get the legal documentation and the exchange of contracts ready before you leave Budapest to return to Munkács. When are you leaving Gabriel?'

'We are leaving on Monday, 25 July. The removal company will arrive on Sunday morning to collect my belongings on Sunday, 24th. I am leaving this copy of keys for the apartment so would you please release the keys to Mr Krenczberger when the exchange of sale contracts are signed.'

'That is all in order Gabriel, and I will transfer the fund of the sale of course minus my expenses.'

'Of course, that is in order Dr Schwartz, and this is my bank account with the Móric Uhlmann Bank the Pesti Magyar Kereskedelmi Bank, Munkács Branch. (Pesti Hungarian Commercial Bank).'

'Well, this was well timed, my darling Rebekah.'

'Yes, Gabriel, it is so well arranged as if it has been done above us. Everything is well in our plan. But I am so surprised that our good deeds got noted and appreciated so positively by the community.'

'Yes, my darling, when people keep their heads down and get on with their everyday jobs and most of them just really concentrate on their day to day problems and count every *'Fillér'* (Pennies) which is so precious that they have, and very little to give away on charity. I know this is a big help to Mr Krenczberger family. When I have moved in here, I only could afford to buy for this apartment was a mattress which was on the floor and a very basic kitchen accessory.'

'So I know what Mr Krenczberger family is facing with their traumatic effort, when they have to move out from the rented accommodation, without having any furniture for the family not even a bed to sleep in or a wardrobe to store their clothing in a much social manner.'

'Well, Gabriel, you have come a long way from that and hopefully we don't have to start from that basic ever again. We are a team now, and we will aim for the best of everything in life.'

'Well, darling, we have to move on as you know we have an important meeting in the synagogue which is concerning our new life together in Munkács.'

'At our arrival to the Grand Synagogue on Dohány utca where we have been welcomed by a secretary, he asked Rebekah to join him in his office while I was involved with this scheduled meeting.'

I have been accompanied by the secretary into a committee room then he went back to his office to entertain Rebekah while my meeting was going on.

I have recognised some members, but I have never met other members around the table. They must have been very important people, the way they have dressed, and the size of their cigars they were smoking.

I have been introduced to the committee by the Chief Rabbi Immánuel Lőw who has sat at the centre of the panel he told me that he is chairing this meeting. There will be no minutes taken because the confidentially of our discussion has to be maintained. Also, most importantly these gentlemen on the panel are all members of OMZSA and JDC like yourself, Gabriel.

'Chief Rabbi Lőw asked me if I have understood his introduction and the importance of privacy and asked me to me to proceed with my presentation to the panel.'

'In my opening speech I have greeted the members of the panel and politely asked if they have been briefed on my works in the Transcarpathian Region.'

Chief Rabbi Low commented, 'Yes, Gabriel the panel have been briefed, and they are familiar with your mission in Munkács and also of your character report. Please proceed.'

'Firstly, I have explained the outcome of the meeting I had at the Ministerium. I would like to present the minutes which have taken of that meeting at a request of Grof Teleki, and here are the official minutes of that meeting' (N 56).

I handed the copy of the minutes to Chief Rabbi Immánuel Lőw who has read it through and passed it on to the other members of the panel. They faces were altered with a kind of smile and a nodding of approval when they have read my report they have asked questions one by one that if I would need any legal adviser to support me in Munkács as my political background is not adequate enough to deal with such experienced politicians.

Minutes of my presentation to the Ministers:

There was four officials whom I have never met before. They all introduced themselves, and I began my presentation. As I've got halfway through Grof (Count) Teleki, walked into the room, and he has sat at the side of the table.

As I have finished with my presentation, and I was waiting for questions from the panel of officials they all looked in Count Teleki's direction waiting first for his reaction.

He has thanked me for my diligent and helpful contribution to their agenda's and for all the useful reports I was sending them every week.

Count Teleki told me that he has read my reports, and it was encouraging for their plans for that region. It was very comprehensive and encouraging to further develop it and adopt my method for other regions like Erdély (Transylvania) and the Délvidék (Slovenia).

Count Teleki suggested that he will visit Munkács and Transcarpathian Regions. He asked me is that true that I have just recently married to a local woman in Munkács?

Yes, Sir I have, and hopefully I am moving and settling in Munkacs to be with my wife and also, I have been offered a position at the Munkács—Beregszász County Hall to be the Officer of Art and Culture. Which I have accepted, and I will take up that position on my return to Munkács. I was hoping for this opportunity to bring to your attention that I will be in position to promote Hungarian Culture and Art of course in Hungarian language right through the Transcarpathian Region.

'Count Teleki walked to the table joined the other officials and told them I like his approach and his ideas, that is very good and very helpful to our agendas this is what we are planning for that regions.'

Then he has continued to the officials and said, 'I do want this young man to be promoted from a ministerial level to be helped in financial ways and with access to artist we are promoting for this agenda.'

'I want to minute these words we have just discussed at this meeting. I want the minutes to be sent to me and to the officials at the Foreign Ministry. I want to issue him with a ministerial command and with all the official endorsements on government document. I will consult with the officials and with my friend the prime minister.'

'I am pleased to meet you Gabriel, and very encouraged with your fertile pro Hungarian patriotic drive. I think I will be going to visit Munkács in the near future, and of course, I would like a welcoming of a pro Hungarian entertainment to be organised by you. Well done, Gabriel.'

All the officials were very upbeat after the approval comment of Count Teleki...

In response, 'I told them, 'I have no political experience at all as I have always been involved with entertainment and yes, I feel to deal with politicians is a different world that I have experienced before, so I don't feel confident enough. In the past, I have always sought Dr Sándor Fried advice which was adequate for me to carry on with my mission.'

'One member of the panel who is the director of a major bank Mr Segal, asked me if in my estimate there a future influx of foreign investments and companies is who are showing any interest to move into Transcarpathia after the changes?'

'Yes, sir, as you know it is the tariff at the Custom and Excise which is the major progress in any business growth in particular import and export. I understand there is an organisation who are in the process to establishing a Transcarpathian Industrialists Alliance, their Chairman is Mr Aladár R. Vozáry.'

'Let's see Munkács; there is wood, salt, tobacco, and much more natural minerals in the region. Mostly there are many very bright well-educated people who are capable to do any trade or business activities and most of them who speak several languages and mostly they are local, and the cost of labour is very competitive. As you know many well educated Jewish graduates are ending up to found works in Budapest. Not to mention of the major investments are to modernisations for Transcarpathian Region by the Hungarian Government plans like for the River Tisza Project.'

'Well, it looks to me Gabriel your main interest is not just in art and culture, but you have a good sense of business as well.'

'Thank you, sir, but when you entertain people, and this is not just in the theatre or concert hall stage but in life generally you sense what would sell and what would flop. My wife Rebekah who has just recently graduated at Lvov University and who is a talented accountant and who is very much in touch with the banking, taxation laws and regulations. She is my partner not just in marriage but in business as well.'

'Another gentleman named Mr Rosenthal a member of the panel who is from a major company who asked me; Where did you get this information regarding the regulation of the River Tisza?'

'I am very sorry, sir, but this information is confidential, and I cannot help you with that neither of my source of this information.'

'That is fair enough, Gabriel.'

Then he turned to his colleagues on the panel and said, 'Gentlemen, this major project is very confidential as it is one of the biggest investments and improvement which is still discussed behind closed doors at the Agricultural and Finance Ministers of Hungary.'

'The project is excavating the riverbed on the River Tisza and clearing the riverbed for a logistical plan to en able the shipping from the River Duna to all the way to Huszt. This program also, part of this plan which is the irrigation program to excavate watering channels for the Hortobágy (region of the Great Plain of Hungary at the Town of Debrecen).'

'Gentlemen, we are getting ready for this changes my father in law owns an engineering company which is a small company, but we are gearing up to manufacture conveyers to elevate water from the river Tisza to these irrigation channels.'

'That is very smart, Gabriel. Does your father in law have a good steel supplier for this project?'

'This is my mission while I am here in Budapest to finding reliable suppliers for this project, and we are going to tender to manufacture these machineries.'

'Well, I can help you with this part of your project.'

'Thank you very much, Mr Rosenthal. May I invite you gentleman to come and visit Munkács and basically the Transcarpathian region to see for yourselves the opportunities for business as the changes are already on the way. I would prepare all your interest of meetings with various business counterparts you would seek to make contacts with.'

After a good constructive meeting Chief Rabbi Immánuel Lőw called the end of the meeting. He thanked the panel members for attending and turned to me.

'Well, Gabriel, you are only here for some four day, and I can hear your name mentioned everywhere in the community. Rabbi Simon Rozenberg from the Rombach utca Pray house- Synagogue called in here yesterday and told me what you have done, and he just wants to give you his blessing to you for your charitable gesture to donate you entire furniture to Mr Krenczberger who has just bought your apartment. Well, Gabriel. What you have done is truly a humbling gesture. Mr Krenczberger is truly deserving of your gift it will tremendously help his family to prosper. He is a good and loyal member of our community.'

'Thank you very much for all this fuss, but Mr Krenczberger story has reminded me when I bought an empty apartment and remained empty as I couldn't afford to furnish it and Mr and Mrs Krenczberger have a small child who would deserve a comfort to enjoy his younger years.'

All the members of the panel have come to me and shaken my hand and praised me for my generosity. Then Chief Rabbi Lőw tapped on my shoulder and said, 'I am proud of you My Boy, I will going to miss you being around.'

Then he suggested that we should have a lunch at the Hotel Astoria, which is only three minutes from the Synagogue, it is on the corner of Kossuth Lajos utca and *Múzeum Körút*.

Everybody has agreed with Rabbi Lőw's suggestion, and Mr Segal asked me if I would introduce him to Rebekah, as he would like to talk to her about the practices and of banking rules and regulations in Munkács.

Before I could answer to Mr Segal, Chief Rabbi Lőw asked me to bring Rebekah along with us to the restaurant.

'Well, Mr Segal here is your wishes it's answered Rebekah will join us for a lunch at the Hotel Astoria.'

As we were walking out of the room Rabbi Immánuel Lőw called into his secretary's room and invited Rebekah to join us for lunch.

As she walked out of the room then Mr Segal stopped and asked me, 'Is this is your new wife Gabriel? She looks like a goddess, Mazel tov my boy.'

I have introduced Mr Segal to Rebekah, and I have left her to talk to him all the way to Hotel Astoria.

At the same time, I have been companioned by Mr Rosenthal who was very keen to learn more of our project with this conveyor idea.

Our group arrival at the Astoria Restaurant I was very impressed by the waiter who knew all members of the panel by name, and he has led us into a private room. Rebekah whispered to me, 'Gabriel, this place is just magnificent, the look of building on the outside and of the inside is just splendid. It must be an exclusive place for the very wealthy elite?'

'I don't know my darling I have never been inside, so I don't have the experience. Yes, it has a good reputation it has been known to be frequently visited by the rich and famous.'

As we sat around the table, I have ended up sitting next to Mr Rosenthal, and Rebekah has ended up sitting next to Mr Segal who was impressed with Rebekah's knowledge of banking.

I have heard some members around the table were asking Rebekah's knowledge and her confidence to deal with businesspeople and the subject is not just fashion but a well-educated conversation in business and commerce.

'You know I am member of The Union of Jewish women and Committee for the Equality of Women.'

Some of the gentlemen around the table stopped talking when Rebekah has explained the reason for her confidence, and they all looked at the Rabbi waiting for his comment on Rebekah's involvement with such a women's organisation.

Rabbi Lőw recognised the pause in conversation and quickly responded in Rebekah's defence and said, 'Well, gentleman, there is nothing against in the law of Moses that women shouldn't be involved with businesses at whatever level it is. After all we are living in 1938 and the times are rapidly changing. If she is for our community's benefit than my blessing on them. Just look at those very talented actresses and movie stars in Hollywood. Many of them Hungarian Jewesses.'

The atmosphere has become more relax as Rabbi Low approved Rebekah's involvement with a university graduation and her activity to defend women's rights.

'I have come to the help of Rebekah as well; You know gentlemen the Union of Jewish Women committee is a charitable organisation who are supporting Jewish women's. Helping them in their needs in the poverty-stricken situations wherever they are in need in financial or offering protection in their domestic hardship. The Ex Rebbe of Munkács, Chaim Elazar Spira only daughter, Chaya Fruma Rivka who married to Baruch Yehoshua Yerachmiel Rabinowicz the present Chief Rabbi of Munkács. She is one of the leading members of this non-political and noble organisation. I believe these ladies deserve every support from our establishment to carry out their works.'

'I believe, gentlemen, it is our duty of we should help our communities as I have met many poor Jewish people in Transcarpathian Region during my mission there. Their children need to be educated properly. Helping them to be ready for their adult life not just with the Bar mitzvah but with education as well.'

'You have said it well Gabriel, we have to help our community so they can help us too. If we don't help our people so what can we expect from the other societies?'

'Thank you, Chief Rabbi Lőw.'

I have received applause from the committee members, and the conversation went back to the more relaxed atmosphere.

During the meal we have exchanged contact details and with the promises that they will definitely visit Munkács in the near future.

As the time was pressing me and Rebekah to attend to our next engagement, 'I have to apologise to the gentlemen around the table as we have to leave as we have a theatre ticket to support our friend Miklós Radnóti who has a poetry evening at the Ódry theatre.'

'Everybody encouraged us to keep up with the good work, and they have asked me to express their regards to Dr Sándor Fried.'

Chief Rabbi Lőw said, 'Come and see me after the Sabbath Service, Gabriel. And enjoy the evening with Miklós company.'

'Yes, of course, Rabbi Lőw. I will come and see you after the Sabbath Services.'

We both stepped out of the hotel restaurant and the heat has just overwhelmed us after being in a cool restaurant room. I have suggested, 'Darling, we should take a tram to *Deák tér* and our apartment on Király utca is not far from the tram stop instead walking all the way from the Astoria to our apartment.'

It was 2:15 by the time we got home to relax and get changed and get ready for the evening engagement to meet up with Johanna and Zoltán for a drink before we are going to the theatre to support Miklós at 6 pm.

I feel after this busy day with the meetings with all these VIP's and having a heavy meal in the heat like this. Well, we both needed some rest which has turned into a very passionate time with Rebekah, and at the end, we ended up just lying on the bed in total exhaustion.

We were meeting with Zoltán at the Uránia Film Theatre's bar at five and then walking to the Ódry Theatre on Vass utca.

Rebekah was very naughty again she was behaving like a young schoolgirl who has just achieved her first hugs and kiss, and she wanted to practice it all the time.

'Darling, we wouldn't be ready to meet up with Zoltán unless we stop kissing all this afternoon.'

'My dear, Gabriel, I am just so happy for today I feel like I am just being dreaming to meeting all these important and very influential people, having dinner with them and the way they have treated me in such high respect. They have recognised me as a serious businesswoman which I am, and they promised that they will come and visit us in Munkács in their fact-finding mission.'

'In particular, Mr Segal who is I think a very powerful man in the banking business he talked to me the most.'

'Yes, my Rebekah, you are a very bright and strong-willed businesswoman, I noted the way they have responded when you told them that you are member of those women organisations.'

'You see these people are still a conservative minded 'old guards' of society. They believe the women's job is staying at home and taking care of running the household problems and joining their husbands for entertaining guests at social events, and they are worried at losing their control over their household power when they meet with a charismatic women like you are.'

'But I am very proud of you, Rebekah. You are truly an amazingly talented person, and I am very lucky man because you are my wife.'

She kissed me and adjusted my bowtie and said, 'Well, I am ready now my lucky husband.'

I have complimented her on her looks and said, 'My goodness, Rebekah, you look like a movie star in this dress.'

'You look strikingly beautiful in that new dress from Klára Rothschild.'

Chapter 39

Party Time with Miklós, Zoltán and Kávéház

We walked down from the Király utca on Kazinczy utca all the way to the Uránia Film Theatre and café house on Rákóczi ut. By the time we arrived on time Johanna and Zoltán had been sitting on the terrace under a parasol and waving to us.

We have greeted each other, and I said, 'I hope you didn't have to wait for long as we are on time.'

Zoltán said, 'Of course not. We just came into the town centre for window shopping.'

Rebekah and Johanna were complimenting on each other's clothing and the rest was all girly chat.

Zoltán was telling me that he is sometimes missing a small and quiet town of Munkács comparing it with Budapest. But this is where he came to study at the Corvinus University, and he had a hard time to get on with life generally. He told me he was entering into competitions for advertising companies to create an easy to remember slogans to advertise various products. One of these slogans became very popular, and he got paid handsomely well for that advertisement slogan. The product is a well-known chocolate called 'tibi chocolate'.

The meaning of TIBI is: 'The word tibi is used in Latin meaning to you, for you'.

'I didn't know that Zoltán, that was your idea, but I like that chocolate. I like it very much.'

'I hope that money has helped you financially during your time at the university.'

'Yes, Gabriel, as you know we all went through a very 'lean years' that time in our life.'

'I guess you were in the same shoes as many of our generation were after the Great War.'

'We all appreciate what we have now and just try to help those who haven't had the opportunity to go forward with their dreams and with their hard work.'

'By the way, Gabriel just going back to our conversation with your enquiry about the electric motors and electric generators that are our company's main products.'

I have explained to Zoltán the concept of our product and the variety of specification we are looking for is a fitting for all specification of a standard electric motor with a control unit, and it has to be reasonably priced.

'What made you to open up to this ancient Greek technology to revive and create this system as a multifunctional tool for this modern time technologies.'

'Basically, using a perfectly simple and well tested mechanism invented by the great Archimedes as his principle which is power it with a strong enough motor to move any kind of liquid, semi liquid or a solid material either in horizontal or vertical elevating situation. There is a company in England who is in business in manufacturing these systems, and I believe it is very profitably business.'

'Look, Gabriel, I have some idea of the specification you are looking for, and I can promise to you that I will send you a couple of these electric motors with its control unit for you to experiment with them. I can get it shipped to you to your factory in Munkács, free of charge. With the promise from you that for the future we, will by Ganz Works – Kandó Electric of Budapest, will supply you exclusively for all new and replacement units. Also, we would be more supportive for you if you would set up an agency to represent us in Munkács for the whole Transcarpathian region.'

'Look, Zoltán, I can promise you that we will use Ganz – Kandó Electric as our main supplier exclusively.'

'Also, I will represent Ganz – Kandó Electric as a main agent for the Transcarpathian Region.'

'Here is my hand as a guarantee for our agreement.' We have shaken our hands over this agreement as our seal to respect our Gentlemen's Agreement over this deal.

'Johanna warned us about the time as we have ten minutes left to get into the theatre.'

300

Zoltán paid the bill, and we walked into the theatre which is just five minutes from the Urania Film Theatre.

'I made a comment on the theatres late start, you know they are very flexible as every performance they put on they always starts late with the performances.'

As we arrived, we have sat in the last row in this small theatre but at our arrival we have made some heads turn from the rest of the audience. I am not surprised on this curiosity as Johanna and my Rebekah looked absolutely stunning like true Movie stars. Zoltán and I have sensed this reaction, and we looked at each other smiled and were very pleased with the audience reaction to our late entrance.

Rebekah sat next to Johanna and Zoltán and I next to our wives on both sides. Suddenly Fifi has tapped on my shoulder she was standing behind the last row in the theatre I winked at her and said hello. And the performance began.

I have breathed a sigh as I thought this is my last time here in this theatre where I have spent all those unforgettable times of joy and fun. But now that is in the past and my destiny is taking me away from the 'mask of being someone else' to reality. I suppose I have matured now, and I have a future with the most beautiful wife that anyone could wish for.

The performance was a typical Miklós Radnóti, the true entertainer with all of his flamboyant charisma he had the audience in his palm.

At the interval many of us went outside of the theatre as the heat was just getting uncomfortable.

Fifi rushed to us hugged and kissed with Rebekah then Rebekah has introduced Johanna and Zoltán to her. Fifi was in her exciting form and was bubbling as she does each time Miklós is performing.

The three girls have instantly clicked, and they were chatting away until the theatre bell interrupted us and called us back to the theatre.

In the second half Miklós has been joined onstage by some actors and actresses. I knew some of them but there were some very talented new commers. It was a very interesting arrangement the way Miklós arranged his poems and short stories.

At the end of the performance Miklós and Fifi joined us and six of us walked from the theatre to the New York Palota. The three ladies walked in front of us, and they were giggling loud enough in the almost empty Rákóczi ut.

As we walked past the National Theatre the crowd were growing as well. Rebekah said what a beautiful building it looks like the Opera House. It looked as the National Theatre was finishing with its performance as there was quite a crowd who was leaving the theatre, and they were desperate to grab a taxi in front of the building.

We crossed *Rákóczi út* at the Emke Coffeehouse to the *Erzsébet kőrút* and surprisingly the entrance to the New York Kávéház was very busy with people. We thought that all these people want to get in, and we will have difficulty to have access to the place at all. We later learned that a famous guest prima donna Miss Hanna Honthy who was performing at the National Theatre will be going to the Kávéház and all these people just wanted to have a glance or collect autograph from the star.

Miklós with a loud voice requested access through the crowd which has parted, and we had free access to the Caffe House. At the door Józsi welcomed us and called Marci the bell boy to take us to our table which has been booked by Miklós. I asked Józsi what is going on here why is this chaos?

'Oh, Gabriel. We have Miss Hanna Honthy, and she is having a party with some VIP's who are her guests and as you see is everything is in a chaos now.'

'By the way, Józsi your cousin Mihály from Ungvár sending his regards, I have seen him some weeks ago, and he is a very nice man like you.'

'How is he, Gabriel?'

'Oh, he is very happy and doing well. There was a gypsy band called—' I just couldn't finish the sentence as Józsi finished it.

'Yes, it's Tibor Rácz who is now playing here tonight.'

'Well, Józsi, this world is not big enough as you are meeting with people who know you or the people you know in some other part of the world.'

'I know what you mean Gabriel just go, inside and enjoy the evening. I will make sure you'll get the best service for tonight.'

'I have thanked and given a tip to Józsi just give us the best table for tonight.'

We've got Miklós favourite table with the good view over the rest of the restaurant and the band.

Józsi went to the gypsy band and whispered something to the *Primás* (leader of the band) Tibor Rácz who has looked up to our direction and waved to us.

Miklós asked me, 'Do you know this primas? They only booked here for the summer while you were away.'

'Yes, Miklós. I have met them in Ungvár in the Theatre Csárda.'

'Well, my 'Marco Polo'. I am amazed by you. You always spot the talents anywhere, typical of you.'

'What an entrance a young beauty has just walked in with Miss Hannah. Who is she?' I asked Miklós.

'Oh, she is the new starlet her name is Miss Sári Grűn. Sorry she has changed her name to Zsazsa. It's a hobby that her father has changed his name from Grűn to Gábor. They are the friends of Miss Hanna.'

As all six of us were getting a bit high on the drinks when Tibor Rácz walked to our table. I have introduced Tibor to our friends, and he kissed all the ladies hands and specially kept Rebekah hand for a bit longer and said, 'With a typical gypsy charm, it is good to see you again Rebekah may I play your favourite song to you again here in this beautiful establishment.'

Rebekah blushed at Tibor's charm and said, 'Yes, please, Tibor, take me back to Ungvár to that special evening.'

Then Tibor signed to his band and played the Monty Csárdás with such emotion that his violin bow almost touched Rebekah ear. Many people around us turned their attention away from Miss Hannah and Miss Zsazsa and asked the questions who are these ladies dressed in the latest Parisian style with Miklós and Gabriel?

Then Tibor kissed Rebekah's hand again and said something to her in gypsy which we didn't understand and moved on to play for the party at the table where Miss Hannah was sharing with her friends. Miss Hannah was sitting with Miss Zsazsa, and she has started to singing some of her famous songs from an operetta *'Legyen a Horváth-kertben Budán and Hajmási Péter, Hajmási Pál'*. Tibor and his band followed her on violin. The whole Coffee house guests have sung along with her favourite songs.

Then when Tibor the gypsy Primás moved on to other tables Miss Hannah with Miss Zsazsa have lifted their glasses and turned to our table and saluted all of us at our table.

Miklós got really angry and said, 'This is the cheap modern culture that they are selling to the 'patriotic people' who are always looking for a cheap entertainment and a cheap drink.'

'Well, they have it with her.'

Fifi and I have tried to calm Miklós who has really got offended on these 'prima donnas' influences on the public.

Beside of this angry outburst from Miklós, Zoltán and Johanna are really enjoying themselves and the three girls never stopped chatting to themselves were having a good time. I have to say Zoltán, and I have joined into the girls conversation and when Fifi has suggested to Rebekah and Johanna to show them around the coffeehouse they have jumped on the opportunity. I said to Miklós, 'Look I am going to marry Rebekah at the Hoif Complex Synagogue in Munkács, and it would be great if my old friend with his wife would attend at my proper Jewish wedding under the Chuppah.'

'I have turned to Zoltán and made an invitation to both of them too. Just think of this Zoltán it could be on opportunity for you to come on a business trip to Munkács.'

'Both Miklós and Zoltán thanked me for the invitation, but they asked me when is that exactly, Gabriel?'

'Oh, I am so sorry it will be on Sunday, 11 September. I will take care of the hotel rooms for you both for the time you are in Munkács.'

They both accepted my invitation and Miklós said, 'I am dying for a good kosher plum brandy from Munkács.'

Zoltán said, 'It looks as if we could do with some more drink, and he has ordered more bottles of champagne from the waiter.'

The girls have come back from their tour around the coffeehouse just in time as the champagne has been served.

Miss Hannah walked to our table and greeted us with a false smile, and she addressed Miklós, 'I know you Mr Radnóti I like very much your poems and writings there is so much passion in them.'

'Then she called her new friend and introduced her to us as Miss Zsazsa Gabor. She is going to be a major international star she is already performing in Vienna and there are movie directors who show much interest for this beauty.'

'Miklós thanked Miss Hannah for her kind praise and returned her appraisal Miss Hanna your voice is still magnificent and very elegant.'

'Then he turned to Miss Zsazsa and said I know your parents, Joli and Wilmos, they are members of the Great Synagogue, both of them good members of the community. I have seen you there with your sisters Martha and Éva sitting in the balcony you must know my wife Fifi. And these are my friends Dr Zoltán, and Johanna Hacsek, and you probably know Gabriel and his wife Rebekah from Munkács.'

Zsazsa said hello to Fifi and said, 'Yes, I know you both well you two have a reputation among the theatrical community.'

Miklós and I said to Zsazsa, 'We are sending our regards to your parents. Miss Hannah said to Miklós please visit me sometime at the National Theatre I would like to discuss with you about a story for on operetta as your stories are full of passions and romance.'

'Yes, of course, Miss Hannah, I will come on see you.'

Then she has moved to another table full of people where she was introducing Zsazsa, as the future movie star. The evening turned into dawn, and Zoltán said, 'I am so sorry, but I have to go to work in the next four hours. So I have to thank you all for this fantastic evening.'

I said, 'Well, Miklós, my dear friend we have to go as well as we had a very busy day yesterday, and we feel tired as well.'

'Zoltán has offered that they will give us a lift to our apartment which on the way to their house on *Rózsadomb* (Rosehill). We both welcomed Zoltán's offer, and we all said goodnight to Fifi and Miklós.'

I said to Miklós, 'I will see you on Saturday at the Synagogue.'

Yes, goodnight to you all and thank you for your support and company today at the theatre and here in the coffeehouse. Goodnight to you all.

In the taxi Zoltán asked me if we would accept an invitation for an evening meal at their house on Saturday.

Rebekah and I said yes that would be wonderful we would look forward to that.

'By the time, we have got to our apartment on *Király utca* it was already in the early hour of 2:30 in the morning and thanking Zoltán and Johanna for their company, and we said we will look forward to see you on Saturday at your house.'

'We have waved goodbye to them as the taxi drove off with them.'

At last finally, we have managed to get upstairs to our apartment and fallen into bed.

I have thanked Rebekah for her fantastic support for today at the business meeting and for the rest of the evening with our friends. 'You have looked so beautiful tonight, and I was so very proud of you the way you looked and with the confidence you were wearing that new dress I can understand why people have looked at you all night at the theatre and at the New York Coffeehouse.'

'Thank you to be my wife Rebekah, I love you. Goodnight, my love.'

'Thank you to be my husband Gabriel and thank you for this memorable evening. I love you too, goodnight.'

She has buried herself into my arm, and we just both drifted to sleep.

Chapter 40

It Is Friday, 22 July, Packing for the Last Time in Budapest

After an eventful day and a more tiring night we have slept in a little bit longer than usual as we have no other commitment for meetings or sightseeing activities for this day.

It was already nine in the morning, and we were still in our pyjamas and housecoats. Rebekah has prepared some breakfast for us omelettes with cheese and some salami with fresh bread. Just try to empty our ice cubed full of food as we are leaving on Monday. I have to organise a taxi for early Monday morning as our train leave from Keleti Main Station at 7:23 in the morning. I thought that I will do that when we are going to do some shopping a presence for friends and relatives in Munkács.

I know that there is a major Taxi rank at the corner of Király utca and Deák Ferenc tér. We have packed almost everything what we are taking with us with the exception of clothes we are going to wear for the weekend and for all the engagements like going to Zoltán's house for a Saturday super and for Sunday when the removal company come to collect box full of small sculptures from my artists friends, my books, and other heavier things what we cannot take with us as hand luggage.

I thought that I will leave some beddings like bed sheets, duvets pillows and things I thought that for a start it will help the Krenczberger to settle. Then in time when they can change it for their taste. Also, as I have promised that I will leave my Mezuzah with the scripture on the doorpost, and I will get one for our new house in Munkács. I have only taken down my engraved name plate from our front door which is really not much use for them.

At least their synagogue on Rombach utca is just a short distance walk.

I am really blessed by Mr Krenczberger's, Rabbi Simon Rozenberg who was so nice that he called in to the Dohány utca Synagogue, and he has been praising me to Chief Rabbi Low for I've been so helpful.

Well, Rebekah has finally got ready for the day I know we weren't in a hurry as we have no other official engagements just us for a change. She has taken my advice to wear a low heel sandal for today as we are going to walk much of the day for the presence that we are going to get for our friends in Munkács.

Just walking towards Deák tér to organise the taxi and then we will take the underground from Deák tér to Octagon stop and started to walk towards the New York Coffee house way where all the good shops are for the ladies and for all the furniture shops are where we could get some brochures to take with us which will giving some ideas how to furnish our new house in Munkács.

Our plans were to visit; Parisi Nagy Áruház, Corvin Nagy Áruház, Divatcsarnok, Góya Áruház.

Each time I have passed this building a couple of blocks away from my apartment I always been fascinated with this Reményi Mihály music shop on 58-60 Király utca which is advertised that the largest music shop in Hungary. With all those beautiful grand and upright pianos but I have never been inspired to go in as all the instruments were shiny black polished. I always been looking for a natural wood polished finish cabinet after all we are in the modern style of Art Nouveau with much more modern styles.

When we got to the Música Rt. Zongoraterem on 49 Erzsébet Körút which is next to the Royal Szálloda (Hotel) just looking through the shop window I was fascinated with those beautiful grand pianos. I felt I have to go inside and just touch them, and I thought that how beautiful it would be in our new house in Munkács. The salesperson showed me all those nice pianos, but one particularly has stood out and has caught my attention was an English made Baby Grand Piano in an Art Deco style called Strohmenger. I looked at Rebekah and I noticed that she has fallen in love with this stylish modern instrument.

'Gabriel, are you thinking of buying of this masterpiece grand piano? But none of us play piano.'

'Yes, my darling I know but we could learn on it. Just think Rebekah our children could learn to play on it.'

'That is true, Gabriel, and I don't know if anyone would have anything like this in Munkács.'

'But we have to match our furniture to this beautiful case.'

'But I know your Papa's friend's company can.'

'Do you mean Sutyai Béla Furniture Company of Munkács?'

'Exactly, that is what I mean they can make anything just remember the Parliament Building in Ungvár they did all the furnishing for them?'

'Yes, you right as we have commissioned them to do our kitchen and our bedroom furniture already so they could do our lounge furniture as well to match it up with the grand piano style of Art Deco. Or pick something out from these brochures we have collected from furniture shops and from Bauhaus Magazine.'

'But do you think we can afford this piano Gabriel?'

'Yes, Rebekah, we can, as I have calculated already with my successful meeting and contracts I have secured during this trip and all of our finance will cover much more than just the cost of this piano. We have just sold my apartment here in Budapest as well.'

'That is true Gabriel, yes that is true my love.'

'Yes, I like this piano, and I really would like to have it in our house.'

Then she gave me a hug and then I said now, 'Just leave it with me I will make a deal with the owner of this Piano Salon.'

I have asked the salesman to call for the owner of Musica Piano Salon a gentleman greeted us, and he introduced himself as Károly Neuhold.

Mr Neuhold was very nice and knowledgeable of pianos and the gentleman told me that the company is manufacturing new upright and grand pianos as well in Vendel utca 7å9. In District 9. Budapest.

After I explained to Mr Neuhold that we would like to move the piano to Munkács he said he has a very good friend who is a piano tuner and technician who lives in Munkács too, and he has been an agent for Musica Rt. for some years and Mr Neuhold will send our piano with his piano transporting company which he does deliver already to Munkács and to Ungvár as well.

After as I was promising to Mr Neuhold that as the Officer of Art and Culture for the County of Munkács and Beregszász that I would promote his business in this region.

And furthermore, I have promised that I will organise an exhibition for his piano company in these regions if we could do a deal on this piano.

Mr Neuhold liked the idea, and he told me that he will sell this grand piano to me at cost as a discount if I would honour of our future business commitment. When I told him I wasn't a hurry to have them delivered just yet because the builder is still working on our house.

Mr Neuhold suggested that he will get in touch with his piano tuner friend and Mr Neuhold will send a lorry load of pianos, and he will included our piano along with the other ones for this suggested exhibition and sale in Munkács.

'I told this news to Rebekah that we have just bought this beautiful piece of furniture and piano with a matching stool and furthermore Mr Neuhold will deliver our piano to Munkács.'

We have made an agreement on the sale, and I have told him that I will instruct my solicitor Mr Schwartz to settle the bill next week as we are going back to Munkács on Monday morning.

I have given him our home and my office address where the piano should be delivered and then Mr Neuhold gave us a brochure and an instruction booklet of how to keep and maintain the piano. We said goodbye to Mr Neuhold, and he indicated that he might come along for this piano exhibition sale in Munkács.

This was helpful as we could show Mr Béla Sutyai the style of furniture we would like to be made to match our new Strohmenger Baby Grand Piano.

After we left the Musica Piano Salon Rebekah got excited on the street she has put her arm in mine, and she was behaving like a little girl. 'Gabriel, we are going to have a piano in our house and not just any piano it is an English made piano with such a unique cabinet which the kind you only see in Hollywood movies.'

'Yes, darling I don't think anybody would have anywhere such a piano in the whole region.'

Rebekah was in her form with the shopping she had to stop in front of every ladies dress, hat, and shoe shop. By the time we got to the *Blaha Lujza tér* we were both very tired and hungry. But I was mainly thirsty in the baking heat. We passed the New York Kávéház entrance and Rebekah asked if we could go inside just one more time before we are going back home. I thought it was a good idea, and we ordered a soup and a salad. Rebekah said I just would like to smell the distinct strong smell of the tobacco and the ground coffee one more time.

When we walked in, we have managed to bump into some of my old friends from the press as they were writing out their reports for the evening typesetting to get it ready for the street sellers by the morning.

Some of them couldn't believe that I have married, and I am moving to live in Munkács.

Rebekah said, 'Gabriel, this place looks fantastic equally as at night when all the chandeliers are in fully illuminated.'

'You know Gabriel I don't know why but I do feel here home as I feel in Munkács too.'

'Yes, my darling this place is very bohemian and active 24 hour long. But there are many parts of Budapest where I deliberately didn't take you not because they are the working-class districts of Budapest, but it isn't glamorous, like where the Musica Piano Factory is based is on *Vendel utca* is called *Ferenc Város*.'

'But I suppose every town and city around the world has the same kind of working-class area, but where I just didn't want to take you to such areas when we have just been married and really, we are on our honeymoon, I want you to take back home nice and interesting memories with you.'

By the time we got home with all the extra shopping what Rebekah managed to find that she really missed or couldn't get in the many shops of Belváros.

After our arrival someone was knocking on our door when I have opened it a nice old Orthodox Jewish man stood there along with Mr Krenczberger. He introduced himself as Rabbi Simon Rozenberg from the Rombach utca Pray house – Synagogue.

Then I have realised this is the Rabbi who has praised me to Chief Rabbi Low about my good-hearted action towards the Krenczberger family.

'Please come inside, Rabbi. It is our blessing to welcome you in our apartment, of course until Sunday. May I present to you my wife Rebekah.'

'Oh, it is very good to meet you, Rebekah.'

Rabbi Rosenberg said, 'I can't stay long as I have to prepare for the Sabbath. I only came to give my blessing for both of you for helping Mr Krenczberger and I know that you are leaving your Mezuzah behind, and we thought that we should replace it to you so I would like to present you with this blessed Mezuzah for your new home in Munkács. Also, I would like to give my blessing to both of you on your journey in life together as husband and wife.'

Rebekah and I felt very good while the Rabbi prayed for us and when he finished with his blessing he looked at the table where he saw two candles and the wine with the Kalács which was prepared by Rebekah to celebrate our Sabbath he said, 'Now I must go to prepare the celebration for my congregation.'

'Mr Krenczberger handed over a small package to Rebekah and both of them wished us a Good Shabbes. Rebekah and I responded to their good wishes with our Sabbath Shalom.'

After our visitors had gone Rebekah opened Mr Krenczberger parcel, and she unpacked it then she became emotionally touched by the presence of ladies lingerie underwear and stocking of Bear Brand Hosiery made in Great Brittan. 'You know Gabriel this is very exclusive and good quality brand only the rich people ware this brand of under wares and nylon stockings.'

'Well, darling, it is very nice of them but the main thing that I can see that they have gave you something special which each time when you wear it, you'll remember them.'

'Yes, I will Gabriel, but compared with the quality what I have bought in the shop in Váci utca this brand is the most expensive and superior.'

'That is good I am very pleased for you darling but now it is time for us to celebrate our last Sabbath here in this apartment. It was some time ago when we have celebrated our first time and now it looks as we are going to celebrate it at the last time here in this apartment.'

Then we both went to the bathroom, to clean ourselves then we came back to the kitchen and prepared for the Sabbath celebration.

After Rebekah's lighting of the candles, she waved her hands over the candles, welcoming in the Sabbath. Then she covered her eyes, so as not to see the candles then she recited the blessing:

Barukh ata Adonai Eloheinu, Melekh ha'olam, asher kid'shanu b'mitzvotav v'tzivanu l'hadlik ner shel Sabbath.

She removed her hands from her eyes, and she looked at the candles, which has illuminated her face and completing the mitzvah of lighting the candles.

Then I held the Kiddush cup and thanked The Lord for the wine:

Baruch Ata Adonai Eloheinu Melech Haolam Borei P'Ri Hagafen.

Then I removed the cover from the two challah loaves, lifting them while reciting the blessing:

Barukh ata Adonai Eloheinu melekh ha'olam hamotzi lehem min ha'aretz.

I have ripped the challah into pieces and gave a peace to Rebekah then I said, 'My darling Rebekah this our last family meal together here in Budapest.'

'Sabbath Shalom, my dear wife Rebekah.'

'Sabbath Shalom, my dear husband Gabriel.'

We have enjoyed the food which Rebekah has prepared for the Sabbath and finished the rest of the wine, and at the end of our meal, then we did the washing up of the dishes together then went back to our lounge for a relaxing chat.

The whole evening was so emotional, we didn't really speak much only the one which was concerned of the day's event with shopping and or our tomorrow's planned engagements or commitments after the Sabbath Service at the Grand Synagogue in Dohány utca. We have to collect Rebekah's new passport form Mr Schneider then probably will have a last drink with Fifi and Miklós somewhere in the Belváros.

'I guess we did have a good time with Miklós and Fifi during the past week.'

'My Lord, I will miss them.'

But then again it is everything with our lives now will be in Munkács. So let's concentrate on that. As many people count on my leadership and direction, effectively my drive and vision to take things forward in Munkács.

It was a strange feeling moving from room to room to see bare walls with a clean patch on the wall where the pictures hung and protected the wall from stains. Even Rebekah's cheering up attitude wasn't making me much happier. She just walked to me and sat on my lap, stroke and kissed me on my head, and she said, 'My dear Gabriel, I hope this sadness will be left behind on Monday as we will have a much brighter and prosperous future to look forward to. I will be there for you, and I always love you whatever is the circumstances will bring in our way.'

I felt I shouldn't be like this particularly on the day of Sabbath. I felt guilty in a way to feeling pity for myself which has been picked up by Rebekah as well. I felt she had a guilty feeling to taking me away from my well-established existence here in Budapest.

I don't know if the physical effort of walking or the alcohol which made us both to drift into sleep. But we both slept with our protector Angels.

Chapter 41

Last Saturday with Friends and Supper at Zoltán's House

Having slept well I have try to sneak into the bathroom without waking Rebekah who was still sleeping with angels but she must have smelled the coffee which I have put on a tray and served it in bed for her with a kiss.

'Are you still sad about you a selling this apartment?'

'No, I don't. I have thought of it this morning, and I have realised it that this sale would come sooner or later. This is just a place to sleep and the rest of the times you are all over Budapest doing your job. But from now on I will have a beautiful wife and a home to go to which is much more than this apartment or any other place in the whole wide world.'

'I am so pleased for you Gabriel that you take this moving with a better attitude.'

On our way to the Dohány utca Synagogue I have praised Rebekah's new hat with a yellow and green bow that was hanging down at the back of the brim.

Fifi and Miklós were at the entrance of the synagogue already again as usual. At our arrival he stopped the conversation and welcomed us with a smile and jokingly telling his friends that look out here is the 'another one who has bite the dust' and leaving us.

Fifi rushed to giving a big hug to Rebekah than they have gone upstairs to the balcony and Miklós and I just put on our Kippah and Tallit and walked into our usual seat at the back of the synagogue.

At the end of the service, I asked Miklós if we could meet up somewhere like at the Pilvax as Rebekah and I have some last-minute business with Chief Rabbi Immánuel Lőw.

'Yes, no problem, Gabriel, just don't be too late.'

We have met up with Mr Schneider at Chief Rabbi Immánuel Lőw's office and Rebekah has signed the final document and also her new Hungarian Passport in front of Mr Schneider and Rabbi Lőw which both of them countersigned to make it official.

They both have congratulated Rebekah to be an officially registered Hungarian Citizen.

After Mr Schneider left, Chief Rabbi Immánuel Lőw asked me to stay behind just for a few minutes.

'Look, Gabriel, I have to admit that I have an uneasy feel about your ability to carry out a task we have appointed you with. You had a reputation of a bohemian and flamboyant individual, but I have to say that I have misread you and, in the end, you have carried out your mission with distinction.

'I was very impressed with your presentation to our organisation meeting on Thursday which all members of the panel shared the appraisal of your quality in confidence. One thing which notably impressed the panel members was the way you find yourself around so well in any circumstances. Also, we have been very impressed with you, Rebekah the knowledge and your leadership quality.'

'Your marriage has been made in Heaven and arranged by Angels of the Most Eternal one.

'Looking back what I have experienced with your professionalism will be a loss for my Synagogue membership, but it is a definite gain for your new community in Munkács. Our organisations will still count on your expertise, and we will accept your judgement on any recommendations with regards to our organisations. Also, we will continually give you all the support you will require in the Transcarpathian region.'

'Now let me pray for you two and may; The Lord God of Israel protect you from your enemies, and he may bless you with wisdom to serve His people with all your mind and your soul, Amen.'

'Hopefully, I'll see you soon both of you, now Rebekah and Gabriel go in peace the Lord be with you. Shalom.'

As we were walking away from the Great Synagogue to catch up with our friends Fifi and Miklós none of us has spoken much as the Chief Rabbi Immánuel Lőw's words were still on our thoughts and our hearts.

We didn't even feel the heat as we walked hand in hand like two teenagers. The Pilvax is just some ten minutes away from the synagogue, but we got there in a minute.

'Miklós on our arrival said jokingly thank God you are here I thought I have to drink on our own. I hope everything is alright with you as Chief Rabbi Immánuel Lőw called you in for a meeting?'

'Yes, Miklós everything is just fine it was only his blessing for our journey.'

'Oh, that is very good of him. Rebekah would you like a spritzer? I know what you are having Gabriel, it's a pint of cool Dreher beer. Yes?'

'Yes, of course, after all we are brothers in arms with Dreher. We both laughed and placed our orders with the waiter. During our meal Rebekah and I have reminded them that we expect them for our wedding which is on 11 September.'

Fifi said, 'Trust me, Gabriel, I will remind him well before of that date.'

'I know you will, you are truly a great couple we will miss your company in Munkács.'

'But I could organise an event for you Miklós in Munkács either before or after our wedding. What you say to that?'

Fifi and Rebekah become very excited, and they have already started planning for that event.

'Yes, Gabriel, that would work out well. I like your idea.'

'Miklós, you could get a government sponsorship for this promotion of Hungarian Culture in Munkács.'

'I suggest you should talk to Chief Rabbi Immánuel Lőw ask his advice, and I know he will advise you where to start from.'

By the time, we have left the Pilvax and were heading towards Gerbeaud on Váci utca as we have done this routine on many occasions, I just felt that this is the last time that I have walked this street with friends. I just didn't know why but this feeling was very strong. May it will be as I am moving to Munkács? I didn't have answers to that. But now we are among friends, and we are having a good time together. The girls were still looking into every shop window along till we got to Vörösmarty tér. Miklós was telling me of his financial situation, and he just doesn't know which way he should approach to settle down like I have.

'I think Miklós my situation was down to faith and destiny.'

We've only found a table for four of us under the great Platan tree all the parasols were occupied.

It was a well-planned routine to have a full meal than work it off with a gentle walk into our favoured coffee house where we have a relaxed coffee with soda water and a most delicious cake in the whole world.

I have to look at the time as we have a dinner engagement with Johanna and Zoltán on Rózsadomb.

We walked together as far as Deák tér where Fifi and Miklós got on the tram, and we crossed the road to Király utca and were heading home to our apartment. I have called into Mr Katz shop to get some more food for tomorrow's breakfast and a couple of bottles of champagne one to take with us to Zoltán this evening and one for us to drink for our last evening in our apartment and in Budapest.

I have wrapped the bottle into a nice wrapping paper and then I was getting ready for the evening.

'Is it far away the Rózsadomb, Gabriel?'

'No, it's only on the other side of the River Danube. Will get a taxi at Deak tér where I am going to get a nice bouquet of flowers for Johanna.'

'You know, Gabriel, I like Budapest very much to see the strong Jewish community and you know everybody and everything here I feel that everybody treating me well in respect not like in Munkács where your ethnic affiliation has been challenged.'

'Look, my darling Rebekah, here in the big city which is the Capital of Hungary there are many different ethnic origins living together. The population is such a large number that nobody knows each other, and therefore, they are too busy getting on with their life, so they don't care if you are Jewish or German or originated from any other national background. They don't know how much money you have or where you live. But in a smaller town like Munkács everybody knows everybody and also how wealthy you really are.'

'Rebekah just put her arms around my neck and said; you know Gabriel to see so many beautiful buildings and some magnificent wealth even the Danube is much greater than the Latorna, and I have been treated by everybody so well, but I feel that I am homesick and after one week away from home I miss Munkács and the people I know there, mainly Papa. Rita and everything which I feel is familiar to me.'

Then she kissed me with such passion which I felt was just cover up her insecurity. When I felt her tears on my face, I felt really sorry for her being in a strange city where she cannot identify herself with.

'It is just one more day darling, and we will be back home to Munkács again.'

'Then she looked at me and said, But we wouldn't be able to sleep together again until our marriage has been completed under the Chuppah.'

'Yes, that is true, but we still have our new house which will give us all the pleasure that we seek.'

'You know I have never thought of that. Yes, you are a genius, Gabriel.'

'Now just look at the time my love we really have to get changed and move on. You know I don't like to be late. You are respecting people with your timekeeping.'

We got the flowers and the taxi up to Zoltán place in Rózsadomb. Just looked at his business card, and I asked the driver to take us to 5, *Vérhalom tér*. He has driven us through the Chain Bridge down on Fő utca, up onto the hill to Vérhalom tér.

'What beautiful houses are here, Gabriel. This must be the wealthier part of Budapest.'

'Oh, yes, darling. This is where the middleclass elite of the Hungarian society live.'

'So you say Johanna and Zoltán are really that rich?'

'I don't know my darling, but we will soon found out that.'

The taxi stops at Johanna and Zoltán house which is a beautiful two-story villa with roof bedrooms and a sloped driveway to the garage under the property in the heart of Rózsadomb. A large park in front of the property and an equally large garden in the back completed with a well-designed park style garden.

I rang the bell and a maid let us in, and I felt that I have been in a situation before, and I know there is wealth and class. I thought there must be a butler as well if there is a maid. I was right he welcomed us and led us into the drawing room where Johanna and Zoltán welcomed us.

I have presented the bottle of champagne and the flowers to Johanna. I felt there was a very friendly vibration from both of them which means that there is an inherited wealth and not a pretensioners attitude behind the welcoming.

We've been welcomed by our host and the butler served us with a cocktail which was a kind of Gin-based I've been told it's called Gin-Martini. It was quite a refreshing cold drink in the Summer heat.

Zoltán said he has learned the mix of this drink when he was on business in England.

Johanna has put her arm into Rebekah's arm, and they went out to the terrace then into the garden. The back of the building which has overlooked their well-

317

maintained garden was very impressive. While the two ladies went into the garden and left Zoltán, and I stayed on the terrace and sat down into a comfortable garden chairs, and we started talking business.

'What is the approximate specification of power rating for your conveyors Gabriel?'

'Well, I have very little of this kind of machinery but the only knowledge I have learned on the conveyor that there are three major specifications they are working with is: Bolt density, capacity, and 1000 kg per speed. It depends what kind of materials: Liquid, semiliquid, or solid materials you would move. So the RMP is vital which should be able to be adjusted with a gearbox control. I would guess we would need for our conveyor elevators in power rate between 20kW to 40kW electric motors.'

'I don't expect you to know but a major Governmental Initiative project has been planned by the Agricultural Ministry and of course by the Hungarian Government as well over the regulation of the River Tisza and of the irrigation project on the Alföld.'

'Look Zoltán this information is very confidential indeed my contact could be in grave trouble if this information would go public.'

'On my return I am going to get in touch with a company in England who is manufacturing this kind of method machineries and hopefully I could get more technical information with regards to this manufacturing and tips on its operation.'

'This information you have just given me I know Ganz Works have already a good line of production line finish electric motors. It is true we don't have the gearbox attachment to the motor but that wouldn't be a problem to design to the motor as we have the facility within our factory.'

'Well, Gabriel, I can promise you that I will keep this information that you have given me in confidence, but I will keep my eye on this development over the Tisza program. As you can expect that we have our well 'oiled' confidents at the Hungarian Ministries.'

'I am surprised, Zoltán, that the ministry has not been consulted with your company over this major project.'

The butler came to the terrace and advised Zoltán that the dinner will be served in fifteen minutes.

I commented on the standard of their lifestyle it is really exquisite.

'Thank you, Gabriel, but all this has been inherited from Johanna's grandfather Mr Donát Bánki (N 58) it was his residency.'

'Do you mean the Donát Bánki one of the greatest Hungarian inventors?'

'Yes, that is right. I was working for Ganz Works, and I have met Johanna at the company's Christmas Ball and just like you we have fallen in love and here we are, we have been married for two years now.'

We went to join the 'girls' in the garden and told them that the dinner will be served in 5 minutes.

Rebekah and Johanna walked in front of us still chatting away. The temperature was cooler now.

We've been served the finest wines from Eger and Tokay and the meal was truly delicious.

At the end of the meal we have retired to the drawing room where Zoltán served his favourite champagne Hungária, and the social chatting has continued between four of us till late.

'This is my favourite champagne as well as Zoltán's.'

I have noticed it Gabriel when I have opened your present. It just shows a good taste.

The time has been running away with us it has passed midnight already, and we thanked Johanna and Zoltan for being such a great host for tonight. They faithfully promised that they will come to our wedding for 11 September.

They have ordered a taxi for us, and we were getting down from this beautiful part of Budapest into our little apartment on Király utca.

Chapter 42
Last Day in Budapest, and Evening at Gundel

On our way from Zoltán and Johanna's house none of us made any comment on our hosts and on their wealth as we just absorbed the beautifully illuminated villas, by the time we got to the Danube's Margit rakpart we had the full view of the illuminated Hungarian Parliament building and this romantic picture we would missed out from our very full and busy sightseeing week in Budapest but now it was there before us in full.

Then we crossed the River Danube on *Széchenyi Lánchíd* going down on *Gróf Tisza István* utca to Deák tér and up on to 31 Király utca, to our small apartment. Which is still ours for two more days then we have to say goodbye to it and to my yellow canapé and as well to all with those memories.

I just managed to open the front entrance to the apartment block, and we were making our way up to the first floor. The summer breeze kept the courtyard very pleasant and cool away from the choking heat of the street. The first thing we did when we entered our room was to open all the windows for a short time while it refreshed the room and removed the stale air. I remembered that we have to close it before we go to bed as Évi néni always wanted to hear what we are doing privately.

I have looked at my ice cabinet, and I noticed that only one bottle of champagne is left on ice which I was going to keep till Sunday evening which would be our last night in our apartment and in Budapest as well.

Neither of us really wanted anymore drink as we had quite a bit this evening at Zoltán's house, so we just settled with an ice cool soda water from the 'ice box'.

Rebekah sat back in the armchair and gazed out of the window and said.

'You know Gabriel I have always dreamed of living in a house like Johanna and Zoltán with their own staff and a privileged lifestyle.'

'My darling Rebekah, you have a very loving family too. Your Papa has given you so much, and he has supported you all the way with your education and in a lifestyle which a lot of people would wish for to have or just a half of that.'

'I know, Gabriel, but Johanna doesn't have to do anything as her maid will do it for her.'

'I hope you have noted during our supper that both of them 'cried out' for someone like us, as they have very few friends, because their wealth is holding others from associating with them socially. They are very rich, and the same privileged people are much older than them.'

'Johanna was absolutely excited at you as someone who she can have a conversation with you as both of you are well educated and have the same interest in this modern world.'

Zoltán told me that they had a fantastic time on Thursday with Miklós Fifi, and us. They were walking on the streets of Budapest with a group of people whom they have just met, relaxed, and they were just having fun. And at the New York Kávéház where we have met up with all those famous people. 'You know they always wished to have something exciting like that.'

'Just come away from their stricken world where they are locked in.'

'I know, Gabriel, as Johanna told me that she feels like a bird in her 'golden cage', but she wants freedom and fun with her own aged girls. She is a Jewess like me, and the people are very conservative around her. I told her that I felt the same thing until I have met you, Gabriel. Then my life has changed you have released me from my 'cage'. I am glad that you have invited them to our wedding, Gabriel.'

'Yes, I like both of them very much too. But Zoltán has to come to Munkács on business as we are going to be supplied with electric motors for our new venture by Ganz Works. Then each time they will come to Munkács we will meet up with them again. After all Zoltán is originally from Munkács.'

'Yes, that will be great we can plan much more fun with them when they come and visit us in the future. We can go skiing in the Wintertime to the Carpathian Mountains around us. Or we can have great parties in our house.'

'I can see that new baby grand piano we've just bought will be in the great centre point. Just let you know, Rebekah, that I have told Miklós when they are coming to our wedding. I will be able to organise some poetry evening with Miklós in the county of Munkács and Beregi—Ugocsa major towns. Of course, this is within the Hungarian Educational and Foreign Ministries initiatives of whom is promoting Hungarian Culture and Language in Transcarpathia.'

'That is a very good point and great idea, Gabriel. But now let's go to bed my darling it is half past one already.'

I have closed the windows jut to stop others from sharing our enjoyment of life behind closed doors.

'You know my angel Gabriel I am all ready for an enjoyment, please take me to heaven again.'

Next morning Rebekah got up before me, and she prepared a breakfast for both of us. She has used up all the eggs and salami she has find in the ice cabinet.

At 12 noon, prompt the removal company knocked on our door to collect all my boxes full of documents, photographs, books, and paintings along with my other clothes. I have left all bedding, towels, and other household necessities for the Krenczberger's. Rebekah has made a fresh cup of coffee for the delivery man and within one hour they have removed all my worldly goods.

There was really nothing else to do until 7 o'clock in the evening as we have booked a table at Gundel's Restaurant for our last day in Budapest.

Rebekah ask me for as she would like to walk one more time on the *Ferenc József Sétány* (Parade) from the *Lánchíd to Petőfi tér*. She has been mesmerised with the vast space of splendored view of the Old Town of Buda.

'I thought that is a very good idea as I could have another of my favourite cakes at Gerbeaud, who knows when I shall have the opportunity again to taste my favourite cake.'

We walked far as Chain Bridge, Rebekah still can't have enough of the scenery, and I suggested jokingly that she should move over here into Budapest.

Then she looked at me with such an eye that I have never seen her before and with such on emotion what I have sensed in her anger.

'I was just joking my love. So sorry.'

Then Rebekah has realised that her reaction was spontaneous but unusual in our relationship which I have never experienced this kind of response before from her and as she has responded with her quick temper.

'Rebekah in a much quieter voice apologised when she realised the way she responded and told me that her body time of the month just has started now.'

I thought that makes sense of her behaviour. This hot weather doesn't help her emotional state.

'Would you be alright to take this long walk, or you would like to stop at Gerbeaud for a coffee?'

'Yes, Gabriel, I would like that.'

'She put her arm into mine and walked on the parade as a lady who has no troubles at all.' But I think deep down she was struggling greatly with the uncontrollable situation and with the heat.

We called into Gerbeaud for a coffee and a cake then she went straight to the Ladies Powder room, when she has come back to join me at the terrace she has felt better already.

Then I suggested to go back to the apartment and have a rest. Walking by the taxi rank I asked the operator to book a taxi for 6:30 from 31 Király utca as our train to Munkács will leave at 7:30 a.m. It gave me a reassuring feeling that we won't miss our train in the morning.

As we got back to our apartment Rebekah went into the bathroom to take care of herself, and when she came out, to join me she was smiling again and looked more relaxed.

'You know Gabriel this is the worst time for a period in this heat and away from home where you can take care of this very uncomfortable situation. Thank you for your understanding.'

'Will you be all right tomorrow my love? It is a long journey to Munkács.'

'Yes, Gabriel, I will be prepared for that. Unfortunately, this just happened as we walked in the very hot cobblestoned street, and I was unprepared for it.'

She laid down on the bed, and I went to the bathroom to get a cool wet towel for her forehead.

'Oh, this is good I am feeling better already, Gabriel.'

I sat in the armchair, and we both have fallen asleep. When I woke up just after five and noticed that Rebekah was getting ready in the bathroom. When she realised that I was awake she said.

'I didn't want to wake you up when you were sleeping so peacefully.'

I just looked at Rebekah, and I thought I was must of still dreaming as she looked an absolute stunning in the new dress she got from Clara Rothchild. She has that star quality as she walks just like someone out from the silver screen.

'Darling, you look strikingly beautiful! you will turn heads in the restaurant this evening.'

I stopped her just for a minute as we have to say farewell to our neighbours.

And particularly to Évi néni as we would probably get back home late from the restaurant. 'Évi néni emotionally asked me if I ever will come back and visit her.'

'In reply I said hopefully, God willing I will.'

I broke away from her hugging and said sorry, but our taxi is waiting for us.

We got into the taxi, and I felt easier as I have said goodbye to Évi néni.

As we have a grand arrival at the restaurant with a taxi which has pulled in front of the restaurant's entrance the doorman opened the taxi door and welcomed us into the Gundel restaurant. (N 59)

Morris Hofmann, the Headwaiter, has recognised our arrival. (How could anybody not notice one like Rebekah in that dress tonight) and he walked us to our table in the Kerthelyiség (Restaurant Garden). Morris said I hope this table will be cool enough for you then he pulled the chair for Rebekah and whispered into her ear how beautiful you look. He said, 'Just look all those people here they were following you from the minute you have entered the restaurant.'

I thanked him for his charming words.

It felt so romantic as the dimmed coloured lights and flickering candles on each table sparkled on the crystal glasses and the rest of the light was supplied by the moon. So how much more romantic surroundings could you wish for?

The gypsy band was playing some beautiful song which lyrics was a kind of compliment to my wife her entrance and to her look.

Rebekah has enjoyed the attention that she was getting, and she just fitted in well into the top Hungarian Restaurant's designer decoration.

'Gabriel, what is the Primás singing about with such passion?'

'Oh, you don't want to know that my darling he is just admiring your stunning look.'

'I didn't know that you are speaking Gypsy as well.'

'No, my darling I don't but I know this song and the lyric is very naughty.'

Morris came back to us with his waiter and served us with a welcome glass of French champagne.

He recommended a three-course menu for us and of course with the signature desert which is the Gundel Pancake. He has recommended the best wine from Tokay the Hárslevelű.

I have appreciated the Primas discretion, as he didn't came to our table while we had our meal.

He walked to us and introduced himself as Mihály Ráduly and in a typical Gypsy manner asked us if we have a favourite song?

Rebekah and I both replied, 'The Monty Csárdás, please. We have been played this '*nóta*' (music) in Ungvár by Primas Tibor Rácz and that music is reminding us to a very special night in Ungvár.'

Mr Ráduly asked us if we know Mr Tibor Rácz?

'Yes, of course, we do, in fact. We have seen him three days ago playing at the New York Kávéház.'

'Ah, Tibor is my best friend, as we are both originally from Debrecen. I will get in touch with Tibor at the New York Kávéház, as I haven't seen Tibor for a long time. Thank you to letting me know.'

That evening Mihály Ráduly has played for two of us for free which has impressed Rebekah very much. The *Prímás* got into Rebekah's ear so close that he almost touched her hat. All his song choices was very romantic. At the end of each nota we all with the other diners were applauded enthusiastically. As the *Prímás* walked from table to table you could see that people pulled some money into his violin bow while he was playing.

Morris happily commented on the Gypsy band performance, 'You know Gabriel I am happy when the diners are happy.'

They have been well entertained by the Gypsy band. I can measure this on the success on the alcohol consumption of the diners.

By the end of the night, the temperature has dropped, and the waiters were offering a blanket to the ladies in the restaurant just to keep them warm.

As we were leaving the Gundel Restaurant I suggested to Rebekah to walk through the Hősök tere (Heroes Square) and catch the underground at the corner of Andrássy út Hero's square.

Rebekah said, 'Gabriel, I thank you for this wonderful experience that I have had tonight. I will remember this romantically beautiful night for ever which is our last night here in this wonderful City.'

The Hősök Tere was fully illuminated along with the Art Galleries on both sides of the square this was even more impressive than in daylight.

'You know Gabriel it looks as this ten day we have spent here would have been one month of full of excitement that I have been involved with. And mostly you were with me all the time holding my hand and you have flooded me with all the worldly and Heavenly gifts what anybody could wish for. Thank you!'

'You more than welcome, any time my love, and my beautiful wife, I love you, Rebekah Grósz.'

At home, we have put our travelling clothes on the chairs with Rebekah's new Hungarian Passport, then we have packed everything else which we were going to take with us for the journey.

Then when everything was done, I have opened the last bottle of Hungária Champagne which was helping us to sleep better. Or just an any excuse for us, just to have that drink.

Unfortunately, we have to respect Rebekah state, and we have to postpone our cuddling in bed for some other time. We have a passionate goodnight kiss, and we wished each other a goodnight.

'Sleep well, my darling Rebekah.'

'Yes, my darling Angel, you too. Good night.'

Chapter 43

Journey from Budapest to Munkács

I just couldn't sleep well despite the champagne we have drunk with Rebekah last night I've reacted to every single noise of the night. I was worried that we would have overslept and would miss our train to Munkács.

I keep looking at Rebekah who slept in my arms like a little girl curled up and holding me over my chest with one arm and holding onto her duvet with her other arm. Really it looked comical, but I have enjoyed the view of my beautiful and loving wife.

As I was drifting in and out of sleep suddenly, I have woken up by the alarm clock at 6:00 am.

Rebekah got ready first with her shower and then I, as she needed more time e to get ready.

I have walked from room to room just to absorb and store the memories of the past many years as this place was my home and refuge. I felt very emotional to see it at the last time.

We have left a geranium plant on the table with some encouraging words and wishing them a blessed home for their family.

Rebekah came and touched me on my shoulder and said, 'This is your past Gabriel and here I am your future. Come we have to go as the taxi is waiting for us.'

I have closed and locked the door for the last time picked up our suitcases hand luggage, and I have put the house keys in an envelope and put it through the letterbox as we were leaving the apartment.

As we have arrived at the *Keleti* Main Station this has brought back some memory just as I have been leaving Budapest and Hungary some month ago. I didn't know where I was going to land and what was waiting for me there in the unknown part of the world. But this time is different I know where I am going to, and I know what is waiting for me when I am getting there.

We hired a porter and collected our tickets for the first-class coach.

As soon as we have settled into our compartment the train has started to move out on time at 7:30 a.m. heading to our first stop of Záhony.

The train pulling out slowly then we got to Rákosfalva it has started picking up speed and by the time we've got to Zugló it was running with full speed. When the guard called into our compartment to check out tickets, and he was inviting us to the diners coach.

The train was running so effortlessly and evenly. If they are going at this speed, we should be in Záhony by midday. 'Would you like to have a breakfast my love?'

'I would like a cup of coffee, Gabriel.'

Alright then let's have a coffee in the diners coach. I have locked our compartment just to be safe.

Some passengers have already occupied the diners coach but there was a table for us which was included in part of the ticket with a reserved table.

I ordered a smoked salmon with scrambled eggs and toast.

Rebekah said it sound good, and I would like the same for me please.

'What would you like to drink?'

'We both ordered coffee with milk.'

Just looking through the window we noted as we have left Budapest, that there are less and less built up areas. We are travelling on a different route this time then when we came to Budapest.

After an hour we have finished with our breakfast and went back to our compartment.

Rebekah kept looking at her new Hungarian Passport and with a smile on her face she said, 'This is just wonderful Gabriel I am a Hungarian Citizen with a Hungarian Passport.'

'Yes, my darling and soon you will have the benefit of it when we are going to cross the border at Záhony.'

'This is all thanks to you and to your friends in important places. You have foreseen this well in advance. Looking back now I can understand why you wanted our marriage certificate so quickly.'

'Yes, Rebekah, I hope you don't regret it.'

'Far from it we are married, and this trip was our honeymoon as well as other business.'

'I had a wonderful time with you in Budapest, and I have met with all those very important people as well. It will take a long time to tell all these experiences I had with you and with your friends as well to all of my friends in Munkács and in Lvov.'

'Forgive me my darling but I am going to have a sleep for one hour or so.'

'That is alright my love I will have a bit of sleep too.'

We must have slept about two hours as the guard was knocking on our door, he advised us that we will be arriving to Záhony soon and there will be a check on our passports.

Rebekah was getting excited as this is the first time, she would be using her new passport at the Hungarian and Czech border.

A Hungarian Custom and Border Officer came into our compartment and checked our passports then he thanked us with a salute and moved on to the next compartment.

'You see my darling it takes only this much. I know they have never questioned your Czechoslovakian passport when we were going to Budapest, but we will see on the Czech side if they are happy with your new passport.'

It was a short journey crossing the border from Záhony to Csop which is on the Czechoslovakian side of the border stop.

You could see more solders standing on the station platform on the Czech side.

Two officers came on board, and they were checking our passports. They handed back our passports welcomed us into Czechoslovakia and left from our compartment. Rebekah breathed freely as the border guard made no remarks or questioned her new passport.

After about forty minutes the train started to move out from the border crossing town Chop, and it was picking up speed again.

'Well, my darling, it is another five hours, and we will be at home in Munkács.'

'Oh, Gabriel, I am getting more exited as we will be home again soon. I have missed Papa and Rita too.'

'You know Rita was looking after me since my mother died, and I always knew that there is something much more between my Papa and Rita than just as they have pretended. I wish if Papa would marry Rita, and they wouldn't have to hide their feeling in front of other people.'

'I agree with you my love. Yes, they should do that.'

'I will talk to Papa over our wedding at the Hoif Complex.'

After the crossing of the Hungarian border we both went back to the diners coach to our table for lunch before we would get into Munkács. The diners coach waiter told us that our arrival to Munkács from the border is about four hours so it still plenty of time to have our lunch.

I noticed that Rebekah was getting more inpatient for our arrival, and I think really, she would like to be at home already and telling all what happened to her in Budapest in the past ten days.

'You know Rebekah I can't wait to see our house I hope all that work has now been completed as Mr Klein promised to us.'

'Yes, Gabriel, I am anxious to see that everything is working well in the kitchen and in the bathroom, and it looks like just as we have planned them.'

'Darling, I don't think Mr Klein would let us down because his reputation is on the line if he is providing us with a shabby work.'

Just looking through the window and a much more familiar landscape appears on the horizon.

'Look, Rebekah, in the distance. It is the beginning of the Carpathian Mountains. We are not far away from Munkács now. Let's get back to our compartment to get ready to leave the train.'

We began to see the outskirts of Munkács as the express train has started slowing down and finally stopped, we have arrived at Munkács Main Station.

Rebekah has waved to Isaack from train carriage window, and she grabbed her little case and rushed off first to meet her Papa. I was still organising with the porter to remove all the luggage from our compartment, and finally, I have disembarked the train as it is moving on to Lvov.

'Isaack, gave me a fatherly hug and said, It is good to have you back home Gabriel, we missed you both. Rita couldn't make it as she is preparing the welcome home dinner.'

The porter has taken all our cases to the taxi which has been organised by Isaack.

'My goodness, Rebekah, you had just a half of these cases before you went to Budapest.'

'Yes, my dear Papa but there is so many very nice shops in Budapest, and I just couldn't resist to do some shopping there.'

Isaack looked at me and just briefly asked, 'Was it a successful trip Gabriel?'

'Yes, Isaack. It was and much more than I expected. So now we are in business. You need a much bigger factory as your works on 7 Partalja utca is far too small for this project.'

I think those words were his biggest present that anyone could possibly give to Isaack was that 'we are in business'.

'Gabriel, we will discuss this after our supper.'

Rebekah has been holding on to her father's arm since we have got off the train, and she kept saying, 'It is good to be back home Papa, I have missed you and Rita.'

'I have missed you to Rebekah. Isaack told us that Rita couldn't make the welcome at the station because she was cooking Rebekah's favourite food at home.'

As we got through Isaack's apartment door Rita rushed to embrace Rebekah. Both of them instantly burst out crying on each other's shoulders. 'It's good to have you back home, Rebekah.'

'Thank you, Rita. It is good to get back home again.'

Isaack called us to sit at the table and have our welcome meal before it is getting cold.

Rebekah has never stopped telling stories, and she quickly grabbed her handbag and pulled out her new Hungarian Passport, and she was showing it to Isaack and Rita.

Isaack looked at the document looked at Rebekah then me and said, 'Mazel Tov to you both.'

'Thank you, Gabriel. All that planning before you went to Budapest you were promising me that you will make Rebekah a Hungarian Citizen and here, we are, my only daughter is officially a Hungarian Subject. Well done. I am very pleased and happy for you both. But 11 September wedding at the Hoif Complex Synagogue is still going to happen, yes?'

'Absolutely, Isaack. I am looking forward to it. We have invited some of our friends from Budapest for our wedding.'

Both of us were speaking half Yiddish and half Hungarian as we have mainly spoken on Hungarian in Budapest. But that didn't bother Isaack and Rita as both spoke Yiddish and Hungarian.

After the lovely food Rebekah has retired into her bedroom with Rita as Rebekah was showing off with her new dresses which she walked back to us in the lounge and twirling like a fashion model.

She told us that she is going to show only to Rita her new wedding dress. She said, 'Both of you will see it on our wedding day under the Chuppah.'

Both Rebekah and Rita have retired to her bedroom and Isaack, and I stayed behind in the lounge to update Isaack on my achievements.

'I am very curious Gabriel what you have just told me at the station over my business is not big enough to manufacture this new project you have brought from Budapest.'

He poured me another glass of plum brandy, and he behaved like a little boy who want to know all about his present.

I have told him briefly the irrigation project for the river Tisza then I told him that we have all the suppliers for our project, and it looks like we are well ahead of any company who would be able to manufacture these essential machines for the Irrigation Project.

Isaack was absolutely excited, and he was on 'fire' with his plans and with the setting up the new base for this new and very ground-breaking project and the opportunity of exclusivity we will have with this machine on the market.

'Tell me, Isaack, how is our house? Has Mr Klein completed the work as he promised to us?'

Isaack called Rebekah and Rita to join us in the lounge than he picked up a small box, and he handed it to both of us and said, 'Well, children here are the key for your new house. It has been completed, and it looks an ultramodern villa. I am very impressed with the workmanship of Mr Klein and with the style of it as well. Mazel Tov my children.'

Then Rita kissed both of us and said, 'I am so very pleased for you it is truly a show room standard place. But it only needs furniture.'

'Yes, Papa. We have to go to see your friend Sutyai Béla Furniture maker commissioning him to make furniture which would match the case of our new baby grand piano.'

'A Grand piano? Both Rita and Isaack asked the question in unison, and they have looked both of us.'

'Yes, Papa, look this is the piano we bought in Budapest.'

'Well, yes, this is a beautiful furniture but none of you can play on it.'

'I will learn it, Aapukám.'

'Look, Isaack, now it's getting late, and I have to get to my rented accommodation at Elisabeth Schwartz place. Then I will meet up with you tomorrow.'

'No, Gabriel, from now on you will stay here with us until your new house will have furniture. Of course, you will sleep in the guest bedroom until 11 September. Then you both can share the same bedroom.'

'Well, thank you, very much Isaack this is very good of you. I promise that I won't be disappointing you with my behaviour.'

'Thank you, Gabriel, I know you won't do anything like that, you are a true gentleman.'

'Thank you, Papa. This is very good of you. I love you.'

Rita kept drying her eyes with her handkerchief and smiled at both of us then to Isaack.

Isaack asked Rebekah to show me the room I will sleep, and she said, 'It's only for seven days my love it will fly so quick we won't even know, and we are going to be together at our new house.'

'Goodnight, Gabriel. Tomorrow, we will have a family meeting here over your finding and possible contract through your connection in Budapest.'

'Yes, I will be ready for that Isaack. Good night to you all.'

It will be such a strange feeling to sleep under the same roof without my legally wedded wife.

But if this is the house rule well then, I have to accept it.

Chapter 44

Back in Munkács, Conveyor Company
Info Planning Begins; Inspection of Our House

Rita was already up and preparing our breakfast in the kitchen.

'You know, Gabriel, I haven't seen Isaack in such an excited mood since his younger years after his wife Rebekah's death. He is upbeat and regained his energy with all those planning for our new chapter he says.'

'You know Isaack is very fund of you, Gabriel. While you were away in Budapest Isaack kept saying to me: you know Rita, Gabriel is reminding of me when I was younger. Keeping his head down and always looking for a new business opportunity what other people hasn't even thought about. We will be a great team together. He has a great plan with you and for Rebekah as well.'

'And what do you think, Rita?'

'O my dear, I like you very much. I know Rebekah since she was a little girl since her mother died. I was worried about her over the years as she had no serious boyfriend and that is it, she wouldn't be get married until you have turned up. You have injected energy into Rebekah, and she became a life at last. The tree which has become blossoming again, twice within one year. Isaack, and I have noticed her transformation and that gave us hope for Rebekah's future.

'Then she has introduced you to us, and we understood what made the changes in Rebekah. You are charming and a true gentleman with a very strong will to succeed in your carrier. I as a woman I can see why Rebekah's has fallen in love with you, I like you too. She was praising you last evening so much that Gabriel did this and that for me in Budapest. He introduced me to all those very important people in high society and of the artists among your friends.

'Also, the kind deeds you have made for the poor family who have bought his apartment. She said everybody loves Gabriel and you have treated her like a movie star.'

334

We have stopped our conversation as Isaack came into the kitchen then he joined us around the kitchen table with a cup of coffee and asked me, 'I hope you have slept well, Gabriel?'

'You know I didn't my mind was going around of the 'secret' what you have for me about for our new venture.'

Rebekah have joined us she was still in her dressing gown with a sleepy eye as she still hasn't properly awake yet. Pecking a kiss on each of our cheek and sat down with us with a cup of coffee in her hand. Isaack suggested that lets talk some business while Rebekah get ready than we as a family will sit down and talk about our plans for our future.

Isaack and I moved to the lounge I got all the relevant information's in order one by one as I have made my presentation over the contacts I have made for the conveyor manufacturing concepts and founding a suppliers for the materials and for the controlling systems like electric motors and so on.

Isaack particularly has been impressed with a possibility of the main agency for the electric motors for the whole regions. At that point Rebekah has joined us, and she have turned into a very serious businesswoman from being a daughter.

'She was telling about our dinner meeting with serious businessmen from industry to banking executives at this very exclusive Astoria Hotel. Rebekah told her father that these people will come here to Munkács to investigating of the possibility of their investment into this region and said they were asking my cooperation to helping them in their fact-finding process.'

Isaack said jokingly, 'This is just too much for me to hearing all of this. You have only been a way for ten days so how did you managed to be achieving to gather so much information's and contact in such a short time?'

'You know Papa Gabriel know many important people and now many important people know, Gabriel. And his connections, are important and mainly they know his ability to recognise where to invest their financial interests.'

'Well, my children, I can see and feel the energy what is flying in a speed of the hurricane and the opportunity is now here with us. I am very proud of you both, after all my dreams which I thought would have never happen but now I can see it now will become a reality.'

After our breakfast we all went to Isaack's factory on Partalja utca, and I have presented all the technical details and drawings of the conveyor and elevator principles to Isaack's factory foreman to Samuel Steiner.

Samuel looked at the drawings and his first question was that these 'spirals' are all in a different angle, why? What determine them to be like that?

'Well, Samuel, the only answer I can give you is the one I know but I am not sure if that is the specification for every category like what do you intend to move with the elevator.'

'Well, Samuel, I have very little knowledge of this kind of machinery but the only knowledge I have learned on the conveyor that there are three major specifications they are working with is: Bolt density, Capacity, and Speed per 1000 kg.'

'I guess the speed is depends what kind of materials per weight: Liquid, semiliquid, or solid materials you would move. So the RMP is vital which should be able to be adjusted with a gearbox control connected to the electric motor. I would guess we would need for our conveyor elevators in electric power rate between 20 kW and 40 kW electric motors.'

'This technical information is in English, Gabriel.'

'That is no problem Samuel I will translate them for you later on.'

Samuel turned to Isaack and said, 'Then where sell we get a supply for these materials like electric motors and gearboxes and so on.'

'That is no problem, Samuel. Gabriel have made a deal with the main sales executive of the Ganz Works who are coming to Munkács very soon, and he will bring along two of these motors with a ready fixed gearbox.'

Samuel with a relief said, 'My goodness, Gabriel you are making us work in overtime to produce a working model for the test trial when the motors will be delivered to us.'

I went back to Isaack office with Rebekah, and I suggested to Rebekah that you should write a letter to this company in North of England and explain that we have to manufacture of a conveyor on a request from a local farmer, and we would need some guidance from them with regards of specification. I will translate that letter what you, Rebekah, going to write in Isaack's name and will see if they will be able to help us to take this project further forward.

These are the details of this company:

Conveyor and Elevator Co Ltd.
Lower Bridge Works
Accrington
Lancashire

Director; Mr Charley Wood
His Financial director; Miss Jennifer M Wood

'Also, Rebekah would you please send a letter to Johanna and Zoltán with our thanks for their kind welcoming to their house for that wonderful dinner they have organised for us. And also, to remind Zoltán that we are look forward to welcoming them here in Munkács in the foreseeable future.'

Isaack said, 'Well, I am amazed on both of your energies and professionalism you are putting into this project already. I don't have to worry about our future I can see that you are a great team and Rebekah you are a good leader. You have inherited from me this quality and the beauty of your mothers. My God if she would have seen this transformation in you.'

'My Mama is, see it Papa, and she is very proud for both of you.'

Then Rebekah walk to her father and give him a hug as he tries to hide his emotions.

Then he recovers from it and suggest; let's have a lunch at the Star Hotel I will pay for it.

As we were walking away, I noticed that Samuel was studied the brochures which we have left with him.

It was good to be back to the *Csillag* (Star) Hotel restaurant to see some familiar faces.

The waiter already brought our Kosher Plum brandy to Isaack usual table, and he has offered the local newspaper to Isaack.

Isaack declined of having the newspaper and jokingly said (with a showing off attitude), 'I have all the latest news from all the way from Budapest. Rebekah just brought it back with her.'

Isaack asked about the kind of factory base we should look for and how much money should we expect to be borrowing from the bank.

'Firstly, I think we should need a warehouse type of base where we would have access with lorries a spacious work base for the shop floor and a facility for storing the electric motors as we are going to be Ganz Works Budapest main agency for Transcarpathia.'

Isaack stopped and looked at both of us with a face who has just seen a ghost.

Rebekah helped Isaack to understand what we have just told him. 'Yes, Papa. We are going to be very busy not just in manufacturing but as an important trading company as well as stockholder of electric motors for all the business for the whole of Transcarpathia.'

Isaack just drunk Rebekah's plum brandy in his excitement.

'Look Isaack Ganz Works are the best quality electric motors in the world they exclusively supplying their products for Western Europe as well into Asian countries.'

Isaack voice has changed as he has just won a million Dollar and said, 'This is it my children, this is what I was dreaming branching out to other product and going big. Anyone who is thinking small will never be successful. Here we are three of us, and we have energy and imagination.'

'But, firstly, we have to work out the cost for the new base and how much money we have to barrow from the bank. You know the Bank Manager at Moric Ulman Pesti Magyar Kereskedelmi Bank he is not the most helpful person.'

'Look, Papa, I will take care of the financial part of our new venture. I have met with a director of the National Hungarian bank Mr Segal, and he asked me at that dinner meeting to help him when he comes to Munkács for a fact-finding mission to open a new branch for his bank which would be start here as a base in Munkács.'

'Rebekah, I just cannot believe what I just hearing from you, since you have been with Gabriel you have opened up with such confidence as a true businesswoman.'

'This was the University which has gave me the confidence Papa you help me financially to complete my education. And I am now ready for business, Papa.'

'Thank you to getting me out of my shadow, someone who has resigned to his faith and all the business I have built up in the years would not be dying out with me, but I can see that there is a very bright future not just for you two but for my grandchildren too.'

'Talking about grandchildren when do you planning to have children?'

Rebekah said, 'Papa not for another two years as we have to have everything in order what we have set out for.'

'Just don't leave it to late you know how much I am looking forward to have a grandchild.'

'We both smiled and felt that there is a kind of detective work from Isaack if Rebekah is pregnant yet.'

After our lunch, Rebekah and I went to see our house and Isaack gone back to the factory.

As we were getting nearer to our house the woo dogs started to be barking in such an exciting way that Elisabeth has come out to see what has happened with the dogs.

We went straight to our courtyard and the two dogs were coming through the gate between Elisabeth and our house. They have made a fuss of us until I gave them their bones.

We walked into our house at the very first time we looked around from room to room then Rebekah embraced me and kissed me, and I shared her thought exactly the same what a beautiful modern place it has been transformed from a farmhouse. This is just perfect this is how we have planned it. 'Well, darling, I have to say that I am very impressed with Mr Klein workmanship.'

'Yes, Gabriel, this finish is exceed my expectation. Just look at the kitchen and the bathroom both of them just like as we have seen them in the brochure at Mr Zloch showroom.'

Elisabeth knocked on our door and with a beaming smile, she said, 'Welcome to your new home neighbours. This house is just like the one you see it in the movies.'

'Thank you, Elisabeth, but it is not completely finished yet. We still have to get furniture's to fill these empty rooms.'

'Elisabeth, I would like to thank you for all your care and support that I have enjoyed at your house as a lodger but from now on I will staying at Rebekah's house until we will complete our house furnishing which will be in a liveable state. I hope I don't ow you a rent if I do please let me know that I don't want you to be without money at all.'

'O no, Gabriel, you ow me nothing for rent. The dogs will be happy as you are coming back to them.'

As we were walking back to Rebekah's house we were planning our shopping trips to get kitchen wares and beddings for all the bedrooms, and we have to go to your fathers friend, Mr Sutyai Béla to complete all the built in furniture for all the bedrooms and for our lounge in the style of our grand piano's case.

By the time we got home Isaack was sitting in his armchair and having a Kosher Plum Brandy.

'You know my children that you have gave us a very exciting day at the factory as everybody was talking about of this new project.'

'May I ask you Isaack to tell them not to tell this project to nobody as this could bring us into a competition situation with other engineering companies.'

'I have told them already Gabriel I have made them to swear on the Talmud that they will not talk about it anywhere outside of the factory.'

'Isaack told me that he has some readymade factory building in his mind which we have to visit and to decide on the one which would fit our specification.'

'I agree Isaack but tomorrow I have to report back at the town hall and start to make arrangement with employment contracts and so on for my new position as an Officer for Art and Culture in Munkács and in the County.'

Chapter 45
New Job, Factory, Furnishing the House and Setting Up Agency

My first task was to report at the Town Hall to Deputy Mayor Dr Sándor Fried that I am now ready to start working for Munkács Town as an Officer for Munkács – Bereg County Council as an Officer for Art and Culture.

Dr Sándor's secretary has announced to the Deputy Mayor that I have arrived for my appointment. She showed me into Dr Sándor's office then she left us alone. I handed over the letter to Sándor which I have received from Chief Rabbi Immanuel Lőw at my last meeting with him in his office in Budapest.

'It is good to have you back again Gabriel we've missed you. I hope you have managed to achieve everything what you two have planned for that trip.'

I was reporting all the outcome of the meeting I had with the members of OMZSA at the Dohány utca Synagogue, which will be followed by a visit from a delegations for a fact-finding mission for a possible major investment based here in Munkács then it will branch out to other parts of the region.

'Also, I updated him on my personal achievement of selling my apartment, Rebekah's Hungarian Citizenship and her new passport and our new business arrangement for Isaack's Conveyor and Elevator company, also Zoltán and Ganz agency. I told Sándor that having met Count Pál Teleki Minister for Education and his initialisation of the irrigation project for the *Alföld* (The Great Plain) and the Tisza program, which would allow the Tisza to be suitable for shipping as faraway to Huszt.'

'Count Teleki indicated that he will come and visit us here in Munkács during his tour in the Transcarpathian Region.'

'My goodness, Gabriel, how long did you go for? It seems to me that you have done as much in ten days where other people would have to spend a whole month. I congratulate you for all these achievements you have just told me it is truly extraordinary, well done my boy.'

'I guess you have seen your new house already. I have to say again I am very impressed with your taste for luxury.'

'Thank you, Sándor. I am just like you that we have to dream bigger and bigger. If you do something you want to enjoy it as well as you worked so hard for to get it and don't settle with the second best because you are cheating to yourself.'

'Now, some serious part for this day's meeting. I am going to take you to the Council's chief officer of administration, Mr Jakab Grűnewald and he will officially appoint you into this position as an Officer to Art and Culture. I will be there while this process will take place as an official political authority to overseeing that the process has been carried out correctly.

After a successful initiation we have all signed the document of employment agreement, and I have been told that this appointment will be put on the next Full Council Meeting's Agenda.'

After we left Mr Jakab Gerő office Sándor said, 'Well, congratulations, Gabriel. Now, you are officially employed by the local Authority of Munkács. I think you will be able to keep your old office, and I guess you still would like to work with your old helpers Andre and Viktoria.'

'By the way, that Andre is a very good boy, I had a long conversation with him regarding our organisation, and I am impressed with his ability and his loyalty. Now let's have something to eat Gabriel as I have had no breakfast this morning and you can tell me more about your meeting with Count Teleki.'

'Why don't you go to your old office and arrange whatever you would need, as I have to let my secretary know what I am going to do for the next couple of hours, and I will meet up with you at the Star Hotel Restaurant.'

On my way out I asked the administrator lady, Veronika to ask Andre and Viktoria to come to my old office for a briefing at three this afternoon.

I was hoping to see Isaack and Rebekah at the restaurant as well, but they weren't there on my arrival. I just read the headlines of the local paper when Sándor just walked into the restaurant. The waiter brought us our drink of plum brandy than he took the newspaper from our table to be ironed.

'So what is really happening in Budapest Gabriel? What have you decided at that meeting at the Dohany utca Synagogue?'

'I was telling Sándor the unfair taxation law against the Jewish communities, uncertainty, and uneased willingness of investors, as there are a lot of restrictions on the way and investors are looking for new territories and new marketplaces outside Hungary. This new Jewish law brought out by the Darányi government in May this year is not helpful.'

'Yes, you are right Gabriel I have heard some very nasty alarming stories from my contacts from Vienna.'

'We couldn't continue with that conversation with Sándor as Isaack and Rebekah have just walked into the restaurant and straight to our table. Isaack's face was beaming with happiness Rebekah greeted us with a kiss on our cheeks and both of them showed exhaustion in their body language just crashed into the chairs.'

'Sándor jokingly asked Rebekah, so, how does married life suit you, Rebekah?'

'Oh, I enjoy it, Sándor.'

Isaack quickly commented that, 'Not until 11 September.'

'I am so sorry, Isaack. This is just on unofficial enquiry.'

Rebekah smiled and gave Sándor a cheeky wink.

'So what happened, Isaack? You look so excited and look as if you could do with a drink.'

'Just one drink, Sándor? I need a whole bottle to relax me from this meeting.'

'Isaack was telling us that they have been at the Móric Ulmann bank discussing this project we are going to be involved with. I have told him that we need some financial support for this project and to just cut the long story short the bank manager just wasn't helpful at all.'

'Then Rebekah has mentioned that she has happened to dine with Mr Segal, and they are willing to invest in local businesses here in Munkács. Well, you should have seen the bank managers face he turned white as my Rebekah with her confident businesswoman's attitude completely destroyed his superior behaviour.'

As we were getting to leave his office Rebekah said to the bank manager, 'Look Mr Gerő there are other banks on the way to Munkács, and they are willing to lend money for companies for expansion of their business or on the new business projects, goodbye Mr Gerő.'

'By the time, we got to his door he said I am sorry that I was not aware of the scale of your project. Please come back and let's talk it through. There must be some tolerance with our lending regulations but as you know this is such a substantial amount that I have to have authority from my superiors.'

'Rebekah came into the conversation and explained the way she has turned the tables on him.'

'Look, Mr Gerő, we always believed that you are a business banker and not just the one who is only dealing with the public. If you cannot see the potential, then you shouldn't be in this chair as a business bank manager.'

'I am so sorry, Miss.'

'No, Mr Gerő. I am Mrs Goodbye.'

Sándor commented on Rebekah's firm attitude, 'My goodness, Rebekah. I don't think this bank manager will have a goodnight's sleep tonight. He may well be back to you tomorrow with your approved request.'

Sándor said, 'Don't you worry there is always another day, and he will come back to you.'

'Then he turned to Rebekah and asked her. Would you please update me with your meeting with Mr Segal?'

'Do you believe in that he was really serious with his move or just considered.'

'Yes, Sándor, and he asked me to help him here in Munkács to setup his new base for his bank. Well, it is not his bank he is just one of the director.'

'What do you mean he is just a director? This man is one of the most influential and most powerful men in banking and financing in Hungary.'

'We all looked at Sándor and what he has just said and awaited some more information from him.'

'So sorry but this subject should be discussed in private. But tell me how you like your new house?'

'Oh, Sándor this is our dream come true now only we have to furnish our house to match the style of our new grand piano.'

Sándor looked at us and with a surprised face asked me, 'A Grand Piano?'

I said, 'It is not just any grand piano it is, an English made Strohmenger Art Deco style Baby Grand Piano.'

'But none of you play piano.'

'I just couldn't resist Sándor. You will see when it will arrive here, you have never seen one like this before and think of those concerts and parties that we are going to have this grand piano.'

'I was telling Sándor and Isaack that I have made a deal with the company owner in Budapest, and I will organise a days of piano sales and piano recitations her in Munkács. This will be my first organised classical event for the people of Munkács as part of my project for 'Art and Culture' programs.'

'This will have no political or ethnically divert approach which any ethnic community would object to this promotion. It's purely art and business.'

Sándor commented on this approach, 'You are very smart, Gabriel.'

'Isaack with a confused face asked; but how are you going to get support for this, Gabriel?'

'Sándor came to my help and announced to Isaack and to Rebekah that Gabriel today has been officially appointed as the Officer for Art and Culture by the Authority of Munkács Town Council.'

'I have to assure Isaack that I am still in the family business. But I don't have to sit in your office all the time when I don't need to be there. I will be still in with the family's business interest.'

'Just trust Gabriel, Papa. He knows what he is doing. You are still running the business Gabriel is only in the background, and he still working for you but in this position, he will be able to achieve more business for the company than just being a salesman.'

'Sándor is trying to calm Isaack down to say; Look Isaack Gabriel is the front man of your business who is bringing all important information, contracts for the benefit of your company.'

'Papa, I will explain this to you later.'

'Sándor and I apologised that we have to go to attend a prior engagement in the town hall.'

'As Sándor and I were walking back to the town hall he made a valuable point; you know I feel that Isaack thought that you will be sitting behind a desk and trying to draw up some contracts for him.'

'Yes, Sándor, you're right. I don't think we have really explained this to him properly. But I hope now Rebekah will do that after this misunderstanding.'

By the time, I got back to my 'old' office Andre and Viktoria was there already and greeted me with an enthusiast welcome back home, Gabriel.

'You see I have told you that I won't let you work for anybody else but only for me.'

'I have briefed them over their job description and asked them if there are any questions? The only question was when we shall start working, Gabriel.'

345

'Both of you are now have officially been allocated to work with my department. Do you remember what I have told you that you will work with me again in a much more glamorous job anyone can wish for.'

'Well, a big smile from both of them has registered my confirmation.'

'That is good. I am happy that you are coming along with me in this kind of entertainment world. Away from politics. Into the world where you have to deal with 'Prima donnas' and with genuine artists in the entertainment world. Always be polite and even if the so-called artist is wrong just remember of that they are always right.'

'As long as they are happy, it means the audience will be entertained, and they will be happy. You must remember the audience is the one who pays for your wages, not me or the Council. Both of you will deal with the artists and with their agents. You are responsible for their accommodation and for their refreshments in the dressing rooms.'

'I want everything registered in a notebook for your future references and a proper bookkeeping system for the authority of finance and a monthly report on our previous monthly achievements and also for our proposed projected plans ahead for the next six months. We will have a weekly meeting here in this office. You have to go to all pubs, cultural and musical events and go to local theatres to find out what makes people laugh and how much applause the artists are getting from the audience. I suggest that both of you should go out to any events in your evenings as you want to be entertained but also to learn the trade! We will pay for your expenses like tickets or cups of coffee. Understood?'

'Good.'

'I don't think I would expect you to turn up in the office from 8:00 a.m. to 5:00 p.m. It is a flexible job, but I want you to report everything what you two are doing. We are going to share this room as this is our office. So please get all the equipment and stationery you require. Also get yours and my business cards to be printed with the Council's printer and this is the text for these cards with your individual names on cards. When you are dealing with agents or venues you will use this card.'

'Now, I have to go but I'll see you tomorrow morning.'

'Thank you, Gabriel, it is very exciting time, in our life. We have a job that many of our friends will envy.'

I was walking back home (to Isaack apartment) and I felt absolutely exhausted at the amount of work with my new employment position and training

Andre and Viktoria in my office. Well, I think that I will ask Rebekah out for a drink after our supper.

'Isaack and Rebekah were home already, and Isaack came to me and shook my hand and said, I am very sorry Gabriel for my behaviour at the restaurant, but I was a bit confused there but Rebekah has explained everything to me and now I can understand everything.'

'That is all right Isaack there is no need for apology. It is understandable that you are concerned for all these ideas we brought back to you to progress forward and here we are leaving you on your own.'

'Trust me, my new position at the Council will not interfere with your company's interest. Far from it, it will help in the promotion. It will give you a free advertisement.'

'Ah, that is alright. A free advertisement is always welcome.'

'After the meal, I asked Rebekah if she would like a drink on one of the cafeterias on the Corso. It is still warm, and it is still daylight I could do with a relaxed evening together with you.'

Isaack said, 'Yes, you should have a drink together you've been working hard for it today.'

We have decided to go to the Homdi Café sitting outside on the terrace in front of the coffee the temperature has dropped a little.

'Rebekah compered this coffee with the Parade on the river Danube, in Budapest. We have a beautiful memory that we have brought with us from Budapest, where it was only you and I and the moon.'

I held her hand and said, 'Yes, it is a fond memory my darling that is purely ours. I love you!'

Chapter 46

View of the New Factory Base; Organising the Furniture

On Wednesday morning three of us and Samuel jointly went to see the new factory which is just a few hundred yards away from Isaack's factory still on Partalja utca which is a newly built warehouse/factory unit with all the latest technology power cabled and with a large front easy to access it with any transporting facility. The entrance to the factory is big enough for a truck to drive in for a delivery. The whole unit is much larger than Isaack would need for the manufacturing base and for the Ganz Works Electric Motors storage and show room. Isaack was telling us that he requires 8000 Sq. Feet (750 Sq. Meter) floor space, but there is room for expansion if we need it.

I said, 'It looks impressive Isaack as it is new, and any visitor would have more trust in a company when the outlook of their premises looks professional. Well, I can see that you have to employ more tradesmen for the near future.'

'That is no problem Gabriel I had a meeting with Samuel over this already.'

Samuel said, 'We have to move all those heavy machines like turners and benders and arrange it the way as the new product requires in a much spacious and practical way.'

Rebekah asked Isaack, 'But what about the cost to rent this base, Papa?'

'We will discuss it later, Rebekah. She understood that Isaack didn't want to talk money Infront of Samuel.'

'I walked to the other side of this warehouse and tried to work out the size of the space we would need to rent for the Ganz Works agency's showroom. It would impress Zoltán when he comes with these two electric motors for a test trial.'

I said, 'To Isaack that I would need about 3000 sq. feet for the storage space and also, we would have the room for our offices along with the show room fitted with telephone. You have to include this space along with your factory space Isaack, and I will get the finance for that part of the building. Which has to be separate from your engineering company. Keep the two in separate administration, but both companies are still owned by our family.'

Isaack commented on my proposal, 'It sounds good to me, Gabriel.'

Rebekah looked at me with an angry face. 'And where the finance will come to it, Gabriel. I will not put our new house on the line as collateral at the bank.'

'No darling, we don't have to do that. I will discuss it with you later on.'

Isaack went back to the factory with Samuel and Rebekah, and I went to get our furniture and doors and other wooden parts for the house manufactured for our house.

As we were walking to our house from this new factory on Partalja utca Rebekah asked me, 'And where is that fund coming from Gabriel?'

'Well, partly, a loan from the Ganz Works company as a main representative for the whole Transcarpathian Region and some money I will raise through the bank.'

'But what about the cost of works what Mr Klein did on our house?'

'Rebekah darling, as you know we have sold our apartment very profitably in Budapest. It is so much better than I could buy our new hose four time over as the exchange rate of that money is much more than I expected. This will cover all the work which has been carried out on the house already and will cover the work for the Sutyai Bela's cost for all the necessary work. Furthermore, I can pay back the money your father has lent me to buy this house in the first place. Beside the point your father will need money for this transition from a small place to much larger premises.'

'Yes, my darling, but we need money as well. How are we going to get everything for the house if you are borrowing all this money for this electric motor agency?'

'I agree with you, Rebekah, but we are a young couple who have just got married and all the banks in the world would lend money to younger people than to a much more mature one.'

'They know that we have time on our side to trade our way to repaying the loan what they have lent to us in the first place.'

'Anyway, I have contacts, and I trust my connections who are all looking for investment through me here in Munkács. You remember that meeting at the Chief Rabbi Immanuel Lőw's office? You were there at the dinner table with us when Mr Rosenthal a member of the panel who is from a major company asked me to help him to find opportunities for an investment here in Munkács.'

'Yes, darling I can see your point and your enthusiasm.'

'Please trust me, Rebekah, we have to think big and whatever we are going to do it has to be the very best in quality and workmanship. If we would think in a smallish way than no one would be interested to do business with us. I believe this is how the world works. They expect you to be near to their standard. I hope you see my point darling. We have to think BIG.'

While we were occupied with our thoughts we got to our house. As we stepped inside of the entrance door Rebekah was amazed how spacious this house has become since we have the alterations, and we had enough time to look at those brochures which would match the style of our grand piano.

'I thought that we have to find out with Rebekah if there is a telephone line in the street as I would like to have a telephone in our house just for necessity.'

Then we walked to the back of the house where the fruit and vine garden starts and for our joy there is still strawberries on the bushes, we quickly picked some for us and the taste was like honey.

I have noticed that there will be a good harvest of grapes at the end of the summer. It will supply us with fresh fruit and vegetables for our use.

The bell ringing shortened our time in the garden, then I let in the two men from the furniture company. We showed them the brochures of Bauhaus Magazine latest style of furniture that we would like to have in all of the bedrooms, a built-in wardrobe, and a matching double bed and with the finish on the wardrobes doors we want the same as on the room doors. Also, I have showed the grand piano's brochure, and we asked them to build all the lounge furniture in that style, matching with the piano case of walnut veneered finish. On all the solid doors should be coloured with a matt pale green and a pale brown decorative frame should be fixed on each door surface. The bedrooms and the lounge floors should be natural coloured 'redwood' in glossy lacquered finish.

The foremen called *István* promised that he will take measurements and will work out the cost on the project and will bring it to your father's factory. 'I hope that will be alright with you, Rebekah.'

'That is alright István, but could you give us some idea how long everything would take as we would like to move in on 11 September please. After István left with his colleague we called into Elisabeth's house just to say hello to her.'

By this time, it was well passed 2:30 in the afternoon, and I asked Rebekah to come into the office and say hello to Viktoria and to Andre.

As we got to my office door and to my surprise, I noted that a painted board was fixed on my office door with an Art and Entertainment Department and my name was written on.

When we walked into the office Viktoria rushed to Rebekah and gave her a hug and a kiss on her cheek. Andre said hello but his hand was full of papers, so Rebekah said, don't worry Andre.

Rebekah said, 'But this office is your old room, isn't it?'

'Yes, it is it will be helpful as we don't have to look where to found it.'

Viktoria was admiring Rebekah's new summer dress. She asked, 'Did you by this in Budapest.'

'Yes, and I have a present for both of you, but I wasn't anticipating coming in today so I will bring it to you tomorrow.'

Rebekah was still chatting to Viktoria while I was dealing with the day's achievements with Andre.

I said, 'To Andre and to Viktoria that I am going to have an early day today and I'll see you both tomorrow morning.'

'As we were walking out of the Town Hall, we bumped into Mrs Maria Cohen she was very pleasant and asked us if we had a nice honeymoon in Budapest.'

Rebekah replied, 'Yes, thank you, it was very tiring, but it was beautiful. I can recommend it to you.'

By the time we got out onto the Corso we called into the Homdi Café for a drink before we went home for Rita's lovely supper. Next thing we noted was that Isaack pulled a chair at our table and said, 'I have seen you here, and I thought that I could do with a cold drink too.'

'Absolutely, Papa, you look very tired is it the heat or just the worries with this new factory's financial situation of you facing?'

'No, Rebekah. In fact, Mr Jakab Gerő personally called into my office, and he wishes to discuss the finance we wanted to borrow from the bank.'

'I have almost choked on my beer as I heard this news from Isaack.'

'Well, Rebekah, I think you have rattled this man's cage as he got back to you so soon. Well done, my love. You are a real hard bargaining professional businesswoman!'

'Yes, my darling daughter, I am so very proud of you, I don't know how I would run my business without you. Mr Gerő wants us in at ten in the morning to finalise our loan agreement.'

'This is just unbelievable Papa; did you tell him we shall be there?'

'Yes, of course.'

By the time we got home Rita had the dining table set for the meal after we had finished in the bathroom and Isaack said the Kiddush we all had the pleasure to enjoy Rita's cooking, and we were celebrating the success over the bank loan agreement with Isaack mature *Egri Bikavér* (Bulls Blood) red wine.

At the end of our meal three of us settled in the lounge, and I gave a handwritten letter to Rebekah and asked her to sign it.

'What is this Gabriel?'

'This letter is for the company in Accrington, England, in which we are asking some advice for screw conveyors mainly technical details on the angle of blades on the shaft and what materials would they recommend for the blade itself and what type of industry do they manufacture these conveyors for?'

'This is very good Gabriel, but do you think they will reveal their secret?'

'Well, look at this way Isaack if they won't then we have to go down on the hard road to get this information. I am not asking for a trade secret only just advice. If they refuse my request, then Samuel will have to experiment on several screw conveyors before we would have a successful result.'

The next morning we have parted at the Town Hall as I have gone into my office where I still have to organise my team workload and to learn from the youngsters their age groups interest and balance our direction which would be supported financially by the Cultural and Foreign Ministries in Budapest.

I trust my enthusiasm will have some impact on them. I keep saying we have to promote and deliver what the people want not what we like and want to put on to an empty auditorium. That is not the way we work we have to satisfy firstly the audience than our employer, in this case it the Town Council. We have to show them success in entertainment and in profits.

'I think Andre in the next weeks you have to travel around the County's major towns and introduce our selves to them and explain to them what we can do for their communities. Viktoria if you want to join Andre on some of these trips that is alright with me but not on every occasion understood?'

'Yes, of course, Gabriel, we do understand it, that is no problem.'

'Viktoria, I would like you to come with me across the Square to the Drama Theatre, and I will introduce our selves to the manager and ask his cooperation with us at the Council.'

'Can I join you, Gabriel?'

'Yes, of course, Andre please come along but I don't want our office being left unoccupied for a longer period in the future.'

'The theatre director Mr Robert Aron welcomed us, and he told us that he has been notified by the council about the new department at the council.'

'I have heard much about you Gabriel mainly from my friends in Budapest, Ódry Theatre.'

'I hope it was a positive one.'

'Yes, it is a positive one, and on that experience, we believe that we will have a very good business relationship for the future.'

'Mr Aron, I would like to introduce my very talented associates from my office Viktoria and Andre.'

'I am very pleased to meet you both, but Gabriel I think that I am the oldest one so please call me Robert.'

'Very good, Robert. If you have any questions, please call any of us, and we will be more than happy to see to your needs. And now I would like to ask about your programs for the next six months just to see if there is anything that we could put on in your theatre. I will have access to many acts and artist and movies to bring out from Hungary which would probably help your theatre's turnover.'

'Well, that will be very helpful anything which would bring an audience to our theatre is more than welcome, and I do support those kinds of promotions coming from the Town Council.'

'Walking back to our office as I have found a note put through the door that the Deputy Mayor Dr Sándor Fried would like to see me and Andre.'

Andre panicked as he thought this is it as he just started his dream job and now it will be taken away by the Deputy Mayor.

'As Andre and I got into Sándor's office he offered us some apple juice and went straight into his speech why he called for us.'

'Thank you for coming so promptly both of you. I have read Chief Rabbi Immanuel Löw's letter you have brought for me and there is much information which concerns me of the present political situation that is happening Europewide, and it probably will happen in Hungary too.'

'That OMZSA meeting where you have attended, they are asking our branch of a maximum help and assistance with their effort to take care of the poorer Jewish populations to help them to find jobs and basically support their families life with health and social support.'

'Also, you have whetted their appetite to look for an opportunity to invest here in the Transcarpathian Region. I believe that your new wife Rebekah already has invited Mr Segal here to Munkács for a possible new banking service.'

'Furthermore, there is a note in his letter that you have become a kind of hero in Budapest over selling your apartment.'

'Oh, that is really nothing Sándor, I have just given all of my furniture and the household textiles free of charge to a poor immigrant shopkeeper who has bought my apartment.'

'That is very commendable, Gabriel. We are all proud of you and when you need help, we will give you all that support. We also have plans with you. Andre and I will come and see you over that.'

'With relief Andre has taken a deep breath and said well I thought I just going to lose my dream job.'

'No, Andre, please don't even think about that, we have very important plans for you in the future.'

'We both went back to our office and a worried faced Viktoria asked Andre; is everything alright with you?'

Andre jokingly replied, 'No, I've just lost my job.'

'I have to defend Viktoria as she was on the point of crying at Andre's silly comment.'

'No, Viktoria, he hasn't lost his job in fact he will never lose his job while I am here. But if he treats you badly like now, I will fire him. We all had a lough and Viktoria told Andre off not to do this thoughtless joke anymore. Andre felt bad about it as he never thought it through, and he sincerely apologised to both of us.'

'Look I am going to the Star restaurant to meet Rebekah and Isaack, and I will be back after two, so see you later.'

'Again, I have arrived fifteen minute earlier to the restaurant so hopefully this time I will be able to look through the headlines in the local newspaper. Rebekah arrived with a very happily smiling Isaack.'

'Gabriel, we have all the money we have asked for.'

'That is great, Isaack. then I should make an appointment with Mr Jakab Gerő. I have to call into the bank anyhow as I have to draw money out for Mr József Klein for the building work.'

'I'll buy your meal today my children so we can celebrate.'

'I would rather not celebrate Papa until later at our supper time as we still have a meeting this afternoon with the landlord over the new factory's rental agreement.'

'I will come along with you to this meeting as I have to discuss with them the extra space for the Ganz Works Agency's storage and for the offices as well. I want to make sure that our offices will have access to telephone facility as well.'

'That is all right, Gabriel. I am glad that you are coming along with us. It makes more effective if three of us attend this meeting. May well be you will ask questions which I wouldn't think of.'

After the lunch, I have to go back to my office to let Andre and Viktoria know of my change of plans for this afternoon.

Three of us have turned up for the meeting with Mr Itzhak Steiner at the new factory base unit to discuss the rental agreement. Mr Steiner was a very helpful person as much as you can expect from businesspeople.

'Firstly, we would need a high-powered cabling for the premises and a good support for the overhead roof as we want a heavy crane for lifting and moving parts from place to place. Mr Steiner told us that the power cabling and the crane are in place already, so is the telephone line.'

'I was clearing the office and their storage facilities What about the security. We are planning to store very expensive electrical equipment.'

'Oh, Gabriel. I can guarantee the security is paramount. As you can see it is a new building with a secure fence covering the whole area also, we will have a security man at the main gate who is the porter as well. We are trying to attract companies with a much up to date standard and one which will fit in well with our high standard.'

'Will it be a stockholder of a more high-tech foreign product?'

'Yes, Mr Steiner, it is a well-respected Hungarian company who has representation in countries worldwide, and one of our companies main interest is representing this company's interest with their product for the whole of Transcarpathia.'

'But what about your side of business, Mr Grósz?'

'It is general engineering with a specialised product for the Hungarian Government.'

'Mr Steiner, but I cannot tell you any more of the product as it is confidential. Only information which I can tell you is this company is a family-based business with much credential in the trade. This is my daughter Rebekah she is in accounts and finance and my son in law Gabriel is in sales and promotions, and I have a long well-respected history in the trade for many years.'

'Of course, Mr Grósz I understand it. I know of your background I have heard about your activities Gabriel but not in the engineering trade.'

'Of course, not as I have been employed by the Hungarian Government.'

'Your face is not familiar to me Mr Steiner which synagogues are you a member of here in Munkács?'

'I am from Ungvár Gabriel that is where our company is based.'

'So you must know Chief Rabbi Yosef Elimelech Kahana.'

'Yes, of course, I know him I am member of his congregation. Now I remember you Gabriel you have come to our Synagogue and given your presentation to us some months ago on the changes for Transcarpathia.'

'Yes, Mr Steiner that was so I am sorry for not recognising you today.'

'No, not at all, now it all makes sense to me of your whole involvement and to the connections you have mentioned. I think our organisation will have a different view on your rental agreements.'

'Mr Steiner, are you staying at the Star Hotel tonight?'

'Yes, Gabriel but may I ask you why.'

'Well, Mr Steiner, we would like to invite you for a meal this evening in the hotel restaurant just as a general business dinner if you like. Would seven o'clock this evening alright?'

'Yes, it would be convenient, I would be delighted, Gabriel. Thank you I look forward to it.'

'On our way home, I had to book a table at the restaurant. Isaack looked at me and said that was a shrewd move my boy I think you have impressed him with all your connections.'

'I hope you don't mind me inviting him for tonight's business meal.'

'Can I come, Papa, as well to this dinner?'

'Of course, my darling Rebekah.'

'Absolutely, my love. I would insist as you are one of the partners in our business.'

'After we got refreshed from the sweaty summer clothes we made our way to the restaurant we bumped into Dr Sándor who had just finished in his office at the town hall and asked us; would you like to join me for a dinner at the restaurant?'

'Isaack just explained to Sándor the reason we are dressed for the evening as we are having a meeting with our future landlord.'

'Would you like to join us Sándor? After all, you are our legal representative in our interest. Yes, Isaack I would like to meet Mr Steiner.'

'When we met Mr Steiner at the restaurant Isaack introduced Dr Sándor to Mr Steiner and Itzhak and Sándor greeted each other by their forenames. I thought this is not a coincidence this is a much greater plan which has been arranged by our Angel.'

Sándor said, 'Well, Gabriel, this is faith as Itzhak is one of our men from OMZSA.'

'Well, the evening was a great success, and our future new factory has been sealed by Sándor intervention. This dinner event will be remembered for a very long time.'

Chapter 47

Finalising Deal on New Factory Lease and Progress on Our House

After a very successful day we had a most successful evening regarding our new factory's leasing.

'Sándor's input with his negotiating skill was a real breakthrough. He asked questions from Mr Itzhak Steiner which we have never thought to enquire, and he asked for some amendments to the contract as well. This is where a professional attorney is needed to get the best deal for us.'

'It is a Friday we have only arrived on Monday, 25 July and the month is the 29th already.'

'Mr Steiner has gone back to Ungvár to consult his partners over our offers for a big proportion of their warehouse unit. His early morning departure from Munkács was due to updating them with his findings over our offer and to decide on the deal before the Sabbath began. He told us they will send us their reply within four days. Personally, I think they will give us the best deal as I understand this warehouse been empty for a long time with no income to their company from this unit.'

Rebekah went to the factory with Isaack to get the books up to date. I went into my office which I feel I don't spend enough time in to get the calendar right and show some progress towards my officers above me.

Viktoria was in the office already and her face was as white as chalk. I was worried that something serious thing must have happened to her.

'Are you alright, Viktoria?'

'She just handed me an envelope which had come from the Minister for Faith, Education and Culture Count Pal Teleki.'

'After I read through the contents of the letter I have smiled and told her; don't panic Viktoria, I have met the Minister in Budapest at the Báthory utca

Education Ministerium. He promised that they will send major Hungarian artists and cultural performances for us to organise and arrange a booking for them. The first theatrical group they have sent already is performing for ten days in Ungvár and when they are finished there they are heading to Munkács and Beregi County's venues.'

Viktoria's face recovered from the shock which was caused by the sender's name of Count Teleki.

'Well, our work has now officially started with this letter. I have this program booklet with the well-known names in the cast of: Sereghy Andor director's touring theatrical group with Muráti Lih, Törzs Jenõ, Vaszary Piri, Gellért Lajos, Beregi Oszkár, Dayka Margit, Lázár Mária.'

'Andre just arrived, and I said to him would you please collect all the contacts we have on our records for the whole of Munkács, Beregi, Ungi and Máramarosi County Councils and cultural centres, and we will send a letter which we are going to compose after I come back from the Theatre across the square with Viktoria.'

'I turned to Rebekah and asked her to keep her eyes and ears open to learn the way we conduct our negotiations with the theatre or cultural centre directors.'

At our arrival, Mr Robert Aron asked me, 'Don't tell me that you have a project to offer me already.'

'Yes, Robert, as a matter fact that I have all the way from Budapest.'

'He was very impressed with the play and with the great names in the cast of the theatrical group.'

Robert they are performing in Ungvár till the fourteenth of August than they can perform here in your theatre for a week to ten days.

'That is no problem Gabriel I can do all the promotion and if nothing else but the name like Miss Margit Dayka will bring the audience in. But what about the cost of this production?'

'Don't worry Robert they will take only 25% of your gross and the rest will have been sponsored by the Hungarian Cultural Ministry.'

'That is a good deal, Gabriel. I like it, and I would be ready for them by 17 August. And this is a deal.'

We shook hands over the deal and Robert said, 'I hope you will drop me a contract later today or by next Monday.'

'On the way back to our office I turned to Viktoria and asked her if she learned something out of this deal we have just set up with Robert.'

'I think I will need a couple more of your examples, and I think I have got it. You are a good teacher, Gabriel. Thank you for being patient and the way you are supporting me with Andre.'

'It is my and Rebekah's pleasure to help you two to have success in your future life.'

Back in the office Andre was busy making a list for a potentially targeted area.

'Andre here is a map with all the major towns of the Region and here is a list of possible venues with their interest of different levels of entertainment: Drama, Opera, Light Operetta, Comedy and Classical Music Recitals which we could offer them. Also, I want to promote my poet friend Miklós Radnóti from Budapest, after 11 September.'

'Do not arrange anything for Sunday, the 11th as that is my wedding day. Please make note of that date which both of you are expected to attend.'

'Viktoria and Andre, I want to take you to the National Theatre on Rákóczi street next Monday, 1 August, so this afternoon on your way home would you please call into the theatre and make an appointment with the Theatre director. It is embarrassing I don't even know his name.'

'His name is Mr Jakob Zinger.'

'Thank you for helping me out Viktoria.'

'Now I will let you finish earlier for today, so you'll have enough time to get ready for the Sabbath.'

I just realised in my mind that Rebekah and I have been back from Budapest for five days which seems like a month with the amount of work we have managed to put in just five days. I just looked at my watch, and I realised that I am running late to meet up with Rebekah and Isaack at the Star Hotel restaurant.

All three of us shown with our body language the extensive workload we have put in basically just in four long days as we just ordered our meal without a long chit-chat which we usually do at our lunchtime.

'You know Papa and Gabriel I have to see our financial projections to work out how much money we have to make and to be still profitable after we have moved into our new factory. Also, I have sent off the letter you've translated for me to the Conveyor and Elevator Company in England.'

'Thank you for that, Rebekah.'

'Isaack, we have to have a serious meeting with Samuel over his findings on what machinery we would need to manufacture these conveyors. I don't want to upset your existing customers and their orders with you, but we have to work out the number of new workers to be employed for this new project. How about taking on more apprentices from this September?'

'Yes, your right Gabriel we have to employ more people for this project, and also I would like to extend the number of apprentices with us. I have been contacted by Vozáry Aladár from the Trade and Commerce's Munkács Branch, and he told me that there is a major Czechoslovakian owned engineering company which has just closed down as the Czech owner is moving back to Czechoslovakia because of the Hungarians influence on the region is making them more nervous about staying. So I will going to that auction next week with Samuel to see if they have the kind of machinery which we need for our new base like press, a large turner, circle cutter, guillotine welding tools and gas cylinders.'

'I would like to come with you, Papa, as I would like to find out what is happening to their orders as someone will have to fill in with their customer base.'

'That is a very good point Rebekah. Yes, please come along with us.'

'Thank you, Papa, then I will take care of the finances at this auction.'

'Yes, I thought that you will just do that.'

After an extended 'Family business dinner meeting', we felt that we should walk home and have some relaxing time in the lounge and get ready to celebrate our Sabbath.

All night, I couldn't sleep well probably the from the Summer heat or just so much was going on in my head to organise the most important things I have to do like; I have to go to the bank on Tuesday to draw money out for the builder Mr Klein and transfer the money to Isaack that he has lent me to by our house on Latorca utca and also to arrange an overdraft for my side of the electronic motors agency with Ganz Works.

'Next morning, at the synagogue, I was welcomed by many friends and congratulated on my new job at the town hall but tactfully none of them mentioned our speedy marriage at the town halls registrar. After the service coming out of the Synagogue some people started to call Rebekah a Mrs. Some looked at her, and they said, 'Oh my dear Rebekah you do not really look as if you would expect a baby'.'

'No, I don't expect a baby just yet, but I'll let you know when I do, she replied.'

'Munkács is just a same as Budapest everybody knows everybody, and they know everything about you and what they don't know they will make up to a nice story.'

On Saturday afternoon four of us went to see our new house, as Rita hasn't really seen it since Mr Klein has completed all the alterations on the house. As we got to the house and opened the main entrance door to the courtyard both dogs have appeared and were giving us all their fuss and happy barking.

Rebekah led our 'expedition' to the entrance hall and showed our newly built in kitchen and the bathroom which both were tiled and fully fitted with the latest designed style.

Rita was very impressed with everything, and she kept saying this place is just so spacious and looks so modern.

'Rebekah was telling Rita and Isaack where the piano will be placed and where all the built-in wardrobes are going to be, and all the woodwork will be done by Sutyai Bela's Furniture company.'

'Then we all went to the vegetable garden and to the grape vineyard at the back end of the house. Strawberries are still on the bushes and the grape vines are full of bunches of grapes. It looks as if we are going to have a good harvest this year, so we will have to get ready for a *szüret* (grape harvest). Rita said, we all will be here to help you with that.'

'On the way back home, we didn't go into the apartment Rebekah has suggested let's have a cake and a coffee at the Homdi Café, as we were sitting outside on the terrace in front of the cafe the temperature dropped a little bit. The Corso was full of people in the early on Saturday evening. Rebekah has made a comment; just look at those lovely young people some of them about fourteen or may be sixteen, well they are just looking for a partner for life. You remember Papa you have always looked through the curtains spying on me when I was walking around the Corso with my friends. Some of them founded a partner for life very quickly, and I always knew that my partner 'Prince on a white horse' will come for me. Then she looked at me and said, 'Well, here is my prince finally arrived for me'.'

'Rita eyes become moist, and she wiped them with her handkerchief and said, I do remember those days well. It feels as if it was yesterday.'

Isaack gave a sigh and said, 'Yes, Rita, you are right just as if it was yesterday. And now soon are we are going to be grandparents.'

Rebekah quickly responded to that comment from Isaack, 'Not just yet, Papa. At least not for another couple of years or so. Firstly, we still have our business to build up and our life is just at the final stage as we are settling down to our new house. We all have much to achieve and much to be enjoyed with Gabriel. The world is big and beautiful Papa, I have only been in Lvov and Budapest. But to be in Budapest I have realised that is much more to see than just having children around me and that is it. I want more from my life Papa.'

'Yes, you are right Rebekah I hope you will achieve all your dreams with Gabriel.'

The evening slowly moved upon us, and the temperature started to become much cooler, so we just finished our drinks at the cafeteria and walked back to our place where we had one more drink for the day.

'Early on Monday morning, I had a quick briefing with Andre and Viktoria about our plans for the week. Andre told me that Mr Jacob Zinger is expecting us at 11:00 a.m.'

'Very good, Andre, so please bring all the typed-out programs that we are going to offer to theatre directors all around the region.'

'Three of us went to the National Theatre which is on Rákóczi utca. Mr Zinger welcomed us in the foyer which is a beautiful architectural building equally inside and out. He show us around the theatre, and one particular ornamental decoration in the auditorium has reminded me of the Budapest Nemzeti Színház. It is very impressive Mr Zinger your theatre have a very modern stage with a deep Fly loft and a good-sized orchestral pit too. What is the seating capacity of your theatre?'

'The seating capacity is 500. Yes, we spent quite a lot of our budget to modernise the stage as many touring companies are bringing their scenery set with them and you have to provide an impression on the audiences and also on the touring companies too. We have to have our theatre rewired to carrying such powerful equipment and stage lights.'

'After the tour he invited us to his office for a drink where we had the opportunity to explain the reason for our visit. He liked that we could offer him good Hungarian theatrical touring companies with famous stars which are mainly sponsored by the Hungarian Cultural and Educational Ministry.'

'I would like to congratulate you on your new position at the town hall. It really long needed a professional who knows what the audience need and keeps the artistic standard.'

'What you are offering me Gabriel is very attractive, and I will take the opportunity to stage any of those shows you are suggesting.'

'Also, I would like to have a Piano exhibition with a sale in my theatre at the end of September. How about the 21–22 September, and we can have a two-day piano recital with an international concert pianist Dezső Zádor. He will demonstrate pianos which will be exhibited in the foyer and Mr Zádor will perform in the evening in the theatre hall.'

'This is a fantastic idea, Gabriel. Everybody knows Dezső Zádor who is a well-known local artist he will fill the theatre and also will draw customers for the piano exhibition.'

'Dear Mr Zinger, I am so glad that we are aiming for the same thing which is bringing big stars to the theatre and making good money. For the future if for some reason you cannot get hold of me here is Andre and Viktoria who is well capable to deal with you.'

'Yes, I will remember that Gabriel but as I am the eldest so please call me Jacob. And look forward to seeing you soon with some exciting productions.'

'On our way back to the office Andre thanked me for giving them so much opportunity and trust for both of them and elevating them into the VIP status in Munkács performing art world.'

'Look, this is for both of you, I know you will make mistakes, but I will be here to help you out of that mess what you are going to make in the future. But you always have to focus on one thing you are not going to promote anything that the audience rejects or do not want. Do not forget that 'the public is the one who paying for the show' and eventually your wages.'

'After a successful Monday it was my turn to visit Mr Jakab Gerő at the Móric Ulmann Bank to arrange an overdraft facility for setting up the Ganz Works Agency in the same building with Isaack's engineering factory. My appointment was at 10:00 am, and Mr Gerő welcomed me with a beaming smile on his face. This made me think what on earth is he smiling for? Anyway, I will find out soon.'

'Mr Gerő told me that the bank has received a substantial fund in Hungarian currency in Pengő for my account. (so, this news made him smile).'

'Yes, Mr Gerő, I have sold my property in Budapest, and I think that is the fund that I was expecting.'

'The real reason I requested this meeting with you is that I have this business plan which I need to arrange an overdraft facility to finance it.'

'Ah, Mr Gabriel, your wife and your father-in-law were here last week for an overdraft already.'

'Yes, Mr Gerő I know that but that is their separate arrangement for their business and this one is my own business.'

He has studied my business plan, and he asked me, 'But you have a very healthy deposit account with us so why do you need to borrow money for your business?'

'Look Mr Gerő I have just bought a property on Latorca utca which needed some work to modernise it, and I have barrowed the funds for the property from my father in law. So I want this amount of money to be transferred to my father in law's account also I want to draw out this much for the builder. Then my request is this much as shown in the breakdown in my business plan. I hope as a long-time member of Móric Ulmann Bank from Hungary you should have all my records available for you to see that I have always been a trusted and responsible customer of the bank.'

'Gabriel, please allow me some time to properly study your business plan which looks very impressive with a direct connection to such a major company like Ganz Works Budapest. I will transfer the fund to Mr Grósz bank account today, and I will get your cash from our cashier while you are waiting.'

'Thank you for your time Mr Gerő.'

'I will speak to you about your overdraft on Thursday.'

'In the afternoon, I had a meeting with Mr Klein at our house where I handed the money for the building work in Pengő as he requested, and I thanked him for an excellent job he has done on our house on time. I asked him to landscape the courtyard and make a new fence between the house and the garden as this is not in a great urgency, but I would like it done before 5 September.'

'Back in the office in the morning, at 11:00 a.m. Mr Gerő called into my office with a smile on his face I thought that smile is favourable news. Andre has offered his desk and chair to Mr Gerő while Viktoria has offered him a cup of coffee which he has accepted. Andre and Viktoria has gone to the basement canteen in the town hall for a coffee.

Mr Gerő was enquiring of my job description at the Town Hall. 'As I have walked into your office, I have noticed that you are the officer for entertainment. Is there a great need for it?'

'Yes, there is, as the Hungarian Government's programs is encouraging the Hungarian culture and language to be promoted through this office.'

'So why are you getting involved with an electric motors' agency for such a prestigious Hungarian company.'

'Because they have offered it to me, and beside the point if you are selling electric motors or a theatrical show it is the same thing. It is called business, and you never put all your eggs into one basket. Now the question Mr Gerő can I have the overdraft from your bank, or I should turn to the Hungarian Royal Bank in Budapest.'

'Well, Gabriel, it is difficult as the bank would need collateral of your property against our loan it is a substantial sum of money you are asking for, you know I am putting my job on the line if I have no collateral support against the loan.'

'I understand your worries, Mr Gerő, but one thing I will not do is put my house against your loan. Furthermore, I will transfer all my accounts at your bank, and I will find another more understanding bank to lend me the funds which I need. Perhaps your bank centre in Budapest would like to know your unhelpful attitude towards new business in Munkács. Or should I ask advise from Mr Segal which bank would he recommend me for a bank loan.'

'I didn't mean that Gabriel I would not give you that bank loan far from it, but the bank would need some commitment from you.'

'Well, Mr Gerő, I just can't offer you any more commitment to you than my reputation and my connections. I feel we are both wasting each other's time. Thank you for your visit.'

'No, I think you are misunderstanding me yes, the fund is available for you as you have a good credit references from Hungary and here in Munkács as well.'

'Thank you Mr Gerő so when can I have the overdraft fund available for me.'

'From tomorrow, Mr Gabriel.'

'Thank you, Mr Gerő.'

'After the bank manager gone Viktoria and Andre came back to the office and asked me if everything is all right with me as I look exhausted.'

'I had sighed, yes. I am but it has worth it. I have got what I wanted in the first place, and I think I need a drink just to calm me down.'

'I have met up with Rebekah and Isaack at the Star Restaurant I had a drink in front of me already before Rebekah has arrived.'

'Rebekah looked at me and with a panicking motherly way and asked me if I was alright? She said you look exhausted my love.'

'Yes, my love, I had a very long and tiring meeting with Mr Gerő in my office over my overdraft.'

'Did you get your overdraft? Have you offered our house as collateral against the loan?'

'Yes, and no. Yes, to the loan and No to the collateral commitment against our hose.'

'Both of Isaack and Rebekah were jubilant, and she kissed me on my lips which was a spontaneous reaction from her, but I noted that Isaack face changed to our emotional reaction with a kissing.'

'I just had a confirmation from the director of the National Theatre over the piano exhibition—sale and the Piano exhibition and sale at the National Theatre of Munkács by the courtesy of Musica Piano Salon, Budapest will be held on the 21–22 September 1938. With the international concert pianist (N 62) Dezső Zádor. He will demonstrate pianos which will be exhibited in the foyer and Mr Dezső Zádor will perform in the evening in the theatre hall. Tickets will be available at theatre box office or at Town Hall Cultural Office.'

'Well done, my boy. You have really speeded up our life with your energy and with your ideas. I am so glad that I have a son in law like you, Gabriel.'

'But let us have something to eat as I feel hungry, I guess you as well. I hope Rebekah you could join me and my helpers for a drink at the Homdi Coffee?'

'Yes, my darling of course I will be there with you.'

Chapter 48

Moving into the New Factory; Our House Furnishings

Isaack and Rebekah went to this auction to hopefully furnish the new bay with much more up to date machines which will allow us to complete each phase on the work process much quicker and finish it to a professional standard.

I arrived home before Rebekah and Isaack and had a chat with Rita.

'I hope you will join us for some of the events that I am organising. At least that will bring you out of the house and bring the family into a much more relaxed unity and also, we can have fun as well with all these acts I am going to bring and be staged here in Munkács.'

'Oh, Gabriel, if I don't do the cooking than who else would do that?'

We always can dine out before or after the events.

'When was the last time when you went to the theatre, Rita?'

'Well, I can't remember, Gabriel.'

'From now on I would insist that you should join us at various shows or events which you would be interested in and mainly would entertain you.'

An exhausted Rebekah and Isaack arrived and the first thing they did was to open a bottle of wine.

'Well, we deserve this for today, we managed to buy all the machines that we need,' said Isaack.

'Yes, Papa, and we ended up with more than we went out to buy in the first place. I have to convince you to bid for the office furniture and equipment as well.'

'Office furniture does not earn money, Rebekah.'

'Yes, Papa I know but don't forget that our administration will grow as well as your shop floor as we are going to employ more tradesmen and workers in our new factory.'

'So did you get the office furniture, Rebekah?'

'Yes, we did Gabriel, Papa has finally realised that the office is our frontage of the factory, and it has to look professional.'

'I agree with you darling I will contribute to the furniture as the Ganz Agency will be sharing that office with you as well, so it have to look professional and up to date with all the modern office equipment which is available for the administration.'

'Not to mention to satisfy the customers and the Ganz Works Factory's expectation on the agency's looks as you are selling a very high standard product.'

'Rebekah went to the kitchen to help Rita to prepare our supper Isaack turned to me and said; It was very naughty of you Gabriel, you have transferred the money to my bank account the one I have lent you to buy your house.'

'I know Isaack I should of have told you that I've done it. After selling my apartment in Budapest, I have made a good profit on the sale. As it has been transferred to the bank into the Munkács branch after the Pengő exchanged into the Korona, it worked out well that I have made much more money which is now available to pay for what we would need. So that is what I have done I have honoured my promise. Besides the point you would need every 'Fillér' to pay for your new factory.'

Rebekah and Rita have served the supper and the conversation changed. Rebekah said, 'How sad it was as to see that the owner of that factory had to give up his business because political pressure force him to do that. He told me that after the Czech's took over Transcarpathia from the Hungarians the Czechoslovakian Government encouraged a well-established company like his to move into this region. The Czech officials even gave them a governmental grant and now this change is forcing him to sell up and leave.'

'Isaack contributed to Rebekah's story that this company has been racist in the first place as they have only employed people from the Czech ethnic minority, and they were under cutting every job in the trade because they were working with a very healthy grant from the Czech Government.'

'I didn't know this Papa. Then it makes sense why this company was able to have the most modern machinery and office furniture as well because they have been funded by the Czech government. But now I am so glad that I was so adamant to knock down the prices on this office furniture.'

'Rebekah asked me to go out with her to our new house as she wanted to discuss something important which we have to discuss. And when she secretly gave me a wink, I understood her motives.'

'Rebekah has called into my office at midday with the intention to go to our house. On the way she held onto my arm so tightly that I have felt her heartbeat through her chest.

When we got into our bedroom which was still empty without any furniture, she just couldn't hold it back anymore she said; this is our very first opportunity to make love in our house right now in our bedroom and on the floor.'

'I didn't need any encouragement as we haven't made love since Budapest and that was over ten days ago. We embraced and kissed so passionately that some of my shirt button been ripped off in the hurry of freeing ourselves from our clothes until I felt her velvety skin on my bare chest and the increasingly pounding heartbeat through her firm breasts. It was an irresistible desire we felt which has overtaken our passion to gift each other with all of our love that we have.'

The room temperature was cool, but we were sweating as if we were getting out from the swimming bath. What an experience it is to make love on the wooden floor. She said, 'Do it again as who knows when the next time is when we could be together again in such excitement and in a perfect state of satisfaction under such conditions.'

'Ah, darling, you don't know how much I have been waited for this lust of pleasure with you, being in your arms and making love to you. It was painful to hold my desire down I have felt for you I believe that was a punishment or just a test on my patience.'

'Yes, my darling Rebekah, often I was toying with the thoughts that I will sneak into your bedroom over the nights and dreaming that we would make love there, but I remembered what I have promised to your father that I won't do this while I am in his house. Then I have to divert my thoughts from the desire of lovemaking, so I was planning for new business opportunities for all of us where else could we make our portfolio to be increased and make them more profitable.'

'We must have spent over one hour on the floor together when we felt how uncomfortable the wooden floor really was. Luckily, we have running water and some towels which helped us to clean ourselves from our lovemaking.'

Walking back to my office together with my wife with her arm in my arm happy and light just as we would be walking on clouds.

Rebekah said, 'Let's do it again more often my love, I really want your love all the time, but darling we have to have a bed and new curtain to keep our time of pleasure in much more privacy and comfort.'

'Yes, my darling, I would like to go down with you on Rákóczi ut to look for some beds and some sitting and dining furniture. Also, for some household textiles, kitchen, and tableware accessories.'

'That will be a good idea Gabriel, will do it together tomorrow at dinnertime.'

The following day, I went to see some of the furniture shops with Rebekah she has brought her Bauhaus Magazine and the piano brochure just to try to match the furniture which should be in the Art Nuovo style.

I left all the household textile to Rebekah as she has a much better taste for those things. We both chose the other furniture together. Rebekah has agreed with the store owner to go to our house and measure all the windows to custom make lace curtains and heavier lined velvet curtains too. Rebekah has made an appointment with a lady called Katalin in the textile shop to meet up with her there and tell her what kind of curtains she wants.

The time really has speeded up since we got back home it is Friday again, and we are getting ready to celebrate our Sabbath, with my favourite clear chicken soup.

Next morning, back at the Hoif Complex Synagogue. Now people are saving the seats for Isaack and for me. I don't have to sit in the back row in the room anymore. But I always enjoyed it as often we had a late night with Miklós, in Budapest, and we could nod off for a minute or two and nobody bothered with that.

After the service Rabbi Baruch asked me to stay behind for five minutes as he wanted to ask me about the piano show and concert which I have organised at the National Theatre.

'You know Gabriel since you came to Munkács many things have changed I have to say that you have brought some energy with you and some buzz and interest which is going on all ready.'

'You know we would like to have a piano for the synagogue. I hope you could help to get a good one for us.'

'Rabbi Baruch, did you say that there is a big interest going on for those pianos. Do you think if I would have at least twenty pianos than I could sell them all?'

'I think you would, Gabriel.'

'Then I will get in touch with Mr Károly Neuhold and will make a deal with him to bring at least twenty five pianos and with the transport company so they don't have to go back empty to Budapest, but they could deliver some excellent quality pine and hardwood timber with them an return.'

'Gabriel, your mind is very fertile, quick to recognise a business opportunity and you run with it.'

'I tell you this, Gabriel. I know good people in the timber trade, and I will have a word with them over pricing which you could work with, also I will promote this piano event for you.'

'That will be just perfect Rabbi Baruch and I can guarantee that the Synagogue will have the first option to choose from those pianos. A piano would look well in this room, don't you think?'

'Yes, Gabriel, I can see one standing at the side of the room which would look very well there.'

I have joined Isaack and Rebekah who were waiting for me in front of the synagogue and as we were walking home. Rebekah asked me the reason why did the Rabbi hold me back. And when I told them the news Isaack congratulated me for my quick-thinking Mazel tov my boy, and asked me; is there anything else you wouldn't do Gabriel?

'Yes, exporting timber to Hungary as well.'

'Timbers Gabriel?'

'Why not Isaack, if there is money in the timber, I can get a customer for that. Business is business.'

The following Monday I have sent a letter with a proposal to Mr Neuhold at The Musica Piano Salon regarding the numbers of pianos we would require for this exhibition and sales and a suggestion that the removal lorries could take excellent quality timbers with them to Budapest. May well be his piano company would be able to use some of this timber for his pianos.

Well, the time is flying with us it is 8 August already. I am back in the office where Andre proudly updated me with the news that he has managed to get booking for Miklós. Firstly, here in Munkács, then Ungvár, Counties.

'Well done, Andre, but twelve evenings is quite a lot don't you think?'

'So the first evening for him is here in Munkács on 12 September just after your wedding and the rest of his poetry evenings will be after 14 September. One evening he is performing and the next day he will be travelling to the next venue. So he will perform on every other day.'

'Well, Andre, I know he will enjoy it, but I don't think that Fifi will, but let see how she is going to feel about that.'

It looks as if Andre and Viktoria well and truly have the feel for the art of booking, and they are good at it. They always ask for the confirmation in written form and the name of the responsible organiser at venues.

I have settled with Mr Klein over the works he has done on 11 August. He has done a marvellous job on the fence for the vegetable garden and for the landscaping of the courtyard as well. He told me that the telephone line will be brought into the house in October.

'I hope you are satisfied with everything Gabriel, and many thanks for the payment in Pengő.'

'Yes, József, we are very happy with everything, but we are looking for a good gardener for our back garden and for the vines as I know nothing about them. I hope you could help me with that.'

'That won't be a problem Gabriel as my brother in-law Samuel he is widowed recently, and he is very good, and he would do everything for you around the garden.'

'Thank you, József, I would like to talk to him about doing this gardening for us on a regular basis.'

Isaack has the letter of acceptance from Mr Itzhak Steiner for the base unit of our new factory.

'He asked us to counter sign the contract and send it back to them then all will be in order.' They will send the keys for the factory then we can move in immediately into our new base. That is really well timed as the haulage company would like to deliver the new machines and furniture which Isaack and Rebekah bought in the auction last week.

Isaack and Samuel went along to the new base and marked the place out for all machines for the newly bought and the ones Isaack's old machines on the floor of the new bay as it have to have an enforced electrical power cabling for all machines. This is a very exciting time for all of us as the new factory is getting into shape. Isaack is not very happy as the production has been delayed because of the moving process.

'I have received a reply from Miss Jennifer Wood from Conveyor and Elevator Company in Accrington England… Miss Wood advised us on the kind of fields of industry they are supporting with their products and some important technical details for conveyors in general.'

Dear Rebekah, In England they use screw conveyors for moving powders and dry food stuffs for the food and brewing industry as well as liquids and semi solids. They can be used to load ships with cargo of raw materials such as coal, flour, and grain. There are all kinds of applications for moving raw materials between level in manufacturing. One of their biggest customers are concerned with the movement of water and other liquids…………

I went with Rebekah to The Handelsman restaurant and reception hall to book our wedding reception for 11 September. This venue is just a short distance from the Hoif Complex where our ceremony will be held under the Chuppah.

'I had a letter from my friend Móricz Hlébly, at the Agricultural Ministry and giving me an advise that I must send our product information on our conveyors and elevators to the Ministry of Agriculture with wording of: 'We are a company who is based in Munkács, and we are manufacturing custom made conveyors for industries in agriculture and industries like water works elevations for sewage and water irrigation.' But you must do it now Gabriel!'

At home, this evening we all are late due to our engagements with our business and the four of us have a family meeting over the commitments that we are committing ourselves to financially and physically to this new business that we are involved with. Isaack was breaking down the financial strain which will affect all of us. Rebekah has her profit predictions and figures in front of her from the books in pre and after taxes. I have to say it is not very encouraging.

My input is still not a 'hands on figure', but I believe this information which I am giving them is the part of the foundation of our 'business' we are building now. We have moved from manufacturing from day to day with a steady income to transforming it into a much bigger and much more profitable era with a respectable promised future.

Isaack said Gabriel I have to say that you and Rebekah are driving us into this new field with such speed. I have been respected for the standard of jobs I have produced from my factory, but I feel that this is far too fast for me.

'But Papa we do not want to destroy the standard and your respect within the business communities we are working for you to take it into a much bigger and productive organisation. You are still the head of our family and also the head of the Grósz and Family's Company. We are still now, and we will be a family unit as long as we are alive.

'Now it is me and Gabriel who are taking most of the financial burdens, but it is still you who are the leader of us as we do not understand engineering, we only recognise an opportunity when it's there to take Papa. We have the fresh energy, and we are working with that speed, which we feel comfortable with and that is here now, and I think you should sit back and relax a bit more with Rita. I think you should marry her after so many years she has been there for you, and she was a mother to me in all these years.'

My goodness, the atmosphere suddenly dropped. I thought Rebekah just spoke from her heart.

'Isaack just looked at his daughter and said quietly did you mean what you have just said to me Rebekah?'

'*Aapukám*, I am moving out from this house with my husband. Not far away just to down the road to Latorca utca. You are going to be with Rita as she has always been there for us. Both of you looked after me like a mother and a father, she always been there for you Papa and for me. Rita deserves a recognition and a respect in Munkács.'

Rita was in tears, Isaack was embarrassed, and the atmosphere was icy in the room.

'Look, Rebekah, I have sacrificed my life for you I have worked from seven in the morning till seven in the evening. I know that without Rita I wouldn't have been able to provide you the standard of life which you have enjoyed. I am still a respected member of our community, but I have never thought of this that you have just told me.'

Isaack turned to Rita and told her, 'I never thought of that Rita that we should ever get married. Rebekah is right when she says that you were the most loyal and supportive person in my life. You've been the carer and mother for my daughter Rebekah just as if she would of your own. As I have come to this ripe age, and I am slowing down next to this younger generation and accepting the fact my daughter has grown to a woman and leaving us with her husband, and I realised that this is the time when I should realise that she is right. I have overlooked of the fact that I have should of have married you Rita long time ago. (It wasn't a broken man's speech but the one whose eyes have been opened).'

Rita has burst into tears Rebekah has comforted her, and she said, 'Very sorry Rita if I have made you cry but I felt it had to be said.'

Isaack turned to Rita and said in a gentle voice, 'Rita Goldberg would you marry me?'

Rita looked at Isaack and said, 'Yes, Isaack Grósz, I would be honoured to be your lawful wedded wife.'

Both of them stood up and embraced in front of us. Rebekah and I spontaneously applauded them and joyfully shouted Mazel tov!

I said, 'I think this is the time now to open that Hungarian champagne to drink and celebrate this occasion. Rebekah was hugging both Isaack and Rita and kept repeating herself Mazel tov to you both.'

The rest of the evening thanks to Rebekah's diplomacy was a very special and an uplifting family atmosphere. Mainly happy and joyful.

The next morning Isaack went to see Rabbi Baruch before he went to his factory. I guess something to do with his marriage arrangement with Rita.

I have sent out letters to various organisations locally and regionally offering the new way of moving liquid, semi liquid and solid materials. Also, the other part of our business which is reminding the trade of the Ganz Works agency for electronic motors and generators which are available now from our premises. Also, to Zoltán to say we are ready for business, and we would need some electric motors and generators on a sale or return basis for the start then of course we will pay for the future stocks. Also, we would need permission to use the Ganz Works name above our office.

All of our plans have started to be speeding up in a much faster way then we anticipated. Rebekah had a dinner with Viktoria which I have feared that I would lose her for Rebekah.

I didn't mind as Andre was such an asset for me. He is a natural born organiser; he just has natural feel for the 'entertaining market' he has a good future. But until that he is working with me, and I would not let him to be taken away from me.

'Rebekah told me at our evening meal that Viktoria will work with her in her office from the beginning of September.'

'Well, darling, you have got a very hardworking and very knowledgeable young lady who will be your right hand in every way.'

'I know Gabriel what I have done but sorry I have to take her away from your office.'

'That is alright my darling after all she is still working for me as well in our office.'

'Well, yes, in a way, but she is my employee.'

The following day I went with Isaack and Rebekah to the local Trade and Commerce office and registered our new company with them and asked them for some kind of support in a promotional way and also we would like to have an open day at our new bay's opening party. Mr Aladár Vozáry was very helpful, and he has assured us of his full support for our efforts to make it a success.

'My darling Rebekah, we are going to be very busy as we have István coming from Sutyai Béla Furniture Company he is going to install all the doors and the built-in furniture for the bedrooms and for the lounge. At least we will have our bed at last.'

'Yes, Gabriel, I cannot wait. Also, the lady from the textile shop, Katalin, is coming with the finished curtains to hang them all around the house.'

'We are getting there, Gabriel. When is Samuel coming to start working on our back garden?'

'I am glad at last we are going to have those curtains up as Elisabeth was telling me that some neighbours have started looking through our windows.'

'Samuel is there already and telling us, as you know we have only some more weeks to go to have our first szüret.'

'We have to celebrate that don't you think darling?'

'You know, Gabriel, it is time again for us to see the progress on our house sometime tomorrow. How do you feel about that?'

'I am absolutely starved for it my love and to being with you again there.'

'Me too.'

Chapter 49

House and New Factory Are Completed and Their Blessing

Andre presented me with a leaflet and a poster he has designed for Miklós and Fifi: 'Please come along end enjoy on Evening with a Poet Miklós Radnóti and his wife Fanni Gyarmati Fifi.' I have left the date and the time of his performance space empty for the organisers to fill in the time they are planning to arrange it. 'What do you think Gabriel?'

'It is excellent Andre, it looks professional and tells just enough to the audience which would 'whet their appetites'. This is the photo I am using for Miklós poster.'

'That is very good, Andre, I like it, would you please go downstairs to the printer's copier and make some 600 leaflets which we will send out to all venues.'

'What about the posters, Gabriel?'

'Well, let the cultural centre produce them. It would be more expensive if we have to get them printed at our expense by the printers in town.'

'Gabriel, I have spoken to Viktoria, and she told me that Rebekah has offered her a job at your new factory. Is that true?'

'Yes, Andre, that is true. She will start working at Partalja utca new factory. Rebekah has offered more money and the two girls like each other's company so that is the reason. I will miss her too, but she will still working for me also as I am running the Ganz Works electric motor's agency so she will still be with me in the office.'

'You know what we are going to do Andre it will make us much better off financially. It is demanding hard work, but it will pay at the and make us much more comfortable. I know that I am all over the place, from entertainment to electronic motors agency engineering business to timber exporter.'

'You have forgotten your involvement with pianos.'

'Yes, as well on top of all those other things. There is an old saying Andre, 'never put all your eggs into one basket.' So please stay with me Andre you will not regret it what you are doing is very good you have the talent for this kind of business, and you will be successful in your career. Remember the dressing is very important, the bowtie and a hat are essential for a theatrical agent in the artworld.'

I am sending some of these flyers to Miklós and the dates for his poetry evening with Fifi. Also, the invitation for our wedding and make the point while they are in Munkács they will staying with us.

Also, I have sent an invitation for Zoltán and Johanna. I promised that I will book them into the Star Hotel for the duration of our wedding and if they wish to attend Miklós Poetry evening which is on 12 September. I can arrange that too which would give them an opportunity to come and visit our new factory on Partalja utca.

István has finished with all the bedroom furniture, doors, bedside cubes and the wooden panelled wall in the entrance hall, dining room and in the lounge. All these lacquered finishes with a hint of lime green shading and the curtain rails are coloured in the same tone as the doors and wall panels.

Rita was helping Rebekah to choose all the kitchen ware accessories, plates, cutlery, pans and so on.

Also, Katalin has hung the net and the heavy velvet curtains at every window around the house. She have dressed all the beds with sheets duvets and pillows and left the extra bedding in each bedroom wardrobe.

Mr Klein told me that he will come and show me how to operate the central heating system when the oil will be delivered next week to the oil tank which he put in underground next to the front gate. Mr Klein showed me all the main switches for water, electricity and the central heating boiler in the cold room.

'After checking over the finished woodwork with István from Sutyai Furnishing company, I have to say that as all the work is now in place to a satisfactory standard. Even he has covered all the pipes with the same finished wood. I have to say that our house really looks like a film set in a Hollywood movie. It has been worth it for the long wait and for all the cost of refurbishment.'

Finally, at 6:30 pm, I managed to get back to Isaack's house. The food was already on the table, and I felt a bit guilty that they have to wait for me with the supper. After Isaack finished with the Kiddush, then we started our supper and started our conversation with updating each other on our day's experiences about the new factory bay and Rebekah's shopping with Rita and with my endless day's experience at our new house as it is almost completed. We still need chandeliers and wall lights for all the rooms. And then after our wedding we can move in into our new luxurious house.

'Yes, we have created something very luxurious out of a farmhouse. But we have to ask Rabbi Baruch to come and bless our house. Of course, then we will have a housewarming party.'

'Isaack told us that the haulage company has delivered all the machines which have been bought in the auction and from Isaack's factory, and they have put them into places where Samuel and the other tradesmen will fix it to the floor.'

'Rebekah has told me that she has designated a desk in her office.'

Isaack jokingly commented on Rebekah's statement, 'So that is your office only?'

'No, Papa, it is ours, but I am the one who is running that office. I have a desk for all of us for you Papa and for you Gabriel at the back of the office and for Me and Viktoria. At the front of the office we have a reception area to welcome customers. You should have seen the amount of office furniture we have had with all the filing cabinets, and I didn't realised it when I did my bulk bidding that a very large security safe was included in that auction lot.'

'Even with all the office accessories like ink wells and a comptometer L. C. Smith's Typewriters, and telephones with a complete telephone PBX board and the clocking in clocks for the workers. This now looks like a modern and a much more professional office compared with your old very small office, Papa. I know you will say that office doesn't make money only the shop floor. But now you have an equally modern machine park as you have just dreamt of, and you have always said, 'One day my love, I will have the most modern factory'. Now, Papa, you have it, it is a spacious and a very modern one. Your dream has come true. You won't believe this Papa what I have found; an order book and a delivery book of this company, this was left in the bottoms of the filing cabinet.'

'That can be useful Rebekah I have to read through their existing customer base and see what kind of jobs they supplied to their customers and what did they charged for it. Then we just have to write to them all to let them know that we can continually supply them with their orders.'

'Well, my dear daughter, you are an angel, what you have just found is a goldmine.'

We didn't realise the time as we were on a high discussing the business opportunities which excited us and that it was already midnight. Rita and Rebekah have gone to bed, and we have been left behind just for one more drink.

The following morning, we have met up with Dr Sándor at the synagogue and discussed some social political things as we always do. Isaack invited Sándor for a dinner at his house where we could talk more in private.

'After the Sabbath service, I told Rabbi Baruch that I have ordered the largest upright piano for the synagogue.'

'Thank you, Gabriel, and I have had a word with Kleiner at the timber plant who told me that they have an agent importer from Hungary already, but he could supply you as a one-off shipment.'

'When you see, Mr Kleiner, just tell him that Rabbi Baruch has arranged it with him.'

'Thank you very much, Rabbi Baruch, I would like you to come and bless our house as it is now ready to move into, but we wouldn't move in yet until the day of our marriage here at the Hoif Complex. We will be staying continuously s at Isaack's house, but I would like to have it blessed before that day please.'

'Do you have a Mezuzah Gabriel?'

'Yes, Rabbi Baruch, I have been given one with the Shema inside by Rabbi Simon Rozenberg from the Rombach utca Pray house—Synagogue in Budapest because I have left behind my Mezuzah for the Krenczberger family when they have bought my apartment in Budapest. I have told him the story about the furniture and Rabbi Rosenberg gifted me one for my new house here in Munkács. But we would like to have a Mezuzah for our new factory before we are moving into that base.'

'Well, that was a noble action that you have exercised with your fellow Jew.'

'When would you like me to come to recite the shehecheyanu blessing on your house and on your new factory?'

'Whenever is convenient for you Rabbi Baruch?'

'Well, I know that I am free this coming Wednesday, 24 August I will come to your house first at ten in the morning then I will do it at your new factory at 11:30 am, and I will bring you a Mezuzah.'

'That will be perfect Rabbi Baruch, so I will see you on Wednesday at ten at our house.'

'Mazel Tov. Well done, Gabriel.'

After Isaack said the kiddush five of us with Dr Sándor have started to enjoy Rita's delicious cooking and Isaack's great wine from his admired collection.

'After dinner, Isaack firstly thanked Sándor for the help he contributed towards getting a good deal from our new landlord and with Sándor's contribution with Mr Itzhak Steiner. Isaack was telling us his and Rebekah's successful auction purchases and the mistake that the previous owner has made when he didn't look through the filing cabinets, and he has left behind those important company books.'

'Sándor was suggesting that he knows some very good engineers who are Jewish and have worked for this company and now they are redundant. It would be helpful if we could employ them in our factory.'

'Yes, Sándor of course I will.'

'Mazel tov Isaack so when is the mayor opening of your new base.'

'I am hoping for the first of September. Like you have heard from Gabriel that Rabbi Baruch is coming to bless the factory next Wednesday then soon after we will be ready for full production. I hope you would be able to attend in your Official role as The Deputy Mayor of Munkács to the blessing recite of the shehecheyanu.'

'Of course, Isaack I will be there as an official from the Council. I will bring the local press as well it should be promoted as a local businessman is expanding his business, and he is going to employ more people in Munkács. I think that should help Gabriel's new agency for Ganz Works as well.'

'Isaack, it's called free publicity and also will bring some appraisal for the Council of Munkács Town that we are an inspiration for foreign investment and attracting foreign businesses to move into our prosperous town like Ganz Work of Budapest. I know this sounds very political, but it is going to bring more positive attention to our work at the Town Council and of course to your companies as well.'

'My goodness, Sándor, you sound like Rebekah and Gabriel full of energy imagination and hope.'

'You know the old Jewish saying Isaack? Like a pebble in the shallow lake you will be covered in moss but if you are in a fast-moving river you will be polished like a diamond.'

'Yes, Sándor you are right. Fortunately, I have two precious stones in my hand, and I feel that I am truly blessed with them.'

'And what about this piano and timber business Gabriel you are now involved with?'

'It's just happened Sándor, I cannot help but thank the Lord He brings all these opportunities my way, and I just cannot resist to take up those challenges.'

'I believe that you have invited Mr Rosenthal and Mr Segal to Munkács.'

'Actually, that was I, Sándor who made that invitation.'

'So it was you, Rebekah? Do you know that both of them are coming here to Munkács with a delegation for a fact-finding mission to bring investment here and in the Region?'

'I didn't know that Sándor, I have just pointed out to them that we have much natural energy and minerals which they could help to develop them and of course which would help our economy as well.'

'Well done, my girl, you are a borne businesswoman. You have impressed Mr Segal at the Astoria restaurant in Budapest, he has praised you for your eloquence in business and in finances.'

'My goodness, where does that come from Isaack, I thought Rebekah was studying a human subject at the university and not business?'

'And you Gabriel as only a teacher?'

He added jokingly, 'Have you both been a successful businessman and businesswomen in your previous life? This is just marvellous.'

'Well, Sándor, these two youths who are feeding each other with challenges of growing bigger and better in every way. You should see their new house that is the reflection of the future they are aiming for.'

'Yes, now you mentioned your new house, so when can I see it?'

'So why don't we walk to have a look at it now this afternoon?'

So we all five of us went to see our house as Isaack hasn't seen the completed and finished state.

'As we got to our house Sándor said, I like your new wooden gate.'

'Thank you, Sándor, all the wood works has been, done by the Sutyai Furniture Company.'

As we let them into the house and walked from room to room both of Sándor and Isaack have been very impressed with the finished house.

Sándor said, 'Well, I can understand what Isaack was telling me about your high standards and imaginative life expectations not just in business but also in a taste for a luxurious standard.'

'Well, I would love to see your children what they are going to be like with your energy.'

Rebekah quickly replied to Sándor's hint, 'Not just yet Sándor, first we have to settle with all this chaos that we have started with the business then a couple of years later we both promise you we will have some offspring.'

'Good thinking, Rebekah.'

'Isaack pulled me aside and asked me if I would need some money. As I look at this house now it must have cost you a fortune to have it done to such a high standard.'

'Thank you, Isaack, but I have enough left to carry on finishing what we have planned with Rebekah.'

'After a very exciting visit to our house walking back to Isaack's house Sándor pulled me aside and asked me the same thing as Isaack. You know our organisation would help you if you would need that.'

'Thank you, Sándor, but at this time I am well organised. But going back to the suggestion you have made to Isaack about those redundant workers. I have brought up at the meeting with our leadership of OMZSA that we will recruit more young people and will help them to find work and to help to make up some 'gift package' full of clothing, schoolbooks, toys for children and food for them to celebrate the holydays.'

'I have contacted some textile shops and clothing shops and asked them if they have some of these items that they could contribute to this effort to support the poorer new arrivals from outside of Transcarpathia.'

'I like your idea, Gabriel, why don't you come and see me in my office in the town hall then we will organise it properly with a team of delivery of these gift packages.'

My Monday morning started in Sándor's office where we discussed our gift package situation for the poor Jewish families with prosperous contributors and delivery services. 'Sándor will get in touch with all the Rabbi's in Munkács and Ugocsa County and will ask them to provide us with the numbers of families who would need our gift packages and also, they would do the distribution. All these have to be completed for Rosh Hashanah, 26 September, and Yom Kippur, 10 October.'

'Look, Gabriel, I will come to the factory's blessing in my Official capacity as Deputy Mayor, but I won't be able to attend your house at all for that day. I hope you understand.'

'Absolutely, Sándor, I do understand your position.'

'Well, I'll see you there.'

On Wednesday Rabbi Baruch and his wife Rivka have arrived at our house where only Rebekah and I attended. Before we went into the house, I have put our Mezuza on my Tallit. Rabbi Baruch spoken on Hebrew with a humble tone:

shehecheyanu
Baruch Ata A-do-nai Elo-heinu Melech Haolam she-hech-e-ya-nu v'ki-ma-nu v'hi-gi-ya-nu li-z'man hazeh.

Blessed are You, L-rd our G-d, King of the Universe, who has granted us life, sustained us and enabled us to reach this occasion.

Then Rabbi Baruch fixed the Mezuza on our doorpost then we all touched the Mezuza with our Tallit then Rebekah and I followed Rabbi Baruch and his wife into our newly blessed house.

'Rebekah showed all of us around in every room of the house which impressed Rivka very much indeed. She said that she had never seen a modern house which has been equipped with all the latest technologies and the colours of the wooden panes on the wall which matches with the door panels.'

'Rabbi Baruch said, It is like being in the American movies.'

After the blessing, the four of us walked to our new factory which is almost at the back of Hoif Complex Rabbi Baruch Synagogue on Partalja utca.

When we arrived at the factory there was quite a crowd waiting for us. It was great to see Dr Sándor Fried and Vozáry Aladár from the Munkács Trade and Commerce and from the Munkács based newspapers; a reporter Pál Rácz with a photographer from the *Kárpáti Magyar Hírlap* and Béla Róth a journalist from the *Független Újság* (Independent News Paper) was among the guests.

Rabbi Baruch Rabinowitz has blessed Isaack's Factory then the reporters have photographed Isaack and Dr Sándor Fried and the Rabbi and Aladár Vozáry together and the reporters have interviewed the four men. I have stayed in the background with Rebekah and Viktoria. We all felt that this was Isaack's big day, this is his company and his dream so he should have the attention.

'Then Mr Simon Menyhért and Béla Róth walked to us and congratulated us on our marriage and asked Rebekah and me if they could interview us sometime in the near future.'

We agreed that next week here in the factory would be the best place for that interview.

At the end of the celebration and of the blessing of the factory Rabbi Baruch has fixed the Mezuza on the main entrance of the office doorpost than Isaack invited everybody inside into the office for light refreshments. I helped Rebekah, Rita, and Viktoria to serve the refreshments to our guests.

After some two hours when all the refreshments have been finished, we finally sat down in the office and relaxed after the very busy and tiring day we had today. 'I suggested to Isaack let me invite everybody to the Star Restaurant for a meal to celebrate a very successful opening of our new factory. I think Rita was the most grateful to that invitation as she didn't really have time to prepare our supper for this evening.'

At the restaurant Isaack asked Rebekah and me to have a word with us before we sat down for a meal.

'What is the problem, Papa?'

'We I just couldn't keep it any longer from you that I had a word with Rabbi Baruch Rabinowitz about I would like to marry Rita on the same day as your wedding.'

'Rebekah embraced Isaack and with tears of joy in her eyes she said I am so very glad for both of you. Mazel tov my dear Papa. I have shaken Isaack hand and congratulated him too.'

'Thank you, Rebekah, I thought that would make you happy.'

'Thank you, darling, but please both of you not a word to Rita as she doesn't know yet, I want to tell her tonight at home in front of you only.'

Andre came to join us, and we were all very happy for the successful day. Rebekah and I have more things to be happier about as we know what Isaack is going to do later on.

When we got inside the house Isaack asked Rebekah and Rita to get some glasses for the Hungarian Champagne because he had an announcement to make. Please all sit down and hear my big news.

'I have asked Rita to marry me, and she accepted my proposal and furthermore I have agreed with Rabbi Baruch Rabinowitz to marry us on the same day when we celebrate your wedding.'

'Rita didn't know this, and she just burst into tears of happiness stood up and first hugged and kissed Isaack then Rebekah and then she came to me. I felt her whole body was shaking from happiness.'

I could have drank a whole bottle of alcohol and wouldn't feel drunk at all as I was too tired from all this excitement we had today.

But one thing is sure that we all will sleep very well tonight.

Chapter 50

First Conveyor Almost Completed;
Ganz Motors Arrive

Isaack left early in the morning just to open up his new business for the first day of production. He was in a good mood as he was singing a little Jewish song that I had never heard before.

Rebekah followed her father at eight but before she went, she whispered in my ear that she would like to meet me in our house at twelve. I said I will be there then finally at last went to work at half past eight. I pecked a kiss on a very happy Rita's cheek and congratulated her again.

Rita said, 'You know Gabriel I have never expected this in my life that I would ever be married to Isaack. And here I am over fifty years of age, and it is happening. You know before you turned up on the scene Rebekah was like a shell. I was worried about her that she might end up an old girl like me. Wearing old women's dresses and never going out with anybody. Then you came along, and she has opened up like a beautiful flower and she is madly in love with you. I believe that your meeting has been arranged by angels. As I look at you two from the outside, it looks so unreal it is to perfect what humans cannot control. But what am I talking about you know this special blessing on both of you. I am just so pleased for you.'

In the office some letters were waiting for me. One of them from Mr Neuhold at Musica Piano Company, in which he was expressing his happiness at the number of pianos I ordered from him and the concerts I organised during this exhibition. Mr Neuhold personally knew the concert pianist, Dezső Zádor, from the Franz Liszt Conservatoire. He had visited his showroom several times.

'In the consignment are six grand pianos and (one is yours) and twenty upright pianos. With regards to the timber you have mentioned in your letter I am very interested in having them, but these are the kind and the quantity of wood I would need for my piano factory. If there is more available, I can offer them to my colleagues in the trade. I am very certain that we will have all the timber that these removal lorries can carry back with them. Well, this is promising news of my first success for the future.'

The next letter is from Zoltán in which he thanked me for taking our agreement with such a serious manner. He tells me that they are sending four motors with speed control gearboxes and alternators: one 20kW, two 30Kw, and one 40kW electric motors free of charge just for our experimental purposes.

'Also, Ganz Works Budapest has approved your agency and we will be supplying your agency on a sale or return basis of 250 electric motors with the most commonly used specification. These goods have left our factory today by rail freight directly to your company in Munkács.

'Also, Johanna and I are thanking you for your kind invitation to your wedding and we are both delighted to accept your invitation and let you know that we will attend your wedding. Also, it will give me an opportunity to visit my old hometown Munkács.'

Well, I never expected such generosity and trust from a person whom I have met only three times. Zoltán suggested that he was going to make a booking for an apartment at the Star Hotel for a week and Ganz Works will pay for that expense.

Back in my office with a sad-faced Andre and Viktoria; both of them were unusually quiet. Andre was not happy to lose Viktoria from the office.

'Look Andre there are times in life where one in partnership would recognise that he or she have to take the opportunity to step up on the stepladder with their career. Look at me I am a qualified teacher and I have got myself in the industry which I have never learned but I have adapted to it.

'Rebekah is very fond of Viktoria, and she has recognised her talent in accountancy, and she has offered to Viktoria a chance to work with her in the office with much better wages than I could offer to Viktoria. So please do not be harsh on Viktoria as we all have to move on and adapt to the work which is taking you further upwards with a better financial position. Both of you can carry on as very close friends and hopefully both of you still remaining in that state and eventually you will be married at the time when both of you feel ready.'

'I know Gabriel but at least I still can see Viktoria any time during the day, and I will miss that closeness with her.'

'Look Andre as this office commitment often will take you away from Munkács you have to travel all over the region on business at this time you wouldn't be with Viktoria probably for days. So just think of that would you leave Viktoria alone in the office while you are away?'

'No, I wouldn't like to do that. Yes, I can see your point Gabriel and I accept it. Sorry Viktoria for my attitude but I miss you all the time.'

The two embraced each other and I was happy to see that peace has been restored between them.

'Now both of you back to work please.'

'Yes Gabriel. Thank you Gabriel.'

My mind was occupied with the fact that I was going to meet up with Rebekah at our house where now we have a proper bed and bedding available for our pleasure. Well that is really luxury. Just can't wait, I feel impatient like Andre.

Rebekah was in the house already as I walked through the door, she has flown into my arm and embraced me, and we kissed as if we have never done it before. As we recovered from our travel to heaven and back, we decided to stay a bit longer in bed and with a joyous mood acknowledged that how peaceful and spiritually filled this house has now become. 'What a treat,' I said, 'we have now a complete and beautiful luxurious family home and this is now ours, Rebekah, belonging to two of us. It has been blessed by Rabbi Baruch and you feel the blessing and the presence of the Lord. And when the time comes, we will have the joy of the fruit of our greatest love, our children. If it is a girl, she should carry your name Rebekah!'

'Yes, my darling and if it is a boy, he should be called Gabriel.'

'It's a deal my darling. Yes, we have become husband and wife when we have seen each other the first time in Lvov. Our future has been sealed then by the Lord.'

'I made my commitment to you Gabriel at the moment when I gifted you my innocence. That was our pledge we have made to each other on that night, as we were kneeling before the Lord God.'

Then we got dressed and walked from room to room in the house. Rebekah has her arm in mine then she put her head on my shoulder and I kissed her on her head. It was a very uplifting romantic moment, and that has drifted into reality when we have realised that we have to go back to work.

It was a declining feeling but there is a positive fact that at least we always have a hideaway place to be on our own here until our wedding.

I asked Rebekah to collect all the names of her family and friend who she would like to be invited to our wedding as these invitations have to be sent out.'

'Yes, Gabriel, I have done it already sent out the invitation to my friends and relatives two weeks ago.'

'That is good, so hopefully we will have some idea how many guests we should count on to accommodate them at the Handelsman restaurant after our wedding ceremony.'

'We will work that out tonight at home Gabriel.'

Next morning, I went to the new factory with all the information that I received from Miss Jennifer Wood and sat down with Isaack and Samuel as I had to translate the technical details from English to Hungarian.

'Well Isaack and Samuel, what can you make out this information? I can't so I hope you don't mind that I will leave you to figure out all these technical details. I will be in the office if you need me.'

'It is straightforward to me Gabriel, but I will come back to you if I need some help with the translation.'

'But the main points of law with the conveyors is that we have to put into the principle of the designer is: : **Bolt density, Capacity, and 1000 Kg. per Speed. And they are powered with 20kW to 40kW electric motors.'**

I was arranging my position in the office. My desk is at the right-hand end of the big office where Rebekah has allocated a couple of filing cabinets for the Ganz Works client orders, sales, and delivery records. She is good and well understands bookkeeping practices. Also, in front of my desk nearer to the front windows there are some comfortable armchairs with a coffee table for entertaining business associates and guests.

She gave me a standard notebook and a dipping pen with an ink well and that is it. I will still use my fountain pen that I have been given in Budapest by a good friend.

She had two desks one is with a lockable roller shutter where she keeps her financial records and the other one is like mine and Isaack's a director type with nothing really on just some three draws on either side if the desk.

Viktoria had a desk with draws like the one Rebekah used for accounting purposes. Both of them had a comptometer machine and an L. C. Smith's Typewriter. Every desk had a telephone including one on a metal desk on the shop floor for Samuel. The telephone PBX board and the clocking in clocks for the workers were also on the shop floor. Sometime later after I settled behind my desk, I went to see Isaack and Samuel, they were still discussing the breakdown and costing of a standard conveyor and the time the tradesmen have to spend on each complete unit.

At dinner time thee of us went to the Star restaurant and Isaack gave me some idea of the cost of materials and motor for a standard conveyor unit and Isaack worked it out that we should put 35 to 40% profit on each unit. Of course, if there is a multiple order, we can give some discount to the customer.

By the time we got back to the factory, Samuel had some much better figures for us which with I could compose an information flyer and the letter to The Agricultural Ministry on Kossuth Lajos tér. My friend Móricz Hlébly had advised me to send it to him personally then he will hand deliver it to the competent person in the Agricultural Ministry.

I told Isaack that the four motors with speed control gearboxes and alternators were one 20kW, two 30Kw, and one 40kW electric motors free of charge just for experimental purposes.

'Also, Ganz Works Budapest has approved my agency and they will supply our agency on a sale or return basis of 250 electric motors with the most commonly used specification. These goods have left the factory today by rail freight directly to your company in Munkács.'

'Well we are in business already. Well done Gabriel.'

Next morning after the service at the synagogue Sándor reminded us that the delegation from Budapest will arrive this Monday the 29th of August. They will come straight to his office, but they had specifically asked for Rebekah and for me to attend. There will be four gentlemen Mr Segal from the Magyar Királyi National Bank and his colleague. Mr Rosenthal from the Associated Trade and Commers Office and his colleague.

'They will be staying here for one day then they are going up to Ungvár. I believe they are coming here to Munkács because of your excellent presentation at that meeting at the Dohány utca's Great Synagogue and Rebekah's invitation at the Astoria Restaurant dinner meeting you two had with them.'

Isaack just looked at us and asked Rebekah, 'What else have you done in Budapest that you haven't told me.'

'What do you mean Papa?'

'Well, Mr Segal one of the directors of the Hungarian National Bank asking for your presence and your guidance here in Munkács?'

'Ah, yes Papa, I promised him that I will show him around all the banks in Munkács.'

'Well, I am very proud both of you. I would have never thought that you my daughter will become such an important businesswoman in Munkács.'

Chapter 51
Business and Banking
Delegation from Budapest

Monday morning before we were due to arrive at the Deputy Mayor's office, I called into my office to collect some paperwork which I had prepared for today's meeting. Andre and Viktoria were in the office already. Andre was showing me those big boxfuls of Hungarian Movies which had just arrived this morning from the Hungarian Cultural Ministry.

I said, 'Look, I just can't deal with them, right now I am very busy, but I'll deal with it later on.'

So, at 8.30 am Rebekah and I arrived at the Deputy Mayor's Office in the Town Hall. Sándor invited Mr Aladár Vozáry (who is in a process to be elected as the *Kárpátaljai Gyáriparosok Szövetsége Elnöke* (Director of the Transcarpathian Trade and Commerce) was there already.

He kindly greeted us and congratulated us on the excellent opening of the Isaack Grósz and Family Engineering Factory last Wednesday. 'When will your Ganz Work's Agency start trading Gabriel?'

'I am hoping by the end of this week Mr Vozáry as soon as the electric motors will arrive to the main freight station of Munkács.'

'Look Gabriel if you need some help with the haulage, I can recommend you a local firm.'

'Thank you very much I do appreciate your help it will be very useful for the future as well.'

The delegation from Budapest has been booked into the Star Hotel I can see through Sándor's office window they have just walked across the street, and they have now arrived promptly at 9.30 am so we can prepare our presentation programs for them.

'Where shall we start our introductory trip in Munkács: there is wood, salt, tobacco, mining of natural minerals, pharmaceutical and chemical plants in the region. I have organised some taxis to take us to visit these companies.'

Sándor welcomed the delegation members and introduced us and Mr Aladár Vozáry to the guests.

Mr Segal thanked Sándor and told him, 'But we know Rebekah and Gabriel already from Budapest.' He greeted Rebekah and I then he introduced his assistant, Mr János Koch a Bank Clerk.

Mr Rosenthal introduced his assistant József Walt who is the director of import / export for his company. Then Sándor offered us some refreshment which none of us took up.

Mr Segal suggested that they have a busy day today so they would like to get on with their plan, then later they would like to have some private meeting with Rebekah, Sándor and with myself.

Mr Segal asked Rebekah if she would join two of them and visit some banks in centre of Munkács where Rebekah could recommend some properties for a possible future bank building to be opened for the Magyar kir. Nemzeti Bank branch in Munkács.

So, Rebekah showed them around in the town centre and also, she took them to Móric Ulmann Pesti Magyar Kereskedelmi Bank, and she introduced Mr Segal and Mr Koch to meet Mr Jakab Gerő, Bank manager. Mr Gerő knew Mr Segal from his years with the bank in Budapest. He was very surprised to see them in Munkács with Rebekah.'

I joined the group of Mr Rosenthal, Mr Walt and Mr Vozáry and we started our visit at Latorca RT. Forest and Timber Plant Director Mr Kleiner, than we moved on to the Chemical Plant, the Tobacco Factory, The Salt and Coal Mining RT. Co. and then we ended up at Isaack's engineering factory.

Mr Rosenthal got out of the taxi he stopped in front of our factory building and looked at the large sign on the building, of Ganz Works Budapest Main Agency. He looked at me and smiled and tapped me on my shoulder and said, 'Mazel tov my boy, you are on the right direction working with Ganz Works RT.'

I showed them around the shop floor where Mr Rosenthal asked me, 'How are you progressing with your conveyor Gabriel?'

After I showed him our first working prototype, he was impressed with it and said, 'I will make a recommendation for your product on our return at the Agricultural Ministry in Budapest.'

At the end of the day we all gathered at the Star Hotel Restaurant for a drink first then our guests have invited us for a meal.

Mr Segal and Mr Rosenthal asked Sándor and me for a short private meeting where we were discussing some important issues that are happening in Western Europe politically and about the increasing dominance of Germany in banking and with investment in Western Europe.

Sándor updated us briefly on our plans for our gift aid for the poor Jewish families through OMZSA.

'Would you consider bringing this point to their attention at your next meeting when you visit the Jewish community of Ungvár?'

'Yes, Sándor we are going to encourage this "Gift aid" program with OMZSA members of Ungvár.'

'It looks as if the Hungarian Government and the Foreigner Minister István Csáky is increasingly encouraging Hungarian businesses to invest in Transcarpathia and in their industry and also in the banking sector as well. It's a big possibility that *Gróf* (Count) *Pál Teleki* will be the new Hungarian Prime minister and he is really pressing the investment into this region.'

'Thank you very much to you all for your help and the introduction of these lovely historical town and please make yourself available for us in the future as we are going to ask for your assistance which it looks will be much sooner than we anticipated it.'

We went back to our group and the conversation was very upbeat among the company of business associates around the table drawing up a lot of plans for a promising opportunity for the future.

At late evening before we all are leaving the restaurant Mr Rosenthal stopped us and said to Rebekah that they were really grateful to us for inviting them to Munkács as they had seen the true potential of investing here in Munkács and generally in the Transcarpathian Region. 'You know this interest among the ministers and the of the business community has been triggered off by our meeting with you in Budapest. With regards to your business with this new kind of simple machines of conveyors and elevators will be a very important part of the Hungarian Government plans for the River Tisza Project. We will be lobbying on behalf your company to say you are manufacturing this vital tool for this project.

'Just a word of advice to you both; gear up for this project with materials parts for a big order which will coming your way. This will make you a very wealthy and prosperous company.'

Rebekah pecked a kiss on Mr Rosenthal's cheek and hugged him then she said, 'Thank you so much for all your support for our little company we will be grateful for your continued support.'

Mr Rosenthal was a bit embarrassed as he didn't expect this kind of emotion from Rebekah then he said in reply, 'I can see you are willing to invest and put your energy in this project which is unique in a way, and you are exclusively manufacturing these machines. We do like you both very much at our organisation and we will supporting you whatever you need to make it to a success.'

We left Sándor behind as he was still engaged in a conversation with Mr Segal and Koch over purchasing a property for the bank and Mr Segal asked Sándor to find a building for him in the centre of town.

By the time we got home it was almost midnight, but Isaack and Rita were still awake waiting for us just to find out what was the result of our meeting with these very important people; Isaack asked us, 'So what happened?'

Rebekah was telling all the excitement of the day's events and she emphasised to her father, 'The guests have confirmed that they will be behind our project and will support our products in every level of government.'

We just wanted to get to bed as this day has taken much of our energies so we just said goodnight and promised that we will tell more about it tomorrow.

Rebekah whispered in my ear, 'I have smelled Rita's perfume on my father's shirt.'

We both smiled and we kissed goodnight.

Next morning in my office at the Town Hall we were trying to work out of the kind of movie films we had momentarily stored in our small office when Sándor came into the office and said: 'Gabriel I would like to have dinner with you at lunchtime.'

'So, let's see the list of these movies: We've opened the boxes and there was a letter and a list on top of the metal film storing trays.'

Bánk Bán, Directed Kertész Mihály (Michael Curtiz): Mihály Fekete, Mari Jászai, István Szentgyörgyi

Az Ezredes Dir. Kertész Mihály: Cläre Lotto, Béla Lugosi,
A Kuruzsló, Dir. Kertész Mihály: Gyula Csortos, Tivadar Uray
Nebántsvirág,
A Víg özvegy, Dir. Kertész Mihály: Mihály Várkonyi, Berta Valeró, Id. Árpád
Latabár,
Egri Csillagok, Dir. Pál Fejős
Csak egy kislány van a világon, Dir Bela Gál: Pal Jávor Gusztáv,
Hyppolit a lakáj, Dir. Istvan Székely: Kabos Gyula, Gyula Csortos, Pál
Jávor, Gyula Gózon
Rakoczi indulo, Dir. István Székely: Pál Jávor, Margit Dajka, Gyula Csortos
Meseauto, Dir. Bela Gaál: Jenő Törzs, Zita Perczel, Gyula Kabos
A királyné huszárja, Dir. István György: Lili Berky, László Perényi
Ez a villa elado, Dir. Géza von Czifra: Rózsi Csikós, Lili Berki, Gyula Kabos
Légy jó mindhalálig, Dir. István Székely: László Dévényi
Szegény gazdagok, Dir. Jenő Csepreghy: Tivadar Uray, Zita Szeleczky

'What do you think Gabriel? I know nothing about these films, they are more of your era.'

'Well, yes, here they are Andre but don't forget that the time delay between in Budapest and Munkács is not just in culturally, but it has been influenced by a politically motivated schism as well and for a number of other reasons it is not just a geographical distance from Hungary which is more up to date with the rest of the western world cultural influence. Number two; Munkács was under a different "Anti Hungarian" sentiment from the Czech's.

'But besides that, the Hungarian Movie Film Industry has been established since 1896. By the way Andre did you manage to get my film developed at the Photo Camera Shop on Main Street? Thank you. Back to these movies, we have to get in touch with the film distribution agents and give them the list of these film titles and offer them for free of charge, but they have to send each individual film to the other *Mozi* (Cinema) outlets in the region.

'In return I want to be notified from each Mozi houses to report back to me on the number of audiences and which movie was the best "box-office success". It is a kind of statistic for us. This report will tell us what kind of movies we should send to these individual towns and villages in the future. I have to report back to the Cultural and Foreign Ministry with this finding.

'Well, Viktoria this is your last week of working together as a team as you are going to work for Isaack Grosz Engineering Company from the day after tomorrow, Thursday 1st of September.

'Rebekah and I decided to take you two out for an evening meal as a thank you from my part and a welcoming part from Rebekah for your dedicated work. You have supported me and Rebekah. I hope you can accept our invitation.'

'Yes, thank you this is very good from both of you Gabriel. Where shall we be going Gabriel?'

'To the Handelsman restaurant, I want to experience their menu as we are going to have our wedding reception there in two weeks' time. So, 7.30pm on Thursday the 1st of September at Handelsman?'

'Thank you, Gabriel we will be there, we look forward to it.'

Viktoria just picked up our mail from the Town Clark's office. I had a letter from Mr Károly Neuhold from the Musica Piano Salon Budapest, and he was notifying me that the pianos will arriving on the fifth of September. That was fantastic as I will have a piano in our new house for the day of our wedding. That will just complete the furnishing of the lounge.

This letter now urged me that I had to make that deal with Mr Kleiner at the Latorca RT. Forest and Timber Plant. This afternoon I have go to the office of Mr Kleiner and pass the list of wood that Mr Neuhold requires of fine spruce Pine and other hardwoods in various thicknesses. The removal lorries will be arriving with the pianos they will take it straight to the Nemzeti Theatre and they will deliver my grand piano to our house on Latorca utca. Then the lorries will collect the ready cut timbers from the Latorca RT. Forest and Timber Plant, and they will take the load back with them to Budapest. It is good news as Mr Neuhold indicates that he will be coming in person for this exhibition as he is planning to travel on to Ungvár to organise a similar exhibition in the Ungvár's Theatre.

Zoltán organised that the electric motors will be arriving at the Munkács Railway depot this Friday on the second of September.

My goodness, I am going to have a very busy week ahead of me.

Sándor called into my office, and we walked across to the Star Restaurant for a private dinner meeting. During our dinner Sándor asked me to help him to find a building on Fő utca (Corso). 'You know in my official status I cannot be involved with such activities.'

'I know that Sándor you have to be very careful not to give any opportunities to your enemies. I have promised that I will go to enquire at every estate agent in Munkács.'

'That is good Gabriel they are very serious with this move to open a branch for the *Magyar kir. Nemzeti Bank* (Royal Hungarian National Bank. Try to make the estate agents to be more active to finding a suitable property. If you have information on a suitable property, would you please go along and view it with Rebekah then get back to me with as much information as possible. Our friends in Hungary are eager to be the first ones to open a branch before other banks will prevent them to set and influence the market.'

'But we have Móric Ulmann Commercial and a smaller side of public Bank the one we all are using at this moment.'

'That is true Gabriel, but I believe that the Royal Hungarian National Bank is much more influential, and they are also able to offer better bank rates on borrowing and more beneficial on saving bank rates.'

I promised Sándor, 'I will investigate all his requests and we shall have another meeting in private like this one.'

After this meeting with Sándor I went to see Mr Kleiner at the timber factory with the list to arrange for them to be ready for collection for the sixth of September. To avoid the misconducting over the export license I volunteered that I would pay for the timber and organise all the export documentation at the Tax department at the town hall.

On my way back to the office I called into our new factory where I was full of surprise that Mr Jakab Gerő was in the office and having a discussion with Isaack and Rebekah. With a smile he greeted me as I walked into the office and asked me to join their meeting.

I said, 'I can't really stay long as I have to go back to my office in the Town Hall.'

Mr Gerő was full of praise for our new factory and the agency with Ganz Works and he really would like to offer a better deal than the one we have fought for. I suggested that he should talk to Rebekah as she is the financial director of the company and I excused myself as I had to rush off to my other office.

I got back to my office where I penned a reply to Mr Neuhold and to Zoltán.

Viktoria had already typed a thank you letter to the Cultural Ministry in Budapest for sending these boxes full of films which we had to distribute to all move houses in the counties.

It was well past seven by the time I got back to Isaack's house. Rita welcomed me with a glass of Chardonnay, and she said, 'Well my dear you look as you as if you need one just to calm you down.'

I pecked a kiss on her cheek and sat down with her for a chat. In the next fifteen minutes a very tired father and daughter arrived, and Rita offered them a glass of wine as well. Both of them looked tired but they were very happy. Rebekah was telling me the story how Mr Gerő turned up in their office without any announcement and he was asking us if we would like to borrow more than we have originally argued out with him in the first place. Rebekah was laughingly telling that Mr Gerő was very impressed with her friendship with one of the directors of the Hungarian National Bank.

'I just replied in a very professional manner that yes Mr Gerő I have dined with Mr Segal at the Astoria Restaurant when I was in Budapest a couple of weeks ago. And when you told him that he should talk to you only as I am the financial director. Well, he has just lost it as I am so competent and having all this connections and authority that he has to deal with me, with a woman.'

'I am very pleased the way things are turning out in our life, this gives me much confidence that I need to negotiate with businesspeople on the same level and be respected for my knowledge.'

'I think he was panicking over that we will leave his bank for the Royal National Bank of Hungary.'

'You just wouldn't believe what happened Gabriel, this man whom we all fought for a bank loan some days ago and now he walks into our office and is offering us more money to borrow than we would need for our business at the first place.'

Isaack got into the conversation and said, 'I think you two with your connections made him report to his head office and tell them that you Rebekah have guided the biggest bankers of Hungary into his little bank in Munkács. I think he has been instructed from the head of Móric Ulmann to find out as much information as possible and offer much more money to us than he originally has given to us in the first place.'

'I think you are right Isaack they are, mostly Mr Gerő is feeling that his monopoly is being challenged by the big banks from Hungary.'

I told Rebekah what I had agreed with Sándor, and we had to make some serious enquiries with estate agents. According to Sándor's estimate that the

Royal National Bank of Hungary would like to open its branches here in Munkács and in Ungvár as well by January next year 1939.

'Well if this is true Gabriel then I will take my "debt" bank account to them. I'll be the first customer for them.'

'Papa please leave that to me as you know I am the financial director of the company.' We all burst out laughing.

'I have almost forgotten to tell you that I have received a letter from Mr Neuhold with regards to the pianos. Mr Neuhold told me that our piano will arrive on Monday the fifth of September, and he will be coming to Munkács to attend for the piano sale / concert for the 21-22 of September.'

'That is fantastic Gabriel it's well-timed for our wedding day. I can see all those guests will admire our beautifully furnished house, and that piano will be just the jewel in the crown.'

'Well children the time is getting nearer to your big day.'

'Yes, Papa and for you and Rita as well so don't forget that.'

'Of course not, I can't forget that we are all going to have a wonderful wedding!'

'I have forgotten to tell you Gabriel a reporter came into our office today, Mr Béla Róth from the *Független Újság* he said it is a newly established local newspaper and he would like to make an interview with you when I told him that he should look for you at the Town Hall.'

'Thank you darling. Yes, I do remember him he came to our factory's opening and blessing ceremony.'

I said, 'I will give him an interview some time when I am not as busy as now.'

'What it is all about Gabriel?'

'He would like to know more about the ever more exciting art and cultural program and of the future plans we are aiming for.'

'Right, goodnight to everybody but I am going to have a bath and a good night's sleep and tomorrow I will be fresh again. Goodnight Papa, Rita and Gabriel.' Rebekah kissed everybody on our cheeks, and she went to her room. I stayed a little bit longer and had one more drink with Isaack then we all went to our rooms for the night.

Chapter 52

Build-Up to Our Wedding, Pianos and Conveyors

On Thursday morning the first of September, I asked Andre, 'Would you please go across the square to the Scala Cinema and take a copy of this list of films which will be available for him immediately.'

When Andre came back from the Scala Cinema, a man came into our office and he introduced himself as Béla Róth, a journalist from the *Független Újság* and told me that he has spoken to my wife who had suggested that he should call in to my office today as he would like to interview me over the art projects that we have planned in Munkács for the future. He said it is a newly established local newspaper and he tries to write mainly local stories for local people in Munkács.

'I thought this is a good opportunity and mainly as it is a free advertisement for our events.'

As a typical journalist he tried to trick me over my views on politics and religion, but I made the point that I am not a politician just a civil servant who has been employed by the Munkács Local Authority to promote art and culture.

I presented him with the programs that we have for theatrical acts and musical recitals that we are organising with Andre in this office, and also promoting Hungarian and foreign films as well which is part of our program. I gave him some of Miklós event's leaflets and the forthcoming Piano recitals at the National Theatre by Dezső Zádor Concert Pianist.

But I think it would be much easier if Andre could send him all the latest events to his newspaper monthly it would help him and help us to get the latest stories to the people of Munkács.

'I have heard many stories about your career in art and theatrical events in Budapest, Gabriel. It would make a very good story for my readers.'

I agreed with him that I will give him an interview but not before our wedding.

'But I thought that you are married Gabriel.'

'Yes, I am. We got married at the registrar's office which makes our marriage official, and it has been registered by the authority. Our wedding will be at the Hoif Complex Synagogue on the 11th of this month.'

'Oh, I see. Can I come to that celebration but of course not officially as a journalist just as a bystander. But I promise you that I will only take photos of your wedding which would save you having the extra expense to hire a photographer.'

'Yes, you are right that would be a saving for us.'

'So, is that a deal Gabriel?'

'Yes, it is Mr Róth, it is a deal. May I introduce to you Andre who is my right-hand man so in the future if I am not available please get in touch with him.'

When Mr Róth had gone, I pointed out to Andre how to recognise these journalistic tricks and how to respond to them.'

'Thank you for this advice Gabriel I have noted the way you responded to his tricky questions.'

The telephone rang and it was the station master letting me know that I have two rail wagon loads of goods arrived from Ganz Works from Budapest.

I told him that they will be collected by tomorrow morning. I organised it with the haulage company the one which was recommended to me by Mr Vozáry.

As I was walking to Isaack's new factory to make sure that the shelves are ready and in place to welcome the electric motors from Ganz Works. I noticed that Mr Gerő the bank manager from Móric Ulmann Bank was walking away again from the factory. Deliberately I slowed down my steps just to make sure that I don't have to get involved with him.

As I got into the office, I found both Isaack and Rebekah laughing.

Rebekah was telling me the reason Mr Gerő was visiting them for was with an even better package deal for Isaack's company than the one he offered in the first place. Rebekah said, 'Well. I knew this would happen when we were leaving his office with Mr Segal and Mr Koch from Móric Ulmann two days ago. And I was right about it.'

Isaack chipped into the conversation, 'I tell you something; you two "impostors" you have rattled the banking scene here in Munkács when you invited these very important people from Budapest.'

'Thank you Isaack but these people are just like you and me the only difference between us that they have a better job, and they like to deal with people who have confidence and knowledge.'

I greeted Viktoria at her new job and asked her if she was happy to be working here.

'Yes, thank you Gabriel. I am very much.'

'Good, I hope you haven't forgotten that we are taking you and Andre out for a meal this evening.'

'No, I haven't Gabriel; we are both looking forward to it.'

'I have really come to see if the shelves are in place as all the electric motors will be arriving tomorrow morning.'

'That is fantastic Gabriel so hopefully the four-custom made motors with the gearboxes for our conveyor are included.'

'Yes, Isaack of course they are on the list. I have 250 electric motors with the most commonly used specification and your four motors with speed control gearboxes and alternators: one 20kW, two 30Kw, and one 40kW electric motors free of charge just for our experimental purposes.'

'My goodness Gabriel 250 electric motors will you have enough room for them?'

'Yes, Isaack I have worked it out that is the maximum that I can have in the warehouse.'

'Come Gabriel I want to show you around the factory we are getting there slowly but the production with my old engineering customers are now came back with appraisal and they are impressed with the standard and the new machine shop floor.'

'I am pleased to hear that Isaack. I can see your happiness on your face the joy and satisfaction is written all over on you.'

'Gabriel you have mentioned to Viktoria that you and Rebekah are taking Viktoria and Andre out for a meal to the Handelsman Restaurant? Then, I have to tell Rita that you will be late home. Yes?'

'Yes, of course Isaack, we will be home probably around ten this evening. Will that be alright?'

'Thank you, Gabriel, you are a gentleman and a friend.'

'Isaack before I go back to my office at the town hall I would like to find out if you have managed to employ some of those Jewish engineers who have got made redundant from the company where you went to the auction.'

'Yes, Gabriel I have employed some but many of them found employment somewhere else.'

'Thank you, Isaack, so hopefully will see you later. Yes, much later.'

When Rebekah and I arrived at the Handelsman Restaurant, Viktoria and Andre had arrived earlier, so they have waited for us in front of the restaurant.

'Have you been waiting for long?'

'No, we just arrived a couple of minutes ago.'

As we were been escorted to our table, Rebekah tried to comfort Andre while I was entertaining Viktoria at the table. Andre handed me the developed photos which he had collected from the photographic shop.

I thanked him for to collecting them, but I didn't have time to have a look at them there. After this delay we ordered our meals and went back to our original conversation on the changes with Andre and Viktoria's separation. Rebekah contributed to it, and she agreed with my explanation to the two young ones.

Viktoria and Andre offered their help with the organisation of our wedding which was very good of them as basically we were treating them as our younger brother and sister.'

I said to Andre, 'Look I couldn't discussed this subject with you in our Town Hall office as I believe that just wasn't the right place for it. I am offering to you Andre a deal that could earn you some extra money through your travelling to the towns and villages in the regions on council business so you could promote or even sell our electric motors and our new conveyors what we are manufacturing. Do you think you could do that?'

'Yes, that is a good idea Gabriel I will do that, but you have to tell me more about those products.'

'I will tell you more about these products.'

After the meal Andre and Viktoria apologised but they just wanted to have some time together and they left soon after the meal. We agreed as we had been in that situation not long ago. We both found the food was good enough. The restaurant manager Mr Zak Hofmann joined us, and we decided on the menu for our wedding reception. We were tasting some various local and Hungarian wines. The manager asked us the number of guests they would have to cater for.

'I am not sure what the latest figure is, but we will let you know that.'

'At least four days before the wedding as we have to have the ingredients together.'

'Then we will let you know by next Tuesday. I hope that will be acceptable.'

Rebekah studied the menu and eventually we managed to decide on the whole menu. At the end the manager confirmed that they can cater this menu for up to 150 people.

On our way home I told Rebekah, 'I thoroughly enjoyed the meal at the Handelman, and I am very impressed with their wine list as well. I think all of our guests will be pleased with this menu don't you think darling?'

'Yes, my love I enjoyed the food and the company of our helpers too. Gabriel I was going to ask you, did you send an invitation to your relatives in Hungary? I have seen nobody else on our wedding list.'

'No, I haven't my love. My parents are dead, and my elder brother has died in the Great War, and I am not in a communication mode with my sister and with my middle brother. They always been jealous of me for my ambitions as I always wanted to be more than them.

'I have never fitted into that family as from my childhood they have dismissed me as an eccentric. The only people whom I have as my new family in Hungary is Miklós, Fifi and now Zoltán and Johanna. The only other one's are here in Munkács, Sándor and "these two problem children" Andre and Viktoria and my adopted sister Elisabeth. My goodness I have forgotten to send an invitation to Professor Mihály Schlesinger in Lvov.'

'I haven't forgotten our flamboyant friend from Lvov University. How could I, after all he was our Shadchan. Without him we would have never met darling. Yes, I have sent him an invitation.'

'Thank you darling. I have so much on my mind Rebekah sometimes I don't really know what day it is.'

'You are doing far too much Gabriel I hope after this "madhouse" we will have some time for ourselves.'

'So, do I darling. Yes, these days are very chaotic, but we just cannot let others down neither your Papa.' I looked at my watch and realised that it was ten minutes to ten and I started to slow down with our walk on the shiny black cobblestones.'

'Why are you slowing down Gabriel; is there something wrong with you?'

'No, my darling but I have promised to your Papa that we won't be back home until after ten.'

Rebekah has burst out laughing, even tears appeared in her eyes.

'You say that my Papa and Rita needed some time for themselves? That is brilliant at last they have discovered themselves like every healthy person in the modern world well after all they are humans just like us with some physical needs in their life.'

Rebekah held on to my arm tighter and with a cheeky smile asked me, 'And when are we going to have some time together in our own house?'

'Let me see it in my diary, Hm. How about a tomorrow appointment at lunchtime madam, I can book you in, I can guarantee that you'll be satisfied.' We both laughed at my silly comment.

'Actually, my dear lady I am desperate for precious time with you, as it's well overdue now.'

Rebekah gave me a kiss and said, 'Darling I will be yours again on that journey to heaven and back.'

'Thank you for that my love I won't disappoint you. I promise you that.'

As we finally got home Isaack and Rita had gone into their rooms and there was a pretended gentle snoring audible from their rooms. So, we pretended that we know nothing about their private time together. We kissed goodnight and we both went into our rooms.

Next morning, we find both of them in a good mood and as we finished with our breakfast and were ready to leave home, Isaack held me on my shoulder and said, 'Thank you for your discretion.'

'Don't mention it Isaack.'

I hired a taxi at the Star Hotel and went straight to the Munkács Railway Station to collect the electric motors from Ganz Works Budapest and also my personal belongings like my books, paintings and clothing from Király utca apartment. As I finished with the customs and excise papers, I pointed out my wooden boxed goods in the station warehouse and asked that they be taken to our factory in Partalja utca and to our new house on Latorca Utca.

These men were very strong, and they carried all the boxes effortlessly without any damage to the motors. I gave them a tip and they said, 'Gabriel, we will do anything for you at any time at all just please ring us first.'

It was only still eleven in the morning, and I have all the motors in the warehouse. I asked Samuel to help organise to open these boxes and put them on these shelves and make sure that all the same marked technical detailed motors will be together. 'Don't get them mixed as it will be a very chaotic way of finding them on the shelf.'

Now I had all my motors in the warehouse and at last I am in business now as well. Isaack came to see all these motors and also the ones Zoltán sent to Isaack for the conveyors to be experimenting with them.

Isaack tapped me on my shoulder and said, 'I am a very happy man Gabriel. We as a family will be successful and very prosperous at the end of the day. I know we have invested a lot of energy and money too into this project.'

I asked Viktoria to type out this promotional letter to these companies on the list, and I will sign them when I get back to the office then post them before the Sabbath began. I telephoned Mr Béla Róth just to place an advertisement into his newspaper. He asked me, 'Is this product part of my portfolio as well?'

'Yes, it is.'

'The newspaper will be coming out next Thursday the 8th of September.'

'In that case I will need to put in another advertisement as all those pianos will be arriving for the piano exhibition and sale, from Budapest and the dates for the sale/concert will be 21 and 22 September.'

'Just take your time Gabriel I can accept them as late as next Tuesday the 6th.'

'Right that is good I can compose a well worded catchy advertisement for both products.'

I asked Rebekah to come out with me to see this painting I had seen in a shop on the Corso. She understood my "coded" message and grabbed her handbag and her hat then we were heading away to our house. We sneaked in just to avoid the attention of Elisabeth's dogs as every second was precious from the time we planned to be together.

Just going through our front door was an exciting experience to see this modern furnished house and this is us, it somehow looks sexual and shows so much taste that has been amassed in it.

Rebekah again just couldn't control herself, she was stripped naked from our dining room to our bedroom. I was just halfway through taking off my clothes when Rebekah was in the bed already. What a beautiful scene it was to see her like that even Michael Angelo couldn't have painted a more strikingly beautiful and perfect body then Rebekah's. My heart was beating like a bass drum increasingly louder and louder as I have embraced her in bed, and we kissed like two teenagers then we eagerly wanted to feel each other's love to build it up to the climax and just aimed to remain filled with that emotional and physical satisfaction as high up as we could reach.

At the end when we both were exhausted, she buried herself into my arms and played with the hair on my chest like a little girl. Looked into my eyes then whispered into my ear, 'I love you Gabriel!'

'Remember this my love, I will always be loving you forever. I love you!'

Chapter 53

Positive Interest for Our Business and Countdown to Our Wedding

On this Saturday 3 September at the synagogue Rabbi Baruch asked me to stand up and he announced our wedding to the congregation.

Rabbi Baruch was encouraging and supportive as he pointed out, 'Isaack has made this special day to share it with Rebekah's long time adopted Mother Rita, for all these years bringing her up from a younger age she was grooming her into a wonderful young woman and now Rebekah is ready to establish her own family. Personally, I salute both of them, Rita and Isaack. Both of them lived their life according to the Law of Moses.' Rabbi Baruch asked Rebekah and Rita on the balcony to stand up and he encouraged the congregation to congratulate them to their forthcoming weddings which will be here on 11 September – 15th of Elul 5698, two weeks before (29th of Elul 5698) Erev Rosh Hashana on the 25 September 1938.

I felt a gentle warm feeling after this announcement and to the equally warm good wishes from the congregation as they all shouted Mazel Tov to four of us.

At the end of the service I thanked Rabbi Baruch for his genuine support to our wedding and advised him that the piano for the synagogue will be delivered sometime during the day on Monday the 5th of September. 'Would you be able to organise that somebody will be available to let the delivery men in and to show them where the piano should be placed. As you know it is a very heavy instrument to be moved around.'

'That is very good of you Gabriel. Certainly, I will organise that. It looks as if we will have piano music to entertain your wedding guests. Would you and Isaack come and see me before the wedding to discuss the wedding ceremony.'

'Yes, of course Rabbi Beruch I will come in to see you with Isaack. Would Thursday 8th be convenient?'

'Yes, it would be good, so 9.30 am on Thursday morning.'

This weekend went very quickly the only real event that happened was that Rebekah and I went to our new house to make sure everything will be ready for our guests Fifi and Miklós. We went over to Elisabeth with our invitation for our wedding and just let her know that she is going to have a new neighbour from the 11th of September.

'I can't wait for that Rebekah and Gabriel. I just can't control these two dogs as they keep coming back from your house to me with sad faces. They are really missing you two.'

'We will be here Elisabeth full time like Gabriel said from the 11th.'

'Thank you, Rebekah, at least the fruit will not be wasted as there is nobody to pick them.

'I noticed there was a man coming to do some gardening his name is Samuel, did you hire him?'

'Yes, Elisabeth, he is our gardener, and he will come once a week to look after the flowers in the courtyard and in the garden at the back of the house.'

'He seems to me a good man, doing an excellent job around the house, he said that he is the brother in law of the builder Mr József Klein.'

The two dogs just wouldn't leave Rebekah they were shadowing her wherever she went.

'Elisabeth, there will be a removal lorry will come this coming Monday and they will deliver our grand piano, would you please let them in as I am not sure of the time of the arrival so I will be very busy with other businesses.'

'No problem Gabriel I will keep my eye on them and let them in. Where would you like them to put the piano?'

'Here in the corner of the lounge Elisabeth. And later on, Monday afternoon Rebekah and I well come down to see the instrument is in the right position.'

'Yes, I look forward to seeing that beautiful instrument.'

On Sunday we had a family meeting discussing our forthcoming wedding arrangements and drawing up the list of the wedding guests at the dinner reception.

Rebekah said, 'Father and Rita will walk me to the Chuppah so who is going to be your best man Gabriel?'

'As you know my parents are dead, so I asked Miklós to be my best man and my witness to the Ketubah, and Andre will be my "Ring bearer".'

Rebekah said, 'These are my guests: my mother's sister from Huszt, Rachel and her husband Robert my father's brother Itzhak and his wife Lilla from Beregszász. On Rita's side her two brothers and their wives: Solomon and Rachel, and Daniel and Bori.

'My only other guests are old school friends Éva and Rózsi with her husband Emil Neumann, Samuel from the factory of course Rabbi Baruch Yehoshua Rabinowitz and his wife Fruma Rivka, my friend Magda from the Lvov, Union of Jewish women organisation, it's looks as about altogether twenty-five relatives and friends.'

'My side of guests are Fifi and Miklós, Johanna, and Zoltán, Dr Sándor Fried, Professor Mihály Schlesinger, Elisabeth Schwartz, Andre, and Viktoria.

'I will call in to the restaurant to arrange the time we will arriving at 12.30 and a sit-down meal starting at 1.15 in the afternoon and also pay the deposit for the meal for fifty people. The manager Mr Hofmann was confirming that they will cater for fifty dinner guests at Handelsman Restaurant. We can probably add some more people to the list, but I don't think they would object to a possible extra guest.'

Rebekah asked when I will be going to Latorca RT. Forest Timber Plant and to Mr Ernő Ungár's Goldsmith shop to collect our wedding rings.

'It will be in this morning my love.'

'Gabriel would you please collect Papa's wedding rings as well, it has been fully paid in advance.'

My first thing was for today I have called in this Monday morning into my office just have some quite time of reading my mails in peace which I have received from various cinemas and Kultur Ház (Cultural centres) to responding to our letters of offering these Hungarian movies which we have received from Budapest. I was very impressed on the number of these enquires. I have to stopped reading these letters as the director Mr Shlomo Meyer of the Scala Cinema walked in with an apology for coming to see me so early, but he has seen me walking to the Town Hall and he wanted to be the first of having an opportunity to go through the list of films which I still have in house. Mr Meyer was praising me for bringing Hungarian and Hollywood movies to Munkács.

I have to explain to him that these films are on the distribution system that after every week he have to send it on to the next cinema. We are setting up a rota system so every picture house will have a program which they can advertise for on a monthly basis, then they have to send it on to the next cinema on the list.

'This program will be sent out to every participating cinema so there won't be any misunderstanding over who has what movies and for how long they can hold onto them before they have to send it on to the next cinema on the list.'

'I understand it Gabriel, but would you be good enough to let me see the lists.'

'Yes, Mr Meyer here they are, we can offer you the first of your own choice to choose a list you think would bring a bigger interest or should say "more bodies on the seats". Other word is I would like to know from you what film has attracted the biggest interest and what kind of movies your audience would be interested in in the future like drama, musical or comedy.'

'Look Gabriel I promise you that I will put a questionnaire to the audiences, and I'll report back to you with their interests. I believe that we can help each other to get the best impact for our effort.'

'Look Mr Meyer, this is Andre who is my deputy, and I would like to advise you to sit down with him and work out what you in the Scala Cinema would like to have for the start make sure it should be a successful one with a good promotion.

'Andre will report back to me anyhow so please let us work fairly together and everybody will be happy and prosperous. I am so sorry, but I have to receive my pianos for the exhibition /sale at the National Theatre.'

'I can offer you a promotion in my cinema for any of your events Gabriel.'

'Well Mr Meyer I think if we are going to help each other in the future then we wouldn't regret our business relationship. So here is Andre who has my full support and trust for his judgement.'

As I was leaving from my office I asked Andre to come out with me for a second, as we stepped out I gave him a word of warning, 'Be careful with this man as he can be a help for us, but I do not trust him at all. Say nothing about our plans or our setups.'

'So why are you still dealing with him?'

'Just find out from him what does he know about us and promise him nothing.'

We both went back into the office, and I noticed that Mr Meyer was looking into the papers on my desk. 'Mr Meyer, have you found something interesting on my desk?'

'Ah, no Gabriel just a bad habit.'

'Well, Mr Meyer some moments ago I asked you to play a fair card with us and in return I will work with you in a much more favourable way, but it looks as if you don't know how to play a fair game. So, my verdict is now, you are not welcome in this office in any form at all. Please communicate with us, either with Andre or with me. Please respect my advice and contact us on the official way by post or by telephone.'

When Mr Meyer left, I was almost shaking from anger because I had misread his character and I was ready to treat him in a more beneficial way.

'Well Andre, this was lesson number 1, to your experience you will meet with characters like Mr Meyer. Be on your guard at all the times. Look I have to go to my house to arrange the drop off places for those pianos as they are arriving today to various locations. Then afterwards I have to take them to the timber place, at the Latorca RT. Forest, and Timber Plant and asking the Director Mr Kleiner to give permission for the lorries to have access to his plant for loading those timbers what I have ordered on behalf of Mr Neuhold Musica Piano Factory.'

'Mr Kleiner told me that I have to pay for all the timbers before he would release the goods.'

I felt so embarrassed on his request of payment as I am in debt already with the pianos I felt that I have to ask some short-term financial support from the bank to pay for everything. I went to our house from the timber yard to meet up with the piano delivery man, then Elisabeth came around and she asked me if we would need some food to be put into our new refrigerator.

I said, 'That would be great as Fifi and all are going to arrive on the Friday midday's train from Budapest and they are going to stay in our house so they would need some food like some eggs and some paprikás szalámi and some spring onion and fresh bread. Here is some cash for the shopping Elisabeth would you please tell me if those foods will cost more.'

We had to stop our conversation as the three-removal vans have just stopped in front of our house. I let them in, and three men were carrying the piano, they were complaining that such a small piano and it is so heavy. They have placed the piano into the corner near the door of the lounge on a diagonal as the keyboard was halfway facing to the room showing the beauty of the instrument and of the cabinet as well.

Elisabeth just couldn't get enough of the beauty of the piano just as the brochure you've shown me.

'But look Elisabeth it matches with all the furniture in the room as it been designed for this room.'

After they were finished with my delivery I took them to the Hoif Complex Synagogue where they have offloaded one large Musica upright piano then we went to the National Theatre on Rákóczi ut and they offloaded all the pianos in the theatre.

After that, I guided them with the three lorries to the Latorca RT. Forest and Timber Plant and I organised with the Director Mr Kleiner to load the timber into these lorries so it will be ready for the drivers for tomorrow morning. Also, I left some information with him about the new electric motors, generators and invited him to come and see my agency I have opened from now on. I told him that I'll bring the money for the timbers at this afternoon.'

I took the drivers to the Star Hotel where I booked them in for one night, and I told them I had ordered the three of them an evening meal and some drinks within a reasonable budget.

I told them that I will settle the bill and asked them if they would take back with them to Budapest a small parcel to Chief Rabbi Immanuel Lőw. Sándor will bring it along in the morning. In the meantime, they can have a sightseeing around in Munkács and I will see them in the morning.

After I finished with the haulage company drivers, I went to see Sándor for the loan.

By the time I arrived at the factory it was after 6.30 pm, and I only find Isaack and Rebekah still working in the office. I looked at my desk which was full of messages and unopened envelopes.

I kissed Rebekah and greeted Isaack then I sat down to look through the messages. There was quite a good response from the companies I had approached not just in Munkács but other companies in the region. I had forgotten the time and it now had turned 7.30 pm.

Rebekah told me, 'Come on Gabriel we have to go home there will be another day tomorrow.'

On the way home I told Rebekah that the piano had arrived in our house, and it looks fantastic. It really blends in well with the furniture which has been made by Sutyai Bela's furniture company.

'I can't wait to see it Gabriel but not tonight as Rita has been cooking for us and we just cannot be any later than we are already.'

'Of course not. I haven't had anything to eat at all, as the day just went on, I didn't have a minute to grab a sandwich. By the way, my personal things from my Budapest apartment have arrived as well which need to be arrange in the house. They are all over the floor as the haulage company has just taken them out of the boxes and put them onto the floor as they needed the boxes.

'Isaack was telling me that he has been approached by Mr Mór Grünwald a farming landowner from Ung Vármegye (Ung County) and he would like to order some four conveyors. He will come to see a working conveyor sometime next week as he wants to understand the benefit of having machines like the conveyor on his farm. He has a vineyard and also a dairy farm too.'

Rebekah looked at me with her tired eyes and said, 'I will come and see the piano and gave me a wink (which is our silent communication) in reply I said yes please as we have to get some food and drinks to our house for Fifi and Miklós as they will arrive on Friday midday with Zoltán and Johanna.'

'Isaack volunteered that he would like to see the piano and he can ask his wholesaler friend to fill up my cellar with good wines and Hungarian champagne. We have to have a house worming party.'

Rebekah looked at me with her lips down and accepted that her father was going to spoil our time together.

I thanked Isaack and said, 'That is a great help Isaack and I hope you will be able to see what a difference has been made to our house since you've seen it last time.'

Well, we left it with our "Angels" to have a miracle to allow us to be together somehow.

Next morning all three of us went to see our house. To our great surprise Isaack loved our new grand piano. He went to the piano and stroked the cabinet then pressed the keys and made out a simple tune and he said, 'Well I do not know anybody in Munkács who would have an instrument like this one. This is just very impressive. Mazel tov to you both.'

'Yes, Isaack it is a limited edition piano the company has made only a 100 of this piano for the Great London Musical instrument and Art Nouveau Furniture exhibition in 1937.'

Rebekah was very pleased with her father's comment then she has walked him from room to room just to show him the progress on our house.

She said, 'You see Papa this is like a baby swan; it is in a chaotic state but when we have put everything on place it will show its true beauty.'

Isaack looked his watch and said, 'Oy vey, I have promised Samuel that I will be in the office to discuss his quotation for a job. So sorry Rebekah I have to go I'll see you in the office later.'

When Isaack had gone Rebekah just jumped into my neck and passionately kissed me and jubilantly shouted "Thank you my Lord for this miracle"! This time of our time for pleasure had slightly delayed us, but we managed to get to the factory with a short delay.

Both of us went straight to our work as more and more enquiries were flooding in for fabrication engineering works and the conveyor had developed quite an interest from various businesses and from agriculture as well. I suggested to Isaack that he should employ more fulltime welders and try to use the modern way of electro welding to fix the conveyor blades to the shaft by an Electric Fusion Welding.

'Look, we have generators from Ganz Works already, so we have everything for this method. Many modern engineering companies are using this method.'

'Yes, that is a good point Gabriel I can see that we could save time and money if we would use this method. You have these sophisticated Ganz generators here in house already.'

'You just pick one of these electric generators and have a test trial.'

Rebekah was happier than usual, and she was chatting to Viktoria about her plans for her wedding and the arrangements at the synagogue and with a great enthusiasm explaining what her wedding dress looked like the one she had bought in Budapest.

Viktoria was showing me some orders which have been received for the electric motors, but the generators were creating the biggest interest. In reply to their enquiries they want to come and place orders with us.

'Well Viktoria it looks like this business will become very successful indeed. You do have the price list for each unit, and now we can take orders for the customers own specification as well, but they have to wait for they custom made units to be manufactured by Ganz Works RT Budapest. We are taking of 40% deposit for each special orders.'

I was advising Viktoria to keep her eyes on our stock as soon as about twenty motors have been sold of each unit with the same specification we should order the same amount from Ganz Motors as I don't want to be without or low on that specific item and keep notes on the most popular specification motors or generators.

After three in the afternoon as I was finishing at the factory, I went up to my office in the Town Hall to consult with Andre on the movies and if he had a planned rota between cinemas around the region.

Andre told me that Mr Meyer had brought a bottle of wine and he had apologised for his yesterday's behaviour.

'Well I do appreciate his apology, but I will not accept any gift from anybody like this is a kind of extortion from him and I will take it back to him later on this afternoon.'

I was going through my mail, and I found one in particular who offered some historical privately recorded silent movies from 1896 about life in Munkács and its surrounding villages. This gentleman congratulated us for our effort to restart the interest for a wider audience of our historical heritage and he urged me to establish a movie makers association. With this club we would encourage cinema goers to project on some unusual or historical valued films from the yesteryears.

I gave his letter to Andre and asked him if he would like to front and run this "Munkács Film Club".

'Yes, I would like that Gabriel it interests me very much.'

'Alright so this project is yours alone. I will set it up for you, but I won't be involved with it as I have far too much on my shoulders.'

Back at home with our ever-restless mode as we are getting nearer to our big day; it made us more worried that everything will happen the way we planned it, and everybody will enjoy our wedding. What about the musicians; will it be a happy occasion?

Next morning on Wednesday the Full Council is in session and I had to present our achievement and our future plans which involved a theatrical performance with a Hungarian touring company, several movie films were ready to be distributed, a piano recital and we are in a process of establishing the Munkács Film Club which will be run by our office, specifically Andre.

I think we impressed the full council as they approved our reports and they gave their full support to our office directions, in particular to establishing the new "Film Club".

We left the meeting as we had no other items to report to them and we went down to the Moskop Restaurant downstairs in the Town Hall building for a cup of coffee.

'Well Andre now you have a recognised and well supported position by the Full Council of Munkács.'

'Ah, thank you Gabriel. I hope you'll be there for me when I need some help.'

'Yes, Andre of course I will be there for you any time.'

The next morning on Thursday Isaack and I had booked an appointment with Rabbi Baruch in his office at Hoif Complex Synagogue to finalise and settle the cost of wedding arrangements, like musicians, flower decorations and so on.

Isaack wouldn't let me chip into the cost, he said, 'Sorry Gabriel but Rebekah is my only daughter, and it is my duty to pay for her wedding.'

Rabbi Baruch was taking us through the running order of the wedding ceremony, and he suggested that Rebekah and I should get married first under the Chuppah then we are going through the traditional ceremony then Rebekah and I will support Isaack at their vows.

We all agreed to his plans. After we finished with the running order of the ceremony Rabbi Baruch told me how pleased he was with the piano which had been delivered to the synagogue on Monday. He asked me about the cost and in reply I told him that was my contribution for the benefit of the synagogue.'

Isaack and the Rabbi looked at me for what I just said, then Rabbi Baruch shook my hand and said, 'Gabriel, this is very generous of you and you will see the appreciation from the members of this great synagogue. Thank you very much.'

Leaving the synagogue and on our way to the factory Isaack said, 'I cannot find a word to say how proud of you my son what you have demonstrated at the synagogue it was truly remarkable and noble of you. Mazel Tov, my boy, I am proud of you.'

Back at the office some customers were waiting for us; at that moment I felt what we are doing is right and blessed. We will work hard to make our business a success.

Chapter 54

The Wedding – Nissuin

On Friday morning, I moved into our house on Latorca utca from Isaack's house as is customary. I went to collect Miklós, Fifi and Zoltán, Johanna from the midday express train from Budapest and I took Zoltan and Johanna to the Star Hotel as they preferred to stay in a hotel for a week. Then I took Miklós and Fifi to our house as they will be staying there for a week too.

As we all walked through the front door, I showed them their bedroom and the bathroom, we passed the grand piano and Fifi immediately dropped her luggage and went straight to the piano and started to play on it. It was very interesting to see the two dogs stood up on their hind legs and stared through the window I think it was must be Fifi's playing of the music that made them to do that.

Miklós said, 'Well Gabriel she is happy now. But tell me where you got this magnificent instrument it must have cost you a fortune.'

'Yes, you are right but I made a deal with Mr Neuhold.' I told him the full story.

'My goodness Gabriel what happened to the flamboyant bohemian man I used to have good times with all over the theatre and cinemas of Budapest. I can see you have found your forte of making money with your good business instincts.'

Fifi walked to us from the piano put her arm into Miklós's arm and said, 'Darling, when can I have a piano like this you know how much I love playing on it.'

I felt that I just had to change the conversation. 'Look, why don't you two settles into your room refresh yourself than we could go to have something to eat at the Star Hotel Restaurant. Then we can catch up with Zoltan and Johanna, as they are booked into the hotel.'

'Good point Gabriel.'

Both of them settled into their bedroom and refreshed themselves and Miklós was ready for a drink. Before we left the house, I have showed them the fruit and vegetable garden at the back of the house.

Miklós commented, 'Well Gabriel, one more thing which I would have never expected from you to be working in a garden. You really surprise me.'

'I don't work in the garden Miklós I have a gardener, but I admit I do pick fruit from the garden. It is fresh tasty fruit; it's natural and real just feel the clearness of the air, which is flowing down from the Carpathian Mountain, it's healthy lifestyle.'

'Well I have to give it to you my friend you cannot compare it with the dusty and smoky air of Budapest.'

By the time we got to the Star Hotel Restaurant, it was 5.30 in the afternoon and Johanna and Zoltán were having a drink on the restaurant terrace enjoying the mid-September sun. They greeted us on our arrival and asked if we would like to have a drink.

'I can recommend this locally brewed beer called Ungweiser, you can have a choice of light or dark beer.'

Miklós and I settled with a dark Ungweiser while both girls Johanna and Fifi ordered Fröccs. We had a couple of more drinks before we had our evening meal. The evening meal had turned almost ten at night. Zoltán said, 'This meal will be on my hotel bill.'

We thanked him for the meal and drinks and said that we will see them at the synagogue tomorrow morning.

Johanna thanked us for having such a relaxed evening among good friends and then with Miklós and Fifi we walked back home to my house. Miklós and Fifi looked very tired as they were travelling from Budapest. They had managed to sleep on the train which is not the most comfortable way as we all know it.

Next morning, we met up with Zoltán and Johanna in front of the synagogue and went in together. Rebekah had taken Fifi and Johanna upstairs where they met up with some of Rebekah's girlfriends. At the end of the service Rabbi Baruch introduced Zoltán and Miklós to the congregation and welcomed our guests from Budapest. Then he showed up with the new piano and thanked me for my generosity to gift it to the synagogue.

Also, he reminded the congregation that Rebekah and Gabriel's wedding will be tomorrow at 10 in the morning here at Hoif Complex Synagogue.

I went home on my own as the rest of our friends went to Isaack's house with Rebekah for a light Sabbath meal; as is tradition, I can't see my bride until our wedding day Badeken, also I am fasting till the wedding dinner of **S'eudah Mitzvah.**

At last I had a time of peaceful prayer without any disturbances. I covered myself with my Tallit and just prayed for wisdom and all the guidance from the Spirit of the Lord God of Israel.

I didn't realise the time, but it was late when Miklós and Fifi arrived home in absolute exhaustion.

'You are a lucky man Gabriel you have a great future wife and a lovely family; they think the world of you, Isaack is so very proud of you as his son-in-law. I can see the attraction of settling down here in Munkács and having a family, she is a great girl and a partner for life.'

'But Miklós you have a great girl too who happens to be your wife since 1935. I have known you for a long time; we have been through many exciting things and as much that we cannot be proud of.'

At this time Fifi walked to Miklós and sat on the armrest of Miklós's chair put her hand around his neck and kissed him on his head.

'You see what I mean? I was there for your wedding, and now you are my best man who I am truly grateful for, from the bottom of my heart.'

I opened a bottle of Hungaria Pezsgő and three of us drank for old times' sake. Fifi just couldn't resist the temptation of the beauty of that grand piano and she played Mozart Eine Kleine Night Music with so much passion. We both looked at Fifi and I said to Miklós, 'You've got a pearl on your crown Miklós you should get her a piano. I can get you a good deal through Mr Neuhold Musica Piano Showroom.'

Miklós asked Fifi, 'Is that a hint my darling that we should go to bed with Mozart?'

'Yes, Miklós I am feeling very tired, Mozart was a gentle reminder to all of us we had a long day today and we are going to have an even busier day tomorrow.'

Next morning, I was awake before Matyi Elisabeth's rooster. I just couldn't sleep. I was worried (like a good agent) that everything was going to plan as we, Rebekah and I had so precisely planned it. I went out to the garden at the back of the house and walked up and down and prayed. Szuka joined me she kept looking at me just trying to catch my eye if she has sensed my anxiety. How much feeling in a dog who senses your emotions and just tries to calm you down with her uncompromised loyalty.

I set the dining table for Fifi and Miklós, but I apologised to them as I will not be joining them this morning. I only had a cup of tea then I went to my bedroom to get ready for my wedding. I put on my dinner suit which I had only worn for premiering theatrical events or some cocktail parties in Budapest. But it still perfectly fitted me.

On our way Elisabeth joined the three of us, I introduced her to Fifi and Miklós as we were going to the Hoif Complex Synagogue for my big day. I was surprised to see that Elisabeth was so elegantly dressed as she was wearing a nice summery hat. I have to say she looked attractive, and she didn't look her age at all. We got to the Synagogue at 9.30 am. and we went straight to Rabbi Baruch office to sign the Ketubah and witnessed by and countersigned by Miklós and Isaack in front of the Rabbi.

It was good to see that Béla Róth, a journalist from the Független Újság, had arrived early and started to take some photos already. I thanked him for being prompt and extended an invitation to our S'eudah Mitzvah, Wedding Dinner, as well.

Rabbi Baruch promised that he would conduct the whole service in half an hour as he had to conduct a shorter one for Isaack and Rita as well. By the time we all signed the Ketubah, it was just after 10 am.

Miklós and Fifi walked me to the front of the Chuppah. Andre was standing there already. He gave me an encouraging wink and a big smile. While we were waiting for Rebekah to arrive with her father and Rita, Rabbi Baruch whispered to me, 'Just calm down Gabriel everything is going well.'

Then the cantor started to play on the new piano as Rebekah appeared with Isaack and Rita. I can't remember the music as I was mesmerised with Rebekah's beauty in the dress she had bought from Jakab Rothberger shop in the Váci utca with the help of Fifi.

Rebekah stood next to me in front of the Chuppah following the tradition of Badeken: *which is a custom that derives from the biblical account of Jacob's first marriage, when he was deceived by his father-in-law to marry the heavily veiled Leah instead of Rachel, his intended bride.*

I lifted Rebekah's veil to uncover her face then she gave me a wink which made me more relaxed. I replaced the veil to cover her face then we both faced Rabbi Baruch who led us under the Chuppah, Rebekah on my right side.

We stood under the Chuppah, Rabbi asked the guests to be seated and started the ceremony by explaining the significance of the Chuppah as it signifies our future home.

The chuppah represents the shelter and privacy of the home that the bride and groom will create following their marriage.

Then Rabbi Baruch, in Hebrew and Yiddish, read out our Ketubah and explained the significance then he gave me the signed Ketubah.

The Ketubah document is reminiscent of the wedding between God and Israel of His beloved bride. It is this precious marriage contract.

After Rabbi Baruch read the ketubah, and it was handed to me then I gave it to Andre for safe keeping for the duration of the wedding.

Rebekah circled around me seven times. *As the custom of the bride circling the bridegroom seven times has been interpreted as the symbolic building of a wall of love around the relationship of the bride and groom.*

Then Rabbi Baruch covered us with a Tallit before we had wine symbolising our becoming one. Then Rabbi Baruch asked for the ring. Andre came forward and placed the ring on a small cushion.

Rabbi Baruch continued, 'By Jewish law, this ring represents the wholeness achieved through marriage and a hope for an unbroken union.' I put the ring on Rebekah's right hand index finger and declared my betrothal vows to her.

'By this ring, you are consecrated to me according to the law of Moses and Israel', formed the essence of the marriage service. The circle of the ring is a symbol of the eternal nature of the marriage covenant.

Then I declared, '*Behold, thou art consecrated to me with this ring, according to the law of Moses and Israel.*'

Blessings of Betrothal (Kiddushin)

Rabbi Baruch offered us a drink of wine. We both drank from the cup.

The betrothal blessings express the resolve of the bridegroom and bride to create a Jewish home, dedicated to God and to the wellbeing of humanity.)

Then the Seven Blessings (Sheva Brachot) were recited over the second cup of wine by Rabbi Baruch. He was telling us, 'These blessings are very ancient and set the bride and groom into a wider social and sacred context. They are arranged as follows:

1. Blessing over the wine – symbol of joy
2. Blessing praising God to whom all creation proclaims praise

3. God is praised as Creator of humanity

4. God is praised Who created humanity in the Divine image

5. Hope for the messianic future

6. Prayer for the happiness of the bride and groom

7. The individual hope for happiness for the couple is combined with a prayer for joy in the messianic future

After the seven blessings, Rebekah and I shared a second cup of wine.

Then Rabbi Baruch wrapped the cup and placed it on the floor and asked me to do Breaking of the Glass. I stamped on the glass and smashed it under my foot.

Rabbi Baruch explained the crushing of the glass we have just drunk out of symbolises the destruction of the Temple in Jerusalem some 2000 years ago.

The conclusion of the ceremony, Rabbi Baruch declared, 'Now Gabriel and Rebekah you are husband and wife according to the Law of Moses.'

Rabbi Baruch congratulated us, 'Mazel Tov to you both.'

Everybody shouted 'Mazel Tov'.

We were now a married couple and we proceeded out of the ceremony area to the final part of the order of service, which was the **Yichud**.

I held Rebekah's hand as a proud married couple; we walked past the guests and went into a room next to the main hall to have a passionate time for each other.

Chapter 55
Wedding Reception – S'eudah Mitzvah

Rebekah and I, we must have spent longer in Yichud than we would have expected when we heard the guests congratulating Rita and Isaack, shouting 'Mazel Tov'. Then we came back and joined the guests to celebrate, and we let Rita and Isaack have their Yichud time in the room next to the main hall.

After the wedding ceremony, we all walked together from the Hoif Complex Synagogue to Handelsman Restaurant for our Wedding Reception – S'eudah Mitzvah.

At our arrival to the restaurant the waiters offered a finger buffet of smoked salmon with baby pickled cucumbers on matzo *bread* to our guests and a glass of champagne when everybody had a drink, we four of us "newly wedded" thanked the guests for their support at the wedding then we all drank for the health and happy future of the new husbands and wives. L'chaim!

At our arrival, our good friend Gyula Galambos Gipsy Primás welcomed with un upbeat music. Then he played through the dinner some romantic gipsy music.

The waiters placed more plates of the finger buffet on each table as the guests were looking for their seats on the name board to find their tables.

When we all were seated Isaack and I stood up and declared the meal is begun with our blessing over a wedding challah. After we have the blessing over the challah then we have given a piece of challah to each table. This action has allowed us to greet our guests.

It was a great surprise to see Professor Dr István Pritcz, my old professor, sitting at Professor Mihály Schlesinger's table, it was good to see my two favourite professors from the Rabbinical College from Budapest.

We shared our table with Rabbi Baruch Yehoshua Rabinowicz and his wife, Fruma Rivka, and Miklós with Fifi and Zoltán with Johanna.

Isaack shared the table with Dr Sándor, Professor Mihály Schlesinger, Dr István Pritcz and Rita's relatives.

It was a great reunion with Rivka and Zoltán as they both had been students at the Sugár ut Hebrew Gimnazium. They both had much to catch up with, particularly Zoltán with his further education and career in Budapest. He was telling Rivka that he will come here more often as Gabriel is now the sole agent of the Ganz Works RT in the whole Subcarpathian Region.

Rivka suggested that next time when Zoltán comes to Munkács he should bring Johanna with him so they could be entertained by Rivka and Rabbi Baruch.

'Yes, we are planning to come here more frequently because my plans to establish an agency for Ganz Works in Lvov and in Kiev.'

Then the waiters started to serve the food to the wedding guests.

Somehow, I didn't feel hungry after my fasting but now I have seen the food on the table, and I have become very hungry. I kept looking at Rebekah's dress. I whispered to her, 'Darling, from now on we don't have to "steal the time" to be together. We can do that anytime when we want it day or night as we are now legally husband and wife, and we have our own beautiful home where we are going to live "forever".'

'How about tonight, my husband?'

'Definitely the night is tonight.'

Then Rabbi Baruch stood up and said the Kiddush and then the next overwhelming noise was dominantly made by the guests' cutlery. We had music right through the reception by Gyula Galambos which I know is against tradition, but we are in the 20th century; we can make compromise with the choice of music.

And now it's all celebration for the **Hora**! Let the musicians into their form or traditional dance of celebration is done.

The dance most widely known is when the bride and groom are lifted in chairs on the shoulders of their guests and dance with the bride and the groom individually as well.

Also, it was an opportunity to catch up with friends and relatives about their life and their future plans and I had an opportunity to promote Miklós' performance tomorrow evening at the Drama Theatre.

Dr Sándor was a great help, he had entertained many people before and after the Nissuin mainly he entertained the two Professors and Elisabeth as they sat at the same table.

It was seven in the evening by the time we finally finished with our big day at the restaurant and we five of us with Fifi, Miklós and Elisabeth who joined us were heading to our new home to spend the very first night together.

At our arrival Elisabeth excused herself she said she felt a bit tired, and she had more drink than she was supposed to and went to bed.

Just as we were going to walk through our front door, I picked up Rebekah into my arms and carried her into our house. Then we kissed for a minute or two while she was in my arms.

Miklós and Fifi stopped and laughed then Miklós said, 'What a romantic person you really are Gabriel!'

I put her down and we all laughed at our "performance" together.

Fifi said, 'Do you remember Miklós you've done the same thing to me at our wedding. Then Fifi went to Miklós, put her arms around Miklós neck and they had a passionate kiss too. When they stopped, Fifi said, 'You see we haven't forgotten that night either.'

Then she went to the piano and started to play the wedding march by Mendelssohn; we all laughed at Fifi's sense of humour.

I opened a bottle of Tokay dry Szamorodni and we sat back and had a very relaxed chat as friends would say, just spontaneous and being natural.

Rebekah was given us a twirl in her wedding dress and she asked us what we think of her dress.

Fifi followed her with, 'I hope you like it Gabriel?'

'I have been mesmerised by you, my darling. The dress definitely complimented you.'

Fifi said, 'We spent the whole morning at Jakab Rothberg's shop in the Váci utca where we both chose this wedding dress.'

Miklós and I said, 'Yes it was a good choice, and it's a pity you can wear that beautiful wedding dress just once in your life.'

We all burst out laughing, then Fifi went to the piano and started playing again some of the songs we were dancing at the Hora. Rebekah joined Fifi at the piano and they started to sing along to Fifi's piano playing. I asked Miklós if he was ready for tomorrow's performance at the Drama theatre.

'I have received your Poetry Book last week which you've sent me by post. I will sell your books in the foyer, and you have to sign them at the interval and at the end of your performance.'

'I am very grateful to you Gabriel you have done me a great favour organising this tour for us and also with your advice I've got in touch with the Cultural Ministry in Budapest, and I had financial support from them for my travelling and for my hotels expenses.'

'That is what friends are for Miklós we have known each other for a very long time so this is all that I could have done for a friend. You are very talented Miklós, Fifi is worshipping you; just don't spoil it.'

We all felt tired from this exciting day and finally, I can have my special **Yichud** with my new "officially" wedded wife, Rebekah. Rebekah and I woke up in a much more tired way than when we went to bed last night. And what a night we had together. I just hope we didn't keep Fifi and Miklós awake.

Rebekah said, 'Don't be silly; the guestrooms are in the front of the building and our bedroom is at the back of the house. You know my "new husband" I have enjoyed this first night officially together that I don't really want to get out of bed.'

'But darling, I have promised to Zoltán and Johanna that we will show them the new factory and the Ganz Agency base we have completed recently. I will call into their hotel at 11 am.'

Fifi and Miklós were already in the kitchen fully dressed and they were having breakfast. I greeted them and went back to our bedroom to get dressed. Rebekah started to get ready too, so we weren't going to be late for our appointment at the hotel. Miklós and Fifi decided to stay home to get ready for this evening.

Finally, Rebekah and I made it on time. Zoltán and Johanna were already in the foyer of the hotel wearing comfortable shoes ready to walk on the cobblestoned streets of Munkács.

Rebekah was arm-in-arm with Johanna and the two ladies walked in front of us and led the way to the new company base. You could hear the chatting and the giggling over Rebekah's wedding dress and Viktoria's bridesmaid dress.

Zoltán said, 'You know Gabriel here I am in Munkács where I have grown up which was the memory of my childhood I know exactly where I am and how many times, I have walked these cobbled roads. This place has still remained the same but somehow, I feel like a foreigner here.'

'I know what you mean Zoltán that's how I have felt recently in Budapest, now as I have no property for me there. On the train back here to Munkács I felt that I was going home this is where I am belonging now.'

While we were discussing about our preferred home we have arrived at the factory. Zoltán has stopped in front of the building, and he's got his camera off from his shoulder and has taken some photos of the sign above entrance of Ganz Works Agency and said, 'Well, Gabriel, it looks very impressive indeed. I will show these photos to the management board as some members of the board didn't want to give credit to you as you have no record of being in this business at all. But I have put my reputation and my conviction in my argument that we need a salesman not an electric engineer. I have to say that my instinct and judgement was correct you have a feel for business you will give the promotion and the sale to Ganz Works Rt product here in Transcarpathia.'

'I have some sales Zoltán already and many enquiries mainly for generators which I can see that is going to be the most popular product. We have an opportunity to benefit business and for the public as a useful tool to bring out people from the dark age of oil lamps to the modern world of electricity. The future is "mobile PowerStation" with steam and belt driven or a petrol motor driven electricity generator as a life changer for a small village community in the remote areas as they are not on the national power grid. We have to bring them out of the 19th century to the 20th century.

'You know I have been commissioned by the Hungarian Cultural, Educational and Faith Ministerium to prepare the community leaders to get ready for the administrative changes. I have met many of them during this time and I have seen at many schools that they have no books at all. They were still using slate tablet with chalks and abacuses during their exercise of reading and writing. These children deserve a better education in the first half of the 20th century.

'I have been lobbying at the office of Count Pál Teleki and I have mentioned to him when I have given my presentation on my Transcarpathian mission. He liked my ideas, but his excuse is as always, there is a financial situation comes into the argument.

'Do you think Zoltán if you could make a proposal to the Ganz Board members meeting that you could supply these generators to the poorer rural communities at cost and the Hungarian Government would install these generators to these needy places by their contractors it would be a political and humanitarian goal; for the Government and for Ganz Works Rt.

You know I have all the necessary information you would need and also, we can distribute them through our organisation of (N 37) OMZSA and (N 38) JDC.

Look I am here in Munkács already as an established agent for Ganz Works, I wouldn't charge for the storing and distributing these generators to these places.'

'Gabriel, this idea is not just a noble act but a great advertising opportunity for Ganz Works as well. I will definitely call a meeting with this point on the agenda on my return.'

As we walked into our office, Zoltán liked the idea of the engineering works and the Ganz Works Agency together. It will work well for both businesses.

Isaack showed Zoltán around the factory, but they spent more time at the up and ready working screw conveyor. Samuel was explaining how this machine worked and described and counted how many different fields and business can benefit from this system.

Rebekah entertained Johanna with Viktoria in the office. Johanna was praising Viktoria for her look at our wedding as Rebekah's bridesmaid. The conversations were in a fast flow among the girls on all kinds of subjects.

I got to my office desk, and I was reading my mail which many of them were good wishes for our wedding. Also, there was a couple of orders for generators and some more enquires for electric motors. I left a note for Viktoria to deal with these two orders delivery notes and regulations on collection of goods.

At midday Isaack invited Zoltán and Johanna for lunch at the Star Hotel Restaurant where we tried not to talk business but there was no chance not to do that when we have so many ideas on the table.

Halfway through our lunch, Dr Sándor walked into the restaurant with his friends, Professor Mihály Schlesinger, and Dr István Pritcz. Zoltán and I both of us stood up and we both greeted the guests.

Dr Pritcz asked, 'What are you doing here Zoltán?' And Dr Pritcz introduced him to Sándor and Professor Schlesinger,' Gentlemen this young man was my best student at the Corvinus University, he is Dr Zoltán Hacsek.'

Well, what a small world. Dr Pritcz knows Zoltán, then we needed to move jointly the table next to ours as the group had grown. We all have much to catch up with each other as Zoltán haven't seen Dr Pritcz and Professor Schlesinger for many years. It was like a kind of school reunion.

At the end of our meal I had to remind everybody that Miklós will perform this evening at 6 pm across the square at the Drama Theatre and he would need some support from friendly faces. Everybody was very upbeat with the idea of meeting up at the theatre later on and maybe a drink or two after the performance.

I went home with Rebekah to get changed for this evening performance of Miklós. I told Miklós that some of his books are already at the theatre, so we don't have to take them with us.

Miklós was getting more exited which is understandable. To calm his nerves he was chatting to Rebekah and he was telling her that his mother's name was Ilona Grósz.

'I am not sure that she was your relative at all?'

'I don't know Miklós I have to ask Papa later on.'

Miklós was telling her story to Rebekah: 'Ilona Grósz was my mother, she was born in 1881. She was 28 years old when she died from twin births in 1909 with one of her foetus. I could never recover from this tragedy, which only I, alone who have survived, I could never live without remorse, so I must write it out of me in this poem: Twenty-Eight.'

Then Miklós started to tell that story in his poem that he wrote to his mother:

"You were twenty-eight then
now I have become the same
twenty-eight years since you are dead
Mother, bloody fugitive!
Mother, bloody victim,
I grew up in manhood
the sun is very hot, dazzling,
butterfly with your hand wave to me,
that it is okay that you know
and that I do not live in vain."

Everything had gone quiet as Miklós finished his poem to his Mother. Rebekah and Fifi's eyes were wet, and the tears just rushed down their faces.

I had to admit that I had never seen my friend in such an emotional state, even I had a tear in my eye. I thought yes, this is my friend Miklós. But I thought this emotion will get through the hardest person's heart tonight.

It was so sad that Miklós still blamed himself for his mother's death.

Chapter 56

Business Promises and Successions

Miklós had a full house at the theatre and an overwhelming success. Both Miklós and Fifi got a ferocious applause at the end of performance. He had so much demand to sell his books that I had to ask Andre to help me out with the sale. I had to remind Miklós to ask his father-in-law (Fifi's father) to print more of his books as they are on demand and get them posted to me so I can distribute them in the regional bookstores.

At the end of the performance at 7.30 pm, he was signing his poetry books with Fifi. By the time they were finished with the dedications and talking to the audience, it was past 8.30 pm.

Rebekah went to the Star Hotel restaurant with our guests while I stayed behind helping Miklos and Fifi to deal with the fans when the theatre director Mr Robert Aron called me a side shook my hand congratulated on my yesterday's wedding and he thanked me for a well thought out program with Miklós to present a real higher quality event not just a commercial easy to please program.

I said to Robert, 'Look, I have promised you of all kinds of programs for your theatre. This is a much more subtle kind of act with a deeper emotion and standard, but our aim (yours and mine) is to get the audiences into your place. Filling seats and getting a good revue in the press. I have invited him over to the Star Hotel if he wanted to talk to Miklós, but he declined my invitation as he paid Miklós fee for the evening and his excuse was that he had to count the money and put it into his safe.'

In the end we managed to join the rest of our friends at the hotel restaurant for a drink.

Miklos and Fifi were interviewed by Béla Róth from the Munkács based Independent Newspaper at the hotel restaurant and taken his picture Miklós with

Fifi. Miklos and Fifi were the centre of attention that evening. Looking back on the evening, I think the after party was a successful one, everybody was talking, the restaurant pianist was giving us very atmospheric background music and it was a great send off for Miklós and Fifi as they were traveling to perform in Ungvár tomorrow then all over the towns we've organised for him in Transcarpathia.

Rebekah was telling Miklós that she asked her father if his family was originally from Beregszász. 'But he doesn't know if there was a relative called Ilona, like your mother's maiden name, and Papa's brother Itzhak after the wedding has gone back to Beregszász so I cannot ask him if he would know your mother side of the family. But who knows Miklós we may well be related. There are so many coincidences happening in my life since I have met Gabriel so this relationship with your mother's side would not surprise me at all. So, we may well be cousins, but you have to investigate that.'

We had an emotional goodbye with Fifi and Miklós at Munkács Station and then we got back to carry on entertaining Johanna and Zoltán again in the evening. They were visiting relatives in Munkács during the day.

Rebekah went back to the factory where I will join her later on, but now I went to my office to try to get back to normality as if nothing has happened with us in the past week. Well, yes, a very important thing has happened to both of us yesterday; our marriage has been Blessed by The Lord God. We have made a covenant before Him and before Man.

Back in the Town Hall I had many congratulations, and good wishes and Mazel Tov from colleagues.

Andre was in the office already, he just said good morning and he went back to the work he was doing. I thanked him again for his assistance and support for my wedding as a ringbearer and I brought him and myself a cup of coffee and I buried myself as well into the mounting mail that I had to reply to. I will take some of these more important letters home with me where I could respond to them in peace. Later on, I had to go to the factory after lunch where I can expect a lot more letters there that I had to deal with.

I know also that we had committed to meet up with Johanna and Zoltán as they were travelling on tomorrow further onto Lvov.

As I arrived at the factory there was a small lorry, and I had no idea who or what was it doing in front of our loading bay. When I went into the office there was a gentleman sitting at the reception corner and this man was talking to

Isaack. I greeted everybody in the office, and I thought this man was Isaack's customer, so I walked straight to my desk to get on with my work. Rebekah brought some coffee to them and joined them.

Isaack then introduced him to me as Mr Móricz Grünwald. Mr Grünwald had come to purchase a conveyor, so we were just discussing the technical details at this moment.

Ah, that was very good. Then I went back to my desk and opened the letters and tried to organise them in my letter trays system by their importance of enquiry or actual orders for mine and for Viktoria's benefit to know where to look for a file when we needed them.

Then Isaack took Mr Grünwald onto the shop floor to demonstrate the conveyor in action. Rebekah walked to me, pecked a kiss on my cheek and told me that this man came with his lorry to take away the conveyor as he didn't realise that every conveyor is tailor made. But hopefully, he will order a conveyor.

'That is fantastic darling this is the first one, hopefully many more will follow this.'

Rebekah told me that she had bumped into Zoltán, and Johanna and she had invited them to our house for a drink before we take them out for a meal. Rebekah went home before me to clean the house and change the bedding in the guestroom after we had Fifi and Miklós staying there so it will be all presentable when she will show Zoltán and Johanna around.

Ten minutes later as Rebekah had just gone Zoltán walked into the office with a visibly very tired Johanna. Viktoria greeted Johanna with a hug, and she offered both of them a cup of coffee. Then Viktoria sat down with Johanna and entertained her while I was showing Zoltán all the enquiries and the orders which I had received already after a week of trading since we have just opened our business.

'Well Gabriel, you must have done a good promotion for our product.'

'Yes, Zoltán I have done it, but the credit is not all mine as I am selling the best product which is available on the market with the most respected name of Ganz Works on the sign above the factory entrance, so it is not so difficult to get an interest as such.'

I invited Zoltán to join Isaack and myself on the factory floor to tell him about a gentleman who has driven here to buy a conveyor from all the way from Ungvár.

Mr Grünwald thought that these machines can be bought just off the shelf and not as an individual "tailormade" machine to a strict specification to be designed and to be built. Isaack was still on the factory floor with Mr Grünwald, when we walked in with Zoltán, but Isaack was too busy to be explaining the benefits of this system to Mr Grünwald.

Zoltán said, 'Look Gabriel I will see you later and we can talk more about business but what I have seen here at your factory I have to say it is very impressive indeed. I like your conveyor; I think it is unique and it will make you a very wealthy family. I know how hardworking a family you are, but you will deserve all the benefits you will get from these businesses here.'

I gave him my address where to come later on then they went back to the hotel to get changed from the extensive sightseeing exercise and visiting relatives in Munkács.

On my way home I picked up some flowers for Rebekah who had cleaned the whole house, and everything looked just great. We had to change from our work clothes as well, but as usual Rebekah again made the effort to look beautiful in her new dress, the makeup, and the ever-favourite hat too.

When Zoltán and Johanna arrived and we looked at the two ladies, then Zoltán and I just smiled as Johanna looked and dressed exactly the same and beautiful, she had the same style dress on with the hat like Rebekah. I said to Zoltán, 'Well, these ladies look as if they have stepped out of the Vogue fashion magazine. They should be walking on the French Riviera Corso rather than the one here in Munkács.'

Rebekah was showing Johanna and Zoltán around the house, but the star attraction was our Strohmenger Art Nuevo grand piano. Johanna asked us if she could play on it.

Rebekah said, 'Yes please as we are not the best pianists at all, but it's good to have someone who can play it. It has a great sound and a very responsive touch of its English system with a repetition mechanism.'

When Johanna sat down and played the piano sounded like an orchestra then she stopped just for a minute to comment on the touch of the action, and she said, 'It feels like playing on my *Bösendorfer* Grand Piano then she went back to playing Fantasy by Franz Liszt that she have performed so well.'

I offered a drink to our guests but neither Johanna nor Rebekah wanted a drink. Rebekah just leaned on the piano and enjoyed Johanna's performance. I poured a glass of Kosher Plum brandy for Zoltán and for myself and we both sat back in our chairs and enjoyed Johanna's playing.

'You know Zoltán your wife is a very talented pianist; her fingers move on the ivory like as if she would be a concert pianist.'

'Yes, you are right Gabriel she was studied as a private student with the great Ernst von Dohnányi Professor of the Piano Faculty at the Ferenc Liszt Academy.'

After a while Zoltán told Johanna that we had to get to the restaurant before it would be too late to get a table. With sadness she stood up from the piano and said, 'What a pity I have to stop playing.'

Rebekah made an invitation to Johanna, 'You are always welcome here to enjoy this pretty thing.'

I recommended to our guests two restaurants to choose from, one is the Moskop Restaurant which is downstairs in the Town Hall building which offers mainly lamb and veal dishes or we could go to the Haupt Restaurant, on Rákóczi utca, which serves traditional Ashkenazi Jewish dishes such as gefilte fish and other fish food like carp dishes.

Johanna and Zoltán settled with the Haupt Restaurant. On our way to the restaurant, Johanna and Rebekah were walking arm in arm in front of us and chatting about the beauty of the Winter activities like skiing on the nearby ski slope.

I was telling Zoltán where I have purchased this piano and I was telling him the deal I had made with Mr Neuhold at the *Musica Zongora Szalon on Erzsébet Kőruton*, and the sale and concert I had organised at the National Theatre on the 21st and 22nd September with Dezső Zádor concert pianist.

Zoltán asked me, 'How do you cope with all the different kind of businesses? I am definitely impressed with your energy and tell me what is driving you Gabriel?'

Johanna told Zoltán that she would like to spend some days here in wintertime. 'Well Johanna winter is not all that far away as it is the 12th of September already. Let's plan it this evening. As you have now seen Munkács and you know what it is like and also, we have become very friendly with Gabriel and Rebekah and with their company you would enjoy the winter holiday here in Munkács.'

By the time we arrived at the restaurant we were lucky and managed to get a table at the Haupt Restaurant, where we had a fantastic meal and an enjoyable evening together with Johanna and Zoltán. At the end we agreed that we are going to keep in touch with each other not just in business but as friends as well.'

We walked with them back to the Star Hotel and said an emotional farewell to them as they were going to travel further on tomorrow lunchtime to Lvov on business.

Rebekah and I walked to our own home arm in arm. We both felt a little bit tired, but this is our second night together as husband and wife.

Rebekah looked at me with a mischievous smile then I knew that I won't be doing any work on those letters that I have brought with me from my town hall office.'

But it was worth it as we had the whole night before us and yes, we used up passionately every minute of that steamy night.

Chapter 57
After Wedding Normality and Financial Problems

Having survived the wedding and gotten over the commitment to our visitors we were exhausted not just physically but financially as well.

Most of my "reserve" was invested in the pianos, as I had to pay for the pianos and for the timber as well upfront. Not to mention paying for the transportation of Ganz Works electric motors from Budapest.

I was hoping for a successful sale of the pianos and the payment from Mr Neuhold over the timber that should put me back in credit at the bank.

Sitting in the town hall office on my own as Andre is out of town promoting these Hungarian Movies. I am trying to work out my financial situation and I feel that all the profit I have made from the sale of the Király utca apartment has been eroded dramatically as I have paid for the house, the restoration of the house to Mr Klein and to Zloch Plumbing, Bathroom & Kitchen Company and for all the furniture to Sutyai Furniture Company Munkács.

I really have to sit down with Rebekah and share my financial situation with her as we are a family now and we shouldn't keep secrets from each other particularly financial ones.

Sándor came into the office he brought us a wedding gift for our house. He looked at the notes on my desk and asked me if there was something bad happening with my finances. 'Are you in some kind of financial trouble Gabriel? Have you committed yourself to far too many kinds of businesses deal?'

'Quite honestly Sándor I have, but I had no choice because the opportunities have all happened at the same time and it would of have been a mistake to miss out on all of these opportunities.'

'Is it much Gabriel?'

'Yes, Sándor it is.' I was telling him about the pianos, the timber and the deal with Ganz Works. 'I have to have an emergency loan from the bank. And on the top of this we had our wedding expenses at the same time. By the end of this month I will be back in credit. It is the 14th of September, and I am having the piano sale on the 21-22 September and that is just a week away.'

'Look my boy, if you are desperate for this week, I can help you out with your needs. Our organisation as you know you as are the member of that too will not let you down.'

'Thank you Sándor I appreciate your help, but I have to discuss it with my wife Rebekah, that was my agreement with her, and I will come back to you after we have discussed this situation. By the way Sándor I have found two properties in a very prestigious position one is on Rákóczi utca and one is on the Main Road for the Magyar Kir National Bank. I think the location of the building and the state of the building should be suitable for a bank.'

'That is very good Gabriel, I think if you would get all the details on both property you should send it directly to Mr Segal in Budapest.'

'I will Sándor, but I wanted to discuss this with you first.'

'Very good Gabriel. Now here is my wedding present for you two, it is a very important one and you can use it this evening.'

I unwrapped Sándor's gift which was a pair of beautiful silver candlesticks.

'These are truly exclusive Sándor thank you so much. We were thinking of buying one for tomorrow, but you have read our thoughts with these magnificent, enchanting candlesticks.'

'I got it from our friend Mr Ernő Ungár's shop.'

'I will keep these on our new grand piano, Sándor.'

'Well, have a good Sabbath, I will see you at the synagogue on Saturday. And don't forget my offer to you.'

'Yes, Sándor I'll look forward to it. No, I will discuss your offer with Rebekah tonight.'

Rebekah was out in town with her friend Magda, from Lvov, they were having a meeting of the Ukrainian Women's Union. Magda came to our wedding, and she has stayed longer for this meeting with the members of the Union's Munkács branch.

Finally I've got on top of my paperwork by midday, and I have collected a sandwich from the downstairs Moskop Restaurant and rushed to the factory to carry on dealing with the orders and I am still working on the promotion letters to other areas of the region.

Viktoria was very helpful as she has arranged the orders and piled all the new letters, in the trays that I have received from businesses whom I have approached already.

Isaack was on the factory floor with Samuel working out the order he has received from Mr Grünwald for five conveyors.

I was just looking through my mail when I have received an order from the Agricultural Ministry, Kossuth tér with a serious enquiry for a number of conveyors for the Tisza Program particularly the irrigation and water control project. Among their many questions if waters could be moved in a muddy / murky situation without jamming the systems. As it has had many breakdown situations with water pumps that they use at present and the time they are wasting on rectifying these blockages is costly. An important question is also are these systems mobile or fixed, what is the maintenance situation on these systems.

This gave me a great hope in the long-time project, but I have a financial situation now as I have stretched my cashflow to the limit. I know that Mr Neuhold should be transferring my money this week for the timber I have sent, and I have paid for including the transportation both ways. I know that I have a good deal on the transportation but nevertheless it has cost me dearly.

I just hope those piano dealers, piano tuners and music teachers will come along to that sale at the National Theatre for the 21-22 September.

As the end of the month is approaching, I have to have a new order of units of electric motors and generators to upkeep our stock all the time, but I have to pay for the new units.

I know I have a good profit margin on each unit but eventually I have to pay for these stocks which have been sent by Ganz Works in good faith.

While I was meditating over the financial situation Isaack walked into the office and asked me if everything was alright.'

'Yes, thank you.'

'Well, I have received this letter of enquiry from the Agricultural Ministry with all these questions which I cannot answer.'

'At last Gabriel there is a much more promising sign and hope at the end of the tunnel that we will have some contract with them at the end of it.'

I handed the letter to Isaack then after he read it, he went back to the factory floor to talk it over with Samuel. When Isaack came back to the office he said,

'Well Gabriel it is six o'clock already we should go home and get ready for our Sabbath.'

'Ah, I didn't realised the time Isaack. Thank you to reminding me of that.'

'Well Gabriel now you are going to celebrate Sabbath in your household with your wife.'

'Yes I look forward to that Isaack.'

As I walked into our dining room Rebekah was ready with the food and drink to celebrate the Sabbath. I gave her the flowers then kissed her and I unwrapped the two silver candlesticks. When she held the two candlesticks and looked at the engraved sign that said to commemorate Rebekah and Gabriel's wedding from Sándor. As she read it out loud, she became emotional and she could only say: 'Shalom Sándor. May the Lord God Bless you for your big heart.'

She took the old sticks away from the dining table and placed Sándor's wedding gift with two white Sabbath candles then she stepped back and looked at the table which is already set for to celebrate Sabbath then she asked me, 'Please Gabriel get ready for the Sabbath as it is time now.'

After I washed my hands, I joined Rebekah at the table. I stood on the opposite side of the table and I said to Rebekah, 'Darling, this is our very first Sabbath in our own house as wife and husband just let's make it special. Praise the Lord God of Israel for gifting us with this beautiful home.' Then I asked her, 'Rebekah Darling, let us say the Shema together.'

Hear, O Israel the LORD our God, the LORD is one. שְׁמַע יִשְׂרָאֵל יְהוָה אֱלֹהֵינוּ (יְהוָה אֶחָד):

After Rebekah's lighting of the candles, she waved her hands over the candles, welcoming in the sabbath. Then she covered her eyes as she recited the blessing:

Barukh ata Adonai Eloheinu...

... I ripped the challah into pieces and gave a piece to Rebekah then I said, 'Sabbath Shalom, my dear wife Rebekah.'

'Sabbath Shalom, my dear husband Gabriel'

After the blessing I noticed that Rebekah was so overwhelmed that she supported herself on the table. I just walked to her embraced her and kissed her on her forehead and pulled her head to my shoulder and whispered into her ear, 'Darling, this is now ours alone and also belongs to our future children to share.

This gift which I have received from our Lord is the seal which will never be broken until the time comes to return to our Creator.'

She held me tight, and I felt that she was shaking by the touch of our Lord. I have celebrated Sabbath many times in my life, but I have to say this one is so special we are feeling the spirit of the Lord upon us with this feeling is from the Eternal's peace.

As I was watching her, she looked like a real Angel as her head was covered with that pure white lace scarf. I just can't have enough of watching her she looks strikingly beautiful.

After the meal when we cleared our dining table, I was telling Rebekah about my financial situation and how much I have stretched my bank account to paying for all the bills for the purchasing and on the alterations of our new house the wedding and all the business that I have made.

Rebekah said, 'I thought that my Papa who paid for the wedding cost.'

'No, he is in the same financial situation as I am with moving into the new factory and the machinery, he bought at the auction with you.'

'My goodness Gabriel is it very bad? I thought he rented the whole new factory including your warehouses for the electric motors.'

'No, my darling I paid the rent for my corner of the warehouse floor area. Look, I will have much of our money back next week from Mr Neuhold as he will be transferring the cost of the timber which I have sent to him. I have made a healthy percentage profit on top of the cost on the timber. I will be very much in profit when we have sold all those upright and grand pianos after the 22nd of September. But at this moment I am in debt at the bank. Sándor offered me a loan, but I don't want to lose a friend over money.'

'Well my love I know what you are going through, what you have provided to me in this house, it is just a dream and thank you for this. We are a family now and we will work out this financial trouble together. So, you say we will be back in profit again in a fortnight?'

'Yes, hopefully but I need to place a new order with Ganz Works to keep up our stock. Yes, we have sold so many units which I have cashed in very well but the way the demand is progressing, I have to hold much bigger stock.'

'My goodness Gabriel I feel we are growing far too fast. You are juggling with too many businesses from the musical instruments and entertainment business to engineering and manufacturing business as well. You are burning yourself out darling I want a husband not a crippled man next to me. I love you so much Gabriel.'

'Thank you very much Rebekah for your concern but I have signed the Ketubah contract before the Lord and before man and I will honour that contract at any cost In the meantime, we can live on my wages the ones which I receive from the Town Council.'

'Don't worry Gabriel I have some savings so we wouldn't be without money for buying food.' Rebekah walked over to me then she embraced my shoulders and kissed me with such passion like a young girl does to her father. 'Look my darling we won't be going out for dinner every night until we will be back on our feet.'

I stood up and picked her up in my arms, then she held my head in her hands and kissed me on my lips which felt for an eternity. She whispered in my ear, 'I hope all the doors are locked, my love?'

'Yes of course.'

'Then please carry me into our bed in your arms, darling. The night belongs to us, my love.'

Chapter 58

Next Year's Entertainment Plans and Interests with Banks

The next morning, I was walking arm in arm with my wife Rebekah to the Hoif Complex Synagogue and we received many greetings and well-wishes from people who we don't even know and who are not members of our synagogue but many of them have heard of our wedding from the Independent Newspaper article on our wedding.

Isaack and Rita were talking to Sándor in front of the synagogue on our arrival, he said, 'We've been waiting for you,' so we joined them, as we all went into the synagogue together for the service.

Three of us sat in the same place where we usually do and were quietly chatting to people around us mainly about our last Sunday's wedding. The conversation stopped when Rabbi Baruch Rabinowitz came in and he has started the Sabbath Service. His lessons were:

Exodus 20: 4-5-6

"Thou shalt **not bow down** unto them, nor serve them; for I, the Lord thy God I am a jealous God, visiting the iniquity of the fathers upon the children unto the third and fourth generation of them that hate Me; and showing mercy unto the thousandth generation of them that love Me and keep My commandments."

'I have a message this morning from the Lord; do not worship or bow down to money or their keepers, just keep your focus on the Lord!'

At the end of the service Rabbi Baruch welcomed the newly wedded couples to his office. We had to wait for Rebekah and Rita as they have been kept back with all the well-wishers on the balcony.

At the end Rabbi Baruch and his wife Rivkah offered us a drink and they told us how much they enjoyed our wedding and the reception S'eudah Mitzvah.

446

Sándor joined us outside of the synagogue as Isaack and Rita invited us for a Sabbath dinner at their house. We had a very pleasant afternoon. Only Rebekah felt a little bit confused as this household now belonged to Isaack and his new wife Rita. Rebekah now had one of her own.

I reminded everybody that the Dezső Zádor Piano recital will be on this coming week, Wednesday the 21 and Thursday the 22. This program was placed on the synagogue notice board and many public places as well.

'Do we know the program Gabriel what is Mr Zádor going to perform?'

'No unfortunately Mr Zádor has not disclosed the program in advance. Probably he will detail it in his program book.'

After our dinner engagement when we arrived home Rebekah suggested we should have some fresh fruit from our garden. As we were picking some grapes from the vine I noticed that the wasps have been attracted to the ripened grapes so we have to organise a family and friends supported szüret (grape picking) party before the wasps and the starlings would clear them all.

'Rebekah do you think that next Sunday morning would be right to organise the szüret a day before Rosh Hashanah?'

'Yes, I think that would be an opportunity for us to celebrate our new year in our new house. It is an excellent idea Gabriel. Welcoming the new year with *Must* (freshly pressed grape) sweet new wine, apples, and honey. We can give grapes to our guests to take home with them as we have so much on these vines.'

'You know Rebekah neither of us have done this kind of activity before in our life, so we have to ask our gardener Samuel to help us with the Szüret and borrow some harvesting tools like " a grape grinder and presser". We have some barrels in the vegetable and wine cellar in which we could keep the new wine.'

'Yes, that is a good idea Gabriel, but you have to organise that.'

I went over to Elisabeth to ask her over to us as we would need some advice from her. I asked her where could we borrow these harvesting tools.

Elisabeth said with a smile, 'I have got all these tools in the barn which have not been used for some time. You can use them for some new wine as payment for the szüret-i tools.'

'That is a deal Elisabeth we both agree to that.'

'I will clean them up and make them ready for the szüret. It would be better if you would fill up your barrels with water as they must be dried out not having been used for some time which would close the cracks on the barrels. Soon after that you have to treat the barrels with sulphate to kill all those harmful fungi which have stained the wood as it not been used for a long time and that would protect the wine from going off.'

'I will ask Samuel our gardener to do all these technical things, Elisabeth. I am sure that Samuel will know how to do all these things as he has a small holding and vineyard just at the outskirt of Munkács.'

Then we had a cup of coffee and some nice cake that Rebekah had baked in her new modern kitchen and some freshly picked grape with a leftover kalács from last night Sabbath meal.

Rebekah came up with a Szüret Party slogan to invite friends to celebrate Rosh Hashanah:

Shanah Tovah Umetukah have a Good and Sweet Year with our "sweet grapes".

'That is fantastic Rebekah I like it, well done. I will get it printed in the office with Andre first thing on Monday morning.'

On Monday morning, the 19th of September, I was getting my plans together for the next theatrical season together to discuss it with Andre today.

Andre was back in the office from his travelling in the Munkács and Beregszász Counties promoting and organising the rota for the movie films that we've received from the Hungarian Cultural Ministry to promote Hungarian culture.

Andre was telling me that the political mood in the countryside has become more openly vocal and nationalistic. Some places where he has been people criticised him for the way he was dressed in particularly as he is wearing a bow tie and not just a normal tie.

I wasn't very comfortable with these people who only want "cheap entertainment options" and they were not interested in any of the classical culture or the much more up to date cultural trend.

'Look Andre it is my fault that I have sent you to these places on your own. I should of have been there with you giving you my support in dealing with these situations what you have described to me. I know that the changes have arrived already which I have been involved with at the beginning some month ago but that does not allow or encourage this kind of behaviour.

'We have a request, Andre, from the Drama Theatre after the successful evening we've organised for Miklós. They would like to have a mixture of Poetry

Evening, Comedy, and Theatrical programs from Hungary. I have pencilled in some artists and acts who we could promote here in the Region.

'Firstly, we have to research each town and village by their population and ethnic structure so we will not promote Hungarian culture to a mainly Czech populated settlement and visa. Our job is to make a profit and make sure that the theatre or cultural centre will be a sell-out audience. So, these are the names I think will be suitable for the region.'

'Before you go further on, Gabriel, I have been approached by the Jewish Gimnazium Theatre Group who would like to put on a production of an evening with the poet Endre Ady.'

'I agree that is a good idea to give an opportunity to a local youth to perform. One thing; there will be a guaranteed sell out as many family members will support their children or grandchildren who are going to perform on stage. Ady is a very good in fact one of my favourite poet and writer. So, these are my acts which are follows.'

An evening with the authors / poets:

So here is another Erdéyi writer after Ady, is Áron Tamási, with his book of Trilogy of; *Ábel a rengetegben (In the forest), Ábel az országban (In the country)*, and *Ábel Amerikában (In America)*, and the *Ragyog egy Csillag (One Shining Star)*

We have a comedy writer of many novels: Jenő Rejtő (His artistic name is P. Howard) his books are (*Menni vagy meghalni* (To March or Die and Dirty Fred)

Pap Károly Jewish Author; latest book; *Azrael*

Milán Füst, Author: Latest book; Advent (A great author and loyal to his belief)

Ferenc Molnár, Author and playwriter and his wife Lili Darvas actress.

He is a journalist for Pesti Hírlapban, and Budapesti Napló.

Introduction of newly published books by the Budapest Publishing Company:

Gyula Illyés: Ki a magyar? (Who is Hungarian?),

Gyula Ortutay: Rákóczi két népe; (Rákóczi's two nations) and many other new writers

Comedy.

An evening with actress, Katalin Karády and Pál Jaros, actor

Latabar Brothers (Árpád and Kálmán) and Manyi Kiss (Comedy)

Sári Fedák Actress (Prima Donna / light opera singer and movie star, born in Beregszász)

<u>Theatrical Performance for next year 1939s Seasons</u>

Budapest Theatrical Touring Company; János Kodolányi: Földindulás (Landslide Play, with lead Movie actor; Antal Páger, Piri (Piroska) Vaszary, Movie actress)

For the Opera enthusiasts: By the cast of the Hungarian Royal Opera house performance of Pongrác Kacsóh: János Vitéz; daljáték. (Valiant János, light opera) Conductor; Emil Ábrányi,

Director; Dezső Zádor.

Endre Ütő Theatrical Company's presentation of József Katona's master peace drama:

Bánk Bán

'Well Andre I think that is all for this new Theatrical Season of 1938-1939. I think we will have enough homework to do approaching these company's or their agents to get a fixed booking so we can advertise it promptly in the press and arrange the dates with various venues / theatres in Munkács and around the towns and villages in the counties. Look Andre, I have to go to the National Theatre just down the road to arrange all the pianos for the next Wednesday and Thursday's sale.

'I have managed to catch the director of the theatre Jacob Zinger, and he told me that the piano removal people have started to bring the pianos into the foyer and into the corridors and I have the theatre's resident piano tuner David Kunzberg who is checking through the pianos and tuning them and whatever they need in the way of a touch up.

'Mr Zinger told me that Mr Dezső Zádor the Concert pianist will be arriving tomorrow morning. He is going to stay in the Star Hotel where he would like to meet up with you.'

'You know Gabriel we are receiving a great response from the public not just for the piano sales but for the concert as well.'

I felt a great big stone rolled off my shoulders as this sale should recover me from this heavy burden which has been created by my financial situation. I was checking the way the pianos have been arranged all the five grand pianos are in the main hall and the nineteen uprights are in the corridors. I heard that the piano tuner was checking and tuning the pianos as the corridors echoed through the theatre.

I introduced myself to Mr Kunzberg and I thanked him for the work he was doing to get all the pianos into good working order and tune them. I made a deal with him that I will pass all the maintenance and tuning work to him after the sale and also all the people I know who have a piano in the Munkács area. He will come and tune our new piano on Friday morning.

'I have to ask Rebekah, Andre and Viktoria to help me with the sale to take the money and arrange the deliveries for each sold piano. I know that Mr Kunzberg will be there helping us as the piano tuner, so he has an expertise in this field.'

By the time I managed to get to the factory it was three in the afternoon already and I haven't had any food at lunchtime. The only food I had was a couple of coffees.

I couldn't stop I just have to get on without food till the evening with Rebekah. Viktoria reminded me that there is some matza in the coffee cupboard which should kill my hunger till the supper in the evening.

When I've looked at my desk, I was surprised to see so much mail which was piled up in the enquiry tray. I thought that I was going to be late from home today again. Rebekah won't be happy. But I am just setting up my business and this just has to be done. But when the business is up and running, I could employ someone to manage the business, but until then I am not in that position, so I am afraid I have to put the time into the business as it demands.

Isaack told me, 'You are working too hard.'

'Yes, Isaack that is true I have started at the town hall first than I went to the theatre to oversee the arrangements of the piano sale. And now I am here to manage this part of the business.'

'Look Gabriel you are stretching yourself to the limit don't you think? You are doing so much you may doing some harm to your health. I need a son-in-law and a grandchild. Rebekah is really worried about you.'

'Yes, you right Isaack I am stretching my energy to the limit, but these things have to be done. You have done the same when you got married. As soon these pianos will be sold, I will only be interested in the entertainments at the town hall and this agency.'

'Well, I understand you Gabriel, I have done the same when I started my business, but I have to say in regret that I have been neglecting my wife Rivkah and as you know she has died I neglected her at the time when she needed me the most. I do not want this to happen to you as well this sad same fate could be regrettable.'

I paused for a second or two and said, 'Yes I know what you mean Isaack but when I've signed the Ketubah in front of you I have promised that I will be the provider for my wife and my family's welfare, and I will honour my promise that I've made there.'

'I know Gabriel you've meant it and you'll honour your promise, but I like you very much and I don't want you to make the same mistake that I've made all those years ago. I can see you have a great response from your future customers. It is a good sign my boy.'

Isaack said, 'Come on Gabriel it's 6.30 in the evening we have to close for today and you should spend some time with your Rebekah as well whatever time is left from the day.'

Rebekah had kept the food on the cooker to keep it warm. She only said that she just can't wait for this week to be over and done. 'This piano sale is taking a lot out of your energy Gabriel. I hope after the sales of these pianos you will be spending more time with me.'

I had no answer to that as I know she is right, but you have to take the opportunities when they are there to be taken. If you don't, you have missed out on a financial reward for your effort.

Next morning at the town hall office, Sándor's secretary stopped me and told me that the Deputy Mayor would like to see me at 10 am in his office.

I looked through my mail in the office and I told Andre where I was going, '…so if anybody is looking for me just tell them I should be back within an hour.'

Sándor looked at me and said, 'My goodness Gabriel you look like someone who has not slept for a week. Is it still your financial situation that is bothering you?'

'No Sándor I have received the money transfer for the timber from Budapest and hopefully the sale of the pianos will put me well into profit. This is the only different things that I am involved with which is taking much of my energy. Both Isaack and Rebekah think that I should cut back on my commitments and concentrate more on the family business.'

'Yes, I think they are right Gabriel. But the reason I wanted to talk to you is that I have received a telegraph from Budapest that a delegation is coming from Budapest next week from the Hungarian Royal National Bank to finalise the purchases of the premises for the bank and they want you to supervise their management team with your local knowledge and connections. Of course, I will be there behind you Gabriel, but I just cannot be seen to be involved with a commercial venture in my position I know that would be a political suicide.

'As it is now a very big possibility that the Full Council of Munkács will elect me to be the next Mayor of Munkács and I just cannot mess that up with the possibility slander or corruption.'

'Mazel tov Sándor, that is fantastic news. Of course, I understand your delicate position.'

'Yes, it is delicate Gabriel, but please keep it to yourself not even to Rebekah's or Isaack's ears. Anyway, but the follow up of the National bank's move to Munkács and to Ungvár there is a firm request coming from our associates that there is another bank who are looking for premises in both major towns in Munkács and Ungvár too.

'Who is it Sándor?'

'It is the Budapesti Magyar Kereskedelmi Bank (Budapest Commerce Bank) they want to open in Munkács by April 1939.'

'Well, we just can't have the two banks next to each other.'

'You right Gabriel, but you had suggested me two locations last time, one on the Fő utca and one on Rákóczi utca if I am right. Mr Segal from The National Bank has told us that they prefer the Corso, the Main street property so we can offer the other building to the Commerce Bank. What do you think?'

'Well I think Sándor if the National Bank is in the position that they are coming here to purchase the building on the Corso than they will be in a much-advanced position to open their branch by mid-January 1939.'

'Then there will be a delay of three months of the Commerce Bank opening timetable. I think in all possibility that they could open they branch by mid-April 1939. I will send a telegraph to my contacts and will tell them the news that we are waiting for their delegations and we will assist them with the transaction here in Munkács. But they have to apply for a banking license in Budapest for the whole of the Transcarpathian regions. Now how you getting on with this piano sale and recital?'

'Hopefully, I am organised now with everything and all in all it should be a success one.'

'I will come in my official position as Deputy Mayor Of Munkács to open the concert.'

'That will be a great help Sándor, I appreciate it. Thank you. By the way here is an invitation for our *Szüret* (wine picking) party which will be held from, 9 am on Sunday the 25th on this weekend.'

'I will be there Gabriel, I like Must (newly pressed wine). I look forward to it.'

Leaving Sándor's office, I collected some important letters from my desk and told Andre that I would be at the factory, if he wants me, he can phone me if something is very urgent.

Back at the factory again more letters are waiting for me there was an order for ten electric motors and two generators. This made my day and quickly I have to check the stock on the motors and make a list of how many units have been sold and the numbers of new orders I have to place with Ganz Works Rt.

Also, I had to remind Zoltán of the conversation that he had with me over supplying me with the generator which is built together with a small petrol motor powered engine as a complete unit. I would need at least 100 unit of this specification units to replace the ones that have been sold.

Chapter 59
Piano Sale and Recital; History of Musica

On Wednesday, the 21st at 8.30 in the morning Rebekah and I met up with Andre and Viktoria at the National theatre. We have to have a briefing before the opening of the sale, so we all have the same pricelist on a clipboard, and I am looking through the list of pianos which I priced up yesterday with the help of the piano tuner Mr Kunzberg.

It is a big and exciting day for our new venture for the sale of Musica Pianos.

I had put a number on the back of each piano which will help us to identify them on the list and also it will show the price of individual model. I can offer 4 or 5% discount depending on the price of each model of piano. Like for grands it is 4% and on uprights 5%) but only if they are paying for the instrument on the day in cash. We can offer five years manufacturers guaranty on all the pianos directly by Musica Rt Budapest.

The first tuning is free of charge and will be carried out by Mr David Kunzberg Piano Tuner and Technician, only if they are in Munkács. If Mr Kunzberg has to travel outside of the district of Munkács then he will charge for travelling expenses which is not included in the free tuning.

If any of you would like some help or technical advice Mr Kunzberg will be in the sales area but only if a customer would need some technical query that you cannot answer.

I have to say Mr Neuhold sent some beautiful instruments with equally attractive veneered in different styles like modern or Chippendale leg high gloss French polished finish cases. We've been supplied with some large posters and some smaller A4 size photographs of the models with their technical details on the back of the glossy finished promotional leaflets by Musica itself.

The larger posters have been hung by theatre staff on the walls which names the range of Musica pianos like: Ühlmann, Ühlmann Luxus, and Musica. The

Neuhold and Neuhold Musica was the most expensive one but those are the Grand pianos.

After our briefing it was time to open the theatre for the piano sales.

As we opened the doors the public were just rushing in as if we were offering some cheap musical instruments. I asked Mr Kunzberg why this rush was so overwhelming?

'Well Gabriel, September is the new academic year and the children who have decided to take up piano lessons their parents are rushing to get a new instrument for their children. But this is not just a piano that they are choosing, it is furniture as well where families will put their photos on top of this furniture, but this it is an investment as well. So, September is the time to sell pianos for this reason you have well timed this sale Gabriel.'

Firstly, the grand piano was the one which has been sold first. I thought I should have ordered more grand pianos. I was very surprised as they were the most expensive instruments and people didn't even try to negotiate on the price. There was two beautiful walnut veneered Neuhold grand pianos, one straight grained mahogany and two black Neuhold Musica grand pianos. By at 11 am all the grand pianos were sold to wealthy customers.

As the day went on, I was worried that we wouldn't have enough pianos to sell for tomorrow. By five in the evening I had to close the sale as we were all exhausted from the very busy day of piano sales. The main reason is that the piano recital will be starting in the next hours. I collected all the cash and put it into a larger box and placed it into the theatre's large safe. I kept the keys just for security reasons as it was quite a lot of cash that we have collected from the sale.

I couldn't meet up with Dezső Zádor at the hotel as we have to concentrate on the piano sales today. But he came into the foyer introduced himself to us and he started to test some of the pianos which has attracted attention among the customers. It was a good advertisement for the day as such a famous concert pianist is attending the sale. He is a very nice person and talented concert pianist.

I invited my crew, Rebekah, Andre, and Viktoria to the Star Restaurant for a meal after a very busy day. We had a relaxed supper and after the meal four of us went back to the theatre to enjoy Mr Zádor's piano recital.

We had reserved seats at the back of the theatre just to be there showing ourselves as the organisers of this concert, so we have taken the "cheap" seats the last row in the stalls.

456

Sándor kept his promise, and he has officially opened the concert as he promised as the Deputy Mayor of Munkács. He was giving a good promotion to the piano sales and praised me for organising this piano recital with such a distinguished Concert Pianist then he introducer Mr Dezső Zádor and he sat in the front row in the auditorium. It was good to see Rabbi Baruch and Rivka were sitting next to Sándor in the front row together.

By the time Rebekah and I managed to get home the only thing we wanted was just get into bed and relax. My mind was still spinning over the unexpected interest and a successful sale that we had right on the first day of the two-day sale.

Next morning, we were checking through all the pianos and basically there is only four pianos left without a sold ticket stuck on the back of these instruments. I have to let Viktoria, and Andre go back to their jobs from the sale as I could managed to sell those four-upright pianos on my own. Rebekah had to stay home to let Mr Kunzberg in to tune our own Strohmenger grand piano.

By midday I have sold the remaining four Musica Ühlmann upright pianos as well and have collected all the cash from the theatre sale and I have taken it to my Town Hall office to count. I have worked out the profit that I have made at the end of the sale. I was very surprised on the final figures as it has well exceeded my expectation on the net profit that I have made with this business venture which I have no previous experience with pianos. But business is business, you just sell whatever is there and make profit out of that.

I have put some cash a side and paid Andre and Viktoria for their hard work and with the rest of the money I have walked to the Moric Ulman Bank to pay it into my account.

Mr Gerő came to the cashier desk and welcomed me when he saw me with the large bag in my hand, he invited me into his office, and he called one of the bank clerks to count the cash. I was paying all the money into my account then he congratulated me on such a successful business venture.

Then he tried to offer me a much larger overdraft loan for my business which I turned down.

I thought that I would open my account with the Hungarian National Bank when their branch will be open here in Munkács then I will be able to get a better interest from them after all I am the one who has brought them here to Munkács in the first place.

After the bank I met up with Isaack and Rebekah at the Star Restaurant for dinner.

I was telling Rebekah and Isaack the staggering amount of profit that I'd made with this piano sale.

'Look Gabriel I am very pleased to hear this great achievement, but I would like you to end this piano business for the future as I need a husband next to me and not a very tired and constantly worried man next to me.'

'I promise you Rebekah that this will be the last time I will organise such things.'

'You know Gabriel, when Mr Kunzberg saw our grand piano, he just couldn't have enough praise for the instrument, he said that he has never ever worked on such a magnificent small piano with a powerful concert grand piano sound. I have tried to pay him for the tuning, but he declined my offer, he said you have given him so much business at this sale that he will tune our piano for the future free of charge as a thank you for getting all these jobs for him through the sales.'

At four in the afternoon I suggested to Rebekah we should go home to get ready for tonight's concert and a short celebration following at the Star Restaurant. Rebekah looked at me and she has understood what I have meant and said, now as you say it, I have to get my clothes arranged for tonight then she gave me a wink with a smile. Viktoria just looked at Rebekah, she winked at her and smiled.

On that Thursday evening four of us went to hear Mr Zádor's recital. He was performing a different set of music mainly romantic like Tchaikovsky and Schubert. I thought he has the same background culturally as these composers. I think I will book him to perform here in Munkács and in Beregszász as well. I made a point to Andre during the interval that we should work out some programs for the next theatrical season for Mr Zádor. While we were chatting in the foyer, I have given an envelope to Viktoria and one to Andre. I was telling them there is some appreciation cash inside the envelope and thank you for helping me with the sale.'

After the concert Mr Zádor was telling me that he has spoken to the piano tuner who just couldn't stop talking about our Strohmenger grand piano.

He asked me if I would allow him to play on my piano.

I thought that this would be an opportunity for me to discuss possible future concerts series here in Munkács with him.

I asked Mr Zádor, 'Would you accept an invitation for our Szüret Party the one we are organising for this coming Sunday? Only some good friends which some of whom you have met already at your concert who are going to attend at this party, and you could play on the piano as much as you would like.'

'Well thank you very much for your kind invitation I haven't planned anything else for this weekend so why not, I always liked a good Szüret-i party it is a good fun. Thank you I will be there Gabriel.'

When the piano sale and the concert finished, I have worked out the profit I've made from the total takings minus my expenses. I was very pleased with deal that I've made with the theatre who gave me the use of the foyer to sell my pianos free of charge, and the theatre is to pay Mr Zádor's fee for his performance from the ticket sales and the profit is kept by the theatre. Well I think at the end everybody is happy, and it was fair deal for all of us, and it has created a very good future relationship with Mr Jacob Zinger and with the National Theatre of Munkács.

On Saturday on the way home from the synagogue I discussed with Rebekah that we should ask Elisabeth to help us prepare some food for the Szüret-i party. 'I'll give her some cash to get all the ingredients for the party and to make a kind of finger buffet type of "cold plate" with fresh bread.'

'I will ask her for our Sabbath dinner Gabriel then we can discuss it with her during the meal.'

'That is a great idea Rebekah, she's always been there for us, and she is a very loyal neighbour to us.'

Rebekah was one of those women who always cooked for more than we need. She always said, 'You just never know Gabriel if a stranger would visit us unexpectedly, we should be able to provide them with food.' I agree with her, that is the very least that we can do to strangers to offer them food and drink. You never know that you might welcome an Angel into your house like Abram did.' *Genesis 18: 4-5*

Elisabeth was very excited that we were getting her involved with our szüret-i party and she said that she had most of the ingredients—eggs, salamis and so on for the szüret-i party only what she has to get this afternoon is fresh bread.

I gave her some cash more than she would need for the food, but I know she does not have a great income, only the one she makes at the market every Monday at the local marketplace.

Chapter 60
Szūret

On Sunday morning, we were wakened by our friend Matyi the rooster. Rebekah asked me about the bell ringing which came from the main road direction.

'What is this cowbell ringing at this time every morning Gabriel? I was going to ask you but as the day went on, I have forgotten to ask you about it.'

'Oh, that is our "Kanász" (herd man) who leads all the animals (cows, sheep and geese) every morning to the pasture to graze them then he brings them back from the field in the evening.'

'So why is he sounding the cow bell?'

'Well, he is letting all the residents know who have livestock that they should open their main gates to let the animals join the herd. Then in the afternoon on the way home he is sounding the cowbell again when he is bringing the animals home so the residents will open their gate and the animals will leave the herd and go back to their own barns where they live. This exercise is repeated every day accept Sunday as that is the herdsman's day off.'

'Well, you know Gabriel I've been living here in Munkács all in my life, but I never knew this very Interesting practice. But how do the geese and other animals know where they live.'

'I just don't know my love, I guess they just learned it from their adult animals and now they are just accustomed to it. It was new to me as well until Elisabeth has explained this routine to me.'

I had the Kosher Plum Brandy from Kecskemét ready for the day I have kept it in the refrigerator to start the day with our appetiser for the hard work we are facing today.

Elisabeth has brought all the cleaned-up harvest tools over from her barn and we were ready to welcome our friends (helpers for the day). Andre and Viktoria have arrived first than Samuel our gardener arrived and Isaack and Rita. Rita was helping Rebekah and Elisabeth in the kitchen to prepare the finger buffet for the guests.

Then Samuel (our gardener) has arrived with his expertise, and he was telling us about the order from clipping the grapes from the vine and putting them into a "puttony" (a wooden pannier) then we bring the grapes into a large wooden vat and then all the ladies crush the grapes with their bare feet.

After Samuel's demonstration we all started with the grape picking. There was a kind of hazard to do that process as we have to negotiate with the wasps as they were all over the grapes.

Then Sándor arrived with Dezső Zádor and they joined us and got straight into the process of picking and carrying the grapes from the vineyard vine stock to the large vat in our courtyard.

Rebekah and Rita just stood by the vat and were a bit puzzled as to what to do. Elisabeth said to Rebekah and Rita, 'Just tuck your skirt into your knickers, then get into the vat and start stamping on the grapes. This is how it's been done for centuries; just follow me.'

Well, Rebekah particularly liked the idea and she followed Elisabeth and she tucked her skirt into her knickers and got into the vat and held Elisabeth's shoulders and started to stamp on the grapes. To see the fun of it, Rita and Viktoria did the same and got into the vat joined Elisabeth and Rebekah stamping on the fresh juicy grapes. There was a lot of laughter among all of us to see the ladies were falling about laughing so much as the grapes were tickling their feet.'

We fellows all stopped and watched the girls dancing, stamping on the grapes with great fun.

Halfway through this wine stamping, Rabbi Baruch arrived with his wife Rivka and this fun immediately clicked in with Rivka; this spontaneous "ancient ritual" of wine making szüret-i traditions. Elisabeth swapped places with Rivka in the vat. Elisabeth brought out the food to our guests.

Then Samuel scooped the crushed grapes into the wine press and started the pressing process which can take some time as the grapes have to be drained out from the winepress completely without any waist of the precious "must". All the "must" (grape juice) has to drip into a smaller vat then it will be poured through a filter leaving the bits behind then poured into the ready prepared barrel.

After we have picked all the grapes and it has been crushed by the ladies Rebekah has organised some precooked *töltött káposzta* (stuffed cabbage) for all of us and Andre was looking after serving drinks to our "workers".

461

At this time, I was showing our new grand piano to Dezső who sat down at the piano and tested the touch of the keys saying, this is beautiful Gabriel these keys are covered with real ivory. And the regulation of the action and repetition is just perfect. As I opened the top lid of the piano it has given an even louder tone. Dezső started to play some Franz Liszt piece and said this piano play and sounds like a big concert Bösendorfer. Then he went back to play on this piano by that time we were all just finding a chair or something to sit on or just standing in the lounge with a drink in our hand and being mesmerised by the piano playing of this great talent.

A little later Samuel and Elisabeth joined us after they have cleaned up the winemaking tools and they were equally taken by the performance of Dezső Zádor.

After about 40 minutes of performance Dezső stopped playing as he just realised the audience he drove with his playing and with a spontaneous concert we all asked him to play some of our favourite music. 'Rabbi Baruch asked Dezső if he could play a song as Rosh Hashanah begins tonight and it would be a great opportunity if we could all join in and sing it together of Hine ma tov u'ma na-im which he just started singing:

Hine ma tov u'ma na-im
Shevet achim gam ya-chad

Then we all joined in, singing along with Rabbi Baruch and as Dezső was slowly speeding up the tempo and we were getting more vocal and clapping to the beat to the greatest speed that I have ever sang this song only a concert pianist can play it to that speed. All the men and the women started to dance to it, and we all ended up as a true Jewish party as a build up to Rosh Hashanah. Finished with our all-time favourite:

Hava nagila hava
nagila hava
nagila venismecha
Hava neranena
hava neranena
hava – hava venismecha
uru achim

ur achim belev sameyah
ur achim belev semeyah
ur ahim ur achim
belev sameyah

Later on, after we were exhausted from the singing and dancing Samuel came in with a couple of large "*kancsó*" (clay jars) of *must* (freshly pressed grape) and Rebekah with Elisabeth's help brought in some freshly baked *kenyér* (bread) and the finger buffet. Everybody enjoyed themselves and the new wine that we all are being part of.

As the Sun was getting lower our energy was following the Sun's setting mode and we felt quite tired after the very physical exercise that we had today to enable us to complete our szüret.

Rebekah and Elisabeth made "Szüret-i gifts" to all of our guests in small wicker baskets which included a bottle of freshly pressed must, new wine for the New Year, apples, pears, and plums from our trees and Elisabeth's baked honey and ground walnut cake. Everybody has pleasantly enjoyed themself on this spontaneous event. I think they will talk about this event for a long time.

We thanked our friends for their help and said goodbye to them, wishing Shanah Tovah to all. At the end we finally managed to have a long bath and retire to our bed in a totally exhausted state, and we fell asleep immediately.

Chapter 61
Holidays, Rosh Hashanah and Buying a Car

On Monday, the 26 September (1 Tishrei 5699), the first day of Rosh Hashanah we all celebrated together in the Synagogue with a full congregation. After the special service at the Synagogue Isaack and Rita invited us and Sándor for a dinner at Isaack house where Rita has prepared a meal to celebrate the first day of Rosh Hashanah.

We all bore signs of the yesterday's szüret tiredness and mainly the drinks we had particularly at the end of the evening when we all sang and danced together.

Sándor told us that he had a meeting with Aladár Vozáry President of the Munkács Trade and commerce who told him that Transcarpathia Trade and Commerce will have its own special Freestanding Pavilion at the forthcoming Budapest International Trade Fair in April 1939. Aladár Vozáry asked me to suggest a company with a unique product that would represent Munkács and be part of this team of companies for this trade fair.'

'I have suggested you Isaack with this new Conveyor system you are manufacturing now. It is unique even by the Hungarian standard of products and it would fit in well with the exhibition organisers regulations. And just think Isaack what an opportunity it is for your business at such an International Platform where the trade would acknowledged this product, and you never know what trade it could bring you.'

'What would it cost us Sándor?'

'Nothing Isaack you only have to pay for your accommodation and expenses. But I know the Transcarpathian Trade and Commerce office has negotiated a discounted rate for corporate accommodation for all the exhibitor members.'

'I think Isaack this opportunity is not to be missed.'

'I know Gabriel yes; it is an opportunity but what about the business I would have to be away for at least ten days.'

'Papa, here we are with Gabriel, we can run the business without any difficulty. I've been your accountant for so many years, Gabriel can manage the orders and run the production. So why are you hesitating Papa? You could take Rita with you as you have never had a holiday together for a very long time. And please take my word Budapest is beautiful in, particularly in the late Springtime.'

'Well, all right I will apply for this exhibition.'

'You don't have to Isaack; I have applied for you already. I knew you would be interested to participate in this great opportunity.'

'Thank you, Sándor you are a true friend, I will show my appreciation to you.'

'You don't have to Isaack you are helping our boys with employment and that is a great help.'

Rita put more nibbles on the table as we were having a relaxed time. I asked Sándor if he could recommend me an automobile dealer. Everybody stopped drinking and they all looked at me with surprise written on all over their faces.

Rebekah broke the silence first, 'Did you just say "an automobile" Gabriel?'

'Yes, an automobile. We are wasting so much time with walking and we find it difficult to get a connection with public transport to travel outside of Munkács and an automobile would give us that flexibility and mobility to all of us for our business sake and also for our comfort sake. Look I have made a very healthy profit with this piano sale and with exporting timber to Hungary so we can afford it Rebekah. Why should we have to walk or to use taxis to get faster and more in comfort travelling from A to B?'

'Yes, you right Gabriel I know automobile dealers here in Munkács I will let you know by Thursday.'

'Thank you Sándor I appreciate your help.'

'But I have forgotten to tell you darling that we are going to have a telephone in our house from Thursday the 29th of September.'

'Well this is just fantastic Gabriel.'

'Which one, Rebekah? The automobile or the telephone?'

'Both Gabriel. Absolutely I am excited for both news. So, we will be becoming equipped with the latest modern household facilities for our comfort. Thank you darling.'

'Sándor said goodnight to all as he felt a bit tired.'

Rebekah said, 'Yes, we have to go as well, thank you my parents for today's happiness and for a lovely dinner. We will see you after the holidays. I hope darling Gabriel you are not tired tonight.' She looked at me with her distinctive naughty smiley eyes which were sparkling in the flickering gas lights.'

'No, I am not tired my love I will be yours all night long and all day tomorrow and forever.'

What a great feeling to wake up with your wife still sleeping in your arms. I don't have to disturb her just remove her body from my arms. I have no engagements for today, so I am just making the most of this peaceful experience of looking of my beautiful wife who is just like a little girl who is curled up in her father's arms. I just closed my eye and remembered the sheer pleasure to be with Rebekah. We've managed to sleep through Elisabeth's roosters crow and the herdsman's cowbell, we must be exhausted from the past week's workload that we have gone through. Thank the Lord for the Holy days that we can enjoy.

Then I drifted back to sleep and woken up to find Rebekah was kissing me on my forehead.

'Would you like my darling your breakfast in bed or will you join me in the kitchen to have our breakfast together.'

'I'll come to join you in the kitchen Rebekah. How beautifully peaceful the life can be for us.'

During breakfast, Rebekah asked me, 'Are you serious about buying an automobile Gabriel?'

'Yes, my love, I am. Just think of the lost hours waiting for public transport to visit customers for Isaack and not to forget that he is getting older and mostly it is most impressive to turn up at your customers with your own automobile.'

'But my Papa cannot drive an automobile, Gabriel.'

'No, he can't, I can but you will.'

'What do you mean Gabriel I can't drive either I know you can, but I can't.'

'I know darling, but I have booked you for driving lessons then when you've passed the test you can drive Isaack to see his customers and also you can go shopping with your friends.'

'But the automobile is very expensive Gabriel.'

'Yes, it is but I have made so much money with the pianos, with the timber and as my Ganz Agency is making good progress too. But I would purchase the automobile on the business account. You are the accountant Rebekah so you should be able to claim it back from the tax office from our company's profits. This is a luxury item in some people's eyes, but it is a necessity for our business.'

'Yes, you are right Gabriel I can claim it back from our profit against our taxes. Well, I have never thought of it. You are my clever man. Yes, I can see myself wearing my big hat and all my stylish dresses as I am sitting behind the steering wheel and driving around in Munkács.'

'Yes, my darling I can see that too. You would look just perfect indeed my love.'

'You are spoiling me, Gabriel. I love you so much. You know what Gabriel as we don't have to go anywhere no commitments so we could just stay in our house coats without dressing up for the day. What do you think?'

'Yes, my darling you are right we can be lazy for this day and just stay in our night dresses. Have you thought about how much help and comfort it would give you to carry our baby child in the automobile it would be better than just pushing him in the pram.'

Rebekah looked at me with her usual naughty eyes when she is fired up to fly into a higher and physically most pleasurable status. 'Did you just say that we should start practicing extending our family, to having our own children?'

'Yes Rebekah, that is what I meant. It would be the greatest gift for both of us to have a family on our own. And hopefully with God's blessing the children would be just like us. Beautiful and smart like you and crazy and articulate like me.'

Rebekah just jumped into my arms embraced my neck with tears running down on her red, rosy face then we passionately kissed while I've carried her to our bed. We didn't get out of our bed till supper time.

On the following day Wednesday 28th September, we have to stay home as we have to let in the telephone technician who was installing our new telephone into our house. It was exciting as we could speed up all communication with our business partners and with our friends. We didn't have to walk anywhere to speak about business or being reached for all these reasons.

'You see Rebekah, this is what people would call as a luxury, but it is just like to having an automobile it is a necessity in life, after all we are in the end of 1930's. These things are part of modern life, just look back to the time when we were in Budapest, these things were a normal everyday life in a modern society. We don't have a good public transport system in Munkács, but we are a very well of community with many wealthy people. I have really recognised the number of wealthy people when I had the piano sale. Many people who bought an expensive piano from us never even bothered to negotiate on the price of the pianos just paid the price we are asking for them.'

'Yes, Gabriel you are right why shouldn't we have the same luxurious items that the people enjoy in Budapest when we have the wealth to pay for these goods.'

After the telephone technician left the first thing that we did was to phone into our factory and told Isaack that we have the telephone now and we gave him our new telephone number. I could hear him shouting, 'Mazel tov, my children; now I can communicate with you any time.'

Then we phoned Sándor and arranged a dinner with him at the Star Hotel Restaurant. 'Well my boy you have brought many "Bourgeois" and "materialistic" ideas with you from the "Big town Budapest",' Sándor laughed, and he congratulated us for getting back on our feet financially and with confidence. 'Mazel tov, my boy.'

At the restaurant Sándor told us that he had a word with his old client Mr Czerny who has a Škoda agency in Munkács.

'Mr Czerny will get you a good price and a nice automobile just what you are looking for.'

'Thank you, Sándor that is very helpful, but I would like to discuss with you another important thing which is for the benefit of the Jewish communities. I have placed a large number of petrol motor-driven electric generators from Ganz Works, which we could distribute to these communities in the small villages with the help of OMZSA or JDC.

'It would help the communities either Shul's or Synagogues and Shtibelach, to generate electricity for them mainly to bring the children out from the candles and paraffin lights era to the 20th Century, in particular now as the longer darkness of wintertime is approaching. All people should have an opportunity to see a movie film in their small rural villages not just only the ones in towns or larger settlements.'

'I like your idea Gabriel I agree with you this is the time now for us to act on these communities as we have the tools available which is very mobile, to achieve our effort to help the next generations to not to miss out on the future technological advantages in their life. I will send them a message to get the backings for our initiatives. It is a very noble thought Gabriel, and it should be supported by our organisations.

'I tell you what Gabriel I'll take you to meet up with Mr Czerny to have a look at his stock and dealership to see the automobile that he was telling me about. He is a good man, and I am sure you could make a deal with him on this car as this wouldn't be an official engagement for myself.'

'That is alright Sándor we can hire a taxi to take us to his garage.'

Rebekah was getting excited that she could have the opportunity to see and chose the colour and the style of the car we are going to buy after all she's going to drive it as well.

This very nice garage with a hand operated petrol pump in front of the building and a servicing workshop in the rear on *Sugár út* where the taxi has brought us.

I had passed this garage before many times on my way to the main Railway Station, but I had never taken any interest as I have never thought that I will ever be able to purchase one of these automobiles, and here I am with my wife and my friend to purchase one.

Mr Czerny welcomed us to his garage. There was room for three cars in the showroom and one has stood out which I noticed that Rebekah had picked one already as her eye stayed on this nice two-toned black and yellow four door automobile. I picked that as well as it stood out from the other two black ones.

Škoda Superb Luxury and Škoda Favorit Limousine

I left Mr Czerny to give us some technical details on the performance and the differences in luxury between the three cars. Also, he told us the retail price of the vehicles. He quickly added to these figures that of course as we are friend of Sándor, he can offer us a much better discounted price. All three of us sat in all the three cars and we have decided on this Škoda Superb Luxury model. I have agreed a good, discounted price with Mr Czerny we both shook on the deal and then he gave me the receipt of sale for the car. I told him that I will bring a cheque from the bank for the amount agreed to his account prior to our collection on the 3rd of October. Then he drove us back to the Hotel Star and with a polite gesture, he gave one of the car keys to Rebekah in a nice box wrapped with a pink bow on top of box. Rebekah was very emotional and then we walked into the restaurant for a drink to celebrate my big purchase of this beautiful automobile.

As we walked in, we noticed that Isaack was having a business dinner with his client. After he finished with his client then he joined us for the celebration that we have just become a proud owner of an automobile.

'Well my children I can't find a word to express my joy for both of you. Well, Gabriel since you have come on the scene my family has lived a relaxed steady middle-class lifestyle. Firstly, you fired up my daughter made her to become a beautiful butterfly even you have woken me up from every day's grey monotony and now I am having so much enthusiasm for life and for businesses we are involved with.'

Sándor agreed, 'Well, my boy you've brought so many new ideas with you from Budapest that the whole Jewish community is benefitting from. Rabbi Baruch keeps praising you for that new upright Musica piano that you've gifted to our synagogue. You are truly a gift for us Gabriel.'

'Thank you, Sándor and Isaack for your appraisals but I didn't want to take up the job that I was offered in the first place, but it is faith or destiny that has driven me to this move. But I guess I have just stepped out in faith and in that package, there was a beautiful girl who become my destiny and I've just accept it as my future place to be with. It's an old proverb which has become my motto: *God grant me the serenity to accept the things I cannot change. Courage to change the things I can and wisdom to know the difference.*'

'This is so beautifully profound Gabriel and there is so much wisdom in this proverb. It's just like it happened to me that I have just accepted my fate as supporting my father for the rest of my life until our angels have brought us together at the university in Lvov and our future was bonded from then on. And here we are sharing the gift of our Lord God which He has been arranged for us through his angels and here we are and just trying to understand His wisdom and learn from it.'

'Yes, Rebekah we are nothing without him as He who made us for his plan to serve and worship Him by faith.'

Chapter 62

Celebrating Sabbath / Shabbes at Our House and Rosh Hashanah (Shanah Tovah)

Rebekah invited Rita, Isaack, Sándor and Elisabeth to our house to celebrate our second Sabbath at our house. After the great szüret-i party we had last Sunday the must was slowly transforming into a new wine. The smell of the fermenting grape is creating some level of dangerous gas which can be fatal equally for animals or humans, so we have to go to the cellar with a candle as safety tool to detect this fermented gas, if the candlelight dies the level of gas is overwhelmingly dangerous. So, we have left the cellar window and the door open, so the room will have a draft to clear these bad gasses from the room. I brought some clay jarfuls of new wine to celebrate Sabbath together with Rosh Hashanah.

After Rebekah's lighting of the candles, she waved her hands over them, welcoming in the first Sabbath of the new year of 5699 then she recited the blessing:

Barukh ata Adonai Eloheinu, Melekh ha'olam, asher kid'shanu b'mitzvotav v'tzivanu l'hadlik ner shel Sabbath. Then we ask the Lord Blessing for the food and wine then we have started to enjoy the fantastic food we all corporately put together for this special First Sabbath of the new year.

The atmosphere was very relaxed and joyful. I had to go to the cellar two more times as the new wine was very popular particularly when served chilled.

After the supper we fellows moved to the lounge for a chat while the ladies cleared the dining table then they joined us in the lounge.

Sándor was telling us that today the 30th of September the Czech government handed over its Sudetenland a big part of Czechoslovakia to the German's demand according to the Munich agreement.

Also, 'I've been hearing disturbing news from Berlin, and Vienna about many Jewish business owners and Jewish Communities have been molested and boycotted by the local Germans for no reason and they encourage those Nazi brown shirt army uniformed youth who wear the armband with the swastika to cause trouble.'

'But you say Sándor this is happening only in Austria and Germany.'

'Yes, Isaack it is I know it's far away from Munkács but nevertheless it is happening in central Europe. It is all about the German "Nordic or Aryan races" (master race).'

'Well, I hope this movement just won't happen here in Transcarpathia just like Isaack said we are a long way from Berlin or Vienna.'

'Yes, Gabriel let's hope we won't be affected like our friends in Austria and Germany.

'After all we've just established our business and it has taken off in such an unbelievable way and importantly as we are providing a livelihood to so many of our workers. We just can't let them down they have supported us in the past all the way.'

'Yes Sándor, Gabriel is right we just can't let them down we are just like a big family. This news you've been getting may be only local to Germany and Austria.'

'Yes Isaack, I hope it may well be just a local infight.'

'But let's forget this subject and talk about your new automobile Gabriel. I have to say I like that car very much it is truly luxurious with red leather seats, very comfortable. I can see your Rebekah driving that car you will have a lot of pleasure out of that automobile.'

'Yes, Sándor I still have to have some driving lessons as Gabriel has found a local taxi driver who will teach me.'

I was so glad we changed from politic to other subjects in our conversation like the factory fitted petrol motor driven dynamo's which could provide people in the little villages with electricity.

'By the way Sándor I am expecting these generators/ dynamos arrival next Wednesday the 3rd of November.'

'Gabriel, please let me know when those units will arrive at your warehouse, I would like to see them to be able to understand the way they work.'

'And how is your "Exhibition" conveyor is coming on Isaack?'

'It is coming on well, but we keep having to put it back as other orders are demanding priorities Sándor. But we will be ready for the exhibition as I have to be ready with the complete working conveyor by the first week of March next year.

'I have a confirmation from Mr Aladár Vozáry the Director of the Transcarpathian Trade and Commerce office that they have accepted my application and they will transport the conveyor to Budapest along with the other chosen exhibitors from Transcarpathia.'

'I am so glad that you have applied to be part of this exhibition. I know there is an interest coming from the Hungarian Agricultural Ministry over this conveyors as Gabriel has received a letter from them telling us that their officials want to come and have a test on the machine when they are coming to Beregszász to set up their offices there. But Gabriel can tell you more about it.'

'Yes, it is a definite move from the Hungarian Government to set up this Civil engineering base in Beregszász which really makes sense as Beregszász is the nearest major town to the River Tisza.

'You know Sándor we are working very hard to set up this production line as we will not just be manufacturing this machine, but we have to do the maintenance or repair the existing conveyors, so they won't have a breakdown situation with their work progress. What about you Sándor, how is your career getting on?'

'Well, I don't really want to talk about it as it may never happen.'

'So, can we celebrate our friend as Mayor of Munkács?'

'No Gabriel not just yet. But keep those bottles of champagnes on ice.'

'I will do that, but we are the happiest people to hear this great news Sándor.'

As the night went on so well, I suggested that both Sándor and Isaack with Rita should stay overnight at our house and go to the Synagogue in the morning together.

Rabbi Baruch Rabinowitz welcomed us all for the first Sabbath of the year— the 6th day of Tishrei 5699.

One of the Cantors in the synagogue followed the tradition as rituals for **Rosh Hashanah** he was blowing of the shofar. The sound of the shofar starts a ten-day period known as the Days of Awe, which ends with **Yom Kippur**.

Rabbi Baruch made this day a special one and he told us that the Lord God has created heaven and earth in six days. His main teaching was based on *Exodus 20:11… "For in six days the LORD made heaven and earth, the sea, and all that is in them...on that day He rested from all the work of creation that He had accomplished...That is why the LORD your God has commanded you to keep the Sabbath day."*

At the end of the service, he invited everybody to the assembly room and he has served us with new wine and honey-coated apple to celebrate the new year men and women together.

It was an opportunity to catch up with friends and some of the members whom I have never met at the synagogue. Even Cllr Cohen came to me with his wife Maria and wished Shanah Tovah. Cllr Cohen pulled me aside and said, 'Look Gabriel, I judged you too harshly when you did your presentation on the changes in education and the dominant language of Hungarian will be in practice. Now I can see that these changes are going to happen in a matter of time as I can see here in Munkács the teaching is in Hungarian already and I can hear there are more and more gymnasiums and schools are changing the teaching from Czechoslovakian to Hungarian language. Please accept my apologies Gabriel.'

'Look I have not carried my grudge against you from that day when you have challenged me over my presentation. Just let's shake hands on the past and move on.'

'So, we are friends now, Gabriel?'

'No, I wouldn't say that we are friends but definitely we have no bad feeling for each other.'

'Thank you Gabriel I can accept that and hopefully we can build a better relationship for the future.'

By the time we managed to get away from the synagogue it was well past half past three in the afternoon Isaack with Rita and Sándor went home earlier. As we were walking home Rebekah has made a point on the weather that has suddenly changed. Can you feel the chill wind blowing down from the Carpathian Maintains.

'Well Gabriel this is your first winter here in Munkács and trust me it is much colder than in Hungary, I guess.'

'Yes, you are right my love as you are reminding me of this, I can feel it already. After all it is the first day of October and you could feel the sudden change in temperature.'

'I am so glad that we have completed our szüret last week well timed it.'

'You know I still haven't heard any news from Miklós I hope he had a successful tour with his poetry evenings. I think if he would have failed than I would have been told by the theatre directors.'

When we got home the whole house was a little bit cold and I had to study the user manual of the central heating boiler. After a few minutes I managed to start the oil burning boiler then it slowly warmed the whole house evenly.

'I am very pleased for this central heating Gabriel. I don't have to feed the fire in the stove like at our house. I never liked to do that I was always covered in soot and smelt smoky.'

'Come here my darling I will teach you how to operate this central heating boiler.'

We both sat down to have some chicken soup with dumplings and finish the crushed honey cakes which were left over from the szüret. As we relaxed after the dinner, the telephone suddenly rang. We both looked at each other as we just had no idea who would know our telephone number as we just had it installed a week ago or so. I answered the phone, and it was Béla Róth, the journalist from the Independent Newspaper on the other end of the line. I asked him where did he get my telephone number.

'Look Gabriel I am a journalist, and this is our job to investigate stories for my newspaper.'

'And how can I help you, Mr Róth?'

'I believe you have had a very successful sale of pianos and an even more successful concert with Mr Dezső Zádor. My readers would like to hear a story of this unusual event in Munkács. May I ask for an interview Gabriel, perhaps I could come to your house and interview you.'

'Look Mr Róth I would prefer if we would do that interview in our factory office, and you would be able to write something new that you have never seen.'

'What is that Gabriel?'

'It is called conveyor and elevator system.'

'Yes, that is very interesting; when can I come to see you?'

'How about ten in the morning on Thursday the 6th of October.'

'Thank you Gabriel. I will be there with a camera.'

Rebeka and I just relaxed for the rest of the day catching up with our books which we had been neglecting due to our busy life. It was quite a relaxing experience just amusing ourselves with an exercise which I used to do a lot in my little apartment on Király utca. It seems to me as we have been staying there a long time ago, but it was only three months ago.

Then I have fallen to sleep in the armchair I have woken up as the book that I was reading has slipped out of my hand. Rebekah laughed at me.

'You looked so comical Gabriel your head nodded forward then when your book has slipped out of your hand your face was so panicky as if you didn't recognise where you were.'

'Yes, you are right my love I was dreaming of my little apartment on Király utca, Probably that was the reason why I was so surprised on the furniture and decor.'

'It is late now darling let's go to our bed. I promise I will sing you a lullaby and will spoil you.'

I just lowered my head into Rebekah's arms and within minutes I was fast asleep.

I felt Rebekah's gentle hand as she was stroking my face and my hair but the next thing I remembered was that impostor Matyi, Elisabeth's rooster, which woke me up from my dreams. I looked at Rebekah as she lay next to me with a smile on her face. I thought she must be playing with angels. She looked like a little cherub.

Footnotes / Glossary / Pictures
History of names, events and places

(N 1) Chief Rabbi & Scholar, Simon Hevesi. Source: opensiddur.org

(N 1) Chief Rabbi Imanuel Löw: Sources: szegedfolyoirat.sk-szeged.hu

(N 1a) New York *Kávéház*

(N 2) Mission to *Munkács*

(N 3) Odry Theatre and *Barlang Mozi / Film Muzeum*

(N 4) Dohány Str Great Synagogue of Budapest

(N 5) Nyugat (West) Literary Journal

(N 6) Magyarország (Hungarian Nation) newspaper
Zsidótörvény 1, - Jewish Law 1 (proposal)

(N 7) My mentor in Munkács, Dr Sándor Fried

(N 8) Andre and Viktoria, my helpers / secretaries

(N 9) Hoif complex Synagogue of Munkács.

(N 9a) Chaim Elazar Spira the old Rebbes of Munkács

(N 9b) Grand Rabbi Baruch Yehoshua Yerachmiel
Rabinowicz of Munkács. Source:
commons.wikimedia.org

(N 10) Mrs Elisabeth Schwartz house

(N 11) Munkács, *Kárpatalja* Transcarpathia

(N 12) Town Hall of Munkács

(N 13) Corso/Fő utca

(N 14) History of Hebrew *Gimnázium*

(N 15) This act is: The 1843/44 2nd Act ordered Magyar to be the official language of Hungary.

(N 16) The Ukrainian Women's Union

(N 17) 1938, under the First Vienna Award Annexation of Transcarpathia

(N 18) The Sztuka coffeehouse

(N 19) Lvov sightseeing/Grand Hotel

(N 20) Rebecca, the meaning of the name is "captivating beauty".

(N 21) As Gabriel, the meaning of name is "God is my strength".

(N 22) The administrative-territorial division of the region
(*Vienna Arbitration)*

(N 23) The First Jewish Law, the Balance of Life , 1938: XV.tc (29/05/1938)

(N 24) Homdi Café on the Corso

(N 25) April 1938. Konstantin Hrabar establishing the National Scout movement

(N 26) Rabbi Yosef Elimelech Kahana.

(N 27) Great Synagogue of Ungvár

(N 29) Miss Annie Fischer, world famous Hungarian concert pianist

(N 30) Transcarpathian Parliament Ungvár

(N 31) Andrew Bródy Member of Ungvár Parliament

(N 32) Franz Joseph a visionary leader of the Austro-Hungarian Empire

(N 33) Miklos Radnóti and his wife Fanni Gyarmati

(N 34) History of Zserbó

(N 35) Czechoslovakian Korona and Hungarian Pengő

(N 36) New bathroom, kitchen furniture from Zloch & Partner on Rákóczi street

(N 37) OMZSA: The Országos Magyar Zsidó Segítő Akció

(N 38) JDC Jewish Joint Distribution Committee

(N 39) Ábrahám Ganz

(N 39b) Kálmán Kandó

(N 40) Budapest Elisabeth Bridge

(N 41) Széchenyi Chain Bridge

(N 42) Royal Castle Buda

(N 43) Mátyás Templom, Mathias Church. Source: en.wikipedia.org

(N 44) King Stephen's statue and the Fisherman's Bastion Source: trip101.com

(N 45) Hungarian Parliament Building

(N 46) Our apartment block on Király street

(N 47) Opera House Budapest

(N 48) The Old National Theatre Budapest. Source: commons.wikimedia.org.

(N 49) Budapest Földalatti (Underground)

(N 50) Hősök tere (Heroes' Square). Source: commons.wikimedia.org

(N 51) The City Park (Hungarian: Népliget). Source: flickr.com

(N 52) The Budapest Zoo and Botanical Garden

(N 53) Vajdahunyad Castle (Vajdahunyad vára)

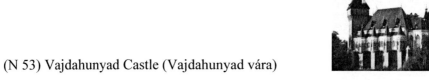

(N 54) The Original Corvin Castle in Transylvania

(N 54a) Váci utca

(N 55) It's Gabriel at age four in his first new suit

(N 56) Minutes of my presentation to the Ministers

(N 57) Reményi Mihály music shop on 58-60 Király utca

(N 57a) Música Rt. Zongoraterem on 49 Erzsébet Körút

(N 57b) Strohmenger Baby Grand Piano in an Art Deco style

(N 58) Donát Bánki a Hungarian Jewish mechanical engineer and inventor. Source: en.wikipedia.org

(N 59) Gundel's Restaurant for our last day in Budapest. Source: en.wikipedia.org

(N 60) Conveyor & Elevator Co.

(N 61) National Theatre Munkács on Rákóczi utca. Source: mukachevo.net

(N 61b) Isaack Grósz Conveyor and Elevator Factory

(N 62) Dezső Zádor concert pianist. Source:
eo.wikipedia.org

(N 62b) The story of the Hungarian Cinema begins in
1896

(N 63) Ketubah "Marriage contract"

(N 64) Seven Blessing - Sheva Brachot

(N 65) Gabriel & Rebekah under the Chuppah

(N 66) Musica Piano history

(N 67) Szüret (Wine harvesting): Source:
sorokmogott.blog.hu

(N 68) *Škoda.* Source: skoda-storyboard.com

(N 69) Rosh Hashana

(N 70) Yom Kippur

(N 70b) Sukkot

(N 71) Kristallnacht

(N 72) Synagogue of Beregszász.

(N 73) First Vienna Award

(N 74) Hannukah Channukah

(N 75) Budapest International Fair / Spring Exhibition

(N 75b) First sign of open Antisemitic Campaign

(N 76) Passover – Pesach

(N 77) The Second Jewish Law

(N 78) Arrow Cross Party

(N 79) Gendarme – Csendőrség

(N 80) Miklós Horthy de Nagybánya

(N 81) Baron Zsigmond Perényi de Perény

(N 82) Brit Milah (Circumcision)

(N 83) Hangya Szövetkezet / Co-Operative organisation. Source: commons.wikimedia.org

(N 84) BBC Announced Germany Invaded Poland

(N 85) The Second World War

(N 86) The Treaty of Versailles

(N 87) Soviet Union invaded Poland

(N 88) Nimrod

(N 89) Jewish Newspapers in Munkács
(N 90) The forced labour Battalions Law

(N 91) KEOKH

(N 92) Governor Vitéz Miklós Kozma

(N 93) Ration book

(N 94) The Tragedy of Man Theatrical Play

(N 95) Germany declare war on Soviet Union

(N 96) The Kaminets-Podylskyi Massacre

(N 97) 3rd Jewish Law

(N 98) Cattle Wagon

(N 99) Auschwitz – Birkenau

(N 100) Zyklon B Pellets Killer gas: Source: bbc.com

Acknowledgement to my Research

https://www.yadvashem.org/

Munkacs - USHMM: https://encyclopedia.ushmm.org/content/en/article/jewish-community-of-munkacs-an-overview

Mukacheve - Kehila Links:

https://kehilalinks.jewishgen.org/Mukacheve/default.htm

https://kehilalinks.jewishgen.org/Mukacheve/images/Mukacheve-Town-Map-1.jpg

https://en.wikipedia.org/wiki/History_of_the_Jews_in_Carpathian_Ruthenia

Fedinec Csilla; A kárpátaljai magyarság történeti kronológiája 1918–1944

https://mek.oszk.hu/01800/01843/01843.pdf

Raz Segal – Days of Ruin / The Jews of Munkacs During the Holocaust

https://en.wikipedia.org/wiki/Raz_Segal

Great Synagogue Budapest: http://www.dohany-zsinagoga.hu/

Wikipedia: https://en.wikipedia.org/wiki/Doh%C3%A1ny_Street_Synagogue

Yad Vashem Valley of the Communities Memorial to Munkács:

http://citeseerx.ist.psu.edu/viewdoc/download?doi=10.1.1.738.9520&rep=rep1&type=pdf

OMZSA, Mare Magnum Dan Wyman Books LLC Brooklyn, NY 11211, US :

http://www.marelibri.com/t/main/3301701-shoah/books/AUTHOR_AZ/1900?l=ru

JDC:

https://www.jdc.org/about/

https://en.wikipedia.org/wiki/American_Jewish_Joint_Distribution_Committee

Kálmán Kandó:

https://en.wikipedia.org/wiki/K%C3%A1lm%C3%A1n_Kand%C3%B3

Széchenyi Chain Bridge:

https://en.wikipedia.org/wiki/Sz%C3%A9chenyi_Chain_Bridge

Buda's Funicular:

https://en.wikipedia.org/wiki/Budapest_Castle_Hill_Funicular

Mathias Church: https://en.wikipedia.org/wiki/Matthias_Church

Fisherman's Bastion: https://en.wikipedia.org/wiki/Fisherman%27s_Bastion

Hungarian Parliament Building: https://www.google.com/search?client=firefox-b-d&q=Hungarian+Parliament+building

Király utca: http://www.multesjovo.hu/hu/aitdownloadablefiles/download/aitfile/aitfile_id/435/

Adverts: http://muzeumantikvarium.hu/upload/szmcppp.pdf

Electric Motors:

https://en.wikipedia.org/wiki/Ganz_Works

https://en.wikipedia.org/wiki/%C3%81brah%C3%A1m_Ganz

Bánki Donát: https://en.wikipedia.org/wiki/Don%C3%A1t_B%C3%A1nki

Gundel Restaurant: https://en.wikipedia.org/wiki/Gundel

Fórum Intézet, Lilium Aurum Könyvkiadó - Galánta–Dunaszerdahely 2002

https://karpataljalap.net/2004/10/15/zenei-elet-kivalo-karpataljai-kepviseloje-zador-dezso

https://karpataljalap.net/2004/11/26/adalekok-munkacsi-nemzeti-szinhaz-tortenetehez

Conveyor and Elevator Company Accrington: http://www.conveyor-and-elevator.co.uk/

Hungarian films:

https://en.wikipedia.org/wiki/List_of_Hungarian_films_1901%E2%80%931947

https://en.wikipedia.org/wiki/Cinema_of_Hungary

Jewish Wedding: https://sites.google.com/site/jewishweddingtraditions/home

Szüret: https://sorokmogott.blog.hu/2017/09/18/szuret_falun_avagy_ahogy_nagyszuleink_csinaltak

Rosh Hashana: https://toriavey.com/what-is-rosh-hashanah/

Yom Kippur: https://toriavey.com/what-is-yom-kippur/

Sukkot: https://en.wikipedia.org/wiki/Sukkot

Kristallnacht: https://en.wikipedia.org/wiki/Kristallnacht

Orion Radio: https://www.radiomuseum.org/r/orion_99g_99_g.html

Synagogue in Beregszász:

https://dbs.bh.org.il/place/berehove-berehovo-beregszasz

First Vienna Award: https://en.wikipedia.org/wiki/First_Vienna_Award

Hanukkah: https://en.wikipedia.org/wiki/Hanukkah

Arrow Cross Party: https://en.wikipedia.org/wiki/Arrow_Cross_Party

Csendőrök Munkácson:

https://www.yumpu.com/hu/document/read/18805767/a-m-kir-csendorseg-elhelyezese-magyar-kiralyi-csendorseg

https://www.yadvashem.org/odot_pdf/Microsoft%20Word%20-%206245.pdf

Regent Horthy: https://en.wikipedia.org/wiki/Mikl%C3%B3s_Horthy

Zsigmond Perény:

https://en.wikipedia.org/wiki/Zsigmond_Per%C3%A9nyi_(1870%E2%80%93 1946)

Brit Milah: https://en.wikipedia.org/wiki/Brit_milah

BBC announcement:

https://www.bbc.co.uk/archive/news--invasion-of-poland/zmd68xs

PM Chamberlain BBC Speech, "We are at war" with Germany:

https://www.theguardian.com/world/2009/sep/06/second-world-war-declaration-chamberlain

Treaty of Versailles:

https://www.history.com/topics/world-war-i/treaty-of-versailles-1

Brief History of Hungary at WWII:

https://hu.wikipedia.org/wiki/Magyarorsz%C3%A1g_a_m%C3%A1sodik_vil%C3%A1gh%C3%A1bor%C3%BAban

Soviet Union Invade Poland:

https://en.wikipedia.org/wiki/Soviet_invasion_of_Poland

Photos of Ernő Ungár and details of immigrants from Poland:

http://citeseerx.ist.psu.edu/viewdoc/download?doi=10.1.1.738.9520&rep=rep1 &type=pdf

Vogue Magazine: https://archive.vogue.com/article/19391201168

KEOKH: http://degob.org/index.php?showarticle=2019

Governor Kozma: https://en.wikipedia.org/wiki/Mikl%C3%B3s_Kozma

The Tragedy of Man: https://en.wikipedia.org/wiki/The_Tragedy_of_Man

Germany at war with Russia:

https://en.wikipedia.org/wiki/Declarations_of_war_during_World_War_II

Zyklon B: https://en.wikipedia.org/wiki/Zyklon_B